The Promise of the Witch

The Promise of the Witch

Steve Oates

Library of Congress Control Number:		2019920170
ISBN:	Hardcover	978-1-9845-9290-3
	Softcover	978-1-9845-9289-7
	eBook	978-1-9845-9288-0

Print information available on the last page.

Rev. date: 01/21/2020

To order additional copies of this book, contact:
Xlibris
800-056-3182
www.Xlibrispublishing.co.uk
Orders@Xlibrispublishing.co.uk
806101

This book is dedicated to my dad, Sydney Oates. He showed me what was possible with a bit of imagination and a lot of application.

The story concerns a young Wren in the Royal Navy, who everyone expected would do her duty as a sea-going witch (just like her nana) - only someone forgot to brief her.

When I was a kid at school, I seriously considered the Royal Navy as a career, but instead I created a fictional career for a young Wren who was fated to transform into a witch. The received wisdom is that you should only write about what you know, but it will now become apparent that I did no such thing. So, none of what follows should be taken to represent what it is like to serve in the Royal Navy or any of the armed forces, at any time in the past. Instead, what I have written comes mainly from my own, erratic imagination.

The historical and geographical framework should just about be recognisable, from 1940 to the present day, but most of the buildings, facilities, ships and people, are fictitious. The character of the Wren is based on someone I met at the finish line of the Great Galley Hall Pram Race in November 1979 - she enchanted me but she was almost certainly not a witch.

Prologue

A shimmering green leaf sea, ebbed and flowed in the breeze,
In this steep-sided valley, cut through with trees,
Gnarled limbs of oak, birch and alder, swishing with leaves,
A shimmering sylvan sea, punctuated by a symphony,

A symphony of song: the sweet, descending trill of the wood warbler; the truncated warble of the redstart, the excitable opening by the pied flycatcher, the chiming of...

...a piercing shriek that broke the calm!

'Nana, Nana, it's a harpy!' The girl came scampering down over the brow of the heather strangled hillside, towards the leaf sea, her hair flying behind and the hem of her smock flailing against her legs. Breathless, she reached her nana's side and grabbed hold of her apron. 'It's coming for us!' gasped the young child.

'That is no harpy, that is a bird of prey' was the firm reply.

'Oh, oh, is it preying on us, Nana?'

'No, it is a fork-tail and it's searching for carrion.'

'Oh, oh, what's carry on, Nana?'

There was a deep sigh. 'Carrion. It's dead meat. You are quite safe.'

There was a long pause while the child thought: 'Oh, oh, are you safe then, Nana?' she asked. The child ducked easily below the lazy admonishing swipe that came her way, swept her long, off-brown, wavy hair back with her left hand so that wooden ringlets chattered together in the cool, billowing air.

Her grandmother sighed and looked down quizzically. 'Do you have anything for me?'

She offered a sheaf of herbs to her grandmother but they were rejected with a sage shake of her head. The child decided to ignore this advice and put them in the basket anyway. 'Nana, that thing you asked me to do for you?'

'Yes?'

'It sounds very hard.'

'Yes, it is, but you promised me faithfully! It is the final stroke in a conflict that has lasted many years!'

'I know' the child replied in a sing-song voice, 'you want to be made whole again, don't you Nana?'

'Yes, and you will do this for me. You promised me!'

'All right Nana I will, but how?'

'You will find a way.'

'But how, Nana?'

'When you are able to...fulfil your promise!'

'Oh, when's that, then?'

'You will know. Your body will call on you. This will guide you. The triskelion!' Grandmother gently brought a pendant from inside her smock and placed it over the child's head and held it so that the light danced rainbows through the endless, triple spiral.

'What's this for then, Nana?'

'I'm loaning it to you...'

'For fighting?'

'No, it is not a weapon...'

'For trading?'

'No, and it is not an ornament. It is a symbol that you have reached a certain level of womanhood and...you are nearly ready.'

'Oh, nearly ready for what, Nana?' the child asked. There was no immediate reply. 'Nana?'

'Nearly ready to...fulfil your promise!'

'Oh, that.' There was another pause for furrowed brow thinking: 'It's not actually worth a sheep's fart, is it Nana?' the child murmured quietly.

'It is valuable in other ways. Protect it with your life!'

'Oh, all right Nana.' She sniffed the pendant and dangled it towards the sun. At least it made pretty patterns against the sunbeams. 'I'll call it Tris!'

And then it was time to resume her meander behind her grandmother, gathering a further harvest of pods and stems from the hillside meadow. Now, she had another question. 'Nana, where do we all come from?'

'Who us, or everyone else?' her grandmother replied. She straightened herself very slowly to gaze at the hump of the sacred mountain above them, that balked the sun, and as she stretched out her sore back, her lined face crinkled in pain.

The fork-tail flew close towards them but with a twist of its tail, it disappeared over the crest of the hill and left them alone in the valley.

'Y'know, Nana, us, our people, all the funny talking ones' replied the child. She chewed hesitantly on a pod, grimaced then spat out what was in her mouth. 'Eurghh, it's nasty Nana!' Her tongue lolled out of her mouth, coated in partly chewed mush.

Her grandmother took a corner of her white apron and patiently wiped the child's tongue clean and looked with disdain at the green stain. 'We arrived in wooden boats from the Western Sea, many years ago, when the lands to the east were still covered in ice. These became our homelands.' She stooped slowly to look into her granddaughter's wide, flashing blue eyes to see if she was placated by this, but she wasn't.

'How many years ago?' asked the child.

'Many, many thousands of years ago' came the reply.

'How do you know that, Nana? You don't look that old?' She ducked the lazy admonishing cuff that came her way but she was clipped inadvertently in the ear on its return. 'Ooft Nana!' she cried out in indignation.

'We have a story that we hand down from generation to generation. It tells us where we came from, how we got here and what we had to do to survive.'

'How do you know this story is true, Nana?' the child replied, rubbing her ear.

Her grandmother thought for a moment and considered how best to sooth this child's incessant and irritating curiosity. She was satisfied with her reply: 'Because, no one in their right mind would invent a story that was so utterly ridiculous.'

Chapter One

0800 Saturday 10 May 1940 - Bahnhofstrasse, Zurich

Mademoiselle Abgrall opened her satchel and checked the contents in the cool of the shade made by the arcade of solid, block-built monuments to the prosperity of the Swiss. In the distance, to the east, there were sharp peaked mountains which even now, heading into summer, had caps of snow. She wondered on this crystal clear day if these mountains were across the border with Nazi Austria. Yes, they probably were.

Inside her satchel there was a porcelain encased mirror; a stubby, palm sized blade, triple spiral crowned; a small silvery ingot of precious metal that sang; a stiff backed notebook and a leather bound book of poems by Paul Verlaine, always with her. Rozenn thought back to the two poems she had recited to herself while she lay in the bath this morning, titled 'Spring' and 'Summer' and she gave a short shiver of guilty pleasure.

More worryingly though, tucked inside her notebook, was the heart-breaking letter she had received from Christoph saying that his unit was joining the conflict. On a more positive note, the string of garlic bulbs looped around the handle of the satchel was maturing nicely.

Rozenn checked her face in the mirror and was pleased with what she saw: her wide cheeks were in sharp relief; her turquoise eyes made bold by shadow; her auburn hair was teased out in a sensible but stylish ponytail, secured in a leather collar. All of this was crowned with a simple, black cap. No adjustments were necessary. The tram was here. She stretched upon her toes to look through the ranks of passengers to see if the gentleman was present. He was! Her heart surged in relief and then excitement.

Rozenn climbed the two wooden steps to board the immaculate blue and white tram, saw a red and black handbill of a serious, stern looking face. She tore it off the metal partition on her way to the fourth row of seats and stuffed it into her satchel. There was a space of a buttock and a half next to a forbidding, dark gowned woman clutching a wicker basket. “Bitte?” she asked and got a scowl in return. This was enough. She squeezed in and their arms, shoulders and thighs reached a tight and awkward equilibrium. “Danke” she said to her close companion. There was no reply.

Rozenn paid the fare to the Parade Platz, further annoying the old woman by invading her space. So, she busied herself by bunching her hair with one hand and re-securing it adeptly with the engraved leather collar and a delicate bone pin. Her close companion still seemed uncomfortable and the prettiness of her flowery, wide-brimmed hat was more than offset by the sour look on her face.

In the wicker basket there were more handbills of a man with this little, idiotic, square, moustache and a ridiculous wedge of slicked down black hair over his left eye. Rozenn slid a handbill out of the basket and stared at it, considered it for a moment and then crumpled it into a ball. She placed it back in the old crone’s basket. The old woman stared back in disbelief. No matter.

The man opposite Rozenn was wearing a brown felt hat and a copy of the majestic Neue Zürcher Zeitung newspaper. He seemed amused by the transaction going on opposite him but he settled back and hid behind his newspaper. Her seat bounced as the tram turned into the Bahnhofstrasse. The man seemed too absorbed in his newspaper to respond to her presence but the eyes of the man in uniform on the front page seemed to follow her, whichever position she took on the wooden tram seat.

“Excuse me sir?” she asked.

“Yes, frau” he replied, “may I help you?”

"I apologise, but who is that man on the front page of your newspaper?"

He folded the newspaper and flipped it over. "That is Herr Adolf Hitler, the Fuehrer of Germany."

"Ah, I see. There is something about the way his eyes follow me. Is he a fanatic of some kind? He seems very cross about something!"

He acknowledged her question with a curt nod and looked admiringly at the picture of a man in the uniform of the German Heer, distinguished by a neatly trimmed moustache and by an immaculately brushed wedge of black hair across one side of his face. "In some ways frau, yes, you see, he is the leader of the new Germany, a modern day messiah. He will lead the Germanic peoples into a new age of peace and enlightenment and provide a shield against the hordes from the east!"

"Oh, but hasn't he started a war!"

"Yes, frau, but he had no choice. He had to correct the injustices of the Treaty of Versailles and this he will do."

"I see. And was there no other choice, other than starting a war?" Rozenn leaned towards him, eager for his answer. She flicked her eyelashes and gazed intently at him and then treated him to an ever-so-slow blink and a gentle pursing of her lips.

"Herr Hitler tried diplomacy but his neighbours chose not to negotiate. They chose war instead" he said, seemingly a little flustered, "but it is a fine May morning, we are not at war here in Switzerland and I am sharing my journey into work with a beautiful, intelligent young lady."

She flushed brightly. "That is very kind of you, sir. May I ask where your journey into work will take you?"

"You may. I am in charge of the legal department of the Bank of Zutter & Co."

"The legal department! At a bank! You must be a very important gentleman at the bank. May I ask your name, sir?"

"Yes, you may. My name is Herr Zutter. My father owns the bank and I manage it for him."

"I am very impressed, Herr Zutter."

"And you?"

"My father does not own a bank!"

"That is not what I am asking you!"

"Ah, I see, you want to know what it is I do?"

"Yes."

"I... work at the Hotel Zurichsee"

"As a housekeeper?"

Rozenn hesitated. "No sir, as a maid."

He seemed shocked. "I don't believe you! That is absurd! You are far too well dressed to be a maid!"

She flushed again. "I like to look my best, even when I am travelling to work. I think standards are very important." So, he hadn't recognised the maid's uniform or the feather duster concealed beneath her raincoat.

"Yes, I can see that." The tram clanked merrily along the Bahnhofstrasse. All the passengers seemed happy and at ease, apart from the grim looking woman sitting next to her as she was now attempting to straighten out the crumpled handbills in her basket.

"I apologise, I must alight here" Zutter said. She looked into his eyes and gave him a long lingering smile that was as lingering as she thought she could get away with. "This is my card" he said, "call for me at the Bank of Zutter on Am Schanzengraben today. I will find you a post that is far more deserving of your talents. My name is...Herr Hermann Zutter." He paused and stretched towards a posy of flowers inserted into a brass cup at the end of the teak seat. He presented these to Rozenn with a broad smile and a curt nod. "And what is your name?"

"I call myself..." She paused for a moment. "Ya, I call myself...Frau Rozenn Abgrall" she laughed, "and I thank you for the bouquet!"

"My pleasure, Frau Abgrall" he replied, as he jumped off the tram and stepped onto the pavement.

She called out after him, "Pleased to make your acquaintance, Herr Zutter!" So, his name is Hermann. Just repeating it sent a slight shiver up her spine.

The tram seemed to take an eternity to approach the Zurichsee. As it clanked to a halt, Rozenn alighted and raced up the steps of the hotel, with the rough fabric of her uniform flailing against her legs and cut flowers scattering behind her. She pushed past an elderly couple remonstrating with her as she ran to a Telefon booth, lifted the receiver and dialled quickly. "It's a Zurich number, the French Embassy, quickly, quickly."

At first, she didn't recognise the voice at the other end. Maybe it was the new telephone operator. "I need to speak with Monsieur Pascal urgently."

There was a click and a buzz. She heard him clear his throat.

"Pascal, it's Rozenn. I've made contact with the younger Zutter!" she announced.

"Rozenn? What are you saying?" he replied.

"Pascal, I'm in, I spoke to Zutter on the tram, he's invited me to meet him at the bank' she gasped down the telephone mouthpiece, "today!"

"D'accord, but the delegation is going in this morning. The bank will not change their position!"

"But it's too early!"

"They'll be arriving at the bank about now. The full delegation!"

"I could be there in ten minutes! No, I can do better than that - five minutes!"

"But what will you do?"

"I do not know. I will have to decide when I get there. I'll make a disturbance, that is what I will do. Then, I will call you when I know what's happening, Pascal. Au revoir!"

She placed the mouthpiece back in its bakelite holder, stepped out of the booth and ran down the steps that led to the basement. Here she pushed her satchel into her locker, locked the door and ran back up the steps, pushing past an elderly couple still fretting in the foyer.

Rozenn took three large breaths, skipped down the steps to the street and started to run.

Chapter Two

0815 Saturday 10 May 1940 - Am Schanzengraben, Zurich

Rozenn turned right outside the hotel and ran up the Talstrasse past the newspaper and tobacco kiosk. At the kiosk, she shouted at the customers, that she had very important information about the Bank of Zutter. There was a coffee house opposite the kiosk. She ran inside.

Rozenn hitched up her uniform so she could climb onto the reception desk, much to the annoyance of the two men in bowties behind it. The hubbub in the smoke filled room eased. “Gentlemen, gentlemen” she shouted, “I have some information that will be of interest to all you. It is concerning the Bank of Zutter, they are awarding an ingot of precious metal to every new customer who agrees to start a new cheque account with them today! See!” she shouted, waving a tiny, silvery ingot above her head.

There was a sudden animated babbling across the room, some calls of annoyance and some alarmed gasps.

Rozenn repeated her announcement very deliberately. “Yes, but that is only for the first one hundred customers!” Two men at the back of the breakfast room slunk out carefully, hoping not to be seen. And then the stampede started. “It’s not a very big ingot of precious metal. In fact, it is truly tiny” she shouted after them.

She held the silvery ingot against her ear and heard it sing it's sad song to her. It was only a little lie that she had told but it still gnawed away at her insides like a hungry mouse.

"Mädchen, what does this mean?" asked a waiter. His grey hair and moustache seemed to bristle at her.

"It is springtime for Switzerland and it is a time for renewal and rebirth" she stated as she looked through the long, wood lined windows to the peace and tranquility of the gardens at the back. "Sir, between you and me, I think they must be in trouble" she confided, "they've run out of money and they are in debt to the tune of millions and millions and millions of francs!"

He dropped his note book, removed his black apron and ran to the swinging door that lead to the street. A small lie she thought, but such an immediate and gratifying reaction. There were just a few coffee drinkers remaining but they were now chattering away like restless starlings. She followed the waiter out into the avenue.

At the crossroads Rozenn turned right, paused at the patisserie and shouted a message to all the customers there. As she ran onto the Bahnhofstrasse, she paused as she came across each group of people and made a shrill announcement to each, concerning the Bank of Zutter.

It was a left turn at the crossroads, onto the Bleicherweg, over the bridge, then right onto Am Schanzengraben along the waterway. And there it was, the Bank of Zutter, a large, concrete faced, edifice, shaded from the morning sun. She took a moment to settle her breathing, and realised that there was an excited and noisy crowd around her. There were children in straw hats and smart uniforms, women in more ornate hats with flowers who chaperoned the children and another woman with an English pram carriage containing a squalling baby, and men in dark suits, neck ties and a range of headwear. The woman directly in front of her wore an elaborate, wide brimmed floral hat: the baby wore a less pink bonnet above it's ruddy, blotchy face. The woman wanted to know what was the problem? Was she in trouble? How could she help her? The children said nothing but their manner suggested that they would rather leave immediately and make their way to school.

Rozenn stood tall, or at least as tall as her frame and sensible brogues would allow and made a pronouncement. “Guten morgen, damen, herren, the Bank of Zutter is a fine Zurich institution. My friend is a teller there. He told me a secret. I don’t know that I should tell you this. He says that they will give an ingot of precious metal to each customer who sets up a new deposit account with them today! Look!” She withdrew the metal ingot from her handbag. See what I have!” There were gasps and then a pause as minds made calculations and decided the next course of action. The crowd, as one, looked down the street and then moved quickly en masse towards the bank.

Rozenn followed them and then pushed her way to the top of the steps that led inside the Bank of Zutter and addressed the crowd below her. They were rapt with attention. Two grey coated guards emerged through the main door. She would need to be quick. “Guten morgen, people of Zurich. I call myself...Frau Abgrall, I am a citizen of... Zurich. Please listen. The building behind me is the Bank of Zutter, and we see it as a...pillar of the Swiss Banking system, known across Europe for it’s principles of...” And now she was struggling.

“The principles of transparency, fairness, honesty and integrity” shouted out a distinguished looking man underneath a black, wide brimmed hat.

“Thank you sir!” There was a smattering of hand-claps. This was an encouraging start. Now for a little lie. “My mother has a long relationship with the Bank of Zutter. She has invested heavily in this bank.” This warranted a further smattering of applause and a short salute of approval for Rozenn. Yes, that was good, think of mother country for mother. “But she needs her money now. She is in great difficulty. She is threatened. She is desperate.” There were nods of understanding from her audience. “But the bank won’t give her back her money! She is in terrible strife but the bank will not give it to her! They say that she is a bad risk. But it’s her money! Why will the bank not help her?”

There were mutterings of disapproval from the crowd. Now for the big finish. “The bank must explain themselves. Why will they not follow the principles of...”

“Transparency, fairness, honesty and integrity!”

"Indeed, sir! Why are they undermining the whole system? Why? Why?'" she cried out, "Yet, yet, they are giving away precious metals to entice new customers! See!" She turned and pointed with her silvery ingot to the two Bank of Zutter officials struggling to repel the first wave of citizens. "They must explain! Why have they betrayed my mother!" There was a shout from a man in a bowler hat, a cry from a women in a head scarf and then more cries of indignation and outrage. The crowd surged around Rozenn, pushed the officials to one side and stormed into the lobby of the building. A man in a homburg hat turned to another man wearing a cap as they pushed his way into the bank. "Do you bank with Zutter?" he asked.

"Of course not, do you?"

"Of course not!"

"But this is our civic duty. They must honour their debts or everything collapses into chaos!" They joined the pushing and shoving throng with their vigour renewed.

Rozenn ran back to the gaunt, anonymous building that merged into the eastern wall of the Bank of Zutter. Two uniformed guards dashed past her. She gripped the iron handle of the still swinging door. Her heart fluttered in trepidation. Now, what was she to do? All she had to protect herself with was...a feather duster!

Chapter Three

0820 Saturday 10 May 1940 - Bank of Zutter & Co, Zurich

Am Schanzengraben is a tree-lined avenue aligned east-west, following one of the zigs, or zags, of the old defensive moat of the city of Zurich. One end of this avenue is anchored on the Bleicherweg, and the other end on Gartenstrasse, with boats for pleasure seekers anchored on the North quay and linen covered tables for takers of coffee along the promenade.

At the western end of Am Schanzengraben is a five storied building, that could be a school if it wasn't for the prison-like apertures set regularly along the floors. Set back from the moat-side frontage there is a separate octagonal tower that looms over the main building. It is capped with a lead cupola. The frontage of the building is so tall and imposing that visitors will experience a sensation of visiting the depths of a canyon where higher plants do not prosper, but lower members of the plant family do. Lichens decorate the pavement on the quay-side of the building and mosses on the North side of the roof. Here is the home of the Bank of Zutter & Co, provider of 'Private Banking Services for Free Nations' in 'Full compliance with the Banking Law of 1934'.

Today, the outside of the building is graced with a shiny, black and silver limousine that sported a limp tricolour on the bonnet and the tiny symbols of La Troisieme Republique on each door.

The occupants reveal themselves as they emerge blinking from the limousine: one is in the uniform of the French Air Force; one is in the uniform of the French Army; one is in the uniform of the Paris banking community, a tight fitting mid-blue double-breasted, pin-striped business suit, with matching hat. The limousine doors are held open by a uniformed officer of the bank, wearing a long grey coat, a black hat and a heavy scowl.

They were met on the worn, limestone steps of the bank by three grey uniformed employees of the bank, thin-faced, hard-eyed and humourless. Their escorts marched them into the grim, concrete-faced building. The vestibule smelt of damp and musty carpet. Thibault asked if he could smoke, but this didn't improve anyone's humour.

Along the back wall, there was a sparse rank of flickering gas lights, that barely lit the room. Below each light was a grimy portrait. If you paid any attention to these portraits, you would have a picture of the long, distinguished history of the family of Zutter's involvement in banking, Thibault reckoned. In the centre of the wall on the left was a long, wood-lined passageway, angled sharply to the right and beyond which a constant clattering noise could be heard. They were motioned towards it.

The source of the clattering became clear. Open fronted, upright coffin-like boxes passed unsteadily by, upwards proceeding on the right side and downwards proceeding below the floor on the left side. Travelling in the upwards proceeding coffins meant they were being raised to the tower, a place that can only be reached by the paternoster.

Thibault Yon hesitated and he paused to straighten the cap of the French Air Force that was perched on his head. The guard closest to him nursed something under the breast pocket of his jacket with his right hand, as if he was armed. He crossed himself at the prospect of what was to come. He was pushed forward until his last hesitant step took him into an upward travelling coffin. His guard came in with him. There was no space for anyone else. The sound of the clattering drowned his thoughts. He knew he was rising up into the tower. An aggrieved shout below told him that Adolphe Rochon had entered the coffin below him. Another shout of protest and he knew that Gaston Legros had squeezed his way into a coffin. The three made their separate ascents, vertically and apprehensively, and alighted on the floor that was signed 'Legal Department of Zutter' in cold Gothic script. It was the uppermost floor of the building, or at least, the furthest that the paternoster could take them. They assembled in a narrow corridor and were then ushered into an octagonal room with ornate chairs, an ornate table and ornate metal-framed windows. There were three officials of the bank arrayed at one side of the octagonal table and three chairs opposite. They sat down opposite their counterparts, unloaded their portfolios onto the table and waited for the official in the centre to speak. It was a very long wait.

"Esteemed guests, welcome to the Bank of Zutter & Co Now, please, I believe we have everyone here who needs to be here to conduct our business today." This must be Herr Meier, thought Thibault. At the side of the table was a space assigned to a clerk. In this space was a typewriter and in front of the typewriter was a man in a grey suit, white shirt and a black neck tie. He was already typing into the machine, with precise but single fingered thumping presses of the keys. He turned to the French delegation and looked unflinchingly at their faces and then turned back to the typewriter.

Thibault nodded curtly and announced: "Sir, I am Air Marshall Yon of the Department of Defence. I am content to make your acquaintance. I am accompanied by Marshall Rochon also of the Department of Defence and Monsieur Legros of the Bank of France." They nodded in turn.

There was little acknowledgement from the men opposite. The man in the centre nodded. "Yes, we all know." He was dressed in a dark grey morning suit and a dark grey tie. Who has died, wondered Thibault.

The younger man on the right, dressed in a brown suit and a yellow waistcoat now interrupted. "Sirs, I am surprised at such a high ranking delegation for such a seemingly straightforward matter. My letter of 25th April makes the legal position abundantly clear."

"Herr Zutter, please...remember your position. It was my letter" said the man to the right. This must be Blum, thought Thibault, the head of the Zurich office of the bank. It was then that they all heard the clamour outside. There were excited and anxious voices, wanting to be let in. "What in God's name is going on out there! Deal with it!" He pointed to two of the guards.

Thibault decided to break the awkward silence. "As laid out in my letter of 1st of May, we are here to arrange the release of certain goods and materials..." There was a nod and this triggered the departure of two guards out of the room. "I am aware of your intents, sirs" said the man in the centre. There was another long pause as papers were re-ordered on the table. "Unfortunately, I have to advise you, the Bank of Zutter & Co has a slightly different position on this..."

"The release of certain goods and materials urgently needed for the French nation to defend itself..." continued Thibault. He noticed that a bank guard was still in the room, at the back wall, and that he had tensed ever so slightly. This now induced a cold sweat to break out in the middle of his back and a drop trickled downwards. There was something wrong here. He got to his feet very slowly. "Please, order this man out while we discuss our confidential business, there is no need..." and his hand moved to cover the pistol holster at his left side. The guard now infiltrated his right hand inside his long grey coat. He must have a weapon in there and was ready to use it. Thibault moved his hand away from his pistol holster.

"Please, please. Let us all behave as gentlemen. Now, Monsieur Yon, sit down. Please, sit down" said the official of the Bank of Zutter. "Thank you. Thank you." He licked his lips before proceeding. "Now, Herr Zutter cannot be here today due to a pressing family matter. I present his apologies. However, his son, alongside me, is here, he is learning the business. He will represent the Zutter family." He nodded curtly to Hermann Zutter to his left. "I also have the Head of our Zurich branch of the bank here, Herr Blum. We are all at your service." He paused. The Frenchmen were very still.

"Now, I have a typed copy of the...transaction between the Bank of Zutter & Co and the Republic of France" he stated as three carbon copy sheets of foolscap sized paper were passed across the table to the French delegation, "and why the Bank considers it to be...not in our best interest." He then waited until they had acknowledged that they had read the document. "As you can see gentleman, we have a problem. The balance of risk is very much against the bank, by a considerable margin, and this level of risk is very, very unpalatable for us. Do you agree with the accuracy of this statement? It is as stated in our letter of the..."

"The 25th of April" interceded Hermann Zutter.

"Non, this is impossible" muttered Gaston Legros. "This is absurd!"

"That is right, Legros" Thibault replied. "But monsieur, we engaged your bank in good faith and because of your reputation for... this type of transaction."

"Be very careful what you say next, gentlemen" said Blum.

"I will. And, as I was going to say, your bank's reputation for facilitating these types of transaction...is well known across Western Europe" said Thibault.

"We will be in breach of our Swiss Banking Law, if we proceed with this...transaction, sir" stated Blum.

"How?"

"These materials are for...the prosecution of war, in our opinion."

"That is absurd! All countries need such...materials to run their economies, tell me that one that does not!" blurted out Rochon.

"The Bank of Zutter prides itself on our total compliance with the laws of Switzerland...and other applicable regulations."

"What about your business with the Nazis?" shouted Rochon.

There was silence for a moment.

"How dare you!" retorted Blum.

"It's true isn't it? The Bank of Zutter helps Germany procure materials for the conduct of war, doesn't it?" shouted Rochon.

"We cannot possibly comment. We pride ourselves on complete confidentiality!" stated Blum matter-of-factly.

"Sir, we do not dispute the...precision of what is written, but you have changed the terms of our business! We are here to negotiate the release of these essential materials, so we may defend our country. Surely, you see the sense of this? Our nation must have these... materials as a matter of urgency! They are waiting at the border but we cannot secure them due to this legal... question. An issue that has been caused by a change of policy of your bank!"

"Gentlemen, gentlemen, the crucial point is that we cannot continue this...transaction with your Ministry of War. We will not commit...until your authorities make a written commitment not to use these materials for any warlike purpose."

"You are asking France to make an impossible choice. We are at risk of invasion. We must have materials to defend ourselves from the Nazi aggressors!"

"Ah, so you admit it!" said Zutter, triumphantly.

"Sirs, the Bank of Zutter is a small, cantonal bank and we cannot afford to...carry that level of risk, gentlemen."

"This is outrageous!" blustered Legros.

"We will hold these... materials until the legal question is resolved."

"But what can the Bank of Zutter possibly do with these materials? This is impossible, you are condemning our country to defeat!"

"Sooner than you think" muttered Zutter.

"What was that, monsieur? What do you know?"

"Herr Zutter, say no more" said Meier sharply.

Zutter continued, mockingly: "France is a very bad business risk at this time. We foresee that you will have great difficulty repaying any debt in the short, medium or even long term!"

There was silence. Herr Meier proceeded to read a statement in a dry, monotone voice. This continued for two of the longest minutes that Thibault had experienced. It merely summarised in legal terms what they had already been told. He watched every second that passed by on his pocket watch, with metronomic precision, each movement of the hand precipitating an increasing realisation that it was his mistake, his responsibility, his honour that was at stake.

"We can have funds transferred to your bank in three working days at most" announced Legros, "tell me what sum will help to... facilitate this transaction?"

"That will not be soon enough" answered Zutter.

"What do you know Zutter?" challenged Rochon.

"I can say no more" replied Zutter, "but the balance of power is changing in Europe as we speak, the old regimes are dying and a new order is coming!"

"You know when and where the Germans will strike, don't you Zutter? How could you possibly know that? Unless you're in league with the Nazis!" shouted Rochon.

"Herr Zutter, please, no more" snapped Meier.

"They will know soon enough! The matador's cloak conceals the sword thrust to the sea and your armies will be split asunder. In a few short weeks, there will be no Third Republic. And we will have the pickings of the French banks!"

"You're in league with the Nazis! Why are you doing this?" shouted Rochon.

"Please be calm! Herr Zutter, no more!"

"The Bank of Zutter has made a business decision, based on the facts. We cannot afford to back a country which is rotten to the core and will not exist in a few weeks!"

Adrenaline started to seep into Thibault's bloodstream. He calculated what could be the next possible actions. Adolphe to his right stood up with his hands balled-up into white knuckled fists. Gaston's face bulged red and swelled, ready to explode, his hands slapped loudly against the table. Eyes and eyebrows across the table raised but their black coated selves did not flinch. They remained seated. But the sullen guard stepped forward, body primed ready for action. And there was silence again, just the ticking of a wall clock and the ticking of heart beats and the beating of another heart close by.

"Gentlemen, it is time for you to depart. Our business is concluded. We will be taking immediate action."

And then they all heard a sneeze, a woman's delicate, apologetic sneeze.

"What the hell was that?" shouted Blum. He strode across to the door and flung it open. A young woman stumbled into the room, clutching a feather duster and wearing a raincoat covering a maid's uniform.

"Who in the name of God are you?" Blum shouted.

"Alors, I am the maid of course" she said as she brandished the duster, "and did you know, that corridor is utterly filthy."

"Who gave you permission, girl?" he shouted.

"He did" said Rozenn, pointing the duster accusingly at Hermann Zutter.

"I did no such thing!" exclaimed Zutter.

"You did! You said I should come here for an interview!"

"But not until midday!"

"Ah, but I came early. I believe punctuality is so important, don't you?"

"You have been spying!"

"Non, non, I am just a maid. I have been dusting!"

"What are you doing here?" shouted Legros. "This is a private meeting! What have you done?"

"Just the corridor so far" replied Rozenn.

"Does she work for the bank?" snapped Rochon at Blum.

And this was the moment when nearly everyone in the room realised that she was probably not a maid.

"All of you, out of here" shouted Meier.

And now there was a hastened shuffle out of the room, with the French contingent being shoved along by the guard.

Chapter Four

0830 Saturday 10 May 1940 - The Octagon, Zurich

There were shouts from the passageway. Rozenn ran to the entrance to the perpetual motion lift. There was a man in a marshal's uniform being manhandled by a guard of the bank.

"Marshal, marshal, what has occurred here?" exclaimed Rozenn.

"France, France has been betrayed! Who are you, what are you doing here?"

"I am a servant of the French people. I am here to help you!"

"You are a maid! How can you help me!" he cried as he was pushed into the clanking paternoster.

"I can make a distraction" she wondered aloud.

"How, how could you do that?" he replied as he disappeared down below the floor level.

"I...can make a commotion!" And she screamed. "Like this!"

The pistol arm of the guard came rapidly towards her face. She rode the strike and kicked away his leg. Her foot smashed his knee and her duster impaled his nostril. She caught the somersaulting pistol with her free hand and pushed the barrel hard against the back of the skull of the guard. "Stay down there on the ground or I will shoot your brains out! I know it will be a lottery trying to find any brains inside, but I will try anyway!"

"You!" cried out Hermann Zutter.

"Ya, it is I. I came a little early, to assist the negotiations."

He grasped her wrists and the pistol was wrestled to the floor. Rozenn twisted her arms, freed them and struck him between his legs. He dropped his hands and tried to grasp her's again. He was too slow. Rozenn's left arm struck downward into his trousers, grasped at what was there between his legs and pulled hard. A sharp howl consumed the space between them and he sprang away. Zutter patted furiously at his crotch to douse the excruciating pain he felt. He rolled in agony on the bare carpeted floor, gasping for breath, his hands thrust down his trousers, trying to massage away the pain.

"Curse you Zutter and all of your spawn! You will all ROT!" Rozenn's scream reverberated around the room, through the building and along the street. The guard was on his knees - she kicked him in the chest and he fell back into the paternoster. The base of the next coffin crushed against his body and the mechanism grated in protest and came to a shuddering halt. There was a blessed silence other than the muffled groans of the guard. She pressed her hand against his stomach. Yes, from the way that his legs shook, he must be in a considerable amount of pain. Zutter was still writhing on the floor and Meier was staring at her.

"Where is the stairway?" she asked.

He shook his head slowly in shock.

"There must be a stairway, quickly, quickly" she shouted, "an escape route in case of a fire or in case of a crisis" she said pointing at the guard.

He shook his head. He was staring at the guard and the blood in his head seemed to drain away leaving him looking like a ghost.

"Fire escape?"

He nodded his head. There was a window, that looked out to the back of the building. Rozenn opened it and looked across and down. A metal stairway leading to the ground! She was swinging outside of the building from a down pipe and then clattering rapidly down the metal steps.

Rozenn was now at the rear, in a yard. A metal door led back into the main building and she was now through it, amongst the crowd on Am Schanzengraben. They had just witnessed the French delegation jump into a waiting limousine. She banged on the window with her fist. It was Rochon who responded. "Find Thibault. Find Thibault

Yon. He's in a bad way. Zutter's guards have beaten him up. I'm afraid he will do something stupid."

"I'll find him. Where's old man Zutter?"

"He's not here. It was just his son. He left this to his lackeys."

"I'll find Thibault and then I'll find old man Zutter. I will put this right, somehow."

"How can you do this?"

"I don't know, but I will find a way. This I promise."

The limousine pulled away, tyres squealing madly.

CHAPTER FIVE

0855 Saturday 10 May 1940 - Klingenzell, Untersee

Georg Zutter received the call from Zurich at 0845 hours precisely. He was in the favourite room of his Klingenzell summer house, that had such a fine view over the grass-strewn slopes leading down to the Untersee arm of the Bodensee. He sat in his favourite chair and gave a thin smile at the news from Zurich. His son and an employee were seriously hurt, the employee, critically.

This would be a bad business for the Bank of Zutter.

He drained his coffee cup, opened the veranda doors and stepped outside and inhaled a breath of the pure sweet air that flowed about the lake.

There was a new order coming, new overlords for Europe, and they would act as a bulwark protecting Western civilisation from the tribes of the East. His Bank of Zutter would take whatever action was necessary to preserve Western culture using financial and political instruments. If this meant that France had to succumb quickly to the German assault, then so be it. The only issue now was how to bring the British to their knees.

His heart was lifted out of his reverie when he saw his daughter, Alina, waving to him from the lawn. Lush green pasture, fruit trees in blossom and fresh pine forest stretched down to the shimmering lake. To the west was the onion-shaped, copper tower of the church, gleaming in the sun. She stepped up to him. He hugged her - she was such a pale, fragile girl in such a fulsome and verdant landscape.

"Are you leaving us again, Dada?" she asked.

"Yes, dear Alina, I have business to attend to."

"When will you come back, Dada?"

"As soon as I have finished my work, dear Alina."

His wife Hanni, joined then on the lawn. "Georg, are you meeting with the Nazis again?"

"Yes, now please don't complain Hanni. I have to do business with many different clients and many different cultures. Today, the Nazi Party is the sole arbiter of what can and cannot happen in Germany. Nazi Germany is a very influential country in today's affairs, my dear Hanni."

"They are not cultured. They make my skin crawl. Do not bring them back here. Are you sure you can trust him? I can't. They are all thugs and gangsters."

"If it's in the best interests of my business, I will bring him to my home and you will treat him with respect, my dear Hanni. You will treat them as if they were the most important people in the world. Is that understood?"

She turned to walk away from him.

"Is that understood my dear Hanni?"

"Of course, sir" she laughed, "of course. Let me see if I can find an appropriate flag to fly above our home and some suitable pictures to deck the hallway! And music! Beethoven or Wagner? You choose, dear husband!"

He grabbed her hand and gently pulled her tight to him. "Any other choices you will allow me to make, dear wife?" Their noses touched.

"No, that is all husband! Alina and I have worked out a set of investments we need to make. The list is on your desk." She planted a kiss on his cheek.

"Grain?" He undid the clasp that held her flaxen hair and he gently unfurled it.

"No, no, no, much too high a risk. Oil, iron, rubber will be the critical commodities. We must increase our stakes."

"Allow me to take a look at your proposal. I'm sure it will make good sense. Now what about our 'Au Pair'?"

"I will attend to her now. I have arranged for Hans to drive you to the guest house at eleven o'clock."

"Eleven o'clock?"

"Yes, do not forget dear husband." She gently undid the hands that were clasped behind her back, kissed him on the cheek and then walked outside onto the upper lawn. From here, she walked quickly to the back of the summer house. It was only a gentle breeze to this side of the building but she felt the need to drag her shawl tight across her shoulders.

Outside, she passed the serried ranks of logs tightly packed on the lower lakeside of the house and then the enclosure where the goats whinnied and climbed up the stockade to watch her progress. Hanni took a key from the set that jangled at her waist and used the largest one to unlock the door at the back of the building. She stepped into the darkness and walked up the three steps to the mezzanine floor cut into the rock that the building was perched on.

"Dear Gabrielle, may I see inside your mouth?" Gabrielle opened her mouth and gagged as she tried and failed to produce her tongue.

"Ah, thank you. That seems to be healing well. Now, may I see your letter?"

Hanni examined it carefully in the light from the small, round window. There were tiny dots below many of the letters. "There seems to be a coded message here, Gabrielle?"

Gabrielle shook her head vigorously.

"Please write down the message on this paper" asked Hanni. Gabrielle hesitated, then picked up the letter and wrote down a jumble of letters.

"Now, what is the message, Gabrielle" asked Hanni, "please translate or tell me what the cipher is?"

Gabrielle hesitated and then took back the paper and scribbled a short message on it. Hanni read and then laughed as she said the message out loud. 'Hostage of Zutter. Rescue me. Gabrielle.'

"You do understand that we had to give you some instruction in obedience? We placed our trust in you and you betrayed us. Now you betray us again. Tell me the cipher, please."

Gabrielle shook her head again.

"Please tell me the cipher, Gabrielle, or I will have to punish you again."

Gabrielle retrieved a book from beneath her mattress.

"Ah, 'The Count of Monte Cristo' by Dumas. How apt! And we're working from the final page of the novel. Very good. Now, please re-write your letter. The message it will convey is that all is well and Herr Zutter has no plans to travel from his summer residence. Yes, that is all your colleagues need to know. I will return in an hour, let's say eleven o'clock. And you will have the letter ready by then, yes?"

The girl shook her head.

"Ah, but you cannot talk. How silly of me! And you're pleading with me - what is it girl? Ah, you do not want to go back in the manger!"

Hanni pulled Gabrielle's hair so they were nose to nose. The big wrought iron key clanked against the other keys at her waist. "Yes Gabrielle, I'm afraid it's the manger for you!"

CHAPTER SIX

0900 Saturday 10 May 1940 -
The Hoffmann Suite, Zurichsee Hotel, Zurich

The Zurichsee Hotel stands close to the Zurichsee but on a wide avenue that heads north from the lake. It is a self effacing building used by businessmen and officials visiting Zurich and is renowned for its utilitarian Swiss cuisine, with a German twist.

Thibault rang the premier of France just before nine o'clock. It was fortunate he had been able to obtain a secluded office in the Hotel Zurichsee. After five of the most humiliating minutes of his life, he had been able to shakingly replace the handset in its holder. The invasion had started and the materials that were so desperately needed were held on the wrong side of the Swiss border - and the premier had made it abundantly clear where the responsibility for this disaster lay.

He took a long draught of cognac from the elegant crystal glass. After this call, he had made a telephone call to his home in Rouen from the vestibule of the Zurichsee and what a catastrophe that had been! He thought that the voice answering the call had been his wife - he tearfully told her what he was contemplating but he hadn't realised, until she started sobbing, that it was his daughter, Juliette. When his wife had taken the receiver from his daughter, she had raged and railed at him and she would not listen to any of his pleading.

So, he returned to his room, known as the Hoffmann suite. This suite was papered in an unusual wall covering, conceived by local artist, Lienhard Hoffmann, with a repeating pattern of green moths at rest, on a beige and brown background. It is rumoured that the moths can be seen flittering their wings if the observer looks too closely or if they have consumed a surfeit of intoxicating substances.

There he extracted the St Etienne revolver from its holster using his right hand and extended his arm towards the light that shafted through the window - he looked down the sight line towards the families promenading alongside the distant, icy blue, shimmering lake. The lake sparkled in an uncommonly beautiful way this spring morning. His bedroom window was framed by long green drapes that languished on the green carpet. He opened the loading gate of the revolver, pulled the catch back with his left thumb and swung it so that the cylinder presented itself for loading. All six chambers were empty. He located cartridges in the pocket of the leather holster on the table and placed one in each chamber. He then swung the cylinder back so it clicked back into the revolver.

He lifted the barrel and inserted it in his mouth - the taste of cordite and gun oil caused him to withdraw the barrel quickly. He looked coldly and calculatingly at this cold and crude weapon - how could he make this more palatable he wondered? That's it, he could wipe it with the old Cognac in the bureau! But he must also make sure there was enough brandy so that he can ease myself into a numbed state. Or would the shock of the bullet's impact jolt him back into this painful reality? He looked at the old revolver. The design had not changed in one hundred years and here we are in 1940, we are still using them to kill. One bullet had to be enough. Yannick had told him that it was a woman's weapon with no stopping power. One bullet had to be enough and it had to be perfectly directed.

He cast his eyes around the suite, with it's grotesquely patterned wallpaper, it's vile, dark-green gilded curtains and mouldy mid-green carpet. Outside, through the window, there was another world and the sun was shining and all the citizens of Zurich were going about their normal, day to day business. The bullet would have to go through his upper palate and through his brain and blood would go everywhere. His room maid would have to scrub the walls clean and that would be impossible with this wall covering. And she was the worst maid he had ever encountered in fifteen years with the French Foreign Ministry.

He drew the hideous green curtains, then walked to the bathroom and opened the door - the enamel steel bath stood proudly in the centre of the marbled floor. This would be better he thought as he stepped into the bath. One bullet had to be enough...

"Bonjour Monsieur, bonjour monsieur, bonjour monsieur, ouvre la porte, sil-vous plait?" It was that infernal maid again.

Chapter Seven

0915 Saturday 10 May 1940 - The Vestibule, Zurichsee Hotel, Zurich

"Bonjour monsieur, ouvre la porte sil-vous plait." Rozenn shouted and hammered on the door.

The door opened slightly and she was through, her eyes were scanning actively around the room. It was too dark, like a mausoleum, so she threw open the curtains with a flourish but she was then transfixed by the wallpaper. Her hands were placed on the wall and she brought her face up to sniffing distance and then pushed out again. There was a moth emerging from a chrysalis and then many moths, unfurling their wings. They flew in circles around each other, each with a human face. Her mind swirled and then she calmed when the pattern was back in focus. "There is something not quite right about this wall covering!" She pushed away again and took a deep breath. "No matter!" she exclaimed.

Now she marched into the bathroom and scoured it with her eyes from top to bottom. The towels that he had strewn on the floor were collected, as was the glass of brandy, and she now returned to confront him.

"It is you!" he accused. "You were at the bank! You were spying!"

"Yes, a maid's duties are never done. But maintenant, what is it that you are doing?" she asked.

"It is none of the business of a maid" Thibault said haughtily. He was staring at her stockinged legs. "Why are you dressed like that?"

She looked down and pulled at the hem of the maid's dress. It barely covered her knees. "This is my uniform. It's a little impractical and a little short for decency, isn't it? But, that is what we maids have to wear to carry out our duties."

"D'accord mademoiselle, but only in a brothel or a bedroom farce!"

"Non, non, non, this is no farce! I need to know what's going on here. I ask out of concern as a fellow citizen of France." She paused and glanced at the photographs on the table and the letter. Before he could move, she had picked up the letter and started reading. "Is that old man Zutter's final word? He is getting himself into more trouble. He needs to decide who's side he is on. Bastard!"

"That is confidential correspondence. Put it down!"

"Non. If it's to do with the defence of France, it is my business. I am a servant of the people." She looked at the photographs. "Your wife is beautiful. Your daughter is adorable. You will go to them now and save them. They are in danger and they need you now. Find your family, make them safe. Make them proud." She strode to the wardrobe and threw the doors open. "Now fill your valise, you must go now!" She found the revolver and the box of bullets and tucked them both in her maid's pocket.

"That is mine" he shouted, and it's no use to you. It is only a woman's weapon!" he exclaimed.

"But I am a woman," she replied, "so that is all right, is it not?"

"Yes, I can see you are a woman, but that weapon will not stop a man!"

"It doesn't matter. I do not need to stop...anyone. I will make threats that will make...him change his mind. That is what I will do! If he does not change his decision, I will threaten to make a lot of holes in him. The holes will be small but if I make enough holes in them, he may be forced to reconsider his position. I will threaten to shoot him so full of holes that he will look like a piece of Swiss cheese. The holes may be small, but there will be many of them. It's his choice. I have enough bullets to make, let me see" she did a quick count, "thirty small holes. That should be enough."

"And what if it isn't enough to make him change his mind?" He finished packing the valise and watched as Rozenn did a sweep through all the rooms of the suite. All was clear.

"If shooting him full of holes doesn't work, I will hit him over the head with it!"

She led Thibault down the ornate stairway to the vestibule of the hotel. "Now go, take the train to Geneva and cross the border en route to France there. I will deal with everything here." Rozenn waited until he had left the hotel in a taxi heading for the Hauptbahnhof. She then skipped across the vestibule to the row of public telephone kiosks, swung her way into the first one and dialled quickly. "Yes, operator, it's a Zurich telephone number, Please put me through to the French consulate. Yes, immediately." She tapped impatiently on the wooden panel of the booth. "Bonjour! I need Monsieur Pascal immediately. Yes, I said immediately!" She thrummed again on the wall of the booth. "Pascal, it is I. Listen very carefully. My pen friend thinks that Whitsuntide is a good time for his Uncle's tour of the Ardennes..."

Pascal garbled a reply. "But Rozenn, the Uncle's tour has already started!"

"Non!" He was trying to get something written down. "The centre for his tour? I think his priority is to take in the towns of Dinant and Sedan and then the coast!"

Pascal muttered a response.

"It is a surprising choice, isn't it? Please pass the message on immediately to the ambassador and then get the limousine and collect me from the Hotel Zurichsee. Yes, now! I don't care if the Minister needs it this morning - I need it now! Maintenant, tout de suite! I will wait for you outside the hotel. Do not let me down. Where are we going? We will go to the Rheinfall for luncheon! That is where old man Zutter will be. Ya, bring a weapon, but do not wait to sign it out. Ya, I have a weapon. No, I will not fire it, I will persuade him to see the error of his ways."

She replaced the telephone, exited the kiosk and dashed downstairs to the basement. She was followed by the house mistress.

"Frau Abgrall, Frau Abgrall. Please stop! What are you doing?"

"I'm leaving. The Nazis are threatening to invade. Have you not seen?"

"You cannot leave, there are formalities we must go through!"

"Dear Frau, take a look at a map. In a few weeks, Switzerland will be surrounded on all sides by the fascists, to the north, to the south, to the east and to the west. Think about what is most important now. The free world is in flames, Switzerland could be next. Then tell me, is it best to pick up a feather duster to join the fight or a gun?" The house mistress stood in shocked silence. "The correct answer is to pick up a gun!" Rozenn opened the wooden door of her dilapidated locker and removed her satchel. "You can forward what I'm owed to the French Consulate, Zurich. They will know who I am." She left the house mistress mouthing a stream of words of little or no consequence.

Outside, Rozenn jumped down the hotel steps, two at a time, to the pavement. She cast around up and down the tree lined avenue - there was no sign of the Minister's limousine. "Zut alors, where are you Pascal?" She paced up and down for five minutes.

Pascal arrived and swung the passenger door open. "We will need to be very quick. The Minister has allowed us use of his limousine but it must be returned tonight. And it must not be damaged. I promised him that I would look after his vehicle."

"Then, I will drive. I am a quick driver."

"No, I will drive. You don't know how to drive. You are a woman."

She cursed Pascal under her breath. "Drive on then. Zutter has a midday meeting in a guest house close to the Rheinfall. There is a rumour that he is meeting with a member of the Nazi Party. It is en route to Schaffhausen."

"Yes, I know it. So what is your plan, Rozenn?"

"I will interrupt his luncheon, threaten him with a gun and persuade him to change his mind. I will then get him to change the letter he sent to the French."

"What if he refuses?"

"I will start shooting, starting with his outer extremities and then working in to his more intimate extremities." She frowned as she tried to comprehend what she had just said. "Pascal, I have a box full of cartridges."

"Do you know how to shoot?"

"But of course - I was the finest shot in my village!"

"With what? A pistol or a rifle?"

There was a long silence. "With a crossbow."

Pascal started to hammer his head on the hub of the steering wheel. The blare of the car's horn could not be heard over his cries of anguish.

Chapter Eight

1125 Saturday 10 May 1940 - The Schaffhauserstrasse

Rozenn surreptitiously lifted her stockinged feet onto the wooden dashboard. A sharp slap to her calf made her quickly withdraw them. Pascal returned to his hunched posture over the steering wheel, his eyes fixed relentlessly on the road ahead. “Talk to me, Pascal!”

Through the window of the motor car, she could see the patchwork of dark forest, red-tiled villages and green pasture leading up to the massif of Tanzboden. A dark, lanky winged bird of prey floated over the closest patch of trees, its wedge-shaped tail twitching, side to side. A plume of a dark cloud rose over the peaks to the East. It seemed to be growing larger and darker. Pascal was still thinking deeply. “There is nothing to say. You have decided on your course of action. It will go badly, I'm telling you, and you will not listen.”

“That is good, Pascal, we are talking but you are still wrong, because you are a stupid man.”

He shrugged and continued his relentless attention to the road ahead. They passed yet another pony and trap, both of them heavily laden. “I will stop here” he muttered as they came to a guest house on the crest of the hill, looking towards the commune of Winterthur, “I need to make a call, wait here Rozenn...”

“I'm coming with you, I need to use the pissoir.”

"That's good Rozenn, but I will find you something much better than a pissoir."

"Oh a bucket! I'm so happy Pascal!"

"No, better than that Rozenn, a bucket in a closet."

"Oh merci mille-fois, Pascal!" She followed him attentively into the guest house. Once she was settled in the closet, he disappeared to the foyer to carry out his business and he was waiting for her, when she emerged. He had a broad smile and a ham-filled loaf, which he tore into two and handed a half share to Rozenn.

Soon, they were back on the road, heading north. "Rozenn, you do realise that old man Zutter will not change his position."

"No, I do not realise this. For all we know, he may have a great respect for the rights of nations and the rule of law and he may have a high regard for the history and culture of 'La Belle France' couldn't he?"

"Non."

"Or he may have finer feelings than we give him credit for, couldn't he?"

"Non."

"So, you do not believe in me Pascal..."

"Of course I believe in you, but I do not think that old man Zutter will bend."

"I see. So, you think nothing can be gained by this? I am wasting my time and yours? I cannot change his mind with threats?"

"Er, non."

"So, what are you thinking? These things our country needs, can we take them ourselves? These things can be saved! But, what are these things, Pascal? Pascal!"

"There are crates at La Chau-de-Fonds, I think...in the sidings."

"Can't we just steal the train?"

"Steal the train? You think we should start a war with la Suisse?"

"But they do not need to know who took them?"

"Not a good idea Rozenn..."

"Why not?"

"Not a good idea..."

"So, we go to Zutter..."

"Also not a good idea."

They motored down the Schaffhauserstrasse until the roar of the Rheinfall could be heard. The Alpine Guest House was in sight to the right, standing on a knoll overlooking the valley. Pascal parked the limousine directly outside. "Have you reconsidered your plan? Should I come in with you?"

"You will wait here and keep the engine running. When I get out, you we will need to make a fast journey to Basel. I will make my way across the border there."

"This is not a very good plan."

"You are right Pascal, this is not a very good plan. But what else can I do? We will soon be in a fight for survival! And I made a promise!"

Yes, she had sworn an oath, but not to any person in the French hierarchy.

"You must not shoot him. We are not at war with the Swiss. Have you considered any alternatives?

"Of course, I could ask him to... meet with our highest political and military leaders?"

"Hmm, yes you could but Zutter would just laugh at you. He holds all the cards in this game."

Her brow creased into a frown. "Why is he meeting with the Nazis anyway? What does he plan to do? What possible interests can they have in common? Unless, unless..."

"It must be to do with money or power. Everything is to do with money or power these days."

"Or sex" she added.

"How can it be about sex? Do you think they are getting into bed with each other?" asked Pascal.

"Yes, that is what I think. I think Zutter will hand Switzerland to the Nazis on a plate. They are not getting into bed with each other but I see that Zutter has been mounted like a bitch by a big, fat Nazi dog."

"You have such a way with words, Rozenn."

She sat in the passenger seat considering the enormity of the task and the danger of what she was about to do. There was no alternative that worked. Just to make matters worse, she was still wearing a maid's outfit that was a little too short for decency. However, she must stay focused on the task and quell the agitation that was niggling her core.

"Pascal, I am going inside. Wish me bonne chance." She got out of the vehicle, tucking the revolver beneath her raincoat.

"Bonne chance Rozenn. But you do realise that old man Zutter will be very upset. He will have heard about what happened at the bank today."

"Do you think so? But all I did was make a suggestion?"

"You must never start a run on a bank. It is irresponsible! But if it does start, the people have no option. The people have to get their money out! You must have money to live!" hissed Pascal.

"I know that" Rozenn replied, "but I cannot be held responsible for the stupidity of people. Pascal, just be ready for me!"

She turned to leave.

"What did you do to his son, Rozenn?"

She turned about. "What have you heard?"

"I heard...he was injured in a fight...with you!"

Rozenn nodded to Pascal. She could hear the roar of the waterfall and feel the plume of spray blooming up from the river. "C'est vrai, but it was a mere bagatelle."

"A game of balls?"

"Exactly!"

She quickly made her way to the guest house and entered through a side door. In one part of her mind she was troubled by the fact that she could no longer hear the engine of the limousine running. Pascal must have stopped it for some reason.

Chapter Nine

1130 Saturday 10 May 1940 - The Alpine Guest House, Rheinfall

Rozenn walked slowly into the black-panelled hallway. The whole of the fabric of the building oozed with the smell of fried food and cigarette smoke. To her right, a rank of photographs of prize dogs led to a large, heavy oak-panelled door and beyond she could hear a family of voices and the clatter of cutlery on porcelain plates: to her left, the passage led to two large, black dogs sleeping on the floor. Doberman pinschers! She stepped carefully over the sleeping dogs, turned a corner and followed the steps upwards until she reached another closed room. She held her breath and listened at the door. There were just two voices conversing and the smell of cigar smoke. She pushed open the door slowly and there was Zutter in a white shirt at one side of the long table and a man in a brown shirt opposite him.

"Ah, at last, the maid. Refill these, will you" ordered the brown-shirted man.

"I'm not here to serve you, I only serve the Republic of France!"

"Nonsense! I call for the maid, you arrive in the uniform of a maid, what am I to think?"

"Herr Zutter, I need to speak with you urgently on a matter of national importance."

"Beer IS of national importance" guffawed the man in brown. His face was ruddy and beaded with drops of sweat. He banged his beer stein three times against the table.

"This is of more importance than beer, Zutter" she walked across the room so she was opposite him and he could not avoid looking at her. The brown-shirted man twisted round and stared at her, his eyes bulging like a toad's.

"Get out maid, this is a private meeting" snapped Zutter in reply.

She pulled her coat up so that the revolver was visible. "Does this change your priorities, Zutter?" she asked. The large, perspiring man in brown bobbed down from his chair and clumsily hid under the table. His panicky breathing nullified the security of his hiding place.

"Ach, put the pistol down you foolish girl, then state your business" Zutter muttered. The muscles around his mouth jarred when he spoke - there was no spare flesh on his face. His collar was firmly pressed and his neck tie tightly knotted.

"You must change this order, Herr Zutter" she said as the letter of the Bank of Zutter was slid along the table until it was in front of him. Rozenn stepped back a pace and levelled the weapon at his chest. "Do it now!" The man dressed all in brown was still quivering below the table.

"Nein! I do not feel inclined to do that." He got up slowly, folded his arms defiantly and stepped around the table towards her. "So what are you going to do now, girl?"

She tracked him unsteadily with the gun and her trigger finger tightened - how much pressure does it take to fire it?

"What are you going to do now, maid?"

His insidious smile quickly undermined her resolve. So what did he know that she didn't? The muted growling of the dogs downstairs didn't help her confidence either. She grasped the revolver with her left hand and lifted it towards his head but she couldn't hold it level. It wavered up and down, in her hand, all of its own accord. He smiled and approached even closer so he could examine her, bobbing first to her left and then to her right.

"I will fill you full of holes Zutter, if you get any closer!"

"No, you will won't. And let me explain to you why. You have been sent to do a man's job, but you are not even a woman, you are a girl!"

"But I have...a weapon!"

"Ja, indeed you do, but you don't know how to use it, do you mädchen?"

"I do! Of course I do. I just pull the trigger!"

"Ach, I see, I see, but before you do anything foolish, please take into account that I have a colleague of yours in my care, and..."

"A colleague? Never, never, never!" she said with more bravado than was actually warranted.

"She says she is your colleague. That is all you need to know. Not a very intelligent colleague, I must say. My wife is...having to attend to her."

"If you harm her..."

"You'll do what?"

"I'll put holes in you!"

"And what do you imagine will happen to Gabrielle?"

"Gabrielle!" Rozenn gasped.

"And you seem to believe that you have all your countrymen behind you."

"But I do!"

"Ah, but you don't. You seem to believe that Joubert is your friend. He is not, he is my...agent."

"Zut alors!" Her arms slumped to her sides.

"But you are an interesting specimen" he whispered in her ear, "I want you in my collection, mädchen." He was holding her right hand firmly and gently stroking the fingers of her left hand.

Her arms tightened and a tingling rushed up her neck and across her scalp. "Listen to me Zutter, there is something wrong..."

"Really?"

"With you..." she added. Something in his breath, the taint of rot. Downstairs, again she heard the growling of dogs.

"Are you sure?" he said mockingly.

"I feel it, through your skin, through your breath..."

"Stop! Say no more!"

"Your coil is damaged, there is a...trickle of madness running through you all." And now the stairs were creaking.

"Shut her up! Shut her up!" Zutter's hands were over his ears.

She was conscious of a presence behind her. Rozenn knew who it must be. "It's you Pascal, thank the Gods!" Pascal's hands grasped her wrist and pulled her arm down gently onto the table. The revolver spiralled lazily across the table and then onto the floor. "Pascal, what are you doing?"

The man in the brown shirt emerged from under the table with the pistol in his hand and directed at Rozenn. "The safety lever was on" he said, "it isn't now!" he said triumphantly. He nodded at Zutter. Zutter nodded back.

Pascal tried to sooth her. "I'm stopping you committing an act of murder!I'm stopping you getting yourself killed!"

"Let the woman go, Joubert!" shouted Zutter.

Pascal complied.

"This will stop now." There was a silvered case in his hand, large enough to encase a long cigar. The brown-shirted man brandished the revolver, not sure where to direct it. Then he settled on the middle of Rozenn's forehead. She gasped at the cold metal screwing into her skin.

Zutter seized Rozenn's left arm and twisted, so her fingers splayed out on the polished table. Her index finger was swallowed up. She jerked her arm back but it stopped abruptly. A sharp snap! She pulled again, her hand was free, but there was something wrong. A pulse of pain shot up her arm. What was the matter with her finger?

"Bastard" Pascal shouted, "you utter bastard, Zutter!"

She shook her arm but it didn't shake away the numbness. She tried to bite back her tears but they streamed down her face.

Zutter pushed her away. "Get rid of her, before I set the dogs on her. The dogs are trained to bite and not let go."

Pascal kicked the table. It slammed against the brown-shirted man's gut. His eyes rolled upwards as he fell to the floor. Zutter clutched the silver case tightly to his chest.

Pascal held a chair in one hand: his other hand pulled at Rozenn's arm and tugged her out of the room. They staggered part of the way down the stairs, the chair clattering against each step, Rozenn's right arm wrapped in her coat. She turned and waved her good arm at Zutter and the German. "This isn't over Zutter! You will sign!"

"Rozenn, Rozenn! Dogs!" shouted Pascal. The pinschers snarled and scrambled to their feet. They bounded up the stairs. He tried to keep them at bay with the chair but the powerful snapping of their jaws threatened the chair legs. The dogs, snarling and snapping, sprang upon them. Rozenn rolled down the stairs with the first hound. She pushed her coat in its mouth. The other hound seized Pascal's right arm. He shook it free. It attacked again. Pascal kicked open the door, leading out, out into the bright sunshine. He pulled open the rear door of the car and pushed Rozenn onto the back seat. She was crying. Blood was smeared on her coat - her blood.

"What happened to your finger?" asked Pascal, suddenly alarmed.

She looked up at him tearfully. "I don't know! That bastard Zutter broke it! I cannot feel it anymore!"

"Keep it wrapped. I'll take you to a hospital where they deal with such injuries." He ran to the front of the car and swung on the starting handle. Nothing happened. He swung again. A cough from the engine this time. He stopped to draw breath. A scampering of feet and then a set of jaws clamped onto his legs. Canines struck into his shin and molars into his calf muscles. Rozenn got out of the car, directed her eyes at the dogs and made a shrill, three note nasal whistle. Their jaws released and they scrambled onto their back legs and waited for her next command. She dismissed them with the command of "Aus! Aus! Aus!" and they raced away to the rear of the building.

Rozenn scrambled into the front of the car. The engine was running but Pascal was whining like a hound, rubbing his shredded legs. His bloodied hands were now on the steering wheel and the limousine was pulling away from the Rheinfall, so painfully slowly.

Chapter Ten

1655 Saturday 10 May 1940 - The Monastery above Alten

"Pascal, did you betray me?" asked Rozenn as she jabbed him sharply in the ribs with her good hand. They had made good time motoring due south and then to the west, keeping the valley of the Rhein to their right. They were now heading up a valley that was being squeezed by forested hills to one side and mountainous crags to the other.

"I saved you Rozenn, you could have been killed!"

"Really Pascal? Who by? You?"

"No, no, no. By the German, or by Zutter."

"Ah, I see. Who was that German?"

"A Nazi..."

"Yes, I thought he must be. He looked just like how I would imagine a Nazi to look - fat and ugly with a big, square head."

"Rozenn, you should not put everyone you encounter into a pigeon hole."

"Ah, I understand you. However, I will need to put the Nazi in a hole for big, bastard swines. You see, it is helpful to me to put people in boxes. Then, I know how to deal with them."

Pascal just sighed. There was a silhouette of a large, long-winged bird of prey following them, flapping slowly and buoyantly, adjusting its height and position with twisted tail. They would out pace it as they climbed up the valley of the Aare.

Rozenn studied his face. He seemed more at ease now then he had been at the Rheinfall guest house. Or at least this is what she discerned, while staring intently at the reduced twitches of his ear lobe. "I feel I should warn you Pascal, I have also put you in a pigeon hole..."

"A pigeon hole?"

"Ya, it is the one for treacherous pig-dog bastards."

"I understand why, but please let me explain..."

"It's too late." She squeezed the rolled up raincoat containing her arm to her stomach but the sharp pain and the numbness were still there. "But where is this hospital, Pascal?"

Pascal stopped for directions in a town perched on an outcrop of rock that overlooked a fast flowing river. The man giving the directions was dressed so elaborately that he must be an important dignitary. Now the limousine crawled slowly up the track to the mount above Olten and then it coughed and spluttered into a crunching halt. Rozenn could not imagine how a hospital could be located in this beautiful but lonely location. "Pascal, why are you taking me to this place?" coughed Rozenn. "Take me to a hospital. They do have those in this country, don't they?"

"It is close by. It has to be. It's a special place where they will look after you properly. They will keep you safe. They will make you better." He secured the hand brake lever tight. "Now show me your hand." He unravelled her blood streaked coat and examined her left hand. "Where is your finger?"

"It must be here..." She flapped the coat like a sheet. There was no finger. They scrabbled across the floor of the car, under the car seats at the front and back. "It must be here! Unless Zutter's dogs swallowed it...as if it were a sausage?"

"But Rozenn, it's gone! It's not broken, it's been cut off!" He looked again around the floor of the car and in the folds of her coat. "It's gone! Zut alors Rozenn! Zutter has cut it off!"

Pascal encouraged Rozenn out of the automobile and wrapped his arm under her arm and assisted her as they staggered together up the track, pausing every few steps as she took deep breaths to prevent her falling in a swoon.

The hill was like the crest of a wave, with limestone cliffs tumbling below. The track veered to the North and they were flanked by the escarpment to their left and pine forest to the right. The first sign of human activity was a low, limestone wall and a clearing of low tree stumps. Across the clearing, the pine trees closed in again. In the trees, there was an old impractical looking building, surrounded by trees. In front of the building, there was a figure cowled in a long pale grey gown. As Rozenn and Pascal approached they could see below the cowl a young woman. Her hair was flaxen and her skin was pale skin, her lips very red. She greeted them, her arms folded, stern, unwelcoming. “Herr Joubert, who have you there?”

“She calls herself Rozenn, she’s lost a finger. She needs your help.”

“Do you still have it?” said the woman.

“Non” replied Rozenn through clenched teeth, “but I will get it back, somehow, someway!”

“You do realise where you are?” said the woman to Pascal.

“I’m not sure. I was given directions to here from an old man in Aarau. I think he was the mayor. He was very helpful.”

“Leave her with us. You must depart now.”

“But, but...”

“Leave us now. You cannot remain here. We will attend to the girl and release her in a few days. We will register her to the hospice and make her comfortable.” The woman examined Rozenn’s hand. “Is she Wiccan?”

“No, I don’t think so. What I do know though, is that she’s of Breton descent.”

“So, she is Gallic. Not of the wise then.”

“No, she’s definitely not of the wise.”

“Pascal, Pascal, do not leave me here! Please do not leave me here!” pleaded Rozenn.

“I will leave you now. When can I...” said Pascal.

“She will be well in a few days. We will bring her to the town of Basel and hand her over to the French prefecture.”

As he embraced Rozenn she whispered urgently in his ear, “Pascal! Pascal! Do not leave me here with these people! Do not leave me! Please, I beg of you! Zutter is here!”

"I must leave you now Rozenn, the battle has started. I will make sure that an official is expecting you in Basel. You are in good hands." He hung her satchel around her neck.

She pulled at his arm. "Pascal, if you must leave me, remember to find Beladora!"

"Beladora?"

"Oui, Beladora, ma bicyclette! Bring it with you to Basel! I will need Beladora in my pursuit of Christoph!"

"If I must..."

"Yes, you must! And you must rescue Gabrielle! She is a captive!"

"D'accord, Rozenn. Bonne chance, Rozenn. I'll see you in a few days."

Rozenn was taken firmly by her left arm and escorted through the trees, into the darkness.

Chapter Eleven

1705 Saturday 10 May 1940 - The Sanatorium

"Rozenn, my name is Ilse. I will look after you." Her face was perfect like porcelain. She had grey glazed eyes and red lips that looked like they were painted on. It was growing dark and Rozenn could not see her way through the wall of trees. Ilse glided quickly between the trees until they came to a tall, arched gateway, grown through with climbing plants. They edged through the gap in the gate and walked up a path that curled steeply to the left. They were confronted by a wall of limestone, but built into this, was a low, white walled building with a steep, red-tiled roof with two tall chimneys. The buckled stucco of the walls bulged out and the red tiles buckled up and down on the roof. She was led into a hallway that was protected by a solid wooden door with no lock that she could see. The walls of the hallway were punctuated by small, square windows that led to another doorway. Through this doorway she arrived in a large, empty high-vaulted room, lit by candles but filled with the overpowering smell of charred wood.

In the center of the room was a stone platform. Embedded in the platform were shackles. Rozenn was told to mount the platform but she refused. Perspiration was emerging all over and her clothes suddenly felt clammy against her skin.

Four people entered the room behind her. Her limbs were seized and she was lifted and spread out on the slab. There were four loud clicks and Rozenn was shackled tight.

Now she could the newcomer's voices, all female. *"Sie est eine faszinierende frau..."* Cold, unfeeling fingers pulled her hair back and traversed her nose, her forehead, her cheeks and her lips. *"Sie hat starke schultern."* And then cold metal points pressed into her face, her temple and her forehead. Her left arm was raised.

"Es ist ein sauberer schnitt..."

"Das ist gut."

"So. Colour of eyes?"

"Blue. No, brown. Wait, they are now... green. No, grey-brown..."

There were mutterings around the table.

"Ach, they are... changeable!"

"Nein!"

"Ja! Now, browny-blue, now bluey-brown..."

"Not possible. Look her straight in the eyes..."

The nun with the register stepped back suddenly. "Nein, nein, nein, she's looking right into my soul!"

"Let me do it!"

"Ach, shine a light into her eyes..."

After a long period of contemplation, a decision was reached.

"Make the entry as so, 'Eye colour: Indeterminate'"

"Das ist gut."

Rozenn sensed that a man had entered the room and he was being greeted with much deference. She strained her neck to get a look at him but the cold hands pressed against her face prevented it. But she knew the voice and the timbre of his voice made her stomach churn.

"Celt?" was the question he asked. The answer given was not certain.

Rozenn strained against the shackles. Dimensions were taken about her head with cold tipped callipers and the results were called out to a nun swishing the pages of an old almanac. Rozenn decided it must be old, as a puff of motes emerged each time a page was swished over.

"Scythian?"

"Romani?"

"Jewess?"

In each case, the answer given was "Indeterminate".

"Cagot?"

"Nein, nein, nein, see the breadth of the forehead, the strong nose and chin, the gracile limbs..."

"Ah, Brit-anni?" The swishing had stopped.

"Ah, Brit-anni - sehr gut!"

A little shudder emerged from her core and fluttered it's way through her extremities. "Non! Non! Non!"

"So, she is hexe..."

"Hexe!"

"Ahhhhh"

"We will cauterise this wound. No need for further amputation" said Ilse. Rozenn gave a shudder in agreement. This was the signal for a pungent smelling cloth to be placed over her nose and mouth. The suffocating smell made her sleepy but the searing smell of hot metal and the hissing sound of a hot implement brought her back into a taut-eyed panic. Rozenn shrieked as pain seared through her half finger.

"We should mark her" said a woman, whose hair was swept back so severely that her facial muscles could not express any emotion, "as hexe."

Rozenn shook her head vigorously.

"The edict is clear - she must be marked!"

"Ja. Pass the tool."

Rozenn saw a brilliantly glowing and sparking tool coming towards her - she clenched her eyes closed, readying herself for the searing pain that must surely come.

"Now we mark her!"

As a witch? "Non, non, non!"

The shackles were released but she was still held tight and a disinfected hand smothered her mouth. She was face down and a burning pain seared through her left shoulder. Rozenn shrieked in fear - they were killing her!

"Do not cry? Be pleased! You know what you are now and everyone else can see!"

Her right leg was pulled taut and a searing pain stabbed through the sole of her foot. Her throat had exhausted all means to scream. Her body was turned over and her clothes pulled apart. A searing pain stabbed into her core. She coughed on the smell of burned flesh, like the acrid sourness of burnt hog skin. Rozenn swooned into a troubled nightmare, that would never leave her.

CHAPTER TWELVE

0755 Thursday 15 May 1940 - The two-wheeled trap

The two-wheel trap, pulled steadily by a docile, long-eared, grey-brown beast, trundled down the track. Rozenn gazed over the tall spires of the town that stood at the confluence of the two rivers below and her eyes followed the outline of the sharp, green hills above. The air was beautifully fresh and invigorating, and along with the musk of the mule, it started to drive out the taint of burning and disinfection that had lain trapped in her sinuses for days.

The grey cowled girl next to her on the seat, cajoled the mule with the reins, and kept her eyes fixed on the road ahead. Rozenn was burning inside with the need to talk.

"May I ask what you call yourself?" said Rozenn. The girl did not even return a glance and just gave a slight shake of her head. "Please, don't be shy. I call myself Rozenn. What do you call yourself?"

They made their way through a hamlet of red-tiled dwellings but there was no one Rozenn could call out to. "What is the name of this village? It is very pretty." There was no answer, just a mute silence. "Oh, this village has no name? That is very sad, very sad indeed. It's a wonder they receive any post here!"

They clip-clopped their way through the village without stopping. "I will call you...Rahel. Yes, Rahel. Would you like to know why, Rahel? No? Oh, I see, you have been given orders not to speak to me and so you will follow these orders, like a little sheep. Well, I think that you are a little sheep. Baah, baah, baah, baaaaah. There now, am I speaking your language now? Yes?" There was still no reaction, but the fists of the girl seemed to clutch the reins a little more tightly and her frown of concentration deepened.

"Rahel, how much longer will you put me through this nonsense? Until we arrive at our destination? Oh, you don't know our destination? You don't know anything? You are just a little sheep, I understand." Rozenn turned to look back at the way they had travelled. From the position of the sun in the sky and the scent of the just warmed air, she reckoned it was mid-morning. In the back of the trap there were several wooden barrels. From the way that they jiggled, and the knocking sound they made when they jiggled, they were not empty.

"Rahel, what time do you think we will reach our...destination?" asked Rozenn. "Oh, I see. You don't know, so you can't tell me. That isn't very helpful, is it? I have an important rendezvous..." This time the girl looked at Rozenn and shook her head, with a deep frown creasing her forehead.

The joint on Rozenn's hand, where her index finger used to be, was smooth and blackened and did not look human any more, but it itched, like her insides itched. The wounds on her left shoulder, over her core and the sole of her right foot still hurt despite the thick poultices that had been strapped over them. Walking was possible but only with a slight limp.

Rozenn cursed Pascal and cursed the women of the nunnery. "Why did you do this to me? Why? You say you are Christians? What order of nuns are you? The order of sadists and torturers?" she said accusingly. "Who is your leader? Is it the Bishop of Basel, or is it the Pope, or is it Satan? I will write a letter to your pope! You will be in such trouble when my letter is received. He will read it and...and...he will lead a crusade, with all his cardinals, and they will stop what you are doing! You have no right, no authority under the sun to do what you are doing. You scheming bitches! He will come for you with an army of minions and wipe out your little nest of vipers, he will clean you out, finish you so that you are barely a memory of the evil that you have done here!"

There was no reply and no motion of recognition.

"Are you listening to me, Rahel?"

The girl fixed her eyes on the road ahead. She was a young woman under the cowl, barely out of her teenage years.

Rozenn tried again. *"Bitte sagen Sie mir, wer du bist? Nein? Was nennst du dich?"* Still nothing. There was a slight watering of the girl's eyes, but that was all.

Two long hours had now passed, and Rozenn amused herself by singing an interminably long rhyme, suitable only for infants, about a bridge over a river. It was now that the girl pushed a paper wrapped package across the seat to Rozenn. When she opened it there was a green apple and half a baguette containing a slice of cheese. Rozenn sniffed at the cheese to check it's ripeness and made great play of eating it with excess gusto. She checked her companion frequently. Still no reaction. Rozenn dusted the breadcrumbs over onto her companion's robe. Still nothing.

"You think I will not write to the Pope, don't you?" After counting how many larks were singing between the next two villages (at least twenty), she became restive again. "I am on first name terms with your Pope. I think his name is Giuseppe? Yes, I think that's it. I will write to Giuseppe, care of the Vatican, Italy. Then we shall see."

The girl hunched even more over the reins and encouraged the mule again.

"Or is it Pius? It could be Pius, could it not? I will write to Pius the Pope, the same address as before. Then we will see."

After a particularly rough passage through an orchard, Rozenn cracked. "You must talk to me, Rahel!"

The girl turned her head to Rozenn, opened her mouth wide and pointed. She had no tongue, just a stump.

Rozenn stared back at the track that wound ahead. What was causing that slopping and slushing sound in the barrels? The sourness of vinegar overwhelmed her sense of smell. And then she gulped - it was a long and hard gulp which made her gasp desperately for breath. Was it the jiggling of the soft and fleshy, the pickled parts of people, the human waste of the nunnery hospital?

Rozenn considered jumping off the trap and running but running was not the best option, with her barely healed foot. She would wait until they were close to the border with France and then she would make her apologies and depart.

Chapter Thirteen

1210 Thursday 15 May 1940 - The crossing into Weil am Rhein

"So Rahel, is this the crossing we need, the crossing over the Rhein? Do we need to cross here?" shouted Rozenn. The cart clattered its way to the bridge, but she wasn't sure it was the right bridge, because this crossing was guarded.

There was a newly built roadblock in the middle of the bridge, made of discarded wooden furniture, patrolled by guards in brown uniforms and brown kappes. They seemed relaxed but intent on smoking tobacco and drinking from their metal canteens. Rozenn's stomach was churning, partly through hunger but mainly through fear. She rummaged inside her vestments until she found her passe-partout and held it ready. Both she and Rahel were beckoned to step down from the trap.

"Frau, mädchen, what is your business in Germany?" asked the corporal. He appeared to be in charge of the border guard. Rozenn looked to the girl but she seemed frozen still in her muteness and in her fear.

"Herr Captain, we are nuns from Switzerland. We have come to Lorrach to procure German sausage for the nunnery." This seemed to prompt much jollity amongst the Germans. Rozenn continued regardless. "We hear that in this part of Germany can be had the finest German sausage in the land!" The corporal turned to his compatriots and thrust out his pelvis towards Rozenn and repeatedly pointed to where his fly buttons were located.

"Non, non, Herr Captain, we need German sausage for the nunnery" said Rozenn as she mimed eating a sausage, "and the nuns are much hungrier than that!"

This prompted even more back-slapping and laughter. Rozenn offered her papers but they were dismissed with a wave. As Rozenn climbed back aboard the trap, she received a hearty slap on her backside. She nestled carefully back into the seat and collected the reins. "Allez, allez" she cried and the mule pulled forward. The mule received a smack on the backside from a guard to accelerate it on its way.

As the mule and trap clip-clopped across the cobbled street they came to a long building with a commotion of people passing inside and outside. They were carrying barrels and boxes - the building was being emptied into a row of carts, with stocky horses waiting patiently at each cart. She approached the first horse and tempted him with an apple. The long-legged, black and white beast was uncertain. Rozenn took a bite and held it for the horse to bite. The black and white beast ate the rest. "What is happening here? Where are you all going?" she asked the drayman.

"Have you not heard? The big battle has started. Where have you been?"

"Schweiz!" she indicated with her arm. Her glance behind, and the warmth of the sun, suggested that the day was now already half way through. She would have to get away quickly. Rahel took the reins and manoeuvred the mule and trap to a set of tall, battered wooden doors that were wedged open. A thickset man in a black cap acknowledged her, swung down the gate at the back of the trap, climbed aboard and threw the barrels down to a lad who caught them with accomplished ease and rolled them into the yard behind the gates. Barrels which must be full, judging by the huge effort needed by the lad to lift them, were heaved onto the back of the trap. Rahel handed over a bag containing coins. These were tipped into a weighing pan and were accepted with a curt nod by the black-capped man. It was time to return.

The man pulled the mule round and slapped its flanks. "Be off with you" he barked as they made their clip-clopping way back to the bridge. Rozenn heaved a barrel so it sat next to Rahel on the seat and they waved back at the guards on the bridge as they passed across.

Rozenn wiped her brow. "This is far enough, Rahel, I will make my own way from here." She reached up and patted the top of the girl's hand. "And take care." Rozenn stepped warily around the parapet of the bridge and descended to the river-side. It was surging its way westward. There was little river traffic, other than two seagoing barges, heading with the flow towards the sea. She climbed up the pier and reached a walkway under the bridge. Then walking quickly, she returned to the German side of the river. There were voices above. They were talking about their next meal, soup and bread. She climbed up the bank and sorted through her papers. If she was stopped by the guards, she should be able to bluff her way out of trouble.

Rozenn walked along the streets, keeping to the shadows on the south side. She found the house she was looking for - above the solid, imposing wooden door there was a nameplate attached to the wooden lintel. The family name of 'de Bourcard' had been overwritten with the name 'Burckhardt'. Rozenn knocked urgently on the door. There was no response. A face appeared at the upper floor window and then quickly disappeared behind closed shutters. There were three storeys to this building even though her friend, Christoph, always pleaded that his family were poor. If that was true, my friend Christoph, you really don't know the meaning of being poor. She knocked again, this time for much longer and much louder. Her left hand was hidden away, still throbbing with pain.

The door was opened by a young frau. "Rozenn, is it you? What are you doing here? Don't you know we are at war with you?"

"I know this. I need to get to Christoph urgently and I need to collect my belongings. You must help me."

"Mother is out at the back. You will need to be quick. Follow me. Mother! It is Rozenn!"

Rozenn followed and there in the backyard was a short, solidly built lady, violently beating a row of eiderdowns, slung over a line. Her white hair peeked out from a green scarf, knotted below her chin. She turned to glare at Rozenn, with the broom pointed threateningly at her. "Madam de Bourcard, it is I, Rozenn Abgrall, you have something for me!"

"Get out of my home, you harlot!" She lifted the broom and pointed it threateningly at Rozenn.

"We need to talk about Christoph, and I need to collect...certain things, and then I'll go. Put down the broom, Madam!"

"Do not order me. Get out of my house!"

"Put down the broom Madam de Bourcard" Rozenn said more firmly, "and help me."

The broom handle was now being prodded at Rozenn's stomach. She wrenched it out of the madam's hands and snapped it over her knee. The two pieces clattered on the ground.

For a moment, Madam de Bourcard seemed incapable of reaction. Then she shouted "Magda, go and fetch a policeman, now!"

"Mama, please, listen to what Rozenn has to say. She knows what is happening to Christoph!"

"How can she know?" She was examining the strange garb that Rozenn was wearing and the strange way she was carrying it. "Have you joined a nunnery?"

"Not exactly" answered Rozenn.

"I think Rozenn knows... because they are in love" said Magda with her hand shielding what she had said from Rozenn.

But Rozenn had heard and she quickly interjected. "Non, non, non. Christoph and I are good friends. We communicate by letter, sometimes. However, as he is my...best friend, we know each other in much detail. I know how his mind works, I know what he is thinking, I know his moods and I know how to...calm his moods."

Madam de Bourcard slumped sobbing to the ground. "He is a soldier, he can't be thinking of you! It could cost him his life!"

"Ah, I'm sorry. That was indelicate of me, but we need to talk... about your son."

"Shall I fetch a policeman?" Magda asked.

"Non"said Rozenn, "put the kettle on the stove, Magda, and boil the water, then make the coffee." Magda left the yard and headed back into the house.

"Please Madam Abgrall, tell me what you know about Christoph. He said very little in his latest letter."

"Ah, please call me mademoiselle, not madam. But sons, they are all unthinking bastards. They leave home and they think that is the end of their responsibilities!"

"He is no bastard! He is my oldest! How would you know, anyway? You are not a mother!" She was staring at Rozenn's clothes again.

"That is true, but I know of men, and I especially know of young men, and I know of Christoph!"

Madam de Bourcard snorted "Then tell me about Christoph!"

"I can't tell you everything, it would put you in danger. There is so much that is secret. I will tell you what I can. What is Magda doing? Is she making coffee? Do you have a cigarette?"

"No, I do not! Women should not smoke tobacco. It's demeaning and unladylike."

"I understand. Then I will smoke alone and I will, of course, be discrete" said Rozenn and then she realised that the scowl meant that this would have to be done outside in the yard, if she could find any tobacco. "I will see how Magda is getting on." She settled Madam de Bourcard on the white-painted window seat and went inside to check on Magda.

The kettle was boiling. Magda prepared a pot with grounds of something that had been roasted, but probably not as coffee, if the aroma was anything to go by. "Are you and Christoph lovers?" Magda asked suddenly as she poured hot water into the coffee pot.

"Absolutely not, but we are...deeply involved with each other. So, we have a relationship as if we were a...brother and a sister. Ya, like a brother and sister." Magda looked disbelievingly at her. "He is the brother and I..."

"Yes, yes, yes, but have you been...intimate with Christoph?"

"Oh, no! But we do share...intimate secrets with each other."

"Oh Rozenn, but how?"

"How? We talk when we meet and we write letters to each other... when we are apart. And Christoph has written to me...secret letters."

"Love letters?"

"Non, non, non! Absolutely not. They are letters to do with...our personal dealings together."

"Please, show me his letters!"

"Non, non, they are far too intimate!"

"Oh, Rozenn!" Magda took a tray and placed it on the kitchen table and went to fetch her mother. Madam de Bourcard sat down at the table dabbing the tear stains trailing down her cheeks with a handkerchief. Rozenn sat opposite and Magda sat at the head of the table. She seemed to have taken on the role of interpreter.

Rozenn started her explanation. "Your son Christoph, he knows me quite intimately, but he has taken me to the heights of...difficulty."

"Pleasure" said Magda as an aside to her mother.

Rozenn frowned at Magda and then put on her clipped, reassuring smile for the benefit of all. "He leaves me fuming with anger sometimes, because he does things without thinking about the consequences first."

Magda gasped. "No! Has he?"

"Has he what?"

"Has he had...relations with you?"

"Yes, I told you! We are like brother and sister together."

"Mother! Did you hear that!"

"You harlot!"

"I am not a harlot! I am..."

"Show me his letters!"

"Non! They are far too intimate!"

"Show me!"

"Non!" Rozenn's nose wrinkled. She realised that Magda was more worldly-wise than the golden locks of hair tied in a bow, or her ruddy cheeks indicated. Now Rozenn's forehead creased in thought. "I cannot show you the letters, as I don't have them. I have spent my last few days in a nunnery and...there, that is it."

'You...you must...tell me the truth!" shouted Madam de Bourcard.

"Ah, I can see... there will be a problem." Rozenn furrowed her brow while she considered what to say next. A little lie was needed.

"Well?"

"Aha, you did not realise that Christoph and I are lovers? Well, we are. But it's difficult as we are so far apart, and now we are divided by the conflict. It's been so many weeks since we lay together, and I can't bear it!"

"Oh, Rozenn, I'm so sorry!" said Magda.

Rozenn wondered how much did Magda know? "Christoph, he took me to the heights of pleasure, then he left me! He left me purring, like a contented cat in front of the fire! He is such a fine lover - you should be very proud of him, Madam de Bourcard!"

"Oh, Christoph, how could you?" wailed Madam de Bourcard.

"And now I need to find him, otherwise I will die!"

"Magda, find his last letter, quickly girl!" Magda scurried to the front parlour and returned, brandishing a hand written letter, in a pattern that Rozenn recognised immediately.

Rozenn scanned through it quickly and inhaled its musk deep into her lungs and then she coughed. It was Christoph's handwriting and his powerful scent! She held it tightly to her chest. "So, he is on his way to the sea, with his comrades!" With his comrades, the Boche, but that did not matter, he was living and he must have been thinking of her when he had committed his pen to the paper. He was alive! And living in her world! Her heart beat to a quicker, more excited rhythm. But now, she wondered, what else can this letter tell me? She recalled their splashing together in the mighty, swirling river, the eddies that could swallow you into their counter-clockwise winding and then make you disappear below into its over-powering embrace. She slumped back as a heavy blanket of foreboding enveloped her - she could see Christoph looking westward, over the dark grey sea and he would be lost to her, in the cold and the dark, alone.

"Rozenn! Rozenn! What is it?"

"I will have to find him, and save him."

"Find him? But how Rozenn?" Magda stood up. "I know, I know, by following the mighty River Rhein all the way to the sea! You will be a river sprite Rozenn, that is the only way to find Christoph!"

Really, thought Rozenn, this ingénue, Magda, knew of romantic things and the totally impractical, but not of practical things. Magda could not see that there were complications arising from the invasion of France.

Magda patted Madam de Bourcard on the shoulder and then followed Rozenn out into the narrow, walled garden at the back of the building. "Are you a witch, Rozenn?"

"All women can be witches, Magda, if we choose to be. We can express ourselves as a witch in very different ways. So, in the spectrum of witches, you can think of me as at the red end of the spectrum; your mother is probably at the other end. All women use their craft to get men to do what we want them to do. You need to understand that it is the womenfolk that make the world go round. Without women, it would be a very different world. The world is going through a bad time now. There are men in charge that do not have a women to guide them. That is why the world is in such a mess. Do you understand, Magda?"

"No, I don't. Leaders and governments decide. We have no say in what they decide to do."

"Ah, but Magda, do you know anything about how the world works? I do. I see in intimate detail how it works. The menfolk and their courtesans are in charge in France. That is why we are in so much trouble." So much trouble, thought Rozenn.

Magda just stared at Rozenn as she took out a cigarette from the pewter case, casually lit it with a match and inhaled deeply.

"Does that burn your mouth?"

"Non, it doesn't. If it did, I would have to stop."

"Can I try?" asked Magda.

"Non, I'm already in trouble with your mother, and if your lips got burnt...well!" Rozenn blew out a smoke ring and watched it disperse into the late afternoon air. "Your mother seems very upset Magda - what is it? If it is the broom, I will make it good."

Magda giggled. "It isn't the broom, it is your relationship with Christoph. She thinks of you as a femme fatale. She still thinks of Christoph as a boy, swimming in the river, climbing in the trees and running through the fields."

Rozenn wondered if this was the time to be completely truthful, but she decided it probably wasn't. "D'accord. I think of him very differently" she said as another smoke ring was blown into the evening, "I don't think of him as a boy, I think of him as... an animal, a beast of the jungle. Pack me some supplies Magda, I will pursue Christoph, like a big game hunter pursues his prize."

"Rozenn, are you going to save him?"

"Ya, I will find him and lay myself down and save him from himself. I promise you this. Quick, quick, quick, Magda!"

Magda's hand clamped over her mouth and she quickly went inside the house, her body quivering, as if she was having some kind of fit.

CHAPTER FOURTEEN

2110 Thursday 15 May 1940 - On the bridge over the Rhein

Rozenn climbed down the bank of the river and then onto the inspection gangway under the bridge. It was a narrow, wooden gangway that led over the river, just below the main structure. Her twitching ears told her that there were men at the far end coming towards her, making guttural calls, as they shouted strident commands at each other. She would come together with them at some point mid-way along, if she was to cross the river here.

She started with her legs crouched, moving slowly at first and then more quickly as she gained confidence. Stopping every few yards to listen, she tried to sense how close danger was. Now, she was at a point which was nearly half way across. She knew this, as the clearance between the structure above and the structure below was squeezing down on her.

The river eddied and swirled darkly below and the heavy stench of algae and burning coke enveloped her. Her legs could not support her - she dropped to her hands and knees and gasped to stave off her dizziness. There was barely room for her on the platform as the beams were so low. She dropped flat on her belly and wriggled her way along but it was now difficult for her to suck breath in. She hugged the wooden beam around her chest but the water still swirled below, ready to swallow her up.

And now there were loud shouts immediately above her and a high-pitched voice that was begging for mercy. She twisted her body so she could look up through the criss-crossed structure above her. There were black boots and grey trousers. A man in bedraggled khaki uniform was being dragged above her. Rozenn stiffened in fear - there was a red face in a gap, with wide, panic stricken eyes staring wildly into hers. Its mouth widened and pleaded to be given help. Rozenn slowly lifted a trembling finger to her lips and her eyes pleaded with him not to say anything. The jackboots were clunking above her now. There was more shouting. The captive struggled to his feet and she heard his toecaps scraping along the wooden boards. And then they were gone.

Rozenn looked through the gap again. There was another eye, a hostile one. A sharp, steel blade slipped through the wood above her. It sliced into her cloak and nicked her waist. She cried and pushed away, her flailing arm trying to grasp onto something solid, but there was nothing to cling on to...

Chapter Fifteen

2115 Thursday 15 May 1940 - Below the bridge over the Rhein

The skipper of the 'Marlene', Wolfgang Breiner, trimmed the Rhein barge onto a more south-easterly course that would take the unwieldy vessel under the rail bridge and to a position where they would be in range for the planned bombardment. He signalled the sister barge, 'Adele', which was eighty meters astern, of his intention and the Adele's skipper acknowledged his signal and conformed.

The sister barges had been extensively modified in the shipyard to accommodate artillery pieces on two high platforms, ready to use ammunition lockers on the new raised deck and ammunition magazines below in the hold in place of coal bunkers. An observation tower for spotting the fall of shot had also been added and skims of concrete to the inner part of the hull. This design was intended to improve the protection of the barge, in case of enemy fire, and to improve her stability, which it hadn't, in Breiner's opinion. The artillery pieces belonged to the Heer and were installed on their platforms in such a way that they could be fired forward, to the beam or to the stern. If they were fired across the beam, the barge would turn over and capsize, in his opinion. This had never been tested. Until now.

The young German officer of the Heer who had marched into the shipyard had given his instructions, and they had been followed to the letter, but these were hasty instructions that made no sense. What they were about to do also made no sense - the invasion of their near neighbours. He tried to work out what he could say in his defence to all the other barge masters that plied their trade along the Rhein in times of peace. All he could do was shrug his shoulders and blame the madness. Nothing made sense any more.

His eye was drawn to a drama being played out on the railway bridge ahead and above. It seemed to be of little consequence - until a body toppled off the structure, followed by an ear-piercing shriek and limbs flailing desperately, trying to gain purchase against the air. His heart jumped - he willed the girl to twist about, to stabilise herself and not to fight the fall, but her plummet towards the river accelerated. He shouted at the girl to save herself; he shouted at the Heer artillery crews to stir themselves; he shouted at the helmsman to cut the diesel engine to half speed. And now there was a commotion on the deck as men ran to the port side of the barge, scattering playing cards and stubbed out cigarettes. Breiner cursed as the barge rolled to port and then, thankfully, settled on an even keel. The barge slewed in the face of the muscular flow of the river.

One of the artillerymen, a sergeant, scrambled down the boarding ladder, seized the girl by the collar and with a roar, swung her over the gunwale and onto the deck. Cheering broke out. Breiner barked a quick instruction to the helmsman, Wilhelm Voigt, and ran to where the girl lay. She was young and pretty but she was gasping like a hooked zander. And there was something else, something that unsettled him, something that could mean harm to his ship.

"Ha, I've caught a nun!" shouted the sergeant. The girl sat up and coughed up river water. The soldier pulled her cloak around her, tightly and in a kindly way, to comfort and warm her.

"Let me see her" said Breiner. She seemed unharmed by her fall, by some miracle, perhaps by the hand of God. He tugged back her cloak so he could see her left shoulder. The sergeant pulled her cloak back around her and scowled at him. Breiner frowned when he had comprehended what he had seen. "Who are you girl and why did you jump off the bridge? You could have been killed!"

"She is mine" shouted the sergeant, "my mädchen!" He lifted her gently but firmly to her feet and wrapped his arm round her shoulders.

"So girl, what game is this you are playing? Are you taking a swim? Talk to your Uncle Hans!"

She blew out her nose and spat overboard. "Please, I am a nun. I need your protection!" said the girl.

Above, on the bridge, there were guards calling out and laughing.

"You are no nun - you are heks!" shouted Breiner.

"Nein, nein. I am a nun!" she said flourishing her nun's gown.

"You say you are a nun? What order are you?" challenged Breiner.

"What order am I?" said the girl, as if this was the most difficult question in the world. "I am of the order of...William Tell" she said indicating the design of her cloak, "a little known Schweitzer order of nuns."

"There is no such order - you are of the order of disorder, heks!"

"Nein, nein, I am a novice in the order of William Tell nuns. There, that is what I am!'

"I believe you mädchen, now come with your Uncle Hans!" said the sergeant.

"This is my vessel!" shouted Breiner.

"The nun is my prisoner. She is my prisoner of war!"

"No, you must throw her overboard, she will bring us bad luck!"

"No, she is mine! My mädchen!"

"Bind her then! Bind her hands! She will cause mischief! She is heks!"

"Nein, nein, I'm his! I'm his!" called out the girl.

"What is it Wolfgang?" shouted the helmsman.

Breiner breathed a sigh of relief. The helmsman wore a sensible cap and sported a sensible, sizeable and well-manicured moustache and a sensible and calm mind. "She is heks - see! Bind her, then throw her over the side - she is bad luck!"

"Never!" the sergeant pulled out a pistol. He aimed it at Breiner's chest. At his side were his comrades and they all had rifles.

"Let it go Breiner. Let us do our job and secure the vessel. Let the Heer do their job!" said the helmsman.

The girl was led to a position on the deck and made to sit, shrouded in a blanket. Above her was a long, dark grey, metal barrel directed to the far bank of the river, the French bank. The girl shivered and pulled the blanket tight over her shoulders. Water seeped from her clothes onto the wooden deck and made little rivulets.

The crew of the gun busied themselves with a well-rehearsed routine as Breiner looked on. Ammunition was readied and so was the human train to bring up the shells from below. The barge was now moving north, with the flow of the river behind, heading downstream until the target was opposite. The stability of the barge would now be tested.

The elevation of the barrel was adjusted, using a wheel, and the direction was adjusted by moving the whole piece on its wheels and securing it in place with rope. A shell was brought up to the breech of the gun, shoved in place, and the breech slammed shut. A young blond-haired boy with smiling, blue eyes motioned that the girl should cover her ears, so she did. The lanyard was pulled, the barrel recoiled with a sudden crack and the shell was speeding on its way. She waited with eyes and ears clenched tightly closed, waiting for the shell burst and then she unclenched when the flash came leagues away. And then again and again, so rhythmically conducted was the routine of the gun crew, tirelessly at work. And the barge swayed over each time, so that the river lapped against the top of the gunwale. But the blond boy was grinning at the girl, ripping his tunic off, flexing his chest and arm muscles at her, grimacing at the sergeant, then returning her wide smile and sharing a long lingering glance, until the next shell, destined for the loading tray, was dropped from his idiot arms.

But, the girl was already moving, as if she knew what was about to happen. In that moment, the gun crew stopped in mid-routine, looked at one other, swallowing as one and looking into the hold, silent, knowing what was about to happen but by contracting to remain statue still, stopping time, they would change the inevitable. The shell plummeted, armed fuse first, down to the serried ranks of primed rounds below and clanged heavily. And there they were, caught in a horror-stricken spell, gawping, as the girl leapt overboard, as if carried by the flash that was brighter and more totally enveloping, than sheet lightning.

There was a collective gasp of relief, then a massive pulse of air, a storm of metal and wood, flying over and beyond, that shredded all fabric and flesh and rope in its path.

The girl tumbled through this maelstrom of air and water, like a river sprite and was then swallowed by an onrush of roaring water and suddenly, he saw that the girl was between the water and the air, as waves slapped at her face and about her arms and flailing legs. And that was the last thing Breiner ever saw.

Chapter Sixteen

2135 Thursday 15 May 1940 - Under the bridge over the Rhein

Rozenn watched as the barge flashed and crackled in the middle of the Rhein, belching gobs of flame and oily smoke upwards to the clear evening sky. As the barge swung and keeled over there were screams and then stiff limbed shapes thrashing frantically in the heavy flow of water, washing them away, downstream. Then there was the screeching of metal against metal as the 'Adele' impaled the burning wreck, and the two barges slewed towards the far bank, accompanied by the whining of screws, scything ineffectually through the air.

Fire spread across the river, moving in stages towards her. There was splashing and screaming and it was getting closer. Rozenn stepped down off the bank of the river so that she could see better. A man was splashing towards her, alternately on his back and then his front, arms thrashing wildly. And then the arms stopped thrashing and he was close to her. She reached towards him but he was struggling against the river's flow. He came again, her insides turning over when she saw the state of his face, no hair or skin. She waded out so the water lapped at her chest and reached out to grasp his hand but his skin came away. A lunge for the collar of his jacket secured him and she could pull the red and brown body towards her. His mouth cried out "Heks?" but it had no lips. It was Uncle Hans.

So, Rozenn bathed his face and whispered that he would be saved and tried to close his eyelids, but he had none. He passed away in her arms with a final choking sob. She launched him back into the muscular stream of the river.

As Rozenn hauled herself out of the river, there was a series of crackling explosions and then a thud as the enmeshed barges ran into the far bank. She tipped river water out of her satchel and looked apprehensively inside - Christoph's letter was ruined. And she was cold, so cold that her teeth chattered, like all the needles at a knitting circle.

Behind her, the sound of a speeding vehicle, springs scrunching and bouncing came rapidly towards her. She turned, and it was close, so close, that she could not get out of its way. There was a screech from the left side of the vehicle and its right flank swung around rapidly, spattering soil from its tracks. She stood her ground, transfixed by the machine, unable to galvanise her legs into action. A soldier in khaki battle dress jumped over the thinly screened metal side of the scout carrier and shouted "Oi you, come with us!"

He was a British soldier, judging by the green saucer shape perched upon his head, the badly fitting tunic and knickerbockers and the khaki puttees wrapped around his shins. He was not alone in the machine. "Who are you?" she stammered.

"Tommy Atkins" he replied jauntily, "now get yourself in or there'll be trouble!" She was hoisted over the lip of the thinly armoured flank of the vehicle into the cluttered hold and squeezed into the space in the corner between boxes of ammunition, a radio set and a coiled camouflage net. There was another soldier with her, a driver and a man with the bearing of a commander in the front of the machine. The engine coughed back into life and the vehicle skidded across the rough hummocks of the flood plain, back the way it had come. She was offered a cigarette by her new companion and tried several times to keep it still while it was lit by the other soldier. It caught fire and she felt the welcome warmth on her fingers. The man who had jumped out to get her was clutching tightly to the back of the armoured compartment, his helmet tilting madly up and down, as the vehicle gathered speed.

"Are you a German, girl?"

"Non, are you?"

"No, do I sound like a Kraut, do I? I'm asking the questions, aren't I? You are a prisoner, my girl!"

This, she could not deny. "D'accord!" she muttered, as her body shivered with cold and fear.

"Name, my girl!"

"Alors, I call myself...Rozenn Abgrall."

"Nationality?"

"I am of the Breton nation!"

"She's French, Jimmy, can't you tell!" shouted the man in charge.

"He calls himself Tommy!" she replied, over the crunching of gears.

"It's Jimmy. What are you doing here?"

"I am your prisoner! You captured me!" she stammered.

"No, I meant what were you doing down by the river?"

"D'accord - I was just watching the boats..."

"Watching the boats! It's not a bloody regatta out there!"

"Alors, there was an accident!"

"What happened?"

"There was an accident, a terrible accident. Can you not see!" She pointed back the way they had come.

"And you had something to do with that, girl?" he jested.

"Non, non, non!"

"Leave it out Jimmy. They'll interrogate her when we get back to HQ!"

"You can do better than that, girl!"

"I am not a girl! I am...a woman!"

"Leave her, she knows nothing!"

"I know many things! I know what happened to the boats!"

"Ah! Come on then! Tell me!"

She closed her eyes. "A shell fell and made...hell."

"A shell? Don't you mean round?"

"Yes, it was round and it fell into the others" she said, slapping her hands together above her head, "and it burst, like that!"

"Let me get this straight, the wrong way round burst in the magazine" the soldier said laughing.

"Ya, ya, that is what happened!"

"And how do you know that?"

"I...was there!"

There was silence while this information was assimilated. "You were there? How did you get away?" They looked back towards the river. "Oh my good god!" There was nothing to see apart from orange flames, licking their way skywards.

"Ya, I saw everything and it was...terrible."

"What's your conclusion, Jimmy?" asked the man in charge.

"She's out of her mind, sir, she's completely bonkers!" The carrier slewed to a halt amongst a host of soldiers running to and fro, loading boxes onto a pair of trucks and into the panniers of two motorbikes with sidecars. Behind them were burning buildings. The man in charge climbed out of the carrier and started an animated conversation with an officer. Rozenn presumed the other man was an officer because he wore a peaked hat and his navy-blue tunic and trousers fitted. And he had a stick instead of a rifle. The two men strode in unison to the carrier, as if they wanted to talk to someone urgently.

"Madam Abgrall?" asked the officer.

"Mademoiselle" she corrected, as she stood up.

"You're soaking wet!" he said, as he took her hand and assisted her over the side.

"Yes, I have been in the river..."

"So I see. Why didn't you go via the Basel consular office, mademoiselle?"

"Huh, so you know of me?" she replied, wondering who the man was. But her heart was beating rapidly now, despite her being sodden and cold.

"Or cross the bridge..."

"It is crawling with Boche." She wondered if he knew about Christoph. "I am in pursuit of my boyfriend, monsieur, and who are you?"

"Poor chap. It's Jenkins, Commander...Jenkins, Naval Intelligence," he said, "and do you have any intelligence for us... Mademoiselle Abgrall?"

"Non, Monsieur" she replied. "How do you know who I am?"

"I know everyone on my payroll...and we are allies, of course" he replied.

"Huh! I doubt that."

"So, do you know where de Bourcard's unit is headed?"

"Christoph's regiment? Non" she replied, "but I am pursuing him." Her arm then made a broad sweeping gesture towards the burning airfield. "What is happening here?" she asked.

"The Jerries got our range. Are you still in contact with de Bourcard?"

"The Boche!" she muttered. "Why won't you stay and fight them? And how do you know that name?"

"I just do. And what about de Bourcard?"

"He has re-joined his unit. I do not know where he is."

"I don't believe you, mademoiselle. You of all people must know where he is!"

"He is travelling with his unit...to les Pays-Bas. That is all I know!"

"To Holland? But the Dutch have surrendered. Why are they needed there?"

"I don't know that!"

"Mademoiselle, why are they needed in Holland?"

"I think it is because...of Hel!" She cursed herself as the realisation came that Christoph's last letter had so many hidden layers that she hadn't unpeeled them all. And now she was telling the Britanniques?

"Hell?"

"Yes, Operation Hel. Hel will be launched from les Pays-Bas!"

Chapter Seventeen

2325 Thursday 15 May 1940 - Crossing the Rhein

Private Lloyd was delighted with the task he had been assigned - he was to assist the French girl 'out of her wet things' and into whatever dry, spare, small-size service dress could be made available. So, he had a blanket, some underclothes, an under-sized tunic, a pair of baggy trousers and plimsolls. And she would have to be quick, as there was a flap on, and they were pulling out. And all the buildings that surrounded them were burning!

He took her to a parked lorry. Rozenn pulled the canvas apart to reveal that the well of the lorry was full to over-flowing.

"No good?" he asked.

"No good" she confirmed.

"Where then?"

"Ici" she said, "behind."

"By here?"

"Oui. Hold the blanket. Avert your eyes and I will... disrobe."

"I see."

"Non. You will not. You will not...dishonour me. Think of me... as your mother - you are holding up this blanket so your mama can change her clothes on the beach. Your mama!"

He held up the blanket and looked steadfastly towards the burning hangar, to his left. He thought of his mother and their holidays on the beach at Rhyll, where his mother had held the blanket for him as he pulled on his knitted swimming trunks. Those long hot summers that now seemed to belong to a different age, an age with endless summers and no cares. The French girl slipped off her cloak, then the clothes underneath, then put on a vest, hauled up some pants, then struggled into the trousers...

"Is that a tattoo you've got there?" he asked. He had glimpsed a rounded shape of whorls, impressed in the skin of her left shoulder.

"Non" she snorted back, "it is the mark of a brand."

"A brand? Like, with a branding iron? Like a farmer puts on his prize bull?"

"Non, not at all like a bull. And you must not be looking!"

"I couldn't help it! And get on with it!"

The girl hauled the shirt over her shoulders and he couldn't help grinning as she squirmed in discomfort. "Mon dieu! This is like wearing the skin of a wild beast! That kind of beast that grubs around in the soil with his nose - do you know this kind of beast?"

"Like a hedgehog?"

"Ej-og? That's it! This is like wearing a sack made of inside-out ej-og!"

"That's as maybe, but that's all we've got, so you'll have to get used to it" he muttered, "we all do, don't we? Just one of life's little sacrifices, isn't it?"

"Huh. I am ready! You take me to les Pays-Bas now?"

And she was ready as well! Somehow, she had removed all her wet things and replaced them with dry, and all he had got was a glimpse of her shoulder! Only her shoulder!

"You take me to les Pays-Bas now?"

"Where's that?"

She waved to the North. "It is that way..."

"Lloyd!" It was his sergeant."Is she ready?"

"Yessir!"

"Bind her hands behind her back..."

"Why, Sarge, she's just a girl!"

"Just do as your told, Lloyd, or we'll all be in trouble!"

"Sarge!"

Her arms were pulled roughly behind her back and her wrists secured with strapping. She tested the knot and wriggled, but her wrists were bound sufficiently tight. "Get her in the lorry!"

"Where are you taking me!"

"Where you'll be safe!"

"Take me to les Pays-Bas!"

"Through the whole, sodding German Army? I don't think so! Bundle her in! Sit right beside her! Make sure she doesn't move. You saw what happened out there on the river!" With this parting shot, he strode away.

"Sarge!" Lloyd guided the hooded girl back to the lorry and hauled her quivering body over the tailgate.

She squeezed her body between wooden boxes and tried to move her legs into a comfortable position but couldn't. "It's not my fault. They should not have shot at my people!" she grumbled.

"She's right. We're at war with the Hun, so no holds barred" shouted the driver. He secured the tailgate.

"What holds?" shouted back Rozenn.

"Any holds!"

"Ah, la lutte, I know of this!" She thought for a moment. "So you will break any rule to win?"

"If that's what it takes."

"D'accord. And then you will leave them to burn."

"They can all burn in hell!" The driver was now thumping the sides of the canvas as he headed to the cab.

"Then, may the gods spare all our souls!"

"Sorry girl, orders. Too much talk." Lloyd pulled a bag over her head and now she started to pant like a hooded hawk. She was now squeezing herself tight into a small gap between two wooden boxes and her whole frame wriggled like a hooked fish. He perched unsteadily on top of a large crate. He rested his rifle, with it's protruding bayonet in the corner formed by the frame and the canvas. This would be a long journey to who knows where. 'Break any rule' she had said and she was right. This would be a war fought to the finish, he thought. No quarter given and no quarter asked for. And what could he do about it, nothing, that's what.

But at least he could admire the wriggling of this girl, who was in his charge, as she tried to get as comfortable as she could.

The hood pressed darkly against her eyes and caught between her lips as she gasped in air, but the gasps did not taste of air, they tasted of unnatural substances and the natural sweat of man. Rozenn tried to breathe in a more measured way through her nose instead and felt a little calmer. She adjusted her legs as they started to cramp - they were now resting on top of the crate - she clenched her buttocks several times so her back was now in a position that was a little more comfortable. Her shoulders were tight so she manoeuvred them in such a way that her arms stopped cramping. There was still a prickling sensation in her fingers and thumbs but a curious absence of feeling where her left index finger should have been.

The man who was sharing the hold of the lorry was still there, judging by the random whistling that came from his direction. He was still positioned opposite her and took the opportunity, every few minutes, to divert his tuneless whistling away from her, to the outside world. Rozenn was lulled into a fitful sleep by the continual skittering of the tremble-leaf trees, interspersed, on occasion, by the plaintive mewing of the lowland eagles. And now they were on a rise, and she felt the sensation of rolling, as if she was going to roll out of the back of the lorry and down the hill. Instead, she wedged her body in behind the planks of the crate and held her breath. It was no good. She had to gasp in air. Now stop that, settle yourself and breathe, breathe, breathe through your nose. That was better. The soldier who called himself Lloyd, was now towards the back of the lorry, probably looking out - the driver was still in the front of the cab, talking to someone next to him. From the voices that she could hear from the cab, she guessed the passenger was a leader and he could have the power to make decisions that could help her. Or not.

Rozenn's bladder was full to bursting so she squeezed her thighs and buttocks tightly together and tried to distract away the discomfort.

Rozenn could see herself rushing down a hill, two wheels rattling wildly between her legs and brakes squealing in protest. There was blue sky above, pocked with white clouds and the green of pastures and orchards all around her - but in front of her was the steep, grey, downward descending road and, ahead, a fall. She would have to veer off this road and tumble to a halt, before the precipice ahead. There was a shout from behind her and a bicycle came past, the rider flapping his arm up and down, warning her to slow down. She shouted that she couldn't.

He came alongside, a blonde haired boy, tugging at her saddle bag to slow her. And now she was wobbling side to side with the bike but he was in control, and she would be safe and she was slewing to a halt, in a shower of pink and grey gravel. The blonde haired boy lifted up her bicycle and put it next to his. "You are hurt" he observed. Bending down, he lifted her so she was sitting and licked away the mess of blood that had formed on her knee. "Spittle is the best antiseptic for scrapes" he said. He wiped the teary stains from her face using a square of white linen and then tied it across her knee. Her insides were now in complete disarray. "There, you look fine" he commented as he stood her up and looked into her, with his deep blue eyes.

The way he acted and held himself suggested he must be a soldier. Her whole body tingled in a warm, spreading glow and, oh, how embarrassing, she felt her cheeks go red and blotchy. He now checked her bike, stood it upside down and repaired the puncture in her front tyre. "I think that is mended" he said.

Rozenn saw that he had a broad smile and fine, orderly teeth. 'How I need you' she thought as she tried to order the turmoil of thoughts in her head. He now took her by the hand and there was an instant shudder that leapt up her back and then across her shoulders. She shrugged it away as she straddled her bike but now his hands cosseted her across the waist. This triggered a surge in her core and an 'Ooh' from her throat. "Are you well?" he asked. Rozenn nodded vigorously.

"And, what is your name?" he asked.

"I call myself Rozenn."

"And your family name?"

"It is Abgrall."

"Abgrall? So, you are...a French girl?"

"Non, non, Breton..."

"You are a long way from home?"

"Ah, I work...there" she replied, pointing in the approximate direction of Basel.

"Allow me to escort you down the mountain" he said, "just to make sure that your machine is working correctly and that you are too." She smiled at his joke and nodded coyly in agreement.

They set off down the hill. He did this annoying thing of pedalling quickly away and then slowing down so she could keep catch up. The hill levelled out and she felt more confident, so she raced him to a cluster of trees on a knoll. Here they stopped, because she was now breathless, and rested under a tree. He presented her with an apple which she chomped through.

He proposed that they should meet again and announced that his name was Christoph. Why not come to my family home, he suggested, and then they could ride together and Rozenn could meet his mother, and his mother would make pack them some food to eat while they travelled together. She agreed immediately but said they should be careful about being seen together.

After they parted, Rozenn cycled back to the boarding house, feeling full to bursting in her chest and empty at the same time in her stomach. She had agreed a rendezvous with a soldier of Germany and this rendezvous was just a short time away while the clouds of war were gathering and they were ready to release a storm.

Rozenn's bladder was full to bursting. "Stop, stop" she wailed, "I need a pissoir!"

"Oi, Morris, she needs to piss!"

"I can't stop here, we're miles from anywhere!"

"We can't stop..."

"You must stop! It will be like the fountains of Fontainebleau in here if you don't!"

"It's not up to me girl, I'm not driving..."

"Give me a bucket!"

"I haven't got a bucket!"

"Anything! Anything! It must be big!"

'Oi Morris, she's desperate!"

"Can't stop! She'll have to hold it in!"

The lorry just trundled on. It had travelled south-west and now was trundling north-west, in her estimation. She sensed that soldier

Lloyd was at the opening at the rear, smoking a cigarette and fretting. Rozenn turned her torso and used her tethered hands to find a container. Her fingers found a cold, metal receptacle. She made several attempts to wedge it in place and level it so that it could act as a bowl; a receptacle that would be stable and could be filled, when she mounted it, like a bed pan. She resorted to sitting on it and at last, it was wedged firmly in the right place. Her sigh was long and caused Lloyd to stop his whistling. The whistling resumed and now she could wrench and twist and grunt her underclothes down past her buttock cheeks. She rolled and wriggled so her core was firmly squashed over the bowl. And now she released with a huge sigh of relief. Rozenn rolled away quickly onto her back and wriggled her underclothes back up over her backside. Success.

"What are you playing at" Lloyd asked, "are you still holding on?"

"I never play. Play is for infants" she replied through the cotton of the hood.

He moved towards her, his feet stumbling over the obstacles in the well of the lorry. She held her breathing - his foot was about to encounter the inverted bowl.

"I am empty, but the bowl is full" she announced.

"Empty? Empty? What bowl?" he shouted, "what have you done?" He stubbed out his cigarette and slapped the canvas tilt. "Come on, come on, Morris, stop, we've got to get her out!"

She heard snatches of conversation outside, as the lorry bounced its way along a cobbled street, and the sound of domesticated animals and carts. All the sounds that you would expect of a sizeable commune. The lorry ground to a halt and the officer got out, whistled his way to the back and called to Lloyd. "Let's get her out, there's a privy just over there..."

Lloyd jumped out and the tailgate latches knocked open. She heard it flap down. And now Lloyd seemed to be casting around desperately for something. "It was here, just a minute ago..."

"Where's your helmet, man?" said the sergeant.

"Ah, it's here..." He sounded very upset. "Oh, Jesus Christ! You dirty, filthy, French whore" he shouted in her direction, "you pissed in my helmet!"

Ah, so that's what it was. But it didn't matter. Most importantly, it was just the right capacity so that it could be filled to the brim, with the contents of a bursting bladder...

"What am I supposed to do with this?" She heard embarrassed laughter from the sergeant and the driver and then a splash as liquid was cast away.

"Just empty it and wipe it out. We've got to get going!" shouted the sergeant.

"You piss head!" laughed the driver. She could hear the clanging of the helmet as it was kicked about in the street. But behind this was the sound of a column of automobiles trundling towards them. And then she heard a loud strangled scream of a human voice that caused everything to stop. Everything that is, apart from the continual chittering of the tremble-leaf trees, and the occasional mewing of the lowland eagles and now, the combustive rattling of petrol engines.

Chapter Eighteen

1135 Friday 16 May 1940 - In the city of Besançon

"Where's your helmet man!" a man of authority shouted. He seemed upset. She could hear the boy Lloyd scrambling to find it, pick it up, and restore it back to where it belonged - on his head. And then Lloyd starting whining that it smelt of lady piss. She heard his two front of cab colleagues scramble to attention next to him. "Where's the girl?" was the next topic on the mind of the man of authority.

Now there would be trouble, thought Rozenn. "Ici" she called out timidly, through the fabric of the hood. She was invited to come out of the lorry, which she did with helping arms to lift her over the tailboard. Now she was standing in front of the shouting man. The others were stood to her left side, rigidly to attention. "And who are you?" she asked timidly. She could hear three necks twist abruptly towards her.

"What the bloody hell have you done to her?"

"She's trouble sir, we had to keep her restrained, sir" offered the sergeant.

"She used my helmet as a potty, sir!"

"Were you wearing it at the time, man?"

"No sir!"

"You were lucky then! If it was me, I would have shat in it!"

"Sir!"

"Remove that hood, untie her!" was the next order he issued. As the boy Lloyd did as he was ordered, he muttered that she had better not get him into trouble, or she would in big trouble. Rozenn gave a curt nod in response. It was an officer to her front, in blue-grey service dress, with golden wings sewn over the left breast of his jacket, and trousers that fitted. A shower of impulses flooded into her nose, ears and eyes and via her feet. Her neck craned upwards so her face could feel the warmth of the rising sun and to breathe in the cool, fresh air of the fields. It felt like she was at the gateway of...

"Papers!" he shouted.

She offered the folder of papers that she found at her hip.

"No! I don't smoke! Your identification papers!"

"Ah, pardon." Rozenn turned away, thrust her hand into the pouch that cosseted her stomach and withdrew a folded wedge of paper and waved it towards him.

He took them and shouted "Turn and face me, girl!" She complied. He had dismissed the boy Lloyd, the sergeant and the driver and told them to get their vehicle off the road. They ran to do his bidding. She was now alone in the middle of the road with this bad-tempered man and a little convoy of vehicles that trailed back towards where the sun had just risen. There were men leaning against their vehicles, taking the opportunity to light a cigarette and to enjoy the views between the tremble-leaf trees.

"Name?"

"It says on my papers..."

"NAME! I know what it says on the papers!"

"I call myself..."

"Spit it out!" he roared.

"Rozenn Abgrall. That is what I..."

"Rozenn Katerin Abgrall?"

"Yes" she replied. His shouting had moderated a little. "You are a very rude man."

"It is you!"

"Yes, I know that!"

"Age?"

"You are a very rude man!"

"AGE!"

"Alors, I have, um, let me think, vingt-et-un years..."

He thrust the papers to within a hands length of her face. "Would you like to try again!"

"Ah, I see. It is written, the day of my birth. In that case, I have dix-huit ans..."

"Are you sure?"

"Oh..."

"I'll give you a clue - happy birthday!"

"Oh, is it really? My anniversary? Ah, d'accord, dix-neuf ans!"

He nodded. "Occupation?"

"I am a servant of the people..."

"Really? It says here that you are a clerk at the French Embassy in Switzerland."

"Yes, I am a clerk for the people. You can take me to les Pays-Bas now?"

"No, you come with me to Paris."

"To Paris? No, I cannot, I made a promise and I have a great hunger..."

The officer clicked his fingers to his rear. Some kind of bread-like material encasing some kind of meat-substance came back to him. He passed it over to her.

She clutched it to her mouth and started biting. "I also have a great thirst..." she mentioned between bites.

"Milk?"

"Milk is no good for me but wine will suffice..." His manner seemed to have improved. Perhaps he had come to help her reach les Pays-Bas?

"Water it is." He passed her a canteen, that when shook, sounded like it contained water.

"Mademoiselle, now, please get in the car..."

"But first monsieur, you tell me what you call yourself and why I need to attend at Paris." She wiped the crumbs from her mouth and took a slug from the metal canteen. None of it was pleasant and she resorted to spitting out the contents of her mouth into the road.

"First, you get in the car."

"No, first you tell me what you call yourself, or you will have to bind me again."

"Very well! All you need to know is that I am an officer..."

"Ah, an officer? I see, yes, I think your family name is then...Kirk? Yes? And you Kirk are a..."

The driver squashed his cigarette butt into the road. "She's good, isn't she sir? Are we going to crack on, sir, there's a bit of a queue behind!"

"A captain in the corps of King's royal flyers..."

"And my superiors want to find out what you've found out about your boyfriend's movements, but God only knows why." He beckoned her to follow him.

"Which one is mine?" she asked. There seemed to be a choice of three; the first looked like a touring car with wooden slats along the side; the second was a car encased in armour sheets with a turret but no windows; third was a smaller open topped car with what looked like the skeleton of a giant's gamp stuck in it. "I like this one" she said, pointing to the open-topped vehicle.

"You'll come with me in the Snipe" said he pointing to the touring car, "back seat, and you will behave yourself, or I will have your wrists and ankles bound."

"D'accord. You take me to Paris now, then I go to les Pays-Bas, our destination is settled."

"The Dutch have capitulated, love" said the driver of the tourer, "so no one is going there!"

"D'accord. That is understood." She hesitated by the door to the front seat of the automobile and then she was ushered into the back seat alongside a young man, also in a blue-grey uniform, also sporting a gun in a holster. He had his right hand over the holster. He introduced himself as Frank. In front of her was the driver Drover and to his side, sat the officer Kirk.

"Get going Drover, we've lost enough time. At this rate, it's going to take another two days to get to where we're going. Bloody country! Good thing if the Hun takes over. They can build some decent, bloody roads!"

As they passed Lloyd's lorry, Rozenn called out "Au revoir" and "Bonne chance". Lloyd and his compatriots just scowled back. She settled back in her seat and wrapped a blanket around her shoulders. It was time to rest. Behind her automobile was the automobile with flat faced armour and two big guns protruding from the turret and behind that, the open-topped car with a tall aerial. She should be safe for a few hours, she reasoned, protected by the corps of British King's royal flyers.

"I thought you were hungry?" challenged Kirk, his hair and moustache bristling in the gentle breeze that was coming from a south-westerly direction. He must get them trimmed before very long.

"There is something missing" she said in reply.

"What's missing?" he wanted to know. She had now become very sullen and she pouted like a sulky schoolgirl who could not get her own way.

"Taste" she replied.

"Go hungry then!" He had noticed over the last few miles that her hands were increasingly twitchy, first in her lap, then over her ears and then under her legs and then under her armpits. And then there were her hooded eyes and the massive pout.

They were approaching a bustling commune, where curly horned cattle with brown hide and swishing tails, hid under trees and further ahead, citizens looked up anxiously to the sky from their homes. The Abgrall girl turned her nostrils to the air and sniffed, and then her eyes closed and her nose twitched from side to side, like a rabbit. She seemed to have scented something on the wind, and then after a few minutes, he could too. There was a food market ahead.

The speed of the tourer slowed to less than walking pace as they threaded their way through the main avenue of the commune and on to the central market place. Both sides of the street were teeming with people, carrying or dragging their chattels, crossing their path, all converging on the centre of the town. Soon, the horn and the shouting from the tourer made a deafening cacophony of sound. The automobile came to a halt. He slumped back in his seat with his arms crossed. "I don't bloody believe this!"

"It'll be quicker to walk" muttered Drover. Lance Corporal Frank was staring anxiously out of the tourer window, slapping the side of the car. There was nothing from the Abgrall girl. "How about firing a few shots in the air, sir? That'll clear 'em!"

"So, 'servant of the people', these are your people, is there anything you can do about this shambles?" He turned to look back, but the seat where she had been sitting was empty and her door was open. Her companion on the back seat was staring aghast at the hollow in the seat where she had been sitting just a moment ago. "She's disappeared!" he muttered in complete disbelief. He patted the leather seat and looked under it. "She was here a second ago!"

"All right, stop the car Drover. We need to find her..."

"We're already at a standstill, sir!"

He cast his eyes to the heavens and cursed under his breath. "Frank, you take the left side, I'll take the right. Use your weapon if you have to! Drover, drive through to the other side of the town and we'll rendezvous there!"

Kirk was now in the crush of people, heading to the town square. His Webley service revolver was held securely in its holster - best not to brandish it or there would be a mass panic to deal with. He now pushed his way through the milling crowd, past hens and struggling around bicycles and carts, looking ahead and to his side. The Abgrall girl was in khaki fatigues, wasn't she? That would make her stand out in this crowd, wouldn't it? And her long auburn hair, piled messily on her head, and those flashing, turquoise eyes...

He now passed stalls with cheese, animal parts (he suspected horse) and bunches of plant leaves that he did not recognise. What was the matter with these people? And then he was through the crowd, on the other side of the square. Frank was across the street shrugging at him. He had trusted Rozenn and she had betrayed him. Rozenn's care had been entrusted to him and he had failed. And now he would have to explain this to his superiors and they would have to explain this to His Majesty's Government.

And then he saw her face. She was sitting on a stone horse trough and then she stood and shouted out: "Ici! Monsieur captain!"

His first impulse was to breathe a colossal sigh of relief but then he felt anger welling up from his gut as he marched up to her. "What the hell do you think you were doing?"

"Eh, voila! Bartering and trading for provisions!" She held a sack full of bread, ham, cheese, pots, fruit and vegetables of uncertain provenance for him to inspect. "See! Dijon!" she exclaimed.

He swiped at her hand so the pot crashed away against the cobbles. She thrust the sack in his hands and ran to where it had landed. She scraped up what she could into the largest shard of the pot. "Oh, non, non, non!" she sobbed, "pour nous tous!"

He came to her side and helped to recover what they could of the mustard. "I'm sorry Rozenn, but you should not have run away." He looked into her tear-filled eyes and suddenly, he felt inextricably bound to her.

"Monsieur captain, you are very angry with me, and I understand this, but you must also understand..." They were facing each other, he with the sack still in his hands and she with the remnants of the mustard in hers. When she looked at him with those eyes full of melancholy, her face looking up submissively at him, her lips in a pout, she was uncommonly attractive.

There was a warm, and uncomfortable stirring in his loins. "Rozenn" he announced. Even saying her name caused him a major tremor inside.

"Monsieur captain?" Her voice, that soft honeyed voice, laden with sweetness.

"Rozenn, you must promise that you will never, ever, do anything like that again!"

"Procuring provisions? Pour nous tous?" She offered him a taste of the mustard clinging to the tip of her finger - he declined.

"No, running off like that."

"D'accord captain, so, I must ask you first..."

"Yes, you must ask my permission."

"D'abord..."

"Yes, Rozenn." Frank was at their side, grinning at their conversation.

"This I will do for you, but I have made a promise that came first, and to a mother. This promise I must also keep."

"So?"

"So, if the second promise stops me doing the first promise, I will have to..."

"Regrettably decline?" offered Frank. "Sir, we have company!" he pointed to the three vehicles that had pulled up behind them.

"We'll take a break. Just ten minutes. Let the engines cool down."

"Yes, sir! Can I take that for you?" Frank took the sack of provisions and strolled away. "Phwoarr, smells of old socks!"

He directed his attention back to Rozenn. She was frowning at Frank. "What promise?" he asked her.

She hesitated. "Alors, I promised a mother that I would find her son and...save him."

"And how are you going to do that?"

"I will go to les Pays-Bas. This is where I will find him."

"Not possible."

"Yes, it is. All is possible."

"And how will you get there?"

"By road, river, or by locomotive or by aeroplane, and if all else fails, à pied!"

"Rozenn, come with me." She followed him to the tourer and watched him as he took out a map of the low countries from his breast pocket and spread it across the bonnet. He accepted a piece of baguette with a slice of ham and cheese from Drover.

"Dijon?" offered the girl. He shook his head. Rozenn smeared it generously over a slice of ham. She would have to concentrate now, because they were surrounded by the captain's men. "What is this about?" she asked.

"You're gonna be shown the tits" laughed Drover.

"The tits?" asked Rozenn. "What are these tits?"

"Yes" he said to Rozenn, "I'm going to show you just enough so that you buy into my proposition."

"D'accord. I must concentrate now!"

He took apart his sandwich. He placed a piece of baguette so it was anchored in Germany and slid it across Holland and Belgium. "The German matador's cloak" he explained.

"I know this, but so far into la Belgique? Zut alors!"

He placed a piece of well-seasoned ham over the region of Artois and Southern Belgium. "The BEF and the Belgian army." He now placed a piece of bread below the ham and slid it over Luxembourg and slowly edged it over Sedan and then Laon. "The German matador's sword..."

"Non, non, non. Where is our army?"

"No one knows, they're in full retreat."

Rozenn made a yellow stroke across the map with mustard and it ran south to north from Paris to Breda. “Then this is the way I must go - en avion!”

“No one’s going to fly you to Holland - our planes have been dropping like flies! We’ll be lucky to get any out...”

“Are you abandoning us?’ asked Rozenn.

“No, we will fight on, somehow...”

“Then you must get me to Paris! Tout suite!”

“Good. I promise you, Rozenn, that I will do all in my power to get you to Paris, as quickly as I can.”

“C’est bon. Then I will use all of my powers to help you. This I promise you, monsieur captain!”

“That’s good, let’s get going then!” Kirk breathed deeply “Men, she’ll be no more trouble! She promised me!”

Rozenn was pleased with the change in the touring car seating arrangements: she had requested a seat at the front; Kirk was now in the driving seat and Frank and Drover were in the back seat. There had been some squabbling while Frank looked frantically for his gas mask and its container. Some other items of kit had also gone astray. Kirk drove on after giving sarcastic instructions about the need to keep your personal kit safe and ready to hand, as you never know when they might be needed. Rozenn kept a discrete silence - she knew very well where these items of kit were - they were in other hands - French hands.

Their convoy had grown - a column of lorries and tracked armoured carriers had joined in behind. Kirk got out and greeted them - she learned that they were soldiers from the Scottish Lowlands, re-deploying to the west of Paris. Her heart plunged into a dark coldness - Christoph was becoming more and more distant from her, more and more out of reach.

It was getting darker as they drove westward, and the conditions clouded and cooled. She pulled the blanket around her shoulders so it was tight. They were approaching another, much more significant commune - the citizens were swarming around the streets, gobbling like a cackle of geese, craning their necks to the sky, not sure what to do. As the tourer rumbled along the main street, Rozenn could see that wooden shutters from the second floor windows had been thrown open. There were girls leaning out, shouting and waving excitedly at the soldiers below. She glanced back at them. Where were their clothes? There were none! The girls were naked as far as she could see!

"Eyes front!" muttered Kirk as he pressed harder on the accelerator pedal. Rozenn stared down into the darkness of the steering wheel well.

Kirk had decided that they must travel through the evening and the night, in order to make quicker headway against the random groups of people and their bicycles, carts and animals. The valley of L'Aube was behind them but they were now in dense woodland. Beams of light from the tourer picked out the road and the trees and the sky too, and they set the limits of the world she was now passing through. Rozenn spent these hours in fitful sleep, imagining the flight of thousands of communities from the lightning strikes of the Hun, and her struggle through this marching mass of men, women, children, bicycles, animals and carts and vehicles of all kinds.

The door came open and she grasped at her seat, but she was falling out of the car, her legs scrambling frantically in the stones of the road, trying not to fall. But she didn't fall. Rozenn was hauled to her feet, her left arm grasped fiercely. There was a cart across their path but no lights close by - they were alone. She felt cold metal against her throat. There was shouting in her right ear, directed at the men in the tourer. She smelt the sweat of fear and the dust of the road on him. He was still shouting and her ear was hurting and her arm muscles pulsed painfully.

Kirk was out of the car. He was shouting from his mouth and remonstrating with his arms. Frank and Drover were out of the car, looking at her and then at him.

"Monsieur!" she whispered, frightened that if she spoke too loudly, the knife would bite into her throat, *"Je suis juste une fille!"* And then there was a hush. She tried again, *"Monsieur, avez-vous des enfants?"*

Out of the ditch struggled a women, with a child in each arm. She had a pretty face, creased in fear. The boy was fast asleep, the girl was squalling into the women's coat.

"Monsieur, je suis française!"

The knife tightened against her throat. She pictured blood bubbling out and then running down her throat and chest. But it didn't - the pressure released. Kirk drew his weapon out of the holster. She motioned him to put it away.

"Monsieur, I am French, like you! I am just a girl, like your daughter." The grip on her arm weakened and the cold metal against her throat was gone. She turned to face him. He was frightened too. Rozenn held his hand. "Monsieur, I will help you on your way, but in turn, you must allow these men through. They are our allies in the fight against the Boche, do you understand?"

He nodded. She saw that a wheel had come off the cart. The white and brown horse between the poles was standing but getting restless, rearing its head and harrumphing. There was a black and white cow, settled in the road, chewing the cud. She snapped her fingers at Kirk. "Captain, please. Calm the horse." She clicked her fingers at Frank and Drover. "Please, raise the cart." She nodded to the man. "Monsieur, please place the wheel." Behind them, there were headlights approaching. This would have to be done quickly. Frank and Drover lifted the corner of the cart; the man placed the wheel on the axle; Rozenn hammered the retaining pin in place. "Eh, voila!"

She asked the man to pull the cart to one side. He pulled his cap back and he kept shaking his head. Instead, the man took the reins from Kirk, motioned his wife to board and whipped the horse into a slow plod, along the road, heading west. Kirk was looking quizzically at her.

"Restez-vous, ici. We start again..." said Rozenn, "in three hours." Kirk walked down the line of vehicles, barking his orders. The headlights were doused and the drivers put their feet up, or stood to, snatching a smoke or making a brew.

He was back. "Come with me Rozenn, I'm going to show you..."

"Show you the tits..." sniggered Drover.

"Yes, I'm going to show you how to use one of these." He held a leather holster in one hand and slowly withdrew a gun with the other. She felt an iciness in her spine, across her shoulders and down her arms. “This is a service revolver” Kirk continued, “and it’s a large calibre weapon that will stop an elephant.”

“Stop an el’phant? What is this?”

“That doesn’t matter!”

“You must tell me!”

A hiss of tea-tainted air whistled through his teeth. “An elephant... an elephant is a massive beast with legs like tree-trunks and a long, long trunk and is very difficult to stop when it charges.”

“The Boche have such creatures! Quelle horreur!”

“No, no, no” he replied quickly. “Ah, you are mocking me.”

She breathed a huge sigh. “Ah, that is good!” She paused for thought. “So, what I need is a gun that will stop...a Hun...but not an el’phant!”

“Exactly! And it will do this. Listen Rozenn. What is important is that this weapon will stop a man...”

Rozenn gasped, “Stop a man!”

“Yes! Now come with me!” She followed him meekly through a meadow and a belt of trees to a lake that stretched out as far as she could see. The sky was cloudless and the lake surface was bathed in light misty pools. The call of the screech owl echoed mournfully across the water.

Kirk showed her the workings of the gun and then he pushed six cartridges into the waiting chambers. She then stood with her feet apart, arms stretched out, holding the gun two-handed but there was a problem. “Change your grip! Use your right hand!” She used both hands to hold the gun, her right index finger ready to pull the trigger, and her eyes aligned with the sight along the barrel. “Your target is that duck to the right of that post!” Sure enough, near the post floated her assigned target - a preening drake with the self-satisfied look that comes from having just successfully mounted a duck.

Rozenn was ready: the index finger of her right hand felt the bare metal of the trigger. The lake was still, the water fowl all calm and serene, but she felt anything but calm. The drake seemed to be blissfully unaware of what was about to happen. Kirk said that she should take a deep breath, hold it in, aim and squeeze the trigger. So, she breathed in, held her breath inside and adjusted her aim to the left.

A shot rang out and there was pandemonium all about. Geese and ducks leapt into the air, honking and quacking in alarm and flying rapidly away. The recoil jarred her hand and arm but she reset her aim by a notch downwards and her target was back in sight.

"Missed!" shouted Kirk. "Rozenn, you've got to make that first shot count!" He peered through his spy glass. Five further shots rang out. "Stop, stop! You're wasting bullets now!" He turned to look at Rozenn - she was still standing firm, her arms extended, the revolver pointing out over the lake and then it was lowered slowly. "That'll have to do, Rozenn, but that was very, very poor shooting."

She offered the gun back to him. "I cannot kill a living thing, captain, unless it is doing me harm. There you have it, my captain!"

Kirk scanned the lake because his nose had started twitching at the smell of freshly shattered wood. There were pieces floating serenely past his field of view. And then he realised what she had done. "Bloody hell, Rozenn!" he muttered. The post had been obliterated and just the stump remained, barely showing above the water. He demanded an explanation.

"That colvert, he was smiling, I could not shoot him!" she said.

"Don't you shoot ducks to eat?" he asked.

"Of course, we trap them but not when they are pairing" she asserted, "and where is your retriever dog, captain" she continued, "to retrieve the dead ducks?"

"It's very shallow, Rozenn, you could have waded out there" he countered.

She gave this due consideration. "I do not want to get my clothes wet, captain" she replied.

"You could have taken your clothes off."

Rozenn pursed her lips, looked up to the clear night sky and slowly closed her eyes. "Then you would have seen my naked body in the moonlight and you would not have been able to control yourself, captain."

"You're right of course, bad idea."

"And you captain, are paired with another."

"Yes, well, it's lucky you missed then."

"Yes, isn't it?" She no longer felt calm, but restless. "Now, we must remember why we are here. We have our promises to keep, do we not?"

Across the lake, there were sharp flashes and then the ringing of gun shots - a flash light was shining up to the sky and then across the lake. She offered the gun to Kirk, but he indicated it was her's. "Wear it. I'll give you six cartridges. Don't waste them on posts!"

She tried the weapon in various positions on her body as they marched. "Alors, it is...difficult to wear!"

So, he stopped to buckle the holster and belt around her waist. She slackened it. He tightened it so it didn't hang too low over her thigh. "You are not Annie Oakley" he muttered.

She had no idea who or what he was talking about. The belt was slackened again, and the belt rotated, so the holster nestled between her shoulder blades.

"That's no good, Rozenn, how are you going to..." He didn't finish his sentence - she had drawn the gun and it was pressing against the middle of his forehead. "Ah, that's not in the service manual. Very good, Rozenn. Let's get back."

Rozenn walked purposefully ahead of Kirk - she now had a weapon, a tool that could help her, a tool that could help her rescue Christoph. Behind her, the wildfowl of the lake were settling back, quacking and honking at each other. Together, they were retracing their steps back to the convoy. The screech owl had started screeching again.

"Where did you learn to shoot like that, Rozenn?" Kirk asked.

"I was the finest shooter in the commune, my captain."

"I see. Tell me about your commune, Rozenn."

"It is a small commune, maybe fifty souls, built into the rocks, looking over the great green sea."

"It sounds...very romantic!"

"This commune is made of rocks and souls. It is borne on the great green, like a wrecked vessel, shattered on the coast, it is not a romantic existence, my captain!"

CHAPTER NINETEEN

1235 Monday 19 May - Ahead of Troyes

Rozenn was at the crossroads. The commune of Troyes was somewhere straight ahead. Stretching away from her in all directions were rows of poplar trees, receding into the distance, flickering in the late morning sun. From one direction, the north-east, there was a slow flood of people, carts, motor cars and animals heading down the road, moving steadfastly away from oily smoke that smudged the sky just above the tree line. These oily smudges were illuminated by flashes of light and licks of orangey-red flames. The stump on her left hand itched continuously, and the itch spread through the skin of her hand and then up her arm, and then across her shoulders, building up to a furious crescendo across her scalp, which could not be soothed by her scratching. Also, it could not be accounted for by the chaos in front of her.

Rozenn was at the head of the spear, with the shaft, a twisting column of honking, drab, dust-covered vehicles full of soldiers behind, trailing through two villages. Kirk's squadron had fallen behind when the tourer had attempted a short cut across pasture and promptly became grounded. A British army fifteen hundredweight truck was positioned to stem the flow. Two of the lowlander soldiers hoisted her onto the cab roof.

The leader of the host wore a dark, buttoned up cloak that finished at his neck with a straight, white collar. He was a tall, substantially built man, with no hat, but with lush black hair that stuck out prominently from behind his ears. There was some kind of shiny band of office suspended about his chest. This was going to be difficult, even though she had the advantage of height, balanced as she was on the top of the lorry cab. She stood tall and shouted, "Monsieur, monsieur, you must make your people turn back! You must make way for the army of the alliance!"

"Mademoiselle, the enemy is coming, can you not see? Let us pass!"

"Monsieur, the Boche will shoot you down like dogs! Go back to your homes! There you will be safe!"

"Let us pass my young lady" he growled, "or will you too shoot us down like dogs?"

Another self-appointed leader cried out, "The Germans are coming, they are coming! Flee before they come! Don't listen to the girl!" She also had a long cloak that flirted with the ground and an insignia of office hanging round her neck.

The officer in command of the Scottish Lowlanders marched up to the side of her lorry and doffed his cap to her. He sported trews that were made of the blue and green tartan of his clan. "Sir, I think we have an impasse" she muttered from behind her hand.

"We'll fire a volley above their heads. That will make them change their minds."

"You will not, sir! You will frighten the animals and the children. There will be a stampede. People will be hurt. Let me try to turn them round."

"I'll give you five minutes, and then we fire a volley!"

Rozenn shouted again, but the man in the long black cloak led the surge around the vehicle and the flood of humanity continued unabated. Her stump felt like it was burning - she put it in her mouth and gnawed at it. And then she stopped.

There was a high pitched whine of rapidly spinning machinery. It was an unfamiliar sound to her - it was not the wind nor a bird. Could it be an aircraft engine? Yes, but there were two separate engines, almost synchronised, two aircraft heading her way at high speed but at low level. They could only be military aircraft, with guns, bombs and cannons. A spasm went through her left arm and then across her shoulders, across her crown and down her spine.

"Get off the road" she shouted, "danger is coming!"

The column of people started an excited and concerned chatter. First one woman and then others moved off the road. The high pitched whine was getting louder and more insistent, and coming at them from over the village. And then she saw them; one plane circling over the village and a second, coming at her, like a fast flying hornet. She withdrew the gun from her back holster and levelled it at the plane hurtling towards her. It was flying directly at her. She had six bullets: her assailant probably had thousands.

She steadied her breath and fired six shots at the canopy. There were flashes in the wings and above the yellow spinner - a staccato rhythm was beating down two trails either side of her - little eruptions burst in the soil behind her. And then it was gone, roaring away on its narrow, waggling wings.

There was a sudden silence - heads popped out of ditches and from behind the trees and then this was broken by screams and moans. Rozenn's heart was thumping violently and her hands were shaking out of control. And then as she slipped from the roof, she was violently pulled to the ground. It was by a khaki clad soldier. He seized her tunic with both hands and tugged her under the lorry. She saw fuel spattering from a metal cylinder to the ground. He was shouting at her but she couldn't tell what he was saying.

"I said, what the bloody hell are you doing?" he screamed.

"I'm trying to stop him" she cried breathlessly as she wriggled back out. The plane had gone with a waggle of the wings and a screaming turn back towards the north. The crush of people had dispersed and they were lying scattered in the surrounding fields, crying and screaming. A girl clutching a doll ran down the road towards her. She swept the girl up and pulled her tight. "Don't cry. I will find your maman!"

She passed the child to the soldier and turned towards a tracked armoured carrier just a few paces away. There was another plane approaching quickly. It was not a friendly plane. Rozenn ran and hurdled over the thin armoured side into the cabin and gathered her breath. There was a long, metal gun on a mounting, pointing impotently to the sky. She swivelled it about so it was directed to the north above the village. The second plane was approaching, like another angry hornet. The wooden rest fitted comfortably against her shoulder. It swivelled easily.

A soldier scrambled alongside her, panting and gripping his helmet. He had another helmet in his hand. 'You'll need this' he shouted above the sudden babble of frightened voices in the fields surrounding them. He placed it on her head but it didn't fit. The plane was closing, there was no time! She slid it back so it covered most of the back of her head and neck.

"Open that metal box down there." He pointed to the floor of the vehicle. "Open it, take out the reel of bullets and thread it in here." It clicked easily into place. The aircraft engine was howling louder. The soldier took control of the gun. The noise of the plane's cannons hammered out - greeted with screams from the road. The soldier set himself and pulled the trigger. "Keep that reel feeding through" he roared through the cacophony of explosions, "I'll get the bastard!" Empty cartridges flew into her face and rattled around the metal compartment. And the roar came to a crescendo with hundreds of rifles and machine guns joining in. Shells smacked into the soil and ripped holes through the cabin. The gun was spun round and continued a stream of fire after the retreating plane. The canister was empty. She found a replacement, opened it and was ready to feed the bullets again to this insatiable weapon.

The soldier gave a massive sigh. "Stand easy love, he's running off with 'is tail between 'is legs!" Rozenn glanced in the direction he was pointing - there was a thin oily trail of smoke marking the plane's direction. "I reckon we got the bastard!" He slapped her back - the helmet slid over her face. "And next time, put it on properly! Adjust the fit, chin strap under your chin, get it level and then it might do some good!" Rozenn shrugged in agreement. The side of the vehicle was jagged with holes. There was an intense acrid smell from the damaged metal, from the burnt cordite and from leaking petrol. "We should get out. It's had it love!" The soldier jumped out first and then held her arm. Her feet crunched on the shells that littered the floor as she vaulted over the armoured side of the wounded carrier.

All the troops were waving their helmets and cheering - apart from one. An officer was striding towards them, his face was purple with barely contained rage and this clashed with the green and blue tartan of his trews. "You! I gave you an order! You must obey orders! If you don't follow orders you put yourselves and others at risk!"

"We got him, sir! See!" The soldier pointed to the sky where there was a dirty oily brown streak heading in a northerly direction.

"You! The French girl!" He chased her towards the fifteen hundred weight lorry. "I'm talking to you!"

Rozenn looked under the lorry but there was no girl. She cast her eyes around about but there was still no girl. "You cannot fight the Boche by hiding in a ditch!" Rozenn hissed.

Now, where was that girl? There were screams and shouts that punctuated the high pitched buzz that swam around inside her head.

There was what looked like a doll lying limply in the ditch, resting on its back, one of the limbs splayed out at an absurd angle. She knelt down by the side of the doll and tugged at the loose limb - it came away easily.

"Allons! Allons! I must get you out of there!"

There was an ugly, jagged hole through the shoulder and through the stomach. The holes were so big, there was little else left of the broken doll - just two holes, shattered bone, charred flesh, clothes mangled into the holes. She gathered up the limp figure but the loose limb fell to the ground. Tenderly, she picked it up and placed it next to the body.

Across the field, there was a cow jumping and bellowing in pain - three men were chasing it, two in soldier's uniforms. There were two shots, a gut-wrenching bellow and then the animal fell heavily to the ground. A whinnying horse was held down on the gravel of the road, and then the crack of a bullet suddenly ended its life.

The limb could not be connected back to the body, because there was some part of the joint missing. Rozenn scanned the bottom of the ditch - it was churned and steaming, like it was alive. She pressed the little limb up tight to the shoulder but it would not connect, so she placed it as close as she could to the torso and it left a scarlet and black streak across the chest.

A pair of blue and green trews went by, shouting orders. The engine of the armoured carrier started and it promptly skidded into the ditch on the far side of the road. The tracks continued to clatter around the bogies. Four men further down the road were lifting the near-side of a lorry, so that a shot through tyre could be mended.

She carried the body along the ditch and then out into the field, were there were people swirling about, shouting, not really knowing where they were going or what they were doing. And then there was a flat patch of soil where six bodies had been laid out, like puppets with their strings cut through.

Rozenn waved the loose limb at the people there, calling out *"pas si bon, pas si bon."* The people did not seem to care. They opened their mouths and spoke but their words could not be heard through the persistent buzzing in her head. She stumbled across the big road - there was a jumble of wreckage there - and made her way towards more people. A woman screamed and started banging her fists against her head. She cried out something that sounded like "Sophie" over and over again. She tugged at the doll and took it away from Rozenn. The woman was now kneeling over the body and screaming.

"Votre poupée?" asked Rozenn.

A man was tugging at her arm. "Kirk, what are you doing here?" she asked, but her voice seemed disembodied, so she asked again. She was being pulled away, her feet scampering to keep pace with the captain. They were approaching the crossroads through a crowd that was moving uncertainly back to their village. The big man in the black cloak looked at her reproachfully as he started to ease his flock back the way they had come, back to their homes.

"Monsieur?" she called out.

"Mademoiselle, see what your war has brought to my commune! Ruin!"

"Monsieur, this is not my war!" Her voice seemed far away, so she stopped shouting.

Kirk had his arm around her shoulder and he was squeezing her away. "There's nothing you can do, Rozenn, the child had no chance."

"But Kirk, there was no one with her when she passed! What happened to her soul?"

"There was nothing you could have done - no one could have survived that! Two cannon shell hits! That would have felled an elephant!"

"But her soul, Kirk! Her soul! Her soul is lost!"

"There's nothing to be done here - we must press on!"

"No, Kirk, in this time, it is not enough to kill your enemies. In this time, we destroy our enemy's families - the old folk, the womenfolk and their infants!"

The convoy was ready to move on. She begged Kirk for more bullets as she had expended them all. Her weapon and her belt were now full again. There was still the incessant rustling in her ears but once again, she could pick out distant sounds, know from what direction they were coming from and how quickly they would reach her. Beyond the plateau and the broad river valley to the north, there was the steady rumble of war machines punctuated by rumbles through the ground. She must press on.

He was now calculating what to do next. "Wait a minute, Rozenn." He withdrew an envelope from his side pack and presented it to her. "Keep this with you. This is a letter issued by my government. Any man in the British Armed Forces, or our alliance, is charged with doing everything that is necessary to get you safe passage to England."

"Mais pourquoi, captain?"

He stared at her. "You really don't know, do you Rozenn?"

"It must be my relationship with Christoph and what he has told me. It must be concerning the ghost division and the Nazi operation known as hell. That is all I know!"

CHAPTER TWENTY

1055 Tuesday 20 May - Before the Gare de Troyes

The Abgrall girl was fretting again, and he understood why. Kirk's squadron had become enmeshed in a slow-moving convoy of Scottish Lowlanders, on their way to a new location, somewhere to the south-west of Paris.

However, Rozenn had followed her normal routine of folding away her bivvy, kicking the ashes of the fire into touch and putting away the urn in the tourer. The coffee she produced each morning was only tolerable with large quantities of sugar and cream, but she had this gift of bringing back treasure from her early morning foraging. They were never short of butter, milk, cheese, bread and bundled roots and leaves of uncertain provenance. The latter were practically indigestible.

But now, they were closing in on the outer reaches of Paris, which seemed to sprawl out from the centre like the tentacles of an octopus stranded on the beach. This particular tentacle stretched to the south-east and ran alongside a railway line. And the chaos that stretched as far as Kirk's eye could see was a direct result of the hustle and bustle of the main line railway station in front of him. And then there was the stench that was ripening in the midday sun.

"Come with me Rozenn. We need your diplomatic skills again!"

"Pourquoi, Captain?"

"You are our chief liaison officer for our expedition - I need you to sort out this mess!"

The stench of horse dung permeated the air around the long line of railway trucks lined up sullenly along the outer-most siding in the railway station. People crowded along all the other station platforms, but not this one. This one was on the edge of the railway station and was overlooked by a large metal cylinder.

"D'accord, my captain!" She held her nose as they marched together to where a small conference was being held out in the open. At the center of it was a man dressed all in black, except for his starched white shirt with the turned down collar ends and a burgundy neck-tie. Arguing with him was a Scottish officer, who called himself Stewart and a private soldier, hanging back.

"Monsieur, I need you to do as I ask of you. Now!" said the officer in green and blue trews.

'Non, Monsieur. I will not allow it!"

Kirk stopped and turned about - Rozenn was chatting to two men by the water tank. She scampered to join the conference, after the taller of the two men had given the cylinder two resounding taps with a very large spanner. This seemed to satisfy her and now she was beaming at him with those beguiling brown eyes.

The railway official continued in the same vein. "Never! I insist that you do not desecrate this structure! There will be a republic after this conflict and we must preserve our national treasures!"

"Pardon Monsieur" announced Kirk, "may I present to you our liaison officer, Madam Abgrall."

"Madam Abgrall?"

"Oui. I thought she could help us to resolve this...impasse...as she is a considerable translator."

"Bonjour monsieur. Comment allez-vous?" said Rozenn, politely.

The official gasped, swept his arm to encompass all the chaos around and then flung his arms up in exasperation, uttering an animal snort.

"Monsieur, I see you are a little busy, so I will keep this short. I foresee two possibilities."

"Madam?"

"She can also tell you your fortune" said Kirk. His buttocks clenched- he hoped no one had noticed his sudden discomfort.

Rozenn continued. "The first possibility is, you will help the Republic and these allies of ours and I will be very grateful for that."

"C'est bonne. And Madam, please, what is the second possibility?'

"I will have you shot, monsieur."

"Madam, that is monstrous!"

"Monsieur, war is monstrous, and so am I, and there is little time!"

"Non, non, non!"

"Monsieur, are those your final words?"

He folded his arms and looked haughtily up at the sky.

"Maintenant, we have the second possibility." She turned to the man in trews. "Shoot him!"

"No, no, no, he's a civilian! That would be cold blooded murder!"

"Yes, you can. He's a cold blooded idiot! He chose the wrong possibility. Soldier, shoot him!" She directed this to the private who had stood uncomfortably by with his rifle at the ready.

"I canna shoot him in cold blood! That's murdah!"

"Yes, you can! He's an imbecile. Shoot him!"

He made no move to shoot. The rifle was still slung limply to his side. So, she wrenched the revolver from the holster on her back and pointed it towards the idiot. She had forgotten that her left hand had no trigger finger, so she quickly swapped the revolver to her right hand.

"Madam! Mercy!'"

There was a click and everyone stopped talking. Several pairs of eyes stared at her.

"Zut alors! The safety catch!"

They all blinked through the flash. The idiot cowered below, his large black top hat thrust towards her. The shot rang out across the station. The hat had a bullet-sized hole in it.

"Zut alors, down a notch!" Captain Stewart looked aghast. The idiot looked horrified. Kirk turned away, his hand clutched over his mouth.

The official got to his feet and examined his hat. He was shaking and so was his hat. "Madam, your first possibility, is that still available to me, please?"

"Yes, but quickly now! Vite! Vite! Vite! There is no time to lose!"

She followed the official as he stumbled along the railway line, barking commands at a crowd of ruffians, scornfully smoking hand rolled cigarettes, spitting in the dust. Suddenly, they were galvanised into action: the hose from the water cylinder was deployed to wash out each truck as it was pulled steadily past; two men were deployed with brooms to scrub each truck clean; squads of soldiers were deployed to load themselves and their equipment on board.

"I say, why are you doing this?" asked Captain Stewart. He skipped over the sleepers in order to keep up with Rozenn.

"Captain, I am a civil servant. It is my job to serve the people! And I made my promise to Kirk. But I am losing so much time..."

"I say! Really! We need people like you back in Blighty!"

"In Blighty?"

"England. You know, green and pleasant land and all that..."

"Ah so, that is Blighty. How wonderful." She could no longer see the railway official - he must have found some other petty travail to occupy his time.

"Rien!" shouted the man perched on top of the tower, his legs straddling the hose, his hands holding a large tool which he used to bang on the sides of the cylinder. The last of the wagons had passed by and was loaded with its military cargo.

"That is all Captain Stewart."

"That's all...mademoiselle. So, where will your duties take you now?"

"Huh?"

"As a servant of the people?"

"Huh?" And then she understood. She brought out the letter that Kirk had presented to her.

"Sorry old girl, we're re-deploying. You can come as our..."

"Chief...liaison officer...expeditionary?"

"Ah, those initials make...Chloe! That's my old sister's name, Chloe!"

"Cloe? No, no, I call myself Rozenn."

"Rozenn, I think we are finished here, old girl. So, toodle pip!"

"Bonne chance, Captain Stewart."

She sensed a commotion and it was closing in. Two men in smart black kepis and tunics were running towards her from across the tracks. Gendarmerie!

Rozenn weighed up the possibilities; there was Kirk and his interminably slow moving touring car; there was Captain Stewart and his slow moving train; and then there was the Gendarmerie.

Her arms were seized and she was dragged away from the wagons, her feet stumbling across the iron rails and the wooden sleepers. So, where was Kirk? She could see no sign of him.

Suddenly, there was a passage made through the crowd and they made quick progress across the tracks. The railway official was standing outside his office and he smugly waved his hat at her as she was dragged by.

And there was a car outside the station, with its engine running and a man leaning on it, in his uniform and kepi. He rapidly stubbed out his cigarette, wiped his mouth and opened the passenger door for her.

Someone was shouting her name. It was Kirk. She turned to look at him running her way as her head was pushed inside. Tears flowed down her face as she waved him goodbye. Their pact had been broken. Her head was pushed downwards and she could no longer see him.

"Rozenn" was the cry, "Rozenn!" It wasn't an angry cry - it was a cry of despair.

CHAPTER TWENTY-ONE

1435 Wednesday 21 May 1940 - The Ministry for War, Issy-les-Moulineaux, Paris

Rozenn straightened herself in the car seat and puffed and huffed - her wrists were tightly cuffed, but now she was as straight as she could get, the odour of sweat, that permeated the stained leather, did not trouble her so much. And, now she was straight, she could see the increasing regularity of the communes they passed through and their steady aggregation into sizeable cantons.

The police car arrived at a white, stuccoed block, streaked with the rust that trickled down from the iron clad first and second floor railings. The door was large and wooden and was flung open as they came to a halt. A little man in a black, white topped kepi, a black tunic, flared blue trousers and black leather boots came running out. He stared at Rozenn, his gaze flicking to a large sheet of paper and then slapped his forehead twice. He then did a little pirouette and ran back up the steps to return to the dark inside.

After several moments, the little man was back, now accompanied by a taller man with gold fittings on his uniform jacket and kepi. This man tapped on the window and now there was a heated discussion outside the automobile between the Gendarmerie. Rozenn calculated that she was going to be interrogated inside.

So, up the steps they went, below the tricolour, into the gloom and across a chipped marble floor to the rear of the building. Now, she was bundled into a large, stale smelling office with a very large, imposing desk. A seat on a quite humble chair was offered and she reluctantly sat down. She could barely see above the lip of the desk, however, the decorative inlay could be seen to great advantage from her eye-line. The senior Gendarme now asked for her papers. She responded that she could not reach them. Before the little gendarme could insert his hands down her tunic, she stood, stepped backwards over the wrist cuffs and shook them once, twice, three times. They fell away with a clatter to the marble floor. She then presented her papers with a flourish and stood with her hands on her hips. The little man pushed her down into her seat, picked up the wrist cuffs and started to examine the locks on them very intently.

"Ho are you?" the senior man asked.

Rozenn frowned.

"Ho are you?" he repeated more forcefully. The size of the dark grey thicket on his top lip hid his mouth and made it difficult to comprehend what he was saying.

"Ah, d'accord. I call myself Rozenn Abgrall, I have nineteen years of age and I am a servant of the people. Most recently, in the service of my country, and the Army of France, I have the most important duty of chief liaison officer with the British Expedition..."

At the mention of 'the British', he dismissed her answer with a grand sweep of his left hand. A pile of papers was sent flying across the room. Another motion of his left hand stopped the little man from stooping to capture them.

"Yo must decide what side yoos on."

"I am on the side of anyone who will stop the Boche. I have a letter which says you must help me."

"Puh!" he mumbled and tried to swat it away but she held it tight.

"Please" she implored him.

And he read, and read, and read. At least, that is what Rozenn assumed he was doing, as the thicket on his top lip moved up and down and his eyes moved from side to side with the rhythm of very slow reading.

"Ah see" he pronounced at last, "yoos must be woman et sez 'ere?"

"Yes."

"Ah see."

"And yoos will do what it sez there, monsieur captain?" she said very deliberately.

"Ah must."

"Yes, yoos must, if that is what it sez."

He stood up and towered above, with a fierce expression like an eagle - just like the eagle carved in wood in the centre of the wall behind his desk. He clicked his fingers and the little man took her arm with one hand and the wrist cuffs with the other and marched her out of the front of the building. The little man whispered that she had been very fortunate as his superior had just enjoyed a very excellent luncheon. He fumbled as he tried to put the wrist locks back on Rozenn, but they decided by mutual consent that there was no point in doing this.

To her left, close to the steps, a dark green vehicle's engine was coughing into action and was being filled with an escort of armed policemen. Just behind this was the automobile she had arrived in. Rozenn was bundled into the back seat.

Nothing moved. Several pairs of eyes looked at her expectantly.

Rozenn chose to break the silence: "Monsieur driver, take me to Issy!" she instructed as she brandished a letter in front of his eyes.

"Ah, Issy-les-Moulineaux, that is in the department of Hauts-de-Seine?"

"Oui, monsieur."

"Oui, I know that. But where are you going in Issy-les-Moulineaux?"

"It says here on this letter. You know the avenue that is by the river?"

"The Seine? Oui, I know it, ..."

"Ah, that is good, so you know of the ministry for war."

"Oui, you mean the ministry of mistakes!"

"You know it?"

"Mais oui, of course! I will take you there."

"Merci monsieur!"

The Ministry for War at Issy-les-Moulineaux is a neo-classical building of the Second Empire, standing back from the Seine.

The colonnade that overlooks the river is distinguished by a row of Corinthian columns, spaced apart following a long forgotten mathematical formula.

Rozenn's driver commented that the armed guards at the front of the building were now provided by the Gendarmerie as the Army of France could not be trusted. He predicted that the Third Empire would end in ruins and be replaced by a German led Fourth Empire, distinguished by order, discipline and honour. Gendarme Abel believed that this would be the best thing that could happen to their country.

She was escorted in through the columns, after her papers had been checked by a gendarme, who said that until recently he had been a duty sergeant in Vichy. He took away her belt, holster and revolver.

Inside, she had time to gaze at the high vaulted entrance hall and then the cell she was led to. In here, she had her clothes removed, was plunged into a deep bath, searched, dried off and then allowed to re-assemble her clothing, her possessions but not her dignity, all under the strict supervision of a female officer, who was in all probability of Alsacien descent, if her manner was anything to go by.

Rozenn was led up a flight of steps. On this level they stopped. Over the metal railings there was a hush - punctuated by the clumping of shoes over the polished stone floor. She saw military caps and civilian hats below.

The Alsacien women explained: "Les Britanniques."

"Les Britanniques.? But why?"

There was an uncomfortable pause. *"La bataille et...vous."*

"But why?"

The Alsacien shrugged and tugged at Rozenn's arm. "Par ici." She was led into a small room and took a seat. Across the table was an official of the ministry. They sat like this for ten minutes as he tried to digest a report by pressing his hands hard against his temples. She peered anxiously out of the window that overlooked the Rue Saint-Dominique in the 7th arrondissement of Paris. There were thin trails of smoke drifting above the pitched roofs. So much paper to burn, she thought.

Rozenn learned that this administrator administrated on behalf of the supervisor that supervised the staff that supported the deputy for the Minister of War.

"Mademoiselle Abgrall, this is very confusing" the administrator announced eventually. "This man, Christoph de Bourcard, is he a French national?"

"He was, but now he is hostage to Nazi aggression."

"Alors, it's not clear to me how you have the...position to access any relevant intelligence."

"I understand, but please let me try and explain..." His waxed moustache twitched up and down as he spoke, like a bat flitting its leathery wings.

"Make a call to the Zurich embassy and they will tell you..." she continued.

"And even if it is true, which I rather doubt, why should I do anything about it? France is finished. The English will be finished in weeks. What is the point of all this? We are at war with the Nazis. We could soon be at war with the Italian fascists. All of Europe will soon be part of a greater Germany. Do you want to spend the rest of your life eating bratwurst and sauerkraut? I do not!"

"I must find Christoph and rescue him, then everything can be made clear."

"Enough Mademoiselle Abgrall. We are going to have to make decisions in the best interests of France. We are on our own now. The British will desert us and make their own terms with the Nazis. They will abandon us. Maintenant, I will abandon the ministry and Paris. Bonne chance mademoiselle." He stood up, collected his greatcoat from the hook on the door and quickly left the room.

Rozenn was now led up a flight of steps by the woman. As they paced her way along the main corridor of the second level, a young, gaudily dressed woman had tottered past, clutching a large handbag, shaking her painted face to and fro. They arrived at a door. A tap on the door and they were called inside. Rozenn took a seat opposite a distinguished looking officer - distinguished by a grey moustache and beard and a chest full of ribbons and medals.

"Sit" he said.

Over his shoulder Rozenn could see trails of dirty smoke smudging up the sky above the roof tops of the arrondissement. Below, in the quadrangle, there was shouting and the shifting and scraping of wooden crates. The whole of the city seemed to be in the grip of a panic.

"Cognac?" he asked.

Rozenn declined but her nostrils twitched at the scent of alcohol and the cigar smoke that filled the room.

He moved some papers around, took a puff from the cigar that smouldered in the ornate ash tray and then took a hefty swig from a crystal tumbler.

"You call yourself Mademoiselle Abgrall, you function as a clerk in the Zurich Embassy..."

"Also at the Basel Legation" added Rozenn.

"On whose authority?"

"The Chef de Mission, of course."

"Of course."

"Also on the authority of the Attaché of the Armée de Terre..."

"Of course. Alors, the Head of the Bank of Zutter has made a complaint to our ambassador...it is regarding your behaviour to him and his family."

"Alors, old man Zutter is a monster..."

"And you have had an affair with a Nazi soldier of the Geist Regiment."

"He is not a Nazi and I have not had an affair with him - he is my friend!"

"So" he continued, forming his hands into a temple, "tell me what you learned from...your friend."

Rozenn pulled a face - her eyes cast around the room behind him and then settled on an especially round blemish on his nose. Should she disclose what she thought or what she knew or what she thought she had understood from his letter?

"I learned from Christoph how to handle a sailing boat, how to repair a bicycle and how a women should be respected!"

"Non, non, non! What did you learn regarding his movements?"

"Ah, his movements? Very little...he is a very private man."

"Mademoiselle, where is his regiment at this moment?"

"Christoph's regiment is moving to les Pays-Bas, that is all I know..."

"What is their mission?"

"I do not know."

"I think you do."

"I think I do not."

He stood up and walked to the map that covered the wall. "What could they be doing in les Pays-Bas?" he muttered, "the Geist regiment, always at the tipping point for the Boche, what is the coup de main that they plan?"

"I do not know this. I have told you all I know."

He returned to his desk and scribbled a three line note. "Sign this Bout de Papier. This is all you will say to the Britanniques. Tout. Do you understand?"

"I cannot sign this."

"You will sign!" He slapped the Bout de Paper to the desk in front of Rozenn.

"I cannot. Jamais, jamais, jamais! I don't know what it is!" His thin smile did not disguise his anger and she was shaken. If she deviated from his script, she would be in trouble.

He turned to the Alsacien woman. "Alors, stay with the girl, if she says anything different to this, bring her back to me, and then we will see..."

They emerged from the meeting in a silence that was intense. Rozenn loosened the leather belt that girdled her waist and her collar button. What did the Britanniques want from her? A reading from the dregs of the tea cup? They descended two flights of cold, stone steps in quiet harmony.

"You should not have said that" said the Alsacien as they reached the ground floor.

"I could not help it! I cannot sign his paper!"

"It is bad enough that you are a girl."

"Yes, that is bad, I realise that, but..."

"Maintenant, none of this matters, the Nazis have reached the sea and our armies are split apart. We have only weeks before they enter Paris."

"You cannot say there is no hope. There is always hope."

"The Dutch have surrendered, Belgium will soon follow, the Britanniques will flee like they always do. All they care about is their rotten empire, they care nothing for our alliance."

"Non, non, non. I met Scottish soldiers - all they care about is having a good fight!"

They walked quickly across the hall to the back of the building - there were men scurrying here and there with no discernible purpose.

"This is a different kind of war. There is no humanity, no honour, no humility, just a casual disregard for what sets us apart from animals."

"The Germans, even the Nazis, must follow the rules of war... because there are consequences!"

"There are no rules, not any more! They attack our people with bullets and bombs. Our people are fleeing in panic, and we cannot stop them!"

They arrived at a double set of doors, beyond which Rozenn could hear many animated voices, some French, some English. Two men burst out through the doors, an English officer and a French officer. She caught a snatch of their conversation:

"Monsieur general, what are we to do?"

"Stand and fight! Bring up all your reserves! Pray for a miracle!"

"But monsieur, what will you do?"

"We'll be right behind you!"

The Alsacien peeped through the doors - Rozenn could see a long table, covered with maps and a row of Britanniques on one side and a row of Frenchmen on the other.

They were ushered inside.

"Bring more coffee, bring cognac" shouted a voice from the French side.

"Is this the Abgrall girl?"

"Oui. Say your piece girl and then bring the coffee! And cognac! And cigars!"

Rozenn sat at the head of the table. A nod from the chair and then from the Alsacien prompted Rozenn to start. Her body quivered as her voice stumbled over what her name was, what her role with the diplomatic mission was and the barest details of her correspondence with Christoph de Bourcard.

"And that is all?"

"That is all, monsieur."

"So, the real question is, what is the mission of the Geist regiment, is it not?" summarised the stout man with the biggest cigar.

"It is immaterial. We need to counter attack and cut off the head of the serpent!" said a highly decorated officer of the French Army.

"Coffee, cognac and cigars!" shouted another.

Everyone looked at Rozenn. She stood up and turned to leave.

"Tea for me!" shouted a British officer over the clamour.

"Tea! We are at war! You Britanniques!"

The British officer pulled out a tea pot and a pouch from under the table. "Let me help you make the tea - it's time for a brew!"

The man with the biggest cigar stalked across and put his hand on her shoulder. "Mademoiselle, I am enchanted." He took her hand and planted a kiss on it. "Major McPherson will look after you."

The major led her out of the room - the Alsacien hesitated and then followed them.

"I do not know. Where are we going?"

"Through here" he directed her to an ante room. It had a row of cupboards, an urn, a metal rack holding bottles of wine and a large bottle of brandy. It had no window but was dimly lit by two gas lights.

"I do not know. What do we do now?" she exclaimed.

"First, warm the pot, like so" he instructed, "and then one, two, three spoonfuls of tea and one for the pot. There you go."

The Alsacien women snorted, took a cafeteria of coffee and a carafe back into the meeting.

He replaced the lid on the teapot and smiled and her knees went weak - she leaned for support against the wall. A cupboard sprang open. "Ah, petit fours, excellent! May I?"

"I know nothing."

He looked at her in surprise: "Bite-sized appetisers, baked in the cooling oven, you live well here, don't you?" He popped a pastry into her mouth; she swallowed it whole. Confiture and cream oozed into her stomach. She beckoned for another; it followed the same path.

"What do you want from me?"

"My name is Sandy. Sandy McPherson. Let's go somewhere quiet where you and me can have a little chat. Would that be all right?"

"Monsieur..."

"Sandy."

"Monsieur Sondy."

"Sandy."

"Son...dee."

"That's close enough. Here, what should we take for our little picnic?"

Rozenn scooped up the remaining petit fours and dropped them onto a sliver platter, and then added a jug of milk. He added the tea pot, two cups and saucers. She put a bottle of brandy under her arm and two bowl-shaped glasses between her fingers. A few paces away they found a small room, and inside the room there was a window looking out to the formal gardens at the rear. All around the grand fountain, there were small bonfires being fed with armfuls of papers.

They sat down side by side on packing boxes and he took her left hand and patted it. She tried to pull it away. He held it up so that the gap amongst her fingers was glaringly obvious. "What happened to you?" he wanted to know.

"Ah, the finger? I lost it."

"In a fight?"

"Yes."

"Must have been vicious."

"He was. And he knew how to damage me!"

"Who was he?"

"Old man Zutter. He is a bastard."

McPherson took off his cap to reveal his sandy hair. His sandy moustache was neatly trimmed and he casually brushed it every time he spoke. And then she started to tell him everything that had happened to her over the last few weeks, and he listened intently, asking a little question on occasion and nodding gently. And when she came to the now time, she realised that a lifetime had passed her by. She looked for something to drink. She dribbled out the tea that was offered in a teacup and instead, took a sip of brandy from a glass. "Ah, bien, but none of this matters, I just need to find Christoph!"

"And, it may be in our best interest...for we British to help you in that."

Her eyes narrowed and she pulled away. The left arm twitched and she had to tuck it away below her leg. "What do you mean, Sondee?"

"Let's see if we can put it all together." He unrolled a chart and held it up against the window. It was a map of Northern Europe. He managed to locate a little piece of Switzerland in the lower right-hand corner. "Your best friend Zutter, is in league with the Nazis - he is sabotaging your country's efforts to procure vital war supplies."

"He is not my best friend - he is my worst enemy!"

"I agree. Zutter has a lot to answer for, including nicking your digit."

"He does, but I got him back!"

"Good girl! But he has access to all the materials he has sequestered, now what could he do with those?"

"I do not know. Could he put up a big sign that says 'à vendre'?"

"Yes, he could do that, but who could possibly be interested? Now, that barge you landed on in the River Rhine - it had been converted, but what for?"

"For the use of artillery and for soldier passengers."

"Yes, you could be right. And your Christoph's letter - an elite regiment is re-located to Holland, away from the Schwerpunkt."

"Ah, but is it?" Rozenn squeezed hard on a pastry and a dollop of jam landed on Basel. "Oh, pardonnez-moi monsieur!"

"Or is it exactly where it needs to be?"

Rozenn got up and ducked inside his arms. Her left hand now traced the flow of the river as it made its way towards the Grey Sea. She closed her eyes: Christoph was looking over the waves to the west, a heaving monster of a sea, taunting him. He was on a craft, floating on the Grey Sea, swaying one way and another, his stomach rolling, but there were flames roaring over the angry boundary between wind and water and then the flames were upon him, his skin blistering and he was swallowed by the cold, angry sea, his limbs flailing helplessly as he was sucked into the huge, seething mass.

A long diagonal streak of jam bisected the map. Rozenn could feel a heart bumping furiously against her back, in unison with hers, and a sudden gasp in her ear causing a rapid chill all over her skin.

McPherson shouted: "Jesus Holy Christ!"

"No matter! I wipe it away!"

"No, no, no, Rozenn, can't you see?"

"Of course! The architect of all this evil is Zutter!"

"No, no, no, Rozenn, the Boche are coming for us!"

"Then you Britanniques had better be ready!"

Chapter Twenty-Two

1535 Wednesday 21 May 1940 - Vlissengen, les Pays-Bas.

"Ach, can you see it yet?" called out Oberst Schiller.

"Das England? Nein, nein. It's just behind that smog!" Feldwebel Rubens stepped away from the tripod mounted range finder and rubbed his eyes. He replaced his feldmütze back on his clean shaven head. "It's a shitty little country anyway, is it worth all this effort?" The lapels of his field grey uniform had the symbol of the 'Geist' picked out in white upon them.

"We have our orders, Rubens."

"Herr oberst, but now I'm so close, I could just step over this pool of piss, take Churchill by the neck and throttle him like an old broiler!"

"Very good, Rubens. That will save us a lot of trouble, if you can get your hands all the way round his neck!"

Schiller tightened his belt, turned smartly and marched along the dyke to the armoured car with its bedstead aerial. A Nazi big-wig was waiting for him impatiently, in contrast to the white belted brown cattle on the pasture below, continuing to chew the cud with complete disinterest in their new arrivals.

"Those men are a disgrace, look at them, I thought we had more pride in the Heer!" Two soldiers were play-wrestling and they were tumbling down the slope to ribald cheers from the top of the dyke.

"They will deliver England to the Fuehrer on a plate, like a trussed chicken, Herr Gauleiter!"

"It's not right. They need to maintain their discipline. How can that be right?" said the Nazi. He was in the full brown shirt regalia of the Munich stein thumpers.

"They will be going into battle soon but with little prospect of returning. I will be instructing my men to write final letters to their loved ones in the next days. Their sacrifice is the ultimate one!"

They were joined by another uniformed man. His uniform was that of an Admiral in the Kriegsmarine, but it was the Kriegsmarine of the last war, and Schiller knew he was no admiral. He fitted somewhere else in the hierarchy, not amongst the Nazis, but the head of one of the German intelligence agencies. The man removed his admiral's cap and the on-shore breeze swept a mane of white hair across his broad, wrinkled forehead. His nose was broad and bulbous, his lips taut and thin.

Apart from the harbour town of Vlissengen, to the south-east, there was nothing much to see apart from the modest waves lapping continuously against the seawall - a flood of grey-green sea, flushing its way into the Scheldt estuary.

And now there was a huddle of uniforms, looking across the grey-green sea. A card table was erected by the ersatz admiral's side, covered with a lace tablecloth and set for tea using blue Dresden china from a leather case. His adjutant placed a burner on a second table behind the man and lit it. And then he filled a copper kettle with water from a flask and placed it on the burner. A crystal glass was placed on the first table and topped up with clear, vinous fluid from a hip flask. The admiral swallowed this in one gulp and indicated that the crystal glass should be refilled.

"The Fuehrer will not be happy. He will think this is treason" muttered the brown uniform. He turned abruptly, gave a cursory long armed salute and started to stride back towards his staff car, a significant distance away. His driver stumbled after him, desperately holding his cap in place with his free hand.

"We will let the Fuehrer know at the right time. He will be grateful when I present him England on a plate. Assemble in the hotel at midday. I will issue the orders for Operation Hel."

"Schneider, Fischer, Weber, Burckhardt!" barked Schiller.

"Herr Oberst?"

"Get your men disembarked and get those letters written! Briefing in the hotel, twenty minutes!"

"Jawohl, Herr Oberst!"

The admiral stood up, brushed down his uniform and replaced his cap, squarely on his head. With a sweep of his long arm, he dismissed those around him and took a heroic pose, looking to the west: "Das Englanders, what a contemptible nation! Das mediaeval class system! Das old Etonians and their bowler hats! Das empire built by slaves! Das gin soaked women and their port soaked gentry! Das twee vicar's tea parties on the village green! Das queers! Das masons with their satanic altars and their... witches."

He paused to drink another shot of Schnapps. The admiral expectorated towards where he thought England should be but the breeze caught it and planted it on his tunic trousers. His aide bent down quickly and wiped it away.

"We're heading to jolly old England, just across this pool of piss and bringing thunder and lightning to their green and pleasant land! With one hard kick at the Englander's door, the whole decaying shit-house will fall!"

"That was very poetic and magnificent, Herr Admiral." The aide lowered the cine-camera.

"Did you get all that on film, Steiner?" He sat back down at the card table.

'Yes, Herr Admiral, I did."

A sheaf of type-written papers were presented to the admiral amongst the crockery. He looked for his fountain pen and it was placed in his waiting hand. Still looking across the North Sea and with nothing but a cursory glance at the papers, he signed with a grandiose flourish.

"This will set the operation in motion. We are at the tipping point Steiner - this is when the British empire collapses in ruins and a new order replaces it. Within a few weeks our leader will be sitting on the lawn at Buckingham Palace taking tea with their royalty and explaining to their shocked majesties about what has just happened!" He took another glass of schnapps.

It was just a signature on a set of orders, but a flurry of activity would ensue: Leutnants would brief sub-Leutnants, sub-Leutnants would brief squads of soldiers, field telephones would tinkle and wireless coding machines would tap into life.

Soon, the diesel engines of a flotilla of motor boats would cough into life and the triple engines of corrugated-sided planes would splutter. Men in uniforms would climb inside transport planes, carrying their weapons and parachutes. And a fifth column had already been infiltrated into the mass of fleeing Englanders and their reluctant allies.

CHAPTER TWENTY-THREE

It's the pattern of the sea witch!

Little Miss Katie creaked her way down the wooden stairs, necklace clutched tightly to her chest, barely daring to breathe. And then her heart leapt up her gullet! Lights flashed and beeps beeped! It was the alarm on her wristwatch! Slap, slap, slap she went until it was beaten into a resigned silence. She slowed her breathing and listened carefully up the stairs and across the landing: There was the gentle wheezing of her much older sister Gwen; the blubbering of Gwen's husband, Mister Hofland; the neighing of her niece, Monique and the moaning of her nephew, Alexander. All present and correct!

She stepped across the stone slab floor and pushed open the sitting room door. The embers behind the iron grill in the place of the fire barely glowed. Now she entered the room slowly, on the tips of her toes and made her long loping walk towards the Norway spruce. Despite all the water she had dripped into the red-papered pot, that held the base of the spruce tree, the outer stems were now drooping like a weeping willow. Tired needles had showered the brightly papered gifts below.

Her heart leapt! There was someone else in the room, waiting for her! Someone had their eyes fixed on her, cloaked as she was in baggy grey pyjamas, capped in a red hat with a white woollen pom-pom and footed in pink fluffy slippers. She stiffened like she was flash frozen in a freezer.

Seized from behind she was pulled gently backwards, and now she was caught between the arms of a chair and a man's arms, pinioned like a helpless minnow in the jaws of a dragonfly nymph. 'Let me go' she squealed, as quietly as she could. She was pulled tight and nuzzled behind the ear. She giggled, 'I want to see!'

'There's nothing for you' he answered. It was the hoarse whisper of their surprise guest.

'But why, Uncle Alec?' she asked.

'Because you are a pagan girl and Christmas isn't for pagans, is it? We celebrated Midwinter with you' he said pointing to her wrist, 'now stop your squealing, before you wake everyone up!'

She wriggled free and slithered like a snake towards the pile of presents.

'You must not touch!' He pulled her back gently.

'But I want to see if there's anything for me!'

'But, there's nothing for you. Your kind do not believe in Christmas, do you? You celebrate other, more arcane festivals of the season, like the winter solstice!'

'Eh, what's that, then, Uncle Alec?'

There was a long, drawn out sigh. 'Ah, never mind, but I do have something for you!'

'You do, Uncle Alec! Let me see!' she squealed.

He retrieved a small, navy blue box from his jacket pocket and flipped it open. Inside, she could see a shiny object, a gold cap badge, with engraved words that she could make no sense of.

He tilted the badge so that it sparkled at her. 'Can, you see that? It's your grandmother's and it is engraved with the legend 'Ultra Mare'. It means above, over and beyond the sea! It's the pattern of the sea witch, those who can see across the oceans, those who can shape the winds and the waves. It means that you could be ready soon!'

'Oh, ready for what, Uncle Alec?'

'Ready to fulfil your promise!'

'Oh' she replied. The disc was flipped in an out of her fingers and tossed from hand to hand with accomplished ease. 'Can I have some chocolate instead, Uncle Alec?'

CHAPTER TWENTY-FOUR

Wednesday 11 May 1105 - Over Plymouth Sound

The venerable, dazzle camouflaged Sea King helicopter, came within sight of the Cornish coast. There were two lines of green berets sitting along the sides of the cabin and one figure in a blue Royal Navy beret, blue shirt and trousers. Leading Hand K.E. Talog (Acting Unpaid) looked around the cabin and then continued writing in the ring-bound diary. The badinage about the hand bandages had subsided at last, but bandages on your hands make it that little bit more of a struggle to get your diary updated.

'Ket, what happened to your hands' shouted Marine Afshan Iqbal, 'did you cut them shaving?' He howled loud like a hunting werewolf then he laughed at what he seemed to think was a well constructed jibe.

'Lembo!' was the terse reply. A recalcitrant lock of wavy brown hair was swept behind an ear and the long pointed nose wrinkled in thought.

'So, what are you doing, Ket?' asked Sergeant Pettigrew, who sat opposite in the cabin of the helicopter.

'I'm plucking my fucking banjo, aren't I?' was the shouted reply.

'So that's how you pluck a banjo, I'd often wondered' he yelled back.

'So, what's the first thing you're going to do when you get back on dry land, Ket?' Marine Jerry Ryan asked. He leaned into Ket from the left side, making it even more difficult to write.

There was a wistful sigh. 'I can't tell you that, but the second thing I'll do is take my pack off!'

'Ha! You must be desperate for it! Come on, you can do better than that. Who's the unlucky one?' he shouted.

'I'm going to shag your brother' Ket replied loudly.

'Ha! No, you're not! I haven't got a brother!'

'Your sister then!'

The shouting stopped abruptly. There was just the constant whirring of rotors as they chopped through air.

'So how old is she?' asked Ket.

'None of your bloody business!'

'Ah, she must be in range then. What's her name?'

'I'm not telling you. Just piss off, will you!'

'She's younger than you, isn't she? She's right on the cusp. That's very interesting!'

'For God's sake Talog, keep it clean!' muttered Ryan.

'I hear you're Welsh, Talog' called out Marine Barry Spence from across the cabin, 'is that right?'

'Sure am, boyo' Ket replied sarcastically.

'You don't sound Welsh, Talog?'

'Well, you don't sound like a twat, which just goes to show, doesn't it?'

'Huh?'

'You heard!'

'So, what are the Welsh famous for, apart from stealing stuff?' Spence came back with.

'Shagging anything on legs!' muttered Lance Corporal Maddocks.

'Kicking your hopeless English arses!' Ket continued scribbling in the ring-bound notebook.

'So, what do you know about kicking English arses, Talog?' asked Marine Ryan.

There was a pause for thought. 'Well, I do know that the English ones are pimply, pink and porky!'

'Nice. So you've seen a lot of arse then?' shouted Ryan.

'More than I would like.'

Private Simon Cotter nudged Ket in the ribs and passed across a photograph. 'What do you think?' he asked.

'Not now mate, I've got important stuff to think about.'

'Go on, what do you think?'

Ket took a glance at the photograph of a confident looking young lady with an incredibly large pair of breasts. 'Blimey, those are massive doops! I thought I'd seen some record breakers in my time but those beat all comers. Ryan, what do you think?'

'Yes, those are massive. Jealous?' asked Ryan.

'No! What you can't see is that she's stepping like mad on a foot pump to keep them up! What are you supposed to do with jahooblies that size anyway?'

'Don't you stick your face in between them and...'

'Suffocate?'

'No, you come up for air on occasion.' He mimed the practice of smothering and breathing like he was a well practiced front-crawler.

'Still sounds dangerous. She should have a warning message stencilled on them, shouldn't she? What if she turned round quickly? She'd knock you out cold, wouldn't she?'

'Do you think so?' exclaimed Cotter in alarm.

'Yes, you should definitely be packing a helmet when you take her out!' shouted Ryan.

'Well, you've got yourself a bucketful there - in fact, two bucketfuls! Much bigger than a British Standard bucketful, I would say' Ket retorted.

'Yes, gorgeous, isn't she! See, I've got her number and I'm going to give her a call and take her up town!' Cotter announced.

Ket looked at him thoughtfully. 'That's nice, you could use her bra as a hammock, in case you miss the last bus!'

'You think so? I hadn't thought of that. I know, why don't you join us?'

Ket felt this idea had to be quashed very quickly. 'Look, it's a date, isn't it? That's for two, isn't it? I think you've got more than enough on your plate already!' There were laughs all around the cabin, with everyone enjoying Ket's discomfort.

'You can take one each' called out Marine Iqbal.

'What am I supposed to do with one of those, when I get on it?'

'Suck it and see!'

'Oh yes, and what do they taste of?'

'Tit milk.'

'Tit milk! Eurghh! Anyway, how do I get one of those in my mouth?'

'I'm sure you'll manage, you gobby slag' shouted Maddocks. Ket jabbed the pencil into the cover of her diary and ground it in until the point broke.

'Anyway Cotter, I think I might have something on? Ket announced.

'Why don't you check?' he asked.

'Why don't I, what?' Ket replied.

'You've got your diary right there, why don't you check, Talog?' came a call from opposite her. It was Sergeant Pettigrew. Ket made a mental note of his intervention.

'Well, let me have a little look then.' Ket opened out the month planner and examined it carefully, accompanied by a series of 'hmms' and 'haars'. 'When was that again?' Ket asked. Cotter pointed to the Saturday of the coming weekend. 'Oh, that's soooo unfortunate.' After more study, Ket looked back to him. 'You my son, are the unluckiest bloke on the planet.'

'Why's that?' he asked.

'Look at that, I've got 'PH' on that evening.

'PH? What's that?'

'Well, in short, it means I can't make it, pal.'

'Can I see what you've got there Talog?' asked Ryan.

'No, you can't!'

He snatched the diary and slung it across the cabin. 'You little prick' Ket hissed, as Spence caught it. 'Give it back now, that's got all my life in it!'

'Let's have a look in here' Spence muttered as he started to flick through the pages.

'Give it back, give it back!' Ket demanded.

'No, let's see what you're going to be up to at the weekend. What's so important you can't make a threesome on Cotter's date?'

'Lieutenant, he's got my sodding diary!' Ket shouted across to Lieutenant James Griffiths. He seemed to be absorbed in something else.

'This is a load of old bollocks, isn't it? What the hell is 'PH'?' said Spence. He showed the pages to Lance Corporal Eddie Maddocks, who was sitting next to him.

'It's the reason why I can't meet up with Cotter and his top heavy bird...'

'Yes, I know, but what is it?'

Ket hesitated: 'Well, obviously its 'power hair wash', isn't it? It's the night I sort out my hair?' There were incredulous looks around the cabin. Maybe that was a little bit far-fetched.

'And that's more important than helping out one of your oppos? That's so rubbish! What in the name of god is a power hair wash, anyway?'

'It's when I wash out all the little creatures that jumped ship when a share a ride with you lot.'

'Careful Talog!' interceded Sergeant Pettigrew.

'Well, Spence, you wouldn't know about power hair wash, would you? You've hardly come across 'wash' before, have you?'

'Oi, watch it Talog!'

'I have been! I think you're trying to preserve what little's left of it!'

Maddocks ran his hand through Spence's hair. 'Talog's right, your barnet has seen better days, hasn't it?'

Spence scowled at KT and then flicked the pages to the back of the diary where the 'Contacts' section resided. 'All right, let's see what we've got here. Is this written in code Talog, this looks like...hold on a minute, what's this? I'm in here? So, I'm one of your contacts then Talog? What's going on here?'

'Oh, shit! This is so embarrassing. Just be a mate and hand it back!'

'What's this? What's this a picture of?'

'What does it look like?' shouted Ket.

'It looks like a drawing of an arsehole?' called out Maddocks.

'That's what it is, isn't it? You're not very quick on the uptake, are you?'

'And, and what does it say here? Here we go, 'Foxtrot Oscar? What's that supposed to mean?' asked Spence, completely flummoxed.

'Give it back and I'll help you out.'

'Foxtrot Oscar? FO?'

'Give him a minute, let's see if he can work it out for himself.' Ket watched him intently and imagined cogs and wheels grinding into action inside his head. 'You seem to be struggling, let me help you. What it's NOT short for is Foreign Office, it is short for...'

His face welled up when he understood and then his face curled down in acute embarrassment. 'Wait a minute Talog, but I'm one of your key contacts? Doesn't that mean you fancy me then?'

'No, you're a total arsehole!'

'Bollocks! Lieutenant Griffiths, can you have a word about Talog's foul language?'

Ket smiled sweetly and winked at the lieutenant: 'I'm in the Senior Service, so technically I outrank all of you!'Jim Griffiths treated Ket to one of his stern looks. 'In other words Spence, I own your arse...'

'The expression is, you own his ass, not his arse' shouted Sergeant Pettigrew smugly, with his apology of a beard, 'and we're all Senior Service!'

'That's rubbish, but just in case it's true Spence, you'll need to hand your donkey over...'

'For god's sake Talog...'

'...or the cash equivalent.'

Spence bridled indignantly: 'I don't frigging believe it, I've been rinsed...anyone got a pen?' Spence started drawing in the notebook and then passed it to Maddocks.

'Sorry mate, but you sleep walked into that.' Maddocks secured the diary and spun it back to Ket. It was caught adroitly and opened to the last entry in the 'Notes' pages - it appeared to be a sketch of an erect prick.

'Is that life size?' Ket shouted and held up the page for everyone to view. Ribald laughter filled the cabin. 'What is it? It looks like a prick only much smaller? If you've really got one of these growing on you, get it seen to, pronto!'

'Lieutenant, can't you keep Talog in order?' wailed Spence.

'Talog, just keep it clean will you, I don't want you corrupting the minds of my men!'

'Men? Puh! Minds? Puh!'

'Anyway Talog, don't we have unfinished business?' shouted Maddocks.

'Look, I've got a load of idiots to deal with, you'll just have to get in the queue, won't you?'

'You need to give me your full attention, Talog' he came back with.

Ket decided to ignore this. Cotter seemed to be mouthing something and there was a danger of him stringing together a recognisable sentence. 'All right so you've got something else on' he whined, 'but it's your loss. I was going to take her to the cinema and then for a fish and chip supper afterwards.'

'Lucky girl!' Ket replied sarcastically.

'You don't know how lucky you are mate, that was a narrow escape' commented Ryan.

'Oi, a bit of respect please. Cotter's not that awful' replied Ket, 'that would be you...'

'So, what do you think Talog?' It was Cotter's photograph, this time just inches away from Ket's nose.

'Well, I think you're punching well above your weight, Cotter, so well done.' Ket had an afterthought. 'Let me know when you've done with her - the local school's organising a children's party and I was thinking they may need a bouncy castle. We could use your girlfriend's chest!'

'Really?'

'No!' Ket's head shook in despair. 'Anyway, Mad Dogs, you were saying?'

'Talog, Talog, I need your full attention.'

'What is it, Mad Dogs?'

'So you really think you can take me Talog, mano-a-mano?'

'What's that? I didn't say that? Unless you mean one on one. No, you're right, you'd better bring a couple of pals. Hold on, you haven't got any pals have you? Oh no! What are you going to do?' Ket resumed writing.

'You might have all the gab, but I've got this.' He pulled up his shirt sleeve, flexed his right bicep and pointed meaningfully at it. Ket couldn't make out what the tattoo said, but it wasn't pretty. This needed very careful handling.

'Are you auditioning?' Ket shouted.

'What are you on about?' he growled back.

'To be my shag buddy' Ket yelled back.

'You're really coming it now, Talog!'

'Let's check this out. First question, 'Is he a man?', it says here. Let's see.'

'Talog!'

'Oh look at that, you're bolloxed at the first question!'

'I demand satisfaction!'

'There could be a problem there!'

'See this...' he pointed out his bicep again.

'Yawn. What's that then, RSI?' Ket asked.

'What are you talking about?'

'Repetitive stress injury. From all the wanking?'

'You're a right gobby slag, aren't you? But can you back that up?'

'Just leave it out, Maddocks, give her a break!' shouted Ryan.

'Just me and you - name the time and the place!'

'All right, I will. Is this a knee trembler then?'

'No! Just you and me, one on one, no interference! We're going to settle this!'

'So, would you describe yourself as a sensitive lover?' This was greeted with more laughter. 'Or just a knob end?'

'Mano-a-mano, Talog!'

'I've told you, I can't do mano-a-mano - we could do boyo-a-boyo, maybe? I thought we...'

'Just front up or shut up!'

'Oh, all right then!' She beat a nervous tattoo on her thighs. The half smile on her face had disappeared completely to be replaced by a frown. 'That's that then' she muttered.

'Are you insane, Ket?' hissed Cotter in her right ear.

'Don't worry, he'll realise he's outclassed long before he beats me into a bloody pulp!'

'Just back off Maddocks!' shouted Ryan.

'Oi, Ryan, are you going to be my champion?' shouted Ket.

'Piss off!'

'You worm!'

'Fight your own battles Talog!'

'All right' shouted Griffiths, Shut up all of you. I don't know what's going on here but it stops now. Talog, Maddocks, enough!'

'No, it's too late for that' shouted Ket.

'I said...!'

'All right. I'm sorry Mad Dogs. I crossed a line there.'

'No one calls me Mad Dogs!'

'What?' She nudged Cotter in the ribs. 'He doesn't even know his own name does he? There's no sodding hope, is there!'

'Leave me out of this, I've got a big date at the weekend!' Cotter muttered in reply.

'Talog!' shouted Griffiths.

Ket inhaled deeply. 'Sorry Mad Dogs, I shouldn't have called you Mad Dogs, or a wanker. I apologise. Are we all right now?'

'Talog, get over here!' shouted the Lieutenant. He indicated the seat adjacent to him by the cockpit. Sergeant Pettigrew rose and she did an ungainly 'pas de deux' with him as they exchanged seats across the cabin.

She sat down hesitantly. 'Don't I get an apology, then?' she asked as she secured herself in the seat.

'What's all this about?' asked Jim Griffiths sternly.

She looked deep and dreamily into his eyes and gave him the ever-so-slow blink. 'We're having an affair, aren't we? Me and Mad Dogs. He wants to go one on one on one on me...'

'No, you're not, he's getting married in a few weeks!'

'That's right, but he wanted a final fling!'

'No, he doesn't, I don't believe you.'

'You're right, it must be a fight then.'

'It's not going to happen.'

'If you say so, lieutenant.'

'I mean it.'

'Of course you do.' There was an awkward tight lipped pause. She turned her attention to Daniel Pettigrew, now opposite her. 'So, who's the passion in your life, sergeant?' she shouted.

He seemed hesitant about responding 'She's called Lizzie.'

'Lizzie, that's a pretty name. And is she pretty, does she miss you?'

'She's beautiful.' He seemed transported to another place.

'It must be very difficult for you' she yelled.

'What do you mean?'

'It can't be easy, can it?'

'It isn't' he said hesitantly.

'So when you rock up with that thing that passes for a beard...'

'Ha! Yeah.'

'And she wants a bit of oral....'

'Yeah?'

'Then your face gets meshed up with her fuzzy pudding!'

'For Christ's sake Talog!' The cabin was full of a cacophony of catcalls, crowing and whistling.

'Looks like you've just been 'Talogged' mate' commented Jim Griffiths. The clamour died down. 'Okay, a bit of hush' he shouted. He adjusted his position on the seat so he was very close to her.

'Hallo, sir. Are you going to have a shot at chatting me up? That's nice...' She felt a little cough inside her, and the blood rushing to her cheeks. 'But, it would be nice if we had a little bit of privacy. Can you get them all to just step outside for a moment?' Maddocks was now engaged in a three-way conversation with Spence and Iqbal, opposite. No one reacted to her comment.

Jim Griffiths turned his attention directly to Ket. Her heart was racing now. 'Just calm down' he asked.

'Look, this is me calm' she replied. She closed her eyes, stretched her arms out in front, her fingers describing delicate circles. She started a slow, rhythmic chant: 'Omm; omm; omm.' She opened her eyes. 'Omm!' Everyone at the front end of the cabin was again looking at her. 'Look, if I wasn't calm, if I was upset, this helicopter would look like a Catherine wheel falling into the sea!'

'It will be all right.'

'No, it won't be all right' she said as she leaned towards him confidingly, threading a long, recalcitrant lock of wavy brown hair behind her left ear, 'I'm in deep dwang - I've just been through it all again and there's stuff I can't account for!'

This triggered a chorus of 'Oohs' around the cabin. She turned round to admonish her cabin mates but decided it wasn't worth it.

'Perhaps they'll make you walk the plank, Talog?' called out Spence. 'I'd really like to see that!'

'It would be good if you could wear a tight tee-shirt!' shouted Marine Boyle.

'I'll start selling tickets then, shall I?' she shouted, 'Twenty each?'

'Twenty pence? I'll have some of that!'

'Twenty quid, I'm thinking...'

'That's a bit steep, you really fancy yourself, don't you Talog?' shouted Spence sarcastically.

'Alright then, bikini bottoms it is for the plank walk!'

'Yeah! I'm in!'

'Me too!'

'Puh! Like that's going to happen!' she snorted.

'Or maybe they'll hang you from the yardarm this time!' shouted Marine Graham Grubb. She dismissed this and turned back to Jim Griffiths.

'I've got a new commanding officer, Nicola Spry, do you know anything about her?'

'I haven't come across her before.'

'Have you got any dirt on her? She sounds like she's going to be a bit of a thruster.' He looked blankly back at her. 'You, know, a bit of a stickler.' She closed her notebook. 'I reckon I'll be pushed towards the paper navy. I'm going to have a long spell on land, so you're going to have to sort yourselves out now.'

'I'm sure we'll manage, somehow' he shrugged.

'I reckon I'm going to get the inquisition about my mum again.'

'I don't understand why, KT, I thought everyone knew you were the unnatural offspring of a Welsh male voice choir and a she-dragon?'

'That would be hilarious, but unfortunately, it's not far short of the mark, is it?'

'So how is your mum?'

'She's fine from what I can tell. She's not been bombarding the Andrew with letters. That's probably a good sign unless she's plotting something really big.'

'So did she ever buy into the postage system?'

'No, not really, she's never used stamps.' She started muttering to herself, when she looked at her spider's web of notes. 'You know what, I'm truly and royally buggered.'

'Is that Welsh, KT?'

'No, its general cursing, for the use of.'

'Just remember what we rehearsed – stick to the line, you can't be criticised. It was in the finest traditions of the Royal Navy!' he chuckled.

'In your mind, I think you're trying to help, but you're really not!'

'Anyway, you know the boys want to initiate you into the Royal Marines' he paused, 'as an honorary member, of course.'

'Of course, how could I forget.' She thought about this for a moment. 'So, what happens at one of these?' There was no immediate response so she thought she would try again. 'I know I'm going to regret this, but what exactly does an initiation involve? A ceremony, a trial, getting drunk, womanising and fighting the locals?'

'Yes, but you don't have to do any womanising if you don't want to.'

'That's good.' She tried to work out what the opposite of womanising was, but she couldn't decide. 'I think we're going to have to set some ground rules then' she said, 'and I'll need a billet for the night in your quarters, I'm not sharing with anyone and you get me back to my billet safely and no funny business. All right?' There was no reply. 'I won't be doing any simulated sex either, or that Suck It And See game, or that game where I have to carry a coin clenched between my arse cheeks.'

Jim Griffiths took out his list of entertainments and started to cross them out.

'I bet you regret asking her now, don't you sir?' shouted Ryan.

'Do we need to get a plank, lieutenant?' shouted Grubb.

Katie took a look around the cabin. 'No, you've got more than enough planks here!' she murmured. 'Anyway, will there be any split at this do, or is it just me' she asked. This was met with puzzled expressions. 'Slot, then?' Still no response. 'Gash? Shaggable girls?' she clarified.

'Just you, KT.'

'Oh brilliant, this just gets better and better' she muttered.

The co-pilot came through to make an announcement, 'Acting Leading Hand Talog, we're dropping you off at HMS Raleigh in two minutes, please get yourself ready.'

'Yes, sir.'

'And just because you've had your hands all over my collective, that doesn't mean you own my chopper!' he chuckled.

'Ha, you're hilarious mate!'

'Did you leave lipstick all over it, Talog?' called out Grubb.

'Don't be dirty! No, I wiped it clean after, didn't I?'

'Toilet mouth!'

'Knob shite!'

'Get her out of here!'

She turned her attention back to the co-pilot. 'Really, three hours to come up with that? Is that what you've been up to in the cockpit? Oh, hold on, is that why it's called a cockpit?'

'Can it Talog, or I'll kick you out over the dry dock!'

'So what do I tell my new CO when I turn up late? The pilot and the co-pilot were jerking each over off?' This led to jeering from the cabin.

'We have unfinished business, Talog' a voice growled. It was Maddocks.

'I know, you miserable scrote.' She flicked through her diary. 'I've got a load of idiots to deal with but I can fit you in...then.' She wrote on a piece of paper from her diary, ripped it out with a flourish, folded it into a ball and threw it at him. Maddocks grabbed it as it bounced off his forehead, unfolded it, read it and nodded in satisfaction.

'You got that Mad Dogs? I assume you can read. At least I saw your lips moving. I'm coming for you and you'd better be ready!'

'I'll be there' he growled.

She put the notebook away and sighed deeply. So that was that. The helicopter was descending.

Someone else piped up, 'That's close enough, you can chuck her out now!'

'Lembo!' she shouted back. The Sea King helicopter hovered a few feet above the yellow lined circle and then settled unevenly on the ground. The main door was thrown open and she dropped down to the unyielding concrete. She caught her rucksack and her blue roll up bag as they followed her out of the main cabin door.

'Wednesday, be ready at six!' came the shout from Jim Griffiths, 'and I'll have a word with Spry – it'll all be fine!' The rotors strained, cleaved the air and the helicopter struggled back up into the azure blue sky and headed inland.

Katie left the bag and the pack where they had landed and climbed carefully down the rusted wrought iron metal rungs to the sliver of sand and shingle below the sea wall. No one would be able see her down here.

She knelt down and inserted her hands into the shimmering mass of sea-soaked sand and offered a small heap of it to the sky. And she quickly dropped the mass - there was something in there and it was alive! Something wriggling and scratching and biting between her fingers! Katie poked the mass with her best finger and a head with twitching feelers and scuttling pairs of legs and a tail emerged. Sharply, she pinged it away and took a few deep breaths to calm herself as it scuttled away over the sand.

A deep breath and another mass of coarser sand was gathered up. Ever so slowly, she let the particles slip from her grasp, grain by grain through her outstretched fingers. The light danced around the grains and flashed a tight, little rainbow in front of her eyes. There was a larger grain between her fore and middle finger and it was soft and malleable and golden, like living ore. She pinched it, squeezed it and examined it critically against the sunlight and then quickly tucked it away in her shirt pocket.

The breeze rippled the rushes to her right and the rippling made a sound, like a voice, and it cried for help. Katie's heart leapt and she stared but all she could see was the fluttering stems, no physical presence.

It was time to check in with Danu, if she could be reached, because that could be her, sweeping through the rushes. She took a long breath so that it reached all parts of her lungs: 'It's me, Katie, I'm back.' And then she waited quietly for a response, but there was none - just the slow lapping of waves against the shore line, the chipping of the wind-hovering terns over the channel and further away, the busy bustling of the dockyard.

'I'm quite well thanks, just a few scratches and I'm a proper matelot now, and this is what we have to do when we return from the sea, isn't it? And what I have to do, of course!' She took her cap off. Katie couldn't recall the next part so she stopped to think.

A tug proceeded down the channel, heading towards the sea. She considered acknowledging the crew on the bridge as they looked in her direction. The klaxon sounded, one short sharp toot, followed by a longer, descending one and a brief cheer, directed in her direction, that quickly was muted by the on-shore sea breeze. They seemed very happy with themselves, she thought, and then the next sentence came to her.

'Ah, thanks for the sun that warms me and lights my way.' And now she could see the pale outline of the moon, like a ghostly porcelain mask in the sky.

'Thanks for the rivers and streams, which water me and clean me.' A plastic carrier bag whirled helplessly out in the tidal stream towards the open sea.

'Thanks for the plants that feed and heal me.' What looked like a bunch of lilies, half submerged, wrapped in cellophane, bobbed past.

'Thanks to your great spirit that created all the worlds and which shapes all things for a greater good.' There was a heightened buzz of activity all around her, especially in the direction of the repair yard. The breeze must have changed its direction, with no assistance from her.

A puff of wind brought the smell of sewage towards her. She snorted her nose clear quickly. 'If you could help me have the strength and the courage to do what I need to do, Danu, that would be good, because what I have to do is a bit tricky...isn't it? A lot of things need to happen, all in the right order and a lot of people will need to do what I need them to do, at the right time and place...'

She listened carefully for the response. There was none. 'And I've lost her pendant' she added quickly and quietly.

There was a roar of an after burning engine inland but she decided that it wasn't a cause for alarm. 'If you could pair me with someone who likes me and wants me for what I am, that would be nice too.'

She closed her eyes and took in the ozone of the air, heard the chipping calls of the oystercatchers on the shore and that relentless buzz of human endeavour behind her. 'So, for all of these things, for taking care of me and for everyone that matters to me, and everything else, I totally thank you.' She wondered if she should make an offering, as she fingered the tiny nugget in her pocket, but decided not to.

There was a calm and then a little tingle in her fingertips which made its way along her arms, across her shoulders, up her neck and on top of her crown. There was a little contra-rotating eddy making its way up the channel. Could she straighten it out? Make it go the other way? She pointed her left arm towards it and motioned it to turn the other way and...it disappeared!

The rippling rushes cried for help a second time and then a third time. She stared at them but there was nothing she could discern other than a noisy little brown bird, clambering nimbly amongst the stems. There was no one she could see who could be in trouble. She lifted her head and took in the tainted air that had been brought in from the south-west.

But then, in the sea mingling with the shingle she could see a spent condom, pulsing like a deflated jellyfish. She turned with alacrity back to the black painted, rusting ladder that lead back to the landing ground and climbed it quickly. With her luck, the next item that would come down the channel would be a giant turd. Instead, a soldier in Royal Marine uniform was waiting for her up top, his cap wedged covering his forehead so only his gimlet eyes showed.

'All right Shitter?' she asked.

'It's Corporal Bricknell to you' he snapped back. His lips were wrinkled into what was the beginning of a snarl - his index finger pointed at the two yellow stripes on his tunic sleeve, outlined in orange. 'You should be throwing me a salute, Talog!'

She acknowledged this with a nod and then pointed to the single, fouled anchor on her sleeve, picked out in gold. 'Can you see that? That's my killick, that is. I think that means that technically, I outrank you.'

'What! Leading Hand Talog? What the hell were they thinking?' He seemed unduly perturbed about this.

'Acting. I think that someone must've thought I was worthy of advancement' Katie replied, 'at least for a short while, now, who knows?'

'Do you have any ID?' he blurted out.

'Yes' she said as she presented her papers and her dog-tag, 'is that all right?'

He held her tag and gave it a surprising amount of reverence. 'It will do. Well done, by the way' he said grudgingly, 'now, follow me please.'

'Ooh, follow me please, he says!' She stuck her tongue out but he had already turned away. She hauled her rucksack over her shoulders and then hesitated before picking up the roll bag. 'Oi, Shitter, why don't you give me a hand with this one?' His eyes swivelled under the brow of his cap. That was probably a big ask!

'You brought them with you so you carry them' he barked. He continued his military march to the set of buildings sprawled across the top of the rise.

She slung the roll back strap across her left shoulder and they proceeded towards the training installation. As they approached, she diverted and quickly and stealthily stepped towards the NAAFI canteen. 'I'll be making a detour here to the NAAFI, Shitter. I'm gagging for a brew!' she said quietly as he marched quickly away in the other direction.

Katie calculated it would take Corporal Bricknell a few minutes to realise what had happened. She paused and then walked quickly towards the restaurant. She really needed a mug of tea. As she crossed the concrete walled walkway alongside the quay, she felt the unyielding solidity of concrete through her feet, through her legs and through her hips. The smell of cooked breakfast and coffee lured her on.

The canteen was quiet but very inviting. A cadet in naval uniform approached her as she struggled between the tables and chairs - he offered her a large photograph and a pen. It was a likeness of her, rampaging down the right flank, hockey stick in hand, ball on the floor. Inter-services tournament she reckoned, three-one to the dark blues.

'Sign please!' he asked, interrupting her reverie. There was jeering behind him from a table of four junior, spotty male rates with awkward chopped hair and awkward laughing eyes.

'Who's it for?' she asked.

'For me!' he answered, the red of his blush now transmitted to his big, awkward ears.

'You knob-head! What's your sodding name?' she asked, in exasperation.

'It's, it's Matthew' he replied and then wondered if he should correct his answer: 'No, it's Matt.'

'You're a bit short for a 'Matt', mate, it's got to be 'Lofty' now. Front or back?' she asked.

'Eh?'

'Front it is' she said as he turned away, grinning like an idiot, to salute his mates. She drew a large triple spiral, with her initials 'KET' scrawled across it. 'There you go, Lofty!' He seemed to dance his way back to the table, with an awkward, incompetent swagger.

She settled down on a high stool and ordered a NATO plus. The girl at the counter didn't seem to know what this was so Katie patiently explained that NATO standard tea is with everything in it. Yes, that means milk and two sugars. Therefore, NATO plus is with three sugars. Apparently you have to help yourself to sugar. Yes, you have a great day too.

Katie settled in her seat, gazed across the sound and reflected on what had happened during her tour of duty and then the urgency of her journey back home. It occurred to her that the French helicopter was still struck down in the hanger of her ship, the HMS Albany, somewhere in the deep blue. The French wouldn't be best pleased, she thought. Landing on the helicopter deck of the Type 23 frigate off the Comoros had been fine, but take off was not a safe proposition. I'm buggered, she concluded.

Corporal Bricknell had still not reappeared. She wondered at what point he would realise that his charge was missing. She had a few minutes yet.

'Welcome back Katie' said the man in full captain's regalia.

'Uncle Alec!' She jumped on her feet and opened her arms wide.

He pointed to his sleeve. 'Now, now, Leading Hand Talog!'

'Oh, sorry, sir!' It must be time, she thought.

'How was your flight?' he asked.

'It was awful sir' she said, 'I had to hitch a lift in a Junglie with the Royal. We had to do a bounce off an assault ship in the Bay of Biscay!' Uncle Alec looked at her sympathetically, 'It would have made far more sense to put me on a Fat Albert out of Cyprus, wouldn't it, sir?'

'Yes, I know, but we all wanted you back as soon as possible. How are you doing?' he said scanning her face and her hands.

'I'm actually doing all right, sir' she answered, as she set her cap over the sticking plaster on her forehead and slipped her hands into her trouser pockets.

'We've got a lot to cover Katie, so gather up your kit and follow me.' He took her roll bag and slung it across his shoulder. They swung towards the concrete administration block, known colloquially as 'The Bunker' squatting between two of the accommodation blocks. Katie adeptly balanced an egg and tomato roll on a NAAFI mug full of sweet tea and held a paper bag containing two slices of toast, pots of butter and marmalade and a plastic NAAFI knife. 'I need to introduce you to your new commanding officer, Lieutenant Spry, and get you two up and running.'

She looked back and saw Corporal Bricknell running into the NAAFI, with one hand holding his cap in place and the other wildly gesticulating to the girl behind the counter. They turned a corner and were now out of his sight. Here, there was a file of ratings, coming at her, led by a CPO. 'Eyes right' the CPO barked, 'and salute!' Katie offered a half salute with her right hand but couldn't be sure if she was following the correct protocol. Oh, well, it was too late now.

'Listen Katie, she'll want to go through what happened to you off the Comoros Islands. We all do, but if you need time...'

'Yes, I expected that. How much does she know?'

'As much as the rest of us, it's all over the French papers. Our press didn't get wind of it. So, how are you really?'

'I'm really fine, really!'

'Have you heard? We've had another batch of letters.'

'No, I haven't. Does she still want me out?'

'We're trying to process them. They're incomprehensible. They seem to be written in old Gaelic, but they caused a lot of upset in the Cryptography Department.'

Katie tried to work out what this might mean. Mum's letters were normally perfectly clear: they were written in plain English; they threatened legal action; they included a curse on all Her Majesty's armed forces and Her Majesty's government. But they had stopped many, many moons ago. There was something here that didn't quite ring true. 'That doesn't sound like my mum' she commented.

'Well, maybe you should take a look at them. Listen Katie, there's something else I've got to ask you. I've just heard a whisper that you're going to fight a marine. Is that right? Because I have to advise you, that is madness.'

'Ah, I heard that rumour as well.'

'And?'

'It was actually me who started it!'

'And?'

'P-lease Uncle Alec, give me some credit. I may be mad but I'm not stupid, am I?' She paused to think about what she had just said. Did I get that the right way round?

'Well, I'm pleased to hear it. We should do what we can to quash that one. It doesn't do you any credit. Quite apart from the beating you're liable to get!'

'Listen Uncle Alec, I can look after myself!'

He fingered his sleeve again. 'No, you can't. They're highly trained elite soldiers, and you're not.'

'I think they're overrated. They're a bunch of pussies from what I can make out' she replied, winking at him.

'I suggest you keep that opinion to yourself, Katie.'

They entered 'The Bunker', introduced themselves to the prim and efficient receptionist at the desk and waited. 'You can go through now' prompted the receptionist. Lieutenant Spry was waiting for her. They shook hands. Spry was that little bit taller than Katie, had a strong jaw and what was probably long blonde hair meticulously gathered and chaperoned and tied back so that it strategically covered her ears. All the features of her face were perfect, Katie noted, but they hadn't quite been assembled correctly. Looking obliquely at her face, she tried to work out what the problem was. Probably of Norsewegian descent, Katie decided, strong jawed and strong browed, a Vikingess probably. 'Please take a seat, Katherine' offered Spry. No desk, Katie noted, so she must have been on an interview techniques course.

Katie took off her rucksack, laid it in front of her chair and sat with her feet over it with a relaxed sigh. Next, she placed a napkin over her legs and placed the roll and toast on top. 'Sorry, I'm famished, I need somewhere for all this. I'm going to need a table.' She held up her tea. Uncle Alec found a chair to place it on. There was still the little matter of her cap - she looked around the room, located the hat stand and spun the cap across the room so it whirled onto a hook - she balled her fists together in silent and gleeful celebration.

There was an uncomfortable quiet in the room, and then Spry spoke: 'My name is Lieutenant Nicola Spry, and I will be your commanding officer going forward. Of course, you know Captain Wicks. He has provided you with... um, pastoral care over the last few years.'

So, no surprises so far. Katie positioned herself so she was a little closer to Alec and at a slightly greater distance from Spry. There was something about her voice and the set of her jaw that brooked no nonsense; none of the nonsense that had served her so well in her time thus far with the Royal Navy. Uncle Alec, is there something you should have told me?

CHAPTER TWENTY-FIVE

Wednesday 11 May 1135 - The Bunker, Torpoint

'Katherine, may I call you Katherine? I thought this would be a good opportunity for us to meet and start building our working relationship, but also get your version of what's been going on off the Comoros.'

Katie shook her head.

'What's the matter, Katherine?'

'That's not my name.'

Nicola Spry frowned but continued straight on. 'Then, I need to talk to you about your family, some behavioural issues and these... letters.' Nicola flicked a glance below her seat. 'Then I need to talk to you about your career progression to date and what the next steps are. Is there anything you would like to discuss?'

'Yes, ma'am, I call myself Katie, because everyone does. It's not Katherine.'

This prompted an awkward pause and a shuffling of papers on Spry's lap. 'I'm sorry, I thought... So, what is your first name?'

'It's actually Katell, but if you just call me Katie, we'll be just fine' Katie replied, 'and, if its all right, I would like to table a report.' She paused and thought for a moment: Can I table a report if there's no table? Oh, well, never mind. 'I made it while I was cruising around the Indian Ocean.' She removed a bound report from her rucksack and passed it across to Spry. It had survived the journey from the Indian

Ocean remarkably well. 'If we can avoid our ships and helicopters spending so much time in transit, we'll start winning, ma'am.'

'I'm surprised you have had time for this considering your other duties' flapped Nicola Spry. This seemed to have unsettled her, which was good.

'It's taken nine months ma'am. It's about how we maximise the time on station of our helicopter on long tours of duty. Nicola flicked through the report. 'Who's idea was this? This is very unexpected, Katherine.'

'It's Katie. My CO on the Albany set it for me as a task. She thought it would look good on my record.' Uncle Alec looked like he was swelling up with pride.

'I see. I see it's signed by your CO - it looks, it looks very well presented, Katie!'

'Yes, ma'am that's her chop. Thank you, ma'am.'

'Is this all your own work?'

'Obviously, I had some help ma'am, to be fair, but Cutie helped me all the way through - you can see her name and all the other names in the list at the back.'

'Yes, it's a long list of acknowledgements. Cutie?'

'Oh yes, that's Big CIS, she's my CO on HMS Albany, ma'am.'

'Hmm, Big CIS?'

'Yes, she heads up the Comms and Info Systems department, doesn't she?'

'Thank you, Katie.' She flicked to the start and then finish of the report. 'Bahrain, indeed! I think you'll find that a lot of this has already been considered and rejected. Is there anything else?'

There was no mention of the Chinese submarine yet, which was curious, but probably for the best. She would keep that up her sleeve just in case, but like a silent running submarine, there was something hidden below Spry's chair that was silent, watching, brooding. 'Nothing else, ma'am.'

Uncle Alec pursed his lips and shook his head. He examined the tip of his pencil.

'I'm aware that you might think there are restrictions on what we can talk about, due to the Official Secrets Act.'

'Certainly is, ma'am.'

'But that's utter nonsense - If there's anything I need to know, you will tell me and it will be kept confidential. Do you understand, Katie?'

'I...I'm not sure. Sir, what can I say?'

'I will intercede' commented Uncle Alec, 'if and when we get to that point.' He resumed his minute examination of the end of his pencil.

Spry stared for a moment at Uncle Alec and then continued with Katie. 'Firstly, let me introduce myself. My name is Nicola Spry, I've been with the service for eleven years, based mainly at Portsmouth. My specialism is human resources. You may have heard of me.'

'No, ma'am' Katie replied a bit too quickly and then tried to stifle a snort of derision and coughed instead. Uncle Alec flashed her a stern glance.

'Katie, please can you summarise your service, in a few sentences?'

'Well, I joined straight from school, just after my birthday. And I arrived at HMS Raleigh for my initial training.'

Spry waited then asked, 'Yes. And then?'

'I passed my initial training.' Uncle Alec chose to snigger at this moment.

'And then?' Spry asked impatiently.

'There was an awful lot of training and square bashing and stuff...'

'And then?'

'I did even more training. There's a lot of training, isn't there?'

Spry's impatience did not seem to be abating.

'Then I trained in communications and air and sea logistics...'

'Yes?'

'And my first ship was HMS Harpy, she's a...'

'Come on...'

'And for the last two years, I've served in HMS Albany, and she's a Type 23...'

'At last! And your role on HMS Albany?'

'I work in the Communications and Information Systems department, ma'am. And I'm qualified as a winch girl - with our helicopter crew.'

'You've done very well in advancing to acting leading rate so quickly.'

'Yes, I thought so ma'am.'

'In fact, it was quite sudden.' There was a long pause. 'So how did you manage that?'

Katie thought for a while and several sarcastic responses flickered through her mind and unfortunately, one of them was broadcast out of her mouth: 'I shoved the previous incumbent overboard, ma'am.'

'What!?!'

'Just kidding, ma'am!'

Spry didn't seem to like that answer. She re-crossed her legs and looked out of the window. Now she was formulating a new question, Katie supposed.

'So, as a member of the crew of HMS Albany, how do you think you have performed your duties?'

'Admirably' said Katie.

'Can you expand on that?'

'Not really ma'am, I think that says it all.' Katie looked away so that she could take another bite from her roll.

'All right, Katie, let's try this a different way. Can you give me three words that summarise the particular qualities you bring to your current role?'

Katie was taken aback. She hadn't seen this one coming. There was a pause while she flicked mentally through the web of symbols she had written down in her notebook. These offered no help whatsoever. 'Well, I'm quite admirable...'

'To whom?'

'Oh, to my oppos and the rest of the crew, to our flyers, and to our fighters in the Royal and to our friends.' She cringed at the last bit because it sounded like complete and utter bollocks.

'And what about the public?'

'And what about them, ma'am?'

'Do we serve the public, Katie, as we have a role in protecting the seaways and their way of life?'

'I suppose we do, but if I walk out of here, head into town I don't think I could find anyone who gives a toss about what we do.'

'A toss?'

'Yes ma'am.'

'So who do we serve?'

'Um, the people, ma'am, but they have no clue about what we do, do they?' For example, there was her family...

'I see, that's very interesting, we could do a better job of communicating what we do' said Spry as she scribbled on the note pad in front of her, 'anything else you would like to add? Any other qualities, Katie?'

'Um, well, I am...quite far-sighted, so I can see problems coming and then we can all work out how to deal with them and this helps get things done efficiently and properly.' She felt she had recovered well and felt relaxed enough to take a long and noisy gulp of tea.

'When you say 'properly', what do you mean?'

Katie paused. This sounded like trouble. 'In the way it should be done?'

'I see. Well, I'll come back to that. My understanding of the word 'properly' and yours are quite different.'

Katie sat up straight and tried to work out where this was leading. 'And I'm quite intuitive...' She watched alert as Nicola Spry flitted through the papers on her lap. There seemed to be trouble brewing.

'I'm interested in your background, can we talk about that, if that's all right with you?' Katie flashed a look to Uncle Alec but he was examining the end of his pencil again.

'So your full name is, is Katell Ebrill Talog? Did I say that right? Is that Welsh?' Nicola paused. 'And, you have two much older siblings, a brother and a sister. Your sister is your next of kin, is that correct? How did that come about? Are you still in contact with your mother and father? What part do they play in your life? Do they support you?'

'Well, ma'am, I heard several questions in there, so I think the best way I can answer all those is just to say, yes.'

'Yes?'

'Yes.'

'Please can you expand on that?'

'Not really.' Katie calculated that this line of questioning was going to get her into some difficulty. Spry seemed to be flustered again. She flashed a look at Uncle Alec, flashed a look back at Katie and started flitting through the papers in front of her. Katie continued 'I don't think it matters what my background is. My background hasn't caused any problems so far, ma'am. I think the Andrew is far more open minded than it used to be.'

'The Andrew?'

'Sorry ma'am, the navy.' I need to re-direct this conversation Katie thought. 'Um, I think it would be helpful to say, at this point, that I'm very excited about the prospect of serving in the new capital ships being built for the Royal Navy. So if you think I could be considered, that would be brilliant.'

'Hold on Katie, I haven't got to that point yet...'

'I think they will help restore our position as a global power, ma'am. What do you think I need to do to make that happen?' There, that should do it, she thought.

There was a flurry of papers, and some urgent strokes made in Spry's note pad. Katie seized the opportunity to munch on a piece of bread and tomato.

'I acknowledge your interest, but I'm not ready to talk about that just yet, so, just hold on to that thought and we can talk about that later...'

Katie frowned at this. 'What do you think I need to do to move things forward, ma'am?' she asked.

There was a pause pregnant with tension. 'You need to perform well in your current role and learn about the new weapons and communication systems, but you can't just assume...'

'Well, that's the piece I think you can help me with' Katie replied.

'Your educational achievement is an issue. You're not a graduate and you don't have an engineering background. You didn't take the opportunity to take day release to compensate for those omissions and you've no vocational qualifications. So, let's come back to that. Let's talk about what happened in your last tour of duty, I think that's the salient point. And I would like to talk to you about your personal circumstances and then bring that all together.'

This is starting to sound very ominous, Katie thought, she's not going to let go of my personal circumstances.

'So, Katie, talk us through what happened in the Comoros Islands.'

Katie looked towards Alec Wicks but he had his head down and seemed absorbed with writing infrequent, notes in tiny script which

Katie could not quite interpret. 'Well, what can I say? It's all in the day report ma'am, everything that happened.'

'I've seen that. It's just a bare statement of facts, but, I want to hear your version of events, Katie. I want to hear what's not in the report. I want to hear how it affected you.'

Katie coughed. Her throat had become very dry. She was aware of the need to be economical with the details. 'Well, we were positioned about one hundred nautical miles off Mayotte when we received a signal from the MoD to assist a French party stranded on an island. We were given the coordinates and...'

'And what was your role in this?'

'I had just finished a watch, but someone suggested that I joined the team that was sent in...'

'Why?'

'Well, I know of the French, I speak the language and...I'm a qualified winch girl!'

'Was this a rescue mission?'

'Not really, but it wasn't clear at the start. I didn't know what it was when we took off. It felt like a bimble before breakfast...'

'I see. A bimble before breakfast? The MoD say differently.'

'Yes, well they would, wouldn't they ma'am?'

'I'm sorry? What does that mean?'

'They see everything differently, ma'am. That's what makes them MoD.'

'And why did you alight from the helicopter?'

'I didn't, I winched down.'

This didn't satisfy Spry.

'Because, I needed to talk to the French face to face so I could understood what was going on and check if it was safe to land. Their radio communications were piss-awful, but I was in always in close contact with my crew and my ship.'

'Whose decision was it for you to go onshore?'

'Um, that would be Flight Lieutenant Hodge. We agreed together as a team what needed to be done and Scodge gave us our jobs to do. I'm not qualified as a flyer...'

'Why did you take the French helicopter?'

'Oh, I'm sorry ma'am, that was much later. It meant we could do the rescue in one lift. I talked this through with the French on the spot, and they agreed. We managed to recover their chopper.'

'Why did they need our help?'

'Their chopper was U/S. They couldn't repair it so we brought them a spare avionics control board.' But it was something else that needed fixing. Was this a good time to mention gremlins in Lynx helicopters? No, absolutely not...

'And what happened then?'

'We managed to get it airborne and then their pilot flew it, ma'am.'

'Only he wasn't a pilot though, was he?'

'Um, no, I did wonder about that out at the time, ma'am, but, he seemed to know his way round a control panel, so I didn't really have any choice, did I?'

'Did you realise the risk you were taking?'

'Yes, ma'am - if something had gone wrong...we would have crashed into the sea. A bit like a Catherine wheel dropping into the ocean.'

'Why didn't you get the necessary authority?'

'There wasn't time. They had...weapons. We didn't have time to mess around. There was an ugly looking crowd heading our way. I did what was needed to get everyone out, ma'am.'

'You didn't follow protocol.'

'There is no protocol for what happened that day, ma'am.'

'You didn't follow protocol.'

'No, I didn't' she answered resignedly. 'I should have waited until the next chopper came along and hoped for the best, ma'am.' She looked towards Uncle Alec. Still no eye contact. She was on her own.

'Why did you go open net with the French?'

'That was at the start, ma'am. They wouldn't follow NATO protocols and... I had to talk to them in the clear.'

'Did you understand the risk you were taking? Anyone could have listened in. You didn't follow protocol.'

'I understood that, but I managed the risk, didn't I?'

Uncle Alec suddenly perked up. 'And how did you manage that risk, Katie?'

'Um, the French lieutenant, he was a Breton, sir, so we worked out how we could go open net safely.' And then in the front of her mind, she saw him collapse back against the wall, his chest wound making a neat blood-red arc on the parched concrete.

Uncle Alec swung back in his seat, gazed at the ceiling and whistled and then there was a long pause. 'Katie, why don't you tell us what protocol you adopted?'

Katie released a pent-up whistle and reverted back to the present. 'We spoke Bretonish because we thought no other bugger could possibly understand that. It was difficult but if we kept it simple we could understand each other. I thought there was very little chance that anyone else could understand what we were saying.'

'And who came up with that protocol, Katie?'

'Well, it was me!'

Spry puffed her cheeks and looked to Wicks, 'That was a big risk, right there. Anyone could have listened in and they could have worked out what you were doing. You should have insisted on following the correct protocols.'

'Yes, ma'am, I'll bear that in mind, next time.'

Two nil to Miss Crusty Knickers.

'And where is the French helicopter now?' Spry asked.

'I imagine its back with the French by now, ma'am. I don't think it could be flown off our flight deck, ma'am, the undercarriage collapsed. It would have to be lifted off by crane in a harbour or onto a logistics ship. Captain Marriott would have it offloaded as soon as he could, because it was a wreck. I reckon it could be on Mayotte or somewhere. It won't be in HMS Albany's hangar any more, she'll be in the East Med, off Crete, on her way back to Guzz...'

'Guzz? What's Guzz?'

'Devonport, Ma'am.'

Miss Crusty Knickers was now well on top. She conversed quietly but insistently with Alec. Katie took this opportunity to dig meticulously and with increasing frustration into the small plastic pot of butter using the plastic knife. 'Are we rationing slide and glitter now? There's not enough to coat the toast!' She looked appealingly at Uncle Alec, with a wide smile that creased her cheeks and he smiled back. He took pity on her, got up, collected her empties and asked if she needed a refill. 'Thank you sir, can I have a Nato plus please?'

'Mister Wicks, please check in with HMS Albany and make sure that the helicopter has been offloaded onto French soil' announced Spry. She thanked him as he left the room and swivelled about so she could favour Katie with a wide, painted-on smile.

'Slide and glitter, Katie?' asked Nicola Spry.

'Sorry ma'am - butter and marmalade.' This woman really has no clue!

'I'm glad we're on our own as I wanted us to talk, woman to woman. Is that all right? I want to know more about where you come from and your family so I can understand you better and understand what's behind your reputation. Are you comfortable talking about this?'

'I'm not sure, ma'am' said Katie slowly and reluctantly, 'I don't see what this has got to do with anything. I want Uncle Alec here with me - there are bits that only he knows...'

Spry's smile was now so wide there was a distinct risk that the top of her manicured head would flip open, to reveal her brain.

'You have nothing to worry about, Katie, if there's anything you're not comfortable with, we'll just stop. Just remember that Mister Wicks is now out of the picture, so your coach and your confidant will be your new CO. Me!'

Katie got up from the chair and sidled towards the door and tentatively pulled at it: It rattled but did not open. As the door was safe, she edged her way anti-clockwise around the room. There was something brooding in the room, like a plague, straining to be released so it could inhabit a body.

'The door isn't locked Katie.'

There was a black brief case behind Spry's chair. 'What's in there?' Katie demanded. There was something disconcerting about the way it was propped up against the chair. It could fall at any moment and spring open.

'Sit down and I'll show you.'

'I don't want to see! It can stay where it is!'

'Don't be ridiculous!'

'I want Uncle Alec in here to support me - you have no right to do this to me! What's in that case?'

'I just want to understand what makes you tick And now I'm beginning to understand!'

Katie continued to edge her way slowly around the room keeping the briefcase fixed in her view.

'Something I don't understand about you, Katie. I thought I knew all the reasons why someone would want to join the Royal Navy: It can be a family tradition; it could be a career choice; it could be a way of making a living; it could be for a life of adventure. But you're different, because I can't fit you into any of those categories. You don't really like all the discipline and the order, do you? You were barely a teenager when you enlisted, why aren't you working in a supermarket?'

'We don't have many where I live, Ma'am. It's a bit behind the times in the Marches, isn't it?'

'Milking cows then, herding sheep, working behind the bar in the local pub?'

'I've done with all that, I needed a change.' She reached the window but it was sealed. She tested it but it wouldn't move. Whatever was in the briefcase, it was stuck in the room with her and Spry.

Spry had turned in her swivel chair and looked on bemused.

'Look, it's going to be all right, it's going to be all right' Katie said to herself. She came and stood before Spry with her hands on her hips, breathing deeply. 'Just ask me what you need to know so I can get out of here!'

'Why did you sign up?'

'To earn a living.'

'There are much easier ways of doing that.'

'There's a family tradition on the Houghton side, isn't there?'

'Ah, yes, but you're not a Houghton though, are you? You're a daughter of the Welsh!'

'Ah, but we're all British, aren't we?'

'And do you have any contact with Alain Houghton?'

'Who, Mister Houghton? No, he's in a home, ma'am, he's troubled. Listen, would it help to clear things up if I said I like to travel?'

'No, it wouldn't.'

'Well, no matter, I'm here now and that's what's important, isn't it?'

There was a long pause. Finally, Spry relented. 'Let's move on. So, tell me about your relationship with your mother, Katherine?'

'That's not my name - it's Katie; K for Kilo, A for Alfa, T for...'

'Yes, I've got it...'

'That's Kilo, Alfa, Tango, India, Echo, ma'am!'

'I've got it' Spry said sharply. 'Now Katie, what's your relationship with your mother like?'

Katie's nose crinkled up and her palms went clammy. 'Well, she's like a mum to me, isn't she?'

'Yes, but what is she like as a mother?'

'She's...different. She's a bit hands-off, if you know what I mean.'

'Pardon?'

'You've no right to do this to me, ma'am!'

'Why not?'

'I'm ready to die in a ditch over this one! I'm not talking about my mum, not to you, not to anyone!' Katie sat herself down in front of Spry and folded her arms in protest.

'Well then, Katie Talog, I'm prepared to wait here until you rot in your ditch!'

Katie's feet tapped together in synchronisation with her heart beat. Spry's pencil tapped a similar rhythm on her notepad. They came to a deafening crescendo.

'All right! All right!' Her feet came together and stopped abruptly. 'All right!' Katie expelled the air in her lungs noisily and Spry's papers fluttered to the floor. They both bent down to gather up the papers. Katie was there first and lifted them sharply. Spry gasped as one sliced into her finger.

'Oh no! Paper cut! Let me get that.' Katie took a clean napkin and wrapped it round Spry's middle finger. After a few moments, Katie removed the napkin and wrapped her lips around the finger and sucked. It was salty, sweet and tart, all at the same time. After counting three, she withdrew Spry's finger and examined it closely. 'There, that's better now.' She picked up the sheaf of papers and placed it in Spry's lap and sat down again. 'Do you need a dressing for that?' She needed a long draught of sweet tea to wash away the taste.

Spry looked aghast. After several moments examining her finger, she relaxed a little. 'Please can you deal with that medical waste properly, Katie!' she said tartly.

'Certainly, ma'am!' Katie placed the napkin in a plastic wrapper but could not locate a suitable bin - she slipped it into her trouser pocket.

'So, where were we? Ah yes, your relationship with your mother.'

After a few moments silence, Katie answered. 'Well, my mum thinks I messed up her life. But I didn't - she did that all by herself. She had everything and then I came along, and then she had nothing!' After a pause to reconsider: 'Well, to be fair, she didn't have nothing - she had a little bump.' Katie got back to her feet and started to traverse the room again. 'That was me!' She now encountered the well seasoned oak panelling and then was back to the entrance door. Katie pulled at it again, and it rattled, but it wouldn't move. There was another loud expulsion of air from her lungs.

'What's the role of Mister Wicks in all this?'

'He must have told you this already? It's not for me to say!'

'I want to understand your perspective on this...'

Katie glared back. 'Aaagh!' she cried out and looked down to contemplate her legs. 'All right, let me try this on you - you know when a ship comes into harbour and it's a dodgy mooring due to the harbour and the tides? You have an old tyre alongside the ship or along the mooring? Well, I'm the ship, Uncle Alec is the old tyre and my mum is the dodgy mooring.'

'This arrangement - it goes right off the scale of irregularity. Why has this happened?'

'I've already said, haven't I!'

'I'm not buying it.'

'You have to! That's all there is!'

'Katie Talog!'

'She's always trying to get at me, or the Andrew, or my CO. She's been doing it since I enlisted. It all got a bit heated. She wants me back, for good. Uncle Alec's job is to fend her off.'

Spry was shaking her head. 'If this happened for every rating, we wouldn't be able to man our warships. This is ridiculous!'

'You don't know my mum!'

'I don't, but she sounds...possessed!'

'Yes, I think she probably is.'

'So, why did your mum and dad split up?'

'What? Why did they split up? I've already said, haven't I! And he's not my dad!'

'Why did they split up?'

'For pity's sake!' Katie pursed her lips and thought. It was no good, her left hand was trembling so she quelled it by sitting on it.

'She said it was down to me again, because when my mum was pregnant with me she was kicked out by her husband.' There was a long, long, uncomfortable pause.

Spry wasn't going to be deflected. 'Why did he do that?'

'I think he thought I wasn't his.'

'Why would he think that?'

'It's difficult for me to say, ma'am, I wasn't born then but I think it was because they hadn't slept together for some time, so I probably could not be his unless...'

'So, who is your real father?'

'Aaagh! I don't know. Could be anyone. We could start looking in Powys or in the Marches or Gwynedd and then start working outwards.'

'You seem to be every dismissive of your mother?'

'Well, she started it, didn't she?'

'Do you want to find out who your father is?'

'Not really, I've managed without him for long enough, he's probably some born again scrote...'

'Well, my father has been a true inspiration...'

'Oh, has he? Well, my mum will tell me when she's ready' Katie interrupted, 'if she knows.'

'So, no father figure in your life?'

'Um, yes, there's Mister Hofland.'

'Your sister's husband? Your brother-in-law?'

'Yes, that's the one. He was quite strict with me. He spent a lot of time with me, he taught me about discipline, in fact... he disciplined me.' (Hold on, that doesn't sound quite right.) 'He instilled discipline into me.' (That still didn't sound quite right.) She turned towards the door and whispered, 'Uncle Alec, where are you? I need you.'

'What did Mister Hofland do?'

'Do?' Katie walked back to the chair in the centre of the room and propped herself up with her hands on the back of the chair. 'He sat me down after school and we'd do writing and numbers every night. He taught me... he taught me what I needed to know to pass exams.'

'You haven't passed any exams, though, have you?'

That was true. 'Well, I got through the entrance exam to the Andrew, ma'am. That gave me a chance...to make good on my promise.' She looked longingly out of the window. There was a blackbird's fluting song outside and the screaming of a swift just around the eaves of the building opposite. 'My PE teachers at Ludlow, Mister Davies and Mister Pratt, taught me how to kick, throw and catch balls. They taught me the rules of games and life. They got me here. They are my...father figures.'

'I see - are you still in contact with your mother?'

'Er, yes of course, she writes me a bluey every now...'

'A bluey?'

'Yes, but I don't get them any more, do I?'

'Why not?'

'Someone in the Brain's Trust decided that I shouldn't get them.'

'I don't understand. Why don't you stay in contact with your mother?'

'I've just told you.' This wasn't working. 'Well, she wasn't very good at looking after me. Others looked after me, like my nana. My sister and her husband eventually took me in, when they found me wandering around in the hills.' Katie gulped and then bit her lip.

'Were you harmed by all this Katie?'

'What? No! I don't know.' There was another difficult silence. There, it was, all out in the open now. 'My mum wants me out of the navy and back with her - she says I owe her that.'

'What do you think?'

'My sister thinks our mum is like a black hole, if I get too close I'll get sucked in.' There was another difficult silence.

'I think you need to see her' challenged Spry.

'I will see her when I'm ready.'

'How long has it been?'

'About thirteen months, ma'am.'

'Why has it been so long?'

'I had a long spell of duty...'

'I see - and what happened to Mister Houghton?'

'I think he's still in a hospital near Cannock Chase. He's been there for years. He had a bad time in the Falklands and his break up with mum tipped him over.'

'Do you visit him?'

'Sometimes - we had a bit of a disagreement. I think he would have preferred it if I didn't exist.' She paused while this sank in. 'But unfortunately, I do' she clarified.

'And how does that make you feel?' asked Nicola.

After a long pause. 'I don't know how it makes me feel, I try not to think about it.'

'I think you need to spend time with your family. You've been away from home for a long time, over the past two years you've been at sea for more than eighteen months. You should spend some time getting re-acquainted with your mother! And maybe that way, the Royal Navy will no longer have to receive all these threatening communications that are directed at you!' Spry gave a wry smile as she brought out the black brief case - she opened it to display a sheaf of letters wrapped in several layers of clear plastic sheet and secured with a red ribbon. 'These have been passed to me by the Cryptography Department.'

Katie took the red ribbon secured sheaf but dropped it almost immediately. There was something wrong here, something unfamiliar about the scrawl on the top letter - not English or Welsh but something older, something more menacing. She swept it to the floor and edged the pile under her chair with her foot and breathed again. 'These must be burnt, I don't want them!'

'Don't be ridiculous!' said Spry.

'They are nasty!' yelled Katie.

There was a bang. It was the door! Uncle Alec arrived back in the room and nodded to Spry. Katie caught his eye. 'Uncle Alec!' she shouted. 'The letters! They should be burnt!'

'Katie?'

'For pity's sake!' She lunged for the brief case, snaffled the wallet of letters in the jaws of the case and barged her way out of the room. In a few strides, she was outside. Now for a few deep breaths. There was the clinic opposite and behind, bins for clinical waste. Katie flipped open a lid, opened the plastic bag inside and tipped in the sheaf of letters. The bag was resealed, the lid closed and now, a pause for thought. What to do with the brief case? She threw it in for good measure. Katie considered what to do with the blood soiled napkin in her hand. 'I'll keep this' she decided. It was a quick walk back inside, a cheery greeting to the receptionist and a sweet smile to explain that she had gotten rid of the rubbish.

She was back in the room - Uncle Alec and Spry were waiting. Katie sat down and crossed her legs. 'Sorted' she announced with a wink to Uncle Alec.

Spry's jaw was hanging open. 'I'll explain later' said Uncle Alec. 'Are we in any danger, Katie?'

'Who's read them?'

'Only a select few in the Cryptography Department.'

'Call them, find out who's handled them - they may need a bit of help if they got anywhere with the message!'

Uncle Alec passed a faxed sheet of paper to Spry and turned to leave the room. 'I'll get on to it!'

Spry gazed at Katie - she seemed to be in a state of shock. 'What on earth is going on?'

'They're tainted and they're written in old witch-script and they've got postage stamps! Mum would never do that!'

'Aberystwyth postmark?' asked Uncle Alec.

'Yes - those women of the Elenydd really hate us! It's an old feud, ma'am and they don't play fair!'

The door banged again as Alec left.

Nicola Spry spent a minute composing herself but the fax fluttered in her hand. 'Ah, that all seems to be in hand' she said quietly. And then she re-read it. 'I understand that something else happened during the mission? Can you tell me about it, Katie?'

'I don't know what you mean, ma'am?' This sounded like more trouble.

'One of the French soldiers was injured...'

'Oh, yes, there were two casualties, ma'am, and one of them was very bad.'

'Tell me what happened.'

'One of their men was badly wounded in the chest, he was all opened up.'

'What did you do?'

'I got him to safety' she said, agonising over what to say next, 'and I patched him up as best I could.'

'Are you qualified to give first aid?'

'No ma'am, but there was no available medical orderly. We all have basic first aid, so, I put him back together as best I could.'

'Was he critical?'

'Um, he wasn't happy with the way I bandaged him up, but he was in a bad way ma'am. I kept him going as long as I could.'

'How?'

'I just did, that's all.'

She had put in padding to staunch his bleeding and bound his chest with the biggest pressure dressing. She had spoken to him in her faltering Breton, and he had spoken back, despite the morphine and his wound. She had soothed him and embraced him as his eyes subsided.

At least he had the comfort of knowing that someone was caring for him, even if it was just this girl from the Marches who had recited meaningless bollocks in a piss-awful accent. 'I didn't think Benoit would last much longer. All I could do was put him back together and comfort him. We got him into the Lynx and Scotty got him back to HMS Albany, as quick as he could. And I topped up his morphine, so he was comfortable.' Katie's heart was racing now and her eyes were welling with water. 'Benoit kept talking to me, trying to help me, trying to help us, until he subsided. He kept calling for his mother, but all he got was me!'

'There are times when we need our mothers, and you did your best for him.'

'I was with him, I did all I could do, it was all down to me. It's what any of my oppos would do for me.'

'You don't know, do you Katie?'

'Know what, ma'am?'

'He made it.'

It was no good, the tears were now rushing down her face. 'I'm sorry, please give me a moment!' Katie stepped across to the door, hammered at it with her shoulder and thigh until it released her into the corridor. She turned to the right and ran, leaving a trail of tears behind her on the shiny, wooden floor.

Uncle Alec found her by the plastic food machine. 'Have you been crying, Katie?'

She turned to him. 'I had a moment.'

The machine juddered into life, advanced one position. Katie took a quick look. The machine juddered forward again and ejected a pie in plastic wrapping. She removed it and started to unwrap it. It was a custard tart, she noted, as she bit into it. 'Uncle Alec, I'm getting pinged from pillar to post in there and just when I need to tag you in, you've buggered off!'

He looked shocked. 'What are you talking about?'

'I'm getting a right pinging...' She paused to wipe crumbs of pastry from her lips and chin.

'Yes, I got that. But I'm not on your team, I have to remain impartial. This isn't a bout of tag team wrestling!'

'What is it about, then? Are you just a spectator, Uncle Alec?'

'I'm not sure that this metaphor is working for me' he muttered.

'A metaphor, is it? I thought it might be an allergy, with Spry the villain of the piece?'

'An allegory? I don't think so. Maybe it's a simile or an analogy...'

'Whatever, it doesn't matter. The point is, if you're not my tag team partner, then you're the referee, and your job is to see there's fair play, isn't it? Well, she's been tugging at my hair and gouging out my eyes. What are you going to do about that?'

'I haven't seen any of that! Do you mean it's been getting physical?'

'Not yet, but I can't promise it will stay like that.' She paused for a thought. 'Anyway, you're no use as a referee because you bugger off when the foul play starts!'

'I went to the fax machine! And then I made an emergency call to the Cryptography Department! They've had two operators off work for months!'

'Never mind that. You buggered off and left me isolated...you've got to keep up with me!'

'Look, I'm getting lost here!'

'Listen, so you're not the referee, you're now my coach. Speaking allegorically, what am I going to do?'

'Allegorically? Stop fighting her!'

'What sort of an idea is that? Do you think you're trying to help because you're really not!'

'You have to realise you're way out of your league! You're going to have to yield to avoid any more distress!'

'You're right, I don't need any more distress, but somehow, I need to sort this out, categorically.'

'So Katie, what do you intend to do, categorically?'

'I don't know, I'm still wondering.' She frowned. 'I'm not going to lie to you, Uncle Alec, right at this moment, I want to zap her one.'

He looked horrified. 'Listen Katie, there must be no physical violence! No touching an officer! Absolutely not!'

'Uncle Alec, there's no touching needed for a zap' she snorted indignantly, 'it's just a bit of channelling!'

'Katie, let's make it a rule that there's to be no zapping.'

'Not even a little one?'

'Not even a little one.' He seemed perplexed but not entirely surprised, which was surprising. 'But Katie, have you zapped someone before?'

'Er, no, no, no...just the once.'

'Aha! And what happened exactly?'

'Well, he looked a bit shocked to be fair...then he hopped off.'

'So just to be clear, Katie' he asked sharply, 'he got a bit of a shock, but you didn't make his leg fall off?'

'Oh, no, no, no, nothing like that' she said, recalling the brown-eyed boy in his red football shirt, staring back at her, with bulging eyes so wide that they should have popped out of their sockets. 'but it was all a bit fuzzy.'

'You should talk that through with your sisters.'

'My sisters?'

'I mean Gwen, of course. So no physical damage caused by this... zapping incident?'

She revealed her finger nails.

'Aha.'

'So, no zapping?'

'Not even a fuzzy one. I must say I've never heard that mentioned in any hand-to-hand combat training manual!'

'I know that now, but I was just talking...metaphorically. So, what you're saying is, as my coach, that I have to give in, tap out, concede to Spry?'

'Yes, one of those.'

'All right then, I'll go back in and say, Spry, you know sod all about anything but in this case, amazingly, you may just have a point.'

'Can we work on the tone of that?'

'The tone? So, I need to be a bit more rhetorical then?' She was momentarily lost in thought. 'It's all right, I've got it!'

'Conciliatory?'

'Totally, but I'm going to turn this around and sort it out, whatever it takes.'

'That doesn't sound conciliatory!'

'It's not, I'm going to find her weakness. Have you got anything on her? Is she doing someone she shouldn't be doing, hypothetically?'

'No, nothing like that. Look, are you all right to go back in? You seem a bit shaken. Was it the letters?'

'No, no, no, it's Benoit, I thought he was a goner, so I did something...'

'Benoit? No, he's very much alive. The French papers are full of it.'

'What are they saying?'

Alec showed her a faxed sheet of paper and allowed Katie to read it. She tried to read it several times but it didn't make any sense.

He put his hand on her shoulder. 'Do you know who L'Ange du Albany is?'

She looked up at him in confusion. 'Who? Angel of the Albany? Who's that?'

'It's you!'

'Blimey! Has anything else been said?'

'What do you mean?'

'I mean, there were things said and done in the heat of the moment, while all the shit and bullets were flying around and has any of that got out?'

'What is the problem Katie' asked Uncle Alec, sternly.

'Benoit knows what happened out there, what I said, what I did...'

'So?'

'It all got a bit...dodgy.'

'He wants to meet up with you.'

'Well, I can't meet up with him, can I? Not until everything has settled down. There could be an enquiry, couldn't there?' The plastic food machine jolted again. 'He wanted me in this sodding bikini' she whispered behind her hand, 'but there was hardly anything of it! Just enough for three eye-patches, that's all! And I'd been eating cake like it was going out of fashion!'

'You're making too much of it - unless there's something you're not telling me?' Uncle Alec gently manoeuvred her away from the vending machine.

'So it's not going to happen, is it? There were things said and done in the heat of it, and stuff I've eaten - and none of it shows me in a particularly good light' continued Katie.

'What things?'

'I can't tell you. They're best left unsaid and undone, I think. Or uneaten.'

'Try.'

'Well, you know that thing that only priests are allowed to do... with the about to die?'

'Not really.'

'Well, I did it with Benoit! I...sent him on his way!'

'What was that? You kissed him goodbye?'

'No, the other thing, but what was I supposed to do? Tell him a joke? Have you heard the one about the bloke who was dying but really wasn't?'

'Katie?'

'The only good thing was, he may have been high on morphine.'

'So what does it matter? He was drugged to the eyeballs! Wait a minute, you didn't overdose him?'

'No, not that I know of, but he had been doing a bit of self-dosing.'

'What's the problem then?'

She looked up at him with her widest, teary smile, her most soulfully deep eyes. 'It's nothing, Uncle Alec, I'm worrying about nothing. I just need to rack out for a couple of days.'

'Okay, I don't think it's a problem but you might want to talk it through with your sister. For now, just accept that there's a strong possibility that he would have died if it wasn't for the action that you took.'

'All right, I accept that, but back to the now-time - I had to step out of the room because Spry was having a go.'

'About saving Benoit?'

'About everything! Weren't you there? Oh yes, that's right, you went off and did some skivvying for her, didn't you? Totally, bloody brilliant!'

'What happened, Katie?'

'She's doing my head in. While you were out, she got on to the subject of my parents.'

'You don't know who your father is though?'

'I know that. I think I've covered that one off.'

'And your mother?'

'Yes, my mum and all those sodding letters...'

'Right.'

'And the first I hear about the letters is when Miss Crusty Knickers waves them in front of my face?'

'It's nothing new, you know the form. If we think it's a threat, we keep them secure until you decide what needs to be done.'

'Well, it didn't happen and there's nothing that can be done about it now. I'll have to sort it out myself. But, what do I do about Spry?'

'My advice to you, as your coach, is to concede. You cannot beat her, she's a wily old campaigner.'

Katie looked down the corridor. Nicola Spry was beckoning them back into the interview room. 'So what you're saying is, Uncle Alec, I should pull up my big girl knickers and get on with it?'

'Yes, something like that. You should also know that you are well regarded by everyone you work with. You're going to be advanced whether you like it or not.'

'Blimey?! Should I be getting more money, then?'

'Could be. Spry will discuss a new land based assignment with you. You will report to her for the next six to nine months where you will be able to demonstrate your ability to lead, train and do as you're told. And you'll be locked into the Andrew for another five years.'

She favoured him with a big frown and a wide smile. 'No one told me, it's been stupid the last few weeks. Mum won't like it, Gwen and Stefan won't like it, especially if the women of the Elenydd are playing up. Another five years - blimey!'

'You need to relax. We're all on your side. Stop being so...bloody difficult!'

She wiped her eyes dry. The tears had served their purpose.

'How are you feeling Katie?' asked Nicola as she settled back into her seat.

'I'm better, thank you. And thank you Mister Wicks for coming to check up on me.' She hoped that Spry had picked up on the intended dig.

'Are you ready to continue, Katie?'

'Yes, ma'am, I am' Katie replied. The room seemed to have a calmness about it which it didn't have before.

'So, I understand that you have been mentoring some of the junior ratings on HMS Albany.'

'Yes, ma'am, I had two 'wingers' to look after.' Spry frowned and looked at Uncle Alec and he nodded in reassurance.

'The reports I've had back are mainly positive Katie. There was one piece of feedback I wanted to discuss with you. One of your 'wingers', as you term them, commented that they weren't comfortable with the amount of bad language used. They didn't realise that it was obligatory on board ship.'

'Yes, ma'am, that's a common misapprehension, but I soon put them straight.' Uncle Alec turned away and smirked.

'Really!' Spry turned to Uncle Alec looking for support but didn't get any. 'Do you not think you have a responsibility as a woman to help moderate that sort of behaviour?'

'Absolutely not, ma'am!'

'I see. I see.'

'This will all become obvious to you ma'am, once you've spent any time in a ship's company.'

Spry breathed out sharply and seemed to be considering a rebuke but it didn't come. They stared at each other until Spry dropped her eyes to the security of her typed notes. 'In much of the feedback I've had, you are known by different names, why is that?'

'Ma'am, it's standard that we don't call our 'oppos' by their actual name in a ship ma'am.' Spry looked puzzled by this. 'So if he's a short rating, we call him Lofty, if he's called Smith, he's Smudger and if he's called White, we call him Chalky and...'

'Isn't that disrespectful?'

'No ma'am. It helps with giving a sense of belonging and team building.'

'So how do you account for all your nicknames?'

'Eh? Well, I'm not a Taffy am I?' Spry's face was shrouded in puzzlement. She really had no clue. 'My initials are Kilo, Echo, Tango, so it became Ket, then Katie? See?' There was a pause while she considered if she needed to expand on this.

'Thank you for that explanation...Ket.'

This jarred badly. 'You're welcome ma'am, but as you're my CO and we're not in a ship, I think Talog is perfectly fine.'

'I see. So what would you call me?' Spry asked abruptly.

Katie was taken aback by this. 'I don't think that would be appropriate ma'am. Even if I had one, I think it would be better to keep it to myself.' Spry looked like she wanted to pursue this for a moment but didn't. Katie suddenly had a vision of frying food and bubbling skin and her whole body shook spontaneously. 'I think 'ma'am' is perfectly fine, ma'am.'

'I believe you're also know as Tally, why is this?'

'That's from the Fleet Air Arm ma'am - I don't know why they have to be different.'

Uncle Alec chose to intervene. 'Why are you so concerned about this Nicola? Where are you going with this?'

Spry addressed Katie. 'Your relationships with other groups interests me. Team working is essential within the Royal Navy, as is respect for others.'

'In which case, are there any others we should know about. Katie?' Uncle Alec was smirking again.

Katie hesitated. This felt like it could be a trap. 'I don't know what you mean, sir?'

'The RFA?'

'Royal Fleet Auxiliary? Oh, yes, they call me 'Littlewoods' and they all think it's hilarious, but I don't get it.'

'Are there any others, Katie?' asked Uncle Alec.

'Oh yes, 'Cornflake'. They also think that's hilarious but I don't get that one either.'

'Any others you are happy to disclose, Katie?'

She looked through the window into the middle distance, above Spry's left shoulder. There were others. 'The Anzacs call me Sheela, but I think they are just naturally rude.'

'Anzacs?'

'The Aussies and the Kiwis, ma'am.'

'I meant, how come?'

'Oh, combined ops, that's all ma'am.'

'I see. Don't you find that disrespectful?'

'Oh, I see. Yes ma'am, it's rude. I should have told them to stop, shouldn't I ma'am? But to be fair, he was the commanding officer, wasn't he?'

'So, how do you think you should be addressed, Katie?'

'Ma'am? I'm happy being Ket, Tally, Littlewoods, Cornflake or Sheela to the dicks - they all work for me!'

'Should it not be Leading Hand Talog?' Spry gave herself a big smile at this point as if she'd said something very clever.

'Um, I'm not sure, ma'am.' Hold on, does that mean I'm no longer acting, but I'm being permanently advanced and no longer unpaid, but paid? Although, to be fair, she had been paid while acting. 'Oh, my gods, ma'am!'

'Do you agree, Leading Hand Talog?'

'Yes, ma'am. You're right, I should absolutely be Leading Hand Talog and nothing else!'

'Good' sighed Spry. 'Good. Now, Katie, your relationships with others. How do you manage those relationships with others in the wider team?'

'Absolutely brilliantly, ma'am.'

'I see. In that case, tell me about your relationship with the artificers.'

Katie hesitated. She knew where this was heading. 'You mean the 'Clankies', ma'am?'

'Clankies?'

'Yes ma'am, mechanicians. Mechanical engineers.'

'And...how do you address them?'

Katie paused to consider how best to respond to this. 'Well, Nico is called 'Thick Crust' and Ray is called 'Bogey'.'

'And why would that be?'

'They're the names they have been given, and everyone else uses them, so it's just standard, isn't it ma'am?'

'It says on your report that you had a serious altercation with them. What was that about?'

'An 'alter' what ma'am?'

'An argument, Katie.'

Katie scribbled a quick mark in her planner. 'That's not totally true...'

There was no response from Spry. She was waiting for Katie to continue. After several moments, she decided to give her version of events. 'Well, I was told that a conversation I had with them was overheard and they say that every other word they heard was a swearing word. There, that's all it was.'

'Was that true?'

'No ma'am, maybe every fourth or fifth word.' Katie paused. Would that be enough explanation or would Spry delve into her state of mind at the time? Katie continued, 'It's how I make myself understood to the 'Clankies' because basically, they're just below deck scum.'

Katie observed that Uncle Alec's face was painfully contorted as he tried desperately not to laugh out loud.

'What do you call them?'

'Below deck...'

Uncle Alec turned away as his face progressed through redder and redder shades of crimson. She glared at him but he would not return her stare.

'That's very disrespectful of your colleagues!'

'Er, yes, you're quite right ma'am.' Katie decided to continue with Nicola Spry. 'Anyway, it may seem to outsiders that we don't get on, but we do. The Clankies just get a bit precious about spare parts, which is quite funny, when you think about it.'

'I see. Let's move on. I'm going to summarise where you are in terms of performance and then we can discuss your advancement. So, overall, your performance has met the standard required as a... leading hand in your current role. The feedback from your immediate commanding officers, including the Royal Marines and from the task group has been in the most part positive. We've discussed areas for improvement which must be addressed. Do you have any comments, Katie?'

'Yes ma'am. It's just that...I don't see how anyone could have done more in a year than I've just done.' Spry just stared back in response to this comment.

Uncle Alec stirred and gave Spry a penetrating look. He leant over, beckoned for the papers in front of her and gathered them up. He fluttered the edges slowly and then looked up ready to make his pronouncement. 'I'd like to add to Nicola's comments based on my own personal experience of dealing directly with you, Katie, and on the many, unsolicited conversations I've had with the people who work with you on a day to day basis. It's important we have the full picture.'

'Wait a moment, I don't think that's appropriate Mister Wicks, let me continue...' Spry replied.

'No, please let me just say this. It needs to be said. The paper record is only part of the story. He riffled through the papers again. 'Just dealing with the facts,' he announced, ignoring Spry huffily crossing her arms, 'just dealing with the facts, you have completed a tour of duty that is close to thirteen months and that is exceptional in this day and age.' Spry sighed noisily and stretched even further back in her chair. 'During this tour of duty, you have served in the crew of two warships and in a multi-national task force. The feedback of commanding officers, and all those working with you is frankly, full of the highest praise.'

Katie groaned inside. Her hands came up to shield her eyes. He was going to make a speech. She dropped her hands so she could see what was going through Spry's mind. Her eyes implored him to stop but he continued resolutely on his way.

'So the facts. Through your efforts and those of the Albany team, the life of a French colleague has been saved, four French hostages and a French military helicopter have all been rescued in the Comoros Islands. You assisted with the installation of two water systems in Madagascar and the building of artificial harbours off Cape Delgado and Pemba Island. In between all this you helped with the capture of twenty hostile craft, over ten million dollars of opium and the action off the Seychelles will go...'

'Sir, please stop...' Katie interrupted.

'What's the matter, Katie?'

Spry picked up her briefing sheet and looked over the front and the back sheets. 'And where's all this, Katie?'

'The stuff off Zanzibar. That leads to the action off the Seychelles. That's all hush-hush.'

Uncle Alec continued. 'Ah, I see. Still, the French CO involved with the Comoros Islands, writes that you were their 'White Queen'. You retrieved a dangerous situation by your own efforts.'

'There's going to be an enquiry about what happened there, sir. The day job, we're all right talking about that, but it's the Royal that goes in and pulls them out. I just find them.'

'What we are trying to say, in our different ways, is that you have performed all the duties you have been assigned with great verve, confidence and efficiency, over an exceptionally long tour of duty. The Andrew hasn't seen anything like this since the days of Horatio...'

'Thanks sir, but...'

'And the way that the team handled the Chinese submarine will become a master class in the art of anti-submarine warfare. How you boxed it in and got it to turn turtle...'

'UNCLE ALEC!' shouted Katie.

'That wasn't in the briefing, Mister Wicks.' Spry snapped.

'No, it can't be ma'am. Official Secrets Act' replied Katie.

'So the facts speak for themselves' Uncle Alec finished lamely. 'There are questions about what happened off the Comoros Islands but there will be a wider enquiry about that. That's not for you to answer, that's for the officers in command to answer.'

'I see sir. So, ma'am, what happens now? Where do I go from here?' asked Katie.

'We spoke before about what your ambition is - what I heard is that you want to join one of the Navy's new capital ships, maybe as a flight controller?'

'Yes, ma'am.'

'But you don't have the experience, the knowledge or the right technical qualifications, do you?'

'I have loads of qualifications and four good years of experience - you can't beat that. That's as far as the plan went...and doing what I'm doing to the best of my ability.'

'Actually, you have no formal qualifications, no GCSEs, nothing. Isn't that true?'

'Er, yes, ma'am.'

'So, this is what we're going to do with you' said Spry. 'I am looking for a leader, someone to assist me in leading a small, shore based installation. I have responsibility for the Navy training range HMS Hawkins at Shoeburyness from September. It involves working with the personnel on site, supporting them in what they want to do and making the site safe for further development. You will report to me. What do you say?'

'Yes, but Shoeburyness? Where's that?'

'It's in Essex, on the River Thames.'

Katie suddenly felt very uneasy. She didn't like the sound of this. 'Oh, I see, HMS Hawkins, a concrete frigate, but what would I have to do there? Am I a writer now? A pen pusher? Because, that's really not going to work, is it?'

'You will need to split your leave, so we can brief you at HMS Hawkins on May 26th. You will arrive at the main site installation at eleven hundred. You will meet Captain Coles and he and I will brief you about your assignment. I will be taking command of the site.'

Katie scribbled furiously in her diary and flipped out the map of the United Kingdom. 'Shoeburyness, but that's not a navy base is it? It's a firing range isn't it?' So, Shoeburyness, opposite the forts in the middle of the Thames, opposite the River Medway and the Isle of Sheppey, all places that she should know because their existence was somehow written deep inside of her, but she didn't know because she'd never been.

'Yes, it is. It's a satellite of the main site there. You will report to me while we assess what's there, catalogue it, deal with any issues, deal with the people.'

'How will I have the authority to do what needs to be done?'

'Through me. We will work up a plan with Captain Coles on May 26th. You will start officially on August 15th and you will arrange weekly meetings to keep me informed about what is happening. Are you on board with this?'

'Yes ma'am.' Katie scribbled a list in her notebook. 'If it all goes well, what happens when I've finished this assignment? Am I finished in combined operations?'

'If it goes according to plan, we will consider your next position. This is just the first step in your development and you must perform it to my complete satisfaction.'

'Oh!' Katie sat back and smiled a tear stained smile. 'Bugger me' she commented, 'I never dreamt...I must tell Gwen, she won't believe this!'

'So Talog, is that a yes?'

'Yes, it is.' She looked to Alec Wicks and then back to Nicola Spry. 'So ma'am, why me? What is it about me that makes me right for this?'

'That's not for me to say. I haven't had time to formulate an opinion yet.'

'You must have some idea, ma'am?'

'It's not for me to say. That decision was made elsewhere...' There was another long, uncomfortable pause. 'I will be completely frank...'

'That's fine, ma'am, I'll be completely Katie...'

'It's apparent that you are highly regarded by the ship's companies that you work with. I'm not entirely sure why. You may have a certain physicality that may be attractive to others, but it doesn't cut any ice with me.' Spry paused to look at Katie and blushed suddenly. Katie filed this image away under 'weaknesses'. 'I understand that you have a certain way with officers that men might mistake for charm. That won't wash with me. I've seen this at first hand. I see it as a lack of respect for authority.'

Katie gasped and her hand went up to her mouth.

The look Spry gave was steely but invalidated by the flush that still mottled her cheeks.

'Thank you for that ma'am. So, is it fair to say that I'm a rough diamond that needs a bit of polishing?'

'Yes, Talog, a very rough diamond that needs a lot of polishing.'

'I'm very relieved by that ma'am.'

'Why?'

'I'd rather be a diamond than a turd, ma'am, yes I would...'

'Well obviously...'

'...because, you can't polish a turd' finished Katie.

'Although you can roll it in glitter' added Uncle Alec.

Spry gave a deep sigh.

'As we're all together, can I give some feedback too?' Katie continued.

'I don't think that's appropriate, Talog' replied Spry.

'Even so ma'am, as we're all being open and honest, aren't we? It's how we want the Andrew to be, isn't it sir?'

Uncle Alec nodded vigorously.

Spry retorted: 'This is most irregular, I suppose so, if you must.'

'Well, first of all, I'm really looking forward to this opportunity to report to you, ma'am. I think I will learn a lot about how to manage our people and how things work upstairs.' She looked across to Uncle Alec. He seemed to be swelling with pride again.

'Thank you Talog' Spry said cautiously.

'So, what is it that you want to get out of our working relationship, ma'am?'

Spry looked to Uncle Alec who was smirking again. 'My objective is to...I don't know why I'm telling you this. My five year plan is to achieve captaincy of a warship, through merit alone.'

'I see, ma'am.' Kate nodded. 'I can see you are a stickler for the rules and you like to follow processes. That's fine in the office. What you will have to learn is that...what's the name of that German who was a master of tactics and all that stuff?'

Uncle Alec smirked to himself. 'Are you thinking of Franz Beckenbauer, Katie?'

'Who?'

'Franz Beckenbauer, also know as 'The Kaiser'?'

'Possibly' Katie murmured cautiously. 'Anyway, what this German bloke said was that you can have the best plan in the world but it will all fall apart on first contact with the opposition. What that means is that in an encounter, you can't call a time out or go back to your quarters and read the manual. You have to react quickly and go with your gut, because if you don't, you will always be one step behind.'

'Have you quite finished Talog?'

'Er, not quite, ma'am, but what I would say is that you can only train your gut by facing these situations...like I've done!'

'I see. Well, thank you for your comments but I don't believe it has any relevance in this day and age.' Spry looked down and made a quick written note on the papers in front of her.

'So, what do you want from me, ma'am?' Katie asked.

'I want you to follow my orders to the letter, without embellishment, addition or any attempt to anticipate what I might want. I want unswerving obedience. You may not be used to this, but's that's how it will be with me.'

'I see. So why me, ma'am?' Any idiot can follow orders, but who will speak up when they know the orders are wrong?

Spry sighed a long and heavy sigh. 'We're seen as having complementary skills Talog, unbelievable as that may sound.'

'Got it.'

'We'll see Talog. That concludes our meeting. I will write to you and confirm what we've discussed. I can confirm that you will report to me as leading hand at HMS Hawkins. All your other terms and conditions remain the same.'

'So, I ought to be getting more pay, ma'am?'

'Don't push your luck, Talog.'

'Well, if I'm a fully paid up leading hand now, ma'am, I deserve a raise! Anyway, I'd better go, the scab lifters want to give me a good going over too. I'll see you at HMS Hawkins on May the twenty-sixth. I'm really looking forward to it!'

'Thank you Talog.'

'Katie, I'll see you out. Just give us a minute' asked Alec.

'Now get some rest and talk to your family. Tell them the good news' said Spry.

'Yes ma'am, thank you ma'am.' She stood smartly, gave her best salute, retrieved her roll bag, cap and her rucksack and pushed open the door.

'And remember Talog, regardless of your back history, you are now a Daughter of Albion!'

Katie stopped momentarily. Did Spry just get in the last word? She strode through the doorway and quickly along the corridor, dropped her bags by the plastic food machine and returned stealthily back to the door of the interview room. As the door opened slowly, Katie pressed her body against the wood panelled door and held her breath. After a moment, the door closed again with the two occupants still inside. She pressed her ear against the door and listened.

Spry spoke in a hushed tone to Uncle Alec in the closed room. 'So, mission accomplished. That all went according to plan. Three things I wanted, three things I got. I don't know what all the fuss is about?'

'Three things?' Uncle Alec asked, 'you don't feel there was some sort of reversal back there?'

'No, not at all. It was all textbook. I wanted her to recognise that she has to follow orders to the letter. Tick.'

Katie sensed that Uncle Alec would just give a shrug in return.

'I wanted her to stop this barrage of letters the Navy has been receiving. Tick, she's committed to doing that. And finally, she will join the staff of a shore based unit where I can mould her into shape. Big tick!'

'Well, she is uniquely talented' Alec remarked.

'We're all unique but she's got the edge on most of us. What did you make of that feedback about her cursing? Is that what we want from our girl leaders? I thought the idea of having women on board ship was to help to moderate behaviours - has that worked in the opposite direction with Talog?'

'Well, Nicola, what it doesn't say in her dossier is that she can curse in many languages - she can hold her own with the Aussies! And the Royal Marines!'

'I have to grant you that Captain Marriott is very positive in his feedback. I think he used the word 'revered' which seems over the top and she's regarded as an old hand by the younger rates but she's still very young.'

'Lieutenant Griffiths said the Royal would be happy to have her in the Royal Marines, if rules allowed. She's quick, decisive and knows what she's doing' added Uncle Alec.

'I still don't understand how someone who is barely literate or numerate can enter the service. How on earth did she get through the entrance exam?'

'Ah, there are three things you need to know. Just excuse me a moment.'

Katie heard the chair move back and then quick footfalls towards the door. She took two steps to the right and squeezed tight against the wooden panelling. Uncle Alec's head was out of the room looking quickly up the corridor to reception. She stilled her breathing and then her heart. After looking in both directions along the corridor, Uncle Alec's head disappeared back into the office.

'Ah good' she heard him say quietly, 'she's not about. Best to check, she has this uncanny ability to hear things she shouldn't be able to. Now?'

'Was that one of them?'

'Ah, good point...four things. But first of all, she didn't enlist. Katie was selected, almost literally, out of a field.'

Katie heard a splutter. It could only have come from Spry. 'Selected? Like an officer cadet? But that's absurd! How?'

'Can't say. She was selected at the age of fourteen...'

'That is just ridiculous. What process is this?'

'I can't tell you, but it's enshrined in a most solemn oath held in Admiralty House, if you want to follow up.'

'Really? Is there anything else I should know?'

'Yes. Nobody's really sure what happened in the Comoros Islands. The main witness, a French lieutenant called Benoit...is still in an intensive care unit in Brest.'

'He's the man she rescued?'

'Yes, something happened but she will not say anything about it. We just know that Katie has knife wounds on both her hands and a graze on her forehead from that encounter.'

'Anything else?'

'Yes, just a cautionary note. She is...' The sentence stopped in mid-flow. It resumed with a whisper that was too low for her to hear.

'Oh, good God! She is surrounded in secrets. How do I get to the bottom of all this?' Spry said.

'You don't.'

'None of that matters. I will treat her as any other.'

'Well, I'm glad that went well for you. She is willing and able, you'll see.'

'But I can't believe how exhausted I feel. I'll need a stiff drink tonight!'

Katie listened carefully from behind the door. She nodded in agreement.

Uncle Alec paused. 'Look, I need to fill you in on what went on outside and more of her back story. But it is the right time to move her on. I'll be back in five. I'll just catch her before she goes.'

'I've got her right where I wanted her. I just needed to get under her skin and then she was just putty in my hands!' Spry crowed to herself.

Katie shook her head and a broad smile spread across her face. That was a woeful summary of what had just happened. She took several quick stealthy steps along the corridor and waited for Uncle Alec to emerge.

'Everything all right, sir?' she asked.

'Yes, that was very well done. Let's get you back to reception and on your way. So, how did you think that went?'

'It went much better than expected, sir.'

'Look, it's all right. Just tell me...'

'I don't think she likes me. She's decided against me and it's going to be difficult...'

'You'll make it work.'

'It would help if I had some dirt on her, but...'

'You'll make it work...'

'So, is this the end for me and you?' she asked.

'Well, no. I'll be in the background, but you'll be fine. No worries. You're not a girl anymore. You're a fully fledged wren. It will work fine with Lieutenant Spry.'

They reached the reception area. 'Well sir, thanks for everything. Will you stay in touch?' she asked.

'Of course. I will follow what you're doing with great interest. Just get in touch if there's anything you need. Anything. I must say, I was impressed with how you dealt with that. Good move. It was a bit cheeky but it got her thinking and you finished on top.' There was a moment where they both stood and wondered what should happen next.

Katie swung up her rucksack and picked up the roll bag. 'I'm off to see the medics. Then I'll go to bed for a few days. To sleep, to dream, mainly.' As she stepped towards the exit to the world outside, she was overtaken by melancholy. As she turned she saw him make a slow, smiling salute toward her. 'Oh, I'm sorry, you shouldn't be doing that!' She returned a stiff, formal salute with her free arm, dropped the bags and rushed to hug him. 'You big idiot!' As he lifted her and spun her around, she felt a surge of energy through her core, a whoop from her throat and a wave of relief from her spinning mind. As she settled back to the floor she breathed deeply and tried to regain her composure. He held her at arm's length by her waist. Her body tingled through her back and along her arms.

'Look, you'd better go' he reminded her, 'I'll catch you later...'

'Yes, and you'd better go and get some work done. I'll give you a shout when I get to HMS Hawkins.' With that she gathered her bags and plunged outside into the early afternoon sun. There were screechers circling high above, shrieking excitedly. 'Yes, I know how you feel' she exulted, 'I know how you feel!'

CHAPTER TWENTY-SIX

Wednesday 11 May 1310 -
The Butcher's Shop, HMS Raleigh

It was a short staccato stumble to the clinic, like a flamenco dance, with rucksack and roll bag, negotiating a stream of navy blue heading in all directions, except hers. Katie passed a sleek, white automobile decorated with a triple spiral on the doors, crowned with the red letters S.I.K.S. and with some other hieroglyphics in black - a name and an address. Her heart jumped. What was that doing here? Two quick ticks in her mind and she remembered that she had to make a telephone call to a Swiss gentleman who called himself Herr Robert Glaus.

Katie stopped in the entrance to the clinic, took a deep breath and pushed her way through the double doors, where inside, her nostrils were assailed with the smell of disinfectant and human. It was like the smell of a school on the first day of term, but lacking the aromas of the kitchen or the musk of exercise books. School was another place where she had been beset with boy rabbles.

As soon as the booking in procedure had been completed by the sour faced receptionist, Katie visited the washroom. She looked at the face looking back at her in the mirror: big, wide kaleidoscopic eyes, becoming bluer, then greener, then browner; a pointed triangle of a nose, like the prow of an Arctic icebreaker. She looked again - her left eye seemed slightly smaller than the right so she exercised the lids apart with her fingers but it made no difference. Her nibbling teeth and her fangs were a little too prominent - would eating more nuts help to wear them down a bit? The rest of her tooth arcade was complete.

Her ears were a touch flappy but readily concealed by her blondie-brown hair, which had now taken upon itself the duty of growing incredibly quickly, just like her finger nails. Was this normal when you reached nineteen years of age? She wished this growing would stop soon. She studied the ends of her fingernails in minute detail as they seemed to be adding more nail as she watched, layer by layer. Despite all this growth going on, there was a tuft of white hair on the back of her head that was difficult to conceal. However, she was pleased with her tanned face and neck but the tan terminated abruptly at her chest. The other thing, no two other things, that were growing, were her doops, after her semolina and cake enriched diet. She eased her blondie-brown hair back to view the sticking plaster on her scalp and groaned to herself. What would the M.O. say? There would be fussing and questions about how this could have happened to her. She would be told that she had not been looking after herself.

Katie sluiced her face with cold water and watched idly as the water ran over her tightly bandaged hands. She shrugged, pulled her gloves back on and gave her teeth a thorough brossing over with toothbrush and floss. With her teeth bared like a hyena, she could see that they were as immaculate as she could get them. From a small bottle of acrid smelling liquid she dabbed a little under her ears, in between the cups and just above the elastic line of her pants. They were the best she possessed but they still left an unsightly welt across her stomach. She took a deep draft from between the wispy tendrils under her left arm and groaned. The scent was just about tolerable.

Katie returned to her seat in the waiting room and decided she did not want to sit, so she paced up and down, circumnavigating the low, magazine scattered table, to the irritation of everyone else and the receptionist. After a further ten minutes of pacing she was called through to the consultation room.

The female nurse tried to put her at ease. 'You are leading hand K.E. Talog?'

'Acting? Yes, that's me, but I call myself Katie.'

'And your date and month of birth?'

'Eleventh of April. How was that?'

'Yes, spot on.'

'Good. Same form as before?'

'Yes, a complete assessment. I'll give you a quick triage and...' She started to read from a sheet of paper clipped neatly to the clipboard and then laughed. 'You have been in the wars, haven't you?' The nurse's face dropped as she read to the bottom of the page. She spun away from Katie and slapped the clipboard twice on her forehead.

'Listen, there's no need to beat yourself up' said Katie.

The words kept coming from the nurse but these were mouthed in utter incomprehension. 'I'm sorry, I didn't realise. You have...you have wounds on your head and your hands we need to look at and the doctor would like to have a chat about how you're coping, and the other doctor does too. Oh my God!' She waved the clipboard at her side and tried to regain her composure. 'The doctors will check how you're dealing with everything. They want to do a complete physical and mental assessment.'

'It's all right, really.'

'The doctor will check you over, then decide. Is that okay?'

'I suppose so. Who will be doing me physically?'

'It's Medical Officer Moore. I believe he knows you and he was quite insistent? And then we have a dietician and a mental health specialist lined up. You do have a busy afternoon ahead!'

'Lucky me!' Katie breathed deeply in relief and her heart trembled for a moment. No detailed explanations would be needed with Medical Officer Moore and he would be kind and gentle and considerate and handsome and would not ask any awkward questions. And suddenly there was a warmth that spread from her core and flooded throughout her body.

The nurse removed the head dressing and expressed surprise. 'That's healing very nicely! I don't think we need to replace this one!'

Katie felt the place where the dressing had been removed. There was a shallow impression in the skin, but this barely protruded. 'Will there be a scar?'

'Only a little one - no one will notice.'

Katie wiped a little tear from her right eye - that was one less thing she had to worry about.

There was now pumping to her side as her blood pressure was checked. 'That seems low but normal-ish, for you at least' noted the nurse cheerfully.

Next the gloves and dressings were pulled away from Katie's hands. There was a sharp intake of breath. 'These are healing very nicely, too.' The nurse disposed of the dressings and asked about the gloves. Katie said yes, she still needed them, mainly to hide the ugly black marks that swelled under her fingernails.

'So' the nurse pronounced, 'have you had any other problems on this tour?

'Do you mean apart from the obvious ones you can see? Well, what you may not able to see is...I've had a bout of the crimson scourge.'

There, she had said it. In fact, it had felt like her core had been tied in a knot and hacked through with a blunt carving knife.

'I'm sorry, I don't know what that is? Crimson scourge, you say, what's that? Do you want me to do...'

'Oh, no. It's just regular girl problems. It's not like I need a blood transfusion, or anything, is it?'

'When did this start? Is this new?'

'Two weeks ago, and it wasn't nice, but I'm over it, for the moment.' Katie swung onto on the surgical bed and laid down. 'The pusser's pants, navy issue have been a boon, haven't they? They're very nearly bullet proof, aren't they?'

'Right Katie, I've got some notes but your medical record is missing. The new people have made a right mess of things but they say they'll recover them soon. They've been an absolute nightmare. Your blood group is special, isn't it?'

'Yes, it's always been a bit of an issue, hasn't it?'

'And your blood's quite feisty, isn't it?'

'I'm not sure what you mean?'

'It doesn't like sharing, does it?'

'Er, no.'

'I see that we've been taking your blood out of you on a regular basis.' The nurse paused. 'Are you okay with me taking a fresh sample of your blood?' She unwrapped a sterile syringe and located a vein on Katie's right wrist.

'Wait up, you already have some of my blood. What's happened to that?'

'I said, didn't I? Your medical record is missing and that means that...'

'I want to know who's got my blood! I'm not letting you have any more until I know! You don't seem to realise how serious this is!'

'I'm sure it will turn up somewhere. It must be with us somewhere. It's not as if it was any use to anyone else, is it? I'm sure it will turn up.'

The up and down lilt of the nurse's high pitched voice was getting quite annoying now. 'That's not good enough. I want to know who's got it now! They could harm me unless I get it back, couldn't they?'

'Look it's nothing to worry...'

'Right, where's Mom? I want to see him now.'

'Mom?'

'You know, Medical Officer Moore!'

'He'll be along shortly. Now let me get on...'

Katie squirmed as the needle approached and her body jerked. The nurse tried to insert the needle but couldn't. She withdrew the needle and examined it closely, as if there was something not quite right with the tip.

'Or perhaps we won't take a sample today' said the nurse, taken aback. I'll just check your vital signs. There's a question about how we keep you at sea when we have such a limited supply of blood that's suitable for you! Medical Officer Moore wants to have a chat with you about that.'

Katie's heart slumped. What could this mean? 'Look, I'm not joining the paper Navy.' She thought for a moment. 'What if I got a paper cut? What then?'

'We'll let the doctor decide. Do you have any other problems?'

'Yes, my finger nails and my hair have started growing really quickly. I mean, really quickly' Katie said with emphasis. She ran her hands through her hair, unlocked it and pulled it down around her shoulders and removed the gloves from her hands to show her nails. 'Do you see? Bits of my body have gone into overdrive and I don't know why.'

'I'm sure its nothing to worry about - it's just growing up, isn't it?'

'No, no, it's all growing out, can't you see?' Her teeth ground in irritation and then there was that taste and smell you get when the dentist drills into your teeth.

'Doctor, please can you come?' shouted the nurse.

Katie was still fretting when the doctor arrived. But this was no ordinary doctor, this was her doctor, the doctor who had been so gentle with her when she had arrived at HMS Raleigh, barely a teenager, so unknowing, so beguiled. Her heart was pounding so loud that he and the white-coated woman with him must be able to hear it. It was her Medical Officer and he smelt so fresh and clean and manly. But there was a gold band lurking on his finger and so her heart slumped. 'Sod it!' she muttered.

'I beg your pardon, Katie?' he said. Medical Officer Moore settled her back down on the couch and gently caressed the nape of her nose to the top of her forehead with his thumb. And she let him. Her arms settled between her legs and she rested contentedly. 'So Katie, when did you last eat?'

'Ooh, it was about two hours ago, Mom' she replied drowsily.

'Please don't call me Mom' the Doctor replied, 'I don't think that's appropriate, do you?'

'I thought everyone called you Mom?' she said irritatedly. So, he was going to be all professional on her now and not caring and tender, like he had been before.

'Yes, but only because you started it.'

'Oh yes! I'm sorry about that, but it fitted so well though, didn't it? I thought it was...just right!' As a nickname it seemed perfectly in line with his fussy approach to his patients, particularly her, but not any more.

'So, what did you have?'

'What did I what?'

'What did you eat?'

'Ooh, I had an egg roll with tomatoes. It was well lush.'

'Anything else?'

'I had some toast with S and G on it.'

'S and G?' Mom asked.

'Yes, slide and glitter, it was nice.'

'Did you have any tea?'

'Yes, I had a NATO plus, it was sweeeeeet.'

He withdrew the needle and now it was full of vibrant red liquid, her vibrant, pulsing blood. And his soft cool fingers had caressed her skin.

'That wasn't so bad, was it?' said Mom.

'What wasn't so bad?' She sat up hurriedly. 'You've taken my blood you sneaky bugger! That was amazing, I hardly felt anything!' She stroked her arm where she presumed the needle had gone in. There was no blood oozing out. 'That was very neatly done, Mom!' And then a dressing was applied by the white-coated woman over the red mark. His hair had receded since they had last met, leaving a sandy tuft on his forehead and he had the look of a married man. Still...

'Plenty of years of practice Katie, now...'

'Wait a minute, did you hypnotise me? You know that's not allowed!'

'That would not have been ethical, Katie Talog.'

'I know! You could have had your wicked way with me and I wouldn't have known anything about it!'

'I did no such thing, Katie Talog, I have to abide...'

'Oh, you mean the oath...I've had to do one of those, but I never had to swear on a hippo...'

'Never mind all that, Katie, I just need you...'

'Oh Doc, you need me?'

'What I meant to say...' he snapped back.

'Listen, you doctors think you're so clever, but you're not really, are you?' she retaliated.

'That's enough Katie, now just strip off to your underwear and put on a gown. I'm giving you a full physical then we can have a chat.'

This was all very sudden. 'Ooh, a full physical' she rejoined, 'but shouldn't we go somewhere...private then?' She nodded at the stern, white-coated woman with him. Her hair was swept back tightly in a brown bun and her tight, round, metal-rimmed spectacles made her look like...a mole.

His hand went to his forehead and he swept back an imaginary shock of hair back over his crown. 'No, Katie, a full physical examination, to check your general condition and physique.'

'Ooh, you doctors and your silvery tongues!'

'Never mind that, just strip off down to your under...'

'I'm not stripping off' she said in as matter of fact way as she could muster. 'I don't see why I should, unless...'

He signed deeply. 'I need you to strip off. I need to make a thorough examination. I can't do that unless you're undressed.'

'That's as maybe, but you didn't say please, did you?'

'Please...will...you...strip...off!'

'Not...if you're going... to talk to me...like that!'

'Please, Katie!'

'All right Doc, but it's just a glimper's charter, isn't it? You just want to see me in my bra and knickers, don't you?'

'No, I do not. I have no interest in seeing your underwear.'

'Oh' she murmured as she studied his face very carefully, 'that's a shame, isn't it?' A thought occurred. 'But you don't know what I'm wearing though, do you Doc? I could be wearing something really saucy, like a G-string?'

'You, wearing a G-string?' He sought for the right words, 'If I find you are wearing a G-string, Katie, I will eat it.' He turned to leave the cubicle.

'All right, give me five. Do you want ketchup with that?' she enquired.

He paused as if to reply but instead he strode out with barely a semblance of dignity and a full red flush on his cheeks. The stern, white-coated woman paused and then followed him. Was she in his charge? Was she a trainee? She had an unfamiliar, yet at the same time, familiar style of lettering on her breast pocket - it read S.I.K.S.

She called out to him from the cubicle. 'I think you need to work on your chat up technique, Doc, I can't see any girl falling for your patter, unless she's a one eyed gronk just out of prison!' And instantly, she regretted what she had said, because it was mean.

Katie undressed quickly and spread her clothes all around the cubicle, as if she had undressed, all of a dither. That would set the scene nicely she thought. She heard footsteps returning and she laid herself demurely on the bed, with her gown wrapped tightly round her waist and her legs exposed artfully. He was back, but he had company, the white mole-woman. 'Hallo, Doc, my name's Katie, you've got me at a bit of a disadvantage, haven't you? And who have you got in tow, there?

'What game is this you're playing, Katie?'

'I thought we'd play doctors and patients. I'll be the patient. So, my name's Katie, what's yours?' Katie turned her head to the nurse, 'That was your signal to ship out, Missy' she hissed.

'I'm not playing this game, Katie' demurred Medical Officer Moore.

'Well, I think you should, if you want to have your way with me...'

'What are you saying?'

'I'm saying that your colleague should push off, because we don't need her anymore...' The white-coated woman looked hesitantly at the doctor, straightened her glasses and turned to leave.

'She will do no such thing. Stay where you are doctor' he said. He now leaned over Katie so he was very close and could examine her scalp.

She took a deep breath of his scent. Her heart bolted and then settled back. Katie whispered confidingly in his ear: 'Doc, I put on my best knickers for you!'

'Never mind that! Sit up please.'

'Nope. I can see what you're up to much better like this.'

'I see, You're going to be awkward. This will go a lot easier if you do as I say.'

'If this is you chatting me up, it's not working. Are you still there, Missy?"

'Sit up now, please, now!'

'Well, that's not very nice!' Katie sat up. 'If you want to chat me up, and I think you do, just be nice to me, be polite to me and let's have some privacy. So, Doc, what's your name?' She should know this but she couldn't recall. His first initial was 'M', so could that be Michael? Yes, Michael, that was it.

'My name is irrelevant, Katie.'

'No, it isn't. It's Michael isn't it? Well, Michael, it's very nice to meet you.' She offered a handshake which he declined. 'I hear you're a doctor, so you must be very good with your hands then?'

'I'm not a surgeon, Katie...'

'I should bloody well hope not, look at your hands, they're bloody shaking!'

'Will...you...just...do...as...I...ask...you!'

'All right, all right, no need to shout, just be nice to me, talk me through what you would like to do to me, and you never know, you might get lucky!'

The white-coated mole-woman turned away, her hand over her mouth, her eyes clenched in what looked like agony.

'So, my name's Katie, I think you want to look me over, and that's fine by me, but how about you tell me just exactly what you plan to do with me?'

'God, give me strength!' he muttered through clenched teeth, looking to the ceiling.

'Listen Michael, a little bit of feedback, this is starting to sound like the worst bedside manner ever. So, let's get this back on track, what is it that you really do, Michael?'

'I'm the poor bloody bastard of a medical officer that has to look after you!'

'Michael, really! That's no way to talk to a patient... and a special patient at that!'

'Katie, can we get on with this please?'

'What, no foreplay? Are you trying to hustle me?'

The mole-woman's body was bent over now. She looked like she was having some kind of fit.

'Please, let me get on. Please! Please!'

Katie sat up. 'All right Michael, just treat me gently, that's all.'

'The other way round, please' he hissed.

'The other way round? Ooh Michael, you want to try me in different positions? That's very naughty of you!'

'I will count to three...' There was now silence in each and every cubicle as ears were strained in the direction of Cubicle 7. 'One, two...'

'All right, all right, you can have me Michael, any which way you want me!'

'For crying out loud!'

She smiled sweetly and manoeuvred the end of the stethoscope so it covered her heart. 'Ooh, ooh, that's cold, Michael, let me blow on it!'

'Will you stop messing around!'

'Well, warm it up before you touch me with it!'

There was a very deep sigh. The stethoscope was pressed to her back.

'Ooh, that's better. Just a little bit more there. Ooh, that's really hitting the spot. More, more, more, more, more!'

'Will you behave!' he hissed.

'Well, don't stop now!' she hissed back.

Security had arrived. A be-hatted official poked their head between the curtains of the cubicle. 'Is there a problem?'

Mom stepped outside and there was an urgent conversation carried out in hushed tones.

'It's Katie Talog, she's acting the goat' muttered Medical Officer Moore.

'Everyone can hear you, even in reception' reproached the security official, 'and opinion is, this sounds like a knocking shop!'

'Perhaps you can have a quiet word. I still need to complete my examination. She's making this very difficult.'

She heard the man from security parting the curtain as she slid underneath the sheet. The man from security stepped inside the cubicle. He pulled the sheet down so he could see her face. She looked out coyly and pulled the sheet back to leave just her eyes and nose showing.

'I'm sorry. Did I interrupt your tea break?'

'What's going on?'

'He's been touching me up with his telescope.'

'I believe it's called a stethoscope and he needs to do that so he can complete his examination.'

'Fair point.'

'No more.'

'Got it.'

Mom returned, looking very sheepish. The woman displayed a tray of dressings and other medical paraphernalia. Nothing sharp, Katie noted, which was comforting.

'All right sir?' asked the man from security.

'He's fine. We're fine. You can tootle off now' answered Katie. She got up and shrouded her body with the sheet. Mom sat down in the bedside chair. 'I'm sorry about getting you into trouble, Michael.'

'It's Medical Officer Moore.'

'Yes, Mom' she sighed, 'I'll do anything you want so where do we start?'

'Remove the sheet and gown and cross the cubicle for me please.'

She indicated the mole-woman with a cursory nod and then shook her head vigorously. He just stared resolutely back at her. Katie sensed he was about to shout. Reluctantly, she removed the sheet and gown and poised to attention, with the corner of the cubicle fixed firmly in her mind. 'This is for your eyes only Michael. Missy, turn away now.' The white-coated woman looked away into the corner of the cubicle and then Katie took a deep breath and turned a cartwheel so she was standing to attention in the far corner. Another deep breath, a reverse of the cartwheel, a sharp intake of breath by Mom and she was back where she started, alongside him. She cradled his waist with her arms and waited for the verdict.

'I wasn't expecting that' he muttered as his pen inscribed some incoherent patterns on the chart, 'not at all.' He turned to the woman whose face glowed red. 'Katie is one of our special patients' he said to the woman. She wobbled her head in agreement. She too had gone the colour of a boiled beetroot. 'We go through this nonsense every time, don't we Katie?'

'Yes, but it's only for you, Mom. I'm not really a patient anyway' she noted to the woman, 'I'm one of Michael's special cases, aren't I?'

'Yes, of course you are. Now, what shall we do with you?'

'Just mark me 'A1' and let's get on with it.'

'I agree, let us get on. Doctor?'

Doctor? Really? The white-coated mole-woman who had no clue? 'Oh, Michael, are you suggesting a threesome? I'm not sure I'm ready for that. I don't think Missy's ready for that either.'

The woman left the cubicle, her body convulsing in some kind of coughing fit. 'I was looking for a compromise' said Mom.

'A compromise? Can I have a bath now, please?'

'We'll talk about it when we're finished.'

'A bath? Really? Together? Oh, Michael!'

A low fizzing hiss came from his lips. 'I'd love to be able to offer you a bath, but...' His voice suggested that there would be no more messing around, which was a pity.

'I suppose you want me to do stationary cycling now? Well, I don't want to. It's futile. I never get anywhere. It's pointless.'

'We do need to measure your recovery rate. You can have a shower after cycling.'

'I think I will have earned a bath. I don't care if it's the Commodore's bath either, providing he's not in it. What you have to realise is that I've just spent an hour getting a grilling from my new CO and before that, I had to endure the Royal ripping the piss out of me for, ooh, let's see, lots of hours...'

'I'd love to be able to offer you a bath, but all I've got is a shower.'

'All right then, how long do I have to cycle to get a shower?'

'Ten minutes, and then you can have a shower.'

'How about three minutes?'

'No, it has to be at least ten minutes.'

'All right Doc, let's do the treadmill, but I want a bath afterwards.'

'Can you do me twenty minutes on the treadmill then?'

'Walking, yes, I think I can.'

'Not walking, running.'

'How about...skipping?'

'Not skipping, just running.'

'Oh Michael' she sighed, 'you just want to see me all hot and sweaty!'

'Actually Katie, yes I do.'

This seemed a sudden change of tack. 'Oh I see. Well I suppose that's all right, then. How about my bath then?'

'Let me see what I can do.'

'Running, you say?' Katie pulled on a black, long sleeved vest and leggings from her roll bag. 'How do I look?'

'Wonderful, like Wilson the Wonder athlete!'

'Who?'

'From a comic strip?'

'What's a comic strip?'

Katie fell in by the side of Medical Officer Moore as they proceeded up the stairway to the first floor gymnasium.

'You know Katie, we could have something done about those old scars. Techniques have improved out of all recognition over the last few years. I can make an appointment for you to see a specialist.'

'Would they have to be grafted over, then? Where would the grafts come from? Somewhere else on me, like my arse?'

'That's right.'

'Let me think on it, but they're not scars, they were put on me deliberately - I'm branded, remember?'

'If I knew who'd done that to you, I would...'

'You'd do nothing, because you're a decent man and you have to abide by your promise, but there are others who think they're above all else, don't they?'

'I still can't believe how anyone could do that to you...what happened to them?'

'Nothing quite yet...'

He looked puzzled but she quelled that with a wink.

'Still...'

'Moving on quickly...'

'Ah, well, those wounds on your head and your hands have healed incredibly quickly. It's actually miraculous!'

'They did a good job on me in the butcher's shop, didn't they?' said Katie. She looked away over his shoulder. There was a lot of grunting and gasping by the super fit, amongst the muscle building machines. The get-out-of-breath machines were silent.

Katie mounted the closest get-out-of-breath machine while Mom watched. The fabric of the running belt on the soles of her feet felt cold and strange. She gripped the handles and powered up the machine to a slow jog. As she started running, in unison with the machine, her head at first moved gently side to side and then she was running more steadily, her head steadied. And then she reached the moving plateau of performance; her breathing was fully in rhythm with two quick and one long breath; the balls of her feet barely touched the rubber; her toes pushed away easily and automatically; her mind disengaged from her surroundings. There was just a sequence of soft patterns of light and colour in the periphery of her vision; her head was now still; her eyes closed. She was a perpetual motion being; she could run for ever and ever. Seconds merged into minutes, nothing else mattered, nothing else mattered...

And now she was kicking her way through the heaths and the ling, following the sheep track that wandered across the pink and purple hill, her body and breathing in complete harmony, just the pipits and the larks flitting and flighting away, marking her path, bursting into song, and the tawny silver-crowned fork-tail, to her side, tail twisting and wing caressing the breeze and her sheepdog, running ahead. And then the fork-tail screeched and the sheepdog broke into a barrage of alarm barks - there was a dark figure ahead of her, face hidden by the cowl, throwing threats and curses...

Katie's eyes sparked open but the treadmill still clattered on.

She started to skip, first to the left side and then to the right. There was Mom, with his clipboard and pen, remonstrating at her. She fell into a short sequence of star jumps and complemented these with sour expressions of displeasure. A forward tumble prompted an agonised shout from her side. She stumbled back into a running rhythm, but her body was propelled forward; Katie jumped, still grasping the handlebars and teetered vertically for a moment, legs flailing up to the false ceiling and in a moment, realising this position could not be held, she tumbled forward over the handle bars. She took a tumble on the floor, hopped and slammed against the big glass window.

Katie opened her eyes, regained her poise and saw through the mist of her breath on the window - it was a posse of cheering ratings outside and below. She pulled a face and stuck out her tongue but withdrew it quickly from the cold glass.

'Young lady, a word please.' It was Mom and he seemed upset, if his double teapot handle pose was anything to go by. He motioned her away from the window. She rested her hands on her hips and looked at Mom attentively. 'A couple of issues' he said sternly, 'for one, the auto stop sensors seemed to have been tampered with.'

'Oh, yes they do, don't they? I think they must have gotten in the way.'

'And, what I was going on to say is that the automatic belt should have stopped at least a dozen times during that display...'

'It should have stopped, shouldn't it? But it didn't and I think that's because...it's all buggered up.'

'Please can you un-bugger it so that it is safe for others to use?'

Katie mounted the machine again, inserted the key and the waistband tag and waited for it to respond. It didn't. She looked coyly at Mom. 'You may have to switch it off and then back on again. I'm sorry about that.'

Medical Officer Moore unplugged the machine from the wall. She jumped down from the treadmill and tried to read what he had written on her report. He pulled the report to his chest, but not quickly enough.

'What does that say?' she demanded.

He flashed the page in front of her eyes but she couldn't make any sense of it.

'Look it's all right. Just tell me, I won't be cross!'

'Superb gluteus maximus muscles, times two...' he muttered quietly.

'Oh Doc! You've been ogling my arse! You naughty doctor!'

'You are going to get me struck off, young lady' he said as he scribbled furiously to mask what he had written, 'and no, I was not ogling your arse, as you put it, I was checking your general physique to see if there were any muscles not functioning correctly.' He pretended to make some notes on the form. 'You are a magnificent specimen, though' he said under his breath. He dropped the clipboard to his side.

'I bet you say that to all the girls' said Katie, as his face became the colour of boiled beetroot again.

He brought himself up to attention, gazed at a spot above her right shoulder and at last announced: 'I think that was the most extraordinary display I have ever seen on a treadmill!'

'Really, do you think so, Doc? It can be a bit 'run of the mill' though, can't it?'

'Not when you're using it!'

'Anyway Doc, if the treadmill was a gymnastics event in the Olympic Games, how many points would I have scored?'

'That's a very difficult question. I think for sheer physicality, I would give you a score of nine point eight.'

'Ooh, sheer physicality, nine point eight? That would put me right in amongst the medals, wouldn't it?'

'Yes, but I would have to mark you down for artistic interpretation. I would give just five points for that.'

'Five? Bugger! Is that all? Was it because I stuck my tongue out at you and gave you the finger?'

'Yes, exactly that. I think any judge would have had a problem with that...'

'Oh well, just mark me down as 'A1' and lead me to the bath!'

Katie knocked tentatively on the door and entered when beckoned. She placed her bags in the corner of the room and sat down opposite Medical Officer Seager, who looked up briefly and continued reading the document on the desk. This room smelt clinically clean, bright and sterile. There were no pictures, no furniture other than a desk and two clinically clean plastic chairs. Katie had a feeling in her gut that the state of her mind was about to be operated on.

'Take a seat, Katie' said her interrogator.

'Thank you ma'am' said Katie and she waited patiently for the interrogation to begin.

'So, Katie Talog, how are you?'

'I'm very well thank you, how are you?'

'I see. Well, Katie, it would be good to have a chat about your last tour of duty.'

'Yes, it went very well, thank you.'

'I see.' Seager continued to read a written report in front of her.

'Are we done now? Can I go?'

'No, we haven't started yet.'

'Oh, I'm sorry. Let's start.'

'How did you cope on board?'

'On board HMS Albany, ma'am? Very well ma'am; I had loads of sunshine so I could top up my tan, miles of deep blue sea as far as I could see, lots of tropical islands and dolphins. And that's just while I was on duty, so you can imagine what my down-time was like! It was like South Pacific every watch, grass skirts and cock...'

'Yes, I can imagine' snapped Seager, 'but there was an incident, wasn't there? Now tell me about it!'

'I don't know what you mean, ma'am. It's not the one where Rating Mulch fell overboard, is it?'

'No, it's the one where you suffered wounds to your hands and your head while on duty!'

'Oh, that one. Well, they've all healed up nicely, so I say, let's just forget about it.'

'But young women don't go through that kind of experience every day!'

'I should sodding well hope not!' Katie muttered and then cursed herself.

'I'm sorry?'

'I said, I should sodding well hope not, ma'am!'

'But it happened to you, Katie!'

'Yes, it did, but worse things happen at sea!'

'But you were at sea!'

'Ah, but this was different, ma'am...'

'Different, how so?'

'It just was, that's all. It was on an island, for a start...'

'Different, Katie. What makes you different from everyone else?'

'Eh? Well, I'm my mum's daughter...'

'And how does that make you different?'

Katie took in a deep breath of the heated, breathless air. 'I was brought up in the Marches. I had to be independent. There was no one I could go to if I got into trouble, was there?'

'So your mother abandoned you?'

'No, she didn't.' Katie blinked and tried to work out the route that would cause her the least damage, 'she sub-contracted.' She would have to concede. The route that led to her mum was much too difficult to navigate. 'All right, ma'am, you win. I need counselling.'

'Counselling?'

'Yes, I need someone to have a natter with.'

'I see, so is this really what you think, Katie?'

'Yes, it is, ma'am. I thought I could tough it out, but I can't, can I?'

'I see, I see. So, this incident, how do you think it has impacted you?'

'Not at all, ma'am. Can I just check, are you counselling me now?'

'Don't you want to talk about it?'

'There's nothing to talk about really, thank you ma'am.'

There was a very deep and irritated sigh from across the table.

Katie felt she had to offer something. 'I had a bout of the crimson scourge, ma'am. When I woke up for my watch, I thought I'd been stabbed in my sleep! And you wouldn't believe the mess! And it came out of nowhere! And it took me totally by surprise, it did!'

'I see, Katie, was this your first, um, episode of the, er, crimson scourge?'

'Yes, it was, which is probably why it took me by surprise, didn't it?'

'It's quite natural, Katie and nothing to be worried about. Having a period is a quite normal process for young women. How old are you?'

'I've just turned nineteen, ma'am.'

'So, you're a bit of a late developer, then? How does that make you feel?'

'A bit sticky and a bit achy down below, ma'am.'

'I meant, how does that make you feel when you discussed this with your female colleagues? They should have been able to give you some wise counsel and reassurance?'

Katie snorted. 'You mean in the 'Wrennery'? I don't go in there ma'am!'

Seager made a house with her long, bony fingers: 'And why not Katie?'

Katie puffed her cheeks. 'I don't like it down there. I prefer dick to split, ma'am.'

'I beg your pardon, Katie? Do you not associate with your female colleagues?'

'Of course I do' Katie snorted back, 'but not in the 'Wrennery'!'

'Why?'

'I prefer dick to split, ma'am. I'm sorry, but there it is. It's too chatty in the 'Wrennery' and most of the time they're chatting about me!'

'Chatting?'

'Bitching, I mean.'

'Do you dislike women, Katie?'

'No, I don't dislike them, I have to work with them, but in my downtime, I prefer to spend my time with the dicks, sorry, I mean the lads, doing 'Uckers' and 'Bulldogging', watching the footie and wrestling.'

Oh, crap Katie thought. What I have I done? I've given her a lead, a lead to talk about my relationship with my mum. Stupid, stupid, stupid.

'So, you don't like being with other women, let's explore this a little...'

'Let's not, ma'am...'

'So, how is your mother?'

'She's fine. How's yours?'

'She's running a mobile library across Dartmoor. She's just planted an Alpine bed in her garden and it's coming on a treat.'

'Oh, how lovely...'

'And, your mother?'

Katie shrugged. 'She's still alive, as far as I know...'

'Have you stayed in contact with her?'

Oh, no, not this again, the well-meaning who know nothing, offering advice about how to handle someone else's problem. My mum! Katie had to stand up. 'You stopped her letters! You stopped her sending me parcels of food! That was you, that was! But I didn't know what to do with it! There were cookies and cakes. I ate them! There was some stuff like dried leaves which I made tea with. I didn't know it wasn't good for me!'

Seager just sat there looking impassively, so Katie sat back down again. Her brain was now reeling and her stomach started to flip over.

'So, how does that make you feel about your mother?'

'She means well, but she really doesn't get it. I'm doing something worthwhile, something good, I can't fix the whole world, can I?'

'So, do you think she understands that you're moving on?'

'Yes, she understands, but no, she doesn't accept it. That's it, that's all there is.'

'You seem very angry about her.'

'I'm not angry, I just realise that she's, she's different from me. I'm not going to be like her when I'm grown up...'

'When you're grown up? But you're already a young woman, Katie!'

'I know that and she's just going to have to get used to it!'

'I see. Tell me about your mother. She seems to be quite a unique individual.'

'No!'

'No, what?'

'No, ma'am.'

'When was the last time you spoke to her?'

'Let me think, it would be over a year ago...'

'That seems a long time to be not speaking to your mother.'

'She hasn't got a telephone and we don't have anything to say to each other. There you go. That's it, there's nothing else to say, ma'am.'

'I see, so you don't know how she is.'

Katie glared back. 'She's fine, I'm fine, we're all fine ma'am!'

'Katie, Katie, you're going to have to deal with this!'

'Deal with what?'

'Your relationship with your mother!'

'Bollocks! We're fine, we're both fine, there's nothing to deal with!'

'Why are you getting angry?'

'I'm not getting angry! I said let's not talk about my mum, now you're talking about my mum and you won't stop!'

'All right, please calm down. Let's try another angle.'

'No! I haven't got time to calm down. I've got lots to sort out!'

'Have you Katie?'

'Yes, I have!'

'And how do you manage all that?'

'The lots to sort out?' Katie took a deep breath: 'I write it all down in my diary and plot it in my planner, ma'am.'

'Please can I see.'

'No, you can't. It's private!'

'Katie, please let me see.'

Katie drew out her ring bound diary, swelling with tacked in sheets. 'All my life is in here, all of it. I cannot afford to lose this.'

'And this works for you?'

'It does.' Katie riffled through the pages and the coloured writing and pictograms flitted past her eyes. She skipped over the picture of a triple spiral, adorned with a sequence of doodles, one of which was a brain, coloured blue. 'It really does work for me. My brother Paol got it for me. He says, I have to accept that I'm scatter-brained' she continued, 'but I can help myself.'

'And what does it say for the 29th of April?'

'April 29th? Let me see, ma'am.' Katie quickly flicked through the pages, found the April 29th, gasped and slapped her diary closed. 'Oh, fucketty, fucketty, fuck!'

'Remember who you're talking to Talog!'

'I'm sorry, ma'am, but you shouldn't have!'

'Nicola Spry tipped me off. Please Katie, what does it say?'

Katie slowly and tentatively opened the diary to that page. She turned it so Seager could see. The diary fidgeted in time with her fidgeting hands.

'Wurst day? So that's fine, is it Katie? Oh by the way, worst is spelt with an 'o' not a 'u', Katie.'

'I was looking forward to sausages for breakfast' muttered Katie, 'then eggs, it was supposed to be my special day.' She turned it round so she could read the red-pencilled words written large in capital letters across a page that had been struck out in red. 'But I've dealt with it. A simple mistake, that's all it was and I promise you, it will not happen again. Me and the Royal, we've had a little chat and it's done, it's dealt with, it will not happen again!'

'And what about you?'

'I'm fine ma'am.' Katie gripped the page and prepared to tear it out.

'Don't you dare, Katie Talog!'

She paused as she stared at Roberta Seager. 'It's done, it's finished with!'

'It happened, it happened to you. It's changed you for the rest of your life. That page stays there, so you don't forget that you need to deal with it.'

'I've already said, I've dealt with it.' Katie tore out the page angrily, crumpled it into a ball and tossed it over Roberta Seager's head. It rattled provocatively in the corner of the room, like the rain that had rattled on the corrugated roofs of the shanty houses, the day she nearly lost Benoit, the day it started to rain and would not stop. Ever.

Katie watched Seager lick her lips, as if she was unable to decide what to do next. 'Can we have a break, ma'am? I need a drink.'

'I see, what can I get you?'

'Nato plus please.'

'I don't think that's one of the available selections...'

'Tea, with everything in it, plus one sugar to make it...three sugars, ma'am.'

'All right Katie, it's just down the corridor. I'll get a water. Just wait here and take a few deep breaths.'

Seager left the room, closing the door carefully and there was the sound of footfalls along the corridor. If Seager continued with this line of questioning, would this end with her being drummed out of the Andrew, unfit to serve?

Seager returned with a glass of water and a mug of tea. Katie took a sip. At least her interrogator had got the tea about right.

'Would you like a longer break, Katie?'

'No thank you, ma'am. Let's get on with this.'

'So, what's your recollection of what happened in the Comoros Islands?'

Katie decided that once again, she would have to offer something. 'It's odd. I can remember some things in tiny detail. Everything else is a blur and I could hear this voice...'

'And how do you think it's affected you?'

Seager hadn't picked up on the voice comment. 'Not at all, ma'am.'

'Well, it's going to hit you in the next days. No one around will know or care about what happened. You will be on your own out there in Civvy Street. You will need to talk to someone. That could be me or someone directly involved. Who do you think would be best?'

'I think it would be... Scott Hodgson. I can see if I can get in touch with him. He was there or thereabouts.' Actually, he might as well have been on the other side of the planet, as he was piloting the helicopter and she was in eye-to-eye combat with two of the locals on a barren and burnt out island.

'Have you cried?'

'About what?' Seager wasn't going to let go, like a weasel with its teeth in the neck of a rabbit, shaking and shaking. 'No, I haven't.' Was that true? She had felt like crying every morning and every night, but no tears had come.

'It's okay to have a cry.'

'No, it's not. It means you're weak and you can't handle it.'

'You will feel the need to cry - don't fight it.'

She blinked away the tears as she searched for something to wipe them away. Her sleeve would have to suffice.

'Is there anything else we need to be looking at?'

'I don't know, ma'am.' She wondered if should say something about the voices. 'You know I said that I heard a voice? Well, I did, inside my head...'

'What sort of voice?'

'Well, it was a low whisper. I think it was the voice of...a little demon!'

'Why would you think that, Katie?'

'A big one wouldn't fit inside my head, would it, ma'am?'

'I meant, why a demon's voice?'

'Because it happened when I was a little bit stressed. And it started having a conversation with me, about what to do.'

'When was this?'

'Once only, during the fight, once only...'

'And what did this voice say?'

'It said spare him, it said spare him...' Katie could see the brown skinned boy, wedged between her thighs, wriggling frantically, like a snared fish, mouth and eyes stretched wide open in panic, his throat panting and his head shaking to and fro. And the handle of the knife, his knife, was now in her hands, held high above them both, poised, ready for the thrust, deep into his right eye socket, plunging, tearing, ripping...

'Katie! Just calm down please, take some deep breaths and breath in and out, in and out, nice and easily.'

The woman in front of Katie was so different, so pale, so calm and in control. The vision of the boy in red evaporated.

'Let's try something different. Let's carry out a little mind exercise. It will give me an idea what state of mind you're in. It's called 'Word Association...'

'Football' Katie replied.

'Ah, you started before me. Right, then. Players.'

'Fags.' Ha! That would throw her!

'Hags.'

A vision sprang into her mind of an old, gnarled woman. 'Mum.'

'Nurture' was the response.

'Torture.' (Why had she said that?)

'Pain.'

'Mum.'

'Grow.'

'Tall.'

'Short.'

'Dwarf.' Katie's body shuddered.

'Handicap' was Seager's precise reply.

'Mum.' (Why had she said that again?)

'Bosom.'

'Tit.'

'Milk.'

'Sour, sour, sour!'

Katie's head slumped to meet her crossed forearms on the table. She pushed hard against her eyes to stem the flow of sniffles and tears. There was a hand caressing her crown through her thick thatch of hair.

'Sorry, Katie'

'Regret.'

'I see. Reflect.'

'Hate.'

'I think that's enough, Katie.'

And suddenly, the lights blinked and the shutters came down...

Katie Talog brushed down her navy blue jacket and trousers. They were as immaculate as she could get them. Her navy cap was placed at the precise angle that Winnie had drawn across her forehead. If the cap did not ride up, her drill instructor would not see the line that was drawn there in eye liner.

'Wish me luck!' Katie called out as she skipped out of the hut and turned for the HMS Raleigh parade ground. There were sympathetic murmurs of good wishes behind her. She quickly realised that she should now be marching and started a rhythmic swing of her arms and her legs. She looked down to check that the 'L' and the 'R' written in pen on top of her wrists were only just visible. Around the corner of the breeze-block built building, there was her drill sergeant stood statue-still, waiting for her. Serried ranks of white painted seats overlooked the parade ground, ready for friends and family - but not her's!

Katie marched up to him and threw up a salute. Try criticising that, you petty minded scrote!

'Talog, do you know why you're her!' he screamed at her.

She blinked away the spit that had impacted on her face. 'Yes, Sarge!'

'And?'

'That's all Sarge!'

A quiet descended on the large empty space that surrounded them both. It was a cold early April day and she noticed tiny flecks of snow meandering aimlessly towards the hard, forbidding ground.

'Today is the day that you pass out from HMS Raleigh, Talog!'

'Yes, I know Sarge!'

'It will be a perfect day. The Princess Royal will be here and your family and friends to recognise the achievements of you and your colleagues.'

'Yes, Sarge!'

'Did I say you and your colleagues? I'm sorry, that's not what I meant to say - I meant just your colleagues!'

'Sorry, Sarge.'

'That doesn't matter! You will be perfect today Talog. When you march and take the salute you will make me and your colleagues and your family proud. Do you hear me?' he screeched.

'Yes, Sarge! Just one thing.'

'What's that, Talog?'

'My family aren't coming so I can only embarrass everyone else. Sarge!'

'Your mother?'

'No, Sarge. She's a pacifist.'

'Your father?'

'No, Sarge. No one's sure who he is.'

'There must be some family coming?'

'No Sarge, they're all bastards.'

'I see. Friends?'

'Well, my half-brother Paol, is coming down, Sarge. He's taking me out for big eats.'

'I see. Do you want to embarrass him?'

'He's not arriving until after, Sarge!'

'Do you want to embarrass yourself?'

'No Sarge!'

'Do you want to embarrass your colleagues?'

'No Sarge!'

'Good. I will now put you through your paces. I will make sure you can tell your left from your right and that you can put one foot in front of the other. Am I making myself clear?'

'Crystal, Sarge!'

He presented his weapon. 'Do you know what this is Talog?'

'Yes, Sarge. It's a... shooter!'

'A shooter!?!'

'Yes, it's the shooter I'll be carting around the parade ground, Sarge!'

'This is an SA80 assault rifle, Talog!'

'Yes, Sarge, with a stabber at the end!'

'A stabber? A stabber? It's a bayonet!'

'Got it, bay'net Sarge.'

She would have to concentrate as fiercely as she could, try and anticipate each evolution he wanted before he screamed it out, and whatever happened she must end up standing to attention in front of him.

And then he started barking her instructions and she followed: 'About...turn. Left turn, left turn, right turn, right turn. Notice anything Talog?'

'I'm right back where I started from, Sarge!'

'Very good! That means you got it right! Left turn, quick march. Quick march. I said quick! I want to hear the squeaking of your minge!'

'What, Sarge?' she asked in alarm. She thought first about her armpits and then where her legs came together. Surely he couldn't mean below her fuzzy pudding? 'Oi, that's rude Sarge!'

'I'm sorry, is that a little tear I can see?' He was right in front of her again, peering with that peculiar squint of his, right at the bridge of her nose.

Her nose wrinkled in response. 'No Sarge, I don't do crying, Sarge!'

'I see Talog, atten-shun!'

And she was off again.

'Get to it Talog! Right wheel!'

Katie stuttered as she looked down to her wrist to check what was right and then wheeled to the right.

'You horrible, crab crawling tart!' he screamed.

'Sorry Sarge.'

'Left wheel quick march, eyes right. Salute. Right wheel. Halt. Eyes right. Eyes front. Stand to attention. Talog, I want to hear your lips smack when you do that!'

'Oi, that is rude, Sarge!'

'Stand easy. Eyes front. Curtsey. Stand to attention. Stand easy.'

She looked in as steely a way as she could muster, straight to her front. He walked around her and scrutinised every part of her uniform, tugging at the back of her trousers and pulling down the back of her jacket. He walked around her again, accompanied by a steady tutting. She pulled a face, stuck out her tongue and then returned them back to their proper state when he re-appeared back in front of her.

'Fine physique, fine turn-out, Talog.' He paused while this sank in. 'You will pass muster!'

'I bet you say that to all the girls, Sarge!'

'Yes, Talog, even my good lady has to work hard to earn that one.' He was deep in thought as he paced up and down in front of her. 'I'm sorry your family won't see you pass out. That's a great shame. When you arrived here at HMS Raleigh, you were nothing but a backward, backwoods trollop. Now I can see that you will make a fine rating, Talog. You are now a Daughter of Albion, so we, we in the Andrew, are now your family. We look after our own in the Andrew. You will make us all proud!'

'Thank you Sarge, can I go for breakfast now Sarge?' The aroma of bacon had entered her nostrils and they twitched in response - a drip of saliva formed in the corner of her mouth and started to migrate down her chin.

'I don't think that's a good idea Talog.'

'But I'm hungry, Sarge!' Turning her head slightly did not arrest its progress. She got ready to lick it up.

The drill sergeant tutted, got out a handkerchief and wiped the drip from her chin. 'All right, but remove your jacket first and wear a serviette down your front. No brown sauce or baked beans. About turn. Quick march, quick march. Right wheel!'

She wheeled to the left, winked at him and scampered away behind the NAAFI block. As she snatched a look behind her, she saw him take his cap off and throw it to the ground in mock rage. Thankfully, he was grinning.

'Katie! Katie Talog!'

She lifted her head from her arms, the arms that had made a pillow while she dreamed. There was a woman at the other side of the desk, in naval uniform, tight, concerned and inquisitive: Medical Officer Seager.

'Ah, you're back. Nice dream?'

'Ma'am? I don't think so, it was all about marching drill.'

Seager was not on her own. She was now sat on the other side of the desk with a bevy of seated brass: Sympathetic Medical Officer Moore, smiling Uncle Alec and another woman. Oh crap, she thought, it was the committee of the concerned.

Medical Officer Summers closed the book and placed it on her lap. Katie craned her neck to read the title. Although the title was capitalised, she struggled to work out what it meant.

'Let me help you, Katie, it's titled 'Beta Testing of Biological Systems'!'

'Oh. Is that a bestseller, ma'am?'

'Not yet, but it gives valuable insight into how we interface our people with electronic systems.'

'I see ma'am, like when I pre-order lunch from the galley?'

'Not quite, but interesting you should mention lunch Katie...'

'Oh, I've had mine, thank you ma'am.'

'Yes, I know. I think it's fair to say that you've been put through the mill, Katie, and you need rest, lot's of it.' There were supporting nods from those alongside her.

'I agree, ma'am. Can I go now?' Katie replied.

'No. Let's have a chat about how things are going. How is your diet working out?'

'What do you mean?'

'I mean, what have you been eating, while you've been away on duty?'

'In the ship? Well, all sorts of good stuff.'

'Good. Let me see your eating record, then.'

'My what?'

'Where you record what you put into your body on a day to day basis.'

'Oh, that.' Katie delved into the side pocket of her rucksack and pulled out a dog-eared record book. It was dog-eared but up to date. Now there would be big trouble. She handed it over, reluctantly. 'I don't understand why I have to do this - no one else does, do they?' said Katie, plaintively.

'You are an important biological system and we need to ensure that your performance is not impacted by your patterns of feeding.'

'My mealtimes, you mean? Well, they're fixed, aren't they and I can have whatever the galley has on offer, can't I?'

'No, you have a meal time plan. It's to ensure that you have a balanced and consistent diet to meet your specific needs. Now let's see how you've been doing...'

There was an uncomfortable period of silence, just broken by the swishing of pages being perused. Occasionally, Summers would show a page to her colleagues alongside her, accompanied by murmurs and nodding. As the periods of silence became longer and longer, Katie decided an interjection was needed.

'I've not been feeling well recently.'

'Oh, really? What's been the matter, Katie?'

'It's difficult to say, but I've felt a bit under the weather and I've changed what I eat to compensate for that. There, that's what's happened.'

'Really? What is 'BFG' Ann?' asked Seager, 'I don't recognise this as a dietary term?'

'It's a special that the galley does for me' intervened Katie, 'and it's a vegetarian dish with fruit, beans and other good things in it.'

'Beans and fruit, what kind of dish is that?' asked Seager.

'It's baked, ma'am.'

'Baked?' asked Seager.

'Yes, ma'am, in an oven.'

'What type of fruit?' asked Seager.

'It has a lot of cherries in it, doesn't it?'

'I see. And these cherries, in what form are they?' asked Summers.

'What do you mean, ma'am?' asked Katie, suddenly concerned.

'Are they raw, unadulterated fruit?' asked Summers.

'Well, no, they've been soaked in something to make them nicer to eat.'

'And the beans Katie?' asked Wicks.

'I don't know what they do with them. I think they might roast them or something. Then they grind them up and add milk and sugar.' Uncle Alec chose to snigger at this moment.

Summers gave a deep sigh: 'Is it fair to say that a key part of your diet over the last few months has actually been Black Forest Gateau.'

'Where a gateau is a cake? Yes, I'm afraid so.'

'You are unbelievable.'

'Oh, thank you ma'am. It's not that difficult. I have an arrangement with the galley.'

'And this after the cookie crisis!'

'Well, as you know, I had to kick my mum's cookies into touch.'

'Yes, and you do understand why that had to happen?' interjected Uncle Alec.

'Is it because they had more calories than a slice of fat knacker pie, sir?'

'No, they may well have done, but there was another reason - the narcotic content. So, what are we going to do with you?'

'I think you should cut me some slack. I'm on leave now for a few months and then I'm shore based.'

'We agree' said Seager.

'You what, ma'am? What happens now?'

'You are a key biological system and like any other system, you occasionally need repair and maintenance!' said Uncle Alec.

She turned to face Uncle Alec. 'I've got no idea what that means, sir?'

Summers announced: 'You need rest and some time away from operations. We think we should relax your dietary controls while you are shore based and then we'll look again when you have another ship-side posting. So, how will you keep fit?'

'I...may do some running' Katie replied.

'Good, anything else?'

Katie wondered if the horizontal tango was considered suitable cardio-vascular exercise. She decided that she would keep that thought to herself. 'I have a hockey tour in June, an athletics event in July and maybe I'll play a little cricket for the village.'

'I see, very good. Athletics Katie?' asked Summers.

'Yes, I do the javelin and the long jump.'

'I see, and a hockey tour?'

'Yes, the RN girls are touring Holland.'

'What position, Katie?'

'It's just across the North Sea, ma'am.'

'I meant, what position do you play in the team?'

'Oh I see, centre midfield ma'am.'

'Good, good, that should keep you fit!'

'Yes, it will ma'am.'

'And will you find time to see your family?' asked Seager.

'Yes, I probably will, ma'am' replied Katie.

'Good. I hear your mother's a bit of a character though?'

Uncle Alec nodded vigorously at this.

'Yes, you could say that ma'am.'

'So, did she serve in the Royal Navy?'

Alec shook his head.

'Oh, no, she's a hardened pacifist' stated Katie.

'So, what did she do' Seager wanted to know, 'did she work as a civil servant?'

'She's never worked in all her life!'

'Professional mother then?' asked Seager.

'Well, no, she was a bit intermittent as a mum. Are we done?'

'Katie, we need to agree what support you will need over the next few months' said Seager.

'I'm fine, ma'am, I just need to rack-out...'

'Will you be able to cope with HMS Hawkins? How do we keep tabs on you?'

'I could call in once a week, as I did before, but don't I need to run this past Nicola Spry?'

'No need for that. This is just your team providing support.'

'So why? What's special about me?'

'Nothing. Nothing's the matter with you. You're just, different, that's all and you've had a life changing experience' stated Seager.

'Different, how?'

'Just...different. Different experiences, that's all.'

'I see. Well, I think you think you're trying to help me but you're really not. I've moved on. There's no need for you to check up on me, is there? If I have a problem, I will report it to Spry. That's how it will be. I'm leaving now. Tell me if I'm wrong?'

She picked up her bags and looked back to see if she was challenged. She wasn't. Katie smiled to herself as she pushed her way out of the office, followed the long, clinically white corridor until she blinked her way back into the daylight.

There was a Royal Marine sergeant waiting for her. He took her roll bag and slung it in the back of a royal blue pick-up truck. Then he offered her a photograph attached to a clipboard. It was an image of someone, very like her, wearing regulation tropical shorts on the flight deck of a Type 23 frigate, and in the background was a Lynx helicopter and the deep blue ocean beyond that. Without thinking, she scrawled a triple spiral on it with her initials in the centre. And now she was in the passenger seat, resting her head against his shoulder, and that's when the curtain descended and the lights went down.

Chapter Twenty-Seven

Thursday 12 May 1800 - Landulph

The gangway rocked gently to and fro as she turned to look back at Great-Aunt Katerin, wrapped tight in a brown shawl, her brown weather-beaten face surrounded with a cascade of tangled long white hair and all crowned with a navy blue cap. Glinting in the sunshine were her watery eyes and the cap badge, that bore the legend 'Ultra Mare'.

'I'll be back' called out Katie.

'No, you won't' replied Katerin, and she started coughing again - the kind of cough that wracked her whole body as if in the next moment, it would turn inside out, 'but send my heart-felt felicitations to my sister and to my nephew...' She stooped over the transom as if she was going to empty her lungs into the mud below the Fairmile motor gun boat. This had been Katie's home when she had started her training at HMS Raleigh. Planks were starting to show through the thick layer of tarry paint on the hull. The conversion of the Fairmile launch to a house boat for her great-aunt had been a successful use of an unwanted Sea Cadet vessel but it seemed so out of place, mired in the mud of this creek, whose only ambition seemed to be a gradual ooze of its way down to the River Tamar, '...and don't make promises...' and she coughed again, 'that you don't intend to keep!'

Another coughing fit was the cue for Katie to leave. She gave a little wave but Katerin dismissed it with a flutter of her arm and now she was turning away. This would be the last time she would see her great aunt. 'Get down below, you old hag!'

'Ingénue!' she hacked back. And with that, Katerin was making her stuttering way to the bow of the boat, below the two pounder quick firing gun, where, as was her custom, she would roll a post-meal cigarette and then gaze for hours over the marsh in a pickling haze of smoke, shivering inside her shawl. The remains of the three-tin one-pot supper would fester in the copper pan overnight. Katie wondered if she should have cleared up but she had just endured a very prolonged haranguing about neglect of her personal kit and neglect of the older members of her clan.

Katie jumped back into the now time - it was the ringing call of an orange-legged mud wader below her. Now startled into taking notice of what was around her, she noticed the ghostly pale, blunt faced owl, quartering the marsh, eyes intent on what was below. And then it plunged to the ground, talons snapping out and it was away with something small, brown and wriggling. She hoisted the rucksack onto her shoulders and hoped that the Dhobie Palace had done the deed with her dirties - she was running short of vests and pants and she would soon have to revert to hand-washing them. But she would have to leave now - there was a navy blue Land Rover below the knoll overlooking Landulph and there was a man in uniform waving his arm at her frantically.

'Hallo Sergeant' she offered as a cheery greeting as she strode up to him. She handed her rucksack over and without a word he threw it in the back. He motioned his head to indicate that she should get in at the passenger's side.

'How was I supposed to find you' he said as the handbrake was yanked off, 'Landulph doesn't really cover it, does it?'

'Well, you found me, didn't you?'

'Landulph doesn't really cover it, does it' he continued, 'now if you'd said down one of the creeks looking over Kingmill Lake, that would have been different, wouldn't it? I wouldn't have spent the last fifteen minutes going around Landulph, like an idiot, trying to find somebody who knows where the hell Great-Aunt Katerin lives, would I?'

'Well, it's a bit difficult to explain, isn't it, if you don't know it, or if you don't have a sodding clue.'

'It will take about an hour and a half.'

'What will?'

'Taking you to Broadclyst, it'll take an hour and a half, and we're running late...'

'Broadclyst' she sniggered, 'who's she?'

'It's not a she, it's a place, innit?'

'Oh, what a shame. Do you think they'll start without me if I'm late?'

'I dunno, do I?'

They had joined the Expressway and the Tamar glittered in the sun below. She decided she would try another tack: 'So what do you call yourself?'

'Sargent.'

'Oh brilliant, so you're Sergeant Sargent!'

'No, no, no! Corporal Sargent!'

'Oh, because that's so much better!'

'But you can call me Nobby!'

'I will, then. So, Nobby - is that because you put it about a bit?'

'Certainly do!'

'Well, Nobby, you sound like you know what's what - what goes on at these initiations into the Royal?'

'Everyone gets pissed, has a laugh and then passes out...'

'Oh, fantastic. In that case, I'm going to rack out now - just give us a poke when we're nearly there so I can put my face on.'

'Eh?'

Katie drew her hands down over her face and out popped her happy, smiley face. She nudged him in the ribs. 'See?'

Nobby just snorted in reply.

The Land Rover crunched to a halt outside a public house at precisely seven-thirty pm. Katie presumed that this was the one. Nobby led her through the busy front of house to a back room which was already alive and buzzing with animated conversation. As she entered, the crowd silenced for a moment and then burst into song:-

Oh, why was she born so beautiful?
Oh, why was she born at all?
She's no bloody use to anyone,
She's no bloody use at all!

A long glass vessel with a bowl at one end and a wide rim at the other was presented to her by a young squaddie - it contained a purple looking liquid.

'Blackcurrant squash?' she asked.

'Not entirely' answered the squaddie. It took her a moment to recognise Jim Griffiths and Eddie Maddocks - they were not in uniform. She then remembered that she had an appointment with Maddocks later.

'So, if I fail, what happens?'

'You'll have to wait and see, won't you? The best advice I can give you is, drink it all in one go!'

So, DRINK chug-a-lug
Drink chug-a-lug
Drink chug-a-lug
DRINK!

She started to gulp it back. It was blackcurrant flavoured but there was something sharp and alcoholic in there as well. Something that was unpleasant. Something that was going to harm her.

And she was in the centre of the room, the glass vessel tilted and turned for her as liquid splashed down her gullet, over her chin and down her front. And then the vessel was taken away. She wiped her chin, shuddered at the wetness down her chest and her hand was raised for her to the ceiling in salute, and then there was tumultuous male roaring, like the baying of hounds. But the baying seemed distant, like it was in the next room, but the baying mouths were in front of her and all about her, but the sound was elsewhere. And now her eyes were hurting and at the edge of her vision, there were flirting fireflies and at the very edge, a cold pint glass that was pressed into her hand and she was sat down, where she then poured cold, icy liquid down her gullet. Griffiths was staring at her anxiously, Maddocks and the others were laughing and clapping at her. She stood up but the room lurched sideways and she had to grasp the counter to steady herself. The man behind the bar with the short black curly hair wanted to know how she was and did she need help. He held her hands. She pulled them back to grasp the wood of the counter again and replied that she didn't know but could she get some more cold water, and then the room lurched to her right again.

He said his name was Nathan and he sounded like an Aussie and he was startlingly attractive, with all his hair and tanned skin, lean muscles and bone. He patted the tops of her hands with his masculine hands and this made her feel safe and wanted, all at the same time. And he was startlingly attractive, with his Australian stature and the calm Aussie twang of his voice and his good hair and his straight teeth and the neatly bristly skin of his cheeks and his chinny, chin, chin. So attractive was he, that all she wanted to do was press her cheek against his cheek, and her lips against his lips, so she could...

The room stopped its clockwise motion for a moment.

'What's your name?' Nathan wanted to know. Oh, that voice, that voice.

'Oh, it's Ket or Kate or Katie or whatever you like' she heard herself say. Her body shuddered and a tingle came up and flashed along her spine and her limbs. The roomful of Royal were bantering amongst themselves. 'I call myself Katie, and I think I've just been poisoned by that purple stuff.'

'Crikey, poisoned? I'll get you an ambulance' he said in his Australian toned voice that caused a resurgence in her tingling.

Australian? How did that go? 'No mate, I'm fair dinkum now. Get us another one of those, mate?' she said, pushing an empty glass towards him. He indicated the two filled mugs alongside her elbow and dashed away to serve someone clamouring in the front bar. 'Oh, sorry' she said to his retreating back.

Jim Griffiths put a hand and her shoulder. 'Sorry Katie, that was a cocktail devised specially for you - how are you feeling?'

'A bit ropey, but Nathan is sorting me out.'

'Nathan?'

'Yes, that Aussie bloke behind the bar. He's Australian, isn't he?'

'Can I get you anything, Katie? We're about to make a start...'

'Oh, you mean there's more? Can you just give me a minute, he's back...'

'A minute then' and he strolled away.

'So Nathan, you're a long way from home?'

'What do you mean?'

'Well, you being Australian and all that...'

'I was born here!'

'What? In the pub?'

'No, London.'

'London? But you said...'

'No, I didn't...'

'Oh, so you're just pretending to be an Aussie?'

'No!'

So that was that. 'But you Aussies like a bit of a rumble don't you?'

'No!'

'Yes, you do. Well, it's all going to kick off here.'

'It had better not!'

'I'm going to rip into this bunch of born again scrotes.'

'No, don't do that!'

'But it'll be alright, because it will just be drunk fighting, like when you've had a few and you're not feeling too good and you have a fight and you throw your arms about, and no one gets hurt but you feel better and then you can start getting drunk all over again.'

'I'll call the police.'

'No, no, no, it'll be just drunk fighting. You Aussie's know how to fight properly don't you? So when it all kicks off, you'll watch my back.'

'I'm going to call the police.'

'No, no, no. Just watch my back. Your mate, is he any good in a fight?' She pointed to the man busying himself in the front bar.

'Who? Kieron?'

'Kieron? That's brilliant, so he's Irish! So when it all kicks off, I'll need you Aussies and you Irish alongside me, because both you lot like a fight, don't you?'

'I'm gonna call for an ambulance too...'

'No, no, no, I think we're going to need three or four...'

She turned around as she sensed that Jim Griffiths was about to make an announcement. 'Hush please' shouted Griffiths and the room quietened. She turned to face the crowd. Nathan had hurried away to do something or other, leaving the serving hatch and the counter vacant.

'We're here this evening to induct Katie Talog onto the ceiling of notoriety!' This prompted some cheering and a corresponding hush in the front bar. She looked up at the ceiling of this narrow, stone built room and there were footprints all over it. How could this be? Upside down people? Is this what happens when you get totally bolloxed?

'As you know, Katie is a key member in the Communication and Information Systems department in HMS Albany and she...and what is it you do, Katie?'

This prompted much laughter. Katie started to feel a little more sober as she realised what was about to happen to her. 'I bale you lot out of trouble, time and time again, that's what I do.'

'But before we start the entertainment, I will invite Katie Talog to say a few words.'

She was lifted onto the counter and immediately she regretted it. Nathan, the bar-keep, was now behind her, his arms raised so he could stop her falling. Jim Griffiths also positioned himself to one side. He picked up an empty wine bottle and started signalling anxiously to someone in the crowd. And then the singing broke out again:-

Oh, why was she born so beautiful?
Oh, why was she born at all?
She's no bloody use to anyone,
She's no bloody use at all!

And then it was all quiet again.

She took a deep breath. 'Well, whenever I hear that old hymn, it reminds of all the happy occasions when the English get beaten at rugby' she said, pausing for effect, 'which is quite often, to be fair.'

'She's not Welsh, is she?' someone wondered from the back.

'Have a care lassie, we're not all English!'

'Ah, the token Jockroach - good to hear from you!' There was muttering from the crowd in front of her. 'It also reminds me of all the times when the Jocks get beaten.' She paused as the taste of blackcurrant seeped into her throat. 'And the Paddywacks of course!'

'Throw her to the Beast of Bodmin Moor!'

'Ah yes, the Beast of Bodmin Moor, a mythical beast, mythical like Royal Marine battle honours, some might say...'

There was a collective sharp intake of breath and the muttering became quite hostile. She congratulated herself on how she had handled the heckle. At the back of the crowd, she saw the squaddie, whose job it was to chronicle the event, lower his camera. Maddocks signalled him to continue.

'I don't know why we need the Royal Marines' she continued, 'we already have the Kate.' She paused again. They all seemed a bit slow on the uptake. 'You know, the Kate, Kate Carney, Army.' No laughs so far, just a palpable hostility bubbling away. She took a deep breath. 'As we all know, you're not proper soldiers, you're just ceremonial - you're just there to guard the ship or toot the trumpet and bang the drums', and now the buzz of hostility was palpable, 'and when I really needed you, you had your feet up, drinking tea and having a diddle in your keks while I was doing the fighting!'

A big finish was now needed to get them all on-side.

'Well, we all know what's really the purpose of this evening – for most of you, this is an opportunity to touch up a real girl, other than a close family relation.' This was received with a chorus of boos and jeering.

She tried to down a jug of water but she almost retched. The remnants were flung over the crowd and the effort of the throw nearly caused her to fall backwards behind the bar. 'I'll hand you back to the MC, that's you, isn't it?' She pointed in the approximate direction of Jim Griffiths. 'If you don't know what MC stands for, let me help you out: the 'M' is for monumental and I'm sure you can work out what the 'C' stands for!'

'Alright, get her down' growled someone.

Katie turned round to Nathan and just managed to keep her balance. She wrenched her jacket off but it stuck over her left wrist and the jug. She pulled and pulled and then it came free; she threw her jacket down and handed the glass to Nathan. 'Right, I'm going in, you watch my back!' She took two small steadying steps, twisted in the air and launched herself into the crowd. They would all be flattened below her, like crackling stems in an expanse of golden barley...only, they weren't. Her limbs were caught by unyielding hands and arms. She was suspended five feet above the floor and couldn't move with the wooden floor looming below her.

'Secure her arms! Make sure she can't use those hands!' It was Griffiths shouting. Katie strained each arm but she couldn't free them - her hands just flapped helplessly! She was in big trouble!

A short wiry figure with a short wiry moustache crouched down and looked up at her face. 'Well caught gentlemen. So Miss Talog, are you drunk? What would possess you to take on a room full of Her Majesty's finest?'

She tested her arms again. 'The odds seemed fair to me' she burbled.

'I admire your spirit lassie, but your common sense is lacking. Now are you residing comfortably, we need a wee chat.'

'I don't feel so good...'

He continued, 'So, I'm a Jockroach, am I?'

'Well yes, you're small, Scottish, obnoxious and...'

'And what, lassie?'

'Should be stamped on.' She gasped as she realised what she had just said. 'Or maybe not...' she quickly backtracked.

'Gentlemen, please flip her over.' She was thrown up in the air and landed again in unyielding limbs; she groaned, opened her eyes and found she was now looking at the ceiling of notoriety and Cummins was peering at the side of her face with his moustache bristling.

'Jockroach. That's a very offensive term Miss Talog - would you like to retract that now?'

'Er, no I don't think so' she mumbled, chewing on her lip. Wrong answer, but his monotonous, condescending Scottish tone was difficult to take. She suddenly felt anxiously sober. Based on his bearing and manner, she decided he was a sergeant major in the Royal Marines. Oh crap, she groaned to herself.

'So where in Jockland do you think this Jockroach comes from?' he asked sarcastically.

She rejected the first idea that came into her head and settled for a timid, 'Glasgow?' Oh please, not the Gorbals.

'Very good. And how do you think we deal with miscreants there?'

Again, she rejected the first riposte that came into her mind and settled for, 'Do you pat them on the head, say there, there, and tell them not to do it again?'

'Nice try wee lassie, but no.' He turned to Jim Griffiths. 'Mister Griffiths, what do you think we should do with her now?'

'I think we should proceed as planned, Mister Cummins, we'll just cut out the ceremonials and the celebrations. Katie has fallen lamentably at the first hurdle.'

Katie flexed her shoulders and wriggled but she could not free her hands. Mister Cummins had already resumed his overbearing diatribe.

'Now we had planned a fun-filled evening, with some sociable activities to demonstrate our appreciation for what you have done for us...'

'Hold on, can I say something?'

'No, please let me finish. We invited you here to honour you, but what did you do? You insulted all your guests and you were offensive about the proud history of the Royal Marines - didn't you?'

'No! It was just banter - don't you get banter?' She looked around at all the stern faces looking down on here and appealed for support. There wasn't any. 'Look you tossers, I know people who are high up in the Andrew and you'll be in deep dwang if you do anything to me!'

Mister Cummins tutted as he took a quick look in the direction of Griffiths who just shook his head. 'That threat does you a great disservice Miss Talog. We know for a fact that you have no friends even in the deepest bilge of the lowliest ship in the Royal Navy.'

That has the ring of truth about it, there was no denying it. Why after five years in the service did she not have a bevy of top brass on her side? Other than Uncle Alec, that is...

'What if I cried little girl tears?'

'Aww, a little cry? We all know they would be just false tears, wouldn't that be right Miss Talog?'

'Alright, alright, what if I appealed to your better nature?'

'We all know I don't have one of those. Remember where I'm from. Now, gentlemen, please remove Miss Talog's boots and socks.'

She squirmed but she was held tight. 'No, please don't touch my feet - not my sodding feet!' Her boots and socks were gone.

'Now, Miss Talog, are you decent down below?'

'What do you mean?' she cried out in alarm.

'What have you got underneath, Miss Talog?'

'Keks, pusser's issue, elasticated top and bottom, bullet proof!'

'Excellent choice, wee lassie. Then I recommend we remove your denims, so we don't get paint on them.'

'What? You're going to paint me? Oh, no you're not!'

'I don't need your permission, wee lassie!'

'Bollocks!'

'Ach, enough of your blether...'

All right, all right, but no glimping!'

'Gentlemen, please remove Miss Talog's denims...but no glimping, mind, treat her as if you're in the presence of royalty!'

Noooo! Despite her writhing, they were removed efficiently. Katie felt the bristles of a brush against the soles of her feet and wriggled in torment as a ticklish wash of paint was applied. And then, mercifully, it stopped.

Katie gasped. She was upended, suspended just below the ceiling, by three squaddies. Noooo!

'Now Miss Talog, we require a wee set of footprints, as if you were walking to church, in a very penitent manner!'

Katie complied, but was feeling nauseous. The soles of her feet had a pungent sheen of blue, oily paint. She was neatly rotated about and blue foot covers were placed over her feet.

'Get me another one of those bags, I don't feel so good!'

Katie shuffled to the counter and drained one of the mugs of water waiting for her. This wasn't helping much, particularly as Nathan and Kieron were laughing at her. Nathan offered her an apron so she tied it on - Kieron was sent away to find some towels and safety pins.

'Police and ambulance are on their way' mocked Nathan, 'but do we need the fire brigade?' He nodded at her blue-bagged feet.

'You think you're totally hilarious, but you're really not' she declared.

'We've put out an APB on your strides' he declared, 'but they've not turned up!'

'They'll have squirrelled them away somewhere as a trophy - probably in the Landy!' Katie wriggled her toes but they were still squelching in paint. 'I said some bad things out there' she declared, 'and I don't know how to put it right, do I? I mean, some really, really bad things.'

'Strewth! You were wasted! You couldn't help yourself! It was hilarious!'

'The only good thing is they didn't have an official photographer, so no embarrassing photographs!'

'No photos! You're kidding, right?'

'What do you mean?'

Nathan turned away, shaking his head. Suddenly, he seemed not quite so attractive. Kieron returned with a sheaf of towels and together they assembled a sarong around her waist, secured with safety pins, and the apron was duly put on over the top.

Jim Griffiths indicated that she should go outside, not a bad idea in the circumstances, so she shuffled her way out into the garden.

She was surrounded by the Royal Marines and Jim Griffiths took her to a bench where she sat herself down. Her legs were safely shrouded in towels, secured with safety pins and her head was lodged sorrowfully in her hands. 'I need to curl up in a corner of the garden and die' she muttered.

'This will just take just a minute, Katie.'

She sighed noisily.

'We've already heard from our Katie. I'm afraid she's a bit worse for wear, aren't you?'

She scowled at him. 'Yes, you moron!'

'But anyway, I've a few words to say - we're here today because of what's not in any citation, or any of the official records for that day in the Comoros Islands...'

There was a huge sigh. 'In your own sodding time' Katie muttered quietly.

'What it doesn't say in the record' he went on, 'or in the newspapers is how she took command of the situation, directed suppressing fire and exposing herself to enemy fire...'

She belched loudly. Something was coming and there was no stopping it. 'She exposed herself to enemy fire to pull a wounded ally out of harms way...'

There was a pulse coming the wrong way up her gullet and no matter how hard she swallowed, she couldn't send it back. 'You're all in my line of fire, get back' she shouted. She cast around behind her for something to contain what was surely coming up. There was a black bag sitting idly on the bench. This would have to do. There was a collective gasp and then groans all around her as she vomited into it.

'That's my bag!' gasped Jim Griffiths.

Katie, suddenly unburdened with the contents of her stomach, checked the contents of the black bag. It was leather and looked expensive. She gingerly extracted his wallet, keys and cell phone from the glutinous mass she had left there. She looked up with moist eyes: 'I'm sorry, I didn't realise that was your handbag! Leave it with me, I'll give all your things a little wipe!'

'Mister Griffiths, I did say to you that the wee baggie was a bad idea' commented Mister Cummins. He peered inside. 'I think that is what is known as a technicolour yawn?'

'What am I going to do with this?' moaned Mister Griffiths.

'Bin it' said Katie and Cummins in unison.

'Take a look at my feet!' moaned Katie, 'why didn't those born again scrotes use emulsion?'

She propped up her feet on a chair. Today's speech and entertainments had been severely curtailed - now the Royal were sitting in the garden, working steadily through all the cider and ale that was on offer.

Nathan brought out a bottle of 140 proof navy rum to her 'Let's see if this will get it off - it's certainly not fit for drinking!'

'I thought you and Kieron were going to watch my back? I'm really pissed off with you, and you an Aussie as well. I think the three of us might have stood some chance.'

He shook his head: 'Crikey, no we wouldn't! I can't believe you just dived in - strewth, what were you thinking?'

'I wasn't thinking - that was the point. Do you get this every time the Royal's back?' He didn't reply. He was distracted by a clamouring front bar. 'Do you need a hand? Get me a couple more overshoes and I'll serve some beers.'

'Are you sober?'

'Don't be ridiculous - of course I'm not!'

'Well, are you capable?'

'P-lease! It's the least I can do, everything considered!' She checked the robustness of her sarong and she saw that it was good. 'I'll sort out the Royal!' And then she shuffled outside with two brimming jugs. She was greeted with jeers. She asked sweetly if there were any takers for ale or cider. There were more jeers. In your glass or over your head, it is up to you, she added. There were several takers. This was an opportunity for much banter at her expense, but she had to take it, grudgingly. She felt a pull at her sarong so she rounded on the culprit. 'Keep tugging at that pal and you'll be tugging your teeth out of the back of your throat!' This threat seemed to have the desired effect.

Mister Cummins approached. 'So Miss Talog, how are we feeling now?'

'Utterly humiliated, very drunk, totally ashamed. About par for a Saturday run ashore.' She looked askance at him. 'If you can get my denims back I'd be a lot happier.'

'They're in safe-keeping, lassie. Now, we have just one more job for you.' She trailed back after him and followed the crowd into the corridor of notoriety. 'Please can you make your mark next to your footprints' Cummins asked as he handed her a red wax crayon. She padded to the table wearing plastic blue covers over her feet, climbed onto it unsteadily and scribbled a rough approximation to 'Kate's Plates' in crayon on the ceiling and some curly arrows leading to her footprints. Whistles and ragged applause filled the back room - she responded by extending the middle digit of her left hand.

The Royal trooped out but Katie saw that Griffiths had hung back. She decided to clear some glasses and return them to the counter. She watched as Jim Griffiths climbed onto a table and looked closely at her footprints. He seemed to be assessing the length and width like he was a fitter of ladies shoes. So, they were slightly longer than the average length for a girl of her height but they were quite elegant and came to a nice point with long toes. He spent some time closely examining the outside of her footprints, as if he could see more than the regulation number of toes adorning her feet. No, there was just the regulation five, Mister Griffiths.

The thing that seemed to take him aback though, was a mark on the sole of her right foot. The weight of paint may have blurred it, but what he should have been able to see was a sovereign sized triple spiral, one of three adorning her body.

He gave her a quizzical look as she topped up a jug with cider, but this may have been due to the sarong of beer towels around her waist. She returned his look but with a forced smile. She left the jug on a table and left quickly to get some air - Maddocks was waiting for her in the furthest reaches of the garden.

'At last, just me and you Ket' Maddocks growled, 'are you ready for this?'

'Ready as I'll ever be, I suppose.' Katie twisted the top of her sarong so it fitted tightly around her waist and placed her satchel between her legs. 'Let's do this.'

'You don't think we need privacy for this?'

She looked around as they walked together into the wilderness of the two acre grounds. 'I think we should be all right...about here. No one's going to hear you scream. It's all down to you. If it goes wrong, it'll be messy. There'll be blood on the grass.'

'Your call.' They stopped by a set of goal posts. There was noise outside the pub and in the car park, but not here, just the wing flitting and peeping of bats. Maddocks took a position towards the penalty spot; she circled around until she found a slight rise. She had the advantage of height here, a launch pad for her charge at him.

'Shouldn't you take that off?' he shouted. He was looking at her sarong of beer towels. 'You could rip me to pieces with those safety pins!'

'Look you knob-head, they're called safety pins for a reason. It's because they're sodding safe. There's no way I'm taking this off, you scrote, unless you're taking your trousers off! Anyway, you should be concentrating on what you're doing, not what I'm wearing.'

'Okay, I just need to picture you in a wedding dress.'

'Yes, well, whatever floats your boat. Look, I should warn you, I've had a drink. My co-ordination isn't all it could be.'

'I've noticed.'

'Anyway, can I take it as read that all the ceremonial stuff is done and I just come at you?'

'Yeah, let's get on with this.'

'Ready? You get this wrong and I could wipe you out.'

'Get on with it Ket.'

She took two steps back, crouched and then ran towards him, her arms and legs pumping. Three yards from him, she leapt in a swallow dive aimed at his head. His arms came up to meet her torso but he grasped her awkwardly at her hips. He swayed and his left arm buckled, all her weight was on his right arm. Her body crashed across his face. Desperately, she threw out her arms to cushion the fall. They both crashed to the soil, but she was on top, her right leg wrapped around his neck. He pushed it away.

Katie got to her feet first. 'You hurt me, you scrote!' She lifted her shirt and showed him the graze across her pelvis. 'Take me around the waist, or I'll come crashing down on you. If you take me around the hips, the dress is coming off, isn't it? How's that going to go look? Sodding awful, that's how it'll look!'

He brushed himself down. 'Come at me again Ket - this time I'll be ready. You didn't have enough elevation!'

'P-lease. There was nothing wrong with my elevation. You just panicked!'

'You were too quick, you came at me like a surface to air missile!'

'All right, you want me to just saunter up and then jump at you? That won't look right. And shouldn't you be practicing this with Flick?'

'Listen, I'm getting married in a few weeks, when do you suggest I do this?'

'All right, I'm coming at you.'

'I'm ready.'

'You'd better be, pal.'

She circled back to the slight grassy rise, took a series of deep breaths and ran towards him again. She leapt and was taken by the waist. Her arms and legs were extended, as a star.

'Take me round, take me round again and...let me down slowly' she called out with her neck extended. Her arms came down to her side. He lowered her slowly and applied a gentle bear hug and kissed her on the cheek. 'That was just right. You've got it. Now let me go before you squeeze the sodding breath out of me and some scrote sees...'

She looked over her shoulder. It was Jim Griffiths. He was shouting at them to stop whatever it was they thought they were doing. They were to stop it immediately. She looked at Mad Dogs. 'You can let me go now, I think you've got it.'

Jim Griffiths pushed between them. 'Just stop it. You can't fight... she's just a girl!'

'It's all right, we're done. Call that quits, Mad Dogs?'

'Never, I had the best of that' he replied.

'Well, to be fair you were a bit handy, but I was all over you at the end, wasn't I?' She winked back at him.

'Will someone tell me what's going on?' shouted Jim Griffiths.

'Down to you mate' she said to Mad Dogs, 'I'm going inside for a drink.' She scampered to the front of the pub and slipped inside with Griffiths in close pursuit.

'Wait a minute Katie, I want to make sure this is sorted out. Now!' He followed her inside the pub and she was cornered by the front bar.

She tried to calm him down. 'It's done. We're done. It's not a problem. It's all sorted.' She ordered a pint and Griffiths passed over the money.

'What were you thinking, Katie?' he asked.

'I made a commitment. I've done what I said I was going to do. We've sorted our differences. All sorted. All done.'

Mad Dogs came in. 'Let me buy you that drink I owe you, Ket - what's your poison?'

'I've had the poison. Just need the antidote. Cider please!'

'Cider? You never cease to amaze me girl!'

'That's good, have a drink together, sort out your differences but no physical stuff!' On this note, Jim Griffiths stalked away, heading for the back room.

'So, is she right in the head? Does she know what she's taking on?'

'It's Flick's favourite movie. She wants us to do this as our first dance.'

'She's a bit athletic then and I don't just mean in bed?'

'Yes, she's fit, does modern dance. Flick's a bit taller and lighter than you. You're a bit of a handful.'

'Oi, are you saying I'm fat, Mad Dogs?'

'No, just heavy.'

'That's the same thing, you cheeky sod! Yes I'm a bit chunkier than I look. They had all sorts of problems getting a read on my weight in the clinic.'

'So, this invite Ket...'

'What invite?'

'To Flick's hen night, but you don't strike me as being part of her stiletto and prosecco set, do you?'

'Oh, so what's that then?'

'High heels and fizzy, white Italian wine.'

'Oh, so you know about all that then?'

'This hen night, I'm really not happy about the sound of it.'

'Oh dear, I'm so sorry to hear that.'

'So, you're going to tell me what's planned.'

'I can't tell you.'

'We're friends aren't we?'

'Not really...'

'You're going to tell me, because I have photographs of you that are very compromising...'

'No!'

'I have pictures of you in your keks.'

'Bollocks!'

'No, no bollocks, but just about everything else you could imagine!'

'No, no, no! Not my under cleavage!'

'Your what?'

'My under cleavage!'

'I have no idea what that is!'

'My pwdin blew!'

'Your what?'

'My fuzzy pudding!'

'Still none the wiser...'

'My chuff, fanny...'

'Alright, I've got it...'

'Clunge, muff...'

'No really, I've got it...'

'Pussy, snatch, cu..'

'Alright! Alright! I've got it...just calm down. As it happens, none of those are in shot, thank god. Not quite, those big pants saved you, but take a look, can you afford this to go viral?'

He showed Katie a photograph on his camera. It was ghastly enough, but she breathed a sigh of relief when she saw that there were no stragglers showing. She sat back. If the phone went in his pint of foaming dark stout, that should ruin it. Her left hand darted out to seize it but he was too quick and smuggled it away.

'Buggery, buggery, bollocks' she hissed, 'you wouldn't do that, would you, not to a mate? Would you?'

'You think we're mates? That's very interesting.'

'Delete...them...now...please' she pleaded.

'I don't think I will' he replied. His smile was wide and broad like a hyena contemplating a particularly ripe, thick boned, carcass.

'Mad Dogs, you have the morals and charm of a hyena!'

'A hyena! And you think that's helping your cause?'

'No, listen, if I tell you, you'll delete them, right?'

'No, you don't really understand the situation do you? I will keep these forever. I have leverage over you, Ket, for ever and a day.'

'Bollocks! Why should I tell you anything, then?'

'I will keep these as insurance for my wedding day and my nuptials. I will make sure you do nothing to mess things up.'

Her mind raced. 'I'm not going to do anything, you idiot, because I haven't been invited, so ha!'

'You're invited to Flick's hen night.'

'Eh?' She clawed inside her satchel and found her diary.

'Yes.'

'When?' She opened her planner - it was starting to look very congested in May. 'Oh no, I'm not! I've got a lot on!'

'Then' said Mad Dogs, pointing to a Saturday, two weeks hence.

'Where's my invite?'

'I'm your invite.'

'Eh?'

'I just need you to do something for me...'

'Sod off!'

'I need you to feed me information about what's being planned. I'll tell Flick that you're coming, because you're a friend of both of ours...and you've unexpectedly become available and you're so good at organ...'

'Have I? Am I?'

'Yes.'

'Blimey! A hen party! What do I wear?'

'High heels, tights, the rest doesn't matter. Check with Flick - this is her mobile number.'

'So it is.' Katie pondered how to get herself out of this predicament. 'I'll tell Flick we're having an affair!'

'I'll tell her you jumped me!'

'She'd never believe that! Bollocks, she might. She'll kill me!' Katie tried to work through all the possible outcomes. None of them were good for her. 'All right, I'll be your spy in their camp. I can't believe I'm doing this. You're a despicable scrote, aren't you?'

'Tough.'

'So where is it?'

'North London.'

'I'm going to need more than that, aren't I?'

'You tell me, Ket!'

'Eh? So how do I pass you the gen? Are we using a drop box?'

'No! It's your job to put together the plan for the evening's entertainments and then accidentally drop me a copy! Easy!'

'Oh, shitty shitty, shit, shit, shit!'

Chapter Twenty-Eight

Friday 13 May 0720 - Lympstone

Jim Griffiths quietly entered the room where he had thrown Katie Talog onto the bed earlier that morning. There was no one in the bed, no bedding on the bed and the windows of the bedroom were wide open. Where was she? He turned back and looked down the corridor. There was nobody there. Then he heard a wheezing coming from behind the bed. He stealthily slid over the top of the bed and looked down. And there she was, cocooned inside the quilt with her brown tousled hair at one end and her dark blue feet at the other. He edged closer until his face was close to her hair and he inhaled deeply. Despite being monumentally drunk last night, her scent was delicately fragrant, like a summer meadow, as an officer's wife's should be. A smile crossed his face and a warm feeling bloomed in his crotch. The blue feet struck a discordant note though. He imagined what it would be like if she...

'What do you think you're doing?' she croaked. The shock of brown hair moved to reveal her face with her eyes still crunched closed. She was uncommonly beautiful, even with her eyes hidden. 'Where's my tea?' she asked. Her lips were pink and plump but set against him.

'I'll put the kettle on' he said.

'Make sure you do. Don't come back unless you have a big mug of tea, not too strong, three sugars and biscuits.' The face disappeared again. 'And the biscuits had better be nice, not rubbishy' she added.

He eased himself off the bed. Maybe she needed some more recovery time.

He returned in five minutes. The bed was now occupied.

A hand pointed from below the quilt to indicate where the tea should be left. 'Leave it there' she croaked.

'I want to chat with you' he said. She struggled upright to a seated position. This time, one eye was open, the other was still glued closed. She was wearing one of his shirts. It nestled stiffly over her chest and was rucked around her waist. He now had a full-blown protuberance in his underpants that was both pleasant but uncomfortable at the same time.

She quickly pulled the quilt around her to conceal her bare legs and then turned her attention to the mug of tea and a biscuit. 'I'm drinking my tea now' she announced. Her eyes were now both open but they narrowed quickly. She dipped the biscuit into the tea.

'You're welcome' he said. He composed himself and then sat alongside her. He noticed that his breathing and his heartbeat had ramped up. She wriggled so there was a sizeable gap between them. 'Katie, what was all that about with Eddie Maddocks? I really thought you were going to fight him!' He groaned inside when he heard what he had just said. That was so the wrong strategy.

'Why would you think that?' she asked between slurps of tea.

'Because of what was going on between you? It looked like real... hatred.'

'He may be a knobhead but why would he risk getting beaten up weeks before he gets married? How would it look if he rocked up to the church with a broken nose, a fat lip and a black eye? He would never live it down, would he?'

He noticed that she had cringed at what she had said. Her sharp, pointed nose was now wrinkled up. 'I spoke to him. I know what was going on.'

'Oh, bollocks goes my reputation then.'

'It was a very, very good thing that you did.'

'It was nothing, really. I was just thinking of Flick...'

'Flick?'

'Yes, Flick, the girl he's going to marry...'

'So, you helped Maddocks get ready for his big day. That was a very kind thing you did.' That was better he thought. He looked carefully down the front of the open shirt and his protuberance responded again at what he saw.

She looked very uneasy as if she was uncomfortable about where this was going. Katie pulled the shirt together and fumbled with the buttons. She could not secure them. 'It was nothing. It cost me a few bruises and a grazed hip.' He paused as he considered his next gambit. She seemed more relaxed with a mug of tea in her hand but the tea was very hot and a potential scalding hazard. He now realised why she could not fasten the shirt, it was inside out, but this was not the right time to tell her.

Was this the right time to ask her a difficult question? Was this the moment? Could he really pose the question? No, probably not. Not after last night. Not after he had seen her in such a drunken state. What had she called him? A monumental...

'I was wondering if there's something I could ask you?'

She turned her head quickly to look into his eyes. The tea moistened biscuit fell with a 'plop' into the tea. 'Oh, no!' She looked forlornly into the mug.

'I was thinking what it would be like to...be with a women...a woman with me, here. A woman who's been through similar experiences, a similar mind set, who knows what it is like to be in action, who enjoys a drink.'

'Oh no, no, no, no!'

'What's the matter, Katie?' he asked, suddenly alert that there could be an issue.

'You've got to be kidding me! Really?' She swirled the tea slowly so that pieces of biscuit slop spiralled up to the surface. 'What am I going to do with this?' she wondered out loud.

'Look, maybe you're feeling a bit delicate, but it's fine' he replied.

'Did you see what happened to me last night? You were there weren't you?' The scuds of biscuit swirled and then settled back to the bottom of the mug.

'I'll make you another' he suggested, 'or you could sip it slowly so that the biscuit bits stay at the bottom.' Ah, humour, that was a sure way to get her on-side he thought.

'Last night, you remember last night? I was shot to pieces' she said as she looked again into the mug, 'a bit like this biscuit.'

He insinuated his hand under the quilt and reached gently for her upper thigh. He found it and squeezed gently. He was very conscious that his breathing was steady and quick. She hadn't pulled away. He insinuated his thumb slowly up her inner leg. Her flashing turquoise eyes fixed on his.

This was a move too soon, especially when she was drinking tea. 'Whoa, hold up soldier' she shouted, 'you're not mounting a dawn raid on me - not in my state!'

He cursed himself for this ill-judged move. She quickly slid out of the bed and took up a position by the window, still cradling the mug of tea.

He circumnavigated the bed slowly and carefully approached her, like he was stalking a shy animal, weapon ready, an animal that could panic and bolt if he moved too quickly. As he got closer, his movements became even slower, minutely deliberate but still relentlessly in pursuit of his prey. She was illuminated now by the sun percolating through the window curtains and silhouetting her body.

She took her eyes off him suddenly as she followed his gaze and her face changed as she realised that the dress shirt she was wearing was not only inside out but it lacked the necessary density to conceal what was underneath. 'This shirt, it's not covering me up, is it? I might as well be wrapped in cling film. Can you see everything?'

Everything, he smirked to himself. He congratulated himself on his choice of shirt. Great job! He came towards her again, raising his arms slowly to embrace her but she ducked quickly underneath and scrambled backwards across the bed.

She stood dizzily and her eyes rolled. The tea settled back into the mug and her right hand settled on her forehead, attempting to massage her brain back into its cranium. 'Crap, I shouldn't have done that.' Her eyes followed the room around as if the walls were swaying in front of her.

He approached her again. 'Are you all right?' he asked softly. Now was the moment, while she was in a swoon. He could hold her and pull her tight.

'I feel like shit and you won't leave me alone to drink my tea!' Katie stood straight and managed a quick sip. 'Not bad tea' she murmured. She drained the mug quickly and put it on the bedside table. 'Now, where are my clothes?' She stepped towards the corner where her makeshift sarong had been thrown last night and bent to pick it up.

His heart leapt with desire as he saw her upper legs stretch and her backside tighten against black elastic. He seized the elastic and pulled her back towards him. He cradled his hands around her as she squirmed but his hands were locked in gently around her waist. She was pulling at his thumbs and struggling to insert her hands inside his to leverage his grip away. She stopped struggling. He turned her and the look she gave him was one of disbelief.

'You are gorgeous' he announced to her. Her expression softened - her left thigh was now nestling between his legs and she was pulling his shirt closer so that her breasts flattened across his lower rib cage. Her eyes closed as he brought his lips to hers. Her lips looked soft and yielding and she eagerly anticipated his kiss. He inhaled the musk of her hair and the summer mown meadow fragrance of the tawny skin on her neck and shoulder. His right hand infiltrated her pants and cupped her buttock, his left hand was now supporting her right breast and palping it gently. 'I want to look after you' he whispered.

'Hold up!' She pushed him away abruptly. 'What about last night?'

For a moment he was taken aback. He moved his arms forward so they could clasp around her waist. 'I beg your pardon, Katie?' He hadn't expected this. She had some recollection of what happened last night? How was that possible?

She grasped his shirt with both hands and pushed him away again. 'Was last night an example of how you're going to look after me?' she asked.

'Why, what's the matter Katie?'

'You got me drunk then...I had to endure that sodding Scotch scrote, Cummins, telling me my fortune, didn't I?'

'No, no, he's either a Scot or he's Scottish - Scotch is a drink isn't it?' he said to correct her.

She looked at him disbelievingly. 'And then I had my sodding clothes taken off me!'

'We didn't want to get paint on your denims.'

'And then...and then you had my feet painted in blue paint.' She looked around the room. 'And it was gloss paint, wasn't it? Now, where are my denims anyway, what happened to them? Where are my clothes?' There was the pile of beer towels in the corner of the room, still spliced together with safety pins. 'You've got my denims, haven't you? Haven't you? And my clothes, haven't you?'

'Sorry Katie, I'll get your trousers. And your clothes.' He groaned. So that was that.

'And then, you thought I was going to fight one of your men. How stupid was that?'

'Sorry, that was a bit of a misunderstanding.'

'And what did you do to stop it?'

'It was never going to happen, was it?'

'It might have done.'

'How?'

'You never know. We were squaring up at the back of the pub and...and...anything could have happened!'

'You were practicing a dance move!'

'You weren't to know that! It all could have gone tits up, couldn't it? We could have ended up scrapping, couldn't we?'

'No, you couldn't. You never intended to fight, did you?'

'No, we didn't, but back to the point. What's the point? Oh, yes, you let me get legless, trouser-less and...in a mess with Mad Dogs, didn't you? So how's that looking after me?'

'Look Katie, let me get you some more tea and biscuits' he responded. His member was still swollen but subsiding quickly now.

'I still don't understand what happened to me - I was only drinking blackcurrant squash!'

'Ah, I found out that there was a bottle of a not so fine Maltese wine in the mix' he announced. Now there would be big trouble.

'SCREECH?' she screeched. She seemed very upset now as she wriggled the makeshift sarong over her thighs and her backside. 'Oh, blimey...'

His member pushed sharply against the flies of his trousers. That hip wriggle, that wrinkled look of concentration and then the release of relief on her face when she had succeeded. It was so, so...

'You mean I drank a bottle of screech? Sodding hell! Don't you know I come with a health warning, it says, 'Do not feed with screech!' It's in my records in red capital letters, a foot high.' She adjusted the skirt of many towels so it fitted more comfortably around her waist.

'Since when?' he asked.

'Since a run ashore in Malta, three years ago' she replied.

The moment had gone. She was wide awake and fretting. Her eyes had lost that look of deep languor, that invitation to lay with her and explore her depths. He shook his head to clear his mind.

She gave an instruction: 'I need to get all my stuff through the dhobie palace; have you got a dhobie wallah who can help me out?'

'It's all under control. We were working on that yesterday.'

'So, someone has been going through my keks!'

'If you mean, did we wash and iron everything, yes we did!'

'All right, all right. There'd better not be anything missing, that's all...'

'What are you talking about?'

'I'm talking about trophies for the squaddies. That's what I'm talking about. I know what you lot are like. I'll be counting them back in!'

'You'll get everything back, I promise.' His mind leapt to another place. Trophies? He imagined what it would be like, the smell of Katie's musk? He took in a deep breath and his mind wandered elsewhere, to the spice islands of the East Indies. Nutmeg, he reckoned.

There was a loud knock on the door and then a call for Miss Talog.

'Miss Talog?' she whispered. 'Who's that?' she shouted back.

'Miss Talog' the voice shouted, 'I'm returning your laundry!' He recognised the bark - it was his sergeant.

'Just a minute' she shouted back. She turned to him, 'You'll have to hide!' she whispered.

'Tell him to go away!' he replied.

'I need my clothes - get under the bed!' she hissed.

'I'm not getting under there!' he said indignantly.

'Get under the bed!' she hissed again.

He paused, looked around the room and then quickly scrambled under the bed.

'Just coming!' she shouted at the door as she moved the latch and slowly swung it open. He watched as the door was opened tentatively and imagined her face craning around the opening and looked askance at the man behind it. 'Hallo' he heard her murmur. For some reason, his prick flicked upwards again. He cursed quietly to himself.

'I have your laundry, ma'am' the man at the door announced. He seemed to spend a few moments assimilating her clothing.

'Bring it in and leave it there' he heard Katie reply. After a moment's hesitation the man placed a rucksack and holdall gently in the room. He heard the man snigger as Katie aimed a kick at the boot protruding from under the bed - his boot. He quickly withdrew it.

He sensed that Katie was quite cross. She would be fixing the man with a steely glare from those flashing, azure eyes. 'So, it's all dhobied up?' she asked.

'Yes ma'am, here's the full inventory' replied the man. There was the shuffling of a paper printed list. He heard her acknowledge this and saw her bend down to unzip the holdall and rummage through the contents. He heard a short whistle of appreciation which was curtailed abruptly by an icy quietness.

'What's all this?' she asked as a flat package was pulled out and brandished.

'It's all as stated as in the memorandum of understanding, ma'am' the sergeant replied. A sheet of paper was produced. 'Is that your mark, ma'am?' he asked.

She seemed reluctant to accept that it was. 'I don't remember anything about this' she countered. 'So, these are all new?' she asked.

'Twenty pairs, standard pusser's issue, black, bullet proof' his sergeant announced proudly.

'And these?' She rustled some paper packages, that did not appear to be standard issue. He groaned inwardly, because he was starting to understand what had happened. 'What do you think I do with them?'

'For that special occasion, ma'am!' replied his sergeant.

'Oh no, you haven't have you?' she groaned.

The sergeant presented a sheet of paper. 'All signed, sealed and delivered ma'am!' he said triumphantly.

'Oh my soul, you have, haven't you!' replied Katie.

He listened as a sealed envelope was presented to her. She squeezed it and the sound betrayed the presence of a thick wad of bank notes. 'It was a pleasure doing business with you, ma'am' the sergeant said. 'Er, when do you think we can repeat this...transaction ma'am?'

'Well, I'm at HMS Hawkins in a few months, and...'

'Where is that ma'am?'

'It's in Shoeburyness over in Essex.'

'Ah. No worries, we can do a click, collect and return in two days, ma'am.'

'Oh, I see, that sounds good. Let's say 15th September...and just to be clear, same terms as this time, you pay me to run my stuff through the dhobie palace and…'

'Yes, ma'am, we do an initial assessment, segregate and destroy items that have seen too much action, replace as new and process the remainder as before. If you have any doubt ma'am, see the 'MoU' and check the terms.' He paused. 'Just one thing, your profile will change if you're shore based so we may have to take another look at that.'

'Yes, I'm sorry about that, but...'

'No worries, ma'am, your exploits off the Comoros Islands should stand us in good stead for another six months, easy. Deep respect, by the way, ma'am.'

'Yes, thank you. That's very kind.'

'Our pleasure ma'am, have a good day' he said with a quick glance under the bed.

'Yes, you too' she replied. She slammed the door as the sound of his parade ground boots clattered down the corridor. He cringed as he waited for the outburst.

'You filthy, dirty, minging, perverted, fornicating bastards!' she shouted under the bed.

He emerged sheepishly from under the bed, dusting himself down.

'I'm very sorry Katie' he said, 'I had no idea...'

'What am I going to do?' she wailed.

'Keep quiet about it' he replied, 'there's nothing else you can do!'

She opened the envelope. It contained a sizeable number of bank notes. 'If this gets out, I'm ruined' she muttered.

'Let's keep quiet about it then.'

'Oh my poor soul! I don't want my stuff ending up in a squaddie's kit bag! I don't want my stuff ending up in the Falklands or Iraq or somewhere! It's just not right!'

'I'll see if I can stop anything else getting out' he said, 'I suppose it's the least we can do after what we've done to you. Shall I return the money?' he said with his hand stretched out.

'Piss off! I earned this!'

Yes, the moment was gone, maybe forever. She was now in full flight, listing a series of tasks that needed to be completed. He wondered about kissing her on the cheek. Her eyes told him that this was definitely not the moment.

He left her in the room still remonstrating about all the jobs that had to be done immediately, if not sooner. He stood and looked up to the heavens. His crotch still tingled with unfulfilled lust and his scalp still prickled. What had gone wrong? He worked through every step of his plan. Everything was perfect. Then she had gone off her head. Who had dosed her with 'Screech' he wondered? Then he realised it must have been Maddocks - he had exposed Katie to her nemesis, the fortified Maltese wine known as 'Screech', so named because of its profound and debilitating effect on the minds of all matelots who drank it.

Katie sat on her roll bag, looking down the road. She heard a roar and then she saw an open topped sports car, which appeared as a scarlet, rearing stallion, in her mind. And he was right on time, outside the barracks at Lympstone, exactly when he said he would be. His hair was long and dark, his skin tanned and tight and his sunglasses exuded a sense of cool on this sun-filled day. When he called out to her, it was the same accented voice she had heard on the telephone last night and all those weeks before. The tightness that had enveloped her brain overnight started to release. The driver was Robert Glaus.

Katie dragged her bags to the car and looked helpless as she couldn't see where to put them. They ended up perched upright on the back seat. She sat alongside Robert, her hair tucked inside a woollen cap, her head wrapped in the collar and shoulder of his expensive open necked shirt. As they pulled away at speed in a splash of gravel, she saw through the wing mirror that Jim Griffiths had emerged past the duty guard, frantically waving his arms.

She flipped open her ring bound diary to reveal the triple spiral - the three tendrils of the body, the mind and the spirit that all came together and nurtured the promise, wrapped at the heart of everything. She snuggled closer to Robert - he did not know this yet but he was vital to her plan.

Chapter Twenty-Nine

Friday 13 May 0830 - Exeter Cathedral

Robert Glaus announced that they had agreed to breakfast in Exeter during their telephone conversation the previous evening. Katie had no recollection of this, but her purse felt light in shrapnel this morning, so she assumed the payphone had gobbled it. So, Exeter was where they were headed.

As they motored along the Exe Valley, Robert explained that the institute he represented had a research facility in Cambridgeshire, which she was aware of and their headquarters was in Switzerland, near St Gallen. They seemed to be involved in the mapping of the genome for Western Europeans, whatever that was. Katie wondered what was involved in mapping a gnome, unless she'd misheard. Robert thought that was hilarious.

Robert had sounded young when speaking on the telephone, with a slight accent, but in the flesh, he was firmly Germanic. Katie resolved to find out more about his institute, the SIKS. Her brother Paol could help with this. For today's breakfast meeting she was going in cold but at least she could find out what Robert and SIKS wanted with her and she could firm up on her own quest. Maybe, she had done all she could in the Andrew and it was time to jump ship. She quite liked this metaphor or allegory or whatever it was.

When they arrived in the square next to Exeter Cathedral, she was taken aback by the venue - it was a tea shop. All the folk behind the lead-lined windows were quite smartly dressed and generally quite mature. She would stand out amongst this set of people. They were led to a table by the window but away from the door. Robert stood, smiled and allowed her to sit down first. He was tall, over six foot and slim with it. He was casually dressed, with his trousers being a daring orange-brown colour but somehow he managed to carry it off. He was also confident and purposeful. His hair was a bit too long she felt, but a quick visit to the barbers would fix this.

She was suddenly conscious that she had dressed this morning with no bra, a rough green tee-shirt, denims and brown boots. 'Bollocks' she muttered. All her essential belongings were in a tatty brown satchel that swung from her shoulder and there was nothing in there that could help her.

'What can I get you?' he asked.

'Just some tea please, I feel a bit doggy after last night.'

However, something greasy would be necessary, Katie thought, as she had only had a biscuit that morning and even that had not been whole. The maid was waiting to take the order. Katie's standard response would be a mug of tea with three sugars in and a fried egg sandwich, but she hesitated. They would share a pot of tea instead. She wasn't sure what type of tea she was being offered, however, Ceylon tea sounded safe. She looked around the other tables to see what they were eating - none of it looked substantial enough for someone nursing a hangover. And she had a right, royal hangover. There seemed to be a prevalence of dainty sandwiches and fancy cakes - Robert offered a selection of sandwiches and cakes - she agreed to this. She explained that she was on a special diet: no not Vegan, whatever that was but with a lot of chocolate in it. Robert was charming and considerate, she thought, so she relaxed a little.

No, you need to sit up straight, just like Gwen said, you can't loll around in your seat like you usually do. He wanted to know what he should call her. She offered 'Katie'. She realised that the disadvantage of sitting up straight was that her chest points were now rubbing against the cotton of her tee-shirt, so she slouched again and crossed her arms. He started asking questions about her career in the Navy - he's done his research she thought. I should be on safe ground here.

But perhaps we can steer this around to sport. What do they do in Switzerland? Mountaineering? Tennis? Yodelling? Don't mention football she thought, the Swiss haven't done too well recently. Best not to talk about rugby, either.

He asked how she kept fit on board. Great question - there is a gym and space on the deck for running. She tried to take a sip of tea but slurped instead. The delicate tea cup was causing her difficulty, so she eased her index finger right into the handle - but it was now stuck. She drained the cup and then quickly hid it below the table cloth. She tried to wrestle it off her finger but it wouldn't budge. I bet this makes me look really sophisticated she thought.

Robert saw her discomfort. He took her hand, smoothed some butter around her finger and eased it out of the handle. She felt her cheeks burning brightly. He refilled her cup and suggested she didn't need to insert her finger so far into the handle. She sheepishly said she would take his advice.

He asked a question about her early life. An intermediate alarm was set off in her head. He's seen my birth papers and he's read that my dad is unknown. Where could this lead? My mum, yes her first name is Maela and that is a pretty name isn't it? But then you've never met her, have you? Yes, she was born in Wales and I know who her mum is, but not her dad. Where? Near Rhyll, so yes, she's Welsh born. But I can't tell you anything about my dad or where he's from. So, Robert knows about my unusual blood group, but how? The alarm bell was ringing loudly in her head.

No, I can't discuss my inner essence, whatever that is, or the essence of the rest of my family. You don't need to know about any of that.

The alarm bell was ringing loudly in her head and now the ship's klaxon had joined in.

She thought about standing up, presenting her body and saying: 'Look, here's my outside! This is how my inner essence and the world has made me. See! What else could you possibly want to know?' Katie decided that would create a fuss so she stayed seated.

But now she felt sick inside. She stood up but had to steady herself with a hand on the table. The room lurched to her left and the floor came up towards her. She took four staggering steps, out through the door, into the outside world, out across the road in front of a horn braying truck and onto a low stone wall. The cathedral was squatting in a sea of green.

Robert came alongside her. He was asking if she was all right. She gave a short nod and tried to stand. The essence of biscuit infiltrated up through her acid burnt gullet. He was caressing her forehead, tenderly. She tried to stand again and this time he held her round her waist, so their hips touched together. His big brown eyes narrowed in concern as he spoke words that she recognised but could not comprehend. She breathed in deep gusts of air into her lungs. And then things started to click back into focus - the facade of saintly statues, the tall, square tower and the moustached falcon perched on top, that suddenly cried, leapt into the air and with winnowing wings flew swiftly down the street.

Katie was blabbering a very long thank you. He bent to kiss her, so she softened her lips and gently closed her eyes. His kiss landed on the tip of her nose. Shocked, she opened her eyes. He kissed me on the nose! But why? Was her nose so big he could not reach her lips? But if he crouched down, and came at an angle?'

Normality was restored, as she was escorted back to the tea room and sat back in her seat. The maid looked concerned but was advised that everything was cool, so she did not need to fuss.

Katie was suddenly troubled by what she had printed on her tee-shirt, the one she had liberated from the Royal. No, don't look down you idiot! Robert's fixed smile had broadened to a wide, beaming smile. Was it something that was amusing to the Swiss? What could it be? Something to do with cuckoo clocks? Or cheese with holes in? Or cows with bells on? Or yodelling? What was it?

He was still chattering at her. No mention of her inner essence or her funny turn. The conversation was meandering like a wide river, heading towards the sea, through meanders and swirling pools. Just keep your arms crossed she thought and we might just get out of this without any harm done. It might make me look a bit strange and uptight but I can't let you read what's written on my tee-shirt. No, I can't manage any more cakes thank you - knowing my luck there's already a line of cream all along my upper lip. She wiped her mouth quickly on a corner of the table cloth and realised this was the wrong thing to do when the crocks all clattered together.

Yes, we could meet again but you should let me know the dress code next time. Yes, I would be very interesting to see your laboratory near Cambridge and learn more about your exciting research. Yes, I am considering my future career but I can't possibly imagine what I could do for an organisation like yours. Apart from that one thing, what did you call it? Oh, yes, that was it, your tissue collection! What collection was that? Oh, bless you! She sniggered at this.

The maid asked if everything was to her satisfaction? She pointed out that it was all very fancy and nice but she wasn't used to such fancy things. She pointed out that the teacups were a bit dainty if you're used to a mug and there was a risk that you could get your finger stuck in the tea cup handle. The maid explained that the art was not to stick your finger right through and then there would be no problem. Katie explained that there was no point in having a handle if you can't get your fingers around it. The maid agreed that the tea china was delicate and could take a while to master. Robert seemed to find this whole transaction very amusing. Now the maid wanted some feedback on Katie's experience today and it should be written on a feedback form. Katie explained that she had already said all this, so there was no need. Robert hastily picked up the feedback form and filled it in quickly. He showed Katie that he had added some commentary on the difficulty of using fine china, if all you have been used to before is mugs: therefore mugs should me more readily available. She nodded her agreement with this.

He's so charming and he's tolerated all my little mistakes. But he went too far when he tried to dissect my origins. But perhaps that was the whole point of all this? She was ushered out of the tearoom in a respectful manner and there was a moment outside when they couldn't decide what the protocol should be. 'Nothing gained' she muttered and so she kissed Robert on the cheek to say thank you. He was so close that a tingle ran up and down her spine. 'That was nice' she murmured.

I must call Gwen and tell her what has happened. Robert acquiesced to this and offered her his 'handy'. Katie declined and went to use the payphone.

Katie rang Gwen's private telephone number and eventually her sister answered.

'How did your hot date go Katie?'

'It wasn't a hot date Gwen, it was a business meeting...'

'Ooh, a business meeting! Get you! So what did you chat about with Roger at your business meeting, Katie?'

'It's Robert. We just chatted about his institution and how I could help them.'

'Um, why are you dealing with these people, Katie?'

'They've got something of ours and I'm going to get it back.'

'But it's no use to anyone now!'

'That doesn't matter - I made a promise and I'm going to get it back!'

'This is a dangerous game you're playing, Katie!'

'It's not a game! Anyway, I know what I need to know now. The more I know, the less the risk...'

'I see. But more importantly, when are you coming to see us?'

'I'll be in Cannock on the 17th, let's say eleven hundred hours for you to pick me up, in the motorway services...'

'I'll put you in my diary. That's good, we can go and see papa after.'

Katie's heart plummeted. 'I don't think so...'

'You must...'

'No I mustn't...'

'I insist...'

Katie tried to recall the last time she had gone to see Alain Houghton - it was many years before and it had not gone well. 'All right Gwen, but what if he asks about Maela?'

'We'll tell him the truth, won't we Katie?'

'I think we ought to hold back a bit...'

'The truth Katie.'

'Oh, all right...'

'So your date - handsome is he?'

'Yes, but he's got this fascination with older women like...Maela and who Maela's been with. Do you think we should warn her not to talk to any strange men?'

'It's a little too late for that...and by the way, we're not talking.'

'Oh, what's happened now?'

'I'll tell you when we meet. So, he's Swiss? What's he like?'

'Robert? He's good looking, he's in his mid twenties and he's very charming, in a Swiss kind of way. He calls himself Robert.'

'Robert? He sounds like quite a dish...'

'Well, his eyebrows are quite distinctive and his hair's a bit long...'

'Oh, wow!'

'And he wears orange trousers...' She listened to Gwen's quickened breathing with alarm - it sounded like she was about to swoon.

'Dreamy!'

'Just stop it Gwen!'

'You must bring him with you, Katie.'

'No, no, no, he's got his own car - it's red and its got a rampant horse on it!'

'Oh my goodness me, not a rampant horse!'

'Gwen! Remember you're a married women!'

'Oh that!'

'Gwen?'

'Yes, Katie, so...did you dress to impress?'

'Not really!'

'Oh, no, you didn't wear that green tee-shirt did you?'

'Gwen, what tee-shirt do you mean?' Katie looked down. She was wearing a tee-shirt and sure enough, it was green.

'You know the one I mean. The one with the Swiss army knife and all those surprising accessories.'

'I did wear that one. What's the problem with it?'

'Oh no Katie, not that one. You've been walking around Exeter in that tee-shirt? Did he say anything?'

'He didn't mention it, but I felt a little bit awkward to be fair.' But this awkwardness could well be due to her brain being in the vice-like grip of a super-huge hangover.

'I'm surprised you didn't get arrested?'

'It's really not that awful, Gwen.'

'What about the diagram on the back?'

'What about the diagram on the back? It's on the front!'

'Oh, brilliant, you've only got it on back-to-front!'

Katie did a quick check with her fuzzy vision. 'Oh, bollocks, I see what you mean!' She could see her name on the flappy label.

'Anyway, I look forward to meeting your Robert...'

'It's never going to happen, Gwen.'

'Ooh, I think it will! Bye bye for now, Katie.'

'Bye, bloody, bye Gwen!'

Katie slammed the receiver down and again and again. A cool tanned hand took it and placed it carefully in its holder. It was Robert's hand.

'Everything all right, Katie?' he asked.

'No, it's my sodding sister and my sodding mum and all their sodding little sods.'

'Ah, families. Oh, I forgot to mention, your tee-shirt is on backwards.'

'Yes. Thank you for that. Can you just turn around a moment?'

'I'm sorry?'

'Just turn around!'

He turned around and covered his eyes.

She lifted her tee-shirt, freed her arms and wrestled it back on the right way. 'You can look now.'

'Ah, good.' He looked around. 'But, where is she? The girl with the Swiss haters tee-shirt?'

She looked at a distant spot in the ceiling above his shoulder, because she couldn't look him in the eyes, crossing her arms very carefully. 'You must think I'm a complete and utter twat.'

'No, not at all. I think you're very funny!'

'Yes, sodding hilarious.'

'So where can I take you to?'

Heaven? No. 'London sodding Town!'

Katie vaulted the fence with Robert dragging behind her, looking nervously about him. She ran through the guardian gate and stood in front of the altar with the bluestones all about her, then closed her eyes and listened. There was just the singing of the larks and their joyous ascending chatter and the constant drone of traffic along the main road but there was something else more distant, many leagues away.

She walked a circle amongst the standing stones, listening through the shadow and light of the soundscape and there it was again, in the centre, a perturbation moving below the aether, a very distant cry for help to the westward of the stone circle and then...it was gone. Katie kept walking and listening but she could not relocate the voice. Robert was looking at her in a most quizzical way.

But she didn't wait to be quizzed - instead, she re-commenced her promenade, skipping and wending her way between all the upright stones in the stone circle, gently caressing each one. She did this three times and then presented herself back to Robert. He seemed very amused.

'What's so funny?' she asked.

'You, you're a delight. You seem to have recovered from your hangover.'

'I have, haven't I?' She squeezed his arm. 'I will definitely do it, I just need to talk to my family.'

'Of course you must, but we are running short of time.'

Chapter Thirty

Friday 13 May 1220 - Wimbledon

Katie descended into the underground with a grim sense of foreboding. She was very grateful that Robert had taken her so far into the suburbs of south west London, but the journey she now had to undertake looked interminably long if the diagram in the tube station was anything to go by. And she was away from the sunlight, in a tunnel, well below ground.

There were just a few passengers in the carriage but she placed her two bags upright by the centre doors. The train left the station and rattled its way to the east of north east. As they approached the centre of London, there were many stops at stations she had never heard of and more passengers came and went, but some, like she, were semi-permanent fixtures in the seats.

For example, here was a man in a mid-grey pinstripe suit, wearing battered tan shoes. He insisted on tapping these shoes to a pacy beat, fed through wires leading to his ears. He frowned at her as she pointed at his shoes. Look at the state of those, she noted, then realised that the whole carriage had heard her.

The lady sitting opposite was fanning her face with a sheet of paper, but she was wearing multiple layers of clothes. Take your coat off, she thought, then you'll cool down a bit.

The girl sitting next to her was probably Japanese - she was hunched over a plastic bag with green leaves inside and she was weeping. The smell from the bag was like rotting seaweed. 'I would be crying too, if I had to eat that muck' Katie commented. The Japanese girl turned to her, gave a look of complete incomprehension and started crying again.

It was at the next station, that the carriage filled. Several of the new passengers looked at Katie disparagingly as they pushed their way past her and down the carriage. A group of girls surrounded Katie. One girl had a sign pinned to the back of her dress with a large, red 'L' on it. Katie wondered out loud what that meant.

'What are you looking at?' the girl blurted out. Her breath smelt of alcohol. 'Mind yours!'

'Does that sign mean you're a loser then?' Katie asked innocently.

'No! Are you a dike? Look at the state of you!'

'What's a dike?'

The fat girl and her friends thought this was very funny.

'You like licking out girls, don't you dike!'

'No, I don't' replied Katie as she tried desperately not to stare. What is this I'm looking at? Is it a barrage balloon stuffed with blancmange? Her hand leapt to her mouth but it was too late - she had broadcast this to the whole carriage.

'What's that, dike?'

'I think I said, you look like a barrage balloon stuffed with...'

'You're just jealous, look at the state of you, bag girl!'

'I think you should have looked in the mirror before you came out!' The girl pushing uncomfortably against her was large, tanned, covered with silver jewellery and had somehow squeezed herself into a very tight fitting white dress. The skin of her arms and legs bulged out from the straps and hem of her dress in all their orange, sprayed-on glory. Her four friends were now pushing uncomfortably close and their acrid scent was all powerful. 'Or your mates should have said something!'

'Go on, slap her Ellie! Show her what for!' shouted one of them.

'Ellie, what's that short for, elephant?' asked Katie. Why had she said that?

'Slap her Ellie, don't take that' shouted the dark haired girl.

'Stay out of it you, or I'll take you by your moustache and throw you across the carriage!' No, no, no!

'Oh, no!' said the girl, covering her mouth with her hands.

'I told you to use pile cream...' shouted the girl in ginger plaits.

'Or get it electrified' said the blonde girl with a face like a bruised peach.

'Look we shouldn't fight, people could get hurt...' warned Katie. She started to slip off her woollen hat and it caught on the plaster on her forehead. There was going to be a fight.

'Let's get her at the next stop!' said peach face.

'Look, before we start, I think I should warn you - my job description says I can kill people, especially twats!' Katie passed her woollen hat to the Japanese girl.

There was a gasp and the girls pushed back, much to the annoyance of the other passengers. 'Look, quit it you girls or I'm calling the police.' It was the man in the tan shoes.

'Take her Ellie' one of the girls cried out, now crouching behind her bulk. Ellie's arm was raised in a curiously crooked way that suggested she would dislocate it if she attempted to deliver a blow. Katie slipped off her gloves and there was another gasp.

'Oh my god, she's only a ninja, let's get out of here!' The girls pushed back and started a slow-motion stampede down the carriage, lubricated with coconut oil and foundation.

'Kunoichi! Kunoichi!' cried the Japanese girl.

'No, no, I call myself Katie, I haven't actually killed anyone yet - I'm a Wren! In the Royal Navy! My job is to protect you all!'

'You should know better - shame on you' said an outraged older woman, 'you young girls have no shame!'

'I've called the guard - they're contacting the transport police. You're in trouble now' was the contribution of a mid-grey man.

'And you! In the armed services! You should be ashamed of yourself!' said the older woman.

'I didn't do anything did I?' she exclaimed to the Japanese girl. Katie's eyes were swelling.

'Kunoichi! Kunoichi!'

'Will someone shut her up, I'm not one of those! I'm a Katie aren't I?' she said plaintively.

The train came to rest in a station. There was a hush. An official muscled his way on board. He was tall, in his mid to late twenties and he cut a shambolic figure in his oversized cap, shirt and trousers.

Several fingers pointed accusingly at Katie. There were several quick conversations with witnesses, conducted by the official, who seemed to be acting as both jury and judge. She gathered her bags and followed the official off the train amongst a melee of passengers trying to get on. 'Come with me please' he asked. She obliged. He gave a signal and the train pulled away.

'So, what am I supposed to have done?' she asked. 'I need to get to Camden!'

'Not on the Underground, you're not.'

'I've got a ticket. You're supposed to take me there!'

'Follow me to my office. I need to ask you a few questions. Can I see your ticket?'

She handed it over.

'I see, that seems to be in order.' He passed the ticket back. 'Navy?' he asked. She nodded.

They took a sharp turn along a narrow corridor which she could barely squeeze through with her bags. He opened a battered metal door and pushed his way into the dark space beyond. They were now sitting in a broom cupboard of an office. There was a small desk the size that you would get in an infant school but it was piled high with sheets of printed paper and well-thumbed manuals. There was the taint of cigarette smoke on everything. His finger tips were tainted brown from cigarette tar.

She squeezed into the spare seat opposite him and sat upright, hands placed demurely in her lap, a thin smile on her lips and a nascent tear in both her eyes.

'Look, I haven't done anything, please, just let me go, I didn't do anything.'

'I have witnesses who say you made threats...'

'Was this the bloke in the tan shoes? He can't even dress himself!'

'I have other witnesses...'

'Like the Japanese girl?'

'Yes, like her.'

'She can't speak a word of English and she thinks I'm a Ninja? That one?'

'Yes, and there are others...'

'They're all idiots...'

'Do you mean paying customers?'

'No, definitely idiots. Don't do this, please.' She became conscious that there was a video camera trained on her. 'I didn't do anything, please...'

'I must. Now I'm going to write you a ticket for affray. You have caused delays to your fellow passengers and to the network as a whole. Your name?'

'Oh, K.E.Talog.'

'Address?'

'Um, it's 23 Albany Place, in Camden.' This was an approximation of a possible address somewhere, but it would have to do.

'Contact number?'

She guessed a number. He wrote it down.

'Mobile.'

'No.'

'No?'

She gave the number of her mobile phone which had ceased to work two weeks ago. No matter!

He struck a line through the form. 'Now what was that all about?'

'I admit I said something I shouldn't have done, and it got ugly. I apologise.'

'I see. It's a bit late for that. You armed forces types, you think you can come back and carry on like you're still in a war zone. Well, you can't. We have CCTV tape, so it would help if you were completely honest.'

'Look, I'm always honest. I'm not capable of lying. My body goes into melt down even if I try to tell a fib.'

'I see, I see.' There was a pause while he worked something out. 'I'm going to present this ticket to you.' He pushed an oblong card across the narrow strip of clear desk so that it confronted Katie. She tried to comprehend what this meant. The writing was big, colourful and inviting. It was a ticket for a Grand Opening of the Camden Lido. The smaller text swirled in confusion as it came in and out of focus.

'I see' she said carefully, 'so, if I attend at this place and at this time it will mean that I can settle this whole affray business?' Coincidentally, it was for this coming Saturday.

'Exactly.'

'I see. Let me explore this a little. I can see me attending at this time and place wearing a sweatshirt and jeans.'

'I think you will need to dress more appropriately for the occasion and the location and indeed, the season.'

'I see, I think if I go all out I think I can stretch to this.' She scribbled 'T-shirt & Shorts' on the back of the ticket and passed it back to him.

'I think you should be stretching yourself a little more considering the situation you find yourself in.'

She took back the invitation and underlined the word 'Shorts' twice and pushed it back. She had an old, faded pair of navy blue rugby shorts with deep pockets and a well worn 'Ten Tors' tee-shirt that used to be white. These should fit the bill nicely. 'Let me just say, you will not be disappointed...'

This triggered an upheaval in his trousers, a rummage in his pants with his left hand and an uncomfortable leg-crossing activity that caused the desk to rock from side to side.

'I see. I think...that...could be...acceptable.' He looked across at her and she caught him with a sweet and innocent smile that creased her cheeks.

She gave him the ever-so-slow blink. 'Now, I think that if I attend for say, thirty minutes, I will have fulfilled my part of this, um, transaction.'

'I don't think that will demonstrate sufficient commitment. I propose two hours minimum.'

She anticipated that this would cause ructions with Paol. 'Let me see. I think I could do one hour.'

'I think we can split the difference. One hour and thirty minutes then.'

'One hour and thirty minutes it is. In which case you will need to provide me with refreshments every fifteen minutes, or so' stated Katie in a quiet, but matter-of-fact way, 'and when I say refreshments, I mean drinks that come into the category of 'happy juice', because I get thirsty really easily.'

'I see, but that would seem very unseemly to me' he replied.

'Hmm, it may seem very unseemly to you but me being seemly will seem, um, let me see, very disappointing for you, considering your...expectations.'

'Ah, I seem, sorry, I see. Refreshments on your arrival only, I thought would be sufficient. Now, let's say every thirty minutes.'

'Happy juice.'

'Of course, happy juice. There is an... outlet for this type of refreshment but even so.'

'That's fine. So, on arrival and every thirty minutes, up to and including the time I leave, you will provide for me a 'happy juice' break.'

'I see, you drive a hard bargain. I would remind you that you're right in this up to your neck.'

'That's interesting, because in my mind I thought I was only in there up to my toes.'

'You will need to demonstrate much more commitment.'

'I think I can go in as far as my knees. How's that? Then let's see how things develop.'

'That will have to suffice then. I think we may have a way forward.'

'Yes, we do. And you will bring all along the paperwork on Saturday and we can then settle all this. And the ways and means to provide 'happy juice' breaks.'

'Yes, indeed. So you're free to continue your journey, but not on the London Underground.'

'But, I've got a ticket to ride to Camden?'

'Even so. Follow me up top.'

She lugged her bags along the narrow corridor, up several short flights of grubby steps and then followed him out into the brilliant sunshine. Blinking, she asked him his name. He replied that it was Robbie. She shook his hand when he offered it and then surreptitiously put it back into her pocket so she could wipe it clean of his sweat and grime. She decided that she would know him as Robbie the Blackmailer.

She wanted to know if he was experienced with girls? He seemed hesitant at first and came back with a very implausible answer. Did he have a girlfriend 'on the go' at the moment? He replied 'no' a bit too quickly. She wanted to know how he liked to meet girls? He said that he met girls in many places where people normally meet socially. She supposed he meant in a pub or a club and not outside a school. She then wondered what was his preferred type of girl? He described his type as being taller and blonder than she was and thinner yet larger as well. She doubted if such a girl could exist but tried to picture what she would look like. Some sort of super girl, a girl re-imagined from his porn collection.

He seemed reluctant to talk any more but seemed agitated about descending back below the ground to his dark cell. He pointed out the direction she would have to go in order to reach Camden.

'Til Saturday then' she said.

'Til Saturday then. I'm looking forward to it' he noted positively.

'And just to be clear, I'm just pretending to be your girlfriend, aren't I?'

'Well, let's see how things develop, shall we?'

'Yes, we could do that, but...'

'But what?'

'Listen, I know that you're looking forward to a grand opening' she said as she looked deeply into his sad dark eyes in that long, thin, forlorn face, 'but you won't be getting it from me, I'm afraid.'

She turned and started walking along the pavement, leaving him with a cursory wave of goodbye. He looked forlorn in his oversized peaked hat and his rumpled white shirt and his unruly, soup spattered, dark blue tie.

As she hauled her roll bag along the uneven slabs, with her rucksack over her shoulders, she quickly came to realise how things worked on these unclean streets. There were no friendly faces and seemingly, no point in what any of them were doing. Her brain felt as if it was being assaulted by millions of pricking needles and she couldn't cope with it.

Katie turned into a smelly shop doorway to regain her composure and take some deep breaths. So, you can be as rude, ignorant, obstructive, pushy and ignorant as you want, providing you say sorry after each physical encounter. Along the street there were fast food shops, newsagents, grocers, betting shops and a melee of people. The rendezvous with Paol was a pub in Camden so she would have to get through. There, she would be able to drop her bags and collapse into a seat. No more progress could be made at the moment, so she settled against the wall. There was a dirty, scruffy man sitting on a sleeping bag, holding out a polystyrene cup with some change in it. She took the cup. 'I'll get us both a brew, what's your fancy? Tea? Two sugars? I'll be just a mo.'

CHAPTER THIRTY-ONE

Friday 13 May 1330 - Camden Town

Katie shouldered her way through the double doors of the pub and sighed in relief. Surveying the wide expanse of the room, there was an island bar and a mixed set of well-used furniture and punters. There was no sign of her brother, Paol. The despicable scrote had let her down.

She dropped the roll bag against the bar, and stood on it so she could lean over the bar. 'Hallo barman, service!'

There was a wolf whistle behind her and a boyish voice exclaimed, 'Wow, great job, natural selection!'

'What was that?' Katie said as she turned and looked at the lad who had interrupted her. She was disappointed. He had the look and the manner of a barrow boy but with none of the charm. 'Are you trying to chat me up?'

He sidled up to her at the bar. 'I said, great job natural selection!' His eyes were following the contours of her body upwards to her chest and then her face. 'Do you know why tits evolved? No? Well, they've evolved to look like a girl's arse!'

'Is that what happened to you then?'

'Eh? What? Are you saying I look like a girl's arse?'

'For pity's sake!'

He was determined to continue: 'Rude girl! Did you know, the female body has been crafted by evolution so it's the perfect playground for men...'

'Were you born an idiot?'

'... and I want to play on yours!'

'So if evolution is so great, how did we end up with you?'

'Come on babe, you know it makes sense!'

'Piss off you idiot, can't you see I'm busy?'

'Feisty, I like that in my girls' he countered.

'Knob-head, I find that really annoying in a man' she said, as she turned back to the barman, 'if that's actually what you are.'

'Look doll, do you need any help? You seem to be struggling!'

'I'm doing fine, I'm just about to start a delicate negotiation for a sodding soda water!'

The boy nodded at the barman and he provided a pint of soda water, with a slice of lemon, two cubes of ice and a miniature umbrella. 'Don't worry, it's all taken care of!'

She scooped her unused money off the counter and put it back in her purse. 'Thanks, but I was doing fine 'til you interrupted, wasn't I?' His name was Wayne, if his name badge was anything to go by.

'Did you know that a great rack is nature's way of showing me where to go for a good time?'

'What for? A tit wank?'

'Oi, that's rude!'

'Did you know that your bollocks are now a natural target for my boot?'

'Come with me doll, we need to talk!' Katie sighed, hauled her rucksack and her roll bag over her shoulders and followed reluctantly. She joined the two of them at a table. Yes, there was another one like him. His pal, seemed to offer even less prospects. They seemed surprisingly excited and attentive to her so she would have to see how this played out.

'So what's your name?' asked Gary, for such was the legend on his name badge.

'I call myself Katie.'

'Oh, do you! And what do you do Kate?'

'It's Katie' she corrected. Gary seemed incapable of handling complex words, like names. 'I'm a shipboard Wren and I serve in the Royal Navy!' she said more brightly than she was actually feeling.

'Like a secretary then?' said Wayne. 'I know a lot of Wrens!'

'No, I serve in a warship and I work in the Communications and Information Systems department!'

'Communications and Information Systems! So you're a secretary! I like it!'

'No, I'm not a secretary, I'm a Leading Hand in the C.I.S department...' she started to explain patiently.

'Ha! You're a ship's secretary! You sit on the Admiral's lap and take dictation!' crowed Wayne.

'No, I don't and I won't take dictation from anyone!'

'Ha, clever girl! So if someone rings up when he's having his G&T, you tell them he's busy?'

'Yes all right' she sighed, 'you win. I'm actually a secretary.'

'Good, I'm glad we've cleared that one up. Have you got a uniform?' asked Wayne.

'Secretaries don't wear a uniform, you fool!'

'Oh, yeah. Still, you a secretary, eh?'

Now it was Gary's turn: 'We're going to the lido tomorrow - why don't you come with us?'

'Because I don't do swimming...'

'But you're in the Navy?!?' they exclaimed in unison.

'Yes, but we don't swim into action do we? If we go into action, it's in a ship. If I ended up swimming into action, something's gone really, badly wrong.'

'You'd look great in a bikini!'

'Sorry mate, no bikinis, it's just service uniform and fire retardant suits for me!'

This seemed to be a conversation killer.

'I've got a deck of cards, if you're up for it' said Katie as she withdrew a pack from her rucksack, 'or dominos even?'

Two young women were sitting at the next table, hidden by a pillar. They were tall and slender, with long, straight, shiny hair, long slender tanned legs and shiny shoes with long slender heels. They were adorned with elegant jewellery and small, discretely positioned tattoos. Katie tried to follow what they were talking about; she started counting the number of times she heard them say 'like'. She counted to twenty-three before she was interrupted.

'What do you reckon our chances are?' asked Wayne.

'What? You and Gary? They're light years out of your league!'

They looked at each other while they considered what their next move was. There was the sad sight of many empty lager bottles on their table and nothing to show for it.

Another game of poker was refused so Katie idly moved a pile of her winnings around the table and hid them under an empty mug. She moved this to the centre of the table.

'How would you like the chance of winning back your losings, lads? Double or quits?'

'Is this a con?'

'No ta...'

'I can get this pile of cash out from under here without touching this mug...' She indicated the mug with a flourish of her left hand.

'Let me get this straight. You are going to get all our cash out of there without lifting...'

'No, without touching...'

'Without touching the mug...'

'Well, I'm in!'

'Me too!'

'And...'

'Oh, here we go!'

'And I'm going to do this in a quite amazing way...'

'Right, off you go!'

She held her cupped hands below the table and strained her face. 'Come on, come on, you can do this!'

'Watch those hands...'

'It's coming!' A coin dropped on the floor and then another and then a cascade. 'Oh wait, this is a difficult one!' The strain she was under was etched across her face. Two five pound notes fluttered to the floor.

'She's pulling it through the table!'

'There's a hole!' Gary lifted the mug; Katie swiped the pile of cash away.

'What are you playing at!'

'Winning the bet!'

'Oh for fuck's sake...'

'Shit! You mug!'

'Pair of mugs!'

She pooled her winnings into her satchel. 'Let's play...dare!'

'Dare?'

'Dare!'

'Go on.'

'We just dare each other to do a dare, for a stake of say...'

'Straight up?'

'Course!'

'I need a drink...Katie, your round!'

'Don't be rude!'

'Your shout!'

She returned with two more bottles of lager, plugged with slices of lime and a mug of water with ice. 'There you go!'

'So, do you fancy me Katie?' asked Wayne, drunkenly.

'Don't be ridiculous' replied Katie.

'What about me, then?' asked Gary.

'No thanks. I'd shag her before either of you.' She indicated with a glance at the lady in the tight fitting white dress.

'So, you're a lezzer then?'

'No, but if my only choice is either of you two or her...'

'So, you would take her here and now?'

'Why not? I'll just need a bit of privacy, though, won't I?'

'So, what's the dare?'

'Go on then, what's the bet?'

'I can get their phone numbers' offered Wayne.

'Is that all? Are you going to hack into their handys?'

'Just watch and learn.' He was back in less than ten seconds. Katie asked how it went. He said he would have another go after some more drinks had been consumed. Katie wasn't convinced the girls would wait that long.

'If I get one of their phone numbers, what's that worth?' offered Katie.

'Nothing!'

'Oh, come on! What if I get to snog her?' Their mouths were wide open, like fish gasping for breath in a drying out pool. 'That must be worth twenty- five?'

'A pony?'

'No, twenty-five. And for a shag, one hundred?'

'A shag for a ton?'

'What if I got pictures? That must be worth one hundred? The girl in the white dress, can you see her buttocks? I reckon I could get her to crack walnuts with those. What's that worth? Five hundred?'

'Blimey! Whadya think Wayne?'

'Nah, its a con. She's already got the pictures!'

'Let's see the pictures!'

'How come you got pictures?'

'Give me your phone!' Katie demanded.

Wayne handed over his handy and showed her how to use the camera function. Katie took a quick video clip of Gary and replayed it for Wayne. That seemed easy enough. 'I'll leave you to think about it - I'm going to primp myself up a bit.' She took her satchel and her drink, walked casually towards the two women and eased her backside into an easy, rocking motion. Her thigh brushed gently against the shoulder of the woman in white. Katie looked casually over her shoulder as she walked past and made eye contact. Her lips were gently parted and she gave the girl the ever-so-slow blink. She reckoned that this would set their pulses racing.

In the cubicle she quickly and thoroughly gave her teeth a going over. But there was a nagging doubt - who could get hurt here? The boys would lose some money, but she would gain it, so that was not a problem. The lucky lady would have an experience to boast about. And what about her own reputation? Could this get out? Absolutely not!

She looked down inside her tee-shirt and wondered how what was below could be made to look tauter and tighter. There was something she'd overhead in the mess deck and it involved ice cubes. She picked an ice cube out of the glass with her thumb and index finger and suspended it above her skin. 'Aaah' she cried as her shocked stomach contracted. She took two deep breaths and slid the ice cube across her chest points. 'Aaah, ooh, ooh, ooh.'

A woman entered the heads and looked at Katie in concern. 'Are you okay?'

Katie quickly put the ice cube in her mouth, 'Yes, I'm just freshening up!' and then quickly spat it out again. Her chest felt cold and wet but her sensitive parts were now pointedly erect.

The woman had left after a quick glance in the mirror. Katie knotted her tee-shirt so it was tight and tightened the belt of her denims by one notch. Just enough of her stomach was exposed. Ready. She emerged from the heads and sidled over to a high table in full view of her target and leaned back against it - this stretched out her legs and her stomach to good effect. Katie now held out the mobile phone and admired the image on the screen and then leered longingly towards the woman in white and lustfully licked her lips.

The two women looked towards her, bobbed their heads down and started whispering urgently to each other. Katie's heart was thumping against her chest - something was about to happen!

'Katie, what in God's name are you doing, you big tart!'

It was her brother! 'Paol, I'd given up on you!'

Katie stood up straight, brushed herself down, dropped her arms to her side and flushed brilliantly. She looked across to the two women - they were giggling now. 'Oh, fucketty, fucketty, fuck!' she muttered.

'Whose phone?' Paol demanded.

'It's not mine, it's his!' she gasped, pointing at Wayne. 'I was just going to call you!'

'Well, you don't need to, I'm here now. Hand it back and let's find somewhere quiet so we can talk.'

'I'll get my bags, and my cash!' Awkwardly, she grabbed the rucksack and roll bag and made a quick apology to the lads.

'Yes, sorry I'm late, little sister, I didn't mean to worry you.' Paol located a quiet table in a corner and manoeuvred her towards it.

She pushed her roll bag under the table and propped her rucksack up. 'I think I was about to do something bad Paol, you know, something really, really bad.'

'Okay, so how are you?' said Paol as he fiddled through his wallet.

'I'm horny' Katie announced.

'Horny?'

'Yes, you know, horny, horny, horny, so horny that I was about to do something...naughty.' Yes, that was good, get your excuse in early.

'I see. And what do you want me to do about that?'

'You should be understanding and sympathetic and helpful.'

'I see, well, you're going to have to help me out here...what do you want me to do about your...horniness?'

'It's just possible that I could just jump someone, anyone, because I'm not too fussy at this time.'

'You're kidding. You're not...'

'Yes, someone close by might have to step into the breach...'

'Ah, Henry the Fifth. And when you say breach, I assume you are being vulgar?'

'Don't be disgusting!'

'You started it!'

'No, I was just talking about normal, human needs...'

'Wait, you aren't seriously thinking what I think you're thinking...'

What could he mean by this? Should she lead him on? Of course! 'Well, you're a good looking bloke, you're not too thick around the waist and you enjoy women, don't you?' His hair was short, dark and curly with wisps of grey around his temples. He was reasonably slim despite his predilection for real ale. 'If the size of your porn collection is anything to go by, that is...'

'There's rules about this! You're my sister!'

'Half sister. Anyway, it's just, normal human needs, not the other...'

'I think you need a proper drink and some decent food - what's your poison?'

'Pint of cider.'

'Fine, and what can I get you to eat?'

'I fancy Eggs Benedict.'

'Haven't you eaten yet?'

'Not recently, but I fancy Eggs Benedict now...'

'So, one cholesterol special coming up...'

'Well, you can't beat it.'

'Well yes you can, you can have your eggs scrambled...'

'Scrambled? Is that allowed?'

'I'll ask.'

'And as many chips as they can get on the plate with scaffolding!'

'Just sit tight. I'll be back soon.'

'Well, I'm heading back to the heads...I need a leak.'

'You're a little sweetie, aren't you?' It was the woman in the tight, white dress and the long, slender legs.

'Oh bugger!' said Katie. A shiver swept up her back.

'You've been giving me the come on ever since you arrived' she said as her eyes swept Katie up and down, 'but you don't seem to be the type?'

'Please listen, I'm not really a little sweetie...'

'Oh, you so are...'

'I don't know what you're talking about' said Katie as she turned to leave the washroom. The lady in white interposed herself between Katie and the door.

'I think you do – what is it you want from me?'

'Nothing at all, I was just leaving' squeaked Katie.

'No need to do that, I've got the entrance covered, so no one's going to disturb us. I'm yours for as long as you want me.'

'Oh, crap, is this going to be a gang bang?'

'Is that you want?'

'Look, it was a dare, I thought it would be a laugh, didn't I?'

'No, it was a bet. I heard you.'

'Oh, bollocks!'

'How big a bet?'

Katie looked all about the space but there was no escape route, just closed doors and plumbing. What if she screamed? 'It was on a sliding scale...'

'That sounds very interesting - tell me more!'

Katie coughed - the pain in her gut told her she was in serious trouble. 'It was, you know, which base I got to and...what proof I could get.'

'I see' murmured the woman in white, looking puzzled, 'so, which base is it where you get me to crack walnuts with my ass?'

Katie gave a sharp intake of breath. 'That's just an expression – it doesn't mean anything!'

'Really? Unless you're in the Navy? I had a squeeze who used to say that. She was...masterful.' The woman in white was alongside now and Katie could feel her breath against her face. It was sweet and peachy and overpowering.

'Please listen, there's a bit of an issue...' Her backside clenched quickly - so quickly it could have cracked a walnut.

'What is it sweetie?'

'I haven't got any walnuts...'

'Really, K.E.Talog, what are we going to do then?'

'How...how do you know my name?' She felt a twinge of panic. Her anonymity was gone!

'Your name is sewn into the back of your tee-shirt!'

'Oh crap!'

'So, you're Welsh, all webbed toes and milk sop complexion!' Her thumb ran gently over the skin of Katie's cheek. 'But you're different, aren't you sweetie? Your looks, you're not Welsh, are you, you're something else. You've got a bit of... mystery in you?' She picked an ice cube from her drink. She held it between her thumb and forefinger and dragged it across the rolling contours of Katie's stomach.

'Aaah, that's cold!' Katie gasped. 'Shit, was that first base?'

'Are you kidding me? No, I've not started yet. So Miss Talog, what's it to be?'

'What are the bases again? I'm new to this sort of thing...' Her breath was coming in short, quick gasps.

'Let's just take this one base at a time and see where we get to!'

'No, no, no, where's that ice cube going!' They were touching noses now, and her mouth was gliding slowly towards Katie's firmly closed lips; their hips were pressed tightly against each other; their chests were jockeying for position against each other. She had one hand across Katie's stomach and a camera poised at arms length, with it's lens towards them.

'Your shallow pants, they're making me feel so HOT!'

'Sorry!' said Katie as she tugged her trousers up.

'No! Your breathing, you little idiot, not your...panties!'

Her lips pinched tenderly at Katie's upper lip which was firmly clenched against her lower lip, and a strange 'Mmmm' came from her mouth as she held her breath in. The white woman's glossy lips were kissing Katie's, while Katie's hands gripped the counter and her buttocks clenched tightly against each other.

There was a sharp pang of guilt in her soul which was now overwhelmed by the rhythmic pulsing from her core. There was a momentary, scintillating contact of fluids in her mouth, a pause and then a disarray of random, jagged shapes flashing behind her eyes, with no pattern and then there were shouting voices, then a strangled scream, an acute feeling of hurt, despair, burning tears and then complete darkness. Katie shuddered at this feeling of nothingness that came over, no frame, no structure just the never-ending passage of time.

The woman in white recoiled, her hand left Katie's stomach, and her eyes went wide in shock. 'What was that?'

'Blimey!' whispered Katie.

The woman in white took two staggering steps backwards and wiped her mouth with the back of her hand. Her eyes could not focus. 'What did you do to me?'

'Nothing! You did me, didn't you?'

'You can open your eyes now, you manipulative bitch!'

One eye peeped from below her fringe, 'Oi, that was a bit much, wasn't it?'

'You! You make out your little Miss Innocent, but you're not!' The woman in white quickly preened herself in front of the mirror and then stomped her way out of the washroom.

Katie stretched herself out and stared into the distance. What was that all about? What had she seen? There were urgent, loud voices outside and then the sound of two sets of long limbed women clacking their way out of the pub. 'So, I'm not a little sweetie after all!'

Katie left the washroom cautiously and looked all around her. Paol was standing by the table and watching the two long limbed, slender women leave the pub. 'That's a shame' he murmured to himself. 'What took you so long?' he asked Katie.

'I was just having a lesbian experience in there', she answered casually.

'No! You were doing what?'

'The blonde in the white dress - she jumped me in the ladies!'

'Jumped you? In the ladies? Are you hurt?'

'No, when I say, she jumped me in the ladies, I don't mean she went at me boots first...'

'What did she do to you' Paol asked, 'and more importantly, 'how was it for you?'

'It was all right I think, but we didn't get very far. It wasn't all it's cracked up to be' Katie replied coolly.

'But, she's blonde and hot...and you're not!'

'Well, I have to say that blondes are all very well, but there's something wrong with them, isn't there? They look as if all their colour has been drained out of them...'

'What? What are we talking about?'

'The blonde bird, all talk and...no colour.' She thought she'd lead him on a bit more. 'Now, the brown haired girl, I wouldn't have minded a crack at her!'

'You look like you need a drink, Katie. I know I do! You must tell me all about it!'

'Oh, well, I'm feeling hungry now. Where's my food?'

The Eggs Benedict arrived with a side bowl of fries. 'Are you having any?' she asked.

'No.'

'Good!'

'So are you enjoying that?'

'Mmm' she said as she chomped into the bun and a fork full of chips.

'I think you should eat that with a little decorum.'

She searched through the cruet stand and the plastic sauce sachets. What could he be talking about? 'No, I think it's perfectly fine as it is' she decided.

'Hungry?

'Yes, mmm! Drink?' She held out her hand.

So nothing had changed there, he seemed to be thinking. He unfolded a note and put it in her hand, 'It's a pint of Peregrine's Old Worsnip, for me. Have whatever you want. The dark mild is good. Shouldn't get you too squiffy.'

'P-lease' she countered. And then she was headed for the counter, insinuating her way through the crowd and engaging the barman in animated conversation. And then she was back with a pint of cider and several sample size glasses of ale.

'The Old Worsnip's off, and we couldn't work out what you would like instead so I got a selection for you to work through. I've lined them up in order, light to dark.'

Paol seemed annoyed. 'We? I've been coming here for years and I still don't get that kind of service! And you've been here five minutes and he's giving you free beer? I don't believe it!'

'Just calm down, Paol. It's quite easy, because...I'm so utterly charming!'

'I see. Oh, by the way, where's my change?'

'I put it in the kitty, didn't I?'

'You mean in your pocket.'

'That's what I just said. So are you pleased to see me?'

'Of course, but your timing isn't good.'

Her heart bumped and her breathing ramped up. 'Why?'

'I can't put you up tonight.'

'So, what do I do? Oh, this isn't your annual stock take of your porn collection, is it?'

'No, of course not. Anyway, I don't need an annual stock take, it's all carefully catalogued.'

'Oh, so I'm sleeping in the park, am I?'

'You can stay with a friend of mine, Dorina. She'll meet us here.'

'And who is Dorina? Is she your girlfriend? What will she make of me?'

'You'll get on fine, you'll like her. You're quite alike.'

'Oh, so we're both girls?' She looked into his green eyes and tried to sense what the problem might be. She was still inordinately fond of him even though he was going to betray her.

'It's just for one night' he murmured. How did he label her? That was it, a chippy, mesmerising girl who also happened to be his half-sister. Katie looked at him quizzically over her glass of cider. 'Oi Paol, mesmerising, yes; chippy, no' she said suddenly.

'How do you know what I was thinking?' He averted his eyes as it seemed to have become too uncomfortable to return her gaze.

'When you think, you mouth the words - it's quite sweet actually. Anyway, when you say 'chippy', what do you mean?'

'You know, always in your face, giving it lots of banter.'

'I think you think you're trying to give me a compliment, but you're really not quite managing...'

'It's an observation...'

'Well, just for your information, Paol, all of us girls are mesmerising, lovely, loyal, obliging and chippy...it's you blokes that are the problem, isn't it?'

'Anyway, do you want to take a sip?'

'Not really, it looks vile.'

'I think you'll like this...'

'Go on then.'

She took a sip of the dark, malty looking one. It was vile. 'Ugh, it tastes like poison!'

He wiped her tongue with his napkin. 'Do you know what's particularly interesting about this ale?'

'No idea. Is it all beery, then?' She took a long slurp of cider.

'Good try' Paol said condescendingly, 'but it's something even more interesting than that.'

'Is it made from donkey piss? Because that's what it tastes like...'

'No, that would be really extreme and probably very unpleasant to the taste - Peregrine's don't have their own equipment, they hire spare capacity from other brewers and make special brews using their own recipe and supply locally to pubs and clubs. So they could make this beer in, say Nottingham, and it would have different qualities due to the water and the brewing equipment!'

'I wish I could say that was really interesting but I can't, because I would be lying. You don't want me to lie, do you?'

'I suppose not. Maybe as you mature you will get a taste for the finer things in life?'

'Or maybe not.' She stuffed another forkful of mayonnaise covered chips in her mouth. 'So what else is happening?'

'There's a fancy dress party at the college in a couple of weeks - are you in?'

'It depends - what's the theme and are there lots of fit boys?'

'Lots of fit men, raging hormones, gagging for it.'

'I see, what's the dress code? Random?'

'It's comic book super heroes - I thought I would go as this fine chap!' He flashed his mobile device in front of her face,

'His outfit looks a bit tight - do you think you can carry it off? He's got silvery hair though, hasn't he?'

Paol ran his hand through his hair to show the silver highlights. 'It's not a problem, see?'

'So what have you got lined up for me?' She had a sense of foreboding about this. He showed her a picture of a woman dressed in not so many clothes.

'She seems to be wearing a red swimsuit and not much else. Did she forget to get dressed that day?'

'No, that's her super hero attire.'

'I see. Well, that's like no work rig I've ever seen, unless she's a lifeguard or something...'

'She's not a lifeguard, she has magical powers.'

'If she's got magical powers, why doesn't she magic up some practical clothes?'

'They're brother and sister - don't you think that works really well for us?'

'So, just to be clear, you want me to wear a red swimsuit, red leather boots and some sort of red headdress on my head and a cloak, all for the sake of a fancy dress party?'

'Well, yes, if you feel you can carry it off...'

She groaned.

'Anyway, for your information, the headdress is called a wimple.'

'So, what's a wimple?'

'A wimple is a nun's headdress...'

'So basically, you want me to dress as a nun dressed as a tart, wearing a red swimsuit, is that what you're thinking?'

'Er, yes.'

'Do you realise that what you're thinking is what a filthy minded pervert would think, or someone who is deranged? So which one are you, Paol?'

He made a triangle with his hands and pursed his lips. 'Sooooo, what you're thinking is, what's my motivation for doing this? Is that what you're thinking Katie? Where's the quid pro quo here?'

'Ah, Captain Logic has made an appearance. I think you'd be... quite delighted' she replied, 'and you would crack one off at my expense? Am I close?'

'I see. I was afraid you'd think that. So, you'll think about it?'

'Yes, let me think about that before I give you my final answer of, no... sodding...way.'

'And?'

'That's it.'

'So, that's a 'no' is it?'

'You do not listen, do you Paol, even though you're supposed to be brainy? It was actually a no...sodding...way.' She paused to check that he had taken this in. He wasn't going to let it rest.

'So just to be clear, there is no bribe, no blackmail, no inducement, no level of duress I can put you through which would make you change your mind?' He pushed the handy in front of her again.

'Paol, let me think about this.' She pushed the handy back.

'So, you'll think about it then?' He pushed the handy back towards her.

'I'll think about it.' She could wrap herself in the big, red cloak, so nothing would show. That would cover everything. He must have the costumes already. 'Hmm...'

'What are you thinking, Katie?'

'I'm thinking...I could be up for... a little bit of bribery. What did you have in mind?'

'A sum of money.'

'Not just a pile of klebbies from your last tour of the porn capitals of South-East Asia?' She got a pencil ready and steadied a napkin in front of her.

'No - actual, folding money.'

'Oh, good, good, good' she said as scribbled a figure on the napkin, folded it over and slid it across the table to Paol.

He opened it and threw himself back in his chair. His cry of 'What?!!' rang across the bar and everyone in earshot looked towards the commotion. Katie wondered if she had over-pitched it.

And now he wanted to know what her reasoning was for the figure she had scribbled down.

'Well, Paol, this is what I think. If you want me to dress up like a top class London tart, this is the price tag.'

'Where did you get that from?' He crossed out the trailing '0' and passed the napkin back. 'I am asking you to accompany me to a fancy dress party, that's all!'

'Hmm, I see. Well, if you want me to dress up as a tart, I'm not getting out of bed for less than...' She scribbled an amendment and passed the napkin back.

'Don't you mean, get into bed?' He looked at the new figure. 'What?'

'Don't be coarse, Paol, you know very well what I mean.'

'What exactly do you think a top class tart actually does for this kind of money?'

'How would I know?'

'Go on, you must have some idea!'

'Well...' she murmured as her eyes wandered along the beer spattered ceiling above and tried to recall what she had heard in the messing hall, 'do they ponce around in front of you looking like a costumed twat and give you a... cock massage?'

'A cock massage?'

'Um, yes, orally speaking.'

'And, how would that go?'

'Um, rhythmically and accelerating quickly to...vigorously, hypothetically.'

Paol crossed his legs and grimaced as if he was suffering from a sudden and acute pain in his private parts.

'And a nice bit of licking if you stump up the full sum.'

'Well, thankfully, you won't be expected to do anything like that. I think we can compromise on this figure.'

She took the napkin back and considered this revised figure. 'And there'll be plenty of drink for me and food and not a load of student crap?'

'Student crap?'

'Vegetarian noodles and toffee.'

'Don't you mean tofu?'

'I think that's what I just said...'

'There will be proper nutrition and beverages that will suit all of your various and specialised needs, Katie.'

'Oh, good. And plenty of fit boys?'

'Of course. Dressed as super heroes.'

'Then, I think we have an accordion.'

'An accord even.'

'I think that's what I just said.'

'An accordion is a musical instrument...'

'Indeed, so you can play it to accompany the happy dancing I do when I've just scored myself a great deal.'

'Ah, I'm a mug, aren't I?'

'Well, if you let your cock do your thinking instead of your brain.'

'Do you want to shake on it?'

'Don't be vile!'

'I'll take that as a 'yes'. And you will book time?'

She flourished her diary schedule and blocked out the Saturday that Paol indicated with a finger press.

He gave a huge sigh of relief. 'And is there anything else I can help you with Katie? Anything legal, that is!'

'Yes, there is - I've been invited to do a hen do, on this date.' She illustrated the date by pointing to her planner.

'My, my, you are a busy girl.'

'I am aren't I?'

'And what do you want me to do?'

'Help me sort out the itinerary.'

'Not much then - how did you get lumbered?'

'Well, basically, I was blackmailed.'

'Katie!?!'

'So, there will need to be drinking, dancing, games, naked men and big eats, and we haven't got long to sort this out, have we?'

'Let me work on that - where are we centred?'

'I think it'll have to be by here.'

'I see. And when you say naked men...'

'They could be...partly naked.'

'You're allowing them to wear pants.'

'Yes, temporarily...'

'And they'll need to be fit.'

'Obviously.'

'Good, that's all clear. Anything else?'

'Yes, but you go next.'

'There's something I need to talk to you about...'

'Oh' Katie said resignedly, 'this sounds serious, I'll get the beers in...'

'Katie?'

'Yes, what is it?' she replied as she took a draught from her glass of cider.

'I'm running this war game...'

'Oh, are you still doing that? I thought you'd grown out of that!'

'We're re-playing the German invasion of France in May 1940' continued Paol, 'you know, Blitzkrieg in the West.' He allowed her some time for this to sink in, but she decided not to bite. 'There are a group of us involved and I need a hand with running it.'

'I don't see the point of this?'

'Aren't you interested in why the French and their Allies collapsed so easily?'

'Not really. It's a bit late to do anything about it now, isn't it?'

'There's a scenario coming up that I think you can help with...'

Her ears prickled.

'I don't know how to arbitrate it. I thought you could help as you have considerable experience serving in the Royal Navy!'

'I do have some experience with the Andrew, yes.'

'And I don't know anyone else who has such experience...'

'I might be able to help' she relented. 'What do I need to do?'

'Come with me to Loughton tomorrow and I'll take you through it.'

'Loughton?'

'Yes, it's all laid out on the floor of the pub function room...'

'The landlord must be really pleased about that!'

'It's not a very good pub' Paol quickly explained. 'So, are you up for it?'

'I suppose so. My next posting is to Essex!'

'How wonderful! So can you fit this into your manic schedule?'

She took a quick look in her plan - she had an early morning assignation with Robbie the Blackmailer but the rest of the day was clear. 'I can free myself up from 11am I think.'

'Ah, splendid. So, it would be good if you could wear something... befitting.'

'Something befitting? What do you mean? A red swimsuit?'

'Just anything other than what you're wearing now.'

Katie stood up suddenly and her chair grinded back on the floor. 'Oi, what's the matter with what I'm wearing now?' She was suddenly conscious that there were a large number of males looking in her direction. She sunk back slowly into the armchair. 'What are they all looking at? Have I got a great, big, green grolly hanging out of my nose?'

'You really don't know do you?'

'Know what?'

'Never mind.' He paused for thought. 'They may be thinking that I'm too old for you.'

'Yes, too old and too related.'

'So, how would you characterise your...fashion style, Katie?'

She took a look at the green tee-shirt and her denims: 'Eh? Oh, à la mode I reckon or...maybe smart casual.'

'Some might say, slovenly.'

'Oi, have you been talking to Gwen?'

'Absolutely not, evidence of my own eyes. So what's with the gloves?'

Katie flipped off the gloves and showed her palms, whipped off her hat to show her temple and then settled back in her chair and took a long draught of cider. 'I need to have a little chat with Gwen...I do have other tee-shirts, by the way!'

'How did you get those scars?'

'By fighting...'

'You're not made for fighting, Katie.'

'You're telling me!' As she closed her eyes, she saw wide, brown, smiling eyes narrow suddenly, the tip of the long knife dancing in front of her eyes and then the strike and the sharp, searing pain...

'Anyway, I have a post-grad working for me who would like to meet you.'

She opened her eyes and there was still the babble of lubricated conversations all around her and Paol's curious look. 'Oh, to meet me? How does he know me?' A boy, who wanted to meet her! 'Hold up, what have you told him about me?'

'Girl from the Marches, now in the navy, sporty, fit, likes a drink, completely bonkers...'

'Oi, you!'

Paol had absolutely nailed it.

'So now you're pimping me out to your Post Grad students? That's tidy! And what should I know about him?'

'His name is Udo, he's from Germany and he's tall and good-looking. He's doing a dissertation on the politics of eugenics.'

'You what?'

'Eugenics. We're interested in this Swiss organisation which you've had a dalliance with - The Swiss Institute for Keltic Studies.'

'Oh that, should I be worried?'

'Yes, you should - they have some very controversial ideas.'

'Well, keep checking up on them - I've got an invitation to their Cambridge place.'

'Well, just be careful, they need you as much as you need them.'

'I will.'

She wondered if she should tell him about her date. 'I've got a date tomorrow - with Robbie! He's taking me to Camden Lido!'

'Who's Robbie?'

'I met him on the Underground - he's in the Transport Police!'

'That was quick work Katie. So, why would you want to go to the lido - you can't swim?'

'It's not very deep though, is it?'

'Do you want to borrow a red swimsuit?'

'Piss off Paol! Shorts and tee-shirt will do perfectly well.'

'But you'll be ready for Loughton?'

'Yes, of course. Where's Loughton?'

'Essex.'

'Oh, did I tell you, I've got a posting in Essex!'

'Not in Loughton?'

'No, Shoeburyness.'

'The firing range? What could you possibly be doing there?'

'I'll be ordering trainees around!'

'You know the MOD are closing that site?'

'Noooo! Not before I've done with it!'

'Let me check that for you.'

'Yes, you do that...buggery, buggery, bollocks!'

Dorina announced her presence by quickly arriving at Paol's armchair and sliding onto the arm. 'Hello my friend' she said as she ruffled Paol's hair. 'Is this the sister?' she asked.

'Hello Dorina, I'm Katie. I'm sorry about this.'

'Of course.' Dorina had dark skin with long lustrous dark hair, reaching most of the way down her leather jacket. She wore a black tee-shirt with a skull emblazoned on the front and heavily distressed jeans that appeared to have been slashed through with a sharp knife. 'Don't worry about it, he is my friend and it will be excellent to have your company.'

'I'll meet you outside the underground station at eleven, at the entrance opposite the Underworld' said Paol as his parting shot to Katie. Katie nodded as she and Dorina were left dragging two large bags.

Dorina paused outside. 'We walk' she ordered as they scrambled across the busy road and proceeded down the road opposite, Katie in the wake of Dorina's robust passage through the milling crowd. Now, she turned to issue another order, 'Right turn' to follow a street with tall, town houses bunched in a line, shoulder to shoulder and back to back, hemmed in with nose to tail vehicles.

'I work tonight, what plans are yours?'

'Scran down and rack out...'

'No, no, no, my friend, we work this night!'

'Work?'

Dorina paused at the door of number 132. 'This eve, we embrace the city! Tonight we drink, we sing, we dance, we love, we fuck!' The brown spotted mutt on the step next door, that at first looked like a soiled nappy, looked up briefly but then curled back to sleep; a flock of mottled pigeons lifted from the ledges opposite and wing clapped their way over the red-tiled horizon. The smell of dirt, oil and shit mingled uncomfortably with the smell of exotic spices and frying. Dorina burst through the door into the narrow, dark corridor inside and clattered her way up steps that seemed to twist about and ascend forever.

Suddenly, the stairs ended and they were at a battered door. It was quickly unlatched and they were in a darkened space, below the roof. There was a small window, angled into the eaves and sparse evening light illuminating a single room: it had a sink and a bed and piles of bulging plastic bags and cardboard boxes. There was another door leading to a space below the roof that looked impractical for use as a bathroom unless you were a pygmy.

'Where's the heads?' Katie asked as she dropped her bags in the only bit of the floor which was unoccupied.

'Down the stairs, along the corridor' stated Dorina.

'Oh buggery, buggery, bollocks!' The bed was bigger than a single and the sink did have a drainer, but the drainer was taken up with empty tins, cartons, trays and bottles. Although there were many gash bags, they all looked occupied.

'What are you thinking, my friend?'

'I'm thinking this is a bit of a shithole!'

Chapter Thirty-Two

Friday 13 May 1800 - The Underworld

Dorina brushed past Katie, flounced onto the bed and threw the cupboard door open. 'Throw your bags in there; we will share...'

Katie assessed that the bed was just wide enough to make sharing a viable proposition but it was going to be desperately uncomfortable. There was no space on the floor and the landing had a distinct odour of mutt. She would check out the local parks this evening, ring Paol and beg him, do anything but...

'So, we go to work?'

Katie sighed: 'Yes, we go to work...'

Dorina pulled out two items of clothing from a bag and threw them towards Katie. 'Here, you'll need these.' Katie caught them and tucked them away in her satchel. 'And these.' She now had two black bags to carry.

They left the flat at around six pm and walked quickly south bound. They made good progress until they reached a flood of people emerging from below ground. Now there was someone pressing behind her, much too close. Struggling to turn about she was face to face with a youth under a silver hood, narrow eyed, wide curling lips: 'Yo bitch, come with me.'

Katie met his gaze. He was much too close. 'Show me what you've got then?'

'Don't mess with me bitch!'

'Then show me!'

'You mad bitch!' He pushed her away and pushed his way back through the throng, down below, looked back and then vaulted over the ticket gates.

'Oi prick, you left your self respect behind!' she shouted.

Dorina grabbed her shoulders and pushed her towards the edge of the road. A taxi horn blared out. 'Calm down my friend, he's not worth it.' They stood to one side and scanned the surge of passengers emptying through the narrow concourse.

'Someone's following us, I can feel it' blurted out Katie. A middle aged couple pushed past, over dressed. 'There's many people following us, my friend, see? There's nothing to worry about. Anyway, I am looking after you, so don't you worry...' Katie stood and watched the flood of humanity pass by. 'But I've felt something since we left your place!'

Dorina looked up and down the road. 'You are safe, now come with me...'

They emerged onto the main street and skipped across the road, dodging the hooting cars, to the uncompromising black painted doors that seemed to lead below the ground. Dorina flashed an identification card to the two security guards, picked up her two black sacks again and hauled them down a black painted tunnel. Katie followed.

'You can set up over there, opposite the bar. I'll go here' she indicated with a nod. 'There are two tables. The price list is in the bag. You'll need to write up tickets for the tee-shirts and music and lay everything out! Anya will be along soon, she's the boss lady.' Dorina paused for breath. 'Ask if you need anything, my friend.'

The trestle table was flipped open and erected and Katie stared at it. 'I will kill you Paol, and then I will kill you all over again, and then I will rip off your leg and beat your head to a bloody pulp and when you beg for mercy and think it can't get any worse, I will rip off your other leg and stuff it down your neck until it kills you!'

Anya arrived in a whirl of black chiffon. She embraced Dorina and scowled at Katie. 'Who is this?' she asked accusingly.

'This is my new friend, she is sister of my friend Paol.'

'Half-sister...'

'Does she know how this works? Five percent of what she sells?'

'Ooh, five percent of fuc...!'

'Yes, I've told her' interrupted Dorina.

Had she done all she could to make this collection of black, shapeless musty smelling clothing saleable? The garments had been arranged from small sizes to the left in increasing size to XXXL to the right. Music discs were standing in neat ranks and the table was canted at the back on folded boxes. There was an expanse of white sheet taped to the wall behind and Katie was poised with a black marker pen.

'These will never go at twenty quid a throw' Katie stated, holding up a black, shapeless, musty smelling tee-shirt.

Anya stared accusingly at Dorina: 'You must do something about her appearance – she looks like plain clothes police.'

Katie stared at Anya, her face wrinkled in disbelief. She didn't know what a plain clothes policewoman would look like. Tee-shirt, denims and brown boots could be 'de rigueur' for female police officers going undercover for all she knew. She must have some kind of rejoinder for this ponced-up tart? 'I'm a matelot and I can wear whatever I want! I'm not on duty now!'

Anya shook her head. She seemed to be annoyed. 'Is she kidding me?'

'I'll deal with it' said Dorina as she propelled Katie back down the tunnel and up the stairs. 'Listen my friend, Anya says that we are the face of the band while she's on stage, so...we are part of her company, we make our faces like dolls and we dress for the part. Do you see, my friend? Change your clothes, make your face and we are happy, we work, we make money, we sing, we dance, we make love! Get back soon!'

Katie looked at the plastic bag of tubes and vials that had appeared in her hand. All around her in the bar were people drinking and shouting at each other, except for two men in white shirts with an insignia on the pocket and dark trousers and white shoes who turned together to look her way, recognised who they were looking at and then turned back to resume their meaningless chatter and nonchalant leaning against the counter. A quick shiver made its way up her neck and over her scalp - Katie realised that she would clash with them and the odd couple later. Their disguise as a mature couple going for a nice meal was belied by their quick furtive glances and pretence of indifference towards her as she walked on by. Going to the Ladies heads meant walking past them again so Katie circumnavigated the ground floor of the building until she couldn't circumnavigate any more.

A tattered, vermilion curtain drawn across the passage barred her way; Katie hoped somewhere ahead was a place where she could regain control of her breathing and her pounding heart. A woman came from behind the curtain. At least she appeared to be a woman, with her red corset straining and her careworn fish net stockings and her unfeasibly tall red heels. 'You looking for somewhere to change, darling? Just follow me!'

Beyond the curtain were tables, all surrounded by the young men and women, clandestine and other-worldly, waiting expectantly for the show to begin. But what was on show?

'Am I in the right place?' Katie asked.

'You're here to perform?'

'Well, no not really.'

'First night nerves, darling? Don't worry, I'll look after you. You can call me Scarlet. Let's pop you in here and I'll get Tamara.'

She was led through another pair of heavy curtains and now she was in an ante-room with a white chair and a white dressing table and racks for hanging clothes. Kneeling on the chair, was a woman in front of a mirror, carefully applying circles of red lipstick around her nipples.

'There's someone already in here' Katie shouted out of the room.

'Shhh darling, this isn't the London Palladium. Just get on with it. I'll send Tamara in to sort you out.'

Katie looked askance at the changing woman. 'Don't you think you should get some clothes on. You'll get a lot of strange looks when you go back out there, won't you?'

'What's that?' said the woman as she hauled on a big pair of black knickers and a bra that was several sizes too big. She seemed preoccupied with dressing. And then she paused. 'What do you think you're looking at?'

'I really don't know, I think I might be in the wrong place...' Another pair of black pants went on and a diaphanous, white blouse.

And then black stockings and a leopard print skirt. 'Why are you putting on so many clothes? It's a bit warm out there!'

'So I can remove them, of course!' She looked Katie down and then up. 'Are you going on like that?!'

'I'm not going on like anything, am I?'

'What are you doing here then?' the woman said dismissively.

'I've come here to change, haven't I?' The woman seemed to be going through a difficult phase of doing up straps and buttons. 'So, are you on a first date then, or are you just playing hard to get?'

A white leopard print jacket went on followed by a chiffon scarf, knotted around her neck and this completed the ensemble. There was loud, brassy music from behind the curtain - the kind of music she had heard in a Pompey night club during a run ashore, where women take their clothes off artistically, to loud cheers from the matelots. Her left arm started to agitate in response to a dose from her adrenalin pump.

The woman left the dressing room to be replaced by another - this one had a clipboard, an air of authority but an equal lack of sensible clothing. Katie tried hard not to look down but this woman sported what seemed to be a black swimsuit that had got shredded in a rogue washing machine. 'Who are you dear?'

'Hallo, I call myself Katie.' This woman seemed to be in charge, despite her garb, so she should be able to clear things up.

'Oh, do you? Well you're not on my list.'

'Why should I be on your list?'

'If you want to perform, I need to know your details - what music are you performing to?' she asked Katie.

Katie was standing rigidly still with a fist full of clothing in one hand and a plastic bag of cosmetics in the other. 'I didn't think I was performing, did I? I thought I was just selling?' This didn't seem to satisfy Tamara. 'I don't know what music they play; they probably have guitars and drums and a singer, I think.'

'You have your own band?' was the incredulous response.

'Well, no, they're not actually mine...'

'There's not a lot of room out there. Its best if you let me sort out the music. What are you dancing to?'

'I'm not dancing - I'm just selling stuff.'

'Whatever. Let's see you with your kit on then.' She nodded to the knot of clothing in Katie's hand. 'Get it on, quickly!'

'Turn around then!'

Katie turned into the corner of the room removed her boots and then her denims and pulled on the skirt. This didn't seem to satisfy Tamara, so she lifted the teeshirt off and then hesitated.

'No bra?'

'No bra. Not sure that to do with this, either?' Katie handed the corset into Tamar's writing hand.

'It will do. Let me help you with that. No, no need to turn around. What happened to your shoulder?'

'Oh that? I got bitten.' Katie's nose wrinkled. 'Actually, it's a tattoo that went wrong.'

'If you say so.' Tamara pulled the laces tight and the effect was quite breathtaking.

I'm going to have to wear my shirt and my jacket, Katie thought to herself.

'So, how are you going to perform this?'

'I'll need someone to help, won't I?'

'I like it. Audience participation' Tamara commented.

'You what?'

'Now, make up.' There was a raucous cheer outside to a crescendo in the music - something good must have come off. 'Needs to be quick and creative - black lipstick, very 'a la mode' and grey shadow and let's accentuate those brows...' With a few quick strokes, Tamara seemed satisfied. 'I know, we'll call you Goth Girl!'

'Am I ready now?' Katie asked. Her socks and brown boots seemed to be at odds with her bare legs.

'Music? I think I have just the thing...'

'There's really no need...'

Tamara tugged at the waistband of her skirt and looked down below. 'Oh dear, they're not very nice are they?'

'They're perfectly serviceable...'

'I'm just saying, it will be a major anticlimax when you take your skirt off...'

'What! I'm not taking my sodding skirt off! Why should I? What is this?'

'First night nerves - don't worry we've all been there!' she said, trying to calm her by stroking Katie's arm.

'Just back off, or you'll be wearing this!' Katie had a narrow metal cylinder in her hand - she twisted the cap off and pointed it threateningly at Tamara's face. The curtains whisked apart - arms encircled her shoulders and pulled her sharply back. The arms were wrapped in leather - they were Dorina's.

Tamara was hiding behind the clipboard. It now had a streak of 'Witching Hour' across it. 'I get it' she muttered, 'she's one of yours!'

'What's going on?' shouted Katie. There was jeering across the room - a woman in mid-strip had a leg up on a table and a stocking half way down.

'It's burlesque night, tonight, my friend' said Dorina, 'strippers only back there.' She closed the curtain behind her and pulled Katie away. 'I worry that you left me for so long.'

'Strippers? They thought I was a stripper?'

'Yes, my friend, a mistake; wrong girl, wrong place.' She manoeuvred Katie up against to the floque papered wall in the corridor. 'You need to be made up, your face is missing...' Dorina eased back her hair. 'Your hair, it is not good colour, but it is strong.' Dorina moistened a handkerchief, pinched Katie's cheek and removed excess lipstick. 'I can't do anything with your hair but we can patch your eyes and lips. Pucker up!' She seemed to be working away excess make up. 'Just your mouth, not your face.'

Katie closed her eyes and grimaced.

'No, pucker, not pout!'

'Nuhhh.'

'Your skin, it is translucent, like mother of pearl. Stop scrunching up your face, this is difficult.'

'Nuhhh.'

'I think you will do. It's dramatic, plenty of eye shadow and lipstick, but not too much.' She had finished her repair work.

Katie unclenched her face and peeped out under her fringe.

'You have special powers over men, don't you my friend?'

Dorina had finished her work but Katie chose not to review it in detail as she passed the mirror in the corridor. The sensation around her eyes and mouth was like she had a layer of animal grease smeared on her face. A tentative lick of her lips confirmed this. Hopefully it would be badly lit downstairs in the venue; maybe she could find a wide brimmed hat that would shelter her face and then in a quiet moment, wipe the grease away when Dorina was not looking.

'What is the matter, my friend...'

'I feel like a dirty slapper. Why did you lay it on so thick?'

'To give drama in your appearance and drama in your performance...'

'But, I'm just flogging a load of mouldy old tat...aren't I?'

'No! I don't know what you mean? We sell, we make money, we sing, we...'

'Yes, I heard all that, but...'

They made their way quickly through the bar. There was a merry throng of drinkers, with no one seemingly out of place.

'You know how a man thinks my friend and you can change the way men see you, isn't that so?'

'No' Katie replied, 'it's not so, is it? 'She tried to work out what this accusation meant as they marched down the dark tunnel into the bowels of the building. 'Actually, if that's so, it's because I'm so charming, isn't it?'

'You are a threat to all women my friend - you have the power to steal their men!'

'Bollocks!'

'But you no longer look like a plain clothes police woman - I have seen to that! You may have trouble fighting off the men though.'

The doors to the tunnel opened and the bowels of the building started to fill.

'We get ready and we start selling. The doors are open! There will be a flood of punters soon now!'

They both set to work with the gathering crowd of black tee-shirted, unruly haired, ageing men and women. After thirty minutes Katie had acquired a telephone number written on her arm, several beery embraces and featured in half a dozen snapshots. The support band arrived on stage and the first jangling chords rang out.

As the bar emptied in one direction, a man entered from the stairwell, and cast around furtively, scanning faces – he looked uncomfortable and out of place - an unspectacular man in a white, monogrammed short-sleeve shirt and dark trousers. Katie was standing by the wall behind the tables – she leaned forward, caught Dorina's eye and signalled his presence with her thumb. He moved to a position at the back of the room so he could view the traffic in and out of the bar area.

The support band finished and there was a flood of new arrivals at the stand. Anya arrived to help. 'Look' she announced pulling Katie close and pointing at their twin faces, 'we could be sisters!'

After another thirty minutes, the stock on the trestle table had nearly cleared. Anya handed a set of car keys over to Katie. 'There's another two bags in the back of our van, it's the blue camper van at the side, can you get it?'

Katie nodded, 'Do you know the bloke standing at the back. I think he's been watching me.'

'You get all sorts of creeps in her, don't worry, I'll keep an eye on him.'

Katie handed over her tally sheet to Anya, underlined the bottom line and then took the tunnel and the stairs to street level. She smiled sweetly at the security guards and moved quickly around the old Victorian frontage to the van. As she opened the side door there was a reek of stale clothes and food. The black gash bags were where Anya had told her and she pulled them out of the van. She froze mid breath - her stalker was outside talking animatedly on his phone. Her beanie hat was pulled down as far as it would go to hide all her hair, the van was locked with a rasp of metal against metal and she ducked inside the ground floor entrance to the pub. He followed her in. She clutched the bags fiercely and slid between three men nursing pints in their big, male fists. 'How do you get a drink around here?' she wondered out loud as she looked into the smiling eyes of a stocky man who had long, black receding hair and a long forehead and narrow-rimmed spectacles.

'There's the bar' he pointed out.

'Oh yes...'

'You with the band?'

Her heart sank. The two men in white monogrammed shirts were back at the bar, talking into a cell phone, and the odd couple were back. He was short and broad, built like a squat brick outhouse with red skin showing at his neck and cuffs and the most extraordinary shock of white hair: she was in a dark grey suit, with short ordinary, brown hair.

Her triumvirate were talking bollocks about the band they had just seen. 'They were great, it's the first time I've seen them. The lead singer has a great voice, hasn't she?'

'Yes, and doesn't she know it! Great songs too...'

'I've got their discs and tee-shirts here and I can let you have them at a great price' Katie said quietly.

'You still here?'

Katie slipped out from the group and quickly secreted herself behind a pillar. The men were still talking on the phone. 'Yes, she's in the building but she's not alone.' Katie concentrated her senses on their voices, and what they could be thinking. Suddenly, they stopped talking; she sensed they were looking round the pub. She held her breath. The couple walked out quickly. Katie gathered the bags again, turned right past security and ran down the tunnel.

Anya was there with her hands on her hips. 'At last! What took you so long?'

'I was hiding! There's four of them and they're all after me!'

'Four! What have you done?'

'Nothing!'

'Four?'

'Yes, four!'

'Are these two of them?' asked Anya.

'Yes! Yes!'

'First Aiders.'

'They're never first aiders!'

'Look at the way they're dressed!'

'If they are proper first aiders, why are they following me? Do I look like I'm about to have an accident?'

'No, you look like you've already had it - but just in case you're right, come out with us at the end of the gig and jump in the back of the camper van.'

Katie thought about this for a moment. 'Actually, I'll take my chances on the street - Dorina's quite fearsome.'

There was a surge at the stand - the headline act came on. She had no time to consider her predicament. And then the crowd was gone, leaving two men. They stared. Katie vaulted the table and squeezed her way into the throng heading into the darkness, but it was too slow, too slow. She vaulted the stairway to her right, followed the black wooden panelling that led backstage and ran into a wall. But it wasn't a wall. It was a bloke dressed in black shirt and trousers, his arms folded, solid as a brick built bunker.

'Band only back here!' he announced.

The man in black held Katie firmly by her elbows.

'Those first aiders, they're following me!'

'Band only back here!'

'I'm with the band, aren't I?'

'Never seen you before...'

'I'm new, aren't I?'

'Nah.'

'Ask someone in the band.'

His neck rotated slowly, like a capstan hauling up the anchor. She dropped down, pulled her arms free, ducked beneath his arm and she was past him, past tall black boxes and skipping over cables. She was backstage.

'Band only back here!' came a shout in her wake.

'What's up?' asked the boy on the stage with a guitar slung around his neck.

'I'm being chased!'

'Don't worry about him, girl, he's only security!'

'Those first aiders...'

'Who?'

'Look, in the crowd, there's one with stalky crab eyes and one with sneaky ferret eyes! Look, can't you see?' Katie pointed towards two white-shirted figures at the back of the crowd. The boy fingered the fret on his bass guitar.

The muscles of her long bones bumped to vibrations through the air and through the floor. She was drawn towards the source of the pulsing. The bass guitar, the stomping of feet, the rhythmic shouts. She was on the stage. A mass of faces were looking at her. She peered over the mass of heads and saw her targets - they were towards the back, alongside the mixing desk. She stared; they stared back; Anya stared; hundreds stared - at her. Her body broke into an on-the-spot, rhythmic bounce.

Anya was ready to deliver her message. Her arms stretched out to to the bobbing crowd and she shouted, 'I...I...I...I...' The crowd howled and joined her chant.

'No matter what you do,
No matter what you say,
Fight me all you can,
But I will prevail!'

'I...I...I...I...'

'No matter what you say,
No matter what you do,
Fight me all the way,
But I will prevail!'

'I...I...I...I...'

Katie cued the front row, steadied herself and launched herself. In long, languorous strokes, she was carried by willing arms forward and across the sea of bobbing heads. The bass rolled up and down the scales interspersed with chopping guitar strokes. She swatted away hands that explored too much but now she was close. A somersault took her to her feet and she ran at them. They turned, scrambled around and fled in a melee of arms and bodies. They were gone!

The band was still playing the same grumbling riff. She made herself some space, two quick strides and launched herself back into the crowd. She was passed quickly and reverentially back to the stage. Anya stared at her and the bass player grinned at her and the lead guitarist's right hand massaged the strings and the howl split the air.

'I...I...I...I...'

'No matter what you say,
No matter what you do,
Fight me all the way,
But I will prevail!'

'I will prevail!'
'I will prevail!'
'I will prevail!'
'I will prevail!'

The crescendo of wailing strings harmonised with a roar from the crowd.

'Take a bow girl!' someone shouted but the man from security was waiting and he didn't look happy.

'Band only back here!'

Katie nodded to the crowd and skipped stage left. She was back at the trestle table and drinking quickly from the glass she had left there. Time to reconcile her thoughts and the proceeds from the evening. The remaining stock was stashed away and Katie and Dorina cashed up. She pocketed her share.

But, it was no good just seeing off the first aiders - she would have to confront the odd couple too. Katie ignored the shouts for her to join the band on stage for a final curtsey - instead she headed up the dark tunnel with her satchel over her shoulder and a pint glass in her hand.

Katie took the pint of cider upstairs, turned the corner to the right ascended the stairs and stopped. Her heart leapt up into her gullet. He was here, in front of her, with his red tanned, cone shaped head and all his tanned flesh in folds around his neck. But he was wide and carried his width like a weight lifter or a boxer or wrestler. She took several breaths - she wouldn't want to bump into him on a dark night. 'Oh my soul, you scared the living shit out of me!' She took a step back. He took a step forwards. If she took another step back she would be falling down the stairs.

'Ah, Miss Talog, we meet again.' His voice was deep and slow as if he considered each word carefully before uttering it.

'Oh no, I don't think so!' Her heart was pounding against her ribs. But this was the encounter she had to have. She must just pull up her big girl knickers and get on with it. 'I think I would recognise anyone as...special as you!' Bugger, she had meant to say 'as distinguished as you'. She found her arm was in a strong grip and she was being propelled outside the building and now, across the road.

'I'm glad our paths have crossed' he continued, 'I need to talk to you with some urgency. You could be our salvation!' Her stomach started to knot - he was in charge and there was nothing she could do about it. He led her through a swinging door into the kebaberie and they quickly settled at a table - a waiter came to the table but he was shooed away. 'Miss Talog, my name is Herr Letsch, Herr Ulrich Letsch, as you know, I work at the Swiss institute for Keltic Studies - here is my card. I work in the same Institute as Herr Glaus.' He pushed a business card towards her, but she was staring at the large tuft of white hair that grew out of his forehead. If this tuft could be teased into a cone he would be a rhinoceros. She looked down at the card.

'Why have you spelt Celtic with a 'K' - that's wrong surely?' The rest of the words on the card just made a fuzzy mess.

'Miss Talog, do you realise your importance?'

This seemed a strange tack to take, what could he possibly mean? Unless this was his way of offering congratulations on her advancement to leading hand and another five years with the Andrew. And now she realised she was very hungry.

'No, I don't realise.' The waiter came by again; he seemed curious about what they would be drinking. There was still a part full glass of cider in front of her. Ulrich ordered an espresso and a glass of iced water and offered the same for Katie. She wondered about having a chaser for the cider and also some food, so she ordered a lamb kebab with plenty of sweet chilli sauce and fries and some happy juice to follow. Did they have Calvados? There was no Calvados or Armagnac. Another glass of cider would have to suffice. Did she want ice with it? Why does it need ice, she wondered? Perhaps you should keep it somewhere cool? Yes, so you should, but it is best served over ice. She agreed to his proposal.

She turned her attention back to Letsch as he seemed to be getting quite agitated - he had been rattling on about SIKS, the Swiss Institute that could not spell 'Celtic' properly. But now the pauses in his speech were getting longer and longer.

'I have carried out some research that indicates that there is a molecule in your blood that is of...considerable interest to us.'

'Oh yes, and how would you know that?'

'Ah, excellent question.'

'Unless you've tested some of my blood? So, how did you manage that?'

He paused to stroke his chin.

The ordinary looking woman was now standing to Katie's left side, only she wasn't ordinary, not at all. 'Hallo, Missy, fancy us meeting like this!'

The mole-woman just nodded.

'There's something unique about your heritage, your genealogy as it is called. We can make predictions about your biochemical make-up.' She guessed he wasn't talking about lipstick, eye shadow or any other kind of slap.

The drinks arrived and sure enough, there was ice floating in hers - she methodically picked out the cubes and placed them in the middle of the table.

'That's not the point - how do you know that?'

'I have just explained.'

'No, you haven't.' She flicked an ice cube at him and it landed in his lap. 'Do they make this cider strong, so that the ice doesn't dilute the flavour', she wondered out aloud.

The meat kebab and the fries arrived. She squirted mayonnaise over them and offered them across to Letsch - he declined.

He was still busy brushing the lap of his trousers. 'Herr Glaus tells me that you are invited to our Cambridge facility so we can better explain what we do. Is this still agreeable to you?'

'Of course, I've promised, haven't I?'

'Tomorrow.'

'No, not tomorrow.' Her left arm trembled. Were they going to take her by force? Because, she wasn't anywhere near ready for this.

'Tomorrow, you will be collected at 9am.'

'I'm sorry, but I think we need to agree some ground rules - I'll come when I agreed I would come and Robert will bring me. That's one rule.'

'I knew she was going to be difficult' said the mole-woman.

'And second, when I do come, you are not going to stick anything in me.'

'Miss Talog, we carry out clinical trials on patients and we need your permission before 'we stick anything in you'!'

'Ha! So you say, but it's still not right to stick stuff that doesn't belong into people just to see what happens.'

'Everything we do is regulated by your government - there are strict rules we must follow. Come to our facility tomorrow and we will show you everything we do - and how you can help us.'

'I will come when I'm ready...' Katie now realised that she was in serious trouble - the first aid crew were outside the restaurant, having a quick roll-up; the restaurant looked worryingly empty as the staff were busy working in the back rooms, '...otherwise, I don't see how I can help you.'

'If you don't we will have to consider other options, in other parts of your family tree, for example.'

This was rapidly getting out of control. 'Over my dead body!' she said and instantly regretted it.

'That seems to be a bit of an over-reaction, Miss Talog.'

'No, I didn't quite mean that.'

'I suggest a compromise. Allow me to take a sample and we will test it prior to your visit.'

'Oh no, you won't!'

'It will ensure that we do not waste your time.'

'Yes, but I don't like the sound of that.' If the test result was not what it should be, she would not get into the facility, and one arm of the spiral would unravel and break and everything, especially the promise, would be broken. It would be best if it was done on her arrival on the 16th - this should allow her all the time she needed.

'I must press you on this, Miss Talog.'

She moved to catch his long, delicate hand in hers but he moved it away with the speed of a boxer avoiding a quick jab.

'Listen, how about if I came up earlier on the day?'

'No, that will not do.'

She stared into his green eyes but he flipped down a pair of sunglasses - she twisted her neck to get a deep look into them but his eyes darted away under their protective lenses. He was fencing her away like a skilled swordsman, like a boxer evading every jab of hers, every move she made.

'You have led us a merry dance Miss Talog, but now we get down to serious business.' He produced a clear plastic tube, the shape and size of a cigar holder. 'And now Miss Talog, please open wide...'

'Sod that!' Katie responded.

Her arms were pinioned behind her back - the mole-woman!

'Ah, but you are such a fine specimen.' Katie tried to shrug off his hand from her jaw but his grip was immensely strong. 'Say 'Ah'!' She kicked out but her knees crashed uselessly into the unyielding frame of the table. The swab was in her mouth and brushing the inside of her cheek. It was withdrawn and neatly inserted into its container. He let go and she tried to straighten her jaw. Instead, she gagged and a gobbet of yellow bile appeared in her glove. She wiped it away.

'Thank you!' said Letsch. 'Would you like a napkin?'

She was coughing. 'Is that all I am to you, a sodding specimen?'

'Ah, but such a specimen! But you are right, a damaged specimen is a major issue. Should we consider a bodyguard for you? It would be a critical issue if you were harmed or killed?'

Her eyes had welled up with tears. 'Yes, that would be a bit of an issue, wouldn't it?' As she tried to clutch the bread of her kebab tightly, her thumb could not properly oppose her fingers. A chunk of meat fell out of the kebab and bounced on the table, followed by a shower of sliced cabbage and tomato.

'Be careful, Miss Talog, you're losing everything' he noted wryly. He stood up, did a little pirouette and he was out of the restaurant, handing the tube that contained her essence to the first aid team outside.

Chapter Thirty-Three

Saturday 14 May 0013 - Camden Road

Katie waited outside the kebaberie until Dorina appeared. Now all she wanted to do was rest. The inside of her cheek was sore and her bottom jaw ached. They walked back to the flat in silent company, matching each other, stride for stride.

'What happened to you, my friend?' asked Dorina.

'You know those people who were following me? Well, they grabbed me - that's what happened!'

'We go back. I call the polizia. I will make this right!'

'When I say grabbed, I mean they stuck a cotton bud inside my mouth and swizzeled it around!'

'You keep very strange company, my friend.'

They climbed the stairs to Dorina's flat, and now Katie would have to confront the issue of the sleeping arrangements.

They sat in bed, uncomfortably close. Whenever Dorina's naked legs brushed Katie's she inched her own legs away as carefully as she could, so there was enough of a gap. Dorina insisted on braiding two strands of Katie's hair, to frame her face, as they drank the hot beverages that Katie had prepared, NATO style. Her legs now cosseted Katie's hips, pressing in as she worked neatly and efficiently at her task. Katie stiffened. It was agreed that they would sleep top to tail. And now there was the problem of Dorina's chain smoking. Katie flapped away the smoke with the quilt they were sharing. She felt like she was being pickled like a herring. But suddenly, she switched off and she was asleep.

That was, until the knocking on the bedroom window started. Katie turned over and encountered Dorina's sharp-toed feet. She turned again but the noise persisted.

'Who's out there?' called out Katie in panic.

Dorina quickly explained, 'It's Gigi. He has adopted me, he's always here after closing time. His owner must throw him out every night.' Dorina left the bed and creaked the window open.

'Who's cat?' asked Katie. Must be a pub cat she thought.

'He's a ginger tom. I call him Gigi, after one of our national heroes!'

Gigi squeezed in through the window, bit by bit, like a train of furry cotton reels, strung together with elastic. He seemed a very confident and cocky cat. So cocky, he jumped onto the bed and there he concatenated in and concatenated out. But then suddenly, arching his back, he spat and yowled at Katie. She arched her spine and spat back, removed a sock and swatted him. He swiped back and snagged her sock.

'You evil, slit eyed bastard' she howled.

Gigi howled, leapt backwards and scrambled an ungainly exit through the window. The sock was trailing from his nasty, spiteful, little mouth.

Katie grimaced: 'I don't believe it! As if today couldn't get any worse, I'm a sock down to a cat!' She looked pensively out of the window across the rooftops. 'I seem to have this effect on male cats. And also male men' she added. She sucked in a draught of air and listened - there was a voice singing, singing a nursery rhyme.

Dorina had gone back to sleep so she shook her. 'Are you awake?' Katie hissed.

'Yes, I am now. What is it?'

'Did you hear that noise?'

'There are many noises my friend. This is the great city of London!'

'The singing noise...'

'Singing? Drunken singing? There's always singing. It's a drunk outside. You only need to tell me if the singing gets inside the building and the singing starts to come up the stairs! Now sleep!'

'It's a little voice singing.' Dorina was asleep again. Katie pulled a tee-shirt over her frame and looked out of the garret window. The voice was outside, across the rooftops.

The window was small and opened out onto a series of undulating tiled roof tops. She squeezed through the gap, and alighted onto the flat roof. The moon was bright and misted over. A soft light shone all across the roof tops. Katie could see a pale, hunched figure, softly mewling to itself. It was two roofs away. Katie picked her way towards the figure, as stealthily and as quickly as she could. She reached the position but there was no one there. And now she could hear playground chanting - but in the middle of the night?

She saw the figure stretch and jump athletically across a wide gap, but she could get no closer, despite her best efforts to scramble quickly along the tiled roofs. The figure dragged a knitted doll behind her; a doll with a pointed end, body cloaked in wool, face with a long nose; so long was the nose, that it was the most practical way to drag the doll across the roof tiles and through the blackened gutters. Katie wanted to run and rescue the doll, so she jumped the wide gap, teetering on the edge for a heart leaping moment.

They were close to where the railway ran at rooftop height. The figure padded easily up to the line, passed through the safety fence and stood between the hulking, iron rails. They vibrated, subtly at first and then with increasing and threatening vigour.

'Get off the tracks! Run, run!' Katie ran to the line. The train was close and rushing headlong towards them. The doll was draped across the line. The figure smiled as if it knew what was going to happen next...

Katie was through the fence. The train's klaxon blared out its useless, futile warning. The passage of the train threw her backwards against the fence. She slumped on the gravel, grazed knees down, looking across the tracks. The figure was gone; the doll was amputated across the waist, still draped across the iron of the black, corroded rail, strands of wool like entrails, waving pitifully in the aftermath of the passage of the train.

Katie picked up the doll, a symbol of the danger she was getting into, the severed strands of wool like the severed strands of the spiral, and here she was, entangled in a bad dream.

Entangled in a bad dream? No, it was just her sock.

Somewhere, back in the distant reaches of her mind, Katie recalled a stupid rhyme:-

'One: You arrive all bare,
Two: You pretend to care,
Three: We all stare,
Four: You want to pair,
Five: Lose all your hair!
Six: She's a nightmare!
Seven: Scream, if you dare!'
'Scream, if you dare!'

It was from the school playground, children all around, linking hands to encircle her, and as each line of the rhyme ended, a child pulled in the ring towards her, to aim a kick at her legs, or to pull a face. The teachers stood by, arms folded, impassive, tutting at the new girl, frowning at her clothes, the pinafore dress that scraped the tarmac, the tattered buttonless blouse.

'That's nice, they're making friends with the new girl!'

'They've got to keep themselves occupied, haven't they? Anyway her ma doesn't care for her, look at her clothes? Why should anyone else care?'

'Scream, witch! Scream, witch! Scream witch! Scream!' the children screamed.

She was as a cat, surrounded by a pack of dogs, all snapping. Her body straightened, her arms stretched out and she shrieked; they scattered, all screaming, chased by bursts of whirling wind. And then she was alone, other than a shouting teacher and the pile of sweet wrappers that chased each other around in a swirling circle.

Her outstretched arm was seized and she was pulled along, legs scrambling, into the schoolhouse, away from the blessed kids, into a dark, stale smelling room.

'Sit down, girl' he said. She looked around and then settled on the little, yellow painted, small-person's chair. The teacher was nicely dressed, all in black with a neat white collar. Katie gave him her best smile, the one that creased her cheeks and made them go scarlet and made him go scarlet too.

He did not realise this yet, but he was already under her spell.

Katie looked back across the moonlit rooftops, back the way she had come. And there was that sodding cat, Gigi, still taunting her, with his four immaculate white socks and her, with just one and a half grey ones.

Gigi led her way, leaping the gaps with practiced ease and showing Katie the best places to land. The window to the garret was thankfully not secured. She squeezed in after Gigi and they settled together on Dorina's bed.

'Did you get your sock back?'

'Hmm...'

'Can I have a shower' asked Katie.

'Go back to sleep' murmured Dorina.

'Can I have a shower' asked Katie again.

'There is no shower.'

'Can I have a bath then?'

'Down the stairs and along the corridor. Help yourself, my friend. You will need money for the meter.'

'Bath not included?'

'No.'

'What's for breakfast?'

'So many questions...'

'So few answers - what's for breakfast?'

'Coffee and a cigarette.' With that, Dorina turned over and went back to sleep.

Katie spent the next few minutes organising two scrubbed mugs on the drainer, a towel, shower wash, body squirt, brossing brush and brossing paste. She was ready for her expedition to the bathroom.

Down the stairs and along the corridor to the door, where she found that the lock was broken. The meter was outside in a cupboard which no longer had a door.

A man left the bathroom with a loincloth around his waist and a towel wrapped around his head. The room was now clear, apart for the brown staining along the bottom of the bath and the black mould on the walls. No matter. She tinkered with the meter until it recognised that sufficient coinage had been put in.

A large gobbet of gel was squirted in followed by quarter of a bath of barely lukewarm water. No matter. This would be a quick splash.

Katie splashed, stepped out and towelled herself down, her mind trying to work out the coming day's plan. All her mind could work on was her weariness and her hunger. She would have to run all that off.

She was stumbling down the stairs, pulling a training shoe onto each foot, and pushing out of the door into the street. The white and brown mutt looked up and curled back to sleep. Katie looked up and down the street - something about the look of the right angled aspect appealed to her. And she was away, passing the row of Saturday sleeping slums, shiny silver cars and gutter dirt, her legs pattering along the paving stones. Now, she was off the road and running along a canal towpath and onto the grass of a green space with her feet fleetingly pressing the turf, now pushing hard, past the dog walkers and their dogs, the old man on the bench, the couple wrapped in a blanket in the bushes and now, the smell of baking and bacon and coffee.

She stopped. Her lungs were burning and her heart was pounding against her ribs. To do: breakfasting, dress-shopping, lido-ing, war gaming, big eating. She had the weekend ahead all planned, before Robert collected her on Monday morning, so she would have to pin Paol down before then.

A mug of tea and coffee, two bacon rolls and two cinnamon custard tarts paid for with the help of last night's earnings and she was on her way back to Dorina's, along the sun-dappled streets, past the rippling trees, pushing through the door of the tenement and climbing the stairs to the garret. The door was slightly ajar and there was a space on the bed, just right for bouncing on. Dorina stirred, sat up and reached for her cigarettes.

'Coffee!' announced Katie.

'Uhh.'

'Breakfast. Get it down your neck!'

'Uhh.'

'I need a dress and you're going to help me find it!'

'Give me a minute...' The cigarette was in her mouth but with no means to light it, it just hung there. Dorina got up and splashed her face with water from the sink tap. She managed to strike a match, but the cigarette would not light, no matter how hard she sucked on it. There was a deep breath and then a long hiss of exhalation. 'What time is it?'

'Eight, it's late, we need to...'

'Eight! I need to sleep!'

'I'll give you fifteen...'

'You'll give me nothing, I go back to bed...'

'Dress shopping...'

'Dress shopping?'

'Drink your coffee, eat your bacon butty...'

'All right, all right. Fifteen?'

'Yes, fifteen minutes. I found some mugs!'

'I have mugs?'

'You do now!'

'You are the most annoying girl...'

CHAPTER THIRTY-FOUR

Saturday 14 May 0830 - Camden Market

Katie and Dorina emerged out of the door onto the avenue and turned left. It was a short walk to the market where stalls were still being erected along both sides of the street. One stall consisted of a series of mobile coat hangers which were packed with multi-coloured garments.

'Ciao Christina.'

Christina could well be Dorina's sister, thought Katie: she wore a leather jacket, a black tee-shirt and tight, black leather trousers and boots, and despite the time of day, sunglasses. Her black wavy hair waved its way down to her waist and she continually flicked away a wave that kept springing over her face with a hand that seemed to have a cigarette permanently glued to the fingers.

'Ciao Dorina.'

'My friend is looking for a dress to please her brother.'

'I say, buy a dress that pleases yourself, not your brother...'

'I don't know anything about dresses...'

'What size?'

'My size' said Katie, illustrating this through use of her hands to outline the contours of her body.

'How much?'

'All of it...'

'How much to spend?'

'Twenty?' suggested Katie.

This triggered a bout of head shaking and then shrugging by Christina and Dorina. Christina looked up and down the racks. 'I have nothing like that.'

'Paol just wants me to wear something nice today.'

'Sexy nice or nice nice' asked Dorina. She seemed quite irritable this morning.

'I'm not sure what that means.'

'He could mean a corset, stockings and suspenders?'

'I think he meant a dress.'

'What's inside your wardrobe?'

'What's a wardrobe?'

'Never mind.' Dorina lit another cigarette. 'I will help you my friend...'

'Oh thanks. Did you date him for very long?'

'Who?'

'Paol.'

'Date? Yes, I did, but it went nowhere - he was already in a long term relationship.'

'With his porn collection?'

'Ah, yes!'

'He's a dirty sod, isn't he? So, what happened? Did it all get in the way?'

'Yes, you could say that. Anyway, I'm here for you today, my friend. Let's not talk about Paol.'

'Let's not.' Katie decided that she would have to do something about her brother, after she had got what she needed from him. I will set him up with a woman, she decided.

'Where are you wearing the dress?'

'Well, basically, on my shoulders.'

'I mean...'

'Oh I see. Loughton.'

'Loughton?'

'Yes, it's in Essex...'

'Loughton, Loughton, Loughton...'

'Ah, so you want to look like a chav - just wear a track suit then!'

'That's what I said, but Paol said I look slovenly. He said wear something nice. I think he probably means a dress.'

'Do you have any dresses? What length do you like to wear?'

'No dresses.' She looked through the hangers. 'I wear a skirt on dress days, to be fair, below the knees.'

'And you will wear that hat and those gloves?'

'Of course.'

'You are a strange, strange girl. How about this one?'

'There's not much of it is there? And I'm not sure about the colours - orange, brown and white? It looks like buffet night at the local curry shop!'

'Why don't you try it on?'

'In the middle of the street?'

'No, you can change across there.' Dorina nodded at the shop opposite, which had samples of thread and old sewing machines cluttering the window.

'I don't know, I like to keep covered up. Anyway, what happened to all the material they cut off the bottom?'

'What are you talking about, my friend?'

Katie slipped it on in the backroom of the haberdashery shop opposite. When she emerged her hands were firmly gripping the hem, trying to pull it down her legs. 'This is no good - my stuff will be hanging out for everyone to see!'

Dorina and Christina raised their eyebrows at each other and then looked about each other. 'Men will lust after you in that dress. If you wear that dress, men will follow you like a pack of slavering dogs' said Christina. 'See?' Just across the road was a young man who quickly hid his face inside a book. He looked red with embarrassment.

Katie thought for a moment: 'No, I don't think that's quite the effect I'm looking for.'

'What effect are you looking for, my friend?' asked Dorina.

'Not a pack of chasing dogs, slavering all over me.' She wondered how Paol would react if he found a lot of young men slavering all over her. Not well, that's for sure. 'Can we rein it back a little to a lone wolf and a sniff and a wag?'

'Ah, lone wolf; sniff and wag.'

'That's right, lone wolf; sniff and wag.'

'Sniff and wag, sniff and wag, sniff and wag' muttered Dorina to herself as her hands slid hangers up and down the rail. Katie did the same on another rail, but not really looking, as Dorina seemed to be on a quest.

'Aha' said Dorina as she pulled out a dress that looked like it would be suitably modest, 'sniff and wag!'

He watched her from across the street, his face partly hidden by an open paperback book. It was the worst kind of romantic fiction but it had only cost thirty pence from the charity shop. On the lurid cover, a tall dark, hairy man was about to plant a kiss on the lips of our petite, blonde, innocent heroine. But was this image a harking back to the time of the first modern women a hundred thousand years ago and their first, wild encounters with Neanderthal men? Was this genre a recollection of our dark past where our women had swooned over the idea of a bit of rough with a caveman? Was there a bit of caveman in all of us?

Ah, the girl! Above the stale, musty pages he could see the girl with the well scrubbed, pinched face and her thick wavy fringe, which curiously, had two taut, braided strands stretching behind her head. She didn't seem to be wearing any makeup, but her quick and alert eyes and her mobile mouth, twitching nose and lips gave the appearance of an uncommonly attractive foraging feline - despite the black Beanie hat and the fingerless gloves, the tee-shirt and the rugby shorts.

This girl didn't look capable of bringing down a storm though or even a light drizzle; she didn't look like the girl who stood at the epicentre of a maelstrom, bringing destruction and death to the world. She didn't look capable of mustering a puff of wind, yet she did look remarkably like the picture that Belle had sketched, after their impromptu two-person seance last night.

The girl walked with a rolling gait and free ranging arms and legs, along the rows of dresses resting on hangers. Her hands and fingers pawed at the tightly ranked clothes in an impatient way. She seemed to be spending a lot of time searching and now she turned towards him! She had a dress that her friend had picked out! Her eyes had gone from pools of brown and were now flashing green at him.

But it was an unremarkable, yellow dress with small, white and light blue pastel flowers. She walked quickly towards him. He lifted the book over his face and peered intently at the open pages but the words made no sense.

She was standing directly in front of him! The book was taken out of his hands and turned the other way round. Her head was at an angle and her curious greenish brown eyes looked sympathetically into his.

'You might find that a bit easier' she said. 'I have the same trouble, so I like books with big writing, the right way up.' And then she turned and walked into the haberdashers dropping him a curious look over her shoulder.

He quickly fast dialled Belle. She answered immediately. 'Hi Seb, how's it hanging?'

'I think I've found her!'

'Who? My Stormbringer? No way! Where?'

'Camden market!'

'I'll be right there. Whatever you do, don't lose her!'

He retreated to the front of the adjacent shop. Could he get a view of her from there, he wondered? Was there something special about her? He tried to recall her shape. She was average height and build. He closed his eyes and tried to picture her frame. Or was there something he had missed? He threaded his way through the throng of bodies passing along the street and stood outside where she must be changing.

No! She was inside the shop and beckoning. Oh no! He looked behind. It was him she was beckoning to, quite insistently now. He felt his groin squirming. What was he going to do now? He walked hesitantly into the shop.

'You look like you know your way around a woman's dress - can you fasten me up?' She turned promptly and presented her back to him. 'Please?' She had gathered her brown hair into a hand-made pony tail and pulled it to one side. He got closer and noted that she smelt of fragrant talcum powder. There was a button and a clasp to fasten at the top of the dress. Her skin was perfect, along her neck and across her shoulders, but there was a mark on her shoulder that protruded slightly through the cotton fabric of the dress. He got as close as he could without touching her back and peered down inside her dress. She was still wearing the socks and the training shoes.

'Oi, are you having a glimp back there? You're a bit of a chancer, aren't you?' she challenged. 'Anyway, for your information, they're big and black and the kind worn in the black-out, aren't they?'

He hoped she was joking and she didn't think of him as a knicker fetishist. He fumbled around with the button and clasp and eventually pushed them into place. He was conscious that his fingers had pressed deeply, leaving white button size impressions that resolved themselves back into her lightly tanned skin.

She turned round and smoothed her hands over her waist, over her hips and then over her thighs. 'What do you think? 'She seemed to be interested in what he thought. He was now nursing a very uncomfortable strain in the region of his groin. She seemed to recognise this but didn't comment other than with a gentle, wry smile.

'It looks very nice' he said hesitantly.

'That's bollocks and you know it. I look like a banana in it, don't I?' She disappeared back into the shop. He wasn't sure what to do but he waited outside for her. She came back out promptly.

'You think it looks all right? Good, well I'm going to take it. What do you reckon its worth, fifteen?' She walked outside and returned with the dress and some change. She stuffed it in a leather satchel.

'You don't know shit about woman's dresses, do you? I know I'm clueless but you're actually even more clueless than I am.' She gazed expectantly at him. 'So, are you spying on me? Because, if you are, you're not very good at it, are you?'

'I'm not spying!'

'So, are you stalking me, then? Because you're not very good at that either, are you?'

'No, no, no.'

She looked at him curiously. 'No? Well, just to help you out, I'm going to get a brew...over there! And cake!' She pointed to a patisserie that nestled on the corner of the side street, about fifty paces away. 'I'll be there in about five...'

'I am not following you!' he said but the squirming in his nether regions said differently. It was not indigestion.

'Ah, but this is where you say, 'you're totally right, let me buy you a mug of tea and a piece of cake, that's what you say.'

She wasn't joking. He felt inside his pocket. He may have enough change.

'Erm, let me see if I have any money.'

'Oh, come on. Come with me.' She paused to speak quickly to the two women in black and sorted her way back absent-mindedly through a rank of what looked like leggings and parted them in the middle. She stiffened suddenly, eyes wide in alarm and leapt backwards, landing on her hands and toes and gasping.

There was a girl on the other side of the clothes rack, she had big, manic eyes and wayward, long hair brown with blonde highlights streaming in the slight breeze. Ah, it was Belle! She stepped through with barely a bob to get under the rail.

'Hi, I think you've met Seb, haven't you?' she said happily.

'Oh, him' said the girl as she got back to her feet, 'he's something to do with you, is he?'

'Yes! And we're so glad we've found you! Come with us, we need to find out all about you!' Belle was the kind of girl who wore a green child's sized duffle coat on a Summer's day and wore hair that looked like it had been modelled on a scarecrow. Was that straw he could see in her scruffy locks?

'What's her name?' Belle whispered to him from behind her tiny hand.

'I don't know' he said, 'I forgot to ask.'

'Oh Seb!'

The girl looked down to Belle. 'He's just taking me for a brew. You're not invited!'

'Oh, don't be so silly!'

The girl followed behind as he walked awkwardly with Belle towards the coffee shop - it was awkward as Belle insisted on holding his hand and he was worried that to all onlookers, he looked like he was leading a child.

They queued together. 'I guess, you're wondering what this is about? Or more likely, if we're right, you already know?' chirruped Belle. She had this annoying habit of taking over every conversation and every encounter. She had selected two items and put them on a tray. This could be very awkward as he didn't have a lot of money.

'You're going to have to help me out' the girl replied, 'because I think you're talking a load of bollocks?' She just wanted a mug of tea. He selected the cheapest, most ordinary coffee that he could see on the menu. This was still going to be pricey.

'You see, we think your appearance was foretold in...in...something or another. Do you see? But we need to test who you are?' offered Belle. 'If we're right' Belle continued said as she clutched the girl's left arm, 'there will be things you can do that normal people can't do? Do you see?'

'Nope. Who's paying for this lot?'

'Seb?'

'Let me see...'

'Oh, let me.'

They took the only table that was available - the one that nobody else wanted because it was furthest from the windows and closest to the flapping door to the kitchen.

Belle looked intently into the girl's eyes. 'Now what's your name?'

'I call myself Katie.'

'No, it can't be...'

'Well, it is and I do.'

'That's just silly.'

'No, it isn't.' Katie's pools of peaty brown in her eyes had started to flash green and Belle seemed oblivious to this. The gloves were off.

He gulped uncomfortably and looked around - everyone else seemed oblivious to this. The ceiling light above them flashed. Belle was looking somewhere beyond. The girl Katie was looking, no staring, into Belle's eyes.

'So, we've never met, have we? What's my name?'

The girl decided not to answer.

'I'll give you a clue - it begins with a 'B'.'

The girl thought for a moment as her fingers tip-tapped on her mug and then tip-tapped towards Belle's hand and the other disappeared below the table. The girl had a firm grip of his right hand. 'No, it doesn't, it begins with an 'A'.'

Belle turned in utter glee. 'She's good isn't she? Go on, what is it?'

The girl sighed and her lips pursed as she squeezed his hand tight. They were in a triangle with the girl at the apex and they all had their eyes partly closed, peering at one another. The girl had somehow worked out that Belle's real name was Annabelle, and that she calls herself 'Belle'. She seemed to realise that Belle's mum and dad are called Robert and Millicent and they live in North London in a nice, big house, with a long leafy garden and she seemed to know that we're studying art in a college and we both like drawing, photography, painting and writing. She had worked out that Belle has a drawing of someone who looks just like her, in a folder inside her over-the-shoulder bag. The girl took a deep breath, closed her eyes and frowned. She had worked out that the someone in the drawing is wearing a long, white shift and is bestriding the world like a colossus.

And he could tell that the girl has realised that this crazy, little girl called Belle has a longing for this quiet, weird boy who doesn't quite think the same way of her. They spend a lot of time together at the college but they don't share this obsession about an imaginary girl, who can bring down a storm wearing inconsequential clothing. The girl had worked out that he's had his hair cut in a style so as to distract from his oblong shaped head.

'No, I haven't!' he blurted out.

The girl winked at him. 'Belle, why don't you tell Seb how you feel about him?'

Belle gasped and seemed to choke on the girl's sudden announcement. Her chair rocked; his chair scraped backwards. Belle's cheeks went a brilliant vermilion. She tried to hide this behind her tiny hands. 'I'm...I...I don't know what to say' she stammered.

'It's written all over you and inside you.'

'How did you know?'

'Maybe it's the bits we don't say, those little looks and smiles? They can give you away, can't they?'

Belle regained her composure. 'C'mon, what's your real name? It can't be Katie? I think you're a seer!'

'It's Katie.'

Belle seemed very disappointed. 'Do you have any other names, like a middle name?'

'I do...it's Ebrill, isn't it?'

'Ebrill!' There was a little gasp of excitement as Belle exchanged a glance with him. 'And what is your mother's name?'

'She calls herself Maela.'

'Maela!'Another shared gasp and a shared glance. Belle took a deep breath. 'And where were you born?'

'In Wales, a little place called Rhayader.'

Belle got up, ran outside and jumped for joy and slapped her palms together in a joyous salute. Then she looked about awkwardly, came back inside and sat down at the table looking a little sheepish. 'Sorry about that, but I've been looking for you' she explained breathlessly.

'I don't understand' said the girl. But he reckoned she did understand, she thought they were a couple of young dreamers with a slim grasp of reality.

'Do you have any special powers? I'm sorry, I can't call you Katie, that just sounds silly.'

'You should call me Katie, that's what I call myself. And no, I have no special powers, other than the powers that all of us have...'

'Let me see what I can do here' said Belle as she took the girl's right hand, extended the fore and middle fingers and curled the two other fingers below, 'with a little reflexing.' The girl's thumb stuck out awkwardly at a right angle.

Belle said, 'Try to do something with that light?'

Nothing happened.

'Just the index finger then?'

Nothing happened.

'All right, your index finger left hand?'

Still nothing.

'Hmm.'

The girl seemed irritated. 'Look, this is stupid. Just stop it now!'

'Are you right or left-handed?'

'Neither!'

'Don't be silly!'

'I'm utterly ambiguous, that's what I am.'

'Ambiguous! Let me try this...' Belle took Katie's left hand and slowly and very carefully, extended the index and middle fingers outwards. She watched the girl carefully as she made each movement. There was a click as the girl's fingers and then her hand stiffened - her muscles seemed to have a responded to a memory of something that had happened before - something that had caused angst - something that made his neck go cold and start a shiver down his back.

'Let her go Belle!' he shouted. The light above their heads blinked and the bulb seemed to bulge and contract like a living thing.

Their hands pulled apart. 'I'm sorry, I can't do it, it's wrong' shouted the girl. The light glowed, bulged again then shattered in a shower of softly floating shards, like petals in an orchard.

'Right you lot, get out! GET OUT!' shouted the man at the till. He was very angry. They dashed out into the street, clutching what they could, close to their bodies, turned sharply to the left and sprinted to the crossroads. They shielded themselves in a side street, panting together.

'You shouldn't have done that, that was wrong' said the girl. She shook her left arm to try and relieve the discomfort. She had a mug in the other hand, which miraculously, was still half full of tea.

'What was that?' he heard himself say.

'So, no powers then?' gasped Belle.

When his hand had clasped the girl's under the table, a vision of a spiral getting closer and closer came into his head which then resolved itself into a sharp pointed, spiralling knife, that came at him with little threatening darts, getting closer and closer to his eyes and it made his heart flutter and his neck go cold, so cold that his back shivered.

Shocked, he looked at the girl as she extended the fore and middle fingers of her left hand together like a double barrelled shotgun. Her other fingers and her thumb described the corner of a cuboid. They were stiff, charged and throbbing. She shook it loose like she was shaking out the cramps.

'That's the second one I've walked out with today' said the girl, as she drained the mug, 'no wonder he feels mugged off!' She nudged him in the ribs and it really hurt. Belle was flat against the wall, looking like she was about to hurl up her doughnut.

'Which way to the lido?' asked the girl.

He pointed shakily down the street.

Katie was back in the high street, walking quickly along the market stalls towards the canal. She followed this until she reached a queue of people. In the queue was a tall, shambolic figure, craning his neck back and forth, like an anxious stork, looking for danger. A quick tap on his shoulder, a quick shimmy through the queue and she was on his opposite side, chuckling behind her hand.

'I thought you weren't coming' Robbie muttered.

She looked at her watch: 'Look at that, I'm right on time!'

'Oh, well done. Here's your ticket.'

'Oh, thank you. Now what about the ticket for affray?'

'Affray? Oh, don't worry about that...'

'I am worried about it. I need you to tear it up into a million little pieces.'

'I'll sort it out...'

'Sort it out now!'

Robbie groaned, found a piece of paper with official looking writing on it and tore it in two with a flourish.

'How do I know that's my ticket for affray?'

'Do you want the pieces?'

'Not really.' She scanned the pieces but the writing on them was small and official, as if nobody was supposed to be able to read it, and the words just swirled like the eddies in a little trout stream.

He looked her up and down. 'I thought you were going to wear something befitting the occasion and the season' he grumbled.

'It befits all right' she replied as she scanned the line of people in front and behind; they were all wearing scraps of clothing on beautifully tanned bodies and thongs on their feet and lurid bags with their belongings in. Whereas, she had on a tee-shirt, navy blue rugby shorts, running socks and boots. And an old school satchel. Robbie had on a long, luridly coloured shirt and long luridly coloured shorts and sandals. He seemed to be fretting about her shorts.

'You can't go in the pool like that' he grumbled.

'I wasn't planning to, because I don't swim...'

'But I thought you were going to wear something...suitable?'

The queue of people started to shuffle forward. 'These are perfectly suitable' she replied, flapping the pockets of her shorts with her hands, 'for anything I could be doing in the next ninety minutes.'

'What are you wearing under there?' he demanded as he showed two tickets to the overly cheerful young man at the gate.

'Don't be rude!'

'So you're not going in the water?'

'Too bloody right! I'm going to neck some happy juice then I'm going to rack out for an hour!' She offered him a tea-stained mug but he declined and shambled off to the bar. Her pink wrist band entitled her to a sun-lounger and an umbrella which she unfurled so she was in the shade. He returned with two fruit filled spectaculars which he put on the table between them; he moved his sun-lounger so he was in a full-on sun position a long stride away. 'If I told you how much I needed this, I would fall asleep before I finished it!' Robbie didn't seem to be listening, so she swigged the liquid down. The fruit would have to wait. She curled up and closed her eyes. Robbie was muttering something to himself about 'bloody women'.

Chapter Thirty-Five

Saturday 14 May 1337 - Loughton

Paol was waiting for her at the entrance to the underground train station. He was pleased with how he looked in his black denims, a buttoned up shirt, a light jacket and a rucksack over his shoulders and he was pleased with the prospect of spending the day ahead with his sister. He would not look at his watch because, despite her many failings, she was always on time. Always.

And there she was, running towards him, her hair scrunched under a black woollen cap and her tee-shirt flapping against the skin of her stomach and a towel wrapped around her neck. She stopped in front of him with that wide smile creasing her cheeks and her eyes of azure beaming at him.

'What happened to you, did you fall in the canal?'

'No, I've been to the lido with Robbie!'

They entered the forecourt, with Katie expertly dodging those rushing past.

'So, how was your date...with Robbie?'

'It wasn't a proper date - he blackmailed me into it.'

'Blackmailed you? Are you in trouble Katie?'

'No more than usual.' They trotted down the escalator, one after the other, then boarded a train which clanked its way north. His sister settled on the towel and rubbed her legs down.

'Did he throw you in?'

'No, I got a little bit bored and there were these boys playing water polo...'

'So you joined in.'

'Exactly.'

'But you can't swim...'

'But it doesn't matter, does it?'

'Why not?'

'From what I can make out, its all about tippy-toeing, jumping, catching, throwing and wrestling.'

'Wrestling?'

'Yes, it's a bit rough Paol, so I don't think you'd like it.'

'Well, I'm surprised at you.'

'Yes, me too...'

'Was it worth it?'

'You bet! They loaned me a swimming costume and a towel too!'

'Well, that's just great! We can go to the lido together!'

'Is it?'

'You've got all the kit now!'

'I'll have to hand it back though, won't I?'

'Not necessarily...'

'Oh, really?'

'Well?'

'I don't get it - why does everyone want to go swimming with me? I'm not a sodding dolphin!'

He seems to be fermenting a joke in his head. 'Well, everybody's got to have a porpoise in life!'

'What are you on about?'

'A porpoise in life? It's a pun, isn't it?'

'Paol, you're talking bollocks, now stop it!'

As he and Katie traversed the playing field, Katie adopting a leisurely skipping gait, Paol become aware of a small crowd messing around in the cricket nets. As they were wearing anything but whites, he could tell they were only messing around.

And then he saw Katie make a quarter turn towards them, two quick strides, her right arm extending. He heard a crack and what seemed like a red cannon ball heading their way. He ducked, tucking his head behind his arms; she snared the cricket ball, shouted 'Express!', drew her arm back like a javelin thrower and sped it back horizontally. The keeper should take the ball neatly just above the stumps and acknowledge immediately the speed and accuracy of Katie's return: instead he saw two girls falling and screaming and the scrambling consternation of a bevy of boys diving out of the way as the ball bent the back of the net. Now there would be trouble. He walked quickly away, shouting for Katie to follow him and then stood and watched at a safe distance.

Instead of following him, she walked slowly towards the batter. He was tall, track-suited and big. He walked towards her swinging his bat slowly and then doffed his maroon peaked cap. She greeted him with her hands firmly on her hips. He looked down on her and talked sternly; she nodded and replied in a slow and deliberate way as if talking to a child. Only, she was the child and he was the offended parent.

This continued for several exchanges and then the body language softened; they walked together to the nets and surveyed the carnage there. A large girl in an orange dress and black heels was getting to her feet and then limping away supported by two of the boys. What had once been a picnic was scattered about. Katie turned to point back at him and his heart slumped. Now, Katie was walking quickly towards him.

'Katie, we've got to go now...'

'I'm sorry, I can't.'

'Why not?'

'I'm having a duel with Marcus.'

'A duel! For Christ's sake Katie! Why!'

'They didn't appreciate getting the ball back so quickly - I should have rolled it along the ground, hypothetically...'

'I hope it's not pistols or rapiers. Hypothetically.'

'Rapiers? Pistols? No. I bowl an over to him: if he hits me out of the park, he wins; if I knock him over, I win.'

'Okay Katie. What if you lose?'

'Ah. I'll have to pay for all the damage I've caused.'

'You mean, I'll have to pay.'

'Exactly.'

'And if you win?'

'In that case, I won't have to pay, will I?'

'I see. Well, make it quick and make sure you knock him over.'

'Got it.' She turned away and marched back to the nets. A cricket ball rolled her way and she paced out her run up - just seven paces. 'Left arm over' she shouted and then she ran in, set herself and bowled. It rapped his pads as he swung the bat languidly. 'How's that!' Katie shouted behind her to where the umpire should be but there wasn't one.

'Not out' roared Marcus in reply.

She ran up and bowled again. Another massive swing of the bat but the bat missed the ball.

He watched in admiration at the smooth, easy, flowing run up followed by the gather and the arm speed and the yelp as the ball was released. Another massive swing of the bat and a miss.

Another delivery and another miss. Surely one of these big swings would connect and the ball would be lost from sight.

Another delivery, another yelp. There was a rattle. The stumps were splayed over.

Marcus thumped his bat angrily against the rubber matting. 'One more ball! One more for the over!'

'I knocked you over, that's all you get!'

'One more' he roared, 'if I land the ball on the square, I win...'

'Bollocks to that, I can spit further than that!' she shouted back.

'Against the hoardings then - I win!'

'What if I get you out again?'

'I buy you lunch!'

'What, a date?'

'All you can eat. Tablecloths, silverware, everything!'

'Everything? All right, you're on!'

She walked back to her spot, turned and ran in, quicker than before, thump, thump, thump; his bat thumped the rubber, tap, tap, tap; her right arm extended, her left arm swung through, a yelp, an angry heave of the bat, a crack and the ball hurtling back towards her; she was turning back on herself, tumbling arms stretching, another cry from her.

Paol followed the trajectory of the hit ball but he had lost it. Where was it? Was it heading out of the park?

Katie was stretching on the ground, it was a valiant attempt to stop...wait, the ball was in her left hand and she was holding it up high! Marcus sank to his knees, the bat handle pressed against his forehead. Paol got up and walked quickly to her, but Marcus was there before him, getting to his feet, lifting her up, throwing her over his shoulder and slapping her back.

'Come on you' he called out to Katie's wriggling rear end.

'Who's this, your dad?'

'No, he's my brother!'

'You should be proud of her, brother! There's not many that's done that to me! Not ever!'

Katie's satchel was bulging with a bottle of rum and a plastic box full of patties. 'These are really good' she observed, wiping crumbs of suet crust from her lips. They were outside a public house, off the main street, that in her estimation, looked like a bit of a shit heap. However, beyond the tired facade, the pub garden stretched away into an orchard, and beyond this there were fields and hedges, that seemed alive with birds.

Paol led Katie through the front door and there was an uncomfortable silence. They walked quickly past the locals gathered around the centre bar and headed to the back parlour. She could see eight or nine men gathered around two tables to their right by a cold and dusty fireplace. The youngest was in his early twenties and he looked up and smiled at her: the rest of them looked much older and one of them looked really quite ancient. Paol would slot into the middle of their age range, she thought.

'This is Katie, my sister...' announced Paol.

'Half sister...'

'She's here to assist me. Katie is in the Royal Navy as a...what is it you do Katie?'

'Hallo all. I'm a leader in the Communications and Information Systems Department of a Type 23 frigate. My role is...'

'Katie's role is to look decorative on a boat' interrupted Paol.

'It's in a ship Paol, so that shows how little you know!' This was acknowledged with a round of chuckles and then they resumed puddling roast meat, roast potatoes and vegetables down their necks.

'Thanks for that correction - Katie's role is to look decorative in a ship.'

'You bugger' she muttered as there was another round of chuckling. A distinct smell of old coal ash, sour beer and stale males pervaded this end of the pub.

'I'm sure Katie is a valued member of her crew' said the young man. He had the accent and the quiet confidence of a German.

'Thank you' she said as she opened a Tupperware box, 'do you fancy one of my patties?' This prompted a lot of head shaking.

'We'll just go and set up - start in thirty minutes?' said Paol, pulling at her arm and looking at the pub clock.

'That's not right' she noted as she checked against her timepiece.

'Three o'clock start everybody, pub clock time. Synchronise your watches! It's now...two-thirty. All right everyone, let's get to it' Paol announced. 'Katie, you come with me.'

She followed him sheepishly. 'They're not sure about me, are they?' They came to a door which jerked open under protest and they climbed a metal, spiral staircase to a balcony overlooking a wooden dance floor. It was divided down the middle by a tattered set of red curtains.

'What do you think?'

'Who's the lad and how did you get him mixed up in all this?' she asked.

'That's Udo, he's one of my students' Paol confided. 'You make it sound like this is a Masonic lodge or something!'

'So, this lodge, has it got somewhere I can have a bath?'

'Why?'

'Because I'm all sweaty...and I need to put on my dress.'

'I think you'll find that girls perspire...'

'No Paol, it's definitely sweat...'

'You've got the hots for Udo, haven't you?'

'Don't be disgusting!'

'I see, well just hang on a minute...' On one side of the curtains were blue markers and on the other, red markers. She could make out the outline of Western Europe, the English Channel and the British Isles. The Germans appeared to be red and gathered along the borders of France and Belgium; there were markers behind the border and in the harbours with no indication of what they meant. 'So, red and blue take it in turns to move their forces. You and I will move then move the markers. When opposite colours meet, I decided what the outcome of each engagement is.'

'I'll be red then...'

'That's fine, but why?'

She hesitated. 'It's my favourite colour...' Udo would be on the red team surely, she reasoned.

'Anyway, the outcome of each encounter is based on the value of the pieces engaged with each other, historical precedent and luck, as determined by the computer. I have a software programme that simulates 20th century warfare. Are you with me so far?'

'I think so. I know about wargames, don't I? It's not exactly rocket science is it? Unless... there are rockets?'

'No, it's too early for rockets, isn't it? Mind you, the Chinese had rockets thousands of years ago and by the end of this war, rockets were... you don't need to worry about rockets, Katie.'

'Oh, good.' She paused expecting a response. 'Can I see this programme you're using?'

'No, you can't.'

'Oh, go on - where did you steal it from?'

'Katie! How could you?'

She thought for a moment. Who could have this type of software and still be an easy target. 'Not the Ministry of Defence?'

'Ah, the very same...'

'I do hope you're joking.'

He looked at her sheepishly: 'I'm not joking, it was too easy.'

'I see. So basically, you want me to be an accessory to your crime and a croupier in your...casino of corruption!'

'Eh?'

'You heard...'

'Well, yes, but I do need your expertise in certain naval matters.'

'Ooh, expertise in naval matters? And we're not talking belly button fluff here, are we?'

'No, no - In fact, I need your expertise in... amphibious warfare!'

'Blimey, amphibian warfare! And me, just a decoration on a boat!'

'All right Katie, I think I can see where this is headed...'

'Good, your wallet is going to take another battering, isn't it?'

'You are so mercenary, Katie, sometimes I can't believe we're related!'

'Well, we are, so deal with it. I'm off to the heads...'

'Just to the left of the stage...'

'Bath?'

'Washbasin.'

'Soap?'

'Spit.'

'Towels?'

'Sleeve.'

'For pity's sake, Paol! I'm going back to the pub!'

'Just deal with it and get back here as soon as you can!'

Katie felt as well scrubbed as she could be but still grimy. Her yellow dress fitted well but felt a little tight around the waist - she resolved that she would run off the day's excess tomorrow. Her training shoes, with her running socks tucked inside, were perched on a chair somewhere beyond the British Isles; her backside was planted in German Swabia with her bare legs and feet pointed along the line of the River Rhine. All the red flags were clustered to the north of her along the border with France and Belgium. Soon the curtains would be parted and it would all kick off.

On the stage behind her, the red team had made their dispositions - the German lad dressed in tight fitting denims and tee-shirt and his colleagues in field grey German uniform. The portly old man in a white peaked cap seemed to be in charge, based on the way he did his straight-back strut, up and down the stage, barking utter bollocks.

There was a buzz as the green curtains parted and Paol toiled away on the keyboard, trying to work out all the outcomes. This was going to take bloody ages she thought. She was called into action for another three phases of battle. The red team had the early advantage, as in a championship boxing bout - the young upstart in the red trunks had jabbed with his right fist and then landed a crippling hook to the guts of the old pro with a swinging left. A blow to the head with the right fist would finish it. She saw the old pro in the blue trunks fall to the floor, gasping for breath, the young upstart in the red trunks standing over him, taunting him.

'Katie!' shouted Paol.

The German lad was laughing: 'Your feet are interfering with our left wing!'

'Oh, sorry!' She tucked her legs back underneath her and reached for her cider glass, currently situated in the region of Stuttgart. The reds had reached the English Channel and seemed quite triumphant. There was a conversation going on over her head with Paol about the next phase. The blue team were in a huddle, shaking their heads.

'Take a break, Katie, we're going to be some time...' laughed the German lad.

'Let me know when you need me. I'm going to get a drink.' She got up and wriggled her dress down.

'Do you mind not doing that Katie' called out Paol, 'it's almost pornographic!'

'Well, you would know, wouldn't you? Anyway, why can't I adjust my under-crackers without you calling me out?'

'Because it's inappropriate in a public place!'

'For pity's sake!'

'Anyway, I will need you fairly soon, so don't go too far away - this is taking an unexpected turn!'

'You'll find me in the garden, getting me some sunshine.'

'Don't go too far!'

'I'll be in the sodding garden!' She removed a tube of talcum powder from her satchel and waved it over the red flags nestling on the coast. 'Ooh look, it's snowing!'

'Katie! There can't be any snow! It's nearly June!' Paol roared.

She tippy-toed over the Netherlands and the British Isles, gathered her things and strode out of the hall. 'Pillocks!' she shouted in reply.

Katie made her way to the heads and washed down her face and hair, blew them dry with the hot air blower, scattered talc down her front and massaged it into her sensitive places. She stalked out, procured a jug filled with fruit and fizzy cold fizz at the bar and made her way into the garden, past the casino windows and out to where gnarled trees groaned in white and pink blossom and bees busied about them. A handsome red-tail called 'whooeet' to her and then admonished her with a 'tick, tick, tick' before disappearing into the cleft of an apple tree. 'What are you doing here?' she wondered out aloud. There was a 'wheeoo, wheeoo, wheeoo' high above her head and then the fork-tail twisted its tail and flapped its lazy way south.

Between the trees, a plastic chair propped against a tree trunk and a second chair for her feet, served as a sun lounger, and a third chair acted as the convenience table for jug and glass. Katie settled into her make-shift hammock and drifted into a reverie.

CHAPTER THIRTY-SIX

Saturday 14 May 1540 - The pub garden

She was swept along by the mighty river, that flowed muscularly through the narrows, between the wooded hills; she was the sprite, flowing with the river, spinning in the spirals, floating in the slow-moving ebbs, skating over the algae slickened rocks, always moving, like the silvery sewin, riding the flow, heading to the sea.

The river widened and she was in the shallows, deflected by the river flexing and again, another pulse that thumped against her flank. With a muscular flick of her body, she was in the main race of the river, under the thrashing blades of the giants, the flashing above and the zipping of metal stones through the air and water. With all her remaining strength she flexed her body and sped away from the tumult in the river and she was through, soothed by the mighty river, as it flooded inexorably to the great green salt sea, every wide bend bringing new sensations to her gape and her gills.

It became difficult to see, so much silt, the throbbing of spinning metal and the bulging of metal hulls above, the transport of the giants rumbling along the river, now a fleet of them, blotting out the sun. She was through and suddenly felt invigorated by the thick tang of the great salt sea and the waves washing against her, washing her body clean.

And now she was in her metamorphosis, changes happening to her body and her muscles responded in the way they had always done, the rhythm of rippling nerves and muscles. Silt was flowing through her, choking her but with a flick of her tail she rippled through the watery interface with the shining air, and she saw the mighty piers of a tower, dropped by the giants into the estuary, black plumes of smoke billowing upwards, high into the sky, and burning monsters falling, splashing into the river...

All of a sudden, Katie was mainmast upright: 'Sodding hell! Who the hell is Christoph?' she heard herself shouting.

'Katie, it's Udo!'

'Who? Udo? It's you!' It was the German lad, all tall, lean and ready...

'Yes it is! Well done!'

'I'm not a sewin, am I?'

'A sewin? What is that?'

'A trout.'

'You are definitely not a trout.'

'Whew, that's a relief. I thought I was a trout, swimming up the river...'

'You are not a trout, and the river is very distant.'

'Good, good.' Every river has its own peculiar taste and the silt she had tasted, as her journey climaxed, was the filth of the dark river.

'Are you fine, Katie?'

'Yes.' Another draft of rum cocktail would not go amiss, she thought.

'Paol wants you to come.'

'Oh does he?' she said as she gathered herself up and stood rapt with attention.

'There's a situation in the River Thames' he paused, 'he needs your knowledge of warships.'

Paol met them half way: 'The Reds have launched an attack down the River Thames, they're making landings on the Isle of Sheppey and the Isle of Dogs!'

'But they can't, it's the Battle of France!'

'I told you the battle had taken an unexpected turn!'

'Where's the British army?'

'Most of the British Expeditionary Force is trapped against the Channel coast.'

'But it's only the Isles of Sheppey and Dogs? Come on! I think we should be happy to let those go!'

Paol looked appalled.

'No offence meant' she added apologetically. 'So, where's the Andrew?'

'The Royal Navy? Dover, Harwich and Portsmouth. But there's a big minefield that the Nazis have started to lay off Essex.' Udo frowned at this comment. 'Sorry, Udo, the Red Team are laying the minefield...'

'Better...'

'So, what do you want from me?'

'I want you to arbitrate over a naval action off Foulness...'

'Arbitrate?'

'Indeed. Decide what the outcome is...'

'Eh?'

'Who wins...'

'Oh.' Paol handed her a sheet of paper. She would need some help interpreting this.

'Do you need somebody from the Blue team?'

'No, no, I just need Udo.'

'Oh, okay. Five minutes Katie...'

'I'll need ten, maybe fifteen...' She sent Udo to the bar with instructions and they settled at a plastic table on the patio outside. Udo read from the sheet and she placed her glass at one end and two lines of cocktail sausages. She asked him the time of day and the names of the commanding officers: the sun was setting in the West as Commanders Talog (RN) and Sankt (Kriegsmarine) faced off. She manoeuvred the table so that the sun was behind her. 'The sun's setting in the west' she explained. Udo had one line of sausages abreast with a clutter of half sausages behind; Katie's sausages were in line astern. 'Heads or tails?' she asked as she tossed a coin. 'Off you go then...'

The sausages quickly closed to firing range; Katie's handful now turned south in line astern and they were ready to launch torpedoes. The coin toss determined that she would launch first; Katie flicked a peanut with her thumb and forefinger. 'Phwish' she whistled as it hit it Udo's leading sausage amidships.

'What was that?'

'A salvo of torpedoes!'

'That one's hit' he said as she picked it up and swallowed it. Udo's nut flick was off target. In this exchange, Udo lost four sausages to Katie's one.

'What are you going to do?' she wanted to know.

'I will make a tactical retreat.'

'I see. You're going to abandon your convoy...'

'No, they will follow...'

'But these old transports, they're quite slow, aren't they?' Another round of peanut projectiles was fired, after which Katie felt totally sated and the Red Team's invasion force had been wiped out. 'I can't eat any more of these sausages, can you help me out?'

'You want me to eat my own crews? That would be cannibalism!'

'But they're only little sausages...'

'Not very good sausages...'

'Oh, well keep them for target practice. I'll buy you a drink...and some more nuts.'

Katie led the way back into the pub and she could sense his eyes following the line of her frame from her shoulders to her feet. They sat down at the bar.

'So Udo, what's it to be? One of those? That's a bit of a fancy drink isn't it?' Katie asked for a bottle of cider to go with his glass of designer lager. 'And can you see if you can find me a clean glass this time? Thank you. And some nuts please.'

The petite, painted, pouty barmaid frowned and trotted away. She returned with the order, still bearing a frown. Katie turned to Udo and asked, 'Don't you trust me?'

'Sure, but I want to understand the process, so I don't make the same mistake again.'

'Process?' His voice was quiet and confident but he seemed to have been shaken by her skill at launching peanuts with such accuracy. 'Well, you need to get down low and aim. Do not jump up before you've fired and make sure the sun isn't in your eyes.' She favoured him with one of those wide smiles that creased right across her cheeks and lit up her face and her eyes. He returned her smile. That was a good start...

'Don't you want to know how to flick nuts?'

'No, I meant coming to a decision.'

'Well, you need to factor in skill and luck don't you?'

'By flicking nuts?'

'Exactly.'

'I see. Shouldn't we report back to Paol?'

'No need, here he is...'

'Ten minutes, you said!'

'Well Paol, we're all done.'

'And?'

'The Blue force sinks the Red force.'

'Not all of it!'

'Most of it...'

'And how did you work that out?'

Udo seemed to think this was going to be very funny so she gave him a pre-emptive kick to the shin.

'So, you want to see the replay, Paol?' She laid out two lines of peanuts on the counter, 'So, this is the River Thames' indicating the length of the bar, 'this is the Red Team's flotilla and this is the Blue Team's flotilla out of Harwich. This cider glass is the setting sun. The state of the tide is represented by these puddles of beer on the top and as you can see, it's on its way out.' The barmaid scowled at Katie as she wiped away two of the puddles.

Katie looked quizzically at Udo: he seemed very intent on her every word and gesture. She moved the lines of nuts to the position where they engaged in combat and demonstrated each phase of the battle as she saw it.

She continued. 'It's early evening, so the sun is behind the Blue force and in the eyes of the Red force, and they don't know the coastal waters.'

'We have maps!'

'Yes, but the sands are always shifting, aren't they? I thought that a fair exchange was four of the Red Force ships sunk or disabled, pretty much in the first salvo of shells and torpedoes, one Blue Force ship down by return fire and one damaged.' As a ship was sunk, she placed the corresponding nut in her mouth and crunched it. 'So, that's what I think. The Blue Force then descends on the transports like bears at a picnic. Does that make sense?'

Paol thumped the keys on his slimline computer and then finished with a thump to the return key. 'Like bears at a picnic, eh?'

'Exactly!'

Katie took a beer towel and cleared the top of the bar. There was another scowl from the barmaid but Katie just shrugged this off. 'Let me know what else I can show you.'

'I don't think it will make any difference - the Red Team has lodgements on both sides of the River Thames' Paol said quietly. 'I'm going to call it a day. I need to work through a couple of scenarios.'

'Are we dismissed?'

'Yes.' And then Paol walked away, threading his way between the pub customers, engrossed in his little computer.

'We can do what we want now' murmured Katie.

'What did you have in mind?'

'I thought we could...go outside.'

'We could take a little stroll about the garden and find somewhere...pleasant.'

'About the garden?' What was he talking about? Did he mean her pwdin bleu? She gulped noisily and her heart started to pitter-patter - not in fear but in anticipation. Places in her core started to flex up and down and in and out. What did he mean by 'pleasant'? 'That sounds... nice. Just a moment, I've got to visit the heads and get me sorted out for our...little stroll. Don't go away!'

Back in the sanctuary of the Ladies, she took a towel and wiped her face. What was it she needed to do in here? She sniffed under her armpit - that still smelt of scented talc. Nobody had ever said anything like that to her before. What did he mean by taking a little stroll about her garden? What did 'to be pleasant' actually involve? Did it involve... squeezing and feeling and arching and pushing? Her breathing subsided but her heart still pounded. She tampered with the machine on the wall until a pack of assorted flavoured items popped out; she put the package in her satchel and then wondered what would happen if she had to get them out in an emergency. She took one slimline pack out and tucked it into her pants. But what if he found it there?

Would he think that was...a bit tarty? I know, I'll slip it inside my bra, he won't look in there, will he? She sprinkled some more talc inside her dress and felt ready for whatever this pleasant stroll in the garden might bring.

'So how do I look?' she asked when she got back.

'Same as you did ten minutes ago' he replied.

'It was never ten minutes, was it?'

'I was afraid you'd stood me up and I was going to ask this young lady if she was free for a stroll' he said, nodding at the pouty barmaid. She blushed.

'No, you weren't, were you?'

'No, of course not. She was busy!'

'Sorry, you took me by surprise, I wasn't expecting to go for a stroll today' she replied, 'so I was just tidying myself up!' He took her hand and led her to the patio door, 'This is one of those places where you have to wipe your feet before you go out' she laughed as she made a big play of wiping her training shoes before going outside. Udo laughed, which was a good sign. They went past the plastic tables and chairs on the patio and past the hall windows, towards the lower reaches of the garden. The Blue Team and the Red Team seemed to have reconciled their differences and were talking and drinking together, even the portly man in the white officer's cap.

They walked to a grassy area in the garden just before the apple trees. The red-tail flitted past and the heady smell of honeysuckle enveloped her and made her nostrils twitch. She tried to hold back the sneeze.

'I like your direct approach, Udo, very bold, very direct.' She paused for a moment to judge the effect of this on him. 'But it's high risk' she continued, 'because you don't do any reconnaissance, do you?'

Udo looked confused momentarily and then smiled wryly. 'What are you talking about, Katie?'

'I think we both know what I'm talking about' Katie continued in the same vein, 'you see, you don't know anything about the situation and you could be falling into a trap, couldn't you?'

'I think boldness is the best policy...'

'Your little men don't know they're heading into this trap, where thousands are going to die and their bodies will fill the dark river...'

'My little men?'

'You heard me right - I will storm your heart and take your soul, you will surrender your all to me.' Katie shuddered when she realised that she had said this out loud.

'You're very funny' Udo replied with a chuckle.

'I am, aren't I' she said, carefully, 'but just to be clear, I was being deadly serious just then!'

'I think I know everything I need to know' he said.

'You reckon?'

They settled on the grass amongst the daisies, so close that their legs were touching.

Udo watched as Katie nimbly assembled a daisy chain, with her long delicate fingers. The scars across her palms flitted into his view, like henna coloured knitting needles. As she leant over him and placed the chain over his head, he took in her scent, like a summer meadow, and he glimpsed the slight surge of her breasts under the yellow dress and felt the firmness of her thigh against his thigh.

She sat back and looked at him, bemused by his reaction and then there was that slight, knowing frown and then a slight, innocent giggle. And then he realised, that this was all part of the dance, of the girl and the boy, female led, male driven, that timeless dance of sensual courting, of tender touching, fervent feeling and then binding and reaching into each other; pushing, squeezing, pulsing, releasing...

He watched as she stretched out against the ground, artless but artful, the fluted glass of golden, effervescing liquid pulled towards the split of her legs, pulling the hem of the dress up so that first her calves, then her knees and then her thighs were exposed, smooth and golden in the sun, at ease and resting but muscles slightly tensed, ready to engage with another body - his body.

He drained his glass, got to his feet, reached down to grasp Katie's hands and pulled her up, and she rose like a water sprite emerging from the river, as would a maiden rising from the mighty Rhein, his Brynhildr. The surge inside him demanded release, so he lifted her over his right shoulder and carried her towards the orchard with her hands tapping on his back, accompanied by cries of 'put me down, you bugger' and 'I'm quite capable of walking, you caveman' which, to his mind, was all part and parcel of this timeless ritual of sensual courting.

Through the gnarled limbs of the neglected apple trees, amongst the heady scent of the blossom and the buzzing of bees, she was propelled, brushing away twisted twigs, out of sight of the world but in full view of the flitting red-tail and the chiming great tit. Udo placed her on the bench that encircled the girth of an old, straight plum tree and she stood, her arms around his neck, waiting, wondering, wanting.

About seventy-three or seventy-four inches tall she reckoned, in his bare feet. They were so close now, his hands girdling her waist, his thumbs pressing gently into her stomach and his fingers gently massaging the rise of her buttocks; in and out, in and out her breath sucked in to mobilise her body; her spine curved back slowly and gently so that her chest pushed forward towards him; her lips parted softly and her eyes widened to dark pools; dark, peaty liquid pools that invited the man to plunge in and dive into her depths.

Her eyelids closed and she inhaled deeply again and he smelt clean as she sucked in his scent and found a delicate hint of a zesty musk from his cheek. 'Fill me' she sighed, 'my soul is empty, fill me, you're the man to do that, fill me.' Now, her breathing was deeply synchronised with his and inside his open shirt she could feel his pectoral muscle and his neat, symmetrical nipple; his rib cage was notched and she slid the fingers of her right hand along them. She heard the top button of her dress pop and then the next two. 'I have an aching need that needs to be met, fill me.' Her dress was flapping open and his face burrowed in her chest; his right hand burrowing around inside her pants.

Katie's right hand explored his neck and tugged on the rat-tail of hair there; the left hand slid between his shirt and trousers and worked his belt loose. Frantically, she explored inside, in amongst the warmth and moistness of the glands, which she cupped: 'Oh my soul! That's massive!' His trousers fell, half mast. Her lips were kissed and they spread wide to take his mouth, in out, in out, up and down, up and down; he squeezed her inside buttock and she pulled away to gasp: 'But you're so fucking big!'

'I want to be inside you' he muttered, as his fingers massaged her inner lips.

'No, no, no, not up there! Oh, oh, oh, ohhh!' They toppled down, landing together on the bench, she was doubled up, he was astride her.

'God, I love you!'

'Oh, oh, ooh, ooh, no time for that' she moaned.

Their breathing was loud and frantic. She saw the condom wrapper pinched in his lips; she ripped and pulled with her teeth; the condom was in her mouth - banana flavour! The ribbing rubbed on her tongue, the rest flopped from her lips: 'Get it on, get it on' she spluttered. Something big and muscular was shoving against her and it was skating around and around her mound, like a greasy, wet golf ball, destined never to enter the hole.

'Quick! Get it on, get it on' she implored.

'I'm trying!'

'Let me grab it!' She bobbed her head, the condom re-positioned. 'I'll guide it in' she spluttered, gagging. The massive muscle pumped at her, just missing her nose.

'Not too hard, ugh!' shouted Udo. She had it in her grasp, her mouth wide open, gaping with rubber.

There was a shout. 'Argh, it's Paol!' she spluttered, the condom wrapping around her tongue.

'No, it's Udo!' came the anguished cry from above.

In the gap between Udo's legs, above the trouser belt, she could see her brother. 'Argh, it's Paol. Behind you!' she spluttered again.

Paol roared out something that sounded like her name, quite loud, quite strident, quite distant. Katie was aware of the sound of dirty laughing, way back towards the pub. Udo stumbled backwards, frantically trying to push his enlarged member back into his trousers. She got up on the bench that girdled the plum tree and flopped back against the trunk; Udo stood, helplessly, like the school kid caught showing his tackle under the desk to the girl sitting beside. She could not focus her sight, or her hearing or feel the outside world on her skin - something tumultuous was about to happen inside and it would overwhelm her, like she was falling off a cliff!

Her body jolted inside; the condom was still in her mouth, parked against her back teeth like a lump of gum. What was happening now was right in her core and was growing and growing.

Paol marched up, looked down at her and then took two worried and hurried steps backwards. Katie tried to get down off the bench but her body wouldn't let her. The right arm raised itself and covered her forehead as her whole body heaved and pulsed again; the left arm covered her core in a futile attempt to hold back what was inside. Her eyes watered as she chewed on her lip to stop her wail. All she could see in her mind was Udo, his body entwined with hers, undulating in time.

'Danu!'

Not helping.

'Rhiannon!'

Still not helping.

'His Holiness!'

Something.

'The Cardinal!'

Nope.

'The Bishop!'

Nope.

'Sister!'

Nearly.

'Mum!'

Almost.

'Nuns with knives...'

Nearly there.

'Nuns with branding irons...'

Home and dry.

'The verger...'

Slowly, ever so slowly, the urge to explode ebbed away and her body gradually climbed back into itself.

'What do you want Paol' she gasped, 'can't you see I'm busy?'

'What in God's name is happening to you?' Paol seemed to be in dismay at the disarray of her clothes.

'Uh, uh, I was just chatting with Udo' she gasped, 'and uh, I had a funny turn.' She was still puffing like an Olympic weight lifter. He took her by the hand and allowed her to step down.

'That chatting has really worn you out, hasn't it Katie? Do you need oxygen?' Instead, he offered her a sip from a glass of dark beer.

'Yes, yes, that's right, it did!' She took a mouthful. It was bitter and nasty. She spat it out. 'We started talking about bodies, like human bodies...'

'It was more than talking, Katie. Out, please.' He held out his hand but she couldn't work out why. Then she realised. She took the rubber out of her mouth and placed it in his hand. He picked it up with a look of disgust and stretched it out to its full length. 'So, would you like to explain yourself, Katie?'

'Er, not really...'

There was something sticky in her hair, but it wasn't hair gel, because she never used the stuff.

'Please, I insist...' They were now sitting knee to knee on the bench, the tall plum tree spreading above them.

'Well, Paol, let me see...'

Surreptitiously, she ran her fingers through her fringe but her hand stopped abruptly against the sticky stuff.

He settled back in his seat, crossed his legs and if he had any shag, he would now be packing it into his pipe and getting ready to light it. If he had a pipe, that is.

This would need very careful handling - he was going to be all analytical and condescending, like a complete and utter twat. 'Well, Paol, have you heard of a disease called cancer?'

'Yes, I've heard of it...'

'Good. Well, it's a bastard of a disease and if you're not careful, it can sneak up on you when you're not looking.'

'I see' said Paol, who seemed to be taking a long suck on his imaginary pipe.

'So, I read this article...'

'Wait a minute, you say you read an article?'

'Oi, Paol!' she replied indignantly. 'Oh, I see what you're getting at. Well, someone was telling me about this article that they had read, Paol...'

'That's better Katie, the first rule of story telling is to make sure it has some level of credibility about it.'

'Listen Paol, do you want to hear my story or not? Or are you just going to sit there like a big, fat, condescending prick?'

'Sorry Katie, please proceed...'

'Right Paol, now here was I?' she wondered out loud, as she set about the next part of the explanation. 'Oh, yes, cancer. I learned that it's important to have regular check-ups.'

'Uh huh' said Paol.

'And I was worried about my...chesty area.'

'Really? Do you mean your breasts?'

'Don't be vulgar, Paol. Yes, my girly parts. And Udo offered to check them out for me...'

'And what was Doctor Udo's opinion?'

'Well, he says they're in good shape, quite springy and I shouldn't be too worried.'

'I see. And is it considered best practice to do this by mouth?'

'Oi, Paol! Well, yes, absolutely, it has to be done by mouth!'

'You must let me have the reference to this article, it sounds very... practical. So, then you offered to check him out?'

'Oi, don't be vulgar, Paol!'

'You were about to put his cock in...'

'No, I wasn't, was I? Oh, yes, you could be right!'

'And?'

'Well, he's got a full set of bits and they're all absolutely fine!'

'Good, that must be a relief for him.'

'Yes, he did seem quite relieved, didn't he?'

'Katie, you expect me to believe this?'

'Yes, yes, I do. That's what happened.'

'I know when you're lying, Katie, your nose wrinkles up.'

'What?' Really? Was she still doing that?

'The truth!'

'Oh, bollocks!'

'No, the cock.'

'You are so vulgar!'

'You had your hand on his cock and you were about to put it in your mouth!'

'There was a good reason for that! I'd run out of hands!'

'From where I was standing, it looked like you were trying to insert his German sausage into your...'

'Paol! Don't be dirty!'

'Into your mush...'

Katie felt her face curl up into a cringe. 'It wasn't like that, we were just feeling things, that's all.' The streak of sticky stuff in her hair could only be German spunk! Fucketty, fucketty, fuck!

'And I bet there was plenty of German spunk...'

'Paol, don't be disgusting! No, there was no baby gravy, no, no, none of that got inside me, no, absolutely not!' She grimaced as her hand swept through her hair and she wiped the sticky stuff away under the wooden bench.

'I don't believe it - you were trying to do the dirty with one of my students in the pub garden!'

'Well, when you put it like that...' She straightened out her clothes and stood up. 'How did you know anyway? I thought you were busy.'

'It was the noise - it sounded like a donkey being tortured. Eeaw! Eeaw! Eeaw!'

'Nooooo!'

'Yeah, it was just like that - weren't you concerned about having an audience?'

'I thought I had chosen an out of sight spot - wasn't there any sport on the telly?'

'Well, when there's a choice between telly and live sport... You'd better come with me' Paol ordered. She collected her shoes and her jug and her glass of cider and walked with him, side by side, until they emerged from the orchard. There was a ripple of applause from the rut of males outside the pub.

'Do you know what our sister calls you? She calls you that little Welsh tart.'

'That's not fair.'

'So, I'm going to give you some advice, Katie.' He offered her a drink from his glass of stout.

'You're not seriously going to give me the dad speech, are you?' She dipped her mouth into his stout and looked back up to Paol; she felt a creamy, foam moustache forming on her top lip. 'Agh, that's still vile!' she muttered.

'Do you know how old he is?' Paol asked.

'He's not that old! You may not realise this but I'm nineteen now. It's not an unmountable gap, is it?'

'It's an insurmountable age gap, Katie.'

In fact, he's very mountable she thought. 'So, what's the problem Paol?'

'How am I supposed to tutor him if my sister goes and shags him in the pub garden?'

'Half-sister.' Katie looked towards a man shaking hands with Udo in the bar and patting him boisterously on the back.

'And I do believe...he has a verlobte, as they say back in Germany.'

'A lobster? And this lobster's supposed to trouble me, is it?' This did sound like an unusual thing to own, even for someone from Hamburg.

'He has a fiancée Katie.'

'Noooo!'

'They've had a few problems, but I just want to protect you, Katie.'

'You said...'

'I said he wanted to meet you, that's all, and he's got this blog...'

'Oh, I'm sorry to hear that...'

'It's nothing to worry about, but I feel you ought to know...'

'In that case, I think I need a little chat with him then.'

'I'll see you later!'

She got up and walked circumspectly towards Udo. He was draining another glass of lager. 'I hear from Paol that you're engaged to be married, so congratulations to you.'

'It's not what you think...'

'I think it's absolutely what I think, you dirty, fornicating shit-hound,' Her mind wasn't quite back on line yet but something did not quite feel right. 'I do hope you can sort out your commitment issues because, if you don't, I imagine your lobster will not think twice about killing you. I would.'

'Katie, please!'

'Paol mentioned that his tutor relationship with you could get messy if we continue, so I think it's best if we don't. What do you think?'

'There's nothing to think about - I really want to be with you.'

'For pity's sake!' She attracted a mixture of amused and stern looks as she spun on her heels and carried out her march of shame to the ladies toilet.

Chapter Thirty-Seven

Saturday 14 May 1940 - The backroom of the pub

Udo was missing when she returned - probably a good thing. She went to find Paol - he was engrossed in his little computer. Her ring-bound note book flapped at her side.

'You look very pensive, Katie?'

'No, no, no, I was just thinking, that's all.'

'So what are you thinking Katie?' asked Paol. She quickly closed her diary.

'I was just doodling, wasn't I? I was just updating my 'To Do' list!'

'I see. Well, I hope you've crossed off Udo's name!' He snatched the note book and quickly stepped away. She pursued him but he fended her away with his arm. 'You have been busy! What is this? You have a plan for the invasion of Britain?'

'Paol, I've got personal stuff in there, give it back!'

'No, I'm reading. You are a busy little person, aren't you?'

She grabbed his arm and twisted it. As he bent double she tripped him so he fell to the wooden floor. She wrapped her free arm round his neck. 'Drop it or I'll hurt you!'

'Okay, okay. I've dropped it'. She freed his neck and his arm but left her knee pressing firmly into the middle of his back.

She picked her diary and flicked back to her last entry. 'You're right, it is a plan, but I was just messing around. But this couldn't happen, could it?'

'Are you going to let me up?'

'Only if you promise to behave yourself.'

'I promise.' She got off him and he rolled over onto his back. He looked very sheepish.

'You've got a hard on you filthy pervert!' she accused.

'Well, that was embarrassing!' Paol got up and adjusted himself. 'You're a bit of a thug on the quiet, aren't you?'

'Bollocks, I'm absolutely adorable, aren't I? Just ask mum.'

'Ah, she disowned me when I was born...'

'Well you are a male and a monger...'

'It's minger, Katie, not monger.'

'No, it's definitely monger - you mong porn so therefore you are a porn monger! See?'

'Your command of the English language is utterly astonishing, Katie!'

'It is, isn't it! I've always said that!'

'But this is interesting. So this is what Udo's been up to. Why don't we plug this into the simulator and see what happens?'

'You can do that?'

'Sure, I just need you to clarify some points but that should only take a few minutes.' He picked up the laptop and they walked together to the back room of the pub.

'What's happening here?' Paol asked.

'They're going to make a stop line for the German Army along the river here.'

'This one here, the River Seine?'

'That's the one.'

'The army up here is going to stop pushing south. They're going to create a reserve here.'

'In Holland?'

'That's right.'

'The air flotilla in Norway?'

'That's heading south to Holland.'

'And here?'

'There's all these small craft here. They're going from Germany to here.'

'The Hook of Holland?'

'That's right.'

'And what's happening off here?'

'They're dropping mines like confetti to make a corridor across the North Sea here and here.'

'And these are submarines?'

'Yes, they are.'

'Right, so we have a gathering of the German hordes here in Holland.'

'Yes, and it all kicks off in the first week of June, when the British are evacuating out of Dunkirk.'

'So, the first wave is paratroops?'

'Yes.'

'And they're landing here, here, here and here?' He showed her the screen.

'Yes, that's right.'

'The second wave, that's glider borne right?'

'Yes.'

'And the third wave, that's ship borne, right?'

'Aye, aye!'

'Ja, ja! Well good luck to them. I can't see many of them getting through. They're going to get massacred. There will be so many bodies floating in the sea, the Blues will be able to launch a counter-attack without getting their feet wet!'

'Hmm, can we get this bigger? Your one is a bit tiny...' she said, pointing at the screen.

'Don't get personal!'

'Pillock!'

They all gathered around the big screen mounted on the wall. The Red Team and the Blue Team were already there in their separate huddles.

'Alrighty, I've got all that. Let's press 'Play' and see what happens. Everyone turned to look at the television screen; Katie tucked her legs up and peeped over the top of her knees. As the commands were enacted, she had to cover her eyes with her hands as it soon became very real.

The opening moves of the war game were played out. Orange flashes broke out all along the River Thames. The blue forces fought back bravely, but they looked pitifully thin on the ground. Red force paratroops landed on the islands of Thanet, Sheppey, Grain, Foulness and Canvey. As scores of small fire fights were played out, the islands all fell quickly. Counterattacks were made from the south - these were all beaten away easily. More and more German planes landed at Manston, Eastchurch, Rochester and Southend and then the sea-borne troops started to arrive. Although the size of the Red force lodgement along the Thames did not seem to change, the density of colour pulsed threateningly.

'So, what's the line of attack for the Reds, Katie?'

'Why are you asking me?'

'You seem to be all over it.'

'Oh, well, let's try north-west through this gap here.'

'The gap between Billericay and Brentwood? Shit, there's nothing there. No defensive lines, no nothing.'

Katie reached for her glass but could not drink. 'Where's the Home Fleet?'

'I've intervened twice: I sent the Royal Navy south from Rosyth but it got caught in the minefields off Essex and mauled by the Stuka bombers, miles from anywhere; I sent troops from Dover north by bus and train but the A2 and the main train lines have been blitzed.'

'Well, try harder, Paol, this can't be happening!' Her brain started to swim, like it was immersed in a sea of molasses.

All of Kent and East Anglia were in German hands - tentacles of orange were surrounding Greater London.

'What about the pact, Katie, what about the pact?'

'What are you gabbling about Paol?'

'The pact! What are you going to do?'

'What am I going to do?'

'Think of something Katie!'

'I'll set the Thames alight, that's what I'll do!'

'It's too late, you must do more!'

'Paol? What can I do?'

He stood up; she stood up. A chorus of 'Deutschland über alles' broke out from the red table.

They were standing face to face, his hands squeezing her shoulders: 'I call on the ancient pact between the witches of the Britanni and his

Majesty's Royal Navy. I call on you to fulfil the promise of your clan to always protect these shores from invasion!'

'Paol, you're talking a load of old cock!'

'I call on you to bring down the storm!'

'Paol, don't be a total dickhead!'

'Deutschland, Deutschland über alles, über alles in der Welt!' roared the Red team. Steins full of beer clacked together above the Red team's heads and spray swished over her and Paol as they stared at each other.

The large screen behind them gave a loud buzz and a message flashed three times: 'Britain capitulates.'

Katie didn't speak very much in the train carriage. This was partly because her brother was still seething in a seat of his own and partly because Udo was in a drunken stupor and partly because of the sharp glances they received from their fellow travellers. The train clattered along its lonely passage and came to a halt at another station she did not recognise. A quick exchange of passengers followed, the doors closed and they were on their way again, clanking along the passages of what seemed like a giant ant nest, seething below ground, full of human ants with no other purpose other than to forage, to feed, to carry and to be busy.

As the passengers settled into their own secluded spaces, Katie decided to do something that would really annoy Paol. She sat beside Udo and whispered in his ear: 'I want to cwch with you...'

'What is 'cutch'? Udo giggled.

She removed her training shoes, drew her legs up over his, wrapped her arms around him and rested her head on his shoulder. 'It's like this. Give me a few moments and I'll work you up into a right lather...'

'Katie!' hissed Paol. 'Don't you dare!'

She studied the other passenger's faces - after a quick sideways glance they got on with their own business of looking at their busy little screens or counting out how many stops to their destination or avoiding looking into anyone else's eyes. Why did they all look so unhappy? She felt exultant and content at the same time because she would sleep in Udo's bed tonight. Tomorrow, which was a free day, she would rest with Udo and they would spend the day together, doing nothing other than touching, feeling, squeezing, pulsing, releasing. 'I want to be your girl...' she heard herself say.

'Katie! This is our stop!'

'No, I'm taking Udo home.'

'Katie!'

'Piss off Paol!'

He swung his bag over his shoulder and merged with the crowd that poured out onto the platform. 'We will have words tomorrow, Katie!' he shouted as he banged his hand on the window next to her face.

'I'll see. I might be busy!' she shouted back. And the train pulled away. She shook Udo's shoulder: 'Which stop is ours?'

'The next one' he burbled.

'Are you sure?'

'No!' he giggled.

Katie wondered what Paol had told Udo about her and she wondered how much repair work she would have to do regarding her reputation, which was probably shot anyway. And then she remembered - 'Navy girl, well fit, totally bonkers'. That was it. But had he said anything about her family history, like who had had who? She felt her forehead crease in a deep frown - Paol must have said something and that was why Udo was fascinated about her.

She got Udo out of his seat at the next stop and up the escalator and through the wide gate at the top, once she had found his train ticket in his wallet. As they stood together outside the entrance to the Underground station she suddenly realised that getting him home was going to be very difficult - the cool air had washed out the last vestiges of sense he had and he was like three sheets in the breeze.

Katie pulled him into a doorway and shook him by the chin. 'Udo, I need you to concentrate. Where do you live?'

He pointed somewhere down the street - so, he either lived in a tree or on the roof of the kebab shop.

'I see. Have you got your keys?'

He went through every pocket he had two or three times over, saying 'Nein' over and over again. But she could see an awkward looking bulge in the back pocket of his tight trousers, so she deftly felt her way in, pulled out a set of keys and jangled them in front of his face. 'Ah, there they are!'

He seemed to have lost control of his limbs so Katie fed him a nip of rum. This seemed to perk him up and so they strode together down the street, her arm around his waist, weaving from side to side to avoid refuse bins, lime trees and irate pedestrians.

After thirty minutes or so, Katie realised this was not working as they were just staggering past the 'Kulture Kebab' restaurant for the third time. Just to make matters even worse, a police car had pulled up alongside and a smiling policeman was walking up to her. She carefully propped Udo up in a doorway, his face blowing against the glass and met the policeman part of the way across the pavement.

'Evening Ma'am' he said, taking off his cap, 'are you having a bit of trouble there? The three-legged race finished hours ago!'

He looked very pleased with his witty quip - he must have had her and Udo in his sights for at least one lap of the block. 'Evening officer. Yes, we're having bit of trouble finding his bed.'

'Had a good evening, has he?'

'Yes, he's thoroughly hand-carted.'

'Handcrafted?'

'No officer, hand-carted - you know, trollied, sheeted, arseholed. He's well shot away...'

'I see. Had a few too many, sir?' called out the policeman.

She looked back - Udo was ever so slowly sliding down, his tongue leaving a trail of slime on the window of the kebab shop. 'It's no good talking to him officer, he's just spouting bollocks.'

'And can you show me who are you, ma'am?'

'Yes, officer.' She flashed her RN pass.

'Navy, eh?'

'Yes, officer, I'm a matelot.'

'Can I just check who you are, sir?'

Udo managed to extract his wallet and hold it out for Katie to take and pass on to the policeman. 'Are you a street pastor, ma'am?'

'Well, sort of, I do seem to end up with a lot of drunken idiots' she replied, but he didn't look convinced. 'Actually officer, I'm his girlfriend.'

'You're his girlfriend? You certainly know how to pick 'em, don't you ma'am? So, what's your plan?'

'Plan? I thought we could keep walking around in ever-increasing circles until he sobered up...'

'Yes, well you're actually in the wrong part of town...'

'Oh, for pity's sake!'

'You'll need to get a bus or train...'

Her heart sank. 'So basically officer, you want me to carry him back down into the underground, buy two more tickets, take a train ride and start walking him in circles in another part of town? Is that what you're asking me to do, officer?'

'No ma'am, I see your predicament. How about we give you a lift, for you and your boyfriend?'

Katie pushed the door closed with her backside as the jolly policeman left Udo's flat and clattered his way down the linoleum coated stairs. The policeman had satisfied himself that Katie was not a psychopath, which was reassuring, and she would not take advantage of Udo in his drunken state. Udo was now showing signs that his brain could control his legs in a more efficient manner but he kept falling asleep vertically.

She left Udo against the wall, humming 'Deutschland über alles', which was becoming very tiresome, and decided that the second door on the left led to his bedroom. The door immediately to her left was firmly closed.

'I love you Katie' he smirked.

'That's good' she replied.

Incredibly enough, he seemed able to walk unsupported and he made his way to his room, threw open the door so it banged against the wall and flopped on to his bed. He propped himself up on his elbow and gave her a foolish grin.

'Shall I make some coffee?' she asked.

'No.'

'Can I get you a glass of water then?'

'No.'

'Shall we go to bed, then?'

'Yes, but I must undress...'

'Yes, you must.' She pushed the door of his room closed with a backward push of her leg and propped her satchel up against the wall. It was dark inside. 'Keys and wallet' Katie said as she placed them on to a bedside table. She switched the lamp on and it bathed the room in a sickly, yellow light. He was standing upright now, on his own two legs.

'So, which side is your side?' she asked, indicating the bed that stood in stark isolation in the middle of the room.

'The middle!' he announced.

'The middle? So, where do I go then?'

'Underneath!'

She looked underneath but the bed was a divan. 'Oh, I see, underneath, you dirty dog!' There was a squirming in her groin and a churning in her stomach. 'Alright then!' Katie kicked her training shoes into the far corner and stamped her socks off. 'So, what's the form? Do we strip off now and jump into bed, or...'

'You're so funny!' He ripped of his shirt with a rending of buttons and threw it dramatically to the floor.

'I am aren't I? But we're serious, now, aren't we?'

'Yes! With your permission, I will take off your clothes...' and started to kiss her on her lips.

'Mmmmm, you must be feeling a lot better!' She pulled away and looked up into his eyes and spoke in a slow, soft and vulnerable voice: 'All of mine is yours, if you want me!' He came up to her so close that she could hear the panting excitement in his heady breath.

'I love you, Katie...' he said.

There was a convulsion underway in his trousers. Adeptly, she undid his belt buckle, undid his trouser button and he stomped his trousers to the floor. He tried to undo the top button of her dress at her back; she eased the button out for him. Her quizzical expression questioned his ability to competently remove her clothing.

'Don't be afraid of my thoughts and beliefs' she whispered, 'even if they may seem a bit strange to you.'

Udo fumbled at the next button. She watched his frowning face in quiet amusement and then relief as the button was freed.

'Please respect my body and my mind, as that's what makes me, me.' Another button was liberated and the dress hung loosely from her shoulders.

'If you can do all of this, I will try my best to make you the happiest, most contented and fulfilled person that I can.' Another button came free. 'That is my promise to you!' She shimmied her shoulders so that the dress fell away to the bedroom floor and she stood before him with her head bowed demurely. 'And what is your promise to me, Udo?'

'I will fuck your brains out...'

'You animal!' Katie stepped backwards to the bed and climbed onto it, trying a couple of small jumps to test its resilience. 'Let's hope this is up to the job then...' She beckoned him to her, wrapping her arms around his neck, gently pulling him downwards and his passage was marked by a slick from his tongue, which traversed her fluffy pudding and meandered at the top of her right thigh. Her breathing quickened, her neck and shoulders arched back and her thighs squirmed in and out, in an out, up and down, up and down...

A warm, viscous flood was flowing down her leg and there were uncomfortable, icky lumps in this slick and an unpleasant smell. 'Oh my soul, what are you doing down there' she gasped, 'are you not well?' She looked down, there was a trail of sick with Udo at the end of it, curled up on the floor. 'Noooo' she cried out.

Katie lifted her leg, shook it, stepped back and stealthily hopped out of the room. She then hopped her way to the third door and listened: there was a chuckle of water from pipes so she opened the door and looked inside. It was the bathroom, or actually, the shower room. Stepping inside she hopped into the cubicle and rinsed off the yellow bile and watched it swirl down the drain, except the tomato skins.

Next, could she get Udo into the shower? Just how out of it was he? She cursed Paol and his mean-minded sabotage and the rum drinking challenge he had issued just as they were leaving the pub. Back to the bedroom, she found Udo coiled on top of the bedclothes, blowing bubbles from his lips. He seemed as content and as smelly as a belching baby, so she shook him, got her arm under his and levered him up on to his legs. So far, so good she thought.

They staggered together towards the shower, like contestants in a slow motion, three-legged race and clattered into the cubicle. She stood him up, wondering what to do next. As she pondered this, he slid slowly to the base of the shower in a heap. He was moaning about English pub food and how upsetting this was for his poor stomach. She tugged his pants off, got in the shower with him pulled him up so they were in a sickly embrace. Nudging the shower lever, she gently soaped down his hair, his face his shoulders, his chest and his stomach. He was tight to her body while water lapped over them and between them and this aroused something that prodded at her stomach insistently so she kissed him.

Ah, something else that needed doing. Katie stepped out of the cubicle, found a toothbrush and covered it with toothpaste. Back in the cubicle, Udo had slumped to the base again. Katie peeled back his lips and scrubbed his teeth and his tongue. 'Now, spit!' she said as he was now gagging on the paste. Out came the toothbrush, on came the water and she flushed his face as best she could. With the water off, she heaved him out and sat him on a towel across the toilet seat. His mouth still smelt bad, but there was a bottle of mouthwash and a beaker. She filled the beaker and started to dribble mouthwash into his mouth but Udo grabbed the beaker and emptied it down his throat before she could stop him.

Cursing, she damped him down with the big towel, wrapped him in it and then heaved him back up along the wall, into his bedroom and onto his bed. He moaned. This time he was grumbling about his head and the spinning room. Katie laid him out and dabbed him dry and then dragged a pair of his pants up his fidgety legs, but due to the massive, right-angled erection he was now sporting, only to a half-mast position.

Katie wrapped the damp towel around her tired body and watched Udo, wrapped in a quilt, sleeping on his bed. It was going to be a difficult night: he was snoring uproariously and her nose was twitching from the inescapable smell of vomit that hung in the room, but it was too late and too dark to hunt down the source. She lay down beside him.

This is how they spent the night together, together yet apart, her right leg wrapped around Udo's midriff and her arm trapped and numb, under his torso. When Katie woke, she now had the challenge of how to untangle herself. Instead, she examined his back and conjured images by linking his darker freckles together - there was a rampant horse, like the constellation of Pegasus. So he was a horse god. Of course he was!

Katie wondered if he could be stimulated while asleep, so she used her fingers to caress his buttock and then to work gently between his legs. She applied her palm and this had an immediate, gratifying and profound effect. The condom she had tucked under the pillow, just in case, was still present, but its application would need both of her hands. She eased out her left arm, waved it about until the feeling returned and then hooked his thigh and pulled him onto his back. His cock stood tall and proud. Carefully, she eased her way on top of his chest and stomach and poised above, she teased the condom over his muscular erection, in a very seamanlike fashion. Now, she carefully wrapped her legs around him and levered...

A door slammed! She held her breath tight. Footfalls! There was a tap on the door! Katie pulled Udo's pants back up, rolled off his torso, stole the covers and jumped away from the bed.

'Is that you, Udo?' asked a little girl's voice.

'No, it's Katie.'

'Who?'

'Katie, Udo's girl...'

'No! You can't be!'

'Well, I am!'

'Get out!'

'I am out!'

'I meant, get out of his room.'

'Nope!'

The footfalls receded and came back 'I think you should leave.'

'I don't think I should.'

'I'm going out and when I come back, you should be gone.'

'Off you pop then!'

'I'm going to the bathroom first...'

'Good for you!'

The girl was back sooner than expected. 'Whose clothes are these?'

'They're Udo's...are they dry yet?'

There was a long exclamation of surprise. 'They can't be...he would never do that!'

'Let me just check.' Udo was still lying on his back, snorting, with his penis upright like a prize sausage in the butcher's window. 'Hmm, he's only got pants on at the moment so I think they must be! In fact, he's nearly, quite naked!'

'Howww!'

'So, you're off out, then?'

'Yes, and when I come back, you'd better be gone...or I'll call the police!'

'Well tell them it's Katie, they'll know who I am!'

'I'm going out, but I'll be back!' With that, the little girl voice receded and then disappeared with a bang of the outer door.

Udo was still in a deep, contented torpor. How could he sleep through all that? She saw a chest of drawers, opened the top one and found a grey tee-shirt and a pair of socks to put on. She then stepped lightly out of the room into the kitchenette.

There was just instant coffee and green tea in the cupboard above the sink. And no sugar. Milky coffee it would have to be. But there was a bottle of caramel sauce there, which was an excellent find, and a bunch of blackening bananas on the counter and half a loaf of some kind of blackened bread.

While the kettle was chuckling into life, Katie slunk back into Udo's bedroom. He was still sleeping in the same position. She removed her travel bag from her satchel and opened it on the bed to find the little scissors, then slipped into bed alongside him and snuggled as close as it was possible to get against the contours of his shoulders, his back and his backside, her lips pressed softly against his neck, where she could taste him and take in his scent. He didn't stir. Her hands manipulated his breast and his buttocks, probing deeper when he didn't respond, and so she ratcheted up the press, to try and make him respond, but he didn't. Strands of wavy hair in a little piggy tail curled on his neck. She ran her nose along them, pulled them tight and snip! They were in her fingers! He muttered something and then resumed his deep sleep. Quickly, the strands of hair were twisted into a braid as she got out of the bed and meandered her way to the kettle, deep in thought. She pulled a twined tuft of hair from her own head and twisted that into a second braid and the two braids were now twisted together. 'Always mine' she whispered as she kissed the double spiral, 'now our spirals are entwined!'

Hot water was splashed onto powdered coffee in a mug and the aroma that enveloped her was pleasing. It was topped up with whole milk and criss-crossed with a lattice of caramel. Two slices of bread were popped into the toaster.

She needed her planner, so she stealthily retrieved it from the bedroom - should she slip back into bed with Udo? Best not to, as it was now breakfast time, so she padded back to the kitchenette and cradling the hot mug, eased the handle of the door that opened onto the tiny balcony, and stepped outside into the bright, sunshiny morning, giving a sigh of relief. There was a construction site opposite, with scaffolding looming skyward. On the scaffolding, three workmen were slouching and smoking, and along the wide, tree-lined street, there was just the subdued chatter of songbirds and the whirring of a milk float and very little else. Down the hill could be seen the roof of the river-side pub, the river beside and the meadows and marshes beyond. She sat on the window box, put her feet up over the balcony and took a long, slow slurp of lovely, milky, caramelly, coffee.

Katie delved into her diary: the double spiral of hair was swiftly woven between the rings of the binder opposite a pictogram; a quick glance at the pictures told her that she was no further forward, which meant yesterday had been a right-off, but tomorrow was a crunch day. Today was a day for sunning and stretching out and letting the lazy song of Sunday send her into a reverie. And if Paol wanted to go to the lido, that would be fine too.

The builders across the street were shouting and whistling to attract her attention so she made a rude motion at them with her wrist and hand. This made them noisier still so she went back into the flat and pulled a banana from the bunch. She returned back to the door of the balcony, slipped her bare leg around the door and waited a few seconds and eased her way back into full view on the balcony. And now their bellies were hanging over the scaffolding as they stared in her direction. Segment, by segment, she peeled the banana as she held it upright close to her chest. Her mouth opened widely in anticipation as the exposed flesh came closer...

Someone was pushing at the door! Someone was watching from behind! It was Udo! She pulled the banana away. 'Oh, bollocks' she muttered.

'What's going on?' said Udo.

She wondered how much he had seen. 'I was just eating a banana, that's all...'

'I think what you consider to be eating a banana is very different to what other people would consider eating a banana' he said grumpily.

'Well, I'm pleased you're up - you were totally shot away last night!'

'Is that my tee-shirt?'

She looked down at the grey tee shirt advocating the benefits of the gym. 'Yes it is, I borrowed it.'

'And my socks?' He was really on the ball this morning. 'Yes, I borrowed these as well...can I make you a hot beverage?'

Udo frowned as he rummaged in his pants. Slowly, he pulled out a condom, like a third rate conjuror. 'What's this?'

'It's a condom.'

He was frowning in complete incomprehension.

'A rubber, also known as a French...'

'I know what it is! I can't understand how it got there!'

'Well, I can help you there...it was me!'

'Why?'

'Because it wouldn't fit me...'

'What happened to me last night?'

'Well, just about everything you can imagine and a bit more...'

He looked in horror at her: 'Did you take advantage of me?'

'Absolutely, certainly not...'

'So, why did you...?'

'I was worried your prick might prod into me by accident - you had an almighty hard on.'

The girl with the little voice was back. She was wearing a grey track-suit and her brown hair in bunches. 'Udo, are you all right? That girl was in your bedroom!'

'Bed' said Katie, 'I was in Udo's bed, and I'm not 'that girl', I'm Udo's girlfriend!'

'As of when?'

'As of yesterday. So, who are you?'

'I'm Udo's flatmate, my name is Helga.' Then she added quickly 'We're in separate rooms.'

'I need to think' muttered Udo as he stalked back to his room, rubbing the back of his head.

'Nice to meet you Helga. He's a bit of a snorer, isn't he?'

'Really? I don't know. We just share the flat. I'm from the same city as Udo...Hamburg!'

'Oh, that's nice - I was just going to say I don't really do threesomes.' And I've never done a proper twosome yet she thought, but still...

'Oh, no, no, no, it's nothing like that!' There was a tight lipped pause. 'Do you know, he's engaged to a girl in Germany?'

'I did hear that, but I also heard him say last night he was going to fuck my brains out.'

'No!' Helga shouted and dissolved into giggles.

'So what does Udo drink in the morning?'

'Just a smoothie - he's not very good at getting up in the mornings.'

'Really? Based on what I saw this morning, he could have pole-vaulted out of bed!'

The telephone rang.

Helga flushed and then turned to answer the phone. 'I have Paol Houghton here - he wants to talk to his sister, Katie.'

'I'd better get this - thanks Helga.' She crossed the kitchenette and picked up the receiver. 'Hallo Paol' she said brightly, 'it's me.'

'What have you been doing?' he asked quite abruptly and rudely.

'Just Udo so far, and now I'm having a hot beverage and a banana for breakfast.'

'And what exactly did you do for Udo?'

'He's not properly gotten up so he hasn't had one yet this morning.' She couldn't help but giggle. There was a pause at the other end of the telephone.

'What did you do to Udo last night?' came back Paol's biting response.

'I think that's subject to client confidentiality, don't you?' Where on earth had she got that from? It was utterly brilliant though so she winked at Helga. There was silence again at the other end of the line. 'Are you still there Paol...?'

'When are you planning to get back, Katie?'

'Nothing firmed up yet.' She giggled again. 'So, how did you know how to find me Paol?' she asked.

'Well, obviously, I have Udo's number in my mobile.' There was another pause. Katie sensed he was still fretting. 'Can you let Udo know we have a meeting tomorrow in my office at 9am sharp!'

'Let me make a note of that. Actually, wait a moment, I haven't got a pen on me. Or paper. Or clothes!' The phone was slammed down at the other end.

Helga reappeared at her side and whispered 'Udo wants to talk to you, urgently!'

He was now dressed in a tee-shirt and shorts and still feeling the back of his neck. 'Katie, did you...cut my hair last night?'

'Absolutely not!'

'Don't lie to me.'

'I cut it this morning...'

'WHY!'

'Listen to me Udo, I understand you might be feeling a bit doggy after last night, but there's no need to shout!'

'Why did you do it?'

'Well, I think it makes you look utterly ridiculous...'

Helga turned away and dissolved into a giggling fit.

'You had no right!'

'Actually I have a perfect right, because if we're going to be girlfriend and boyfriend...'

'I will never be your boyfriend!'

'Whoa, hold up, what was all that about last night?'

'Uh, I cannot recall, I was drunk...'

'You're telling me!'

'I think its best if you leave now.'

'I see, I think what you need is a bit of recovery time and some thinking time to realise what a big favour I've done for you.'

'I don't believe this!'

Katie shook on her dress and gathered her things. 'Just give me a call at Paol's and we can meet up for...something or other. Oh, by the way, Paol says you have a meeting with him at nine tomorrow, so don't be late!'

'I'm never late...'

'Well, just see how you feel later, eh?'

'Please leave now!'

'Bye bye Helga, nice to have met you...'

'I'll walk you to the door, Katie!'

'And bye bye Udo, take a couple of brain relief tablets and remember to call me!'

'I will do no such thing!' He turned and walked away, still feeling the back of his neck, as if he had lost something of value.

'Listen to me Udo, if we're going to be girlfriend and boyfriend, you're going to have to sharpen up your act' Katie shouted after him, 'so you'll need to get in proper tea, proper bread and proper biscuits!'

She was left with Helga, who Katie realised was quite smart because she always laughed and smiled at the right moments. 'He's a bit pernickety this morning isn't he?'

'Really?''

'In fact, he's a bit snarky too, isn't he? I wonder why?'

'I can't imagine!'

'Me neither.'

'I'll talk to Udo and I'll make sure he calls you.'

'Thanks Helga.'

Out on the pavement, she heard a sweet, short warble from down the street, then a curious metallic squishing followed by a final, rising flourish. She couldn't work out who the songster was, but no matter, she needed to get back to Dorina's and liberate her clothes.

Chapter Thirty-Eight

Monday 16 May 0735 - Cambridge SIKS

Katie opened up the holdall and considered what her options were. She found a pair of black leggings which she pulled on, but it didn't matter how much she tweaked them, her knees still looked baggy. She pulled them off and threw them onto Dorina's bed. Dorina swiped them away with the hand that was not used for holding a cigarette.

Next she tried on a pair of black trousers. These were eased on over her hips and buttoned up. The area around the knees was worn to such an extent that there was an imminent threat of a tear. She removed these and emitted a loud sigh. It would have to be the navy blue skirt.

'Big meeting?' enquired Dorina. 'What happened to the dress?'

'Yes, very important meeting.' This was duly tugged on and secured at the waist. It felt quite snug over her belly but she could just about get her fingers inside the waistband. It would have to be a white blouse, not tucked in, but luckily it was squared off at the bottom. This was put on and buttoned up. It felt tight across her chest. She released a button and allowed her chest to relax outwards. Her bra was not visible, so that would avoid her looking too promiscuous. Dorina smiled approvingly.

In front of the draining board, she checked her face in the hand mirror. She was conscious that Robert was in all probability outside of the underground station, awaiting her arrival impatiently. Her hair was now secured behind her with a leather clasp and a pin. She lifted her left arm and sniffed. It would have to do. She slid her shoes on, grabbed her satchel, slammed the door closed and then jumped down the stairs - she would have to walk briskly to get there on time. There was the silhouette of Robert, fiddling with his mobile device, typing vigorously, hopping from foot to foot. She paused, he smiled and then she jumped into his arms. As she squeezed him tight, she felt safe and secure and ready. He kissed Katie lightly on the left and then the right cheek and they were on their way.

She had sat side by side with Robert Glaus in the carriage, staring ahead, with just an occasional glance at each other and a half smile. No words were exchanged. Up the escalator to the car park, into the red sports car with the rearing stallion on the front and then a pell-mell journey along busy roads leaving the sprawl of brick built buildings in favour of the chalk plateau and then the flat lands of fields, hedges, small villages and smart business parks.

He crunched through the gears and gave a little half smile at her when the engine roared in protest. And now they were passing lumbering wagons with their poisonous breath and speeding through thick, heady clouds of soil dust and tall grass dust. The sun was behind them in one quarter and in the opposite quarter ahead, a park of big, thrown up shells with windows, surrounded by unbroken fences and cameras on tall posts. As they drove through the main security gate, the two uniformed officials gave them a casual glance and got back to their other duties. Robert made a quick aside to her, 'Special privilege for a special guest.'

'Ah, I see.'

Level 1: Two Kelvins, one with a finger wedged up his nose and the other with itchy bollocks. For out of hours, they would assign their top team, surely.

Robert opened the car door for her and she stepped out. 'Ta' she said, remembering to keep her knees firmly together, 'so, how do you keep the local gronks out?'

'Gronks, Katie?'

Level 2: Twenty-four hour patrols by Zen and his Security Men and their guard dogs.

She was taken by her arm and guided into a big, new smelling lofty foyer, where she took receipt of a security pass with her picture on. The two women behind the desk seemed to know what they were doing and had a brisk and alert efficiency about them. She took notice of the sign in the foyer that welcomed her and listened attentively as the senior of the two women described the security measures and the health & safety procedures. There were two levels of security in the inner part of the building: the electronic lock with role specific entry permissions and the 4 digit code, changed daily. Katie had none of these so she wondered if Robert had to accompany her to the 'heads'? If she needed the washroom, then Robert would have to open the door for her and he would have to accompany her everywhere she went and if there was any nonsense, he would have his balls broken, Katie surmised. She signed to acknowledge that had understood the briefing. 'Thanks' said Katie.

Level 3: Bugger, bugger, bugger.

Together, they trotted up the stairs together, turned and found a set of double doors with a big, bold message on the outside declaring that it was booked for Herr Doctor Letsch all morning. 'Are you nervous Katie?'

'Yes, I am. This is serious, isn't it?' Death defyingly serious she was thinking. 'I'll just put my face on before we go in.'

'Put your face on? But you're already perfect!'

She waved her hand in front of her face and brought up a smile. 'How's that?'

'Too comic.'

She tried again, this time much harder. 'How's that?'

'Too constipated!'

'You cheeky sod! All right, how's this?'

'Serious, attentive, business-like and completely engaging.' She smirked at him. 'Oh, you've spoilt it now!'

Katie was led into a long room; in the room was a long table, made with dark, shiny veneered wood, adorned with cups and saucers, glasses, bottles of water, and chocolate biscuits. Yes, chocolate biscuits! In the warmth of the air, the aroma of chocolate entered her nose, made its way along her sinuses and triggered a reaction from the glands that make saliva. Alongside the table were rows of five legged chairs and behind each chair was a beaming, dressed-for-business person. And they were all beaming at her. The man at the end of the table she recognised. He had a forced smile on his face, as if the corners of his mouth had been tacked up against his chewing teeth. The white tuft of hair on his forehead had been swept back into position on his ruddy scalp.

She was led by Robert to a position at the head of the table, pride of place. There was a gentle round of applause as she sat down. Her name was on a name plate in front of her, as was a glossy SIKS brochure. Two people asked her what she wanted to drink. She asked for tea. There were several different kinds apparently, but she opted for a Ceylon tea that seemed most suitable for mid-morning refreshment. This was made in the cup before her using a tea bag as she waited patiently. Chocolate biscuits were offered to her. She took two and placed them on the small plate in front of her, but left them while she considered when it would be polite to consume them. Katie licked her fingers when she thought no one was looking to get that thin sweet and bitter veneer of chocolate in her mouth.

There were too short taps of a long metal pointer on the screen in front. It was Herr Letsch, calling the meeting to order. Everyone looked and sat down in a squeaking of leather upholstery and chair workings and there was a strange silence, as if they were all part of an orchestra, just waiting for their individual cue. A device from the ceiling dropped down and beamed a picture on the screen. The image was clear to her - it was a double entwined spiral.

Herr Letsch stood at the front of the room with his pointer. It traversed the audience, one by one and each individual introduced themselves to her, saying who they were, how long they had been with SIKS, what their role was and how they would interact with her. The pointer skipped over her and went straight to Robert but this left a gap that she would have to fill - she would be expected to say who she was and what she was doing there in this brand new, sparkling facility. Her heart thumped uncomfortably against her ribcage.

'And now, in a break from tradition, I will introduce you to our valued guest, I will say who she is, where she has come from and how she will be the saviour of a poor, sickly child that is in my care.'

He nodded at her and she gave a little nod back, but she had no idea what he was going to say. She pressed her diary down firmly into the table but she feared that her plan was about to be shot to pieces.

'Katell Ebrill Talog was born to Maela nineteen years ago in Wales and she currently serves in the British Royal Navy. You must have enlisted at a very young age?'

She nodded.

'Very good. We have been able to trace back her genealogy over many years and this is what we have found...'

Katie pushed herself up and slowly walked to the front of the room to join Herr Letsch and she pushed aside the pointer. She was at the top of a long sequence of branches that descended into the distant past, a sequence of mothers with strange sounding names, that her fingers could trace back and as Herr Letsch clicked through the ages she was travelling back through scores of generations and hundreds if not thousands of years.

'And now in a more graphic form for you...'

A rash of pink spots appeared all over Katie now, so she stepped to one side. The pink spots were now on the screen; an island of them along the west coast of Ireland, an upwelling in mid-Wales, clusters along the northern coast of Cornwall, a blight of them amongst the western isles of Brittany and a pandemic in the western Pyrenees.

'You seem to think I'm actually French, don't you?'

'No, no, no, nothing as simple as that! Let me show you how we did this...' She had to sit, at the front, transfixed by what was flashing past on the screen as he described the science and then described the molecule, 'a marvellous, magnificent miraculous molecule' as he called it. She had a gene, as all these other women did, that manufactured this molecule in their marrow and this molecule could track down certain kinds of cancer cell and stop them growing.

Or so he reckoned.

'How did you find this all out?'

'Through good science.'

'Good science? Like when you stuck that swab in me?' Someone in the audience sniggered.

He pursed his lips and lifted the pointer. 'You ridiculous girl!'

She turned away from him and walked along the table, looking steadily ahead of herself, steadily ignoring all the gawping faces, left the room, with the metal pointer stopped in mid-gesture, expressions of surprise frozen in the stunned faces. Letsch shouted 'Herr Glaus!'

Katie pushed through the double doors, turned to her left and ran swiftly along a grey corridor.

There was a mistake in the branches of the chart, she was sure of it.

At the end of the corridor was an alcove at the end with white painted boxes stuffed full of packs of hats, gloves, hairnets, face masks and gowns like white kitchen pinafores. She could hear anxious voices emerging from the meeting. There was a keypad sticking prominently out of the wall, which she covered with her hand. A four digit number came into her mind and she keyed it in. The doors swung open and she was into the core of the facility. There were long, clean benches in this room, as clean as an operating theatre, stacked with metal boxes and glass vessels. She put on a white gown and a white panama hat and she was through.

And then there was another room, locked and silent beyond the door. There was another keypad, which she was able to negotiate by entering the same four digit code as before. In the dark space beyond, faintly lit by emergency lights, large metal vessels brooded quietly.

And then there were another set of large white glossy doors, shiny white, with big clunky handles that yielded to her firm, downward push. The door opened outwards and a bell started ringing shrilly and insistently. Lined up in the sliding racking there were thousands of neatly labelled, pristine vials and one of these was pulling her towards it. The aisle at the back of the room was opened up with a big, black steering wheel of a handle. She walked down the aisle, dropped down on her knees to look at the lowest shelf. There was someone rushing towards her. Her hands flicked along the vials and she found the one that was calling for her. It was a very old, dusty looking glass vial, containing viscous amber liquid and something precious. Her hand reached towards it but her arms were grasped and she was drawn up until she was standing. 'Katie please, you mustn't. You're not allowed in here!' It was Robert.

'Please, can I just see, can I just see?'

'No, you are not allowed to see!'

'But I was drawn here, I felt something in here' she stammered as she was dragged out backwards.

Two uniformed guards arrived, puffing and panting and red-faced.

'It's all under control here, boys, it's just a misunderstanding, isn't it Katie?' said Robert.

She nodded quickly as she was pulled back into the clean pristine space behind and then back into the laboratory. The laboratory staff had stopped working and were now gathered around her, murmuring agitatedly. She was perched on a stool and they circled around her, with their white coats making them look like a flock of white flamingos, gathering in a lake, ready to start a courting dance.

'Ah, Miss Talog, Miss Talog, Miss Talog, you have led us a merry dance' said Herr Letsch jovially. But under his forced joviality was a face that frowned, and beneath the frown, a mind that had calculated how to extract what he needed from her, something that he needed desperately and quickly, but something she was equally determined not to let him have.

He seized her arm and squeezed tight and she remembered how he had seized her jaw, in a grip that she could not dislodge and how he had the strength and the speed and the agility of a wrestler, but not a ponced up one in shiny trunks, but one who knew all the vulnerabilities of her body and could seize her around the neck and snap it.

Her body shook and her left arm tightened. 'You're hurting me!' She wrenched her arm out of his grasp. 'Tell me what you've got down there' Katie shouted, 'is it a body part warehouse?'

'You silly girl! Look and listen' said Letsch and his eyes drew her to the blue flashing lights in the doorway and the shrill siren that hurt her ears.

'How could you, how could you? You can raise those that are passed, those that have left us!' she shouted. The eyelid of her left eye flickered and she couldn't stop it.

He motioned that she should be silent. 'Rubbish, Miss Talog, utter rubbish. You have no comprehension at all, no comprehension at all. Do you know the regulations we must abide by? I do! I have to! Your government inspects us. Many international organisations inspect and approve our work here. You have no idea!'

'That's enough Herr Doctor, let us give Katie breathing space. I think a more measured approach would be better for Katie. Let me take her through the regulations so she can understand what we do.'

'Make sure she understands, Herr Glaus! She is your responsibility!' The siren had stopped but the alarm lights still blinked. 'The consequence of what she has done, is that the security services and the local police are even now, arriving at our facility. I will have to explain how a foolish girl has triggered our alarm system by a wanton disregard for our rules!'

'All I wanted...was to see if your security was any good' she said as she rubbed her left arm, 'and it seems just fine!' If he had kept his grip on her arm any longer, it would have become numb and useless.

'Take her in hand Herr Glaus and make her understand. The police may want to interrogate her. So, tell me Miss Talog, what were you thinking, really? And the truth this time.'

She swallowed loudly. 'It was just...my brain-warp.'

'I will see you before you leave, when the police have finished with you! And I will take action now...' He seized her pass, pulled it violently off her body and crushed it in his bare hand.

'Come with me Katie' said Robert as he pulled her away by her right hand and led her out of the laboratory into another clean, grey corridor.

She allowed herself to be led meekly into an office, which had a desk, a table and two chairs and a large window. She sat down, gazed out at the blue sky and the fields of crops and the hedges that stretched to the horizon and nursed her neck and arm as she twiddled with the five legged chair. 'I really pissed him off, didn't I?'

'You have pissed all of us off Katie' said Robert as he prepared a mug of tea for her, spread chocolate biscuits on a plate and sat down opposite her at the desk. Another blunder, she was sitting in his chair. He was married and he had two very young daughters - one of them had drawn a picture of a stick man with long dark brown hair and orange trousers and it was up on the wall. There were no other clues about Robert Glaus that she could see. Oh, yes, he played a bit of tennis during his relaxation time.

Katie made a sandwich out of three of the biscuits, paused to see if Robert approved and then chomped through it, sluicing the residue down with hot, sweet tea. He watched as she settled back into the chair, fidgeting it back and forth, as she scanned the world out of the window.

'How are you feeling, Katie?'

'Oh, a bit sore but I always end up a bit sore whenever I meet up with Ulrich. He's quite forceful, isn't he?'

'Yes, he's very passionate about his work, as indeed, we all are.'

'I'm sorry I had a bit of a funny turn back there. These biscuits are nice. Someone must have tipped you off! It's a lot to take in. And I don't care what Ulrich says, I think this is all wrong.'

'What he says is correct: There are internationally recognised rules and regulations that are applied to our work. We must abide by these and so must you!'

'He wants to stick a needle in me, doesn't he, and suck my bone marrow out?'

'A qualified nurse will do this and you will be in complete comfort all the time. The procedure will take two or three hours and at the end of it, you will have saved a young girl's life. What we learn could save many other young lives so that is why it is so important to all of us here...'

'Hmm. I didn't know about any of that. I think he just sees me as a specimen, like all the others in his body part museum!'

'Well, I am going to now teach you the regulatory framework within which we must work and our procedures' he said as he placed the glossy brochure in front of her, and took her through it page by page. 'Shouldn't you be taking notes?' he asked.

'I think I will keep it all in my head, thanks.' She wasn't sure if it was the sweet tea, the chocolate biscuits or the numbing pain in her arm or the sharp pain in her neck, but she managed to stay awake through all of this. Or, it could have been Robert's eloquent and passionate delivery.

'There Katie, what do you think now?'

'I think I've got my head around it now.'

'So are you ready to take the test?'

'What test?' she asked in alarm.

'The test that assures me that you have been listening and you have absorbed the key messages.'

'But I'm not ready, I haven't got a pencil, or anything, have I?'

'It will be a verbal test and you will mark your answer on this multiple choice answer sheet - you can borrow my pen.'

'Verbal? So no writing, just marking?'

'Yes, Katie, are you ready?'

'Not really. What happens if I fail the test?'

'I will keep you here until you pass it!'

'Oh, bugger! We could be here for weeks!'

'I'm joking of course...'

'Oh, nice one.'

With much chewing of the end of the pen and some check questions by her to clarify what he meant, she was almost through.

'Are you ready for the final part?' he asked.

'Yes, I think I am.'

'Right you are. Please write the name of the most wonderful woman to have ever graced us with her presence here in this facility.'

'Write?' She nibbled at the end of the pen. There was a plaque at the entrance on the ground floor but she couldn't recall the name on it. Would a lady from the royal family have been invited, she wondered? Or a lady from the government? She gripped the pen more fiercely with her incisors. 'Oh, you want me to write my name at the bottom, don't you?'

'Yes, I do, and your best signature and today's date.'

She added her name and the initials and the flourish that would have to pass as her signature. 'That will do' she said as she finished writing the date. 'Wow, that was tough!' she exclaimed.

'Hmm, let me just calculate if you have achieved the necessary pass mark.' Throughout these few seconds, Katie chewed her lower lip anxiously.

'I'm pleased to say that you have achieved a pass with one hundred percent correct answers. Well done Katie!'

'Blimey, how did I fluke that!'

'It was no fluke. You have learned the basics of the human tissue regulations and how our procedures ensure we are compliant with them.'

'Oh, do I get a certificate then?'

'Of course you do.' He printed the document, signed it with a flourish and presented it to Katie in a white envelope. 'So, will you help us?'

'Yes, I would like to come back soon.'

'Can I book you in now?'

'Yes, you may.' She unfurled her diary planner for the following week. 'It will have to be then,' she said pointing to the day after her visit to HMS Hawkins at Shoeburyness.

'Excellent, we'll have our patient and everything set up for you!' From all the documents that had flashed before her on the screen of his personal computer, she had picked out one name and it was a name she was not supposed to have seen, the name of the patient. It was Uschi Zutter.

The family name probably should have triggered a sympathetic reaction inside, but instead, there was an uncomfortable stirring in her loins. 'Just one condition though - I don't want Doctor Letsch anywhere near me when I come back. He scares the living crap out of me!'

'I'm sorry Katie, but he must be here. It's the law. He is our patient's doctor!'

Katie sat and looked at the telephone. It was a drab, beige, impassive looking thing; impassive because it was waiting for a call to come through, a call for her, from Udo. But, it didn't ring.

'Just call him!' Paol said in frustration.

'What if I call him just as he's calling me?'

'It'll work out somehow. So, why don't you call him on your mobile?'

'It's broken and anyway, I could never get the hang of the thing.'

'Just call him!'

'All right. That's what I'll do.' She riffled through the pages of her diary and found his number in the 'Contacts' section. 'Does this look right to you?'

'Just call him and remember not to mention his hair!'

'I'll call him.' She dialled the number and waited in trepidation for someone to pick up. 'Hallo Udo, it's me, Katie!'

She covered the mouthpiece and said to Paol, 'He wants to know who I am? I'm not the only Katie he's ever met!'

'He's never met another Katie like you' muttered Paol quietly.

'It's Katie, Paol's sister we met in that pub in Loughton, remember? I walked you home!'

She turned to Paol. 'He remembers me now!'

'Yes, that's right - so how are you Udo? I was a bit worried about you!'

She listened intently. She turned to Paol, 'He doesn't remember much about Saturday night' she whispered.

'I wonder why!' taunted Paol.

'I had to clean you up in your bathroom, Udo.'

'You want to know why you've got a tender spot on your forehead? Well, you did a somersault into the shower!'

'Yes, I had to take your clothes off.'

'Yes, you were naked.' She turned to Paol and whispered 'What's a bunny boiler?'

She turned her attention back to Udo. 'Anyway, that was back then, would you like to go out for a drink?'

'A date, yes, that's right.'

'I'll come to yours, if that's all right? I quite like the look of that place down by the river...'

'No, why, what's...'

'No, I don't think so...'

'I disagree - I chose you, so...'

'No, I'm not...'

'All right, is that it?'

'Yes, I suppose we can be friends, but I thought...'

'So, who is this Zella?' she asked.

'Can we do what?'

'No, I'm sorry too...'

'I'll see you around then...bye, bye Udo.'

She put the phone receiver down and tried to get her composure back but the hurt in the pit of her stomach would not allow it.

'He doesn't want to go out with me. He thinks it was a big mistake, and we should put it behind us...and who's this Zella?'

'Zella is his lobster, as you put it' Paol replied. He seemed to be able to do anything on his little computer, including pulling up a picture of Udo's significant other.

'What am I going to do?'

'What does your planner say?'

She flicked through the diary. 'It says tomorrow, I go to Clun...'

'There you are then? And what are you going to do about the Herr Doctor Letsch?'

'I'm going to do as he says...'

'That doesn't sound like you Katie?'

'There' she said as she brandished the page of her diary, 'so up yours, Paol!'

'So you'll want to stay with me again.'

'Absolutely. So, what do you reckon about this Zella?'

'Quite pretty I suppose...'

And there she was in a full length shot: 'Oh, she looks quite like me!'

'A plain girl...'

'Oi!'

'About the same height and build - not very imaginative the Germans, are they?'

'What do you reckon to her legs?'

'They're fine from what I can see...'

'They're not very nice though, are they?'

'There's nothing wrong with them!'

'They're like little sparrow's legs!'

'Well, yours are quite chunky...and hollow!'

'Oi! No, they're not, I have good legs, her legs are horrible. I bet they're all bristly. Udo will get cock burn when he shags her!'

'You have such a way with words.'

'I do, but now I need big eats.'

'To fill those hollow legs of yours?'

'Obviously. And if I said to you all the reasons why I need big eats now, I wouldn't be able to eat big eats until tomorrow...'

Chapter Thirty-Nine

Tuesday 17 May 1137 - Cannock Chase

'What happened to your bob?' her sister asked, as she spun the steering wheel with her palm, like she was shining a window, only Gwen had never shined a window in her life, Katie reckoned.

'Which Bob?' replied Katie.

'The short practical bob you left with thirteen months ago...' The parked ranks of lorries were disappearing behind and Gwen was preparing to enter the nearside lane of the motorway, heading west.

'I don't think I know a short, practical Bob...'

'I mean the sensible, practical haircut you had before your last tour of duty!' They had now manoeuvred into the outer lane and the supercharged engine roared.

'Oh, that. It grew out, didn't it?'

'Don't they have hairdressers on board?' Gwen cursed at the slow moving vehicle blocking her passage.

'They do, but my hair went all rampant, didn't it?'

'What happened?'

'I would rack-out with it all under control then when I got up for my next watch, there was enough to make an anchor rope!'

'You do exaggerate Katie.'

'Just a bit.'

'And, you've blossomed...'

'Like a rose, you mean?'

'Not like that, but you've had a spurt...'

'Don't be disgusting Gwen!'

'...in the chest department.'

'Oh those!'

'So, we're going to get you properly fitted for a bra. That would be a good, sisterly thing to do, don't you think?'

'And what's the matter with my bra?' said Katie as she peeked down her shirt.

'That one is way too small, so it's practically obscene and it's a mucky grey colour!'

'It's perfectly serviceable Gwen and its done its time in the Dhobie Palace!'

'No arguments, we will do this' Gwen said.

'If we must...'

'So have you been on one of those funny diets?'

'I've been eating semolina and gateau like they've been going out of fashion.'

'I thought that was an old wives tale?'

'It turns out the old wives were right.'

'And what happened to the infamous green tee-shirt?'

'It needs a wash.'

'It needs incinerating...and what happened to your Swiss fellow, Robert?'

'Oh, I went out with him yesterday.'

'A date?'

'Well, sort of, we went to Cambridge...'

'Ah, wonderful city...did he take you on a punt?'

'Don't be vulgar, Gwen.'

'You know perfectly well what I mean.'

'No, he didn't take me on a punt. Turns out he's married and he's got two kids.'

'Oh Katie, you really know how to pick 'em...'

'We're not having an affair, Gwen, Robert and I are just...doing business together!'

'Business together? What happened to 'I'm a matelot and I have a 'Percy in every port' Katie?'

Katie was pushed back into her seat by the sudden acceleration and gripped the arms. 'That was a bit of an exaggeration.'

'I'm sorry to hear that, Katie, but if you come back to us for good, there'll be so many young men only too willing to give you a good servicing!'

'Oh, brilliant! So I'm having my cherry popped in a haystack?'

'Still unsullied? Well, there you are, just one more reason why you should quit the navy!'

'I'm not quitting Gwen, I've just signed up for another five years.'

There was a long pause as Gwen fretted. 'You should re-consider.'

'It's too late Gwen, I've made up my mind.'

'Change it. You've done your bit. You owe them nothing!'

'But I've been advanced to leading hand!'

'Leading nothing! The money's a pittance, our farm's going to ruin and you're away twelve months at a time!'

'I send back all I can!'

'I know you do...'

Katie glanced at her sister, in her tailor made brown trousers, open checked shirt and red neckerchief, all tall and slim with perfect skin, long hair gathered in and piled upon her crown, business-ready, like she'd just finished in the farmyard, pulled off her green wellingtons and thrown them in the back. 'You look if you're doing really well Gwen. How's it going?'

'Not good, but we're struggling along.'

'You're not struggling along though, are you Gwen?'

'I'm managing. It's my business. Without me there would be no food on the table and Alexander and Monique would have no prospects!' She looked defiantly at Katie.

'How's Stefan coping?'

'That's Mister Hofland to you!'

Katie decided to let that go for now. 'Can I listen to the radio?'

'If you must, but see if you can find something that's easy listening.'

Katie pushed in the knob and rotated it quickly so that a staccato cacophony assaulted their ears.

'Will you stop messing around with it?' Gwen snapped.

'I'm not doing anything! It's temperamental!' The channel changed again. This time it was a Welsh language station.

'So, are you still learning the Welsh, Katie?'

'Yes, Gwen.' Katie thought for a moment. *'Fy hofrenfad yn llawn llyswennod'* she recited, carefully and deliberately.

'And what's that supposed to mean?'

'It means I've got a kettle full of fish, or something like that.'

'Of course it does.' Gwen paused. 'I think it's right just here' as she skilfully manoeuvred the vehicle into the junction. In fifty yards they passed through the entrance to the hospital unit. 'Stay close to me Katie.'

'No worries about that Gwen!' She looked upwards with foreboding at the red stone walls climbing upwards. This was her first visit to see Gwen's dad since she was sixteen and the coming prospect filled her with uncertainty.

Katie and Gwen showed identification at reception, registered and then were led to a seated holding room. The male nurse warned 'You may be upset when you see Mister Houghton, he hasn't been eating well since you last saw him.' This was directed at Gwen. It's been a while, thought Katie, so I'm already prepared for the worst.

They were led down a corridor and then up two flights of sparkling, disinfected stairs. The ward was open and surprisingly busy. They were brought to a pale blue painted room, simply furnished with a bed, a table fixed to the floor and an armchair, also fixed to the floor. Alain Houghton was sitting firmly in the armchair looking out of the window. There was a slight tremble in his left leg which caused the pyjama leg to flutter. He was thin and he hardly filled his pyjamas. His face was gaunt and his eyes were hollow. White stubble was emerging across his cheeks and jaw.

Alain looked curiously at Katie but ignored Gwen. 'Oh...' he slurred, making a vain attempt to sound cheerful. Katie thought he looked very old and frail. She sat down on the arm of his armchair, ignoring Gwen's reproachful stare. Katie was fascinated by a long white hair growing out of the end of his nose and she tried to work out how long it was - when straightened out, she reckoned, it must have been at least an inch long. There was also a thicket of white hairs coiled in his right ear. She resolved to cut this all away.

Katie looked up at the nurse. 'Can he hear in the clear with all this in his ear?' she asked. The nurse and Gwen simply ignored her.

Gwen sat on the table, and reached over to grasp his trembling hands. 'Papa, how have you been keeping? Can you see, I've brought Katie to see you?'

Katie smiled grimly. 'Hallo Mister Houghton' she announced into his right ear.

He frowned and turned to her. 'Ooh?'

'I'm Katie, Gwen's sister.'

He looked puzzled. He snapped his hands back from Gwen's tentative grasp. 'Ooh?'

'No, I'm Katie. I'm from the Welsh side of the family. You know, the ones that caused all the trouble.'

'Aah?'

'Ah, you remember, Maela's kiddy.' She thought about what she had said. Did Maela have any other kiddies apart from Paol and Gwen and her? She was a bit of an earth mother and not particularly 'au fait' with modern birth control measures.

Gwen waited until this exchange had finished. 'Well, Papa, what can I tell you? What news have I got?' She removed a sheaf of photographs from her bag. They were neatly secured so she could flick through them like an old time cinema show.

'Alexander is doing well at school. He's working hard on his revision and he's starting his exams next week.' Gwen nodded encouragingly to Mister Houghton as she tried to elicit some kind of response.

'Is Al doing a bit of acting on the side?' Katie wondered out loud. In one of the pictures she thought she had seen him in crudely made up eyes and lips and black hair that spiked out in all directions.

'His name is Alexander, not Al and yes, he is trying out...different things.' Gwen seemed a little bit prickly about this.

'Like how to look like a scarecrow!' Katie nudged Mister Houghton in the ribs and they sniggered together.

'Alexander has artistic tendencies and he enjoys... drama' said Gwen spikily.

'Perhaps he can give me a few make-up tips!'

'I think that would be a full time job for somebody, Katie.'

'Oi, Gwen!'

'But the natural look would play out well in the Marches, Katie.'

'There's nothing wrong with looking natural, is there?'

'Drrr...' interrupted Alain. Katie filled his tea mug from the bottle in her satchel and placed the mug in his outstretched hands. He drank it down quickly making a strange, gurgling noise as the liquid passed down his throat.

'Monique is doing well, she is happy at her new school.' Alain resumed his steely and unyielding watch out of the window.

Gwen continued 'Monique idolises Katie, doesn't she Katie?'

'Oh, I don't know about that, Gwen.'

'Which is unfortunate but she does seem very keen on the Royal Navy just now but we're showing her that there are other, and better, options for her. Obviously, if she does sign up it will be as an officer cadet.'

'Obviously' said Katie.

'And soon she could be ordering Katie about, couldn't she Katie?'

'Yes, I think she probably will.'

'Kaaat...?' he asked of the figure sitting alongside him. He looked inquisitively at her. Katie shrugged. 'Yes, I'm Katie, Maela's daughter, which makes me...'

'Baa...?'

Katie leaned across to quickly refill the mug with water and sat back. He swallowed the water and placed the mug on the table. 'Ow!' A sharp pain in her right buttock! She got up and smoothed the arm of the arm chair - there was nothing protruding. But Alain's eyes were smiling and his hands clutched in his lap. She nudged him gently in the ribs. He snickered and hid his face behind his hands.

Gwen gently moved his hands away. She was no longer smiling.

'Maaa...' he said and Katie nodded. She quickly pushed his arm away as it crept stealthily behind her.

Gwen had noticed something going on between them and a frown now darkened her features. She stumbled for words. 'We're struggling a bit to keep the farm going, there's no market for sheep, my husband will have to rethink his strategy.'

'What's happened, Gwen?'

'I'll tell you later, Katie.' She put the photographs back in her handbag.

'I'm running short of clients, so times are a little hard. But we'll survive. We always do. No one cares about farmers, do they? And where's everyone's food going to come from then? Are they hoping for manna from heaven?'

'What's manna, Gwen?'

'I'll tell you later, Katie. And now Katie is back, maybe she could help us out on the farm?'

'Noo...!' Alain cried out. There was silence for a moment and then it was broken by footsteps and the door swinging open.

'I suggest you leave' said the nurse, 'he does get tired very quickly.'

'Papa? Do you want us to leave?' Gwen got up slowly, placed a bag of green grapes on the table and wiped a tear away from her eye. She walked towards the door as Katie waited.

'Me too?' Katie asked.

'Noo...' said Alain.

'Do you answer 'noo' to every question then?!'

The nurse interrupted: 'Are you all right Mister Houghton?'

'Ffffine...' muttered Alain.

'Miss Talog?'

'I'm fine. We're fine. We're all fine' said Katie brightly.

'I'll be back in ten minutes Katie' said Gwen, 'I don't want you left on your own with Papa for too long. I just need to talk to the nurse about Papa's treatment. Try not to upset him.' Gwen left the room with the nurse but the curtains that shielded the room were pulled apart and the nurse gave a meaningful look in Katie's direction to indicate where the alarm pull cord was positioned. Katie acknowledged the signal.

'I thought they were never going to go, didn't you?'

'Yooo...' he said.

'Eh?'

'Like Maaa...'

'Like Maela? You cheeky sod! She's ages older than me!'

'Y'knowwww...'

'Yes, I do know. You were always one for the girls, weren't you?' He sniggered at this. 'You're just swinging the lead aren't you? There's nothing wrong with you at all, is there?' Katie moved round and sat on the table facing him. She took out a chewy bar from her satchel and broke off a piece. What was the protocol here? What was the right size? Yes, that was it, bite sized is right sized: dong sized is wrong sized. 'Chewy?' she asked.

He nodded. She placed the piece in his mouth. It slushed around the front of his mouth and she gasped in relief when he swallowed and it made its way safely down his gullet.

'Mmm...' said Alain.

'More? You can't beat a chunk of chewy, can you?' She placed another piece between his chocolate silvered lips.

'Wrnnn...?' he asked.

'Yes, I'm a Wren in the RN. You know I was sent away for a life on the ocean waves, didn't you? They said I should join the navy as soon as I could, so I did. I'm a leading hand now. But there are no Wrens in the Mob now, just ratings and officers.'

'Lllll...?' he asked. She thought he was going to spit out a Welsh place name.

'Llanfair...'

'Nooo...' he replied.

She looked again at his pyjamas. 'Isn't it time you got dressed?'

He shook his head.

'Yes, it is. Let's smarten you up.' She delved into her satchel and came up with a pack of disposable razors, a tube of soap and a small pair of scissors. It occurred to her that the scissors should have been confiscated downstairs. She rose and stood behind his chair. 'So, buddy, how do you like it done?'

Alain smiled.

She waited for an answer. 'All right, short back and sides it is.' She snipped carefully and gathered the cuttings on the table and chatted about her life on the ocean waves. Every so on, Katie paused to bend down and peer into his eyes. 'Not much of a talker, are you buddy?'

Alain was beaming.

'I can trim your eyebrows too if you want? And your nose hairs and your ear hairs.' Next she made a lather with soap and water and rubbed it into his face. 'These are girly razors, so I don't how well they'll work on your face. They should be up to the job.' Katie positioned herself in front of Alain and carefully shaved away the foam along the grain of his whiskers.

'I'm just back from the Indian Ocean. My ship is HMS Albany.'

'Type...?' he stuttered.

'Yes, she's a Type 23 Frigate.'

'Acct...?'

'Yes, I did a bit. Only it was warmer where I was - bikinis were standard issue. The sea around the Falklands must have been sodding cold though...'

'Cold...' He wrapped his arms around his body and gave a big shiver. Katie walked to the closet and found a pair of dark brown woollen trousers and a checked shirt.

'I'll get you dressed in these!' He nodded. She removed his pyjama top and quickly threaded his arms through the sleeves of his shirt and did up the buttons. 'This is the tricky bit, are you all right with me whipping your pyjama bottoms off?' He nodded again. He lifted his legs and laughed as Katie whisked the bottoms off and then struggled to haul his trousers on. 'If you just stand up, I'll hoist your trousers up so they're not at half mast.' After a further struggle, his trousers were where they should be. They collapsed into the armchair. 'There's room for two of you in there and still I struggled to get them on you!'

She settled down in front of him again. 'I've got a posting to Shoeburyness in Essex.' She massaged his temple with the tips of her fingers and then made silvery grey furrows across his scalp.

'Shoe...?'

'Oh, it's part of the old gunnery range. There's a lot of clearing up to do. I was hoping to get a transfer to one of our new capital ships, but...'

'Whaa...'

'What happened? Off Shoeburyness? I don't know.'

'War...'

'War? Off Shoeburyness? I don't think so!'

He paused and made an agonising search through his mind. 'Da...'

'My dad?'

'No!'

'Your dad?'

'Jim...'

'Who? Jim Houghton? Captain James Houghton?'

Alain pointed behind her to a low lying cabinet. Her right arm stretched as far as it could reach and flipped the door open. Her fingers told her it was full of old books and papers. 'Down. Down there...' he croaked.

'Got it' she replied. Her hand had found an old scrap book and a flutter of the pages told her it was full of old photographs. She gradually pulled it towards her, passed it across his head and put it on his lap. 'Bollocks, I'm going to have to move, just bear with me!'

Katie was back on the arm of the chair, her arm around his shoulder and her cheek against his scalp. There was a photograph of a warship, a warship of an earlier war.

'Eag...' he said as he pointed.

'HMS Eager? Wow, she looks a bit racy.'

'Dad...' he pointed to a man in captain's uniform.

'Your dad? Captain Jim Houghton? Wow, he's a good looking man, isn't he? I can see where you get your good looks from!' She flicked through the pages towards the end. 'Oh, look!' She pointed to two colour photographs. They were portraits of a woman, who had bright but dark eyes, tight skinned and with long braided hair, coiled about her waist.

He touched these and looked at them longingly. He pointed and said 'Maela!'

'Yes, Maela!'

He struggled to think and then captured something. 'Eager at Dun...' He paused for breath, 'Fran...'

'And your Dad was captain and he got them back?'

'Chhh...Chat...' Katie put her hand on his knee. 'Scare...'

'It's all right. It's all over. It was years ago.'

He pulled at her hands. 'Baaaad...'

'It's all right. We got our boys back, didn't we?'

Alain flicked back the pages and pointed at a portrait of a pretty young woman in uniform. Something about the depth of her eyes and the length of her nose and the breadth of her smile made her heart flutter.

'Roz...!'

'Rosaline? Is that her name?'

'Fren...'

'Was she your dad's? Blimey, she's a looker!'

He stopped and couldn't reconnect with his stream of thought. And wasn't that just typical of the Navy? Rescue an army from a beach and bring yourself back a French tart! But now, she had the picture of Maela and this French bint side by side and she grinned - there was something about a matelot that snared all the best looking girls. Was it the uniform? Possibly, or was it something about having a man who went away for months on end and only returned when the girl's heart and soul were sick with longing and then they swept you off your feet and pulled you tight. But she was a matelot too, so why shouldn't it be the same for her?

'Roz...' he said pointing at the photograph.

'Listen, I'm going looking for Maela in a few days time - do you want me to pass her a message?'

He sighed and then whispered in her ear.

Katie nodded and smiled. 'Do you want me to bring back a photograph?'

'Yeah!' He was tearful now.

Katie pondered what to do now. Was it possible that Alain didn't know what had happened to her?

'I need to show you something...' She could hear noise in the corridor outside. She would have to be quick, so she got up, reached for the curtains and pulled them across. 'I've got a mark on my body but it's in a very private place. Try not to make any noise.' She looked behind her to the door. She had marks on her left shoulder and on the sole of her right foot but she would have to remove clothes to reveal either of these. There was no one at the door. Quickly she unfastened her denims and slid them down carefully to just reveal a mark above her core. 'This is what they did to me!'

Alain threw his head back and cried a long, desperate howl. 'Maaaa!'

'No, no, no, not Maela, it was...'

The nurse was through the door and at Alain's side, comforting him. Gwen was through the door and shouting: 'What in God's name did you do, Katie?'

'Nothing, we were just chatting!' She turned away and quickly buttoned herself up.

'You know he's not very well!'

'I know that!'

'Have you shaved him?' asked the nurse. He was standing now, doing a double tea-pot.

'Only his face!'

'And cut his hair!'

'Only the straggly bits!'

'Where are the scissors?'

'In my bag!'

'You dressed him!'

'He can't sit around in his pyjamas all day!'

Gwen was trying to comfort him but Alain kept pushing her away. 'He's upset, Katie, what did you say?'

'I may have...mentioned the war!'

'Which one?'

'At least two of them!'

'Oh, no, not the Falklands?'

'I just said it was sodding cold in the South Atlantic!'

Gwen tried again to comfort him.

Katie turned back to the nurse: 'The Royal Navy is something we can both connect with' she explained, 'so that's good, isn't it?'

'Did you get this out?' he said, brandishing the scrap book.

'Yes, I did, but he asked me to...'

'He asked you to?'

'Yes, he did.'

'No, he didn't! He couldn't have done!'

Alain was calm now and sitting back in his chair, looking quizzically at Katie.

'You had better leave now' said the nurse. Katie looked back and returned Alain's gaze until he turned his head and continued his watch out of the window.

Gwen pulled Katie into the corridor. 'We should go now' she ordered. They walked quickly along the corridor, down the stairs, past reception and to Gwen's big green car. 'What in God's name did you do? You're not back in school now showing the boy at the next desk what you've got!'

Katie blushed fiercely. What could she say. 'It was nothing like that, Gwen!'

'Oh no, you didn't show him the mark?'

She wondered what to say now as they got strapped into the car. Gwen fired up the vehicle and they were quickly back on the motorway but the next few minutes were desperately quiet.

'It wasn't like that, Gwen, I thought he had to know.'

Gwen pulled over, got out of the car and signalled Katie to get out. They were on a curve of the Corve, the edge above them to one side and the wide dale to the other, amongst a screen of alder trees. They were face to face in the lay-by.

'Are you going to tell me what's going on or do I have to shake it out of you?'

'I'd like to see you try...'

Gwen's lips tightened and her eyes flashed green. That wasn't a sensible thing to say. A succession of slight twitches proceeded across her face and body like she was a hunter, considering her next move, her prey fixed by dark and beady eyes, but undecided about whether she should pounce or circle around. 'Katie - tell me the truth!'

'I think I probably did...'

'Show him?'

'Yes.'

'In God's name, why?'

There was a high pitched 'peeeep', then another one as a blink of turquoise flashed along the brook.

'I thought he ought to know...'

'How could you possibly think that?'

'I just did...we connected, didn't we?'

'What rot!'

'But there's something else...'

'There's always something else with you!'

'I can smell the rot on his breath...'

'Yes, I know. He's being treated but he hasn't got that long.'

'How long has he got?'

'Months at most...'

'I'm so sorry Gwen.' Katie stared sullenly into the distance - the hills seemed far away now. Gwen was holding her shoulders and then her arms started to feel their way around her and they were close, so that the moistness of shed tears could be felt. An image was slowly forming in her consciousness and then there were other sensations pulling at her mind. There was the smell of burnt flesh, like burning pig skin and then the piercing yell of a child and then there was the searing pain that could not be relieved by the gush of water from the outdoor tap.

And then there was the daily dilemma about how to keep the ugly little marks hidden; the imprints on her shoulder, over her core and on the sole of her foot; that snagged at her clothes and caused the boys to tease and taunt her, whenever they were exposed to the light.

Gwen wrapped her arms around Katie and pulled her tight. 'Oh you poor child, you poor, poor child, how can I make it better?'

Katie looked in Gwen's eyes. 'You can't, I'm marked and that's the beginning and the end of it.'

'I'll take you back home and I'll make you tea? How does that sound?'

It was the mournful howl that made Katie instantly alert. Her ears and then her other senses reacted. Gwen seemed to have sensed it first and then inexplicably, ignored it. Her eyes were fixed on the road ahead, as the car climbed out of the village, but Katie's eyes were scanning the hillside to the left of the road. 'Did you hear that, Gwen?'

'No, what was that?'

'You must've heard it? A howling?'

'You're mistaken, Katie, what on earth could that be?'

Katie stared at the side of her sister's face then stared back out of the car window. 'It's Owain, he's running after the car! You're going to have to stop the car, Gwen!'

Gwen pulled over to the side of the road and Katie jumped out of the car with alacrity but it was already upon her. 'Owain, get down! Owain, get down!' A bundle of black and white leapt at her waist. Katie absorbed the momentum of his charge, but she could only stagger backwards. She toppled and rolled down into the ditch, face down in the soft mud. Katie tried to push herself up with her arms but four limbs were stamping frantically at her back. 'OWAIN, GET OFF!', she screamed. Katie twisted around so she could face her assailant - a long pink tongue massaged spittle into her mouth and nose. 'OWAIN!' Her assailant whimpered and scrambled backwards. She struggled to her feet and tried to seize the collar around his neck, but it was no collar she recognised. It was new leather with metal studs. 'Now come with me! Heel!' She looked towards Gwen who was doubled up in the driver's seat, choking with laughter. 'He needs to be kept safe Gwen, he shouldn't be allowed run loose on the main road!' Owain yapped twice, and sat to heel.

Gwen's face was stained with tears. She tried not to laugh but she failed miserably. 'I think that's the funniest thing,' she gasped, 'the funniest thing I've ever seen.' Gwen took several long draughts of air: 'That's better, I think I can drive now. Just set him loose and let's get going.'

'What? He's coming with me!' They scrambled together into the passenger seat. 'You got him a new collar?'

'The dog's not coming in the car...'

'Yes he is, he's coming with me.'

'He's not yours...'

'What are you talking about Gwen, of course he's mine...'

'Katie, we had to let him go...'

'You sold him?'

'We gave the dog away. He wasn't happy, he was pining...'

'Pining? Pining? Why didn't you keep him busy? He's a working dog!'

'And now he's working, with a young shepherdess, over Burfield way.'

There was a very shrill four note whistle. Owain's ears flipped to attention and he whimpered. The whistle came again, this time more insistent. Owain's paws scratched at the door window.

'You have to let him go Katie, it's like I told you, Owain is not yours. We had to give him to someone who could look after him properly. A shepherdess over Burfield way, she has him now.'

'I don't believe this?' Katie gasped. 'He was never yours to sell, he's mine!'

'Not any more he's not!'

'But you can't! You can't!'

'Let him go, Katie.'

She ragged his neck and his ears. 'Off you go Owain, this isn't over, not by a long way.' She opened the car door and Owain sprang out, danced a tight, joyful circle and then scampered up the hill, across the short, sheep grazed turf, barking towards his new mistress.

'He missed you Katie, he ran away several times, sometimes for days. When you left the last time, he just sat howling by the gate for hours. We couldn't go on like that!'

Katie sat silently and worked through her options. She would have to get Owain back, and quickly, because she would need him as her scout and her companion when she entered the wilderness of the Elenydd.

CHAPTER FORTY

Tuesday 17 May 1311 - Clun Cottage

Gwen negotiated the steep and narrow track that led to Clun Cottage, where a welcoming party slowly assembled at the front door: Mister Stefan Hofland, Monique Hofland and Alexander Hofland. It was a bit like a scene from an old time movie, Katie thought. She turned to Gwen, 'What's that film where a Swiss family sings songs in the mountains?'

'That would be 'The Sound of Music', Katie.'

'Not 'Gone with the Wind' then?'

'No, that's something completely different and we're not the 'Swiss Family Robinson' either!'

'I always get those muddled' Katie said as she hauled her bag out of the car. 'We need to talk about Owain, and how get him back, don't we?'

'There's much we need to talk about Katie...like how you're never here to look after your dog.'

'You shouldn't have dressed up for us Auntie Katie' sniggered Alexander.

She turned around to him. 'I didn't' replied Katie. 'Oh, I see, sarcasm!'

Monique clutched Katie around her waist. 'We don't mind how you look, so long as you're here.'

'You've grown again - you'll be catching up with me soon!' commented Katie.

'You look like you've been dragged through a hedge backwards, Auntie Katie. And what's that you're wearing? A face pack?' asked Alexander.

'It's not a face pack, it's what you find at the bottom of a ditch, isn't it Al? Owain bundled me in.'

'Owain?'

'Yes, my dog, Owain.'

'Your former dog' interrupted Gwen.

Alexander offered a tentative handshake. Katie accepted it and pulled him in for a hug. She felt his surprised and embarrassed gasp on her cheek, then a tingling down the outside of her arms and her torso. 'Whoa, down boy, I'm your auntie!' she exclaimed.

Alexander blushed, pushed her away and looked at the ground sheepishly.

'What's the matter?' asked Gwen.

'Nothing Gwen, I just think that Al is pleased to see me' replied Katie.

'Shut up, Auntie Katie!' Alexander turned away and stalked back to the front door.

Monique held Katie's hand as they entered the old farmhouse. 'You're in a bit of shit' whispered Monique.

'I know Mon' replied Katie, 'fifty foot of it. Wait up, you're not allowed to say words like that!'

'You say it all the time!'

'No I don't! How would you know? Anyway, I'm a matelot and I can say whatever I want. So, I'm in a bit of crap, am I?'

'Yes, so why's it all right to say crap?'

'It's a general term for something bad - shit is something that squirts out of your arse.'

'I'll have to let mama know, she'll be very interested in that. You have such a way with words.'

'I do, don't I? I think it's a gift!' Katie frowned - this could lead to more trouble with Gwen. 'Actually Mon, don't say crap to your mum either, I'm not sure she knows the difference.'

'Oh, Auntie Katie, that's something else - you're not to call me Mon anymore. I'm a teenager now.'

'Oh, I see.' Katie considered this for a moment. 'That's all right, I know, I'll call you 'Ique'! Eek!'

'Eek? You can be such an idiot sometimes!'

'I know' smirked Katie.

'Anyway, there's something else you should know - Alexander knows about our 'Yapper' sessions.'

'How? Has he told anyone?'

'I don't think so' replied Monique.

'How can you be sure of that?' replied Katie.

'I threatened him' giggled Monique, 'I have something on him.'

'Can you tell me what it is?'

'No, I can't, it's a bit close to home.'

'Oh, crap. I think I might know what it is.'

'You do?'

'Yes. Is it about rude pictures?'

'Come on you two' chided Gwen, 'what are you conspiring about?'

'We're just catching up' replied Katie to Gwen. She paused at the entrance to the cottage. 'What am I going to do?'

'Yes, Auntie Katie, rude pictures of you' whispered Monique, 'and they're so gross, it's almost like incest!'

'Like incest, oh my soul, it's worse than I thought! Have you seen them?'

'No Auntie Katie, that would make me a lesbian and I don't want to be one of those. Anyway, keep that under your hat.'

'Wait, how did he get rude pictures of me? There aren't any!'

'He's found them from somewhere, he's very creative like that.'

'Oh, bugger. I going to have to get inside his head to fix that.'

'Oh, that. Are you sure?'

'No, I'm not sure. It could be difficult.'

'Yes, he's a bit...complicated.'

'And he's a bit...away with the fairies, isn't he?'

'Hmm, dark fairies. Do you think you can fix him?'

'Oh, yes, I think I can.'

'Oh' said Monique giggling.

'I know' murmured Katie.

Gwen had to intervene again. 'Come on you two, let's get Katie inside and settled.'

'I'll try blackmail first' whispered Katie to Monique.

'You're right. You don't want to mess with his head. He's pretty messed up already!'

'Anyway, Eek, never mind that now, we'll all have to knuckle down until everything's back on an even keel, won't we?'

Monique frowned. 'What are you talking about, Auntie Katie?'

'Oh, nothing. You're not supposed to know that. Anyway, anything else I should know, Eek?'

'Yes, they're going to spring something on you during tea so you'll have to act surprised.'

'That won't be difficult, will it? What is it?'

'I can't tell you that, can I?'

Katie stood bemused. Monique skipped inside.

And now it was Mister Hofland's turn: 'Katie, you are most welcome. It's good to have you back. Alexander, please take her bag upstairs.' He hovered uncertainly, frowned at Katie and then did as he was asked. The bag thumped heavily against each and every step of the winding, wooden staircase.

Mister Hofland took Katie's arm and escorted her into the shadowy interior of the house. 'Katie, please come with me.'

She turned to grimace at Gwen: 'What now?' she motioned with her lips.

There was just a shrug in reply from Gwen.

'Can I have a bath first? she asked Mister Hofland.

'You can have a bath after we've finished. Four fingers of water, remember...'

'A quick shower?'

'We have no shower, Katie.'

'Oh yes, I forgot. A bath then?'

He admonished her with a frown.

'Anyway, I'll get you both a drink?' said Gwen. 'What would you like Katie?'

'I would like a rum cocktail please, Gwen' said Katie.

'Oh, yes, and, how would you like that, Katie?'

'Oh, yes, lots of rum, plenty of lemonade and some tropical fruit please...'

'Tea it is then. Three sugars?' she replied.

'I think I'm going to need something far stronger than that, Gwen!'

'I'll get on with tea. Stefan, Katie knows about the dog - they met on the way up the track.'

'I did say that we should have spoken to Katie first. I also said that he should not be given to anyone in the valley. Much too close to home.'

Katie meekly followed Mister Hofland to his study - well, it was described as a study, but it was actually his bolt hole from the harsh reality of sheep farming in the Marches. The wood panelled walls were hidden by racks of smoke stained books. She recognised some of the books that she had been through with Mister Hofland five or six years ago, in this dark and solemn space of lonely contemplation - those ones with large print and pictures.

'Please take a seat, Katie.' He gestured to the wooden stool that sat opposite the grand, roughly upholstered armchair.

She sat down demurely across the oak table from him. His ginger hair and goatee beard were woven through with strands of crinkled, silvery threads. His face was ruddier than she remembered and a heavy fug of cigar smoke hung over him. 'So, you knew what Gwen was doing with my dog?'

'Ah, the dog. We could not manage him, Katie, so we had to act.'

'By getting rid of him? Owain is part of the family!'

'And so are you, but you are never here!'

'I was serving my country!'

'And all because of a rash promise made many years ago!'

'But it's still a promise, isn't it!?'

There was a long pause: 'Nay Katie, nay. Let us start anew.'

There were loud voices from the kitchen. Katie listened carefully, it was Monique talking very loudly to Gwen. 'Mama, you know what you said, that Katie must not call me 'Mon' anymore?'

'Yes, dear.'

'Well, she's decided she's going to call me 'Eek' from now on! Eek! And it's all your fault!'

'Eek? Oh, I see what she's done, that's very clever. Did you thank your auntie?'

'No, Mama, she's an idiot. 'Eek' makes me sound scary...'

'Well, you can be a bit of a fright sometimes.'

'I don't believe this. She must call me Monique, or I'm changing my name!'

'There's no need dear, 'Eek' suits you very well...' There was a slam of a door and then a knock on the door of Stefan's office. Monique pushed her way in.

'Hello Papa.'

'Hello Monique.'

She stretched forward and pinched Katie's arm quickly and viciously.

'Auntie Katie, that's what you get. I've spoken to Mama and you're to call me Monique, not 'Eek'.'

'Listen Eek, I heard every word of your conversation with your mum. In fact, most of the valley heard you...'

'Auntie Katie, you are an idiot, and that's official!' The door slammed as Monique exited and the door to the outside slammed again in quick succession.

'She seems very stroppy. Is she always like this?' Katie asked.

'Monique will be fine in about a minute. She is a teenager after all. Please call her Monique. It will save a lot of aggravation.'

'I see. Have I got time for a bath?'

'No, I would like to get this over and done with. There's a lot to get through so make yourself comfortable.'

This seemed ominous. She found a handkerchief in her pocket, spat on it and rubbed her left cheek. Stefan had a long, hand written list in front of him which she had difficulty interpreting. It was the length of the list that she found intimidating. It filled a whole page of foolscap.

'I thought it best to discuss and agree with you the parameters for your stay with us' he stated solemnly. 'It's been a long time since we last saw you and much has changed.'

'It has, hasn't it, it's been nearly thirteen months, isn't it? Enough time to get rid of my dog...'

'Why so long?' he asked abruptly.

'What? Well, I explained to Gwen, I did a spell of duty in a French ship for a bit of the old 'entente cordiale'.'

'Why did you agree?'

'It's my duty. I thought it would look good on my record and help with my advancement.'

'But you are back now?'

'Well, partly I'm back, but...then I'm gone again.'

'Please Katie, I must apologise in advance, but this is going to sound like a 'State of the Nation' address.'

'Or, in this case, a 'State of the Katie' address!'

He frowned, a frown that creased his forehead and caused her to sit upright and drop her smile with alacrity. There was something on his mind and it was all about her.

'Sorry' she said, 'that's fine with me, Stefan.'

'Please call me Mister Hofland.' This reply seemed unnecessarily formal.

'How about if I call you Mister Stefan?'

'Mister Hofland, please' he insisted, 'or sir.'

'All right, I'll go with Mister Hofland, but it's a bit of a mouthful, isn't it?' There was another uncomfortable pause. 'I'll go with sir' she added. He took a while to compose himself again. 'Or Mister Hofland. 'Sir' sounds like I'm back at school. Or back in the Andrew. Which I still am, to be fair...'

'How long will you be staying with us?' he demanded.

'Just a few days to start with. I've got a shore posting which will start officially in September. I've got an induction at Shoeburyness on the 26th of May. Then I'll come back here for three months. Then I start full time at Shoeburyness. I don't know how long I'll be there. Maybe twelve months, maybe more. I don't know.'

'That's a pity. I could do with your help here. As you know, Katie, this is a working farm...'

'You can call me Ket' she interjected, 'that's what they call me in the Royal...'

'Why? That sounds very coarse.'

'I'm sorry sir, you're right, you carry on. Let's stick with Katie.'

'This is a working farm Katie, and we will need your help while you are here.'

'It's my initials, isn't it? Kilo, echo, tango.' She ruminated for a moment, and then opened up her diary. She flicked through to her

'Notes' pages and made a pronouncement. 'Would you like me to corral the cattle?'

'As I was saying, this is a working farm and I will need your help while you stay with us. I would like you to attend to the flock in the upper fields.'

'Right, I'll sort out the flock first thing in the morning, at sparrowfart-o-clock. Can I use Owain so I don't have to run after the sheep myself? Oh, wait a moment, you got rid of my sheepdog, didn't you?'

Stefan sighed. 'Are you mocking me?'

'No, I'm not.' Now she struggled to keep her serious face on. What was going on here, why was he being so stern?

There was an uncomfortable pause. 'You can use the Land Rover...'

'I can't drive.'

'But, you should have learned by now, you're in the armed forces.'

'There are no cars on a frigate, Stefan, not a single one, and there's no where to drive them to either.'

'Mister Hofland, please. I'll work something out. Now, the lambing season went badly - we have had very little to sell. A farm with nothing to sell is in financial difficulty, as you can imagine.'

'Nothing to sell at all? So what are we going to do to salvage it? What happened to the farm shop?'

'I had to close it.'

'What about the market in Bishop's Castle? Ludlow market?'

'We have nothing to trade or sell...'

'How can you live on nothing?'

'We cannot. I'm considering my options. We will have to diversify, I believe.'

Gwen arrived with two mugs of tea and a large tumbler clinking with ice. 'How's it going? It's good to have Katie back, isn't it?' Stefan retrieved a bottle of whisky from the shelf behind him and poured in three fingers of spiritous amber liquid into the tumbler. Katie watched entranced as the alcohol migrated its way up the glass and swirled towards her nose and eyes.

'Where's mine?'

Stefan shook his head slowly. 'Yes, but Katie's not going to be here for very long, just a few days to start with' he replied to Gwen.

'I see. Just a few days. But you'll back for a few months in the summer, won't you Katie? I'll leave you to it - you both look very serious. Has Stefan told you about the offers you've had from the local boys?'

'I've had offers? What kind of offers? No, I think that's somewhere down the list!'

'I'll leave that to Stefan - very delicate I think.' Gwen eased her way out of the room. Katie stealthily made a play for the tumbler - Stefan quickly moved it away from her.

'Please take your tea Katie. Now where was I?'

'Farm in deep dwang and you need my help, don't you?' She looked pensively out of the small square window to the west and across the rounded mounds above the valley. 'We could turn the lower fields to crops - we could get in a crop of grain maybe. Beans to follow next year. Or rape seed. The sandy field over on the East side - that's never been any good for pasture. We could plough it up and put in some potatoes and cauliflowers.' She paused and watched for Stefan's reaction. His brow furrowed again, so furrowed it didn't seem able relax back. She reckoned that the idea she had sown was now germinating in the fallow of his mind.

'You may have something there - we'll need a tractor and a plough though.'

'No problem, the Tricketts will have one - let me pay them a visit and start chatting them up. Ben'll help me out. I went to school with him, he was my mucker.' She had wheedled her way into the Trickett family to such an extent that it wasn't clear in her last long hot summer in Clun, where she in fact lived. That was apart from the matriarch of the family, Susan, who thought of Katie as a squatter. It would be best to try out Ben and his old buffer first and keep Mrs Trickett well out of it, she thought.

'Best mates, Katie? Nothing more?' Stefan asked.

'No, just mates. I really fancied him, but...what's the matter, Mister Hofland?'

'The Tricketts want to buy the top field. They put in a bid, I said it wasn't for sale. I think they'll try again, now they know we're in trouble.' He paused to look deep into her eyes. 'But then you already knew that, didn't you Katie?'

'No I didn't' she hissed, 'I don't know anything about that, do I?'

'I think you do!'

'No, I don't!' she hissed, and got up from the stool.

'All right, I believe you. Now sit down, please, and keep the volume down. It's just that Gwen said...ach, it's not material.'

She settled back in the chair. 'You know I can't lie. It's always the truth you'll get from me, always!'

'All right Katie, I believe you.'

'I don't think you do. Listen, it's me, your Katie. I would not lie to you.'

'I believe you, but they are up to something, I know.'

'What about my ideas?'

'I will look at the costs first, before I do anything.' He scribbled a note on his stained note pad and then consulted his list again. Katie slurped at her tea noisily and slushed it around her mouth. Stefan didn't react to this, he was thinking about his next move.

She smiled back sweetly once she had swallowed. 'That's better, nice tea. Gwen might be hopeless around the kitchen, but she can make a good mug of tea!'

Stefan looked under the table and brought out a pile of carefully wrapped and labelled parcels. 'These are yours for your birthday anniversary. Happy birthday' he said mirthlessly.

She sorted them in size while Stefan fidgeted. 'Oh, do you want me to do this later?'

He gave a deep sigh. 'It is germane to our discussion. Please continue. But don't make a...'

A shower of wrapping paper confetti fluttered over the table. 'It's from Eek...'

'Her name is Monique, please use her correct...'

Katie took out a set of tattoo transfers and an eye patch from the wrappings. The eye patch was decorated with sewn on sequins outlining an open eye. The transfers were ship's anchors entwined with mermaids. She gasped, stood up and turned for the door.

'Tattoos!'

'We haven't finished, please sit back down.'

'But I need to....'

'Please sit back down.'

'But...'

'Please.'

She sat back down reluctantly but pulled the eye patch over her face so it covered her right eye. 'I'm back' she announced, 'can I...?'

'Please wait until we have finished. This is already very difficult for me.'

She sighed and put the rest of the parcels on the floor beside her chair. What else could there be?

'Christmas. What happened?'

'I don't know what you mean. It happened as normal, didn't it?'

'We expected you to be back here. It was a reasonable assumption, you were due leave. What happened?'

'I think people bought a lot of things they didn't need with money they didn't have? That's what always happens? Then they eat and drink so much that they can't move afterwards. Am I close?'

'I meant, what happened to you?'

'I was...I was....working. You know, chasing pirates, protecting shipping, putting in clean water supplies, building a new jetty for the fishing boats.'

'Where?'

'You know where!' She emitted a blast of air through pursed lips. 'I've already told you this. All the way down the coast of Africa!'

'Yes, I know that, but we expected you here' he snapped.

'Did you? Why didn't someone say?'

His eyes rolled upwards which was never a good sign. 'We wanted you here because we had something very important and personal to discuss with you. It was an important family matter.'

'I see. Well, you can discuss it with me now, can't you? I'm all ears.' She pressed her ears towards him with her index fingers. This probably looked a bit odd with the sequinned eye patch. Oh well, never mind.

Stefan looked down his list with an even more furrowed brow. Things didn't appear to be going to plan.

'We need a guardian for Alexander and particularly Monique, in case something happens to Gwen and I. So, let me ask you, what would you do if, for the sake of argument, Gwen and I died in an accident tomorrow?'

'Tomorrow? Why are you having an accident tomorrow? Is there anything you can do to avoid being in an accident together? Can you stay in tomorrow and not go anywhere? Or go somewhere separately so that you aren't together? So, don't travel in the same car, try and avoid using an open flame by the oil tank, do not approach any dangerous animals?'

Stefan emitted a very big sigh. 'I was talking hypothetically, Katie. What would you do?'

'I see. Well, Mister Hofland, talking hypothingily, I would resign my commission immediately, come back to Shropshire, contact your solicitor, look after Eek and Al until everything was all sorted. Depending on how things looked, I might ship us all off to Holland or...' Her voice tailed off. Was that too heartless, too detailed and too matter-of-fact? '...or somewhere else.'

'Why Holland, Katie?'

'Why Holland? Well, it's a nice place I hear, with nice friendly people and it's flat. Do you have a problem with my plan?'

'No, but I would like to understand your reasoning.'

'Well, Mister Hofland, that's where your family comes from... isn't it? And you still have family out there don't you? In Groningen, I believe...'

'How would you know that?'

'Ah! Because...because, you told me, didn't you?'

'Did I now?' He folded his arms and looked at her sternly. 'You've been in contact with my family and you didn't tell me!'

'I, I didn't tell you, because...it wasn't supposed to come out like that. All right, you've got me, I've got something for you from Marjolein.'

'My niece, Marjolein?'

'Yep, that's the one. It was going to be a surprise, wasn't it? Oh, bollocks.'

'How come?'

'We played 'em at hockey - inter ship tournament - big girls aren't they?' She took the package from her satchel and slid it across the table.

'How is she?'

'She's very well thanks. They're all wondering why you've not been in touch, but I didn't feel I could answer for you, could I?'

'You're unbelievable.'

'I am aren't I?' She wondered where he was with his agenda - they just seemed to be floating in and out without deciding anything.

'Let's move on. I will need you to help with general housekeeping duties. I propose that you help with cooking the evening meal on alternate nights and with the cleaning and washing on a daily basis.'

'Let's say just one evening and I get to choose what to cook and the evening?'

He puffed out a frustrated breath and continued. 'Alternate nights. You can agree the details with Gwen.'

'All right, if that's how it is, we'll need to get the kitchen garden going again. It's overgrown. It needs turning over. We're talking tractor and plough here.'

'You'll never get a tractor in there.'

'Don't underestimate me.' His pencil was beating a tattoo against the desk. He filled the tumbler with whisky again and took a large swig.

'The sleeping arrangements, Katie.'

'Hold on, we haven't sorted out the housework piece yet! Or anything!'

'The sleeping arrangements, Katie.'

'Yes, I'll need to sleep if I'm working my arse off all day!'

Stefan ignored this. 'You'll sleep in Monique's bedroom.'

'That's not going to work. Where's Eek going to go?'

'You will be sharing her room - I will put up a camp bed.'

'That's not going to work - I've picked up some very nasty habits in the Navy. You can't help it, surrounded by a bunch of despicable, born-again scrotes.'

'Make it work. You will need to be in bed by nine o'clock each night.'

She let out a snort of derision. 'Oh, no I'm not. I've been in purdah for over a year and I'm...very horny.'

'Do you even know what that means?'

'What? Horny? It means I...' she looked up at the ceiling, '...I have stuff going on inside me that needs to get out in the open.'

'Nay, nay, nay, I meant purdah.'

'It means that I've got stuff going on inside me that needs to get out in the open, doesn't it?'

'That is very disrespectful of you!'

'No, it's not. It can't be? It's just banter, that's all it is!'

'No, it isn't. And maybe you should be taught what it really means...'

'It doesn't matter what it means, you're not putting a curfew on me! And I'm not sharing a room with Eek!'

'You will do as you are told, young lady!'

'You are not my dad!'

'While you are in my house, you will follow my rules!'

'I'm a guest here, you are not my dad. If I'm back late, I'll sleep in the barn. I'll rig up a hammock. In fact, I'll do that now.' She got up and the legs of the stool grated horribly against the floor.

'Wait Katie, you will not be sleeping in the barn.'

'You're not imposing a nine o'clock curfew on me. You can't do that to me!'

Stefan sighed and sat back. 'Please, be reasonable.'

'This is me being reasonable! You really want your pound of flesh, don't you?'

'Ah, do you actually know where that expression comes from?'

'It's from a book, I think' she answered hesitantly as she settled back on the stool.

'Very good. Any particular one?'

She guessed it was to do with cannibalism. It must be an old book because cannibalism was against the law now. Why did people eat other people? Was it so that they could...become cleverer?

'We've read this together. It will help if you can remember who the author was.'

Was he Dutch? 'I don't think I know who that would be' she responded carefully.

'He's one of your best known and most celebrated writers.'

'A British man?' She recalled someone on HMS Albany talking about a criminal who ate human flesh with a glass of wine. It was a joke about a plate of meat served in the galley. 'Is it from a book called 'Hannibal the Cannibal'?'

'No, it's not. We read this together, it was the 'Merchant of...?'

'Ships. Yes, It was Ships. You were the merchant...I remember now.'

Stefan shook his head sadly.

'Was I close?'

'Nay, nay, nay Katie.'

'Look, don't fret, you're doing okay, but I'm going to have to earn some cash. I'm going to get the ladies of the Clun valley knitting circle going so I've got something to sell at the market.' Stefan looked at her curiously. 'So, I'm going to invite the ladies around and provide tea. I'll get their stuff in mark it all up, box it and take it to market. But I'll need a lift in and out of town. Is that all right? It won't cost you anything but once I've cleared expenses you can have a cut. I was thinking, say ten percent?'

'Let me check with Gwen.'

'I'll check with Gwen. Just nod. I'll need to use your land-line but I'll only use it evenings and weekends only. But I'll need to use it tonight, all right?'

'Let me check.'

'Good. What's next?'

'I understand that you want to see your mother?'

'Correct, I'm going to see her on Saturday.'

'I think it is not in your best interest to do that.'

'I'm still going to see her.'

'Nay Katie, I must say that is a very bad idea.'

'Tough titty - she's my mum, you can't stop me. And by the way, she's your mum-in-law.'

'Yes, I'm aware. You have become very defiant - I must say I don't like it.'

'What did you say to me on my fourteenth birthday?'

'I'm sure I didn't say, now you're fourteen, you can defy me.'

'I'm seeing Mum and that's it - I'll be back here on Sunday morning. You said, 'stick up for yourself, don't take any bullshit from anyone'. There, that's what you said.'

'I'm sure I didn't.'

'I've parrot-phrased it.'

'I'm sorry Katie, there's a long list of things I need to get through.' He shuffled his papers and attempted to re-order them. She slipped one out and had a quick look. It was a handwritten letter, in a very haltering but linear arrangement. Stefan snatched it back.

'I think you had better get on with it - how far have we got through so far?'

'About one quarter.'

Katie puffed her cheeks. 'Sodding hell. Can I have a break?'

'No, let's move on. I need to talk to you about the money you've been sending to us. None of it has gone to your mother because...we lost touch with her and...we put it in a bank account.'

He slid a sheet of foolscap paper towards her.

'You've spent it all...'

'We can't find her, she's not in the Marches any longer - we hear she's living somewhere between here and Newtown. And that's all we know.'

'You haven't tried very hard to find her then, have you?'

'She has no fixed address. She and Gwen had a very bitter argument.'

'What was it about?'

'She decided she didn't want to live in the room we had found for her.'

'Why? Was there something you could have done?'

'She wasn't a very good tenant.'

'I'll find her, somehow. My Great-Aunt Katerin has given me some tips.' Katie flicked through her diary. 'To be fair, they're very confusing - there you go, she's set up base camp somewhere just over the border. I need to find some kiddy called Dafyd, and he will lead me to her.' She slammed the diary shut and sat attentively.

'You are now nineteen years old. How should we mark this significant event?'

'You could let me have a party in the cottage? And I could invite lots of boys!'

'I don't think that would be appropriate.'

'All right then, we could have a seance...'

'Why in God's name would you want to have a seance?'

'So I could get in touch with some ghosts...'

'But why Katie?'

'To see if there's any prospects for me?'

Stefan sighed. 'Ah, I was thinking of a gift, such as...'

'A chastity belt?'

'Nay, nay, nay, Katie, this is not the Dark Ages.'

'You could have fooled me!'

Silence.

'A new cell phone. Which brings me to what happened to your old phone? Gwen tells me you've... disabled it.'

'Yes, it's here. I don't know what happened to it...' She withdrew the phone from a sock and passed it to Stefan for examination.

He turned it carefully in his hands and then flicked off the battery cover. 'This has been in a microwave oven.'

'No, it has not.'

'Look at it. The electrics are melted!'

'I have not microwaved it. I promise you.'

'A new cell phone then.'

'That's very kind of you, but I can't accept - I'm afraid of what it'll do to my brain. And I need to look after all the brain cells that I've still got and you haven't got any money.'

'What if we have to contact you in an emergency?'

'Gwen knows how to do that.'

'What if you need to contact us?'

'I'll use a pay phone and my magic talk card!'

'I find you very frustrating.'

'Stay with it, you're doing well.' She smiled demurely. 'So, can I have a party here to celebrate my birthday?'

'No, you may not.'

'How about in the barn?'

'No, you may not.'

'I'll do something in the village then - would you like to come?' There was another big sigh from Stefan. He folded his arms and sat back. This seemed quite serious to Katie. She decided to throttle back on the banter.

At last, Stefan came back with: 'Where do we go from here? You have become very defiant.'

'No, I haven't.'

He sighed and shuffled through some papers. They may have come out of a school exercise book. 'You have had two letters from local boys, I have been asked to give permission for you to be contacted...'

'Contacted?'

'With a view to meeting with you and commencing courtship...'

'Courtship? Oh, that's a bit unexpected, who's after me then?'

'On your behalf, I turned them both down.'

'You did what? Why did you do that! What gives you the right? Don't I get any say into this?'

'I'm your guardian.'

'No, you're not! And you're not my dad either!'

'Maybe I was a little hasty, but you can do far better Katie.'

There was a pregnant pause. 'Can I?'

'Yes, you can. We need to be far more strategic about this. After, all you are Gwen's sister and that must count for something.'

'Does it? Well, you were a bit hasty. I'd like to have some say in this!' Katie leaned forward and scanned the upside down scrawl of what was, presumably, a letter. 'Me and Ben were muckers at school and his dad's got a tractor and a plough! Blimey! He asked you if he could do courtship with me!'

'Having said all that Katie, you have matured considerably...'

'Like cheese?'

'No, you have matured into an attractive young woman.'

'Blimey, did I!'

'And I think you are ready to have a productive relationship with a male...a serious relationship.'

'Oh my soul' she shouted as the stool grated again against stone, 'a productive relationship!'

The door opened again. Gwen's elegantly bouffed head emerged from behind it. 'Is everything all right between you two?' she asked anxiously.

'Yes, yes, yes' responded Stefan, 'Katie has just had a little start, haven't you Katie?'

'Yes, I had a little start, that's all Gwen.'

'Go on, what was it?'

'Mister Hofland wants to talk about having sex with me!'

'I beg your pardon?'

'Um, let me try that again, Gwen. Mister Hofland wants to talk to me about having sex, with boys. He thinks, I'm ready to do sex...' Her voice trailed away quietly.

'Stefan, this is not a good time to carry out Katie's sex education. We'll be having tea soon, in thirty minutes time' said Gwen as she retreated out of the room, back to the kitchen.

'Thanks Gwen!'

'Now, where were we? Ah, yes! You, Katie, I believe are ready for a serious sexual relationship...'

'Oh no, please no!'

'...and there are young men in the parish, who if given the opportunity, would...well, relish that prospect.'

'Oh no, please don't do this!'

He carried on regardless. 'I think I may have been remiss in not covering this before now, but I sense the time may be right. I sense you are ready to be sexually active.'

'What?' she gasped, as she stood up and tried to control the dizzying whirl of impulses circling through the front of her mind. She looked at the seat of the stool and the table leg that her legs had been coiled round. 'I didn't do anything!' she cried out aloud.

'No, Katie, no, Katie, I don't mean right now!'

'What did you mean then? Gwen's in the next room!' she hissed.

'You could do much better, Katie. Five years ago, you were a challenging, ill-educated and ill-mannered girl; now you're an attractive, confident, talented young woman.'

'Oh Mister Hofland, but you missed out beautiful and charming!'

'I chose my words carefully.'

'Of course you did.'

'So, Katie, this is difficult, but I need to ask you, are you still whole?'

'Am I still what? What do you mean? I still have all my parts, if that is what you're asking?'

'I mean, have you been sullied?'

'Sullied? Well, there's the marks...oh, I see what you mean. Yes, I am still a whole, aren't I? I haven't been pinned, have I?'

'I see. Good, good, good. That is very good. That will stand you in good stead.'

'Good.' There was a pause while Katie wondered what to say next. 'Actually, can I just check the rules about this, Mister Hofland?'

'Of course Katie, that's why I'm here.'

'Firstly, and this is to do with girls on girls. If I get kissed by a girl, on the lips, that's fine, isn't it?'

'I suppose so. My God, is that your preference, Katie?'

'No, but I had a situation. I got jumped in the heads and she did an evolution on me. And we shared spit!'

'My God Katie, were you assaulted?'

'No, no, no, I don't think so...actually it was partly my fault.'

'Yes, but what happened?'

'I just said, didn't I? She kissed me and then...she cupped me.'

'Cupped you? But where?'

'Er...south of the border.'

'Ah! South of the border' he crooned, 'down Mexico way?'

This was an interesting response. 'Yes, if you like, she cupped my 'Mexico'.'

'Nay, nay, Katie, it's a popular song.'

'Is it? Well it was definitely below the belt, if you know what I mean.'

'Yes, I know what you mean.'

'Oh, how come?'

'I mean, I follow.'

'Good. So, in summary, she cupped my pudding, didn't she? And that's all right isn't it, because, that's as far as it went?'

'I'm not an expert, but yes, I would say that is fine...and there was no penetration?'

She heard herself gulp very noisily. 'No, no, no. And sharing spit - that's fine as well?'

'Yes, that's fine, Katie.'

Katie paused for another think. 'So, Mister Hofland, if I decided to pair with a girl, rhetorically, and we are laying together in bed afterwards, how would I know, if our pairing had been successfully con...consom...consommayed?'

'Consommé is a kind of soup, Katie.'

'Oh, I see.' She thought some more. 'So how would I know if we'd successfully made soup together?'

'Er, I...I'm a firm believer in love being the most important thing here' stammered Stefan, 'and finding the right mate, of course.'

'I see. So if we made soup for fun, I would still be a virgin?'

'Nay, nay, nay, Katie. I...I really don't know how to answer that. You should discuss that with Gwen.'

'I can't, not with Gwen.'

'You should...'

'No, I shouldn't.'

'But, Katie, has this happened to you?'

'Making soup with a girl? Certainly not, I'm just trying to... sort out what the rules are, just in case. So, can we move into boys now?'

'Yes, if we must...'

'Yes, we must. So, if a boy comes at me trousers down, organ leading, and I touch it accidentally, that's not being sullied?'

'No, no, but this sounds like...heavy petting. Is this something that's happened to you, Katie?'

'It was a real situation, Mister Hofland, but I'm just checking the rules. So, if I grab hold of his...dong...and it comes into contact with my Mexico, what's that then?'

'If there's no penetration...you would still be unsullied.'

'Good.'

'Katie, this does not sound like love?'

'Love? I thought we were talking about sex?'

'Love is a verb...'

'Yes, I know, but it's a doing word.'

'Quite.'

'Quite, so, in answer to your question, yes, I am still whole.'

'Good, I'm pleased to hear it. Now, this is quite delicate - has contraception been discussed with you?'

'In the Andrew? Yes, they're obviously worried about the clap getting about, aren't they?'

'And other sexually transmitted diseases?'

'Like the pox?'

'Indeed. So, what method have you chosen to avoid any...unwanted pregnancies?'

'Ah! Well, I've decided that I won't do it with any born-again scrotes. There, that's what I've done.'

'I see. What I actually meant was...'

'Mister Hofland, I know what you meant but I don't think that's actually any of your business really, is it?'

'I just need to know that you will take...appropriate precautions.'

'I see. Of course I will. Mum covered all that, didn't she?'

'I was afraid of that! And what did she say?'

'She said it was down to me. What goes on in my body is totally my affair.'

'I see. I must say that does worry me.'

'Well, it shouldn't, but listen, you've got to trust me.'

There was another prolonged sigh and tapping of the long dead cigar butt in the ash tray. 'You've become very cheeky since you were last here - I'm not sure I like it.'

'Duly noted, but it's called charm and you'll soon get used to it.'

'I'm not sure where this leaves us' Stefan answered.

Silence.

This became unbearable after a minute. She would have to break the silence. She scanned the spines of the dusty books on the age encrusted shelves.

'There aren't any famous Dutch writers, are there? That must be a bit depressing for you all? I can't think of any Dutch composers either. Why are you Dutch so hopeless at anything imaginative? You're all a bit matter-of-fact aren't you?' That should prompt a reaction, she thought. Not the right sort of action though. Stefan might consider this an insult to himself and all his fellow folk. Or maybe this was a well known fact and something they just had to live with.

'There are many Dutch writers.'

'Tell me one I know.'

He was still glowering. 'And there are many Dutch painters of great renown.'

'But they only painted pictures of sailing boats and blokes with faces full of minge hair, didn't they?'

Stefan didn't respond to this. She seemed to have jagged a nerve, but there was something else, something she couldn't fathom from his face, from his aura or from his eyes. But those eyes had just glanced at her temples and looked away quickly.

'There's something else' he muttered as he now tapped a pencil on the table, 'and I don't know how to bring this up.'

She reached across and took the pencil and gently patted the top of his hand. 'Just get it on the table then.'

'Gwen told me this in confidence' he said.

'Oh, no!' Katie's heart suddenly felt very heavy. He was avoiding her eyes.

'But I feel I need to talk to you about it.' He seemed very anxious - a mist of flight hormones came over his skin and his right hand shook. 'Gwen believes that you put yourself in danger while on duty - you were involved in single-handed combat...with a man.'

'That's bollocks - they were boys!' Her right hand went to cover her idiot mouth. Oh, fucketty, fucketty, fuck!

'But Katie! How could that happen?'

'Well, these things happen at sea, don't they? It could have been an argument in the mess deck...' Her head dropped and she examined her clasped hands in her lap. 'Anyway, what does Gwen know, she wasn't there, was she?' Katie's left hand flicked up from his hand to her forehead and swept away the hair there. 'Oh, crap' she muttered quietly. She quickly returned her hand back to her lap.

Stefan rose slowly, leaned over towards her and gently moved the left side of her fringe away from her forehead. He recoiled. 'I see' he said. He sat down again and seemed unable to speak. She knew he was very upset and she tried to reason why. I'm back aren't I? There's no lasting damage. Having a scar on the forehead is awkward, but I can hide it with my fringe. What is the problem?

At last he cleared his throat and asked, 'What do you have to say for yourself, Katie?'

He was very upset. She wrinkled up her nose in a bid to squeeze back the urge to shed tears and she swallowed noisily. 'It was just a nick.' She mustn't cry, there must be no tears.

'And, if it was an inch in the wrong direction?'

'Well, it wasn't was it? And if it hit me square on, it wouldn't have been a nick and I would have had the mother of all brain aches, wouldn't I?'

'This isn't funny - I know you're in the armed services and part of the deal is active service, but this shouldn't have happened to you. Where should you have been?'

'Hard a kip' she said eventually.

'I beg your pardon?'

'Asleep in my hammock, in my banyan basha, racked-out, curled up in the hangar, getting a solid eight hours before my next watch!'

'But you weren't!'

'Er, but my opposite number was busy...'

'So?'

'I had to go...'

'Why?'

'I had to, I was needed there.'

'I don't believe you. Why you, why not a marine? Someone who is trained to fight!'

'I am trained to fight!'

'I know how this works, I've done national service!'

'I know you did!'

'Do you think so little of us that you would expose yourself to harm, even death?'

Her heart lurched. 'Witch!' she muttered as she realised what the problem might be. 'It wasn't like that, but I could hear everything over the net. I was talking to them. I could hear everything, I could hear the cracks in their voices. I couldn't just sit on my hands and leave them, could I? I had to do something!'

'I don't understand why no one stopped you? What was your commanding officer doing? Why you?'

'I knew what had to be done. She could have tried to stop me, but...I had to go. We lifted in. We talked in the open. I found out what the problem was with their chopper. We got the wounded out in the Lynx. We got everyone else out in their chopper, but it was in a bad way, we might well have ditched in the sea. But I did my best to save them all, but...'

'Katie, calm now...'

She stared out of the window but her eyes couldn't focus. 'I can still hear the wailing. The man I dragged out of there was all opened up. I patched him up but I got covered in his blood. I had to burn my overalls, they were all covered in blood. I had to burn them, didn't I? You can't wear overalls that are soaked in someone else's blood, can you? You just can't, can you? It doesn't matter how many times you wash them, the blood might look like its gone, but you still can't wear them again, can you?'

'Katie, you must have been bleeding too!'

'I know, but I didn't care. I mean it stung like buggery, but I didn't know it was my blood down my face, did I? There was blood everywhere, I thought it was all his. I thought it was all his.' Her voice tailed away.

'Let me see your hands.'

'No.'

'Let me see your hands! What are you hiding?'

She pulled the gloves off slowly and placed her hands palm down on the table. Stefan looked intently at her finger nails and then took her hands gently and turned them over.

'What are these marks?' Katie did a quick calculation. He would know if she lied. The truth would get her into more trouble. Was there a middle ground here? A partial lie? She wrinkled her face, then realised this would signal a lie. She put on her most impassive face, devoid of emotion.

'I cut my hands on a knife.'

'How?'

'I caught it blade first, I missed the handle.'

'Your fingernails?'

'I banged them and they went black, didn't they?'

'Was anyone else injured?'

'Um, yes, there was a bloke with a broken leg. I don't think mine counts, does it? Mine were just flesh wounds.'

'Who was he?'

'Who was who?'

'The man you rescued!'

'I can't tell you!'

'Tell me!'

'A French marine - he couldn't fix himself, could he? They were on a mission but it all went wrong.'

Silence.

She felt she had to fill the agonising gap. 'I probably shouldn't have told you any of that. Official secrets.'

'So what now?' he asked.

Her hand spidered it's way across the battered landscape of the oak table, at first hesitantly, and then more confidently, nestled in the red-brown hair on top of his right hand. Tentatively and then more probingly, the tips of her fingers pressed in and engaged with his nerves. 'And worse still, I've gone and lost the pendant.'

'Katie, I am sorry.' He was now staring into her eyes but as the seconds passed his stare moved to the middle distance. 'I can't cope with you not being here, I can't bear you being in danger. You should be here, with me and Gwen and the children.'

'Listen Stefan, I'm doing another five years in the Andrew but I will help you get the farm straight over the summer and if anything happens to you, I'll look after Eek and Al. I'll get the kitchen garden going before I leave and I'm going to start selling woollies again at the market. I will do all this for you.'

'But Katie?'

'But Stefan, I will get my dog back and I will see my mum, and I don't care what you think - I need them now. In return, you will need to straighten yourself out and get all the family working together because this farm will be my forward base for what I need to do. Is that clear?'

'Are you on a mission, Katie?'

'Always.'

'Can you tell me what it is?'

'Nope, it's between me and my own.'

'Is it dangerous?'

'No, it's just a little bit...tricky.' She realised that Stefan was one of a few good men who had pulled her away from a bare existence in the Marches, when all she had was a puppy. 'You more than anyone saved me' she said, 'don't you ever forget that.' She grasped his fingers and pulled them towards her heart. 'You more than anyone believed in me, I will never forget that.'

He stood up and offered a wavering handshake. They were standing face to face.

'Come here, you big idiot!' she said and hugged him. The smell of cigar smoke was stifling. 'How many of those do you get through in a day?'

'It's none of your business.'

'Thought so, but it's too many though, isn't it?'

'And you'll share a bedroom with Monique?'

'Sod that! She's weird!'

'But Katie!'

The door opened and Gwen was waiting outside. 'Please put my husband down.'

'Oh, sorry, we were just finishing up, weren't we Mr Hofland?'

He didn't reply.

'Is everything all right? It sounded like it got a bit heated in there?'

'It's all right now, but I won't be treated as a child' Katie said as she looked accusingly at Gwen, 'and you should keep your visions to yourself, Gwen!'

'Well, never mind that now, tea is ready.'

Stefan sat at the head of the table, then Gwen and Alexander and then Katie and Monique. Katie impaled a potato and was just ready to insert it in her mouth when Stefan interrupted.

'Katie, I would like you to lead us in saying grace.'

'Really?' She put the fork down. The eyes around the table looked at her expectantly. 'It's not really my thing, but here goes.' She recalled a chant that she could use.

'It's me Katie, I'm with my sister Gwen, my brother-in-Law Mr Hofland and my cousins Al and Eek.' She looked around to check the roster as Gwen tutted. The others had their eyes closed. So far, so good.

'Thank you Danu, thank you Rhiannon, for giving us the sun that warms us, for the rivers and streams that water us, for the animals and plants that feed us. Thanks to Gwen for preparing this meal for us. For all these blessings, we thank you.'

Murmurs of 'Amen' rang round the room.

'Was that all right, sir?' she asked.

'That was very good Katie' said Stefan.

'You didn't say 'Amen' Auntie Katie?' said Al.

'You must have been peeking, then' she replied.

'So, what is your religion then Auntie Katie, assuming you have one?' She aimed a kick at Al's shin but missed.

'That's a bit personal, isn't it? I don't think we should be talking about religion at the dinner table, should we?'

'I think it's a valid question' said Gwen, 'so Katie, you should answer.' Katie had already cleared half her plate. Maybe she should let the others catch up. 'So Katie, here's the question for you, where do you stand on Christianity?'

'Well, it's a very major religion which has many followers, doesn't it?'

'It certainly does, Katie' said Stefan.

'Its members believe in one God and they go to church on a Sunday and repent their sins. I wouldn't say I was an expert, as I didn't study religious studies at school, did I?' Eek stifled a snigger.

'You did very little studying at school, Katie. But you were something of an activist in religious circles were you not?' said Stefan.

'Not really...'

'You have been in correspondence with our bishop, haven't you Katie? She sighed and popped the last potato in her mouth.

'Yes, to his Holy Bishopness.'

'Is this the Dear Bish, Love Katie letter?' asked Al.

'Yes, that's the one' Katie answered, 'but the point is, it was a letter I had to write for an English exercise, wasn't it? I had to write a letter about something I was interested about...' And there it was again, the family joke at her expense, the one that always surfaced when she came back home.

Al tittered: 'So you wrote a love letter to the bishop, did you Auntie Katie?'

'So, what did you say to him, Auntie Katie?' asked Eek.

'Well, he didn't get back to me, it was one of his little minions' Katie replied.

'You're such a goofball, Auntie Katie' said Monique sniggering at her fork.

'It was a list of grievances that your auntie had about the Anglican Church, wasn't it Katie?' answered Gwen.

'I'm not a goofball Eek!'

'Yes, you are!'

'Anyway Gwen, I wouldn't put it quite like that...'

'So, how would you put it?' asked Gwen.

'It was a list of things they could do better in, like...'

'Goofball!'

'Like what they think about other religions, how they treat women, and their old fashioned ways and being out of date about everything and that...anyway, let's talk about something else, shall we?'

'So what do you believe in Auntie Katie?' asked Al.

'Elbows, Katie!' admonished Gwen.

'Oh, sorry.' She removed them from the table. Katie puffed her cheeks and looked up at the ceiling. The dried out cross beams looked particularly dusty. There were gossamer tunnels that led to lurking creatures with too many eyes and too many legs. She shuddered.

'Auntie Katie?' prompted Eek.

'I believe that there is one god who happens to be female, in a group of other gods and goddesses and she is not jealous of any of them - her name is Gaia but you can call her Mother Earth, if that's easier for you.'

'That would be like a pantheon of gods and goddesses, would it Katie?' commented Stefan.

'Yes, if you say so Sir' she continued, 'but it's more like a committee. So your god, let's call him God, reports in to Mother Earth, because she is above all other gods. She is like the captain and she sits at the head of the table.'

'Or, chief executive officer, Katie?'

'Yes, could be, though I think captain is better.'

'Captain Earth' sniggered Al.

'I have my own goddesses, in this team of gods and goddesses' Katie said, as she looked at Gwen who seemed uncomfortable with the direction this conversation was taking. She decided to carry on regardless. 'One's called Danu and the other is called Rhiannon.'

'What's Rhiannon like?' asked Eek.

'Well, she's a goddess of water, she rides a horse and her job is to try and make everything fair and good.'

Al snorted in derision. 'She rides a horse?'

'Yes, Al, she rides a sodding horse.'

'I want to follow Auntie Katie's religion, please, please, please!' exclaimed Eek.

'Because you want a horse?'

'Yes!'

'She is also the goddess of rebirth, so she'll look after you when they peg you out, so you don't really need anyone else, do you? If you've got Rhiannon at your back, you've got all bases covered, haven't you?'

'Please, please, please Mama' exclaimed Eek.

'Thank you very much for that, Katie' muttered Gwen, 'but just to be clear, my sister's views are her own and you shouldn't be unduly influenced by them because...'

'Auntie Katie's a goofball!' announced Eek triumphantly.

'I wasn't going to say that, but yes' replied Gwen, 'and you will still be coming to church with us on Sunday.'

Katie's teeth ground together. There was that unpleasant acrid taint of clashed enamel. 'You're welcome Gwen, my conscience is clear. I don't think many priests can say that! And, I am not a goofball, whatever that is, I have a responsible job in the Andrew, and...'

'What is your job?' asked Al pointedly, 'Is it answering the admiral's phone?'

'Well, sort of, I'm a Communications and Information Systems specialist and I look after a little team...'

'Of geeks and goofballs, Katie?'

'You're really coming it now! I'm not a goofball, I have a responsible job, I send you money and I look after you all!'

'Calm down Katie!'

'You're really getting on my tits now!'

'That's enough!' shouted Stefan. 'Quiet at the table!' The slam of his hand on the oak table reverberated around the kitchen.

'Sorry, sir' said Katie. She could see that Al was squirming to make an announcement. This ought to be good.

'Auntie Katie, you are the High Priestess of Goofiness in the Kingdom of Goofdem!' said Al laughing. No one else laughed. They just stared at him. He got back to pushing vegetables around his plate.

'This is slightly awkward, we wanted to ask you something Katie?'

'Oh? What was that then Gwen?'

'We, Stefan and I, would like to appoint someone to look after Alexander and Monique, if something happened to us. We decided, after much consideration, that we would ask you...'

'You want me to be the godmother? Really, are you sure?', asked Katie.

'This wasn't my idea' muttered Gwen, 'but considering the other candidates, you are the best option for us, even if your attitude to our religion is decidedly flaky. But you are their closest living relation and...'

'Did you consider Paol?' asked Katie.

'Yes, we did, but not for very long.'

'What about Stefan's side?' Stefan gave her a stern look. She looked back at Gwen. 'Maela?' Gwen shook her head with undue force.

Stefan decided to assert himself. 'No, this is a legal transaction. We just need to make sure that Katie understands her responsibilities.'

'Will anyone object?' she asked. She felt heavy inside. She had known it was coming but to actually hear the words spoken out loud, weighed heavily inside and started a commotion between her heart and lungs. 'The godmother, eh? What does the vicar say? Do I have to convert? What if, what if...'

'What if what, sister?'

'Let's just hope I don't get struck down by a bolt of lightning then!' laughed Katie nervously.

'You can't seriously be thinking of putting Auntie Katie in charge of us? I won't have it' stated Al quietly but firmly.

'You won't have any choice, Alexander, this is a legal arrangement.'

'So Auntie Katie, let me put this to you...'

'Alexander, don't...'

'How would it look if it became common knowledge that Papa had to bust you out of jail? You're never here and you curse and swear like a matelot?'

'I am a sodding matelot! Anyway, none of that never happened. I was not put in jail, was I? The police were just taking care of me, weren't they?'

'That's not what I heard...'

'Well, that's how it was. Anyway, that was years ago, wasn't it sir?'

'Nay, nay, it was on the occasion of your thirteenth birthday. That was a memorable night' Stefan reminisced. 'Anyway...'

'It was just once, and Mister Hofland didn't bust me out. It was just a chat with the local fuzz' she eventually spat out, 'and I learned from my mistake, didn't I? Anyway, I don't think you should be throwing around accusations, not with your...'

'Auntie Katie, shut up...' hissed Al.

'Alexander? Katie? What is this?'

'I don't think Al should be throwing around accusations, unless he feels that that this is the time and place to confess our wrongdoings. Al, do you want to go first?'

'Shut up Auntie Katie!'

'What? It's not like you've got anything to hide, is it? Or have you?'

'Katie, you dare.'

'Don't you dare me! Don't you dare me! I might see that as a challenge and...I dare! I dare, I dare!'

'Shut up, shut up, shut up! Auntie Katie, don't say anything!' She deftly avoided his kick from under the table and retaliated in kind. Al yelped like a puppy and she sniggered to herself. Got him a good one there! Gwen stared at her and she stared at a part of the wall just above Gwen's shoulder.

'Shall we do a quick look round your room then? I think we may find some things that will be very interesting.'

'It's a lie!'

'What's a lie? You've got nothing to hide, have you?'

'That's enough!' said Stefan sternly.

'Dear sister...' started Gwen.

Something else was brewing in his dirty little mind. 'So, are you going to go and see the Wicked Witch of the West, Auntie Katie?'

'That's my mum you're talking about! And your mum's mum! You're really coming it now!'

'Katie! Alexander! Please. Enough!' Al flicked a glance at her.

'Alexander, don't be so disrespectful' said Gwen.

'I'm not, that's what you all think though, isn't it?'

'Is it?' This time Katie's kick landed squarely on his ankle.

'Bloody hell' he exclaimed.

'Alexander, go up to your room!'

'No, I will not!'

'Go now!' shouted Gwen. There was a clatter of cutlery on his plate and then the strident scraping of his chair on the stone floor.

'WILL YOU STOP IT NOW, ALL OF YOU!'

Monique was standing on her chair shouting. Katie was covering her ears. The others sat and stared.

'Mama, take Auntie Katie outside now and talk to her.' She paused for breath. 'Papa, take Alex in the back room and talk to him. Be back here in five minutes and be ready to apologise to each other and say how much you appreciate each other. We must stick together, we're a family!'

'Thank you Monique, that was a timely intervention. Katie, you're with me and just do as you're told.'

Katie followed Gwen through the tangled kitchen garden through to the crest of the hill overlooking the valley. They sat together on the kissing chair, with a full glass of wine between them. The contents sparkled yellowy-green.

'What should I know about Alexander then? What's he been doing?'

'Nothing you don't know already. Nothing illegal or immoral or bad...'

'What then?'

'He made me angry. I thought he was having a go. And he seems to think I'm not fit to look after the two of them, but I am, aren't I?' She took a slug of wine. 'This is nice, just me and you.'

'You've only been here a few hours and this is the second time we're having a heart to heart.'

'It's what sisters do, isn't it? Even half sisters. And there's going to be a third one, Gwen...'

'Pardon me?'

'What happened to Nana's garlic?'

'I've no idea what you're talking about!'

'It's quite simple Gwen - Nana's garlic has gone.'

'Never mind that. Let's make a fresh start, Katie.'

'I don't see how, you old bat.'

'You little Welsh slag!'

'Oi! That's not fair!'

'I'm sorry, I didn't mean...'

'So, Stefan, he enjoys a smoke and a drink, doesn't he?'

'Ah, so you've noticed.'

'Yes, it took about five seconds. His breath is a bit fierce, isn't it? If I'd had a light, I could've had the table incarcerated...'

'Incinerated, Katie' corrected Gwen. 'So, what are you going to say to my son?'

'I'll say I'm really sorry.'

'Is that it?'

'I'm not a sodding poet, Gwen.'

'So, can I ask what you appreciate about him?'

'I'll make something up. Just kidding, Gwen. I'll make it up to him, I know, I'll buy him a drink down at the pub.'

They trooped back into the kitchen where the others were waiting. Stefan frowned at the glass of wine in Gwen's hand. It was Katie's moment to make an apology.

'I'm sorry Al, I shouldn't have suggested that you were doing things that you shouldn't have been doing.' She picked her way through the next sentence. 'I appreciate your...commitment to your studies...and your interest in dramatic studies...and...your computing skills...and...and that's it.'

'It's your turn now, Alexander.'

'Auntie Katie, I'm sorry I suggested that you couldn't look after us. I appreciate your commitment to your naval career away from us, which must be very difficult for you.'

'Good. I'll do the clearing up, then. Mister Hofland, are you going to give me a hand?' Katie gripped Al's shoulder. 'And I'll see you in the pub at eight...don't be late!'

Chapter Forty-One

Tuesday 17 May 1737 - Llanfair Hill

Katie slipped out of Clun Cottage, while the rest of the family slipped away to their own, personal corners, and headed west of south west, into the hilly pasture land south of the Clun Valley. She resigned herself to a walk of around sixty minutes to take her to Llanfair Hill, where she hoped she would find the girl who had stolen her dog and someone who could rule in her favour. The air was sweet and pure and it rejuvenated her heart and her lungs and her legs.

Her finger and thumb went to her mouth and she blew a loud and piercing four note whistle and after two moments, there were two note whistles in response. She cranked up her pace so that she could barely feel the pack on her back, which contained two flasks of well-mature, sparkly, yellowy-green alcoholic liquid, salvaged from the pantry, and a box of dry, chewy rations.

It was at the standing stone by Cefn Hepreas, that she sensed she was getting close. A black and white collie dog appeared in front of her, panting eagerly, waiting for a command, with a big, doggy smile on the snout. 'Hallo Emmy, how are you' she asked of the dog, 'and where's your mistress?' as she ragged the back of the neck and ears. A woman appeared in front of her, with long unkempt brown hair, a denim shirt, a red neckerchief and a tartan skirt. But Katie knew this was no ordinary tartan.

'Ebrill Talog? You have returned?'

'Shepherdess, I have come for my dog, Owain - he has been taken.'

'Ah, I think that would be by Megan, she has your dog. I understood it to be a fair transaction.'

'My sister handed him over, but she had no right. I've come to take him back. I've had him since he was a pup. Owain is mine.'

'Come with me Ebrill, let me see if we can resolve this for you.'

The Shepherdess turned and started to climb Llanfair Hill with quick, nimble steps and precise propulsion from her shepherd's crook. Katie struggled to keep up and despite her desperate panting, fell behind by twenty paces. They came upon two mature women in animated conversation, who stopped abruptly when they saw Katie. The older of the two, with her head piled high with silvery grey hair, jabbed Katie in the ribs as she went past. The auburn-haired women growled in her throat and spat at Katie's feet - Katie scowled back and shook her foot, but said nothing. The woman leading the way brought her fingers to her mouth and whistled and there were distant whistles in response. The ground sloped less and Katie's lungs sighed in relief. She was in a wide circle, surrounded by low, standing stones and between the stones, the forms of women emerged. At a rough guess, there were just enough for a rugby union team. Only they were no team. There were several dogs, all growling at her. One growl she recognised instantly - it was the muted growl of a Welsh sheepdog, her sheepdog, Owain Madog.

'Ebrill, there is unrest to the west' whispered the shepherdess.

'Yes, I should've guessed' Katie whispered back.

'You will be tested...'

'Let's hope I'm not bested...' She turned her head and winked at the Shepherdess. 'That's why I'm wearing my hex-proof vest!'

'Please do not jest...this is most earnest.'

'I know this, dear Shepherdess.'

'And do not mock...'

'It's hard not to...this is such a load of sheep shite!'

'All the nearby communities are represented...Uplanders from the North, Crows to the East, Seeders to the South and there in the West...'

'Sheep fiddlers!'

'Herders, Ebrill, herders.'

'And where's my lot?'

'In the middle of them all.'

In the middle - where she would be surrounded, nowhere to run, trapped within a baying circle of women. The Shepherdess led the way to the middle and waited for Katie. She placed her hands on the back of Katie's shoulders and slowly turned her like the hand of a clock, so all the women could stare at her, recognise her for what she was and greet her. Each nodded in acknowledgement at each turn, with a stony face or a muttered curse and Katie responded as best she could, with a curt nod of her head. She felt her heart pumping wildly, her left arm swinging to-and-fro, to-and-fro. They all saw her as an outsider, someone who did not belong to any of the clans.

And then there were four younger women in the western quadrant that looked her up and down contemptuously: there was a tall girl with hair like tourmaline, white of complexion and pink of cheek, Megan, the dog thief; a slouching, gum chewing girl at her side wearing rubber boots, worn through denim shorts, a baggy shirt secured with a wide leather belt and long auburn hair piled high and scrunched out to one side; she had a mate who was trying to emulate her, only she was pale of face, with gingery hair and big freckles; and then there was a girl in rat-tails, a cropped top and denim skirt. Their faces and bodies seemed to hold her in contempt and Katie knew in that moment there was going to be a fight and she would be at the heart of it.

'Ebrill is a sister of ours and daughter of Maela.' There was a sudden muttering of voices at this announcement and Katie's heart plummeted - this was going even more difficult than she had imagined.

'She's no sister!' shouted scrunch-hair girl, soft of face, hard of eye.

'Ebrill earned her place here many cycles ago - she is of the Britanni!'

'Piss off Britanni! You don't belong here!' taunted rat-tail girl, who was tall but there was nothing of her.

'That goes for me too!' piped up freckle girl, plump of tummy and flabby of limb.

'The Britanni were here before any of you' interceded the Shepherdess.

'No, no, listen to me, I'm Brit-ish, Brit-ish, Brit-ish. We're all British, aren't we?' implored Katie. Megan looked different from all the other females in the circle - her lips and her fists were firmly closed.

A woman laughed bitterly: 'Why have you brought her here? She is the daughter of Maela, despoiler of our land. See over there!' She was pointing to a smudge of brown smoke above the hills.

'What's a despoiler, anyway?'

'See what she has done!'

'Our lands have been defiled by you and your clan!'

'It's not just your lands, and the border's a bit wiggly up and down here, so how would you know if anything of yours has been de-filed?'

'They have always been our lands until the Britanni came!'

'No, no, listen to me, we're all Brit-ish, Brit-ish, aren't we? The land belongs to all of us.'

The Shepherdess spun Katie around so she could look in her face. 'Maela has offended the sisters of the Elenydd, and she is your responsibility, Ebrill!'

Katie removed the hands from her shoulders and then walked a circle so that she could engage with each women individually: 'I am not my mum, am I? I am not responsible for what my mum does, am I? Can any of you say you have responsibility for your mum? No, you can't, because mums are always right even when they're wrong, but you want me to be responsible for mine? All right, I will go to her and I will ask her to stop the burning. If she is doing something she shouldn't, I will stop her. I don't know what she's doing, but if she's harming your land, I will stop her. But my mum is a free spirit, she believes the land is for the people; she believes that property is theft. You may not agree with that but...' Katie continued until she reached the end of the circle and then walked forward to confront Megan, '... you have taken my dog, and that is theft, you had no right to take my dog from someone who doesn't own him. Owain Madog is mine and now you give him back!'

'He is not yours. I agreed with your sister Gwen that I would take him, and look after him as he should be looked after. You have given away your right to own him!'

Owain laid down in the trampled grass, covered his eyes with his paws and tried to keep as low a profile as he could.

'He is mine! Look!' Katie pulled the dog tag from around her neck and thrust it towards Megan's face. 'See!'

Megan peered at the disk. 'That proves nothing! I paid good money for him!'

'You paid money?'

She hesitated 'Twenty, no fifty pounds!'

'Fifty! Never!' Gwen hadn't mentioned that money had changed hands. But Owain was a lazy-eyed sheep dog, so how could he be worth fifty pounds. 'Prove it! Show me the receipt!'

Megan looked confused for a moment. 'I can't!'

Katie brandished the dog tag: 'This proves he is mine! He belongs to me! Owain, come to heel, now!' The dog whimpered and covered his eyes with his paws. He didn't come to heel.

'You can have him back for one hundred pounds!'

'What? But he's mine!' Her hands slapped at the pockets of her pack. She didn't have one hundred pounds of spare cash, or anything like it!

'One hundred pounds' said Megan 'or fight me!'

There were several gasps and then a breath-held-in silence.

'No, he is mine, there's no need for fighting.' There was a press of bodies closing in and then hostile muttering. There was going to be fighting, whether she liked it or not. Katie slowly inched the pack off her back so as not to provoke a sudden attack.

But Megan attacked.

A flurry of blows landed on Katie's raised arms, her shoulders and her head. She stumbled, fell, pushed back up and grunted when a kick landed in her ribs, Katie rolled backwards and Megan was upon her.

'You've got her, Megan!' screamed a woman.

'Go for the eyes!'

'Throttle her neck!'

'Snap her arm!'

'Tear her to shreds!'

Fingers digging into her face, scratching for her eyes. Heaving breaths in and out; a knee thrust into something that yielded; elbow and fist landed on bone. She was on her hands and knees; Megan was rolling on her back clutching her stomach. Katie shucked off her pack.

They were back on their feet. Megan swung an arm that flailed over Katie's head; Katie's knee lifted Megan off her feet. She was hurt. Her leg drew back and swung wildly at Katie's side. Katie caught the leg and fell; Megan screamed, clutching at her crotch.

A look of horror came over Megan's face as Katie's left leg made a dull thud against her ear. Megan spun round, flattened on the ground.

Katie's hands covered up her mouth, as she muttered, 'Give it up Megan!'

Had she wounded the girl?

'Let her up, you bitch!'

But Megan pushed her way up again, her eyes not right, back on her feet. Her right arm swept Katie's legs away and she fell. Megan was on top, folding Katie's legs on top of her, crushing breath out; Megan's hands grasping at Katie's neck, pulling her up and down, her head thumping dully on the ground. Her eyes blinked three times - she could not see! Must escape this, or I'm finished!

Katie's legs fought for purchase round Megan's neck, her chin jerking out of the way of a right hook. She caught Megan's arm and locked it - she tried to pull it back but couldn't; Megan tried to pull herself up but couldn't. Katie flexed her backside and locked her ankles around Megan's neck and arm and they squeezed and tightened again.

She watched in fascination as the face of Megan went from fierce, to puzzled and then to alarm, as her own arm compressed her neck. She couldn't get free, no one could. Megan's face turned to horror and then pain and then subsided tick by tick into passive, barely conscious defeat.

'Say it, Megan!'

'Let her go!' screeched a woman.

'You're killing her!' shouted another.

'He's yours!' spluttered Megan. Her tongue lolled out of her gaping mouth, locks of tourmaline smothered her mouth and nose.

'Who's mine?'

'The dog, he's yours!'

'Say it so everyone hears you!'

'Please, please, the dog is yours!'

Katie slowly released her legs from around Megan's head but still held tight to Megan's twisted arm. She stood up slowly and then raised her boot high above the joint. Megan's face was crushed in the soil.

'Ebrill, no!' shouted the Shepherdess.

Katie released the arm and stood, her body shaking relentlessly, ready to fight again, the fuel for violent action still coursing through her blood, her left arm swinging to-and-fro to her side.

Two women rushed to Megan to tend to her. She was sprawled out on the soil, her face was red and swollen, her chest heaving in and out. Slowly, she was brought to her feet.

The two girls stood facing each other, the Shepherdess to one side and the wild-eyed, auburn haired woman to the other. Megan bobbed her head, reached for Owain's lead and put it in Katie's right hand. 'Thanks Megan' muttered Katie under her breath. The back of her head was swelling, her lip was sore and all she could taste was dirt. Everything hurt, her lungs, her limbs, her everything.

She lurched downwards but the Shepherdess caught her and kept her up. 'Now stand tall, breath deeee...ply, show them that you are not hurt' she whispered in Katie's ear.

'I am hurt! I'm hurt all over, I can barely stand!' she hissed back.

'Show them how a warrior of the Britanni behaves! She is a fierce fighter but she's magnanimous in victory!'

'Eh, is she?' Katie tried to laugh but it hurt too much. She cut it off so that it became a snort. 'What's that? Warrior of the what? I am not a warrior, am I?' She felt wetness below her right nostril. 'Is my nose bleeding?'

'No' replied the Shepherdess, 'just snot.' She smeared it away with her sleeve.

'My lip's sore and' she paused to wipe her tongue on her sleeve, 'I've eaten dirt.' Katie acknowledged the three women in the southern quadrant, the clan of The Seeders.

'You've turned into a little scrapper, a fighting women. I'm not sure if anyone could defeat you now.'

Katie acknowledged the three women in the eastern quadrant, of The Crows. 'This is all about getting my dog back, that's all. I'm not making a living out of this, 'cos it hurts so much.' She acknowledged the three women of the circle to the north, of the Uplanders clan. This left silver bun lady, making a crude gesture at her; auburn haired lady expectorating at her feet and the three young girls in the west, all in a huddle, as if they were scheming something - The Herders. She saw a red Toyota pick-up at the bottom of the hill, the preferred means of transport for the sheep diddlers of the Elenydd.

'So Ebrill, you've won the battle, but how will you win the peace? I will leave you with that thought' said the Shepherdess. She was also looking to the west.

Miss Auburn Scrunch took a few steps forward, hesitated and stopped to pose with her pelvis thrust out and her arms akimbo. She quickly checked that the freckled girl and the lanky girl were in close attendance. 'You must think you're really something.'

'Better than being a nothing, eh,' murmured Katie, 'so why don't you all just piss off and leave this to the women...'

'Well, you're not something - you're a nothing!'

'Yeah, that goes for me too!' said lanky girl.

'Me too, bitch!' said freckle girl.

'You are wicked, she's just a child, look what you've done to her!' hissed the auburn haired woman.

'Ceridwen, it is all settled' announced the Shepherdess.

'She stole my dog and she attacked me! What should I have done?' Katie realised this wasn't over.

'You are of the Britanni, you are of the warrior caste. She is just a child!'

'She is not just a child! Look at the sodding size of her!' Megan was against the standing stone, staring far into the distance.

'Ceridwen, if you want a trial of powers, I'm sure Ebrill will oblige you! Do you wish to challenge Ebrill? Let us arrange a contest for you two...'

'Take her!' screamed Ceridwen. Katie was pushed down to her knees, her arms pinioned and her head shoved against the ground. Ceridwen had her hair and was tugging it back. 'Look at me girl!'

But she didn't, even though the face of Ceridwen was right in hers. 'We are not finished with you - we have the one thing that is most precious to you in the world, and you will have to come to us, and when you do, we will settle with you, and you will come, after Beltane, but before the Solstice, because you cannot help yourself, and then you and your clan will be gone for good!'

Katie whistled three times quickly, three times slowly, three times quickly: There was a growl, a snarl and the sound of teeth tearing into flesh; Ceridwen shrieked. There were shrill girl screams; thrown-out curses. Katie surged to her feet, her right elbow smashing into a soft mouth, her left fist swinging back into a rigid nose. She was spinning around, her arms and fingers extending, her body coiling and then releasing a burst of wind from her lungs: 'Back off, all of you!'

When she opened her eyes, the crook of the Shepherdess was around a leather boot, Owain and Emmy were playing tug of war with a green rubber boot and there was a limping of witches down the slope, one girl clutching her guts, another trying to staunch blood flowing down from her nose.

The Shepherdess grinned as the cowed women retreated. 'We prevail!' she exulted as she waved Ceridwen's boot in the air with her crook.

'This time, we do, thanks to you and Emmy and Owain but I do need to put this right, somehow. Come with me Owain.'

She approached Megan who was propped up against the standing stone, with two women fussing over her tear-streaked face.

Katie dismissed the two women and brought out a flask from her pack. 'I don't know how to tell you this Megan, but your mum's a bit of a twat.'

'She's not my mum!'

'Oh, well, whoever they are, they're all twats then, aren't they?'

'I thought they were...on my side!'

'Oh, I'm sorry for that and I'm sorry for kicking and choking you.'

She offered the flask to Megan and she placed its cold mass against the side of her face. 'So Megan, where did you learn to fight like that?' Megan hesitated and then mumbled 'With my brother.' She sighed as the cold of the flask soothed the mask of pain that creased her face.

'If I fought like that with my brother, I'd do him great harm.'

'Alex? Is Alex your brother?' asked Megan.

'No, no, Al is my sister's son which makes him...'

'Your nephew? Alex is your nephew!'

'Ah, so that's what he is!'

Megan smiled and looked away. Her cheeks flushed even more crimson than they had been moments before.

'Listen, I'm sorry I kicked you so hard. You're going to have a lump there. Let's get you to a medic.' Katie looked around at their surroundings and couldn't see how an ambulance could reach them - she would have to walk Megan off the hill.

Megan shook her head slowly. 'There's no need...'

She and the Shepherdess clinked flasks and each took a draught. 'What do you think Shepherdess?'

'I think she'll feel better after a drink.'

Katie offered the flask of cider to Megan and she took two tentative sips. 'I think you need to gulp it down quickly' suggested Katie, 'if you want the full effect.'

'You've won this fight Ebrill, but what will happen now?'

'I'll walk Megan off the hill and then I'm going to meet my boyfriend at the pub.'

'Your boyfriend?'

'Yes, my boyfriend, what's so funny about that?'

'Does he know?' asked the Shepherdess.

'He wants permission to court me, so I'm going to say, yes, yes, yes!'

'And are you going to meet him as you are?'

'Yes I am, and what's wrong about the way I look?'

'Oh, nothing at all. And what will you do about Ceridwen and her troupe?'

'She got it about right - I'll have to go to their patch, before the solstice and make good on my promise.'

'Take care Ebrill, she is a powerful witch.' With that comment, the Shepherdess whistled and trotted off the mound with Emmy at her side.

Katie walked to the centre of the stone circle. It was now all clear, except for her and Megan and the sheepdog. There was some kind of calm, but to the west, she could still hear little scratchings of noise, like a distant wireless message, coded into bursts, but there was not enough of it to make sense, but its insistence and its persistence, made it a call for help. She walked back to the standing stone.

'Did you hear that, Ebrill?'

'You've tuned into that, too, Megan? Hmm, come along with me, Megan, let's you and me talk. Yes, Owain, come along with your mistresses. Yes, Owain, do as you're told.'

They headed north then west of northwest, with Katie and Owain leading. The sun was still high and wisps of smoke were gathering in the valley below. Katie sucked in the clean, pure air and snorted up something unpleasant from her nostril.

'So who wins?' Katie said coughing.

Megan looked puzzled.

'When you fight with your brother' Katie explained.

Megan smiled and then her face creased as it hurt. 'I do' she said shyly.

'I thought so. Walk with me, Megan, not behind me. Do I look a mess?'

'Umm, no?'

'Liar.'

They paused at the lip of the hill before the steep descent to the valley of the Clun. 'So, how well do you know Al?'

'I see him in the mornings. I wait for him in the afternoons. I don't know what to say to him.'

'Have you tried saying something?'

'I say 'hallo' to him, and he smiles back at me.'

'Oh, and does he...?'

'No, not really...'

'And does he...?'

Megan looked away. She stopped walking and gazed towards the village. 'I don't know what to do.' Katie opened her satchel. She still had the handkerchief. She wiped Megan's face.

'Write him a note. I'll give it to him. Did you know he plays rugby?'

'No! I see him with a kit bag every Wednesday. I didn't know.'

Wednesday must be sports day, Katie supposed. She offered a piece of paper from her note book, a pencil to write with and turned her back so Megan could write a letter using it as a...rest. She wriggled at the slow languid writing that became etched into her back. It seemed unnecessarily long. Megan completed her letter, just before Katie's back went into spasm. Megan folded it into three, tucked one end into the other and wrote, 'Dear Alex' on the outside. She kissed it shyly and passed it to Katie.

Owain returned after a fruitless scamper through the copse to their left. He waited for a command. 'Did you teach him any signals?'

'I did Ebrill, I taught him all my calls and the signals.' She brought her fingers to her lips and made a two note whistle. Owain paused, looked away and then scampered quickly out to the left in a wide sweeping circle. 'See?'

'Very good, Megan.' Katie made three short, three long and three short peeps through her nose and sinuses. She couldn't tell if Owain had detected these until there was a short, sharp yelp from one hundred paces away. 'Are you ready Megan?' Katie asked. 'Owain and I have an override - you should be on Defcon 3 now!'

Megan searched anxiously for the Welsh sheepdog that was turning and galloping outside her line of sight. 'What was that? An override? What does that mean?'

'I think Defcon 2 now...you need to be at a higher level of alert Megan.'

'What is Defcon?'

'I think Defcon 1 now...'

There was a sharp cry, 'Ugh' from Megan. She collapsed like a felled tree. A bundle of white and black bounced up and down over her back and chewed at the collar of her jacket.

Katie grabbed Owain's collar and pulled him away. 'Down boy, Megan's got the message.' Then she pulled the prostrate girl back to her feet. 'Megan, you are right, I can't look after Owain, I'm away too often and the Hofland's don't have the time.' She took Megan's shoulders and turned her so that they were facing each other. 'So, I have a proposal for you Megan. I will let you have Owain on loan. You will look after him as if he were your own. If you find him a bitch, you will have first call on his pups. You will bring him to me whenever I am back at Clun. But he is mine. If something ever happens to me... then he is yours.' Katie swallowed noisily. This was so difficult, there must be no tears: 'Do you agree?' There were tears flowing down her face.

Megan nodded vigorously and winced again.

'We have a deal. Do you want me to walk you...home. Should I talk to your mum and dad?' She wiped tears away with her sleeve.

'There's just my papa, so there's no need. Can I take him now?'

'No, I will take Owain now. We'll meet in the square at Clun this coming Sunday at eventide. I will hand him over to you then. I'm going to the pub now. I'm hoping to meet up with a boy, who wants to be my boyfriend. Is there anything else?'

'No.'

Katie hesitated and then offered her hand. Megan took it and pulled Katie close. 'Thank you Ebrill.' They both winced as they pushed each other away.

'So, how do I look Megan? Will I pass muster when I meet up with my boy?'

'Ebrill, you look like you've been in a fight!'

'Oh, no. Do I look a mess?'

'Yes, you do!'

'Oi Megan, we're nearly sisters now, there's no need for that!' They stood waiting to go their separate ways, waiting...

'Come with me Megan. Al will be there, then you can give him your little letter...'

'I'm not sure.'

'Be sure. Now come with me.'

They kicked their way through the heather and the rank grass until they came to a single tracked road. This was going well until a car came up behind them with its horn blaring loud.

'Are you going our way, girls?' shouted the young idiot of a driver. Katie recognised him - it was Tonny, Ben's best friend.

'No' replied Katie. They were now being examined closely by the other occupants of the car.

'Look at the state of you!'

'We've been wrestling, haven't we Megan?'

Megan just gave a forced smile.

'I really like the wrestling...'

'Got room for three?' asked Katie.

'Three? Of course we have!'

Owain scampered to her side.

'Budge up then!'

'Unlucky mate!' shouted the driver to his passenger on the back seat. They all squeezed in, with Megan holding Owain on her lap and Katie on the lap of the boy in the orange shirt, occupying the passenger seat.

'What's that sticking in me?' asked Katie, shifting her backside to one side and then she realised: 'Oh, it's you, you dirty sod!'

There was silence as Katie entered the bar, as the buzz of meaningless chat ceased and the chatterers stopped to stare. She looked around the bar. Owain whimpered. She felt a palpable sense of hostility. 'Owain, sit this one out, outside with you, Megan, stay by my side...'

'Look at the state of you two! What happened?'

'We've been rolling around in the grass, haven't we?'

'Shouldn't be allowed' muttered a crinkled old man to his crinkled old wife and they each took a sip from a half full wine glass.

Where was Al? Where was Ben?'

'I would have thought you would have learned your lesson...' came a growl from a weatherworn face, nursing a half drunk pint of dark stout.

'What lesson is that?' asked Katie. 'I think you're going to have to help me out here?'

'You know very well girl...'

'No, actually I don't, but I've got one for you?'

'What?'

'Change your pants once in a while...'

'Katie!' cried out a voice from behind the bar, 'Katie Talog!' The voice and the face seemed familiar.

He slapped his glass on the bar and left, a hunched, shambling figure. Katie walked to the bar and confronted the landlady. 'Hallo Fran, how are you doing?'

Fran waved her arm. 'Brilliantly, as you can see. So what happened to you?'

'I've been at sea, Fran, protecting you lot!'

'I meant, why did you bring in half of Clun hill with you?'

'Oh, it's like I said, I've been rolling around in the grass...two pints of water please? And a big bag of ice!'

A lad swaggered to the bar with his pool cue and looked them up and down. 'Fancy one, girls?'

'Fancy one, what?'

'Game of pool!'

She looked around the bar again and clocked that both Al and her boyfriend had not arrived yet. The lads in the battered old saloon had driven on to the cricket ground but said they would pop in later. These two grinning loons at the pool table would have to do. 'Oh, all right then - let's knock some balls about.'

Megan's cue shot barely nudged the pack, bounced off three cushions and landed neatly back where it had started. 'Sorry' she whispered to Katie.

'Don't worry. Looks like we haven't decided yet...' Katie announced to the boys.

'Don't worry girls, let me sort you out. The balls were scattered and he neatly potted two spotted balls.

'Right, we're the stripy ones. Megan, I think we could be in a bit of trouble here...'

'You said...'

'I know what I said, Megan...'

He looked at the girls while he considered his next shot. 'So, what've you girls been up to?'

'Oh, I went to see a girl about a dog.'

'Ha, good one!' He settled to make his shot.

'It was Megan, But there was a bit of a misunderstanding' Katie continued, 'wasn't there Megan?'

'Yeah?'

'And we ended up wrestling...' His shot skewed to the right and disappeared into a pocket.

'Oh, you made a bit of a mess of that. Two shots?'

'Yeah, yeah. Look, just don't talk when I'm playing a shot, alright?'

'I thought you wanted to know what we've been doing?' She got her head down and potted two of the striped balls. She left the cue ball tight in the jaws of a pocket.

The other lad settled down to make his shot.

'When I say wrestling, it was more full on than that, wasn't it Megan?'

He looked up and then settled back down to make his shot.

'It was no holds barred, if you know what I mean...'

The ball rattled in the jaws of the pocket and settled pathetically, just a hand's span from where it had started.

'Two shots?'

'Yeah, yeah. Look, no chat when we're playing, right?'

'You sound like a right pair of pros!'

'Yeah. So no chat!'

Megan assumed a position to play her shot and Katie assumed a position right alongside her, so their faces were cheek to cheek. 'That tickles!' giggled Megan. Katie adjusted Megan's elbow and received a little peck on the cheek as her reward.

'Chin low, elbow high. Play right through it and keep your head down.' The balls cascaded around the table. Katie lifted Megan up quickly as a ball spun past. 'That was nice. Here, have a go at this one.' The ball was duly potted. 'Now, hit this one.' The ball was hit square on.

'Good. Well done Megan.' They returned to the bar and both rested against it, side by side, to watch the next shot.

'Right, no more coaching. Just play...'

'Oh, all right. It doesn't matter, does it? Once shown, always known, isn't that right Megan?'

'That's right, Katie, once shown, always known!' Megan giggled again.

'I showed Megan some good moves today, didn't I? When we were wrestling that is...'

Another shot skewed wildly around the table.

'Two shots? I reckon I can clear the rest of the striped ones from here, boys. What do you reckon?'

'Really? Want to bet?'

'A side bet? How much?'

'Five says you can't.'

'Let's see the colour...ooh, and there it is!'

'Let's see yours...'

'Oi, don't be rude!'

'Money, show us your money girlie!'

She looked at Megan; Megan looked back at her. She looked around the bar but there was no Al and no boyfriend. 'Best scrumpy' she announced as she produced the stone flask from her pack. Both the boys took a sip as Fran's brows knitted into a frown.

'That's good stuff.'

'Totally is, isn't it? High octane!'

With the bet settled, Katie set to work and cleared all the stripy ones and then paused at the black. 'Local rules?'

'What?'

And promptly potted it into her nominated pocket. 'Do you want to try your luck again?'

'No ta, I think we've just been hustled!'

'Well, just to show there's no hard feelings, you can get the next round in! And I'll get the table set up for the next game - shall we double the stakes this time?'

'I'm playing darts.'

'Me too!' And with that, the two boys sauntered their way to the other end of the pub.

'All right Fran?' Katie asked as she made her way back to the bar. The landlady stopped pulling the pint.

'So, how long are you back for Katie? Are you staying with your family?'

'I am, but I don't think they're very happy with me - I'm doing another five years in the Andrew!'

'Well, good for you. There's no prospects here...'

Fran passed the pint across the counter and tutted at the pile of change that came her way.

'They keep themselves to themselves don't they, you Hoflands? We never see them down here in the village.' She started to count the coins into the till. 'You can stay here, if you like? If you could put in some shifts at the weekend and help at mealtimes...'

'Yes, let's do that. Oh, sorry Fran, Ben's just arrived.' Katie turned to admire his blonde curly hair, the soft, blue of his kind eyes and his tall and strong frame. 'He's a good looking lad is Ben' she whispered confidingly to Fran 'but I need to have a little word with him.' She took a few steps and she was between Ben and the bar, just as he was about to place his order.

Ben was taken aback and stopped in his stride. 'Katie, I....I wasn't expecting to see you!'

'Just back today. How've you been?'

'I'm doing well, thanks. What have you been up to?'

'I've been swanning around the Indian Ocean, chasing pirates.' She side-stepped, as he side-stepped, so she was still between him and the bar. 'So...how's your dad?'

'He's very well, thank you...'

'And your mum?'

'She thinks you're a bad girl' he smirked, 'a bad, bad girl!'

Oh, my soul, that smile: meadows of swaying grass, the sandy banks of the chuckling stream and his oh, so gentle touch. 'Whew! I see. Well, what I would say to you is that the things that your mum thinks make me a bad girl are the very same things that boys think make me a good girl, if you know what I mean...' Katie frowned as she tried to work out what she had just said.

'You mean you're a slag?' called out a dry, cracked female voice from the other side of the bar.

'Oi you, at least my tits aren't dragging on the floor like yours are!'

'Katie!' shouted Fran.

'Sorry about that, Ben. And your sister? What's she up to now?' Katie asked, trying to move the conversation along quickly.

'Yeah, she's well. She's working in Shrewsbury now.'

'Don't you mean Amwythig? Oh, good for her. How old is she now? Seventeen?'

'Yes, that's right.'

'Blimey! And is she courting?'

'Oh!'

'Courting. That's an old fashioned word, isn't it? I think that word used to be used in olden times, didn't it? And still used in Clun sometimes, I think.'

'Oh, no!'

'I'm not quite sure what it means, do you? I think it might mean where some knob-head, writes an incriminating letter to the girl's old buffer, and he doesn't tell the girl.'

'Oh, no, no!'

'So the girl pitches up, she knows she's going to have a bit of a difficult time. She didn't show up for Christmas, she hasn't written much and she's covered in bandages and she's wearing gloves in summer but still, she's got her story straight for each of those.'

'Oh, no, no, no!'

'But the old buffer, he's got this letter, hasn't he?'

'I'm sorry, I'm sorry.'

'And the girl's thinking, it's some pillock from the village, having a laugh.'

'I'm sorry, I'm sorry.'

'But it's not is it? So I'm like this pretty little dove, I've come from thousands and thousands of miles away, I'm flapping along, really tired, minding my own business...and then it's like this great big hawk comes out of nowhere, smashes into me and I'm on the ground, in a pile of blood and feathers and he's got his great big talons stuck right in me...'

'Look, I'm really sorry.'

'So, I'm bleeding all over the place and I know my old buffer's going to tear chunks out of me and eat me alive...'

'I'm so sorry!'

'And it's my best friend in the village. The one who covered my back at school, the one I shared my secrets with, the one who I was desperate for, the one who I always wanted to catch me at kiss chase and give me a kiss and a cuddle with, but he never did. And now he wants to court me?'

'I'm sorry. I should have said...'

'Yes, you should. And you shouldn't have written him a letter, should you?'

'But, it's Mister Hofland. I had to get his permission!'

'No you didn't. It's got nothing to do with him. It's me, it's just me. It doesn't matter what he thinks, does it? It's just me you need to convince.'

'I...I didn't know, did I?'

'Well, it is, isn't it? So, you want to court me then, Ben? So you must fancy me then?'

'Yes, I did.'

'What do you mean, did? That should be yes, I do. So, what do you fancy about me then?'

'Well, you're always friendly and you have a nice smile.'

'Well Fran has all that, doesn't she? But you're not going to court her, are you? Or have you been writing other letters?'

'No, no, it was just the one letter.'

'Good. So, what else do you fancy about me?' She noted that Al had arrived but he was hidden away in a corner, feeding a machine with coins from his pocket.

'Well, you're a working girl and you're interesting and...'

'Do you find me physically attractive?'

'Well, yes, I suppose so.'

'Am I more attractive now than when I was at school?'

'Yes, you've grown up lots.'

'Oi, are you saying I'm fat?'

'No, no, no! In all the right places' he added quickly.

'I think that counts as a compliment, so well done Ben. Well, I've got one for you. You've got a nice kind face and you're tall with big muscles, and...' what she really wanted was to go body surfing on his chest and stomach.

'And you're a good laugh and a good mate, when you're here' Ben added.

'See that's nice, we're chatting each other up now. Perhaps you could buy me a drink?'

'All right, what would you like?'

'Could I have a pint of cider? That would be really kind of you. And could you get my friend Megan one as well, if you could please?'

She gratefully accepted her drink. 'So, when do we start courting properly? When do we get serious and...?'

'Your old buffer said no. He didn't give me permission' Ben replied grouchily. He took a long draught from his pint. 'Anyway, when he said no, I, I decided I had to move on.'

Her heart suddenly sank. 'Look, you don't need permission from him. He's not my dad - it's me you need to win over. I'll deal with Mister Hofland - go for it!' She stood up straight; her arms resting on her hips; her eyes closed and her lips puckered.

'I'm sorry Katie, I've moved on. We all have. You can't just disappear for a year and hope that everything stays the same. It doesn't.'

'Ben! We've got a contract! You can't just back out of that, can you? Can you?' she looked around the pub at the faces set against her.

'I'm sorry Katie, I've moved on...'

'What do you mean? You can't have! You're still here!'

'I'm with...someone else. My mum says it's for the best, she said it was meant to happen, she says I'm lucky to be...'

'Where is she then?'

There was a long pause as he looked about the room, as if seeking inspiration. 'Well, she's called Clara, she's really lovely, she's got a head of blonde curls, she's sweet and she always wants to be with me, doesn't she?' he replied defiantly.

'Hmm, does she walk on all fours and bleats when she sees you?'

'Eh?'

'This Clara, is she part of your dad's flock?'

'No, no, no, she's from the Castle, isn't she?'

'So, she's someone else's sheep? That's not nice Ben, you could at least...'

'Katie, of course she's not a sheep, she's a girl' he said indignantly.

'She sounds like a sheep to me' Katie replied. 'Look, just to be clear, there's no way I'm sharing you with a sheep, it's not nice.' The thought of somebody sheep-shagging a sheep was too awful to contemplate. And how do you shag a sheep anyway. 'Do you take her from behind? Didn't you mind all the dags?'

'For the last time, I am not courting a sheep!'

'You say she's not a sheep. In which case, I need to have a little word with her. She can't go around stealing other girl's boyfriends, can she? Where do I find this Clara?'

'I'm sorry Katie, we're finished. I'm with Clarice now.'

'Don't you mean Clara? Look, I forgive you. I forgive you for the letter and for going off with Sheepy Clara. Let's start again...'

'I'm sorry Katie, I've moved on, so there it is...'

'Oh come on Ben, come on Ben, give me a chance. I could do with a good, hard courting!' She puckered her lips again, leering with just the one eye open. 'Come on Ben' she whispered, 'you know you want to!'

'You don't want to be courted Katie, you just want take the piss, don't you? I can't take you seriously' he said as he turned and huffily stalked out of the pub with his glass of ale.

Katie spread her arms incredulously. 'Has he just walked out on me?' she asked everyone inside the pub. 'But I must be one of the most illegible girls in the district?'

'It's eligible Katie - you're one of the most eligible girls in the district.'

'I think that's what I just said, Fran.'

'Good point - of course you did.'

'Hmm, but was I too obvious? I need to work on that.'

'He's moved on Katie, you just have to accept it' replied Fran tartly.

'That's bollocks and you know it. Anyway, who knows this Clara? Does anyone know where she lives? Swifty, you must know?' She looked at the man sitting near the door, nursing a pint of mild and bitter, studiously avoiding her gaze.

'No, I'm not telling you where she lives.'

'It's not a big place is it? I'm sure I can find her.'

'Just leave it Katie, accept the situation as it is.'

'That's assuming this Clara is a real girl and not a made-up one...'

'So, Katie, how's your mother?' asked Fran.

'I'm not really sure. Has anyone seen or heard anything of her?'

'Yes, she flew over the other night, she was on her broomstick!'

'Oi, a bit of respect please. That's my mum you're talking about!'

'Try Sarah Pagan, she'll know. I reckon your mother is just across the border, Kerry way.'

'So, she's close by. Where can I find this Sarah Pagan?'

'Ludlow market. She's always there, with her magic potions and what not.'

'Mmm, I need to have a little chat with the Pagan girl.' So she would have to got to Ludlow on market day, which would be a chore. 'Well, it's all very well for you lot, but I've been protecting you all, and what thanks do I get? None, that's what!'

'To be fair, I can't see how pirates could get up here to Clun?' said the jocular looking farmer in his tweed coat and rubber boots.

'Well, they can. They're not like old school pirates. They have small boats and automatic weapons and they strike fast...'

'Even so...' was his riposte.

'And before you know it, they've come up the valley and they've had your loved ones away and your cattle' she said and paused before continuing quietly, 'which I realise for some of you is one and the same thing.'

'Can't see it happening, somehow.'

'Well, don't say I didn't warn you, now where's my boyfriend got to?' She went outside with a bowl of water for Owain and a sausage, his snack of choice. He gobbled this up greedily. Ben was standing beside her.

'Got your dog back then?'

'Yes, Ben, I did, now I just need to get my boyfriend back and I'll have a full set.'

'How're you going to do that?' he said as he sat down next to her, draining his pint glass.

'Well, I'm going to track down Sheepy Clara and sort her out!'

'Leave Clara out of this' said Fran as she busied herself collecting empty glasses.

'Why? Because she isn't real?' challenged Katie

'It's for you and Ben to sort out...'

'Right then, Ben, you're going to have to win me back.'

'Eh?'

'Come on Ben, let's have a pub triathlon, for old times sake - you choose one trial and I'll choose one trial and if it's all even, Fran will decide the third trial won't you Fran?'

'Yes, I'll do that for you, but what if Ben wins...'

'Which he won't, but if he does, he gets me all to himself.'

'And if you win?'

'Well, it'll depend on how well he performs, doesn't it?'

'So you win either way?' challenged Fran.

'You haven't been listening Fran: If Ben wins, he wins; if I win, I win. It's all very simple, actually.'

'Are you happy with this Ben?'

'Of course he is, so let's get on with it...'

'Fran, it's one all. What's the decider going to be? Cribbage, bar billiards, dominos, blindfold darts, yard of ale, or what?' Their trial by pool had gone according to the form book with an easy win for Katie. The trial by darts had been closer, as Katie had decided that her right arm was her throwing arm, and even then, Ben had only just defeated her. Al pointed out she was not using her best arm, but she quickly hushed him.

Fran thought for a while. 'I know, arm wrestling!'

'What? That's not a pub game! That's something else! That's not fair!'

'Yes, it is and that's my decision!'

There was a surge out of the pub and Katie was carried along with it. A noisy crowd gathered around a bench out at the front of the pub, looking across the village street.

'So, this is the decider then, the arm wrestling trial?' She paused before they sat down, across the bench from each other. 'Listen Ben, I'm happy to share you with Clara, so long as she's not a sheep. What do you say?'

'Look Fran, this doesn't feel right. It's Katie...' said Ben.

'So, just to be clear, if I win, I win all of Ben, if I want him? That's right, isn't it?'

'That's what we agreed.'

'So Ben, if you win, you get to keep Sheepy Clara?'

'I am not shagging a sheep!'

'If you say so. Listen, before we start, I think I should mention that I've already had a fight today and I'm a working girl and I need both my arms to do my job. So just be gentle with me.'

'Shut up Katie. Just get on with it' snapped Fran.

'And I haven't been particularly well recently...' Katie observed.

'This isn't right' moaned Ben.

'Also, my arms and my hands have been a bit dodgy recently...'

'Just get on with it.'

'Ben, I think you should let me win, as I'm a girl...'

'Ben, don't you dare. Stand up for yourself!'

They took their positions opposite each other on the bench. There was a tattoo of a rose on Ben's arm and the name of 'Susan' inked across it. This was new! Katie stood up and pointed accusingly at it: 'Who in the name of crap is Susan?'

'That's my mum, isn't it!'

'Wait a moment, is that Susan your mum's name or is it Susan, some other tart called Susan?'

'It's my mum, Susan!' he exclaimed indignantly.

'I don't believe it, you've got your mum's name tattooed on your arm - how am I supposed to compete with that?' She looked around for Al but she couldn't see him. Maybe he was getting the drinks in, so no help from that quarter. 'So, is Clara's name tattooed on you?'

'No!' He exposed his other bicep.

'Oh, good - so if I win, where's my name going?'

'On his arse!' someone shouted.

'Bugger that' she replied.

'Your name's not going on my body! Not for this! My mum will always be my mum!'

She turned to Fran. 'I can't go with someone who's got his mum's name tattooed on them. How do I compete with that?'

'You agreed. Now get on with it' Fran snapped back.

'All right, I can't afford to lose this. The stakes are too high' she declared to no one in particular. She worked through the chances of pulling off a win - they were negligible to non-existent.

'Come on Katie, you've got no chance. Give it up!' said a male voice in the crowd.

She turned to her heckler. 'There's always ways and means, isn't there? I've got womanly wiles on my side, haven't I?' This didn't seem to convince anyone. Their hands engaged. Katie wheedled her foot stealthily up Ben's leg until it was in the region of his groin and she was ready to jab her foot in.

'Fran, can you see what she's doing? She's trying to nobble me!' exclaimed Ben. She slid her toes in but Ben wriggled to one side.

'Katie Talog, get your foot out of Ben's crotch' Fran ordered.

Katie pulled quickly on his big hand while she had a small advantage. She had the upper hand for a moment, but Ben grimaced, grasped her hand tightly and levered it towards the table. She held him for a moment. Their arms took the strain again. Katie quickly realised she couldn't hold him with one hand and resorted to two. Her face contorted in pain as she realised she was beaten. As her arm collapsed against the bench her trunk swivelled so she was spread-eagled over the bench top.

She gasped, 'Best of three?' and manoeuvred herself so she was looking up into his blue eyes. 'What d'you reckon, Ben?'

'Admit when you're beaten Katie Talog' came a voice from the crowd.

'Look Katie, stop now, or you'll get yourself hurt' said Fran.

Her arm pulsed as he held it down firmly. She prepared herself to be taken on the table. 'You've won me Ben, I'm all yours now? Where do you want to take me? Better be heaven, hadn't it?'

'You're always messing around, Katie Talog, I'm going to finish my drink' said Ben as he stalked back inside the pub with his glass.

Fran pulled Katie upright and took her by the right hand. 'Come with me young lady.' They pushed their way through the crowd back inside the pub and behind the long wooden counter. Fran was uncomfortably close, Katie thought. She tried to open up some space between them but she was now held by both shoulders. 'Now, we need to have a word. It's nice that you are back, but things change here while you're gone and you can't just barge in and upset my regulars.'

'What did I do?'

'You bullirag the boys.'

'No I don't...do I?' Katie thought about what Fran had said. It sounded ridiculous to her, therefore it was, wasn't it? And why did she deserve a good talking to? A pair of empty glasses were slid her way. She took them and turned them upside down in the sink. 'Same again?' There was a nod of assent. 'What was it?' She nodded at the response. 'Cider it is, then.'

'You know you do' corrected Fran.

She pulled two pints adeptly to the top. 'I don't, I was just playing with Ben, wasn't I?'

'Well, there you go! That's what I'm telling you!'

'That's...' She checked with Fran. 'Ooh, that's a nice price. Will I have one? Oh, yes, a large one. Is that all right?' A note of the realm was pushed her way. 'That'll do lovely, thanks.'

'You were teasing him - he doesn't know what to think about you, I know he's a bit cakey, but...'

Katie's face dropped and her smile disappeared. 'I didn't mean anything by it. It was just banter, wasn't it?'

'You don't know what you do to the boys, do you?' Fran looked intently at Katie and seemed deep in thought. 'Have you got any time over the summer? I can do with a hand behind the bar on weekdays, you'll bring in the lads like bees to nectar.'

'I've got a three month furlong coming up - the high-ups reckon I need a rest after my last tour, don't they?'

'That'll be furlough, Katie, not furlong.'

'Oh, whatever...'

Three lads pushed there way to the bar, pattering their palms on the counter. 'Two pints, darling and a Stellensbosch.' They must've run out of mischief they could do at the cricket ground.

Katie looked at Fran. 'This one, right?' she asked, pointing to the beer engine closest to her. Fran nodded. Again, they were pulled adeptly so the they were brimming with ale. 'Stellens? Can you lob me one, Fran?' Katie caught it and shook it vigorously out of sight below the bar. 'There you go. Seven, Fran? No, seven fifty? Wow, that must be good stuff!' She took his money and scooped the change out of the manual till. 'Take care with that, it could be explosive! Oh, let me open that for you!' She twisted the top off and a spurt of foam sprayed into his face. His mates roared as they massaged yeasty froth into his quiff.

'I could start in a couple of weeks, but it depends on your terms, doesn't it?'

'Board and lodging, minimum wage. I'll pay you for the hours you do only. Anyways, Ben, you've upset him, he was really keen on you but he never knew if you were serious. If you are serious, treat him properly with respect - if you're not serious, let him down gently.'

'He's lovely but he's...he can't keep up. I need a boy I can trust, a boy I can do banter with, a big boy with big muscles and a boy who can shag me senseless. That's not too much to ask, is it Fran?'

'All right girly, how about me?' It was the lad in the Wolverhampton F.C. shirt.

'I said a boy, not a twat! Anyway, you shouldn't be listening-in on my private conversation, should you?'

'You poor girl, you've no idea have you? That's probably three different boys!' said Fran as she served a customer.

'So what's your name?' asked the Wolves fan.

'It's Katie, pin head!'

'Aww, Katie, that's my favourite name!'

'Yeah, bollocks, it is!' She looked towards Fran. 'Let me talk to Ben - I'll put it right. Wait, what happened to Al? Has he left me?'

'Who?'

'Alex, Alexander, Alexander Hofland...'

'He'll be halfway up the bonk now, you'll never catch him!'

'I don't know what's the matter with him? Must be hormones or something, he always looks so miserable. And now he's wearing make-up for pity's sake!'

'Up on the hill, you're all a but odd, aren't you?'

'No, we're not! What do you mean?'

'Well, where to start? You're all stand-offish, aren't you? You think you're all better than us. Your sister Gwen...'

'My half-sister, Gwen...'

'We never see her, when she does drive through the village in that big city car of hers, she looks like she's got a bad smell under her nose.'

'Gwen has a lot on her mind and it's down to her to keep it all together...'

'And that girl, Monique...'

'What's up with Monique?'

'She's a strange, strange girl.'

'But Mister Hofland, he's all right isn't he?' challenged Katie.

'Yes, I suppose so, but then there was that day, the one where he was down here with his shotgun, shouting the odds, looking for someone...'

Katie shuddered as the thing that lurked in her hidden depths leapt out into the front of her mind, like the troll that lurked under the bridge, the crossing that took her to a place of safety.

'Yes, it was the day you got burnt and never got to hospital. Mister Hofland was going to take you... and Gwen was screaming that he musn't.'

Did she? But why would she? But she treated me, I remember now, she treated me and bandaged me. 'I never went to hospital, did I?'

'Which everyone thought was queer. And we never got to find out what happened to you?'

'I got burnt. It was me you heard screaming...'

'It was Gwen as well. She didn't want you to be taken to hospital.'

'She's a vet, isn't she? They have some strange ideas' said Katie.

'Yes, she certainly does...'

'All right, you're right, up on the hill, we keep ourselves to ourselves don't we? But I think we're all right...'

'But you were always different, Katie, you never belonged, did you?'

'They looked after me well, they really did. Look, I'll give you a call Fran. I'd better catch up with Al!'

Katie unhitched Owain and they ran after Alex. He was walking quickly and purposefully up the steep incline out of the village. She shouted, but he didn't turn. She jogged again and she slowly reeled him in.

'Al, stop' she was nearly upon him, 'Al, Al, wait up!' She came up to his side and reaped in big gulps of chilled, evening air. 'What's up Al?'

'It's Lexa, not Al!'

'Right you are Al, but just stop and talk to me.'

He turned to confront her. 'It's always about you, isn't it? You don't care about anyone or anything else!'

'Eh? Has someone done something to you? Tell me who it is and I'll sodding well sort them out!'

'It's you!'

'What do you mean, it's me? What am I supposed to have done?'

'You've got no idea, have you? It's always about you. It always has been.'

'Al, that's bollocks and you know it.'

'Is it? Why does everyone have to drop everything and go to you and do what you want and then they get dropped? Why?'

'I haven't dropped you! I've got loads of stuff on!'

'We've all got stuff to do.'

'But this is important stuff - life and death stuff! I'm the only one who's on a mission!'

'You're such a goofball, Auntie Katie!'

'No, I'm not! And don't call me Auntie, I can't stand all that auntie bollocks!'

'All right then, I'll call you Katie and you can call me 'Lexa'!'

'Lexa? Lexa!'

'Yes, Lexa.'

'I'm not calling you 'Lexa'! That's not even a proper name!' They were now within sight of Clun Cottage and all seemed reassuringly quiet.

'Listen Al, don't go barging up to the front door, we can sneak in at the back.' He walked to the door and was about to knock on it. 'Noooo!' It opened ominously without the need to knock. She hung back, maybe it would be Stefan. There would be a glower and then clipped, steely instructions to get inside quickly and get upstairs, now. It would be forgotten by the time morning came.

Or if it was Gwen, it would be like a whirring fan and no end of shit hitting it and no end to the hurt that would be caused by her glaring eyes and the bitter, hissing stream of invective.

It was Gwen who came into view, as the door opened. She was wearing pyjamas, determinedly folded arms and a steely glare. This didn't bode well. Al was dismissed and sent upstairs. He would be dealt with in the morning. It would involve grounding and a loss of privileges. Al cast a doleful, bitter look at Katie as he stomped inside and up the stairs.

'You, I don't want in my house' stated Gwen in a matter of fact way, 'you, I don't want anywhere near my family.'

'You can't shut me out Gwen, I'm his aunt!'

'He's just seventeen, but you, you...do like you always do and sleep outside with the dog!'

'I need a bath!'

'You can't have one!'

'Three fingers, then!'

'No!'

The door was slammed and Katie's eyelids slammed shut. When she opened them, the door was still shuddering.

'Gwen, there is no guilt in my heart' she shouted towards the upstairs windows, 'I was just trying to perk him up, that's all!'

There was no reply so she knocked on the door: 'Gwen! Gwen!'

Nothing.

She looked towards the barn. 'Buggery, buggery, bollocks!'

CHAPTER FORTY-TWO

Wednesday 18 May 0505 - Clun Cottage

The first, cold, grey rays of morning light caused Katie's eyes to flicker open and for her to remember what had just occupied her dream - the bitter taste of burnt animal skin, the animal scream of pain and the mad pumping of a heart and the furious panting of lungs. It had been her scream. Her hand felt down below her stomach and the tips of her fingers encountered the coarse ridges of the ugly imprint there.

Tubular stems dug into her side and a strong musky smell hung over the stack of straw bales in the corner of the barn. She brushed herself down and her body alerted her to a pressing need for feeding and drinking. Owain was still asleep, coiled in a furry ball. He too had been dreaming if the scurrying movements of his paws were anything to go by.

It was time to move. Katie jumped off the pile of straw bales, landed on her pads and trotted to the South side of the cottage, mounted the garden wall and scrambled up to the ledge that supported the wide kitchen window. The sash window was ajar. She levered it wide, wriggled her way through and adeptly somersaulted to the stone-flagged floor. The kitchen door was opened cautiously and Owain Madog entered, very cautiously. All quiet.

She mounted the stairs. There was the snorting of Mister Hofland, the wheezing of Eek and the flubbering of Alex. Together, they sounded like a chorus of toads, but there was something missing in the high registers.

Katie pushed at the bathroom door and it groaned open, and she groaned with it. Someone was coming up behind her.

'I said you were not to come in here!' It was Gwen, wrapped unnaturally tightly in a pink dressing gown and matching fluffy slippers.

'Please be reasonable, Gwen. I need a bath after my night last night!'

'Have you been fighting?'

'Yes, so I could get Owain back!'

'I'll put you a bucket outside.'

'I'm going to need more than a bucket, Gwen!'

Al's bedroom door came ajar and he looked sleepily through the gap at the drama that was unfolding on the landing.

'There's nothing to see here, Alexander, please get back in your room.' He did not get back in his room. Instead he continued to peer at them from behind the protection of the door.

'Al, me and your mum need to have a little chat, so close the door.' He closed the door but he was on the wrong side of it.

'Do not call him Al!' snapped Gwen.

'Al, get back in your room so me and your mum can argue in peace!'

'I told you - it's Lexa!'

'Just look at you, Katie! You're half naked - what do you expect him to do?'

'No, I'm not! Anyway, he could cover his eyes or look the other way, couldn't he?'

'Cover yourself when you're in the house, Katie. Now come with me.'

'I am covered up!' This made no sense - she was covered up with just her face, hands and feet showing. 'Fine, just let me have a quick bath and then I'll be right with you. Four fingers, wasn't it?'

'Come with me, NOW!'

'Crap! I'm just a sodding scullery maid to you lot!' She turned to follow.

'A scullery maid?'

'Yes, whatever, but that's what you think, isn't it?' Katie paused to ponder. 'Oh, are you going to tell me now that you haven't got a scullery, so now I can't be a scullery maid?'

Gwen was at the bottom of the stairs now. Katie slid down the bannister on her backside so they were facing each other. There was a commotion in the kitchen and Owain was most likely the cause.

'What is your dog doing?'

'He's having breakfast, like I should be.'

'What have you done!'

'He's found himself some meat, because that's what dogs eat...'

'Where?'

'In the pantry...'

'That was Sunday's tea!'

'Oh, bugger!'

Katie watched as Stefan waddled through the kitchen garden, his face grimacing as he concentrated on lugging the pail of water so that it did not spill. He placed it on a straw bale in front of her.

'I brought you a towel as well' he said.

'Oh, thanks.'

'I see you have brought the dog back...'

'He's not the dog - he's the family pet. I got him back, but I realised that I can't look after him so I've decided to loan him out to Megan.'

'Good. So, he's had his breakfast at the cost of our tea!' Owain was playing with the last sausage.

'Don't worry, I'll find something to replace them.' She wondered what this could be and concluded that it would probably be a brace of rabbits.

'Get washed and dressed Katie. We will attend to the flock in the top field.'

She looked about her for somewhere to wash and dress. 'Then turn around Stefan.'

'Please call me Mister Hofland.'

'Still, you must turn around...'

He turned around and lit up a cigar but glanced over his shoulder as she took the bucket behind the chaotic stack of straw. Katie removed her clothes, soaped herself down and tipped the bucket over her head. Her body stiffened - Stefan was close behind her and she could hear his laboured breathing. She pulled the towel tightly round her as his arm encircled her waist and she was turned about. He'd had a shave this morning but his eyes were part closed and his lips were gently parted in the look of a prick-led loon.

'Owww, Gwen!' she gasped, looking over his shoulder. His eyes went wide open, his mouth let out a gasp and he had spun about, dropping his cigar.

'Where?'

'Oh, she'll be somewhere close by, won't she?' Katie doused the cigar with the dregs of water in the bucket. 'Kick it away' she commanded.

He kicked and stamped on the embers.

She looked in his face and was pleased to see that he was back in the real time. It was time to deliver him a lecture: 'In the procession of the piss-poor, that's up there with pusser's powdered potato' said Katie as she racked her brain to think of a good ending, 'and processed peas' she finished lamely.

'That wasn't Gwen, was it Katie?' He seemed to have satisfied himself that his wife could not have seen them.

'She'll be in the kitchen, busying herself, but if she had...'

'Yes, you've made your point.'

'Not yet, I haven't - Gwen is the glue that holds this family together and if she gets narked, everything will go to shit.'

'I know this.'

'Well, then, just piss off while I haul my keks on.'

Stefan retreated to the other side of the barn. Another cigar was lit up and it smouldered while he leaned against the Land Rover. She pulled on clean underwear and then yesterday's clothes, while working out how to get herself a bath. Katie presented herself to Stefan and he threw the Land Rover keys to her: 'Here, you can drive.'

'No, I can't.' She caught the keys adeptly and threw them back. 'I'm not qualified, am I?'

'We're not going on the public road, so you are fine to drive.' He threw the keys back to her. She stuck her tongue out at him and then whistled sharply. Owain emerged rapidly with bounding enthusiasm from the back garden and adeptly scrambled into the cab. Reluctantly she climbed into the driver's seat.

'If this goes wrong, it's all down to you, Mister Hofland.'

'I'm aware of that, Katie.'

The gears graunched noisily into place. 'Sorry, Mister Hofland.'

'Its customary to start in first gear.'

'I see. Well, it must be in there somewhere.' She managed to locate it after a lot of strenuous movements of the stick and a lot of cursing. 'So, you've not had your crutch looked at?'

They bounced their way up the steeply sloped, winding track. 'I think you are referring to my clutch and not my crutch.'

'Yes, whatever...or the suspension?' she added. They bumped their way along until they came to the dry upper meadows. Katie crunched the vehicle to a sudden halt.

'Oh, no' she cried. She jumped out of the seat and ran to an overgrown ditch in a hollow. Four woolly legs were stuck straight in the air. 'She's in trouble, I'm going to need a hand!'

Stefan took up a pose, leaning on the bonnet and lit up a slim cigar. 'You can manage!'

Katie stepped into the ditch, gripped the ewe by the shoulders, dug her boots into the soil and levered the animal out of the tangle of brambles. Still, holding tight, she sat astride it and felt carefully over the fore and hind legs.

'You're all right, on your way girl.' Katie slapped her hind quarters and she stumbled and then ambled away towards the rest of the flock. 'Come on Owain, let's move them into the Westfield.' As the last of the flock entered the far field, she closed the shambolic wooden gate behind them. She returned to where Stefan was still enjoying his cigar.

'The way that you handled that ewe was impressive, Katie. You're built for this job, big backside, strong thighs and wide shoulders.'

'Oi, Mister Hofland, are you saying...I'm hefty?'

He didn't reply immediately and just smirked around his cigar. 'No, but what I am saying is...you have filled out and you are now surprisingly strong and capable!'

She went to the back of the vehicle and threw out the pile of fence posts and a coil of wire fencing. Her cheeks felt hot with embarrassment. 'You never thought I could make a career on the catwalk, did you?'

'I don't think that was ever an option for you, Katie.'

'Well, you're wrong! I modelled the new Andrew clothing system - it's fire retardant and everything! I look brilliant in a beret...' She laid the posts down where they needed to be hammered in to close the gap in the hedge. 'Are you going to leave all the hard graft to me, then?'

'I need someone who's good with the animals and doesn't mind getting their hands dirty. So, yes I am!'

She held up the first post vertically. 'Just give this a few taps with the hammer and make sure you don't clump my hands.' The first post and then the next five were embedded firmly into the soil. She stretched the wire fencing between the posts as Stefan hammered hasps in to keep them secure.

'Well, well, modelling fire retardant uniform Katie! Whatever next?'

'For your information Mister Hofland, I've got a career in the Andrew now, I may have a chance of advancing to petty officer, if everything works out!'

'You've done very well, Katie, much better than anyone could imagine. Please reconsider. I would like you to run the farm for me.'

'So what are you going to do, Mister Hofland? Are you going to put your feet up?'

'I will deal with the business side of it.'

'You mean, smoke and drink the profits away?'

'You've become a hard-hearted woman, Katie.'

'And you've become a soft-headed man, Mister Hofland.'

'I will change...'

'Then, you will have to prove yourself...'

'You drive a hard bargain, Katie.'

'It's not hard, it's just right. Have you spoken to Gwen? We haven't been getting on that well since I got back. I can see it would be a big problem if I was here all the time.'

'Ah, I sometimes wonder if I married the wrong sister.'

She swallowed uncomfortably and then stared at him. 'I wasn't available, remember, and you wouldn't have had Al or Eek. You should count your blessings, Gwen is a good looking, clever and driven woman, even if she's not built like a farm girl. If the farm is in trouble, and I can see it is, the first person you should speak to is...your wife.'

'Nay, Katie, nay, I meant that you are very different, even as sisters.'

The journey back to the farm was made in a comfortable silence, apart from the roar of the straining engine and the bouncing of the Land Rover over the uneven track and the constant fidgeting of Owain. She and Stefan just exchanged quick grins, whenever she made a mistake while driving.

Gwen was at her serene best, preparing breakfast, issuing instructions and then departing on her rounds. She would return at lunchtime and take Alexander to his rugby match. Katie could come to if she completed all her chores and made sure that Alexander's kit was all present and correct.

Katie smiled. The list seemed very long but it would be easily accomplished, leaving her with plenty of time to luxuriate in the bath and have lunch ready too.

Chapter Forty-Three

Wednesday 18 May 1240 -
The playing fields of Ludlow

The car rattled up the gravel drive to the front of the severe looking red sandstone school house. 'This must be the place' Katie thought to herself.

Al and Katie got out from the back seat, and then collected their kit bags from the rear of the vehicle. Katie put on her socks and boots, while sitting in the boot, much to the irritation of Gwen.

Al scuffed gravel as he waited. 'Why did you do it, Auntie Katie?'

'Why did I do what?'

'You know...'

'Oh, you mean sorting out your rugby kit? Well, basically, because your mum asked me to!'

'But I don't feel well...'

'But you'll feel a lot better after running around a field, won't you?'

'But, I could get hurt!'

'No, you won't - I'm here to look after you!'

Al didn't seem to know how to answer this so he picked up his sports bag by one end and dragged it noisily away.

'You're perfectly welcome!' she shouted after him as cheerily as she could manage.

'Just...stay out of trouble, Katie!' was Gwen's parting message.

'Totally!' replied Katie as Gwen's car skidded away in the gravel.

There were boisterous shouts from the right hand side of the building so she followed the path towards the playing fields. Over the terraced pitches the horizon stretched to the west showing the rounded mounds of the Shropshire hills. Amongst the thirty or so young men scattered across the first pitch she picked out the yellow and blue bands of her team - they were sitting around, watching the opposition practising.

They reached a slight female figure in a blue tracksuit, looking lost. 'Hallo, is it Miss Parsons?'

'Oh, hello, yes I'm Stella Parsons. Who are you?'

'I'm Katie, I'm Al Hofland's Aunt...and this is Al.' Miss Parsons seemed satisfied by this explanation but pre-occupied about the situation she found herself in. 'Is there anything I can do to help? Can I get the boys to practice any routines?'

'I'm not sure what it is they're supposed to be doing. I just look after swimming and tennis.'

'I'll see what I can do. Where's the captain?'

'That'll be Frank, he's got a number 8 on his back - he's sitting down with the others. Is there anything you can do? I think they should be doing something!'

As Katie walked towards the loafing of lads on the turf, she heard a call and saw a lanky, rufous bird settle in the oak tree to her right. It stretched out its wings towards her flashing dramatic patches of white and black and made its mournful call to her, three times. It looked like an old fork-tail, judging by the amount of silver in its crown.

'Are you the captain?' she said to the boy in the number 8 shirt.

'Yes, what of it?' he said as he got to his feet. 'Oh, hi Al, I didn't think you were playing?' Al replied with a grunt and dropped his bag to the ground.

'We should be getting your team ready...they need to be doing some drills, don't they?'

'What's the point?'

'Because sweat shed now saves blood later.'

'Oh my god, you're right!' He was a big, tall lad and seemed to know instinctively what was the right thing to do. 'Who are you?'

'I'm Katie - get your scrum scrumming and the hooker, hooking. Do that for a few minutes and then get them jogging up and down and passing. We've got a couple of spare balls. I'll take the backs.'

Frank got his scrum together and she could see they were binding together. What was left must be the backs, she reckoned. Her heart plummeted - Al was amongst them. She split them four and three and joined the group of three which included Al. He seemed helpless in the face of a thrown rugby ball. She split them again into three and three and they continued to run in a staggered line, passing the ball haphazardly to each other.

Katie took Al to one side. 'I think its good that you're here to make up the fifteen and I know your captain's very pleased about that...'

'Are you giving me a pep talk, Auntie Katie?'

'Yes, because basically, I think you need a bit of pepping up.'

At this, Al folded his arms and slouched defiantly. 'But I don't want to play, I don't feel well...'

'What's the matter with you?'

'I feel sick.'

'Well, what I'd say to you is that you're going to feel a lot worse when my boot connects with your arse...'

'You wouldn't dare!'

'Just you try me!' Her firm gaze must have convinced him of the error of his ways because he jogged back and re-joined a threesome, this time making some effort to hold his hands out and clutch the ball thrown at him. And she was very pleased with the outcome of her motivational speech.

Now all she had to do was check out the forwards.

She found that Frank had moved onto passing routines but she needed to see the front row in action. 'How did the hooking go?'

'It was all right, I guess?'

She put her arms around the shoulders of the props and she got them to support her as she pedalled her legs. 'Where's the hooker? See, that's the best way to snaffle the ball. Now we just need to rebalance the scrum a bit...'

'It's time to toss up, see you in a minute.' Frank ambled his way out to the centre of the pitch. Katie decided that he must have lost the toss from the disconsolate way that he ambled back. 'We're kicking into the wind' he declared. 'They're all big buggers aren't they?'

The referee asked Katie to run a line for him, so she agreed and she was duly issued with a little flag to wave when the ball went out. Although she wasn't on the field of battle, she still felt anxious about what was about to occur. Miss Parsons stood above it all on the terraced pitch, her arms astride her hips, providing some sort of oversight.

She signalled to the referee that she was ready and he blew his whistle. Al approached the cocked ball to kick the match off and it puttered a few yards into their opponents half, leading to a free kick for the foul.

In this way, the tone for the first half was set: the scrum being pushed back, the line-out being penetrated and the backs floundering in the wake of their opponents. The score had reached 46 points to nil.

The ball was bouncing to her side of the pitch and inside, she was shouting for Al to get there first, pick up the ball and run with it. He arrived, all limbs tangled, at the same time as the opposition, and he yelped in helpless pain. She ran onto the pitch, waving her flag furiously. Their inside center was all over Al, who was clutching grimly and foolishly onto the ball, and he was punching Al again in the face and the chest. Katie tore her away into the maul and punched Al's assailant squarely on the nose. She staggered back, wringing her fingers. There was a shrill and persistent whistle. The face of the assailant went red and there were tears trickling down his cheeks.

'NO! We're not having any of that young lady!' yelled the referee.

'He was battering our boy when he was down!' Katie yelled back. There were three more long blasts from his whistle.

The referee blew his whistle to end the half and one of the teams dispersed to the opposite half of the pitch to chew on a segment of orange and enjoy the moment - the other team gathered around Al as he lay stretched out on the turf, enjoying all the attention.

'Did you actually punch him?' asked Frank.

'Who?'

'The beast...'

'Yes, I think that was him...'

'You shouldn't have done that - you could get sent off for that!'

'Yes, I think I probably should've been - how're you feeling Al? Can you continue?'

'What happened?' he asked.

'You got in the way of a stampede.' He had a lump on the side of his head, the size of a small exotic fruit, but it would be best not to mention that. 'I'm really proud of you...' She started to check his limbs but stopped abruptly when this prompted a reaction in the region of his jock-strap. 'Does it hurt anywhere?' There were sniggers all around.

'It's my groin.'

'Piss off!' What was that fruit she was thinking of?

Miss Parsons was now in attendance with her blue and silver holdall. 'Is he all right?'

'He's fine' stated Katie confidently, based on the reflex action she had observed inside his shorts.

'Could he be concussed?'

'I don't think so, he's always a bit like this...'

The referee, an immaculate figure in black shirt and shorts, decided to make his presence felt. 'You need to move him off the pitch!'

'We'll move him when he's fit to be moved!'

'He looks fine to me. We need to get on with the match.'

'Yes, about that, what do the rules say about thumping another player?'

'You've got to expect some physical contact - this is rugby!'

'But not with the fist, eh?'

'I saw nothing untoward, apart from your punch!'

'Oh, bollocks. You got me!'

And now he walked away to the centre of the pitch and stood in his 'lets get ready to restart' pose.

Now Frank said his piece: 'We're one short. Can you come on? I'm sorry, I don't know your name. You're Alex's sister?'

'It's Katie, and I'm his aunt. Can't we get Al back on?'

'You can try! I'll talk to the referee and their captain. There's a spare shirt and shorts in the team kit bag.'

'Yes, I was worried there might be!'

Katie and Miss Parsons, taking an arm each, managed to get Al off the pitch - he had now developed a limp that wasn't there before. She turned to Stella. 'If you can get some ice into Al's cold pack and keep it on his head and check his right leg, could we get him back out there?'

'I'm not going back out there. I'm injured!' he protested.

'I think he could be concussed' stated Miss Parsons.

'Look, he's always been a bit cakey...'

'Shut up Auntie Katie!'

'And a bit stroppy...'

Miss Parsons found her a pair of white shorts and a blue and yellow striped jersey. 'Have you got any wide bandage I can use? If the ref says it's okay for me to come on I'll need a bit of a strapping, won't I? Listen Al, you need to get back on. Your team's one short!'

'I'm not going back on!'

The mood was sombre when the team got in a huddle. Katie was now dressed in the kit of the blue and yellows. 'What did the referee say?' she asked Frank.

'He wants to talk to you.' She tucked in the rugby jersey and pulled up her socks. 'Let's see what he has to say. With any luck he'll take pity on me and say no sodding way.'

Katie joined the referee and the two captains in the middle of the pitch.

'Your captain wants to bring you on as a replacement? I don't think that's appropriate. You're a girl and you have already punched a player' announced the referee.

'Yes, sir, you're right, I couldn't agree with you more' said Katie, 'I am a girl and it looks a bit...rough out there.' This reply prompted a frown from Frank.

'However, I've spoken to the opposing captain, and he's happy for you to come on.' In fact, he was so happy, he was smiling all over his stupid, smug, idiotic face. The referee beckoned behind him and the player she had punched made his way to join the mid-pitch conference. His nose and the surroundings were still red, but this helped to conceal the plukes that dotted his big, pale face. This was all framed by short black curly hair and he was quite tall and quite large.

'Hallo I'm Katie, what's your name?' She offered her hand; he refused to shake it. Still sore, then.

'It's Lunt, Chris Lunt, I think you should play.'

Katie frowned as she tried to process this information. 'C. Lunt? That's a bit unfortunate, isn't it?'

The referee decided to impose himself. 'I'm not convinced. Let me do some checks. First, do you understand the Rules of Rugby?'

'Of course; I'm part Welsh. It's the rules on thumping I'm not clear about...'

'And are you fit?'

'P-lease.' She postured like a model with her hands on her hips and her lips in her best pout.

'That's not what I meant.'

'Check. I'm a matelot. They make us play all sorts of stuff to keep fit, like ping-pong.'

'Table tennis?'

'And pool.'

'And that prepares you to play rugby, a contact sport?'

'Ah, but you haven't seen the way I play ping-pong, have you?'

'I see. Now, are you aware that there is special dispensation for women players - you can wear a chest protector and tights.'

'Well sir, I'm really impressed with your knowledge of women's clothing!' She lifted the rugby jersey and did a little pirouette. 'There aren't any chest protectors so I had to improvise with bandages - there's not much bandage left now so if you could avoid injuring any more of our players, that would be really appreciated!' She directed this at their captain and Lunt.

Frank turned to Katie. 'Tights?'

'Yes, but not the kind you're thinking of...'

'And you are not permitted to play in the scrum.'

'Fair point, and I'm good with that, there's all sorts of crap going on in there!' There was a pause while Katie's face creased in worry. Maybe she should try a different tack. 'Listen, I feel you ought to know I've played before, so I'm like a ringer.'

Lunt snorted in derision.

Frank interrupted, 'A ringer? How come?'

Katie frowned at Frank, as this hadn't worked out in the way she had intended. 'Well, actually more like a mascot.'

'Yes, you seem to have a lot of, um, knowledge of the game for a mascot?' stated the referee.

A man approached from behind. He was solidly built, with a straggly fair moustache and a round head like a football, crowned with more straggly fair hair, stropped across the top of his scalp. 'What's the hold up' he wanted to know.

'They want to bring this girl on as a replacement. I'd say it's not appropriate for a boy's game.'

'Oh, hallo sir. How are you doing?' It was Mister Pratt, her physical training instructor at school, former Navy scrum half, former England scrum half and former complete and utter bastard to her.

'Good, Katie, how are you? Still playing?'

'I sometimes come on as a mascot, sir.'

'Bollocks!' His eyes followed the lines of her calves and thighs. She quickly pulled the jersey down. His eyes then traversed her hips and her chest. She crossed her arms to cover her chest and swallowed noisily. 'You've filled out, Katie, you didn't get those thighs poncing about as a mascot.'

'Oi sir, that's rude!'

'Hmm, what position do they play you?'

'Scrum half, sometimes I fill in as fly...oh bollocks!'

'Navy?'

'Yes...'

'Any other offers?'

'Oi, don't be crude!'

'Let's see, Wales?'

'Oh, yes, and France.' Oh, fucketty, fucketty, fuck!

'Ah, so they've worked out the French connection. Very clever.'

'Yes, you certainly are, sir.'

'I can vouch for her. Katie can come on. Let's try her at inside centre.'

'But that means...' She would be up against Lunt.

'All right, on you go. Just remember, there will be no special consideration for you. Mascot indeed!' conceded the referee.

'Thanks, that's very...considerate of you.' Katie and Frank headed back to the team. 'I'm happy to play anywhere where you tell me but I don't want to run around too much' she confided.

'It makes sense for you to replace Alex at inside centre.'

'But that means I'll have to do a lot of running around, and that's really not going to work, is it?'

'Just do as you're told.'

'Okay, thanks skipper.'

She infiltrated her way into the edge of the huddle and listened in on the chatter.

'She's played for Wales!'

'No, I haven't, I just trained with them.'

'So she's Welsh?'

'Totally! Just think of the Welshiest person you can think of. She's Welshier than that.'

'What, like the Prince of Wales?'

'He's not Welsh, he's just got a Welsh title.'

'Anyway, she's Welshier than the Prince of Wales.'

'She's not Welshier, that's not proper English. She's Welsher.'

'It's more Welsh - I'm more Welsh than the Prince of Wales' complained Katie. 'So now we all know I'm a bit Welsh, what do you want me to do, Skip?'

'Right lads. There's no special dispensation for Katie. We just treat her as one of the other backs but we'll have to protect her.'

'Yes, keep close to me when I've got the ball so I can offload it like shit off a shovel, pardon my Welsh!'

'Yes, you lot, tuck in behind and echelon back.'

'Echelon? What's that?'

'Its like Alexander the Great, and the Macedonians, phalanx of spears and shields and all that...'

'Right, right...'

'Damage limitation, Katie.'

'And that's all we're going to do? Damage limitation? For pity's sake, if you'll pardon my Welsh.'

'So, what are we going to do to limit the damage, Skip?'

'We'll make our tackles and if we get the ball, we'll pass it back to Katie.'

'Then what?'

'Katie can kick it back up the field!'

'They'll just run it back then!'

'For pity's sake!' she moaned in exasperation, 'we need to get the ball up their end, pardon my Welsh.'

A woman had taken up a position next to Stella Parsons - it was Gwen. Katie strained to hear the conversation. Gwen mouthed 'What's going on? My sister came to watch and now she's playing?'

Stella looked sympathetically towards Al and his little lump. 'Your sister came on as a replacement for your son. Look, there she is' she said, pointing.

'Are you all right, Alexander? What happened?'

'I got punched!'

'Then your sister went and punched one of them!'

'Oh, did she now?'

'She doesn't look too happy now, does she? Will she be all right?"

'She'll be fine until I get hold of her.'

'Don't you get on?'

'Well, we are sisters, if only half-sisters.'

'Ah.'

'But Katie's quite resilient you know, but she'll go all Welsh on us if she gets upset.'

Frank called out: 'Hey Katie, pull up your socks and tuck your shirt in!'

She turned towards him, scowled and raised the index finger of her left hand. Then, she trotted to the halfway line and positioned the ball, ready for the kick-off. 'Damage limitation, my arse!'

Katie measured out her run up, ran up and met the ball cleanly with her left foot - so cleanly that it went into touch most of the way to the red and black's goal line. A line-out resulted, but the throw in was secured easily by the opposition and their backs were unleashed. Katie was already sprinting back to her own goal line when the ball was punted high up, so high that it hung above Katie like a plunging bomb. She caught the ball comfortably and shouted 'MARK!'. Seconds later she was caught by the black and reds, rolled over and trampled. The referee blew his whistle and awarded a penalty, 'for not releasing the ball.'

'Oi referee, I called for the mark!'

'I didn't hear you.'

'You didn't hear me! There's a bloke called Mark over in Wolverhampton looking up into the sky wanting to know who the fuck wants him!'

'I didn't hear you. Just remember who is in charge and mind your language!'

Frank signed that Katie should zip her mouth.

'Penalty!' The black and reds took a quick tap penalty and surged over the blue and yellow line with Katie clinging ineffectually to the leg of the try scorer. Chris Lunt walked over to her and dragged her to her feet. 'Had enough little girl?'

'I've had enough of you, potato head.'

Katie picked up the ball and caught up with the referee: 'So how can I make sure you can hear me, sir?' She favoured him with one of her best and widest smiles.

'I'll listen out for you. Drop kick restart?'

'Naturally!' Katie waved the blue and yellows into position and hoisted the ball high. A flurry of arms went skyward, but instead of being caught, it was punched backwards, and it bounced and bobbled towards her. She scooped it up and accelerated. A boy came at her tentatively and she side-stepped him. Another boy came at her and his arm struck her full in the waist. She gasped, spun out of the tackle and looked ahead. The posts were directly in front of her. She released the ball and swung her left leg back in a languid arc and connected with the ball as it popped up off the ground. The ball sailed away as she went to the ground. She struggled to prop herself up on her arms to watch its progress. It bounced on the bar of the goal and toppled over apologetically. 'Blimey, that nearly didn't make it!'

The referee blew his whistle and signalled a drop goal scored. Katie was on her feet receiving a lot of slaps on the back. Instead of heading back for the restart, she took five big paces towards the goal and dragged her boot to make a line in the pitch. 'That's the mark then' she confided to the referee as she was motioned back to her half of the pitch.

'That was very impressive' he commented, 'you've played this game before, haven't you?'

'No sir, not this particular one,' she replied, 'but others quite like it!' The referee seemed nonplussed by her reply. She gave him another of her best smiles, the one that said we're both in this together, aren't we?

It was their drop-kick restart and the black and reds gathered the ball, passed and their inside centre surged through the middle. Lunt broke through two half-hearted tackles and ran powerfully towards the right touchline. Katie quickly realised that she couldn't outrun him; she swallow-dived towards his pumping feet, grasped his right boot and pulled him down. As he landed flat on the turf, the ball floated forwards out of his reach and his chin grazed the ground.

'Did that go forward, referee?' she called as she gathered the ball and strode back to where Lunt lay. She offered to pull him up but he refused. He pushed her away, rubbing his grazed chin.

'I slipped' he muttered.

'You should've passed it, potato head!'

He grunted and barged her as he walked back: she decided that was enough to make her fall flat on her back.

'Leave her alone, Lunt' said the boy as he hauled her up, still clutching the ball. It was Frank.

'Thanks mate. Did we get the decision on this one?'

'Yeah, but what are we going to do with the penalty?'

'I'm not sure. How about, I kick it into touch by their goal line, we stack the back of our line-out, then one of you palms it down to me, I pass it and then one of you storms over and touches it down in the corner?'

'That's brilliant!'

'Isn't it? But let's just make it a rule that when I'm running with the ball, everyone gets in behind me.'

'That's brilliant - you'll be Alexander the Great and we'll be the phalanx!'

'Um, yes, if you like.' She recalled the cover of a book in Mister Hofland's collection - the man on it wore a silver breast plate and a short, metal skirt and was on horseback. 'Anyway, get your phallus ready...'

She took the penalty kick but it was a bit further out from their goal line than she would have liked. But here we are at the line-out...

'Okay Katie, keep on your toes' Frank said.

Katie cursed him as she joined the line of backs filed diagonally across the field - he was still insisting that she pulled her socks up and tucked in her jersey. The throw-in didn't go far enough and the black and reds snared the ball. She yelled at her players to move up close to their opposite numbers and directed them individually into each tackle. The ball was moving slowly along the line and it was inexorably heading towards their inside centre.

Lunt caught the ball, fumbled it and made two stumbling steps forward. She closed in on him, ducking below the big left hand aimed at her face, her shoulder crashing into his solar plexus, her hands grasping at the ball, ripping it down and away. It was in her hands and she was running at the posts, with only the full-back to beat, his arms wide open, ready to embrace her. There were pounding steps behind her; a quick glance and there was her hooker, Sam, all arms and legs pounding the turf, like a firefighter, but no hose. She was enveloped in the arms of the full-back, but she twisted and thrust the ball at Sam, and he was away.

'Under the posts' she yelled after him, 'under the sodding posts!' He touched the ball down and then looked about him in amazement - he'd only gone and scored a try!

Katie quickly popped the ball over for the conversion and then took her position ready for the black and red's response. 'More like that!' she said to Frank from behind her hand.

The restart was another towering ball towards Katie. She positioned herself under the ball, waited and then jumped. As she caught the ball in mid-air she was hit and toppled backwards onto her shoulders. The ball spun out to the dead ball line. 'Ref, he's an idiot, he doesn't know the rules!'

'Just get on with it! I've awarded the penalty kick!'

Her right winger hauled her up and she wrapped her arm around his shoulder to get to her feet. 'It's Andy, isn't it? Listen, when I raise my right arm, get going and get ready to catch it...'

The ball was at her feet, the blue and yellows just behind her, the black and reds a respectable distance ahead of her, apart from one.

'Watch her, watch her!' said their captain.

'Piss-off, potato head!' she hissed. He put his boot on the ball. 'Referee!'

'Ten yards Lunt!'

She picked up the ball, paced her way forward to the point indicated by the referee and placed it. Lunt jogged past and kicked it away.

'Ref, he's being an idiot again!'

'Ten yards! You know the rules, Lunt!'

She picked up the ball, paced her way forward to the point indicated by the referee and placed it down. It was starting to open up in front of her but she was still too far out. And Lunt was still there. 'Ref, he's getting right on my tits now!' Too far out for her to run the ball over the line, so she would hoof it high for the winger. She pushed Lunt back, deftly dropped the oval ball onto her foot and then flicked it back into her hands and ran past him. The winger to her right was behind her and getting into his stride; she cocked her left leg and executed the drop kick high up along the right touchline. All eyes followed it, but she was falling back - a heavy blow landed across her throat. All the players had run away from her, towards the black and red's goal line and then there was a big cheer from the blue and yellows.

But she was alone, gasping and wriggling on the ground, like a fish out of water with Lunt staring at her and Gwen shrieking and waving a little flag in his face.

The referee's whistle was blown stridently. There was shouting and swearing and pushing. The whistle shrilled above all this. She was struggling to gasp in air and Gwen was shouting at the referee; 'That big lug assaulted my sister!' Katie pointed urgently at her throat but she could now snort air through her nostrils. Lunt shouted at her to get up, but Gwen told her to stay down. She sought refuge on the soil. It was studded in millions of dimples made by studded rugby boots. It was like an inconceivably gynormous, brown and green golf ball that stretched as far as she could see. Grass stretched as far as she could see but it was all sliced and diced and broken. There was a gentle hand on her shoulder and concerned chatter. There was a forest of young legs around her but she could see through to the hilly mass that overlooked the ground, crowned with a grey-green walled building and a tower and a flag pole and a flag. It was Gwen's hand on her shoulder and there was a buzzing in her ear, like a golf ball hissing through the wind, but above that there was a thin croaky voice calling out to her, a cry from the heart. She saw that Gwen was looking in the same direction she was, to the westward. Gwen closed her eyes and muttered, 'Oh no, not again...'

The referee wanted to know if she could stand up? I suppose so, that shouldn't be too difficult, should it? Katie crouched and she could see the extent of the grass. There was a continuous drone between her ears but she could hear disembodied voices talking excitedly and concernedly. She stood up but this was not as straightforward as she'd hoped. The referee was standing in front of her looking into her eyes and talking to her. He seemed anxious and the tone of his voice was anxious but she couldn't quite get what he was saying. Now Gwen was pushing in front of the referee and pulling open her eyelids and starting to talk. The words started to come into focus. Gwen pulled her close and whispered in her ear. 'Did you hear that?'

'That voice? You heard it too?'

'Yes, like the wind rustling through the tremble-leaf tree?'

'No, it was a cry for help...'

'Katie, do you want to stay on?'

'Yes, I want to settle with Lunt.'

'Ah, in that case you heard nothing.'

'Oh, I heard nothing...got it!'

'Now let's take a look at you' Gwen said aloud, 'how's your head, Katie? Any more confused than normal?'

'I'm back to normal, thank you Gwen!'

Gwen turned to the referee. 'Katie's fine to continue. She's back to what passes for normal. She's always a bit flaky, you know. She's always away with the fairies.'

The referee asked if she wanted to stay on. Katie nodded. He apologised for what had happened. She said no need, but she did wonder if the referee realised that Gwen was an animal doctor, not a people doctor. He commented that her team had scored the try but missed the conversion, so the score was 53-15. She commented that the blue and yellows still had a lot to do.

The black and reds kicked off, their forwards fumbled the ball and the blue and yellows had it. It came slowly out towards her and Lunt was closing in, his little potato eyes fixed on her. She couldn't outrun him, the boy outside her had run in front, but there was a gap opening up straight ahead. Katie kicked the ball high and over and ran to get under it. He bent down and his shoulder met her hip and she spun and crashed to the turf. The whistle blew shrilly.

Katie brushed herself down and walked the two paces to confront Lunt: 'You haven't got the brains of a potato, have you, mate?'

'You ran into me' was the best he could manage. He was annoyed and would need careful handling and she would need to be quick as others were converging from all directions.

'Just get out of my sodding way' she hissed as she strode to pick up the ball. Instead of stepping out of the way, he seized her by her jersey and chest protecter and lifted her so they were face to face.

She cursed him over and over again, while she still had breath; his face became angrier and angrier. Her feet wriggled but they were adrift from the ground and she could get no purchase. 'Put me down, you big...,' she gasped. He threw her down to the ground; she did a couple of backward rolls for best effect.

The referee was now having a very animated conversation with Lunt but the boy just turned around and walked off the pitch and just continued walking.

Her sister whispered: 'You crafty, conniving cow!'

Gwen and Frank were attending to her, but Katie insisted that Frank turned his head away. 'Just help me with these bandages, Gwen, something's slipped out!'

She asked the referee if he had awarded a penalty? He said yes. The ball was still in her hand. Before she could do anything with it, Mister Pratt arrived in front of her, wearing the kit of the black and reds and a scrum cap.

'Let's see what you're made of Talog. You're not up against a boy now!'

She got to her feet. 'Eh?'

'I'm coming on and I'll be facing you!'

'That's not right, their lot are one down!'

'Well, that's hardly fair is it, after what you did?'

'But it is, isn't it ref?'

'Lunt wasn't sent off' commented the referee, 'he just walked!'

'But he should've been - he's an idiot!'

The referee just shrugged and got ready for the restart.

'Gwen?' Gwen turned away and walked off the field with her little flag.

And there she was, on her own, tossing the ball, up and down, up and down, catching it one-armed; an army of blue and yellow behind and an army of black and red in front; the referee to one side saying that there was just time for two plays at most. So, to kick or not to kick, that was the question? Was it better to just take the three points, or to carry the ball into this sea of black and red, and force her body against theirs until one or other yields and if happenstance decides the outcome, in another bruising skirmish, it would be one where her speed, agility and craft might give her the edge until that last body fell away and she was over the line?

'Shakespeare?' yelled Frank.

'No, it's me, but I will lay me on the line, just one more time.'

Katie sensed his long glance, lingering over her pulled up socks and her tucked in jersey, but her hand was squeezing a lump of earth while her other arm still juggled with the oval ball. She was shouting at her wingers to be ready and she was exhorting her pack to greater effort. Was Frank thinking that she was their Achilles, banging sword against shield and putting the fear of god into their enemies, just by the force of her presence? No! But he was shaking his head, seemingly unable to dismiss a vision of her in shiny breastplate, a short pleated metal skirt and with greaves covering her shins.

Katie launched a clod of earth and it shattered against his forehead.

'Oi, Frank, get your phallus ready! I'm your Achilles!'

'Stay sharp! She's going to run it' shouted Mister Pratt.

She scooped the spiralling ball out of the air with her right arm, dropped the ball onto her foot, flicked it back into her hands and started running.

Smack! Her shoulder collided with Pratt and his arms were around hers; Frank was close on her right shoulder and Katie slipped the ball out to him. He took the ball, broke two weak tackles but was brought down. She sent the two locks in and then the hooker and the ball dribbled out. She pounced on it, side-stepped and arrowed a long pass out to the wing. Katie scrambled over Pratt, pulling her leg free. Josh made a few paces and was held up. She sent in Frank and the tight-head prop. 'Keep the ball up' she yelled. They scrambled a few yards in-field.

The ball in the maul wasn't moving. There was a black and red body in the way. She reached in and hauled at his scrum cap. He screamed for the referee to intervene but Sam was free with the ball. 'Peel left, I'm with you!' Sam tucked the ball under his right arm and launched the assault, slipped the ball to Katie and she side-stepped one tackle, left another tackler sprawling and then another flat on his face; she surged through the gap on the left flank running an angle. Andy was free for the grubber kick but no, she side-stepped inside a tackle, ran a line to the posts, back to the pack. The fullback had her in his arms, pulling her down, but the ball was down and nudged back to her pack. She rolled away as the forwards coalesced into a ruck and she added her weight at the back.

Katie exhorted her pack to push over the goal line. Steam poured upwards from both packs. This is the moment, she reckoned, the black and reds are struggling. There was a cry. It was the fork-tail hanging above, triangular tail contra-twisting in the air.

Her pack started moving forward, she manoeuvred them to the right to the better ground. 'They're crumbling, keep tight' she shouted, 'push, push, push!' The ball wasn't coming. 'Ref, there's a sodding hand on my ball!' Her right leg was poised above the ball. 'REF!' She stood on it. 'REF!' She stamped down on it. Pratt screamed but the ball was free. Frank picked it and popped it into Katie's arms and with a step, a stride and a leap she was away from the ruck, just yards from the line.

But she was held up! She couldn't get through! Arms burrowed around her, pulling at the ball and arms came around her back, pulling at her jersey. The two props had her securely between them - she shouted at them to bind her tight as she thrust forward.

She crouched and wriggled forward again. She must be close. Another lunge. Bodies cascaded over her. Her breath was crushed out of her frame. The ball jabbed hard into her chest and she shrieked to be let free.

Relief came gradually as bodies came off her. There were just two bodies covering her. They pulled themselves up and stood away and she could breath again. The referee was standing above her. 'Well, who have we got here? Miss Talog, I presume?' She turned her neck and looked at him quizzically. The referee pulled her torso carefully to one side and saw the ball and the try line. He pointed at the ball which was still cosseted in the middle of her chest, encircled by her arms. His whistle was in his mouth. He blew it and extended his arm upwards. 'Try!' he exclaimed.

Katie shifted her body so that she could sit up. Pratt was nursing his right hand and moaning about his neck - his scrum cap was half off his head. She placed the ball in her lap and pulled at her chest bandage. 'Who's been wrangling with my doops?' she complained. 'You dirty sods!' There were bodies strewn along the route she had taken, getting back on their feet as though a cyclone had just passed through. She discretely tugged up her chest bandage.

The referee pulled her to her feet. 'I think you have been disingenuous with the truth, Miss Talog.'

'Disin-what?' she asked.

'Disingenuous. Look it up!'

She turned to the boy nearest her and whispered in his ear. 'So, what's disingenuous, Frank? What am I supposed to have done?'

The committee of boys around her chattered for several moments and then decided: 'You've not been entirely truthful...'

'But, not a word of a lie has passed my lips, has it?' she replied.

Mister Pratt had recovered enough to approach her and thankfully, he had removed his ridiculous scrum cap. 'Referee, in that passage of play I was fouled twice!'

'Miss Talog?'

'Well, I admit I had to lever you out of the maul, but you were cheating...'

'Lever me? You nearly had my head off! Isn't that cheating?'

'No, it's levers, it's not cheating.'

'For fuck's sake...'

'Look, it's just physics, that's all.' She looked up at the referee. 'Sir, physics can't be cheating can it?'

'No, can we get on with this please.'

'Frank, is there ever a situation where physics is cheating?'

'No, she's right. Physics can't be cheating, can it sir?'

'There you go then...'

'What about my hand?' He thrust the back of his hand right in her face and sure enough, it had stud marks on it, her studs...

'You were cheating, so I thought, if I let him get away with that, he won't respect me!'

'You've become a hard-hearted woman, Katie!'

'Thanks!' Katie walked quickly to where she thought the conversion should be taken from. She made a divot in the turf with her heel and placed the ball, and pointed it towards the gap between the posts.

'So, you're taking this one, Miss Talog?' asked the referee.

'Yes, I am. So, if I score thirty-four points from this kick, do we win?' she asked.

'You can have two points, if you get the ball between the posts and above the bar.'

'What if I get the ball to bounce off the right post, bounce on the bar and then go over, how many for that?'

'I can go as high as two points.'

'I see. Everyone else has buggered off to the half way line, haven't they, so it's all down to me?' The whistle blew once more and she kicked the ball neatly between the posts. 'That must be worth 34 points in anyone's money' she exclaimed.

It was time. The final whistle sounded. The fork-tail had soared and flapped its lazy way to the west.

They all stood in a line to do the respectful and perfunctory hand clapping of the opposition players bit. Katie was left on the field of play as the boys trooped to the changing room.

'I need a shower...'

'You'll have to go after the boys have been' replied Pratt.

'Just remind me who you are again?' asked the referee.

'Don't you remember? I call myself Katie, we met earlier, didn't we?' Gwen had joined them, elegantly green booted and still holding a little flag. Gwen and Mister Pratt seemed comfortable with each other, which was surprising. Katie made a mental note of this interesting relationship.

'Do you know Owain Wyn Davies?'

'Yes, he was my kicking coach.' And Mister Pratt was my coach in all matters relating to devilry and bastardry.

'You have some explaining to do.' He placed his hands on her shoulders which seemed strangely intimate as she still had Gwen and Pratt in tow.

'Please, explain yourself' said the referee. She looked around at Gwen and Pratt.

'After I've had a shower and a gut full of cider and a plate dripping with calories, I'm all yours...'

'You're coming home with me' said Gwen.

'That's no way to finish off a game of rugby!'

'I can offer a shallow bath, a pot of tea and sandwiches.' At this Gwen turned and started marching towards Al, who was standing over his bag and scowling at them.

'Hold up Gwen! Sorry about this and I'm sorry about your scrum cap' she said to Mister Pratt, 'it was a bit mean of me, wasn't it?'

He massaged the back of his neck.

'Does that hurt Mister Pratt?' asked Katie.

'Of course it bloody hurts!'

'Oh, I'm sorry about that.'

'Don't be sorry. The osteopath could do with the extra work.'

'Osteo what?' asked Katie.

'The bloke who will charge me hundreds of pounds to fix my neck.'

'Well, rugby is a contact sport...'

'I know that', he replied irritably, 'but what you did to me was illegal...'

'Sorry, but you started it...'

'That was nothing, it was only a playful jab!'

'Yes, but I thought if I let that go, he won't respect me and he will try it on again, so I...'

'Got your retaliation in!'

'Yes' she giggled. It was something about his whining voice and his size and shape that seemed to be a complete mismatch. 'If it gets too much, maybe you should try something different, like carpet bowls.'

'Anyway, well played.'

'Thank you sir.'

'You've learnt a lot. You've learned to be direct instead of all that fannying around.'

'Oh thanks.'

'And you're a strong runner now...'

'Oh good but it's more like gliding then running.'

'And you're ready to fulfil your promise...'

'I hope so, because that's what I'm all about.'

The blue and yellows had all hung back and they were waiting for her outside the shower block. Her two props hoisted her up on their shoulders and she surveyed the crowd around her.

'Frank, you'd better get all the team to warm down, or they'll seize up! Then tell them how well they did, they won the second half! They were all brilliant!' There was a buzz of excited chatter.

'No, you tell them!'

She started with the boy to her left and praised each one for what they had done. Some names she remembered, some she didn't but she knew what position they had played in and what they had done. She finished with her two props.

'Katie!' shouted Gwen.

'Got to go!'

Frank was standing in front of her and he seemed to have something on his mind. 'Do you want to hook up, after?'

'Oh, I don't know. What did you have in mind?'

'There's this place in Ludlow, all you can eat for ten quid.'

'This Friday at six?'

'That's early...'

'Yes, but I will need to start early to get my money's worth. So, do I need to dress up?'

'Eh?'

'Like a Greek spear chucker?'

'Oh, no, no, no!'

'Oh good, I'll come scruffy. And...how old are you?'

'Seventeen!'

'Blimey! I'm old enough to be your older sister!'

'Katie' exclaimed Gwen, 'get in the car!'

'It's rude to leave before you've had a few drinks with the opposition!'

'Alexander doesn't want to...'

'You big jessie!'

'It's always about you isn't it?'

'Oh, not that again, you great big, tedious twat!'

'Katie! That's enough!'

'Well, he is!'

Gwen had flipped up her sunglasses so she must be ready to do some serious driving now. Katie looked up through the sunroof and thought she glimpsed a fork-tail flapping over the road, but it was left way behind in the wake of the car.

'So Katie, have you heard anymore from the Welsh ladies?'

'Which Welsh ladies?' asked Katie in alarm.

'The Welsh women's rugby association, or whatever they're called?'

'Oh, them. They want me to do a summer school in Cardiff so they can work on my speed and my strength. I'm not sure I want to go, though. They should take me as I am, shouldn't they?'

'Why don't you do some coaching locally?' Gwen passed back a business card which had a number written on it. 'Give them a call.'

'Let me think about it, but it all depends...'

'You could start with Alexander?'

'She's not coaching me!'

'Oh, go on, let me' said she, prodding him sharply in the ribs, 'I'll show you stuff that'll make your hairs stand on end!'

'Leave me alone!' Al now had his arms folded and he was staring out of the window. He didn't seem to be interested in this once-in-a-lifetime opportunity.

'Gwen, I've got a date on Friday so I won't be back for tea!'

'Oh, who with?'

'Um, with some kid I met on the rugby pitch - he's taking me out in Ludlow!'

'In Ludlow, how lovely!'

'So, Al, how's it going with Megan?'

'I told you, it's Lexa!' Gwen got back to the business of piloting the car down the road towards Clun.

'No Al, it was definitely Megan I set you up with!'

'I don't want you to set me up with anyone!'

'You need all the help you can get, mate!' She prodded him sharply in the ribs.

'Don't touch me! Mama, she's prodding me!'

'And she's a top girl!'

'She's got a black eye!'

'That'll fade in a few days but you'll still be a useless sack of knackers!'

'Mama!'

'Katie!'

'I don't need your help!'

'Yes, you do. So, have you contacted her yet?'

'No!'

'You need to grow a pair or all the best girls will be gone!'

He turned to look at her with those deep, melancholic eyes; she gulped noisily in return. 'Katie?'

'Not me, you prat!'

'KATIE! ENOUGH!'

Chapter Forty-Four

Friday 20 May 0845 - Ludlow market

Katie watched as Stefan made his way through the kitchen garden, his face creased with concentration, lugging a pail of water towards her in one hand and a mug of tea in the other. The pail was placed ceremoniously on a straw bale in front of her and the mug of tea in her welcoming hands.

'What a fine morning' he said.

'Isn't it?' she replied. Owain already had his head over the pail and was lapping up the water. 'I really need a bath, sir.'

'I can't oblige, my wife is adamant that you are not coming inside until you are reconciled. It is fair to say that there was a disagreeable atmosphere in the cottage last night.'

'Why didn't you open the windows then?' She drained the tea down her gullet and indicated she would need a refill.

'You know very well what I mean.'

'Oh, do I?'

'We might have had a break-in...'

'But I'm family!'

'Nay, Katie, nay.' Stefan was clean shaven this morning and there was no fug of cigar smoke upon him. 'And, what tasks are you planning to complete today, Katie?'

'Actually, I'm thinking of lazing around all day today as I took a bit of a battering on the rugby pitch.'

'Ah, I have it noted that you will attend to the flock and then run the farm stall at the market.'

'Oh, I see. Then, I will need a bath and a big breakfast, won't I?'

'I can offer you a shower only and then we can negotiate your breakfast.'

'I see, so basically, you're offering to tip a bucket of water over my head and hand me a jam butty?'

'Indeed I am.'

'Hmm.' Katie considered her options. 'I see, then you will need to keep your eyes closed and follow my instructions to the letter and no peeking.'

'Of course...and I brought you a towel' he said.

'Oh, thanks.' She looked about her - she was shielded from the cottage by straw bales and from the wider world, by a belt of tremble-leaf trees. Across the hills, there was just the sound of sheep bleating and the ascending chatter of the skylarks and no smudges of wood smoke. She hauled her vest and pants off and stood with her back to him. 'Just a little splash' she instructed, 'and no peeking.'

He did as he was instructed.

'Aaagh, its cold!' She lathered her hair in a squirt of soap and lathered her intimate bits. 'Big splash now.' She was ready for the shock this time. The flannel was quickly applied all over and she remembered not to bend over. 'Let me have the rest...'

All done. She wrapped herself in the towel and turned to him. 'Did you see anything you shouldn't have?'

'Certainly not.'

'Good. I should hope not!'

'But Katie, what have you done to yourself?' She thought about what he could have seen - there would be the brand on her left shoulder and a plague of welts across her back. His hands were on her shoulders, turning her; her hands were pulling the towel tight around her chest. He sighed and kissed her forehead: 'You are like a comet, you will burn brightly and disappear.'

'Like my mum?'

'No, nothing like your mother. She is like a distant moon, a cold, lonely rock that is out of reach.'

'You're not very keen on my mum, are you? Well, this comet is visiting the moon this Saturday! And this comet needs refuelling!'

'Attend to the flock and I'll have it ready...'

'Two rashers of bacon, two eggs, two sausages, grilled tomatoes and mushrooms, toast and I fancy beans today!'

'Hmm...'

Katie swung the door of the trailer open and saw a wall of plastic containers, stuffed full of woollens. Her pitch was in pole position at the end of the row of small stalls and so closest to the town. At the far end of the long row of small stalls, adorned in blue and white striped canopies, was the squat, grey-green castle and beyond that, a squat, green mound of a hill. Each side of the square was lined with grand, well-to-do buildings and there was the scent of breakfast being cooked and cakes being baked and...

'Katie, help me get this lot unloaded!'

'I'm hungry!'

'You will need to set up first!'

'All right then!' The plastic boxes were unloaded and stacked in the stall. There was a grumpy looking woman at the neighbouring small stall and she had something on her mind: 'What have you got there?' she wanted to know. Gwen pulled out an official looking notice and taped it vigorously to the side of the stall.

'Is that alright Mrs Tricketts?'

Susan Tricketts leaned as close as she could to read the notice. What she read there did not satisfy her. She turned away and muttered 'It's not right, it's just not right...'

'And there's this...' said Gwen to Katie. She took the metal container and placed it on the side of the counter close to where folk would pass by. She loaded solid fuel in the bottom chamber and lit it.

'That's the first job done - get the samovar going!'

'I really don't know why you need that' moaned Gwen.

'Everyone needs a brew on a day like this, I know I do!' The bright sunlight hinted at summer warmth but the cold moisture laden wind said spring chill.

'You know what to do? I can leave you to it? You must remember to pay the pitch fee.'

'Of course. I just need the float and the book, Gwen!'

Gwen handed these over but as she did, they both gave a little gasp - there was a presence behind them, a young woman in a long flowing purple dress and long flowing brown hair with purple streaks. They turned and gave another little gasp - this was very unusual dress for market day.

'Can I help you? I call myself Katie.'

'I know who you are' she said in her little girl voice, flicking away a lock of hair from her face. 'I think it's terrible the way that you mistreat your animals.' She was wearing dark lipstick, purple eye shadow and long pendulous jewellery that hung from her ears and jiggled around her neck.

'The sheep were perfectly happy, jumping up and down in the field, when I tended to them this morning!'

Gwen wrapped her arm around Katie's waist and whispered in her ear: 'Watch her, she's a witch!'

'A witch! Never met one of those before!' Katie whispered in reply.

'What's the matter, Sarah?' Gwen asked.

'A daughter of Satan' she exclaimed, 'in front of me now. That's what the matter is! I thought I'd banished you all!'

'She must be talking about you' Katie whispered.

'That's a bit rich coming from someone called Pagan' retorted Gwen.

'Nice one Gwen' said Katie.

Sarah Pagan turned on her heels and strode away, with the wisps of her dress flirting with her calves and her high-heeled shoes clacking against the cobbles. 'I think you showed her what's what, didn't you? Sodding witch!'

'Yes, we did. I've got to go now; I've got four farm visits to make today.'

'Whoa, wait up, what if she turns me into a frog?'

'We'll scarcely notice the difference, Katie, so you have nothing to worry about. I'll see you at five o'clock, prompt. Don't get into any trouble; I have to work with these people when you're gone. And remember, sell, sell, sell, you'll need to pay the pitch fee.'

'Ribbick, ribbick' croaked Katie in reply.

'Bore da!' said Katie to the mature couple looking through the reels of wool.

'Hello dear' the old lady replied, 'are you new here?'

'Not really. Is there anything I can help you with?'

'That cardigan you're wearing, is that from the same wool?' said the woman, pointing at the balls of wool.

'Yes, same sheep. Would you like to feel it?' Katie presented herself to the old couple. 'Who's it for?'

'Our grand-daughter, Anwen.'

'That's a lovely name. How old is she? I think I have just the thing for her...'

By 10:30 she had only sold three jumpers, seven reels of wool, a dozen pairs of woolly socks and eight mugs of tea.

And then she saw his face. It was Tom - long, gangly limbed Tom, walking head up high, in his dark suit with other dark suited individuals, walking silently with purpose, towards the red sandstone arch, through into the shade of the terraced houses which stretched downhill to the river and to the crossing. She called out his name but there was just a twitch of his earlobe and no recognition. She called again, still nothing and so she scampered after him, leaving the stall in the charge of the noisily irritated Susan Tricketts.

Katie caught up with Tom and the phalanx of dark clothed men and boys. There was the taint of alcohol and cigarette smoke which over-laid the smell of clothing which had only seen the outside of the wardrobe on very rare, family occasions. Katie walked beside him and stared at the side of his face. His earlobe twitched ever so slightly. 'Tom' she asked, 'do you remember me? It's me, Katie, are you all right?'

Their purposeful march terminated in front of a red stone terraced house that had all of the window gaps screened with curtains. They took it in turns to file through the narrow doorway into the dark interior but she hesitated. Her left hand quickly pinched her nose closed, to keep out the smell of the stink plants. Tom turned to her and snapped 'It's a wake!'

She frowned and considered this for a moment. 'What's awake? You're awake, I'm awake, we're all awake, it's gone daybreak!' Her voice had the quality of a honking goose so the released her nostrils. The sickening odour of the flowers forced her to clench her nostrils closed and to gasp through her mouth.

'It's a wake, for god's sake, a wake!' said Tom.

There was a room on her right, where a shuffling rank of dark clothed folk were passing into and after a respectable time, shuffled out, muttering words of little or no consequence.

She felt a presence, contained in a wooden, brass handled casket. 'There's someone in there, Tom, and they're slipping away!'

'What are you doing here' he hissed, 'and what are you talking about?'

'I saw your face, Tom. I thought I would come to you and see how you are doing!' They stood on the threshold of the room, as the soul in the wooden seemed to be hovering on the threshold of the next world.

He seemed lost for words. 'Just wait here' he snapped, 'it's Gramps, we've lost him.' He stepped over the threshold but Katie pulled him back. They both looked into the room. The mourners had moved on into the back parlour to mutter amongst themselves.

She turned to leave but there was a voice she recognised amongst the others. It didn't come from the back parlour, but it came from somewhere closer, but also further away, a high pitched whisper that she could barely discern from the whine of gently vibrating crystal glass or...

'Do not be afraid of who you are...' it said.

'I'm not' she replied. Her hands gripped the sides of the casket as she peered inside.

'Who are you talking to?' asked Tom in an anxious tone.

'I'm not sure' she replied, 'can't you hear them?'

Tom strained his ear in the direction that she was pointing, towards the casket.

'Do not be afraid...' said the voice and now Katie was in a playing field below the walled town, a scuffed white leather ball at her feet, pointed towards the scuffed white painted posts. 'Do not be afraid of what you will become, my girl.' In three steps her left leg swung towards the ball and connected so sweetly with it that it made a gentle, spinning arc between the two upright posts. She turned to him and she couldn't help but smile, nearly to her ears, and then she gained her reward - his wide, toothy smile in return and his double hand grab. It wasn't the sweet, physical rhythm of her boot meeting the oval ball square on, nor the beautiful parabola the ball made; but his wide, watery-eyed grin that charged her. It was Tom's Gramps, the man who had shown her how to kick an oval ball, every schooling day, Owain Wyn Davies, who came from the soil and whose body we now return to the soil, but as he passes, we, who he made into better people, now hold his memory in our minds and so his soul will live on for ever and ever...

'What are you on about?'

'Your Gramps!'

He pulled her away and then into the crowd in the back parlour and through into the narrow garden beyond with the stone outhouse. 'Show some respect!'

'I am! He's on his way! And he's...content!' She had managed to secure a handful of sandwiches and a glass of something cool and fizzy on her way through the parlour and past the laden table. 'And so am I, big thanks for inviting me in, Tom, how're you doing mate?'

'It's a...very sad day.'

'No, it isn't, he's safe, he's content he's had a good passage! You should be happy! Just ditch the stinky flowers and have a proper party!'

'You're not dressed properly!' He was looking at her bare legs below her shorts and her button-up jumper.

'Oh, I'm working up at the market. I know! Come up when your wake is done and take me out to lunch!'

'I don't know about that, Katie.'

'Yes you do, so I'll see you later. Great wake!' She passed quickly through the back parlour, refilled the glass and secured another fistful of sandwiches. Looking in at the front parlour all was serene and quiet. It was time to get back to her pitch and start selling socks again.

The sun was masked by a cloud and Katie felt chilly, despite the cardigan. She saw the dark grey pin stripe suit approaching, clandestinely and then with more purpose. It was gone midday and Tom must have forgotten that he was taking her out to lunch. There was a sudden spate of tea sales and now...nothing.

He must have been in his early twenties, his hands were buried casually in his pockets but his silk tie was slack against his unbuttoned white collar. She waited patiently while he summoned the courage to approach and engage her in conversation.

'Is that a man size cardigan you have there?' She looked down and reassessed it's dimensions. This was a disappointing opening gambit, she thought.

'Umm, it's more of a me size cardigan, if you know what I mean. Who are you buying for, someone special?'

He was quite close, feeling the bottom of the cardigan between his fingers and she gave a little gasp as the back of his fingers touched her thigh.

'Well, y'know...'

'So, who did you have in mind...'

'Are you Welsh, like?'

'I am.' She took stock for a moment. 'Are you looking for something for yourself or for a girl?'

'I'm not married, y'know. Give me a twirl, like?'

She twirled slowly with the cardigan undone and her hands placed provocatively on her hips. His 'Yeah' seemed very appreciative but not wholly appropriate for a medium sized grey, brown and white cardigan with chunky buttons.

'Perhaps, y'know, you could come out into the sun so I can see better, like.'

As she stepped towards him he took her hand and lead her towards him. She was conscious of her slight gasp as their hands touched. Her heartbeat had gone up a notch and a tingling sensation headed up her arm, then along the back of her neck and then on to her scalp. She told herself to get a grip.

'How's this? What do you think?' she asked.

'That's looking proper sound, girl, proper sound...'

'Well, I think it would look...proper sound on anyone and it's warm in winter and cool in summer, too.'

'D'you come with it, like?'

'Umm, no, we come separately, don't we?' said she, fussing around, 'and I can't find a price tag for the other item but it will probably be way out of your price range, pal...'

'Well, y'know, let's negotiate, can you spare a minute, like?'

He started to walk quickly to the inn on the square. 'Look, you may be on a break but I'm still working here' she shouted.

'C'mon, let's you and me have a bevvy and some scran, like.'

'Oi Sue, can you watch my stall for a few minutes? I'm just going with this punter.' She confirmed that Sue had got the message and followed him into the hotel.

'Where are you sitting, like?' he asked.

'On my arse.'

'Sit there, soft lass' he said indicating a table for two just inside the door. She slipped the cardigan off and folded it neatly into a bulging block of wool.

'This is fine. Are you buying?' They settled into a pair of chairs and looked across the wobbly table with the cardigan in the centre. She cradled a mug of tea; he looked suspiciously at a mug of cream coloured froth with brown sprinkles on top.

'So, what's your best price, like?' A bowl of potato wedges had arrived with mayonnaise and brown sauce as accompaniments.

She wrote a figure on a serviette and passed it to him across the table.

'Eee, that's steep - how's about this, like?' He wrote a figure on the serviette and passed it back to Katie.

She took a look and her eyebrows shot upwards. 'You've got to be kidding mate - either you make a sensible offer or I walk away!'

He took back the serviette and wrote another figure. He pushed it back to her. 'I think that's acceptable, but it's cash only I'm afraid.' He ferreted through his wallet and produced the required number of bank notes. She accepted these gratefully and put them in the bag around her waist.

'Where's me bag, like?'

'You're pushing your luck, aren't you? Anyway, there you go. Remember it's hand wash only.' He accepted the cardigan, brought it up to his face and sniffed it with deep reverence.

'It will smell of wool, won't it?'

'Eee, it smells of you, soft lass!'

'It smells of sheep, not me!'

He sighed deeply.

And then there was that sensation up her neck, and across her crown, as someone entered the hotel, someone with her in mind. 'Tom!'

'Who?'

Smartly dressed Tom, curly haired Tom, long tall Tom, stopped at their table and stared and then turned around to walk out again.

'Tom, wait!'

'Oi girl, finish your fries!'

'Got to go after him. Good doing business!' She scampered out of the main door and looked up and down the square. He was walking quickly towards the castle. She caught him quickly and snared his right arm. 'Where are you taking me then?'

'You started without me!'

'Oh, that was nothing, that was just a business lunch. Sold another cardi!' She offered him a potato wedge from a serviette and she took one for herself. 'Sooooo, good send off for your Gramps, then?'

'Yes, but who were you whispering to in there?'

'I was whispering to your Gramps?'

He shook his head. 'How?'

'Like this' she whispered in a very low and deep voice. Her shoulder nudged his and she sniggered.

'Right, well, where do you live now?'

'In a ship, mainly.'

'But you're not in a ship at the moment?'

His logic was faultless. 'No, you're absolutely right there.'

'So what are you doing here?'

She puzzled over this for a moment. 'I'm talking to you.'

'How am I supposed to have a serious conversation with you?'

'Oh!' She drew the flat of her hand over her face and the smirk disappeared to reveal her serious face. 'How's that, Tom?'

He just shook his head in response. Katie took his arm again and they walked aimlessly with purpose towards the lawn that fronted the castle wall, their footfalls in perfect synchronisation, perambulating as if they were meant to be life partners.

'Where are you staying? With the Hoflands?'

'Yes, close by, in the barn mainly.'

'Oh, Katie, why don't you come and stay with us?'

Ah, the cottage by the river, which would be quiet and empty and free from disturbance for a while, and reached via the bridge and along the babbling river to the haven, overlooked by the cliff but by nothing else.

'That would be nice, let me think about that, but I can't quite remember what it was like... will your mum be all right about it?'

'Ah...'

'But that letter you wrote to my old buffer, that was beautiful and I'm so sorry I couldn't have replied to you because I would have gone, 'Yes, yes, yes!'' She must be properly flushed now she thought and her legs glowing pink.

'I thought you weren't interested. I thought you didn't care?'

'Well, my old buffer was out of order but I can put it right now.' She sighed and he sighed and she pulled him that bit closer. They were now heading down the bonk.

She clasped his right hand between her hands and drew it to her chest: 'Tom, I need to ask you, you say I'm beautiful but I'm difficult - what do you mean I'm difficult?'

'I didn't mean difficult like that - I meant you're just always away, which makes it...difficult.'

'Well, Tom, I'm here for you now, so if you want to talk about anything... basically, I'm your girl.'

He looked at her quizzically. She recalled that there was a footpath that curled to the right below the base of the steep grassy mound.

'I spoke to your friend, Sarah...'

'Whoa, whoa, whoa, she's not my friend!' They were only about thirty paces from the snicket.

'She had a lot to say about you...'

'Like what?'

'She says...you are a witch!'

'Oh no, my little secret's out!'

Tom frowned at her so she did another reveal of her mock serious face and made a temple of her fingers.

'So Tom, lets examine the facts: who is it who dresses like a witch, is blinged up like a witch, has long fingers and nails like a witch and has a stall full of potions like a witch? It's not me, is it?'

'You had a conversation with my Gramps!'

'I can hear voices, that's all, like my sister and my mum and everyone, basically.'

'Still...'

'So ipso fatso, I'm not a witch...'

'What's that?'

'It's Latin I think. It means case proved, m'lud.'

'But you had a conversation...'

'Ah yes, I'm not quite sure what happened there - my sister reckons I'm hypersensitive or something and it's rude not to reply if you hear someone talking to you, isn't it?'

'So, you all are?'

She dropped his hand and hid her face behind her fingers. 'I...I don't know what to say.' She looked through her fingers. He didn't seem to be angry or annoyed. He still wanted to be with her.

'Is it true?'

She dropped her hands, dropped her eyes and turned her back on him.

'Well?'

'Who knows, I reckon all women are witches anyway. We just show it in different ways, don't we?' She wrinkled her face in anguish. She decided to take another tack. The snicket now seemed as far away as the moon.

'My brother can prove that the Goddess of Love must be ugly, so you can prove anything with words, can't you? I don't have to be difficult, I can put on the charm if I want to, so what is the truth? It's just words and words are just a screen for the truth, aren't they?' She screwed up her face when she realised what she had just said.

'Look, I don't want to upset you...'

'Well, don't then.'

'I don't think you are a witch, Katie.'

'Oh, that's good.' They were outside the castle, where red sandstone blocks protruded through the wall, on the cobbled road that wound down to the river. 'Listen, I'm going to tell you a story - I think it might be helpful. It's like a para-bowl.'

He placed a hand on her shoulder and turned her round and then his hands clasped her around the stomach. She placed her hands above his as she started to pulse ever so slightly from her core. Her left foot swept side to side on the cobbles as she tried to calm her body by closing her eyes but she just sighed instead. There was still the deep heat over her back and a tingling across her skin.

'So, what were you going to tell me Katie?'

'Well, I don't think it would help now.'

'Why don't you try?'

'Well, when I was younger I came down here with my first boyfriend.'

Tom chuckled and his closeness and his intimacy made her head swirl. 'Now, how old were you?'

She tried to calculate what was the answer that would leave her with the least explaining to do. 'I don't know, thirteen or fourteen. Anyway, I wasn't sure what he thought of me so I thought I would show him what I could do.'

Tom seemed amused by this. 'Oh no Katie, what did you do?'

'So I climbed up the castle wall, right to the top. Impressive eh?' She pointed to the top of the wall.

She felt him nodding in agreement.

'Well, actually, it wasn't. He walked off and left me up there. They had to get the window cleaner's ladder up the wall. That was the only way I could get down. I was properly humiliated.' She snuggled in tight. 'So, if I was any kind of witch, I would have levitated myself up and levitated myself down, wouldn't I?'

'So, what do you think of that boy now?' he chuckled.

She was going to say she thought he was an utter twat then something occurred to her: 'It was you! You left me up there!' The vision of the two of them curled up together upstairs in the cottage by the river suddenly evaporated.

Tom had released her and pushed her away. 'Yes, it was me! How did you get up there? You're no climber!'

'It was easy - look at those massive holds! And I couldn't get down!'

'I couldn't believe it! I thought you'd sneaked up a ladder!'

'They had to get me down with a ladder!'

'You are just too difficult!' With that Tom left her, walking quickly down the hill, walking his way to the cottage by the river.

'Ast!' she cried. She slapped the metal parking fee notice with her palm three more times, 'Ast! Ast! Ast! The last slap felt different. Looking up, there was a hand shaped impression in the centre of the sign and looking down, there were scabs of red and white paint on her hand. She quickly rubbed these away as she walked up the hill back to the market.

The number of punters had thinned out and her return to her stall was celebrated by the clapping of Susan Tricketts. 'I helped myself to tea' she said.

'I hope you put your money in the honesty box.'

Susan grumbled and put in half a dozen coins. 'Been chasing the boys again? My Ben not good enough?'

'Well, Mrs Tricketts, he wanted to share me with a sheep, so I wasn't having any of that.'

'You do talk such rubbish.'

'It's true. Ben reckons her name is Sheepy Clara.'

'Never heard that name mentioned before.'

'No, it's not something you talk about at the tea table, is it? So how's it been for you?'

'Watching two stalls? Tiresome, that's what its been.'

'Well, take a break then.'

'Nah, nearly done now. Everyone's leaving.'

After a decent pause, Katie decided to ask a question of her: 'I'm not difficult, am I?'

'Course not, me little sprout, but you can be, oh, what's the word?' Katie felt obliged to wait for the punchline, 'that's it, a bit of a melon. Sometimes, you would cut off your nose to spite your face.' Sue smiled grimly, 'But we still love you for all that, even my Ben does, despite me cautioning him.'

The big, green car with its trailer, driven by Gwen, arrived just after five o'clock in the market Square. The stall and what remained

of the goods in plastic containers were quickly put away. Gwen did a quick cashing up and concluded that Katie had exceeded all expectations. 'And here's something for you' she said as she handed over a blue beer token and a change of clothes, 'for your dinner date.'

'Gwen, while you're finishing off, I'll just go and have a quick chat with Sarah Pagan.'

Katie strolled back towards the castle and stood in front of the gazebo as Sarah Pagan meticulously dismantled it. But the main part of the stall was still present as serried ranks of coloured bottles, all neatly corked and neatly labelled in a Gothic script and neatly organised in trays that can be lifted out easily and put away simply. 'Wow, this is all utterly amazing' Katie declared after considering the set-up for a few moments, 'utterly amazing!'

Sarah Pagan swirled across to Katie and started describing her wares with well-practiced flourishes of her arms and flicks of her hair.

'How have you done today, Sarah?'

'Ah, in terms of monetary gain, not so well, but in terms of spreading knowledge of the craft and new recruits, so well.'

'Oh good, I am pleased. My mum dabbles a bit in potions.'

'Your mother? I thought she was too busy burning down a forest!'

'I don't think she's doing that, is she?'

'Go to the tower, look to the west and tell me what you can see.'

'Sarah, I really can't be arsed.'

'What you will see is the flames and smoke of trees being destroyed...'

'And where exactly is this supposed to be going on?'

'Kerry Hill of course.'

'Of course...that's just across the border, isn't it?'

'You don't know where your mother is?'

'Well, she does travel around a bit, doesn't she?'

'Like a pikey!'

'No, like a traveller.'

'Like mother, like daughter' muttered Sarah.

Katie thought about the truth of this and then decided to move the conversation on: 'Have you got any spells or potions to help make someone feel that they are in love with you?'

'You have to have love in your heart first.'

'Well, yes, obviously. So you have a potion for that?'

'A potion and an incantation...all of these' she said with a purple sleeved flourish, 'but particular formulae depending on the individuals concerned.'

'But, basically, you just drug them and then hypnotise them?'

'No, no, no, that just betrays your cynicism and mistrust of the natural ways' Sarah Pagan retorted. 'Now, you should leave, I have nothing more to say to you.'

'I think what I'm hearing is that none of these spells are worth a sheep's fart.'

'Disbeliever!'

'Sodding witch!'

There was a hush across the square. Sarah Pagan took a bottle and cast a loop of liquid in the air and it made a circle of wetness around Katie.

Pagan uttered the words of a holding spell that would bind the subject into their self-made prison until every molecule of the liquid evaporated.

Katie laughed, bent down and put her finger in the liquid on the paving and licked it but the slick remained and it soured her mouth and burned her eyes. The ground beneath her feet started to lose its substance; she thrust her arms out but nothing could be seen beyond the finger-tips. The circle around her oozed slowly upwards like flowing lava and she was starting to sink, and the oozing seemed to be alive as her eyes and her whole being slipped downwards...

Katie saw a hand above her - she jumped to grab it with her hands! She was being dragged upwards, past these binding walls and then she was out, back in the square, kneeling, panting like an over-heated dog.

Gwen was at her side: 'Katie, snap out of it!'

'Ugh' she moaned in reply.

'What do you think you're doing Sarah?'

'She's a disbeliever - I'm giving her a life lesson!'

Katie watched as Gwen strode to Sarah, wrenched the bottle out of her hand placed it on the ground. 'You don't know what you're dealing with Sarah' Gwen hissed.

Katie felt her face grimace - her left arm was swinging to and fro - she was back on her feet and her arms and fingers were stretching out towards the pagan girl.

And now, little ripples of air cajoled the vial into a slow spin.

'Spawn of Satan!' Pagan snapped. And then she stooped to stare at the legs of the table. 'What is that? What's happening?'

Something seemed to be ascending the legs of the table and infiltrating its way into the vials of liquid, standing helplessly in ranks, because they all started to wobble and jiggle against each other. Could that be the wind, because it could do strange things, up here on the castle mound?

'There is a spirit here that could shut you down organ by organ' Gwen hissed.

Sarah Pagan clutched suddenly at her heart and her jaw sagged open. 'No!'

The vials vibrated together in a shuddering crescendo.

'And there is a force here that could send your body in a million different directions, all at once!'

The vials popped their stoppers and their over-energised contents spewed slowly over the table like molten sugar.

'Do not underestimate this spirit energy, Sarah! There's something inside that takes over when threatened. You are no match for this!'

And then Gwen and Sarah watched in amazement as trails of froth proceeded randomly across the table and then down to the ground. As Katie lifted her arms and extended them towards Sarah, Gwen leapt to her, wrapped her little sister's arms in her own and dragged her away to the far side of the square. As her panicked panting subsided, Gwen released the pinioned arms and allowed Katie to slump back against a wall.

'Katie! Katie! Please come back!' Gwen ran her thumb along the nape of Katie's nose and then across and over the top of her forehead.

All the onlookers had dispersed and all that remained, were steel skeletons where there used to be stalls. Couples were walking aimlessly across the square with no destination and no purpose in mind.

Katie blinked. 'It's alright Gwen, I'm back...'

'What happened to you? Are you all right?'

'Ugh, I had a funny turn' said Katie as she looked at Gwen with teary eyes, 'and now my sodding eyes hurt!'

'What were you trying to do?'

'When, Gwen?'

'Just now!'

'I can't remember exactly.' She gave a wry grin as Sarah Pagan scrambled around, gathering up glass vials and corks.

'She put a binding spell on you, Katie!'

'Don't be silly Gwen, I'm a matelot! There's nobody in the world who can bind me to anything or anywhere!'

'Oh, is that so? Well now, just take a few deep breaths...'

'And think of England?'

'No, think of something nice.'

'All right then. Cider and cake.' Her left arm still swung slowly, side to side, her fingers stretching in and out, like a feeding anemone, as though the tips were charged, but with no means to release.

Gwen took her bottle of water and looked down in Katie's eyes and then jumped back, eyes staring. 'What's up Gwen?'

'Nothing! I thought I saw someone - there was someone or something looking back at me!'

'Yes, that was me!'

Gwen scrunched her eyes closed and looked again. 'Ah, just a reflection of my face, that's all.' She rinsed Katie's eyes slowly and methodically and dried them with the sleeve of her blouse. 'Tell me what that was all about.'

'Oh, I was asking Sarah Pagan about her potions and then she threw one of them all over me!'

'And why would she do that?'

'I said that none of them were actually worth a sheep's fart.'

'That was very disrespectful of you, Katie, none of us know all there is to know about everything and these potions may provide some sort of comfort or help to the misguided.'

'You mean idiots?'

'Exactly. Now sit up - how are your eyes?'

'They're all soaked!'

'But how are they?'

'They're all sodding wet!'

'Good. I think you need a drink, I know I do.' Gwen wrapped her arm around Katie's waist and dragged her along the square to the hotel. She looked into Katie's eyes and listened carefully to her breathing. 'Are you sure you're all right, or do you need a first aider?'

'I'm fine now Gwen!'

There was a ragged cheer from the crowd clustered outside the hotel.

'You daft bint' laughed the market manager, 'what were you trying to do? Don't you know that the Pagan girl can do magic?'

'It's settled now George' replied Gwen, 'so you can all just calm down.'

'I would've exploded her tits' said Katie defiantly, 'but Gwen stopped me just in time!'

'We'd prefer to see you wrestle!' laughed George leeringly.

Katie replied with a pithy comment in her guttural tongue.

George looked quizzically to Katie, 'What's that supposed to mean?'

'Gwen, you translate' Katie said to Gwen. She accepted the glass of cider that was pushed into her hands.

'On the house, girl!'

Gwen took a deep breath: 'George, she said, go away.'

'Go away? Oh, no, there was much more to it than that!'

Gwen took another deep breath, and turned to Katie: 'Can I just check, I got most of it, but the other bit?'

Katie whispered in her ear.

'All right, I think I've got it.'

Katie watched George as Gwen spoke: 'My translation of what Katie said is, 'go away and have unnatural sex with your nanny'!'

Katie cocked her head and waited for the response.

'Oh, nice!' There was an outburst of ribald laughter.

'Nicely embellished Gwen' acknowledged Katie, 'but just to be clear, any sex with your nanny is going to be unnatural, isn't it?'

'I'm going to need a white wine spritzer!' Gwen handed Katie a large beer voucher.

Katie fulfilled the order and moaned at the barman about how much it had cost her. She was making her way outside when she saw

Gwen, down a passageway, making a phone call. She stopped and listened.

'It looks like Katie will make her own way back. She's holding court in the hotel on the square at the moment...'

'No, I don't know when she'll be back...she has a date, remember?'

'But there was something odd that happened. Sarah Pagan cast some sort of spell on Katie and she just crumpled like a cheap suit. There was something behind her eyes...'

'Yes, she's all right...'

'Seems to be, but it was like she believed that the spell was real!'

Katie waited outside and presented Gwen with her drink. 'These are sodding expensive aren't they?'

Gwen swallowed it in three great swigs. 'Just... stay out of trouble, if you can' was her parting shot.

The boy with the fiddle and the girl with the squeeze box had arrived and set themselves up in the back parlour of the hotel. They wondered if Katie was going to sing with them. She said she would be back later, after big eats.

George was mellowing outside in the late afternoon sun and in the long coolness of his pint. 'Y'know you still owe me for the pitch, me little sprout...'

'Oh, Gwen deals with all that sort of thing.' She flashed him a little blue beer voucher but it clearly wasn't enough. 'She's gone off in a hurry with the rest of the cash - I'll have to owe you!'

'Y'know, I'm minded to let you off after that display you put on!'

'Oh thanks' she replied, 'that's good, but there seems to be a bit of an issue with witches about here?'

'Eh?'

'You know what I mean, witches! Shouldn't the council be doing something about it? There's an infestation of them!'

George just threw his head back and guffawed at the early evening sky.

Katie caught up with Eek beyond the garden and where the pasture started. 'Shouldn't you be in bed?' Owain was asleep at her feet.

'Mama said I should wait up for you - you're sleeping with me tonight.'

'Separate beds?'

'If you like...'

They looked over the lip of the hill over the valley and towards the Clun Forest. The sheep were bleating as usual, but there was an unusual quietness which begged to be broken by a scream.

'What's that noise?' said Monique with a start.

'It's an owl.'

'What sort of owl?'

'It's a screechy kind of owl.'

'Are they safe?'

'Yes, unless you're a mouse.'

There was a hush while Monique formulated a question in her little mind: 'Are you any good at being a guardian?'

'I haven't done it before, so it's difficult for me to say, isn't it?'

'Mama said you got duffed over by a girl at the market today.'

'No, I didn't!'

'She said you were on your knees and crying!'

'She got the jump on me, that's all - she threw acid at me!'

'Mama says it was just water!'

'It must have been really dodgy water!'

'So you went, 'boo-hoo, you splashed water on me and now I'm going to tell my big sister!' You're such a goofball, Auntie Katie!'

'It wasn't like that - she did a spell on me!'

'Sarah? You mean, Sarah, 'just look at me, I fell off a Christmas tree' Pagan?'

'Oh, you know her then...'

'Oh yes, and I know her little sister...'

'Baby Pagan?'

'Yes, that's the one...'

There was another hush while Monique worked out another question: 'So why did Papa make you my guardian?'

'He thinks I would do a good job...'

'Will you?'

'Of course I will!'

'What if you go away again?'

'I'll know something's happened and I'll get back as soon as I can.'

'And how will you know what to do?'

Katie paused to think: 'I'm guardian to the Royal Marines and they're big, tough soldiers.'

'I see, so you should be quite a good guardian then?'

'Yes, if I can sort out the Royal, I suppose I should be, shouldn't I?'

'Auntie Katie, you know we have a pact?'

'Yes' Katie replied hesitantly.

'Can I show you my secret?'

Katie felt her heart riding wild. 'Go on then, show me Eek.'

Monique extended her arms horizontally and directed them towards a yellow tennis ball. It popped up and rolled a few inches along the grass. Owain bounded a few yards, tried to pick it up and but it kept popping away. He came back empty jawed.

'Isn't that cool?'

Katie tried to hide her bewilderment. 'Well, that is cool! Does anyone else know about this? You didn't do this at 'Show and Tell' did you?'

'Whooo, that's a really cool idea, Auntie Katie!'

'No, it's not, they'll all get insanely jealous!'

'You know, I think you're probably right, Auntie Katie.'

'Thank's Eek. Does your mum know?'

'Not yet.'

'Is there...anything else, Eek?'

'There is!' Monique backed into Katie's midriff and stretched her hands out towards the valley. 'Quick, put your arms on top of mine, Auntie Katie and close your eyes!' Katie did as she was told. 'Can you see anything?'

'No, my eyes are closed!'

'Relax a bit, breathe slowwwwwly. Now, what can you see?'

There were streams of fizzy green stretching away, along the lines, as far as her sight could see, never to ever meet...

'That's so amazing' Katie said but that was not what she was really thinking, 'so amazing!'

'Anyway, I think we should go back inside before Mama wonders where we are.' Monique skipped back to the house and gave a little wave as she entered through the kitchen door.

Owain looked up to Katie and whimpered.

'I know!' Katie walked towards the tennis ball but Owain was there first and he snapped it up and offered it to her. It was slightly slobbery but other than that, it was a perfectly normal tennis ball. She looked it all over and shook it. She tossed it in the air with back spin and Owain caught it easily on the bounce. 'That is really...peculiar!'

She heard the screech owl calling and it made a pass at her before settling in the rafters of the barn. She gave a shiver as a cold chill settled over the hill. There was a scrabbling of tiny feet in the meadow beyond the barn and the owl bobbed her head three times and launched into a silent glide, hovered and plunged into the long grass. There was fighting and pained screeching and tearing of feathers. Katie ran into the grass - the owl's leg had been seized by sharp, nasty teeth. She brought her foot down hard onto the dark haired beast. She plucked up the owl and tucked her below her arm but the beast kept coming, with its bare legs running and its bare tail slithering and its sharp nasty teeth snapping. Katie backed away, her left arm pointing at the beast as if that could stop it. She shouted 'OWAIN!'

A black, white and brown blur came in from her right and there was another fierce fight, with fur and teeth, subsiding into squealing and whining. She crouched down as the dog brought her a body, bare footed and bare tailed, brown furred and neck broken. Owain juggled with the limp body and bit through the skull with a teeth-jarring crack. It was the biggest brown rat she had ever seen. She followed Owain's gaze down the valley as she stroked the golden feathers of the owl and gazed into her white, heart-shaped face and the round, dark eyes, frozen in fear. 'Oh Selene' she whispered, probably dead by daybreak she reckoned.

There were crunching noises from the dog's mouth. 'Those bitches over in the Elenydd are stirring again, Owain, and we'd better be ready!'

CHAPTER FORTY-FIVE

Saturday 21 May 1037 - Kerry Hill

The bus deposited her at the end of the Teme valley. 'How far is it from here, driver?' Katie asked.

'Well, lovely, it's about one mile up that track.' She followed the line he was pointing along. It was steep and rutted.

'Would that be a Welsh mile or an English mile?' she wondered.

'It's a Welsh mile. Enjoy yourself, lovely!' The nearly empty bus ground up the hill and bumped over the col towards Newtown.

The sooner we all go to one means of measuring, the better it will be for everyone, she thought. She looked to the north-east and set off up the hill. The track started off as wide as a car but after four hundred paces, petered out into a rocky bridleway. Here she found an official-looking notice, with red printing, nailed to a fresh pine post. She ran her fingers over it and sensed there was trouble for whoever it was who had upset the local council.

Katie traversed a short ridge and looked eastwards - on the crown of the ridge, backed by a dense plantation, were jagged angles of green and brown and grey, fencing with each other, like a living kaleidoscope. She stepped back and tried to re-focus. What was she looking at? An image of a forest? But there was little birdsong, just the sound of metal fracturing wood.

Katie looked back the way she had come, and what she could see was as it should be: there were crows in the meadow, cawing at her; there were rabbits squatting and then running in and out of rabbit holes; there was a mewing buzzard ahead, soaring on the breeze; and two fork-tails, flapping their ungainly way above the trees that crowned the ridge. She looked along the ridge and decided to continue.

Katie saw a lean, bare-chested boy swinging an axe onto a log and flakes of wood flying about him. There were piles of stakes and logs and the smell of smouldering ashes. The boy didn't return her gaze, so she continued, picking her way through the stumps.

The wood thickened then opened out again into a clearing. There was a figure, a stooped crone, shrouded in a brown open necked gown, leaning on a crooked stick and smoking a delicate wooden stemmed pipe with a flattened bowl. Her silvery blonde hair was in braids and black ribbons; her long nose, was up-tilted and pointed; her skin was tanned and tight; her eyes had the quality of the finest apatite and fixed unrelentingly on Katie's face.

Katie approached carefully and cautiously, like she was approaching a viper, keeping her eyes firmly fixed on the other's eyes. They were very close now, very nearly at touching distance so Katie stopped and took a very deep breath. 'Hallo Mum, how are you doing?'

Maela stood to her full height, her hair uncoiled to her waist and shimmered against the taffeta of her smock. Her neck and arms were adorned with wooden beads that clicked gently at her every movement. 'It's been thirteen moons, Ebrill' she said as she tapped the residue out of her pipe, 'I remember it was before Beltane when you last came to me. We have much to discuss. Tell me, why has it taken you so long? Am I not important to you?'

'I've been working, Mum' Katie replied.

'Working?'

'That's right Mum, working. You should try it sometime, you might find it quite rewarding.'

'Don't you dare disrespect me, Ebrill. My life has been a constant struggle, I have brought many children into this world and made every sacrifice for them. And remind me, what is your work? Oppression of the poor and the innocent?'

'How many children, Mum?' Katie did a quick head count - she knew of three. Who were the many? Or was this another example of her mum's lack of any grip on reality?

Maela turned away and walked nimbly farther into the plantation.

Katie tried to keep up with her. 'Listen, Mum, I am not an oppressor, I help to protect people. What do you mean? And please slow down!'

'You work to oppress the poor, the innocent and the weak. You work for the evil and the corrupt and the shameful!'

'I had no choice, Mum! They made me!'

Maela stopped and allowed Katie to get within spitting distance: 'Don't you dare! We are responsible for the choices we make! So, you are responsible for the choice you made! You do not make me proud!'

'I had no choice, Mum! They made me and you didn't stop them! I was just fourteen!'

'Ah, ahhhh, but I campaigned tirelessly for you to come back to me, and I wrote so many letters, so many letters' she said, wringing her left hand with her right hand.

'And what did the letters say, Mum?'

'Ah, my memory does not serve me so well...'

'They asked for money, didn't they Mum?'

'So long ago, so long ago, I cannot remember now...'

'So, you were quite happy for the evil and the corrupt and the shameful to pay you money?'

'Ah, so long ago, so long ago, my mind plays tricks...'

'So, what does that make you, Mum?'

'Be quiet, you sneaky, mean-minded, child!'

'I wonder who I've got to thank for that!'

'Don't be impertinent - I am your mother!' With that, Maela turned away and moved quickly with sure feet through the trunks and the stumps of the resinous trees.

She shouted after her mum: 'What about the promise, Mum?'

'The promise, the promise, I know of no promise?'

'The big promise Mum, the one that's so old!'

'That wasn't a promise, that was a blood oath.' Maela paused and turned to her daughter. 'It was made many years ago and it had to be honoured. You were the means to that end, child, and I'm sorry for that.'

'Are you apologising Mum?'

'Don't be absurd!'

They had come to a shanty-built structure made of lopped trunks, crossed at the apex, set in the hillside. There were piles of cut wood scattered at the foot of the house and an overhang under which animals lay. Katie could pick out two goats and a squabble of hens. Maela turned to confront Katie. 'Did you bring me money?'

'Yes, I did Mum.'

'Good, you're more use than your sister, then.'

'She does her best, but you don't help yourself, Mum.'

'Did Gwenaëlle tell you what had occurred?'

'D'you mean Gwen? Not exactly, she just said that you had an argument. I think it's because you were thrown out of the flat. She says you were a very bad lodger, Mum.'

'The terms and conditions were so onerous, so onerous and it was very cold. I had to keep warm.'

'You shouldn't have burnt the furniture, Mum, it wasn't yours to burn!'

'No matter, no matter, but you have brought me money?'

Katie stopped, opened a pocket of her rucksack and took out an envelope. She handed it over reluctantly to Maela. 'Yes Mum, here it is!'

Maela took the envelope and neatly opened it with the nail on her left index finger. 'Is this all you have Ebrill?'

'It's all you're getting. Can you promise me that you will spend it on provisions and not on shag?'

'How was this money earned, Ebrill? Is this blood money?'

'No, no, Mum, it's properly earned money' said Katie, jabbing her finger nails into her thigh.

'I see. You are a good child but it's no business of yours how I spend it.' Maela pulled her smock down to show her bodice. And there it was, her wrinkled chest, not quite as wrinkled as her turkey neck, but more like a peach that had been left out in the sun. 'You will have wrinkles one day, child. Be proud of them!'

Katie swallowed away the nausea she suddenly felt and looked away - It was a large wad of brown beer vouchers and it made an unsightly bulge in her mum's bodice; Katie shook her head to clear this unpleasant image from her mind.

'And what is your sister doing today that is more important than visiting her mother?'

'I think she's gone shopping.'

'Ah, shopping! Procuring the unnecessary for the unworthy and the undeserving. How marvellous, the preserve of the rich and the envy of the poor!'

'Everyone needs to eat, Mum!'

'Then work the land, grow your own, like I do!'

'They do!'

'But you herders destroy the natural landscape and spread chemicals that poison the soil and the water!'

'Mum, you've got goats and hens, so you are a herder...'

'Silly girl, of course I'm not a herder, I move my animals from place to place to preserve the environment.'

'But not the trees.'

'The trees do not belong here.'

'And neither do you.'

'We all belong to the land, it is the common ground and everyone has a stake in it. Do you remember what I told you as a child, Ebrill?'

'Nope.'

'Property is theft.'

'And theft is theft, Mum.'

'Don't you get clever with me!'

'And arson is arson and wanton destruction is wanton destruction!'

'Be quiet, you impertinent child!'

'Not until you stop it!'

'Never!' Her mum stamped her foot and stamped it again. Her locks and ringlets shook and clacked.

The lad with the axe came running. He stood with it at the ready - he was tall and lean and not at all bad looking. 'What is it, my lady?'

'Dafyd, meet my youngest child, Ebrill!'

He nodded and leant on the axe in such a way that his chest and arm muscles became more prominent. 'A'right, girl?'

'A'right, boy.'

'My daughter thinks that our work to restore this hill to its former glory, and to earn you an honest wage, must stop - what do you think about that?'

'Listen you, work is hard to find and I don't want to go back on the dole, do I?'

'Dafyd's parents have no job and his brothers and sisters wear rags to school.'

Katie gave out a loud groan and hid her face behind her hands. 'I'm sorry Dafyd, I wasn't thinking.'

'And what about your ma, how would she cope without me?'

'I'm sure she could manage, somehow. Thanks Dafyd, off you tootle now - I just need a quiet word with my mum.'

Maela dismissed him with a conspiratorial wink and a smile.

Katie looked at her mum carefully. She was wearing eye liner and purple eye shadow and the edges of her lips were subtly highlighted. She was also wearing some kind of base coat on her face and a smug, self-satisfied smile all over her face. 'You're wearing make-up, Mum?'

'Just a little foundation and some highlights - I think it is so important to maintain standards, don't you?'

Katie looked all about her. 'But there's no one here, Mum!' There were times like this, when she could be having this conversation with her nain, all those years ago...

'Dafyd is with me and I think I should show him the respect of...'

'Hold on, he's not...is he?'

'What do you mean?'

'He seems very...into you, Mum?'

'But that is good, isn't it?'

'I think, if I was his mum, I'd be a little bit concerned.'

'But you are not, are you?'

'No Mum, actually I'm your daughter!'

'But not a good one - a good daughter would be here with her mother, helping her in the autumn of her life.'

Maela was a good looking women, despite her great age. She entered the shelter and swirled a wooden bowl that contained two compressed balls of dark green fodder, that looked like horse pellets.

'Are you going to feed and water me, mum?' asked Katie, 'because if you are, I don't want any of that stuff that looks like it's just fallen out of a goat's arse.'

'Yes Ebrill, all in good time. Let me see what I can gather of nature's bounty. The land has been productive for us, we have been most fortunate. Now, come to me child. Let me hold you.'

Maela stood with her arms outstretched and her palms towards Katie. Their palms came together and their fingers enmeshed. Katie was turned round and her arms bound tightly across her chest. 'Breath deeply child, I want to feel your life force' she said.

'What are you doing, Mum?' Katie asked as she struggled to get in a breath.

Maela spoke softly in Katie's ear: 'Your body is bruised and your soul is damaged, child, I will make you better. I will mend you using the old ways.'

'No, you are not' squeaked Katie, screwing up her eyes, 'it's nothing, I don't need mending, I'm fine.' Underneath her tee-shirt was a set of welts that her mum was pressing against. Best to keep those well hidden, she decided. 'So, where did you find this boy, Dafyd, then?'

'Dafyd is my helper, he looks after all my needs.'

'All your needs, Mum?'

'All my spiritual and physical needs.'

'Oh, I see.' Katie paused as that horrible thought came back into her mind. 'Are you shagging him, Mum?'

'No of course not, that would be highly improper of me.'

'You are then!'

'Certainly not, but for his regular breaks, I make him tea and he makes...'

'Mum! That's dirty! He's just a boy!'

'But he is willing, enthusiastic and has much vigour...'

'But does his mum know?'

'I don't believe so...'

'That's why you're wearing make up!'

'I like to look my best for him - the years have taken their toll, child.'

'You dirty slag!'

'Oh, my, you're jealous!'

'Jealous? Jealous of you! I'm a matelot and I've got a bloke in every port!'

'Name one.'

'Oh, well...there's Robert...' Her left arm was pulled tight across her throat. Her breath was coming in a panic.

'Robert? He sounds a fine fellow and where's he from?' said Maela soothingly.

'Switzer...' Maela's left hand was probing inside and down her underclothes. 'Mum, please don't...'

'Switzerland? Switzerland? Switzerland? Is that the country that has no ports?'

There was a painful jab inside and Katie tried to cry out. Maela pressed up tight against Katie's back, squeezing tightly with her wiry arms. 'Yes, he's screwing me and you're jealous!' She started to chant words that Katie only half recognised, words that came from her throat and curled around her tongue, a rhythm of words of old gallic, as a lullaby. There was another sharp jab and blood drained away from her head. 'Virgin!'

Katie's eyes flittered momentarily and then she was lost in a swoon. Maela cradled her so that her body drooped slowly onto the ground. Her legs twitched and then she was gone into a light, softly panting stupor.

But she did see Maela come to lie by her side, and her hand probing down inside her shirt, caressing her stomach, and her other hand sweeping slowly upwards, over her face so that her mouth could only fall open. And then Maela's mouth closed upon it and a wet gobbet of food was pressed in with her tongue and Katie tried to resist this long, moist kiss but she couldn't and she had to swallow. She tried to cough it up, but the bolus slid down her gullet and it was inside her and unravelling and her mind was unravelling too and soon there was nothing but the darkness.

Katell gathered an armful of arrows and put them in her leather quiver. She had a pouch for flint arrow heads and a sleeve for the yew stems that made the shafts and these were slung from a leather belt around her waist. Her twin daggers were slotted into the diagonal sheaves across her shoulder blades. She slotted her arm into the leather loop that supported her body length wooden shield.

'Stay back, leave this to the men' shouted Arian.

'No, we live and die together. You need me and the other bows by your side!'

A shout came from the woods below leading to the river. 'They're here. Come quickly!'

They gathered into two groups and headed quickly down the slope, towards the banging of swords on shields and the war cries that cold-curdled blood. They were close now. As soon as Katell and the other bows were gathered to the right of the shield line, their enemies were upon them.

Now she could see them for the first time, big hairy beasts of men wearing beaten plates of dark grey metal and animal furs, smashing through the forest, brandishing swords and shields and clubs.

Katell withdrew an arrow from the quiver, aimed for the eye of her target, emptied her lungs and released: 'Die, you dog,' The arrow struck home and he fell silent. She drew another arrow, released and another hit. The enemy crashed into their line and it yielded.

'Fall back' shouted Arian. Those that could moved back through the trees, to the crest of the hill overlooking the sinuous, silver river.

'We must stand here or they will cut us down' Katell shouted.

'Save yourself' shouted Arian.

'No, if you fall, I fall with you!' She planted her wooden shield in the soil.

They turned to fight, but Katell saw there was barely a score of her companions still standing. All had taken wounds but her. The enemy horde attacked in force across the hill. They were led by a huge warrior wielding a metal studded club that smashed armour and bones with ease. He attacked through the companions at the centre of the line. Katell released an arrow, that he twisted to avoid, but it split his nose. Still he came on. A bolt skidded through her helmet, spinning her around and stunning her to her knees, heaving hard in shock. Willing arms pulled her back to her feet and she grasped her shield, but the bow was lost. A swinging axe bit into her shield but she rode the force of the blow, took two yew shafts and thrust them deep into her attacker's face. His scream was cut short by her shield smashing into his face.

'Save Katell!' roared Arian. Two men shielded her but they were bludgeoned to the ground by the behemoth. Her legs were trapped and the giant was striding over her. Arching her back, twin daggers were drawn and slashed across the back of his thighs. He grunted, stared down and stamped but her head jerked away. The right dagger slipped into the back of his knee; the left dagger into his buttock. Katell pulled out the left dagger and re-planted it into the base of his spine and the howl curdled her blood. Two handedly she pulled herself up, pulled out the right dagger and thrust it into his neck. He swung his massive arm but the left dagger had cut the tendon at the elbow. His right arm pushed up and he was on his knees and she was free. Katell gasped, screamed and collapsed onto him with the twin blades buried into his throat. An agonised scream heralded his slow collapse. She gasped at the smell and the flood of warm, gushing blood that poured over her face and mouth.

Coughing out hair, wiping blood away from her face and pushing herself up from his shuddering body; she inserted the blades behind his windpipe and jagged them towards her. His twitching stopped. They lay side by side: he like a tree smashed by a storm; she like a rat drowned in his blood.

The crashing and bludgeoning of the skirmish had moved away to be replaced by the screaming and the moaning of those about to ebb away. Many of the enemy had fled down the hill. Those that could.

The whole of her right side was wet with blood and she could not feel her left arm, but there was something else; a twinge in the pit of her stomach. 'I must get free' she told herself, 'I'm carrying Arian's seed inside of me!'

Katie woke suddenly in a panic. There was no form or structure around her apart from the cold damp soil on which she lay. There was the taste of garlic and anise in her mouth and a deep, hollow feeling of shame through where she was hurting. As her senses came to order, she could see she was in a structure built of resinous boughs and she could stand.

She released a sigh of relief when she heard giggling a few paces away from her. So, she was not alone. She got up, walked towards the giggling and found a screen. It smelt of freshly cut willow. She slowly opened the woven, willow screen and looked inside. Her mum and Dafyd were coiled together on a straw bed. Maela's finger beckoned from under the cover. Katie decided not to accept the offer and left quickly and silently.

Back in the space where she had slept, she felt around the walls and the ground. There was a triangle of tree stumps in the centre of the vaulted space. In between the stumps there was a vessel. In the vessel was something liquid and substantial that could be food. In her pack was an enamel mug; she found it and dipped it in the liquid and put it tentatively to her lips. Could it be food, a stew or something else? Her senses said food so she swallowed the liquid down. She dipped the mug back in the vessel and swallowed again. It was good. She then found something flat and leathery on a stump. It might be bread. Or it might not. She folded it into a parcel and chewed on it. It was almost edible and by dipping it in the stew, it was even more edible. There was nothing else she could find to eat. Katie swung her backpack across her shoulders and staggered outside, adopting a bow-legged gait out of necessity. She felt sore and tired but the air outside was sweet and clean.

The animal shelter had a gently sloping roof that nearly reached the ground so she eased her backside onto it and shuffled her way along it. There were pools of mist gathering in the dips and valleys that spread away to the West. Curls of wood smoke languished above the mist and drifted slowly. In her pack was a ground sheet which she spread on the log roof and then she placed her sleeping bag on top of it.

Was that movement she could hear below? Katie heaved herself across the ground sheet and looked down through a gap. It wasn't a goat or hen - it was her mum, looking up. Her tear dropped onto something below and then another one, into something wooden. Maela was collecting them in a wooden bowl. 'You are bound to me, Ebrill' she whispered. Katie gathered the largest gobbet of slobber she could, in her mouth, and let it go. 'Dirty child!' she hissed, wiping her eye, 'dirty, dirty child.' And then it was quiet below, so quiet, she was able to settle into a new sleep.

Katie woke in a panic - her body was clammy from a blanket of sweat and she was missing her left arm, but she found it still there, hanging uselessly immobile. So, she waggled it around a bit and it started to come back to life. Phew, that was a close one! Now she felt down across her tummy and down to her core with her working hand: it was a little sore down there but she was pleased to find that there was no possibility of a seed having being inserted in her.

It was still dark but there could still be seen the amorphous pools of mist that floated around the hills making them look like an archipelago of green islands that could only be reached by floating over the pools. The bark of the fox and the hooting of the owl reassured her that she was safe. She subsided into another sleep.

At daybreak, light streamed over the crest of the hill. The fox had returned. Katie took a tube of soap and launched it. There was a yelp and the fox scampered back into the woods. And now she was a tube of soap down! Idiot!

There was no more sleep to be had now the sun had risen. Instead she drowsed, working through the list of things she had to tackle her mum about. It was quite a long list.

She rolled out of the sleeping bag and leaned over the edge of the roof so she could look into the darkness below. Her mum emerged from the shadows.

'What did you do to me, Mum?'

'You spat in my eye, you horrible child! It's so sore now I need a special poultice.'

'Stuff your stupid poultice - you were harvesting my tears, you scheming witch!'

'Huuuuh, scheming?' She seemed to have trouble accepting this accusation.

'You heard me...'

'I gave you medication to treat all your ailments, and this is how you treat me! How could you?'

'What did you put in my mouth?'

'It was a medication tailored to meet your special physical and mental needs...'

'You drugged me!'

'But you needed rest!'

Katie peered into her mum's face. No, there was no point seeking the truth in those eyes. She somersaulted down to the ground. 'Well, what you did to me was completely out of order and you're not to do it again. Is that clear Mum?'

'No.'

'Is that clear, Mum!' Katie barked, unnecessarily loudly.

Maela covered her eyes and sobbed once. 'I am sorry, child, but today... you have ruined my karma.'

'Fuck your stupid karma!'

'Huuuuuhhh?'

'You heard me.'

Maela swept the cowl back and her wooden ringlets made that irritating clicking noise, like mistle thrushes make. She spread her arms wide. 'Come to me Ebrill!'

Katie took two steps away. What was she up to? Maela took two steps forward and Katie took two more back. She couldn't keep doing this. Maela took two steps forward and enveloped Katie in a linen shawl and then inside her bony arms. 'No pressing or pushing or gripping or strangling, Mum!'

'I only gave you treatment so you could be healed!' said Maela as she manoeuvred her daughter to an ungainly wooden chair, and seated her so they could face each other.

'You drugged me and I had a bad dream and I was fighting this big hairy bloke and I was frightened.' Those twin daggers she had seen before, the ones that sliced through flesh and muscle with ease, like surgeon's blades.

'Ah, that one. It was just a memory, child, of a past time...'

'Anyway, you're not to do it again.'

'I'm not to help you?' asked Maela.

'Ah, you are to help me, but not to drug me. Is that clear?'

Maela was now kneeling in front of her. She rested her hands on Katie's knees. 'Should we break our fast together? May I feed you, child?'

'It all depends.' If it looked like it had just dropped out of a goat's arse, she definitely wasn't having it.

Maela ducked into the shelter and came back with two jars and a spoon. A portion of white, clotted material was offered on a wooden spoon, Maela's other hand was suspended below, to catch any crumbs.

'What is this?' Katie asked as she too held the spoon.

'It's clotted cheese, made from goat's milk. It's quite safe.'

'Well, you go first then...'

Maela took a crumb of it. 'Mmmm, so good!'

'All right, let me try. It was exactly as her mum had said. 'That's all right Mum, I'll have some more...' She took some more. Katie was offered a spoon dripping with purple, ripe fruit. She tasted this. It tasted as it should, so she swallowed this. She pulled the shawl tight around and her and stretched her limbs out towards the rising sun. 'So, you will help me?'

'If I can.'

'That's good, Mum. Thanks for making time for us to have a little chat together, I really appreciate that.'

They looked deeply into each other's eyes. Despite her age, Katie saw that she was still a beautiful woman, despite the amateurish attempts at applying make-up. Maybe she needed a mirror? 'I met with Alain and we had a little chat, he...'

'My husband Alain?'

'Well, he used to be your husband Alain, but now he's...'

'He still is...'

'Still is? But you're separated? As husband and wife? Split up? Divorced? Aren't you?' She was going to need a mug of tea. She got up.

'Stay. Not as such...'

'What? That's...so you're still married to him. But, why Mum?' She sat down again.

'We never got around to the legal niceties, child.'

'Oh, well, in that case I met with your husband, Alain. All things considered, he's comfortable and he's being well looked after, but you need to go and see him very, very soon.'

'Cannock?'

'Yes, you can, but it will need to be very, very soon.' Maela nodded in such a way that Katie understood that she would do this somehow, someway.

'He would like a picture of you.'

'A photograph?'

'Yes, Mum, do you have one I could let him have?'

'No, I have no recent photograph but I have older ones...'

'I see, only older ones. Can I see what you've got?'

'Yes. Wait here, child.' Maela rose and glided into the trees towards a green painted caravan, which had solid rubber tyres on its rusty wheels.

'Daughter?' called out Maela.

'Yes, Mum?'

'Photographs, for my husband, Alain.' Maela sifted through the photographs. They were rolled up in a ridged, metal cylinder. She fingered a tattered logbook and then quickly pushed it back inside.

'What was that, Mum?'

'A diary of misdeeds carried out by your nana, a litany of warcrimes that means your promise is an abomination.'

'I don't need that right now...'

'You should read it...'

'I really can't be arsed...'

Maela secured a black and white picture, showing a line of coy looking women in swimsuits and presented it to Katie. At the front of the row was a blonde haired woman, in a one-piece leopard skin swimsuit, with one hand resting on her waist and the other holding a cigarette discretely, almost out of view.

'Oh, is this you Mum?'

Maela glanced over. 'Yes, child, that is me, at the start of the file.'

'You're not covered up Mum! I can't give Alain this - he'll have a heart attack!'

Maela just smiled. 'It's where I enchanted my husband to be, Rhyll beauty pageant.'

'Did you win?'

'Of course I won!'

'You look...sexy, Mum! Blimey, Mum, what happened?'

'Ah, children came...'

'Mum, that wasn't our fault. That was all down to you, wasn't it?'

'Then you came...and you shouldn't have done.' There were two haphazard streams of tears making their way down her face.

'I'm sorry about that Mum, but...there's a few things I need to cover with you.'

'Yes, child, but do you have an agenda?'

'No, but I do have a list and there are some big things that have floated to the top.'

'Ah, floated to the surface, as for a cess pit.'

'Yes, like a cess pit with lots of cess, which reminds me, before we get started, I just need...a sit down.'

'There is a place, follow the track up the hill and...'

'I'll take a shovel and a bucket with me. I may be some time.' She picked up a spade, put it over her shoulder, and a bucket of water and tramped uphill through the covering of faded bluebells until she could not see or hear anything of the encampment below. There was no sign of human endeavour around, just the singing of the larks above her and the mewing of a buzzard to the west. This would do nicely, she thought, and she started digging.

With a shovel over her shoulder and a pail in her hand Katie stomped back down the track, past the green caravan and the tethered mule and to where her mum was attending to the samovar. 'I'm gasping, Mum!' She sat down in the ungainly seat, relieved that she had performed her toilet. A mug of tea was placed in her hands and her planner was ready on her lap.

'Ebrill, I am ready...' said Maela.

'Good!'

'I've washed your trousers and hung them up to dry.'

'You shouldn't have done that...I was going to wear those again!'

'I'm sorry, I cannot undo what has been done.'

'But Mum, what do I wear now?'

'Water is such a precious resource, child.'

'Yes, isn't it?'

'So, we should give thanks to Gaia that the living water has made its home on this, the blue planet of the Sol system.'

'That's very interesting Mum, so what happened to the dead water?'

'Dead water cannot sustain life, child.'

'Oh, so we're lucky the living water landed here...'

'Yes, indeed, but man mistreats it, man poisons it...'

'And pisses in it...'

'Of course, but what kind of mother would I be if I sent you away in soiled clothes?'

Katie groaned. 'What am I going to wear?'

'Wear what you are wearing now!'

'This is underwear, not outerwear!'

'I have something, just wait.' Katie groaned. Maela was gone again.

She watched as her mum returned, in a swirl of brown taffeta, stepping nimbly over the shallow stumps and carrying a gown.

'Here' Maela said as the presented the garment. It had a strong odour of mothballs and colourful images of humans and animals performing together, as if in some kind of old time circus.

'Thanks Mum.'

'Put it on then!'

'I...don't think I like it.'

'Don't be silly! Put it on!'

Katie ducked inside the voluminous skirts and pulled her head and arms through the bodice. It was a little tight about the chest but floaty around her legs.

Her mum tapped out her pipe and refilled it. 'Oh, you look a delight!' she remarked with a wide smile.

'Thanks, Mum.' The pipe was lit and Maela was sucking deeply on it.

'What are those people doing?' Katie asked, pointing at her skirts.

'They're playing with their pets.'

'Why are they naked?'

'Pets look ridiculous in clothes.'

'I mean, why are the people naked?'

'It's the Rites of Spring, child.'

'Oh...'

And suddenly, her mum seemed very relaxed. 'Let me show you something. Stand!' Katie stood and opened out her arms as Maela stretched them towards the horizon. 'What can you see?'

'The same as before...'

'Try harder...'

'Oh! Green tram lines!'

'Good, these are energy lines. They are a source of power. They can be aligned and re-aligned, shaped and moved to your will.'

'Eh?'

'You will learn with practice.'

'Have you been taking drugs, Mum?' A puff of smoke prompted a minor fit of coughing on her part.

'Use your power to heal the world, child.'

'I don't know how, Mum, and there's an awful lot of it that needs healing.'

Maela dropped their hands. 'Yes, this blighted planet, there is much to do.'

'It's too much, Mum.'

'That is your destiny, child.'

'Hmm, but what if I decide that I really can't be arsed?'

'You will use your powers for the right reason. You will heal the world. You have a good soul, you are incapable of doing harm to another living creature. That's the way you were made.'

An image sprang into Katie's mind, an image of a lad, in his red devil football shirt, writhing between her legs, begging for her mercy.

'Ebrill!'

'Mum, it's not going to happen, it's too much...'

'You will do this child. Look what I have achieved here, in a few short months!'

'What, Mum?' Katie asked as she surveyed the wasteland of shattered wood and the rough stubble of tree stumps. 'What have you achieved here?'

'The evil, dark plantation of invaders has been taken down. The timber is being recycled into the local economy. See this plant? Gentian!'

'Yes, it's very pretty, Mum, considering it's just a weed.'

'It has a chance now. I clear away the work of the despoilers and Gaia takes over. I have healed this hill, I have created an island of hope.'

'Oh, is that what you've done? Well, a lot of people aren't happy about this. A lot of people say you should not have done this Mum. For them, you are the despoiler!'

'They are wrong! I am the healer!'

'Mum, there's an official sign at the bottom of the track! It's got big, red writing on it!'

'I know.'

'So, what are you doing about it?'

'Nothing - I put it there.'

'Really? Oh, Mum, am I going to end up like you?'

'Yes, if that is your destiny, child. You must remember that there is an infinite trail of happy, irreducible accidents that brought everything to this point in time, for all of us, everything that lives.' Maela sucked deeply on the stem of her pipe.

Katie considered what her destiny might be: Healer of the planet? Admiral of the Fleet? Royal Princess? Mad woman living in a wood? Yes, it was probably going to be the last one. And then it struck her, what would her dad have wanted? 'Have you decided who my dad is yet?'

'You know him.'

'Eh?' She picked up her diary and flicked to the project planning page. The pictograms in blue, red and green coalesced for a moment. 'No, I don't!'

'Now, what have we here' said Maela as she snatched up the diary, 'I think this has been dealt with!' A page was ripped out with a flourish.

'Mum! Give that back to me!'

'And this is rubbish!'

'Mum! No!'

Maela made strides to the shelter and kicked over the embers so they glowed. 'I think this is all nonsense - it should be burnt!' She placed the diary on top.

'You are such an idiot!' Katie kicked it off the fire and beat the smouldering out of it.

'No more questions, child, now we chill...'

'There's no time - start packing!'

'You have no right to order me about' challenged Maela.

'Why did you want me back, then?'

'I wanted to see if you were ready.'

'Ready for what?'

'Ready to fulfil your destiny - but you're not, you're still a child. You go away for many moons and you don't reply to my letters. You don't care about me!'

'I was away earning money. And I've given you a lot of it!'

'It's a pittance!'

'It's a small fortune to me! And what are you going to do with it? Waste it all on drugs?'

'Waste it? Certainly not! I will pass it on to those in greater need.'

'Greater need? That was a hundred pounds! I've put water systems into African villages - they've got fresh, clean water and sanitation. You haven't even got that! And you don't have anywhere to live!'

Maela pointed to the caravan with a wavy flourish.

'That doesn't count - it could roll away!'

'I just need my daughter to come back and care for me.'

'But you've got a home help and you haven't even got a home!'

'I can't talk to you when you've lost all reason.' Maela turned away but she had an afterthought. 'And you wonder why you haven't got a man!'

'You've got two weeks!' Katie shouted.

With that, Katie slung her pack over her shoulders and started to tramp down the rutted track. She reached the official sign and kicked it over. Breath hissed its way out of her lungs and she released it all in a piercing scream: 'Baaaaaaaaaaah!

A buzzard mewled in alarm above and circled attentively. 'Fair point' murmured Katie, 'I need something instead of sausages.'

Katie stumbled to a halt on the track and surveyed the area around her. It was a rabbit warren. She located a hole that was four strides away and whistled. A head and a pair of floppy ears appeared tentatively. Her fingers pinched the neck of the flop eared beast and squeezed slowly. The big, doe eyes closed as the animal subsided into an endless sleep. Katie looked again, another fresh digging, another willing accomplice and another doe rabbit to make a brace. She thrust the second body up in the air and taunted the buzzard; it mewled and circled overhead. You idiot, she thought, I have a brace of rabbits and you don't!

Chapter Forty-Six

Sunday 22 May 0747 - Return to Clun

Katie flagged down the bus for Clun and stepped on board. All the passengers seemed transfixed at the appearance of their new passenger joining from Kerry Hill. 'Bore da, driver!' she said.

'Hello lovely, where are you headed, the Middle Ages?' He seemed too young to have the responsibility to pilot a bus, but he had a senior colleague in attendance who seemed experienced in controlling omnibuses in border zones.

'Why do you say that?'

'Your clothes darling, who was the previous owner?'

Katie wondered what was the best way to handle this. There was no way that did not expose her to ridicule. 'My mum. Is there a problem with the way I'm dressed?' she asked. Katie looked down at her clothes and wondered what the issue was. 'Anyway, it's one to Clun.'

'Women were burnt at the stake for less...'

'For wearing a dress?'

'Ah, but it's the pictures, isn't it?'

'It's a pattern not pictures...'

'And is that livestock you've got in there?' His eyes signalled to the large pouch around her waist. She looked down and there was a lop ear protruding.

'No, it's dead stock.' She pushed the ear back in. Some of the passengers seemed agitated about this. 'You're not charging me for a brace of bunnies are you?' she commented as she handed over the exact money for the ticket.

'No lovely, just hang on tight, we're off.' The bus graunched into motion, bucking as it went.

Katie secured her rucksack in the luggage rack. 'So when do you take your driving test?' she asked, as she swayed forwards and then backwards. There was no answer. He was crouched over the steering wheel and struggling with the other controls. She shrugged, swayed down the centre of the bus and settled in a seat midway along. There were two lads opposite her. 'Alright?' she enquired.

'Have you lost your pointy hat?' sniggered the one sitting by the aisle.

'Oh? No, the bus driver's sitting on it, isn't he?' she replied.

'Haha! That explains the bumpy hill start then.'

'Either that, or he hasn't got a sodding clue...'

'Why not fly on your broomstick instead? Much quicker than a bus, isn't it?'

'I suppose it is, but what about the splinters getting up my jacksie?'

He thought about this for a moment. 'Haha! That does sound like a bus might be the way to go, doesn't it? I know, girly, why don't you come over here and sit yourself on my wand?'

'Oh, what's that then?'

'You know, my trouser wand!'

'That's really not helping. I know, why don't you get it out and wave it at me?'

He seemed reluctant to do this but then he unzipped his trousers and eased them down. She peered towards the region of his purple pants. 'Look, if it's got no more girth than a magician's wand, I'm going to have to say no sodding way.'

He inserted his hand inside his pants and tried awkwardly to rearrange himself. 'I don't think it's right that you brought dead animals on the bus' was his rather weak retort.

'Well, at least they're dead. What's up with your mate?' Katie replied, as she looked towards his companion who hadn't said anything so far and was still staring blankly out of the window. 'He's got a bit of the thousand yard stare going on, hasn't he?'

'He's not that keen on girls' he replied, 'specially the witchy ones.'

'I think that's just stupid. Tell your mate that girls aren't that keen on zombies either.'

'So, are you going to put them in a cauldron with some frogs legs?'

'The rabbits? No, I thought I would chew on them if I got a bit peckish.'

'That's gomping!'

'How?'

'You should cook them first' he replied indignantly.

'And that's what I'll do, after now' replied Katie.

'Haha, so you really are a witch?'

'You idiot!'

'I mean, you could put a spell on me?'

'A spell? I suppose I could. I could change you into a toad, couldn't I? Oh, look, someone's beaten me to it!'

Katie's arrival in the outskirts of Clun was quite awkward: she had trouble gathering up her skirts and getting past the seated passengers who were tutting and muttering comments. She had suggested that there should be a bus stop at the top of the hill but the crew were not having it. Katie stomped up the back lane and then the track and Clun Cottage came into view.

Eek was the first to see Katie and she turned excitedly and ran back into the house, screaming, 'Mama, Mama, it's Auntie Katie, she's come back as a witch!' Al emerged next, did something with his little device and guffawed at the result. 'Oh my god, Auntie Katie!' he exclaimed as he ducked back inside the house.

Katie marched up to the door and pushed her way inside. Gwen came down the stairs and stopped half way. She covered her mouth and tried desperately not to laugh. 'How's mother?' she spluttered.

'Mum's the same as always, if you must know, but now she's got a toy boy!'

'Ah, that must be Dafyd, how did you get on?'

'He's an idiot. He thinks he's her home help! How ridiculous is that?'

'Of course, but Katie, have you joined the Sisterhood? Have you gone all Wiccan on us?'

'Mum washed my sodding denims, didn't she?' Katie walked quickly into the kitchen. Gwen scampered down the rest of the stairs, clutching her gown around her waist and stumbling on her fluffy pink slippers.

'So, are you still all right about making lunch, Katie? Will it be bat's wings and eye of toad?' she asked.

Katie slapped two rabbits heavily on the kitchen counter. 'Rabbit stew' she announced.

Gwen looked as if she was about to throw up.

'Gwen, for someone who is a vet, you're very squeamish around dead animals, aren't you?'

'Most of my patients are alive when I get to them. Oh, that reminds me Katie, do you happen to know how an owl came to be flying around the kitchen yesterday morning?'

'Oh, that? I used the kitchen as a field hospital, Gwen.'

'That's not very hygienic, Katie.'

'It was an emergency Gwen - this is the sort of stuff that happens in an emergency!'

'Did you do the deed yourself?'

'Yes, of course I did.' She looked at Gwen's tousled hair, her flushed cheeks, her exposed legs and the pink bunny rabbit slippers. 'You look very pleased with yourself Gwen?'

'I'm just so pleased you got back safely, Katie.'

'Piss off Gwen' Katie said as she studied the face of her sister, 'you and I both know, you've got that just shagged look, haven't you?'

'You've got such a way with words, Katie!' The flush on Gwen's cheeks spread instantaneously across her face. She clutched her wrap even tighter. 'He's shaved, he's canned the cigarillos and cut back on the whisky. He's started talking about the farm as a business again and what we can do to get it back on track.'

Katie filled the kettle with water and put it on the stove to boil. Next, she took a large pan, threw in some butter and warmed it on a low flame. 'I'll just put the cauldron on shall I? And yes, I'm in charge. I'll bring you both a mug of tea in a few minutes. And I'm very pleased for you and Mister Hofland.'

Gwen leaned on the pantry door. She had a slight frown on her face and seemed puzzled. 'What have you been talking about with Stefan?'

'We just talked about how to turn things around, didn't we?' Katie fed tea into the teapot. 'You look very happy, Gwen.'

Gwen swayed her hips and thighs, like she was dancing with her partner. 'I'm so happy today. I'm going to go back to bed with my husband. I know, why don't you join us?'

'Join you? Please Gwen, not even in jest. I don't know what you're pumped full of, but it will wear off sometime and you'll realise it's the worst idea ever. Remember, I work for the government, which is basically a bad idea generator. I know a bad idea when I hear one. In the Andrew, we suffer from a lot of badly thought out ideas...'

'Katie, Katie, I meant why don't you come with us to church?'

'Church? Oh, I see. Well, I don't think so, Gwen. I need to get on...'

'It's a great opportunity to socialise, meet folk and have intercourse in a friendly and supportive environment. So, why not Katie?'

'One of us should be more than enough for anyone on this planet, so no thanks Gwen. Tell him not to be so greedy!'

'Church Katie, church!'

'Oh, but that's what I meant. The vicar should not be so greedy, I'm not one of his flock, am I?'

'But Katie? Why not? You would have to change your dress though. The Church of England is a broad church but even they're not keen on...satanic orgies and bestiality.'

'Listen Gwen, I'll keep an eye on things here and have it ready for when you get back - it'll be about one o'clock. Shouldn't you be getting ready for church?'

'We've got plenty of time. I know, let me find you a more demure dress and maybe you will reconsider. I'll go back upstairs and find you something...'

'Gwen, please don't...' Katie said. She considered what could possibly go wrong. So much! Katie sloshed boiling water into the teapot. She then slashed the skin of a rabbit and ripped the pelt off. 'I wonder if I can make something out of this? Are you still here, Gwen?'

Gwen gulped again, turned and headed back upstairs. The rabbit was now in quarters. She started on the next one. As Eek entered the kitchen, Katie quickly hid it under a plate. 'Yes, Eek?' It was too late, she had seen the bodies but inexplicably, had not reacted to the sight of naked animal muscle.

'Can I help?'

'Are you any good at butchering small animals, Eek?'

'No! Why would I be?'

'It was just a thought. How about you...er...peel some carrots and potatoes then?'

'That doesn't sound like fun.'

'It's not, but it is necessary. So, how about it?'

'Mama and Papa have been in bed all morning.'

'Yes, they're playing mummies and daddies. It's quite normal, Eek. Tell you what, why don't you pull me an onion?'

'An onion?' How do I pull an onion?'

'Yes, it'll be in the kitchen garden. It'll have long shiny green lives and have a big white bulb sat in the soil. Grab it by the leaves and pull it away from the soil.'

'All right Katie.' Monique shuffled out of the kitchen, on the look out for long shiny green leaves in the near distance. She returned with an offering.

'That's a radish, Eek.'

The Hoflands walked to the church that late morning with a leading rank of Katie, Eek and Al and Stefan and Gwen Hofland following. Eek constantly chided Katie about the pink floral dress she was wearing, secured by a narrow, red leather belt. Her hair was constrained by a leather collar, inscribed with symbols, that was in turn secured by a bone pin. When Gwen had asked about it, Katie explained it was her hair loom. Katie's shoes were flat but eminently suitable for the walk down the cobbled track, that led to the narrow, sun dappled lane, that in turn led to the church.

'The Tricketts have come up trumps! They will loan us their tractor next week!' called out Mister Hofland.

'That's wonderful, sir. We just need to find someone who can drive one!' replied Katie.

'You cheeky young madam!'

'Oh sir, I thought you had retired from work! I thought you were a gentleman farmer now!'

'Did you hear that Gwen! What a cheek!'

Katie skipped ahead of the others and turned to face them. 'Who can do a cartwheel?' she shouted, defiantly. 'Diddly, diddly, diddly, diddloo!'

'Katie, decorum please' cautioned Gwen, 'you're not on an assault course now!'

'Is that a challenge, Gwen? Can you do one? Diddly, diddly, diddly, diddloo!'

'No, and neither should you...'

'Let me show you a forward somersault!' She balanced her hands on the shoulders of Al and Eek and tumbled over so she landed on her feet. Her arms stretched to the sky in triumph.

'We could see your knickers, Auntie Katie!' exclaimed Eek.

'No, you couldn't.'

'Why not?'

'Because...I'm not wearing any! Diddly, diddly, diddly, diddloo!'

'Auntie Katie, no!'

'You're not sitting on a church pew without any knickers on!'

'Yes, I am!'

'No, you're not!'

'Ah, I've got something better on.' She flipped up her dress up so everyone could see what she was wearing. 'Running shorts!' she said triumphantly.

'Sometimes Katie, you take modesty to absurd levels.'

'I'm worried about splinters, aren't I?'

'Ah, the passion killers!' commented Gwen.

'I had to wear them for cross country. I really hated that! My legs were the colour of beetroots by the end!'

'Still doing good service then!'

'Can't beat 'em! Certainly got all the boys hot under the collar! It's got Al all hot and bothered too, hasn't it Al?'

'Shut up Auntie Katie!'

Katie saw that Al was now dragging his feet and had fallen behind, meandering along and studying the contents of the ditch along the right side of the track. She dropped back so she could walk alongside him. She nudged him in the ribs. 'You all right Al?'

'It's Lexa!'

'Anyway, you didn't see anything you shouldn't have done, did you Al?'

His lips tightened and his cheeks were scarlet. 'No, of course not. I wasn't looking' he mumbled.

'Just as well, they're a bit snug.'

There was a long pause as he processed this information. 'What are you on about?'

'So, you were looking!'

'No, I was not!'

She stroked a strand of hair back behind her left ear and perched her right hand provocatively on her hip. 'Anyway, what do you think, Al? Am I a bit of a honey?'

'No, you're not!'

'Ooh, well my hair's the colour of honey, isn't it Al? Do you not like it?'

'It's brown!'

'It's not brown, it's the colour of honey, dark honey.'

'It's brown!'

'Dark honey hair, that's what I've got...'

'Only if it's honey made by African killer bees!'

'Oi! Don't be rude! Anyway, killer bees don't make honey, do they? They eat other stuff like...nice bees.'

'That's you, that is. Made by killer bees...'

'You're wrong Al, I'm made by lovely, friendly, honey gathering bees.'

'Killer bees...'

'Wrong, wrong, wrong, wrong and wrong again...'

'Why do you do it?'

'Why do I do what? Somersaults? Because I can, can't I?'

She studied the side of his face carefully. There was a growing bloom of scarlet in the middle of his cheek that was spreading. 'So, what do you really think Al? Do you like me in my dress, Al?'

'It's not your dress, its Mama's!'

'Go on Al, what do you reckon?' She took a couple of long strides forward, with her right hand cradling her waist and her head swaying. Diddly, diddly, diddly, diddloo!'

'Just shut up, Auntie Katie!'

'Do you prefer to see me in my knickers then, Al?'

'Shut...up...Auntie Katie!'

'Because a little bird tells me...'

'It's a lie!'

'You have pictures of me in my knickers...'

'Shut up!' he hissed.

'Oh, so you have. Oh, have I touched a nerve? Well, as you can imagine...'

'Shut up!'

'...I feel a little bit uncomfortable about this.'

'Shut up!'

'Because basically it's not nice, I'm your Auntie. But if you really want pictures of your female relations in their pants, I think I can help you. So I'm going to write a little letter to your Dutch aunties...'

'Please, no, Auntie Katie!'

'It's going to say, their nephew in England, Al, is going through a bit of a dirty phase where he has dreams about his female relatives in their pants and would they send some photos that could help him out.'

'Auntie Katie, this is blackmail!' There were tears welling up in his eyes. Was he sorry or was he frightened? Katie couldn't tell just yet so she turned the screw a little tighter. 'They're big ladies and I hear the Dutch are quite relaxed about that sort of thing, so I think you could be in luck.'

'No, please no, Auntie Katie!'

'So, I'm going to say, just send them in a big envelope, marked 'DO NOT BEND', but I wanted to run it past Mister Hofland first...'

'No, Katie, please...'

'Because I wasn't sure how any 'esses' there are in tosser!'

'I'll do anything, please...'

'Right then, we will sit down after dinner and go through all the smut on your computer and delete all my pictures and any other stuff I decide is dodgy. Then you will write a little letter to my friend, Megan...'

'You little bitch!'

'Oi, Al, that's not nice! Well, if you're going to be like that, I have a whole set of words for you, starting with wan...'

'Alright, alright, you win!'

'So you'll do as I ask?'

'Yes, yes, yes, just don't...wait, you don't have any letter, do you?'

'Why would you say that, Al?' She drew out a folded piece of foolscap from her dress pocket and waved it at him. He could probably see enough of her large, awkward writing to know that it was ready for proof-reading. She gave him a nudge in the ribs just to let him know it was their secret. Well, theirs and Eek's secret.

They were now led on by the dull clodding of the iron bells, calling them to the cold altar in the isolated church that sat coldly above the village. Al was strangely silent, deep in his own thoughts. She turned every few paces and gave what she thought was a warm, comforting smile.

And then the smile disappeared to be replaced by a frown. 'Oh no, they're expecting me!' She grabbed Al's hand and brought it over her chest. 'Can you smell what they've put out for me?'

'Smell what?' He pulled his hand away.

'Al! The stinky flowers! They don't want me in, do they!'

'What are you on about?'

The single, solitary cloud in the sky chose that moment to blot out the sun. 'Gwen, Gwen, I'm going back home. This doesn't feel right!'

'Don't be silly, Katie!'

Soon they were alongside other folk heading to the same place of worship. Outside the church, the vicar was waiting for her, with a broad, but insincere smile. Her vicar. The one who had opened her eyes to the possibility of a soul. Her soul.

'And who have we here?' he asked Gwen Hofland as they approached in a tight phalanx through the roughly tended graveyard.

'It's my sister, Katie Talog. You remember Katie, don't you vicar? She's just back from a very long tour with the Royal Navy' answered Gwen.

'That's wonderful! Wonderful! Miss Talog? We're always delighted to welcome our serving members of the armed forces, unless of course...'

'Actually, I'm a little bit worried about going inside' murmured Katie quietly to Gwen. She coughed and then took a red gingham handkerchief from her dress pocket and covered her nose and mouth.

'And that is quite understandable, Miss Talog!' replied the vicar.

There were two women on their toes, scowling at her, dressed darkly, as if they were attending a funeral. Maybe my funeral, thought Katie. As the Hoflands passed, they nipped Katie out with neat precision and pushed her away from the aisle and back to the inner stairway to the tower. At the foot of the stairway was a door that led to a small, dark room. Katie was bundled in, and she was in this dark space alone. Or so she thought, but there was a gleaming white collar a few paces away. 'Hallo' she asked out tentatively, 'is there anyone there?'

There was someone else in this space. Her left arm twitched and reached out to a bakelite mounting on the stone wall and a thin, insipid light filled the space. There was a seated sour-faced woman, with a page boy haircut that was both severe and ridiculous at the same time. 'Oh, verger! I didn't see you there!' Her hands were clasped in her lap as if she was pushing something down below her cassock.

'Why have you come here?'

'Your minions brought me in here, didn't they?

'His worship will be here shortly. He will speak with you.'

'I see. What does he want with me? Am I going to miss the first number?'

'Just wait a moment, he will be here.'

'Is this because I'm marked? Because I had nothing to do with that. That was you.' There seemed to be a moment of recognition from the verger and then this was replaced by a mask of pale impassivity.

'You must not enter this church, surely you realise that? Heks!'

'Well, no, I don't. I'm here with my family and you've...'

She heard the footfalls of her escorts quickly returning to the task of handing out prayer books and hymn sheets.

'Take a seat, take a seat, I'll be with you shortly' she heard the vicar cooing to the congregation, 'I have a small, parish matter to deal with.' She heard him stride rapidly towards the back of the church, and she imagined his cassock swirling about him. There was a moment of expectant silence in the church. Katie heard Eek ask plaintively, 'Mama, what's happened to Auntie Katie?'

Gwen replied 'I don't know! Take a pew, let me see if I can find her...'

'Ah, Miss Talog, Miss Talog, Miss Talog!' the Vicar said as he breezed in through the door. 'Please take a seat!'

'Hallo Vicar.' She offered her hand to the Vicar but after a moment, when she thought he might spit on it, she pulled it back. Looking behind her there was just a child's chair available. She tried to ease herself into it, but it was too stiff, too small, too upright.

'Please, my correct title is Reverend Doctor Timothy Trimble.'

'Oh, yes, that's a nice, distinguished title, Vic.'

He sat down in an upright, fabric adorned chair opposite her, which allowed his long legs and his long thin body to slouch. 'This is a most unpleasant surprise. I was thinking that nothing could besmirch this most wonderful of spring days but I hadn't reckoned on this.'

'What's the matter, Vic?'

'We are blighted by your presence, Miss Talog.'

'That's very rude of you, Vic!'

He flirted with his cassock and then came to the point. 'Miss Talog, what in the name of all that's holy would make you think you would be welcome in this house?'

'Well, Vic, I saw a sign outside the church and it says all are welcome, so I thought, that must include me! What's the problem?'

'I see, I see, I see' he interrupted.

'That is not an invitation for Satan or his followers, or the godless...' snapped the verger.

'Listen, I can help you sort this out. Satan does not exist, therefore, I cannot be one of his followers, can I? And by the way, I have loads of gods, thank you very much!'

'Blasphemer! You worship false idols, you take...' cried the Verger.

'That's bollocks!'

'Satan is here!'

'There is no Satan, you ignorant crone!'

The verger paused for breath: the vicar paused for thought. Katie noted that his gleaming, wavy brown hair looked like a thick, wet, brown shammy that had been dropped randomly on his scalp. 'I think we may need to tweak that wording a little - clearly our invitation does not extend to you and your kind, who never want to commit...'

'My kind? Listen Vic, I'm not your enemy!'

'All of you heathen, enemies of the good work we try to do here. In times gone by there would be a moat and a drawbridge, a row of archers and spearmen along the battlements.'

'Why?'

'To keep your kind out. Now we have to use other means to keep you away...'

'You mean the stinky flowers?'

'The lilies? Ah, a medieval contrivance, but surprisingly effective.' His eyes wandered over the outline of her torso as he seemed to search for the right words. 'All this time, your whole female line, warring with our Church for millennia... and now you as well! Maela's daughter!'

'And what am I supposed to have done?'

'Ah, ah, please let me educate you.'

'Oi you, I'm a matelot and I've been educated in stuff that'll make all your hairs stand on end!'

There was an urgent knock on the old, oak door. 'Katie, are you in there?'

'Yes, Gwen, I'm with the vicar' replied Katie.

'Ah, hello vicar. Why have you got our Katie in there?'

'Gwen, I can't go back in, it's the flowers...'

'What about them! They're just flowers!'

'They'll make me sneeze!'

'So what if they make you sneeze?'

'They'll make me sneeze blood, Gwen!'

'Oh, yes of course...'

'Mrs Hofland? Please be so kind as to return to your pew' prompted the Vicar.

'Please tell me what you're doing with our Katie? Please?'

'I'm giving your sister some instruction, so she can see the error of her ways. I can't conceive of any reason why you would bring her to this house.'

'Please Vicar, she's my sister. She should be with us!'

'Please Mrs Hofland, return to your seat.'

And now it was the turn of the head of the snatch squad. 'Vicar, we are ready for you?'

'Yes, yes, please start without me. I must deal with this errant child. I'll be with you as soon as I can...'

There was a pause and then the clacking of Sunday best shoes back to the pews.

'Ah, now where were we?'

'Yes Vic, your church has been at war for hundreds of years...'

'Ah, yes. What nonsense!' He folded his hands to make a steeple and perched his chin on top.

'It's been at war with itself and with women, hasn't it?' stated Katie.

'Please, please, do enlighten me Miss Talog. Why would you think that?'

'Vic, please call me Katie.'

'Of course, Katie.'

'Well, it's divided and it doesn't really know where it's going and it doesn't like women, does it?'

'That's a very simplistic and naive view, so typical of a child...'

'Oi, I'm not a child! I'm a servant of the government, I serve the people! I've just done a thirteen month tour keeping you lot safe!'

'You have the ideas of a child. The church is making great strides across the globe.'

'No, it isn't!'

'Pray, enlighten me?'

'So, where is the big bloke, then?'

'Do you mean our Father?'

'Our Father?'

'Yahweh.'

'Bless you!'

'I did wonder when the profanity would start. Right on cue!'

'Christians are fighting Muslims who are fighting Jews! They all have the same god! How stupid is that!'

'And there it is again. You seem to be believe you are something of an expert?'

'No Vic, I'm no expert, but I have worked there. I've seen the problems with my own eyes...'

'We do have challenges, it's true - global challenges and so much strife.'

'So what is your god doing about it?'

'Our Father? Our Father is at work...'

'Is he? What's he done? He's done nothing!'

'Stop the profanity now!'

'Show me what he's done!'

'He works in such subtle and mysterious ways that a child could not possibly comprehend.'

'I'm not a child! I've seen all the shit first hand! I've seen children's bodies, starving, filthy, dying of thirst!'

'That's quite enough. Remember where you are! And you have the solution to all this?'

Katie's mind chased about to work out what she could say: 'No, I don't, but there are two villages which didn't have clean water six months ago, and now they do!'

'And pray, who is responsible for this miracle?'

'It's not a miracle Vic, it's engineers and artificers and a helicopter and my team. There, that's what I've done. I've earned the right to be here!'

'It's God's work, you poor, deluded girl, he works through us. Can you not see that?'

'All right, so I've done his work for him and I deserve to be here!' she concluded triumphantly.

'You believe that tips the scales in your favour?'

'Yes it does, you ignorant twat, so why don't you piss off back to yodel-land?'

There was an urgent tapping at the door and it was pushed ajar. 'Vicar, it's Mrs Hofland, what are you doing with our Katie?' Gwen eased her way into the room and stood next to the vicar.

'Ah, Mrs Hofland, just in time to hear the catalogue of crimes committed by your sister' muttered the verger. She drew out a notebook with both hands and this had a series of bulleted notes down the open page. 'Mrs Hofland, your timing is impeccable. Are we all ready? Let me begin.'

'Katell Ebrill Talog...'

'I don't need to listen to this bollocks...'

'First, you assaulted the girl Megan and stole her dog.'

'Owain is my dog! She stole him!'

'Secondly, you caused an affray at the pub in Clun and assaulted the boy Benjamin Tricketts...'

'No, I didn't. What's a fray anyway?'

'Thirdly, you assaulted the boy Christopher Lunt.'

'No, I didn't! It was a rugby match! And he was playing like an idiot!'

'Fourthly, you caused an affray in Ludlow market...'

'What's all this a fray business, anyway?

'...by destroying the wares of Miss Sarah Pagan...'

'They're not wares, they're a pile of crap!'

'They were of value...'

'Only if you're an idiot! None of them are worth a sheep's fart!'

'They were of considerable value to Miss Pagan...'

'She's a sodding witch!'

'And the flames still burn on Kerry Hill...'

'That's not me! What is this? Trial by idiots? Don't I get to defend myself?'

'No, Miss Talog. The catalogue of misdemeanours speaks for itself. You've been here less than a week and you have brought a wave of crime to the district!'

'That's bollocks. If I am a one woman crime wave, ring the police and do it now!'

'And your garb this morning was obscene.'

'Your face is obscene, you graveyard whore!'

'Quite obscene.'

'Exactly! And that's all you've got, that's utterly pathetic!'

'Katie, Katie, calm down, please remember where you are!' soothed Gwen.

'Back to family matters, Miss Talog...'

'Yes?'

'Your mother?'

'She's fine. She doesn't send her kind regards, by the way.'

'Too busy despoiling the countryside?'

'No, no, she's actually liberating it. Go and see!'

'I don't follow...'

'She's returning it to how it should be.'

'She's burning down a forest!'

'Yes, but it's a forest planted by filthy rich bastards who couldn't give a flying fuck about anybody else!'

'I'd remind you where you are!'

'Oh, yes, in church, and by the way, they've started without you.'

Through the oak door were the first strains of a hymn. His spectacles twitched on the end of his nose; a bulbous nose with tiny purple veins which came into sharp relief when he was getting angry. Like now.

'Hmm, hmm, hmm. Your mother is an enemy of the church, as was her mother before her...'

'Ah, but Gwen and I share the same mum, don't we, so nah!'

'Gwen's father, was a fine upstanding citizen of the parish as is his daughter and her husband, fine citizens of this parish. Now, what about your father?'

Katie realised she could only guess the answer to this question. 'He wasn't?'

'Um, your conception...was not entirely...natural.'

'So, tell me what you know. What was so...unnatural about my conscription?'

'I would rather not say.'

'So, what is he supposed to have done?'

'It's... his character and his morals and what he represents.'

'But, I do good things, don't I?'

'Really, Miss Talog?'

'Yes, I do. I've done so many good things up and down the east coast of Africa, all the people think I'm a missionary! Who else can say that in Clun?'

'You are not to return to this house.'

'Listen, if there is someone or something causing you trouble, just say. Maybe I can deal with it. I know people, who know people who know other people that have special skill sets that not many other people have!'

'What?'

'Is this about spells and witches?'

'Enough!'

'I can help you. Lose your god, then there are no more religious wars, no Satan and all his little followers will have nothing to follow!'

'Blasphemer!'

'Wicked girl!'

'Centuries of enlightenment, art, music, destroyed in an instant. You wicked, irresponsible child!' said the vicar.

'Wicked, wicked!' said the verger.

'Take it to the council, tell them to talk about it!'

'The General Synod?'

'Katie, you've gone too far!' muttered Gwen.

'Evil, evil child!'

'And I'll tell you what to say...' continued Katie.

'MISS TALOG. SILENCE!' roared the vicar. 'SILENCE!'

There was silence throughout the church as the hymn was halted mid-verse. The blaring of the organ tailed away into a low, tuneless monotone.

'Look at me. Consider your next utterance very carefully.' He peered over Katie's right shoulder, upwards to the stone, cold ceiling and then back to her. 'Look at me and listen, child.'

And there was that word 'child' again. She gazed into his bespectacled eyes and tried to get inside the front orbit of his head. 'What'll you do to me?'

There was such a silence that she could hear three sets of breathing and three sets of pumping hearts. She sat back with a gasp, her own heart pulsing madly and her left arm trembling.

'You'll damn my bones!' she laughed nervously. She saw a body, eviscerated, empty, and smouldering, with blackened ribs and sinewy tendons; a body that used to have breasts and a broad opening in the pelvis, now broken; the body of a girl.

'Oh, my soul, you'll damn my bones!' As the walls of the room turned around her, time jumped forward and in the passing of the seasons, pieces of bone fell away from the cadaver, clattering away in the bitter wind that swept the cold ground.

'You call yourself Christians but you will happily damn my bones!' she cried.

Katie got up, turned away from her accusers, shook at the large metal latch to the darkened doorway leading to the graveyard. The Reverend Doctor Timothy Trimble arose and inserted a key from his waist in the lock and turned it to release her. She pushed hard and stumbled into the light, towards the postern gate, through it and out into the lane. Someone was following her. Katie hid behind the wall and gasped for breath. The air was sweet and wholesome and free of the smell of death. When she felt it was safe, she carefully looked back to the church tower. The vicar saw her, smiled grimly, pulled the door closed and locked it with well practised ease.

Katie felt confident enough to look back towards the church - a figure in black was crouched behind the wall, looking at her. Katie jumped back and landed on her haunches. It was a soft, admonishing voice, calling for her.

'Sit here with me. It is Katell, isn't it' said the voice, 'Katell of the Britanni?'

'Yes, it is' Katie replied hesitantly, from behind the wall, 'but who are you then, graveyard whore? Are you in with the witches of the Elenydd?'

'Katell, it's not a Christian name is it? What manner of name is that?'

'It's my given name! The name my nain gave me!'

'Oh dear. It's not a Christian name is it? It's a pagan name, the name of a godless one.'

'I am not godless! I have gods!'

'And that's the problem, isn't it? You worship false gods, gods from the dark ages of man, gods that need blood sacrifice and arcane ceremonials - are those your gods Katell?'

'No!' She rose carefully, took three stumbling steps into the road and looked behind her. The verger stood at the postern but in the furthest reaches of the churchyard there was a boy she recognised, but not as a gardener of gravestones, but as a Somali boy, in white tee-shirt and denim dungarees slipping from her grasp above the sinking boat and disappearing below the troubled sea. There was no possibility in this life that he could be standing in this Clun churchyard and staring open mouthed at her - unless he was a ghost!

'Get away!' She wasn't sure what she was running from, but it must be away from this accursed place.

Chapter Forty-Seven

Monday 23 May 1035 - Clun Cottage

'Have you got any Tits, Eek?' asked Katie. She threw open all the cupboard doors that she could reach, all seven of them.

'What was that Auntie Katie?' asked Monique. She looked down the inside of her vest. 'No, not really, they're just starting to bud...'

'No, not breasts. Have you got any Tits? Tomatoes in Tins? Have you got any...?' Her voice tailed away. 'Some?'

Monique tucked her vest back into her skirt. 'Yes, you'll have to go downstairs, into the cellar.'

'Why don't you go and get me two tins?'

'I don't want to, it's dark down there.'

'It would really help me...'

'I know, but it's dark and creepy. I'm not going on my own.'

Katie switched off the hob and pushed away the pan of spitting onions. Monique was uncomfortably close now, gazing into her eyes. 'Let's go together then. I'll just get the key.'

'It's in the key safe.'

'Why?'

'So it's safe.'

Katie favoured Eek with her special, bemused look. 'These must be really special tits then.'

'There's been break-ins all along the valley...'

'When?'

'...since the last time you were here.'

'Oh, I see. Is that why there is a big shortage of tits about here?' Katie then thought about her recent visit to the pub in the village. 'Actually, no.'

'Follow me Auntie Katie.' She followed Eek to the main bedroom where they both insinuated their way amongst the rail adorned with so many dresses and kicked their way through so many pairs of shoes. Behind a panel at the back of the wardrobe was a metal hatch. Eek quickly tapped in the combination. The door flung open and Katie could see that the back of the safe was adorned with a range of different shapes and sizes of key. A set of four keys was procured. Eek continued to search inside the void of the safe. 'This is the interesting one...'

'Do we need it Eek?' She shook her head and pretended to put it back. Katie pretended not to notice. 'Let's get out of here, this is making me feel uncomfortable' whispered Katie. 'All this trouble for tinned tomatoes!'

'That's not all there is in the cellar Katie, there's other stuff as well. That's why we need all the keys.'

'I can't imagine why you would have anything worth nicking down there.'

Eek gave Katie a scathing look and then skipped out of the wardrobe, out of the bedroom and down the stairs and out of the back door. She handed a key ceremoniously to her auntie. 'There you are!'

They were through the first door and descending into the cool space below the cottage. There was another locked door. Katie opened this and they were in a large, lightless space. 'Where's the light, Eek?'

'There isn't one. You need a flashlight.'

'Did you bring one?'

'No, you didn't say to!'

'This is ridiculous.' Katie closed her eyes and gradually revealed them again. There was a box of matches on the old dining table to her right. She opened the box and struck one. It went out immediately. She struck another and this time it fizzed into life. There was a candle holder on a table, and a candle. She lit the candle and pulled a face at Eek in its orange glow. There was a cage at the back of the cellar and inside the cage were shelves stacked with tins, with packages suspended from the hooks on the ceiling. To one side there was what appeared to be a very large walk-in refrigerator. Eek was there first. She tapped in a six digit combination code, used yet another key to open the door and went inside. Katie stepped through quickly and pulled her out. 'Eek, no, we shouldn't be in here.' Eek had a bottle in her hand.

'We could have this with our tea?'

'No Eek, that's stealing. Put it back.'

'No, it's not. We do this all the time.'

'You drink wine? That's not right, you're too young! It'll rot your little brain. Put it back, now!'

'Look Auntie Katie, look at the name on the label' she called out excitedly, 'it's got trash in it! It can't be worth much!'

'Eh?'

'Montrachet!'

'You don't spell trash like that, do you Eek? That looks really old and pricey to me?'

'Look Katie, it's a Grand Cru, that means it's good!'

'Hmm, they've just dropped the 'd' off the end!'

'I'm definitely taking it then!' said Eek.

Katie felt her way to the cage and looked through the wire mesh. Monique handed her another key and Katie unlocked the padlock. She quickly located two tins of tinned tomatoes and retraced her steps. She quickly re-secured the padlock to the cage and closed the door of the wine store.

In the last guttering of the candle, Katie noticed a low cage and inside the cage, a metal ring bolted to the stone floor and a dog bowl. 'Oh my soul, you didn't keep Owain down here did you?'

'Yes, only when he was bad, and he was bad all the time!'

'That's not right, Eek, that's not right. How would you feel if you were kept down here in the dark?'

Monique shrugged and then her eyes moistened. 'I would hate it, but I'm not a dog, am I?'

'Let's get out of here. This place gives me the creeps, doesn't it you?'

Al and Eek sat quietly at the table as Katie presented a large bowl containing an orange coloured sauce with chunks of sausage, potato and green beans floating in it.

'What's this?' asked Al scathingly.

'It's called sausage fandango, and me and Auntie Katie have spent hours preparing this for you, haven't we Auntie Katie?' replied Eek. She took a long slurp from her glass and sloshed it around her mouth.

'Yes, we have Eek, and if I had realised how difficult it was going to be...I probably shouldn't have bothered, should I?'

'So, why's it called a sausage fandango, Auntie Katie?'

'Because, it's got sausage in it' replied Katie.

'And why is it a fandango, Katie?'

'Well obviously, it's vibrant with vegetables and it dances on your tongue, doesn't it?' Katie placed a tray of warm bread rolls on the table alongside the sausage and tomato stew. 'There you go, bon appetit!'

'I can't eat this' complained Al, 'it's all muddled up!'

'Well, you're going to have to, because that's all there is.'

'I can't eat this...'

'Just shovel it down your gullet, Al, or else...'

'Auntie Katie, no!' called out Eek. She emptied her glass.

'Or else, what?' challenged Al.

'Or, I'll shove it down your gullet for you...'

'I'd like to see you try...' said Al.

'Oh, I bet you would' replied Katie.

'What's that supposed to mean?'

'I think you would really like that' said Katie, 'because you would really get off on it, wouldn't you?'

'I don't have to put up with this. You can't make me, you're only just older than me!'

'Two years older, and I've been out in the big, bad world and I've survived. I'm working, I've got a career and what have you got?'

'My dignity!'

'No, you bloody haven't...'

'Auntie Katie!'

At this Alexander got to his feet, picked up a baguette and strode up the stairs, two at a time until he stumbled at the top. Katie heard him curse and then stumble into his bedroom and slam the door.

'I'll check up on him when we've finished. He's a bit stroppy, isn't he?'

'It's the food Auntie Katie, it's a bit shit isn't it?'

'It's not a bit shit, it's good scran, so get it eaten or...'

'You'll shove it down my gullet?'

'You'll have to go hungry...'

Eek spooned out one spoonful and carefully put a morsel in her mouth. 'It's just about edible' she commented.

'Thanks Eek.' They spooned the stew about and munched on bread in silence.

'We need some more wine to help wash it down.'

'No, we don't, Eek. Wait a minute, what d'you mean more wine?'

'Go on Auntie Katie. It'll finish it off really nicely!'

'No, you're too young. It'll rot your little brain away.'

'No, it doesn't. Mama drinks it all the time.'

'Well, she's a grown up and she doesn't have any need for brains any more. But you're young and your little brain is still growing, isn't it?'

'All my friends drink wine and cider.'

'I don't think you should be drinking wine - not at your age.'

'Mmm, this Grand Crud is nice.'

'Eh?'

'Can I have a friend around, Auntie Katie?'

'No, Gwen didn't say anything about that, did she?'

'Mama said it was all right. Marcie is around here all the time.'

There was a tentative knock at the door. Katie ignored it. The knock was repeated, more loudly and more insistently than before.

'Marcie?' asked Katie.

'Could be' replied Monique.

Katie got up, walked across the kitchen and observed that there were two young people at the door. She opened the door to reveal a girl with long, curly flaxen hair. Her companion was brown haired and heavily freckled. They both clutched carrier bags to their chests. 'Hallo girls, are you collecting for charity?'

'No, we've come for Monique' they chimed in unison.

Katie sighed deeply in such a way as to convey her irritation. 'Well, she's not going out.'

'That's alright. Can we come in?'

'All right, one of you is Marcie, right?'

'Yes, that's me' said the flaxen haired girl. 'And I'm Rosaline' said the freckled girl.

Katie considered her options. Her preference was to send them packing. Maybe they would keep Eek occupied so she didn't need to follow her everywhere. This could be a blessing, she thought. She still needed to clear up, or could she get Al to help? Loud music with a thumping beat started to reverberate around the cottage. Maybe not. 'You'd better come in then, Eek's just here...' This prompted a bout of giggling.

They smiled in glee when they saw Monique and started their starling-like babble immediately. Katie headed upstairs to curtail Al's noise. She had a peace offering.

Katie knocked loudly at Al's bedroom door, balancing a loaded tray with her other arm. After what seemed like an eternity and a lot of scrambling inside, the door was peeled back. She looked inside tentatively. The volume of the music came down to a bearable level. 'Are you okay Al? I've come to apologise, I shouldn't have said what I said, it was a bit harsh, wasn't it?'

He seemed agitated and uncertain about what to do. He cast his eyes around the room as it he was searching for something incriminating. 'You can't come in Katie...'

'Don't be silly Al, let me in or this sausage fandango will end up all over the carpet.' He stepped back from the door to let her in. She placed the tray on his desk and unfurled a serviette. 'I think you should have something to eat mate, and I need to get away from Eek's friends.' The fandango was in two white bowls, the beans neatly separated in a pile and the bread, crusty and white.

He smiled weakly and sat back down on the bed. He took the cruet that Katie had brought up and seasoned the food in and around the herbs that had been scattered across the bowl of stew. She did the same with her bowl. She offered him half a baguette. They both sat on his bed and started to eat. 'It's all right, when you eat it. It looks a bit intimidating at first but it's good scran really' Katie noted brightly. He ate hungrily and smeared what was left at the bottom of the bowl on a piece of bread and swallowed it noisily. The green beans had not been touched, yet.

'That wasn't bad' he commented. 'You kept the portion of green stuff separate?'

'Yes, you like it like that, don't you? Poor man's peas, on the side...'

'Well done, Auntie Katie.'

'Thanks Al. Look, is everything all right with you? You seem a bit on edge?'

'I'm fine.'

'How's school?'

'It's fine.'

'Are you coping with all the work?'

'It's all fine.'

'I see. Let's try something. We say something about how we feel about something, we talk about it and we take turns. How does that sound? It's called a conversation.'

'I know, how about I ask you something and you answer with the truth?'

'Huh? All right, let's give that a go. The truth, you say?'

'The truth.'

'You have to promise it won't go any further. This is just between us.'

'Yes, alright.'

'You have to promise.'

'I promise.'

'There may be some things I can't talk about because of Official Secrets and all that crap.'

'Got it. Okay, what happened to your hands?'

'I got in a fight but I caught the knife in my hands.'

'Bloody hell!'

'Yes, it was a bit like that...'

'On duty?'

'Yes, on duty, it wasn't a pub fight.'

'How...how did that happen?'

'I got isolated from my buddies, I had no cover. I...'

'Who was it?'

'Some kid who wanted me to stop me doing something that I had to do...'

'But you're not a soldier?'

'No, but I'm in the armed forces. It's part of the deal.'

'How did you get out of that?'

'I saw him off. He was only a kid, he couldn't have been much older than you...'

'Bloody hell!'

'I know!'

'But, you could have been killed!'

'Yes, but I wasn't, was I?'

'But...'

'Whoa, wait, it's my turn now.' He became instantly apprehensive. She wasn't sure how to broach this, it would have to be direct. 'This is difficult. Al, but do you...like me?'

'Of course I like you - you're my favourite auntie!'

'No, I meant, do you fancy me?'

'No! No! No! Why would you think that? Why?'

'So, that's a no then? Good, good, good. Any more questions for me, Al?'

'It's Lexa. Do you have a boyfriend, Auntie Katie?'

'I have loads, I'm a matelot, remember?'

'Oh yeah, of course...'

'Is there anything else I can help you with?'

'Are you any good at physics?'

'Well, I'm a bit of an expert with ropes, pulleys and levers...if that's any use.'

'We're not doing ropes, pulleys and levers at the moment.'

'Oh, that's a shame - what are you doing then?'

Al replied with something that sounded way, way, out of this world.

'Blimey! No idea. Who's the class swot?'

'Class swot? We don't have those any more - this is the 21st century!'

'So it is! What about your teacher?'

'What about him? He set the question!'

'So, he must know the answer!'

'I can 't ask him!'

'Of course you can - we'll have a conference call with him this afternoon! Let's schedule for...fifteen hundred!'

'But how do you find his 'phone number?'

'There's ways and means, isn't there? So, while you're thinking about that, why don't you make your bed up, Al?'

He looked down and realised that his bed was naked. 'I don't know how?'

'It's the duvet cover, isn't it? They're a bit tricky. Let me show you how.' She removed the lunchtime paraphernalia and stacked it on the tray outside the door and then oversaw his application of the fitted sheet - which he seemed to manage with no trouble. And now for the duvet cover. 'The knack is to pretend you're an inside out ghost!' She turned the cover inside out, thrust her arms into the corners, and moaned in a tone that she considered was ghost like: 'Whoooooo, whoooooo'!

She stopped abruptly - a pair of hands were girdling her waist. 'No Al, hands go in the corners, not round the sides!' He pressed more firmly through the cotton. 'Al! Stop it! That tickles!' She wriggled out of the cover. 'What are you playing at?'

He was now slumped on the bed, looking desolate, his head in his hands.

'Listen Al, I think that's enough 'whooooo, whoooooos' for now. Can you handle it from here? Once shown, always known?'

He nodded.

'Oh... wait, can you hear that? I just need to check what's going on downstairs...' At this, she stepped to the door. 'Is Eek allowed to drink?'

'Good God, no, she's only fourteen!'

'Is she allowed friends around?'

'Only if an adult is supervising!'

'Well, I count as an adult, don't I?'

'I don't think you do?'

'Oi! Yes I do! Now, what about the cellar?'

'What about it?'

'Is Eek allowed free range in there?'

'Good God no!'

'Oh crap, I may have messed up then. Did you ever put Owain in the cellar, if he misbehaves?'

'Good God, no!'

'Oh, Eek said something different. Just, just stay calm and I'll get back to you.' She exited Al's bedroom and scrambled downstairs. The voices she could hear, were excited, fuelled by something. She arrived in the kitchen - there were scattered bottles, with garishly coloured dregs in them. She arrived in the parlour - the clamour stopped instantly. 'All right girls, what's up? What's all this noise about?'

'Butt out Auntie Katie, we're having fun!'

'No Eek, I want to know what's going on. So, it's Marcie, isn't it? Where do you come from?'

'The village...'

'Where? Let's give your mum a little call and just check that she knows where you are and what you're allowed to do.'

'I can't remember the number?'

'Yes you can and yes you will.'

'But, I can't...'

'Auntie Katie, you goofball!'

'Eek, shut it or I'll ground you! And put that bottle down!'

'Ground me! Ha! I'd like to see you try!'

'Marcie and Rosaline - get out now! I need to sort out Eek!' They turned to look at each other, laughed and scampered out of the cottage, clutching their plastic bags.

'Katie, you are a big, fat stupid twat!'

'Eek, put the bottle down!'

'No!' She drained the bottle and threw it at Katie. It was caught high to Katie's right and Eek was away, running up the stairs. Katie gave chase up the stairs and they were running along the landing.

Eek pushed open the window that overlooked the kitchen garden and climbed half way out. 'Look at me! I can fly!'

'Eek. You're bolloxed! Get back in here! Al, get a mattress outside, your sister thinks she can fly!'

It was late afternoon and time for a SitRep: Katie put her feet up on the garden wall and savoured the mug of tea in her hands; Eek was sleeping in her bedroom with a bucket of disinfectant by her bed; Al was mooning on his half-made bed like a love-lorn panda. All the tasks assigned by Gwen had been completed and the bedding was billowing in the breeze outside. Tea was prepared, sandwiches and scones, all hand-made, and just waiting to see who had the appetite for them.

The sheep seemed fidgety in the upper pasture during her early morning visit but she would attend to them again in an hour or so - this would also be her opportunity to get out of the cottage and assess what was coming in from the west. There was a knock on the front door.

'Round the side!' she shouted.

The head of the vicar loomed around the side of the cottage.

'Oh, hallo Vic, what brings you here?'

'Ahh' the Right Reverend Timothy Trimble said pensively.

'Ah, I see, you cycled' she commented as she saw the battered red frame leaning on the hedge.

'Miss Talog' he harrumphed.

'Yes, Vic, are you here to do missionary work, because if you are, you're probably wasting your time!'

He interrupted: 'Miss Talog, are the Hoflands at home?'

'No, they're out for the day. Can I help?'

'I'll come back later' he said as he half turned away.

'Come in vicar. I'll pour you some tea.'

He paused. 'I feel I should apologise...'

'Yes, you should, but come inside first.'

She ushered him in through the kitchen towards the sitting room and waved towards Stefan's imposing armchair. 'Take a pew Vic, and I'll rustle up some tea. How do you take it?'

'However it comes.'

'That's not very helpful!'

'Milk, one sugar.'

'That's better. Take a pew.'

'If I must.'

'Yes, you must.'

She walked to the kitchen and got the kettle going, flushed the teapot clear of spent leaves and added two spoons of Ceylon tea. 'Have you thought about what I said, vicar?' she shouted in the general direction of the living room. 'Bugger me!' she yelped when she realised he was just behind her. 'Oh, sorry vicar, I didn't realise you were right behind me!'

'Ah, I'm sorry to startle you.' He gestured at the kitchen table. 'Let's sit down Miss Talog...'

'Oh, all right Vic. This sounds serious!' They sat opposite each other at the kitchen table.

'I apologise Miss Talog. The way you were treated at Sunday Mass was unchristian and unforgivable. I am truly sorry.'

'I agree.'

'I beg your pardon?'

'Unchristian and unforgivable and no way to treat a guest of the church.'

'However, the fact remains, you should not have been there.'

'That doesn't sound very...welcoming, Vic.'

'No, I agree. There has been a failure in our church to... excommunicate!' The vicar covered his mouth so he could chuckle at his most amusing quip.

Her forehead creased in a frown. Perhaps she should be more hospitable? 'Scone, Vic?'

He took the item proffered to him, tapped it twice on the hard surface of the kitchen table and placed it next to his tea.

'They're a bit crusty on the outside but they are fine when opened up and spread with a bit of slide.' She slid the saucer with the lump of butter on it across to him. He made his first failed attempt to open up the scone using the butter knife.

'I wanted to speak with Mr and Mrs Hofland about how we can come to some form of reconciliation regarding...your good self.'

'Oh. I see. What did you have in mind, Vic?'

'Well, let's see. I am happy to help you with your...conversion into our Christian family.'

'Conversion?'

'Yes, Katie. Conversion to Christianity. There, that's my offer.' He chose that moment to make his second failed attempt to open up the scone.

'Oh, what does that involve? Because if you're going to tip holy water on my head, that really isn't going to work, is it?' She noted his look of frustration at what should be the simple task of opening up a scone.

'I was thinking of a more educational approach, as I believe you have a thirst for knowledge and a great capacity to take on new ideas.'

'Well, that's very kind of you Vic, and very, very observant of you.'

'And, your answer?'

'I have a counter proposal. Every other week, we give the church over to ...paganism.'

'That's completely unacceptable, I cannot do that.'

'I thought you might say that and I understand that the high ups in your crew may have a problem with us taking over the church, but I promise we will not leave any mess, no blood or feathers.'

'No' he said in a quite forceful way. She wondered how far she could push this.

'The church hall, then...'

'No.'

'Clun Hill, but we'll need a spot in the church magazine.'

'The Clun Congregational?'

'Yes, you could promote this in your little magazine.'

'I can't do that.'

'All right. What if I arrange to have the curse lifted that is blighting your church?'

'What? What are you talking about?' he replied sharply.

'The curse that was bothering you on Sunday, I could tell something wasn't right. And I saw a ghost!'

He took a long, nervous slurp from his tea and looked around. He seemed to be readying himself to leave. He put the cup down. 'There is no curse on our House of God!'

'Oh, in that case, the curse remains, doesn't it?'

'There is no curse, Miss Talog!'

'If you say so, Vic.' She took the scone from him and ripped it in two and presented the two crumbling surfaces to him. 'It's a twist and separate. You can't just attack it with a knife. Do you see that?' Embarrassed, he took a knife and with trepidation, smeared a thin layer of butter across both opened surfaces. She seized both his hands and the knife clattered to the table. 'You're going to have to reconcile both sides of the community Vic, and stick them together.

There is trouble brewing over the border and it can only be dealt with together!'

'Together?'

'Yes. Christians and others together...'

'I see, I see. Do you mean pagans? Let me consider this...'

'Don't consider for too long, Vic.'

'Ah, and there is something else...'

'Yes, Vic?'

'But it's not entirely unrelated. I...don't know how to say this.' There were scone crumbs sticking to his lips, but he brushed these away. 'I wasn't sure what was best, how to protect all concerned in this.' The surplus crumbs landed on his black cloak and this prompted more feverish brushing away. 'I have a new house guest, he's a young refugee.'

He waited a moment for a response but instead she looked back at him, not quite comprehending what he was trying to say. 'What?'

'I, or I mean we, my household, are teaching him the rudiments of, well, the English language and culture actually...'

'Oh, that will be useful, vicar...and what's this got to do with me?'

'Well, he saw you when you visited our church. He says he recognises you!'

She felt her insides lurch downwards. 'How does he recognise me? How come? How? That's not possible Vic, he can't.' Was he a ghost?

And there was the Somali boy again, in her mind, his big eyes begging her not to let go and the sea raging below, one hand clutching her wrist, his other hand rending the collar of her overalls.

'He claims that you came down from the sky. You came down and pulled his brother from the sea but you let him go. He says you released him back to the sea! But he forgives you!'

Wheels scrunched against the gravel. The Hoflands were back! Katie rushed to the front door, but Eek and Al were already through, racing towards their parents. Eek took Stefan and Al took Gwen. Katie stood and stared, wondering what was coming next. There was animated chatter through the embraces and she realised there was trouble brewing.

Gwen marched towards the door with Al in tow. 'Mama, thank God you're back, she's been a nightmare!'

'Alexander, what has been a nightmare?'

'Auntie Katie has. She's worked us so hard and I haven't had time to finish my homework!'

They brushed past Katie to enter the cottage and she muttered: 'You my son are in deep dwang.'

'Katie, I will see to Alexander, then we must talk.'

Eek was whispering something urgently into Mister Hofland's ear. 'Have you had fun with your Auntie, Monique?'

'No Papa, Katie has tortured us. She tried to throw me out of the window!'

'Katie? Is this true?'

'No, that's a load of bollocks, isn't it Eek? Remember, what I said, Eek? Sir, she tried to jump out of the window, and I stopped her, she thought she could fly!'

'Monique, why would you think that?'

'Auntie Katie opened one of your bottles of wine and made me drink it - it made me very poorly.'

'Huuuuuuhhh' gasped Katie.

'Not the Montrachet?'

'I didn't open it!'

'Katie, you don't even like wine!'

'It was Eek, not me! And she was drinking vodka with her friends!'

'What? I said no parties!'

'It was all Auntie Katie's fault!'

'You little witch!'

'Katie!'

Katie gathered in some deep breaths: 'Mister Hofland, this place is a shambles. No one knows what needs to be done, who is to do it, when it needs to be done and even, how it's to be done!'

'What are you talking about, Katie?'

She took a deep breath: 'No one knows what the purpose is, there's no strategy, no plan and no standing orders!'

'This has gone too far. Come with me Katie.' She marched with Stefan, somewhere, not too far, because she could still hear the squealing of her niece and the whining of her nephew. Owain came to heel but she sent him away.

Stefan gripped her arms tightly. 'Do you have any idea how difficult this has been?'

'Just give me two weeks, Mister Hofland, and I'll get this crock knocked into shape!'

'How dare you! It's nothing of the sort!' And they were on the march again. 'Come with me young lady.' They could now see that the lower field had been ploughed and was ready for planting.

'But none of this matters! No one has any idea of what's going to happen!'

'What?'

'You don't know what the purpose is?' she asked incredulously.

'What is this...purpose?'

'You know! You must do, Mister Hofland! It's why everyone's here!' There was not even a flicker of comprehension. 'There needs to be a chain of self contained, mutually supportive farmsteads along the border' she stated, with the backs of her hands pushed in front to make a screen, 'and this is the linchpin of that chain. When I am ready, in a few days I will go straight though them, that-a-way' she said pointing palms together to the west, 'and make good on my promise.'

She assessed the mounting disbelief that grew across his red-lined features. 'You have no idea what I'm talking about, do you Mister Hofland? Bugger, bugger, bugger!'

'Yes, oh bugger Katie. There is no actual purpose, is there Katie?'

'We're in even deeper dwang than I thought. I'll get my bags, I've got to go!' She went back to the cottage, gathered her bags and put them outside the cottage. The Hofland family gathered outside, to see her off. There were looks of complete incomprehension.

'Eek, keep Owain close at hand and keep watching to the west. Gwen, fetch mum and bring her back here. Al, work on Megan, she knows the purpose. Mister Hofland, make sure everyone is talking to each other, morning orders, daily debriefing, evening SitRep. I'll be back in a few days! Good luck!'

Chapter Forty-Eight

Tuesday 24 May 0615 - North Islington

Katie woke suddenly from her dream and sat up. She was in Paol's flat, curled in the bed. In her core, a slow, deep pulse, more than a sensation, but less than an ache, now always present, a gentle but firm caress in the space below her stomach but across her hips, an impulse to conjoin with another, to feel the thrust of their hips, over hers.

She settled back under the sheet and compressed her hands between her hips, trying to squeeze away this nagging yearning in her body, this yearning that took over all her thoughts and pushed everything else aside.

There was a knock on the door. It opened in stages to reveal Paol with a steaming mug of tea and a croissant. She nodded her assent for him to enter and uncurled herself. Her cheeks must be a glowing red now, judging from the burning sensation she felt.

'Are you having a party in there?' he asked.

'What do you mean?' she challenged.

'It sounded like a lot of writhing and moaning to me' he answered.

'Don't be rude! I was just having a little diddle, that's all.'

'Is that what you call it? It sounded like a full-on...'

'Oi Paol! Shut up!'

She sat up in stages, keeping her thighs as tightly closed as she could. 'Ugh, I feel like a jammy dodger' she groaned to herself.

'What was that, Katie?'

'I was talking to myself.'

'Ah, I thought you were being vulgar Katie. Just for your information, I have plenty of chocolate digestives and this buttery croissant.'

'Paol, what are you suggesting?'

'I'm just saying I've got all those little fancies that you like so much.'

'Thank you Paol, that'll all do very nicely.'

'Good.' He seemed to be deep in thought. 'So, what are your plans for today, little sister?'

'I thought I'd laze around in bed all day.'

'Well, to be fair to you, it was a late one. If you get bored, there's a few jobs you could do around the place, Katie.'

'I didn't get a lot of sleep last night, Paol' she said grumpily. Why wouldn't he just go? There was something pulsing inside of her and she needed some privacy to release it.

'Yes, I can see that...'

'Oi!'

'Well, if you're feeling up to it, there's a pile of laundry that needs doing.' The door closed gently as Paol left the flat. Katie got up, made a pot of tea and made her way back to her bedroom, checking how visible she was from the flats that overlooked Paol's. She pulled the curtains tight in the living room and bedroom before curling up in bed. She would treat herself to a bath.

That sensation in her core was still there. Her hand slipped between her legs and her palm gently cupped her pudding and the tips of her fingers explored the folds of flesh. The stickiness was still there between the lips, now gently parted, and inside her was an urge that needed to be satisfied. Her fingers slid inside and touched the creaminess there and withdrew carefully. She took a very careful sniff. It wasn't unpleasant and there was no hint of wee and she was curious to know how it would taste. She reasoned it couldn't be too awful, if the yarns she had overheard in the mess deck were true, but this was only the opinion of the dicks, and they put all kinds of crap in their mouths.

She brought the tip of her finger towards the tip of her tongue. They touched momentarily. Her tongue snapped back like a viper's and then out again and she spat and wiped her tongue with the back of her hand. They're all idiots!

Katie ran to the bathroom and spat into the washbasin.

And here was the big white, roll-top bath that was available for her own personal and private pleasure. She started the bath taps running and poured a large slug of viscous, violet liquid in. Bubbles surged upwards, all of a froth. She recalled a Wren saying that candles lit along the bath and a large glass of cold, white wine enhanced the pleasure to be gained by immersing your body in hot, clean smelling water.

Katie looked through all the drawers in the kitchen and found two happy birthday candles, some window putty to put them in and a box of matches. She stopped the gushing taps and admired the mound of froth that had been made. The candles were lit, the mug of tea was ready, perched along the rim of the bath. Everything was ready, apart from her, so she closed her eyes and invited two young men into her dream and they removed their clothes when bidden. Now they were ready to fight for her, one fall or one submission or a knock-out to decide. Her lips trembled against each other emitting a cat-like chittering and her heart and breathing had smoothly escalated. Her skin felt moist all over as if it was glowing. She stripped off quickly and slid into the warm, foaming water. The depth and the temperature were just right, as her body was just floating and little ripples lapped gently against her nipples.

Her fingers circled gently around her breasts and her mind was now swimming. She pictured the two boys, bare chested, one like a blonde-curled god with soft, light blue eyes and one, darker skinned, dark brown haired, firm chested, chests bulging with deep rhythmic breathing as they fought for her, throwing crunching blows that rippled muscle, gasping for air...

Her buttocks pushed in a gathering rhythm as her left hand sought frantically for the lips between her legs, her mind now completely disengaged from the outer world: feeling, squeezing, pulsing...

Scratching in the lock, a door flung open!

Intruder! No!

Quick footsteps, a short, sharp call of her name...

Paol! He's back. Shit!

She took three deep, practice breaths and submerged her head.

He's in the bathroom now. He's just there, urgently calling out 'Katie!'

Uh, he's gone out! She lifted her head and sucked in a ragged, watery breath.

No! He's back!

Can't breath, gasping, gasping, coughing!

Arms around her, dragging her up, water sloshing everywhere. She was hauled up, hugged, wrapped, dragged away, legs scrambling on vinyl floor, away and out of the bathroom, tea and candles scattered into the foam.

'Katie, Katie, are you all right?' Paol shouted.

Can't talk, coughing fit, soapy water, choking, choking!

She was out of the bathroom, dripping on the carpet, wrapped in a towel, wrapped in his arms, gasping like a just landed fish.

'Katie, Katie, what are you playing at?'

She coughed away a gobbet of phlegm. 'Stop crushing me!' He let her go.

'What are you playing at?'

'I was bathing!'

'Under water?'

She coughed again. 'I held my breath for over a minute!'

'What?'

'Over a minute! I was on for a record! You stopped me!'

'You little idiot!'

'Why!'

He held her at arms length. He was frowning. Something had just occurred to him. 'Candles?'

'Yes, candles!'

'You were pleasuring yourself! In my bath!'

'That's what baths are for! Pleasuring!'

'You were buttering the muffin, weren't you!'

'Don't be filthy!'

He let her go, took another critical look at her and walked back into the bathroom. He trawled for the candles and the crockery and put them in the hand basin. 'Have you finished in here?' The plug was pulled and the bath water started to gurgle away. She looked around the door and he was shepherding the suds towards the plughole with his hand.

Katie gasped: Feeling; squeezing, pulsing...releasing. No, no! Releasing! They scanned the surface of the water together. The bubbles had receded, but there was something floating that was not water or froth. It was a curious, off-white blob with a short, curly hair attached, a hair that had been part of her fuzzy pudding, just moments ago. She pushed in front of Paol and agitated the water to speed its passage. It was too late, his fingers were mired in it. 'Don't move Paol, I've got this!' She unravelled the shower head and sprayed his hand with a pathetically slow stream of tepid water and scrubbed at his hands.

He looked witheringly at her. 'What...the...hell...was...that?'

'Paol, I have no idea what that was, believe me!' His hand was slime free, so she released it, but it might as well still be there, pulsing like a jellyfish.

'I don't believe you...'

'Paol, Paol, listen to me, I don't know if you realise this, but there is...a presence in your flat!'

'A presence? What are you saying? Are you saying there's a ghost in my flat?'

'Possibly, possibly, yes, yes, YES!'

'And the slime in the bath? That was ectoplasm?'

'Yes! Yes! Yes! Ectoplasm, ectoplasm, ectoplasm!' She didn't know what it meant but it sounded out of this world. 'That's utterly brilliant Paol, I think you've cracked it! That's utterly the best explanation for what's occurred!'

'So Katie, are you really trying to tell me that a randy ghost dropped down from the ceiling, to take you in the bath, and then he dropped his ectoplasm in the bath water? Is that what you're telling me?'

A randy ghost? Could that be it? 'Well, Paol, I think that's simply the best explanation...and you're so clever!'

He swatted this compliment away. 'Or, did you think, Paol's out of the way, I can nip in the bath and have a quick shuffle of the pack before he gets back...'

'Paol!'

'So, this is supposed to be ghost spunk, is it?'

'Paol! No! It's ectoplasm or something!'

'Rubbish!' he roared. He stood and glowered at her. She couldn't return his look. Instead, a ripple of follicles stood up at the back of her neck and swept over the top of her head. It felt like the hair on her crown was crawling up to meet the ceiling. The eyelid of her left eye now started to flicker like a camera that couldn't focus.

'You will bleach the bath clean. You will then clean the walls and floor...'

'Paol, that's ridiculous, there's nothing up there!'

'And the ceiling!'

'Paol, I promise you, there was no spurting up the walls!' She had lost the staring match so she stomped into the kitchen. Two standing stomps signalled to Paol how upset she was. A small dose of bleach was followed by hot water into a bucket so that the smell of acrid cleanliness flooded the flat. He was in the bathroom when she returned with the bucket.

'You will do as I ask you, or you're on your way out!'

Buggery, buggery, bollocks what was his problem? 'Paol, it was an accident, don't be an arsehole!'

'I'm going into college now. I'm going to leave you a list of jobs to do round the flat, as you seem to have anything better to do than... diddle your skittle!'

'Oi! You'll have to do those bits for me' she indicated the tops of the wall with a quick nod. Paol mopped these and then she continued with the bath. 'There, that's all done.' She walked back to the kitchen with the bucket. 'Now what?'

Paol had written a list in big green capital letters on a big sheet of paper.

'Show me' she said grudgingly. It was a punishingly long list. She was going to need help to understand it before she could even start on it. This would mean that she would not be doing anything else that day. Sod that, she thought.

Because, in her dream, she had seen Udo's face. She resolved to confront him about this at his college. She pulled the towel tight around her to gain a feeling of security but it didn't work.

Katie pressed her hand against the key pad and the door sprang open. She was in! Moving quickly along the high ceilinged corridor with a gallery of the gowned great and the good, she merged with the gaggle of students moving along, intent on holding their plastic pots of coffee in one hand, talking into their mobile devices with the other, while continuing a conversation with their companions.

'Excuse me, where's your pass?' The woman who had accosted her wore a light blue coloured suit and a pearl necklace and pearl earrings and her smile was wide and earnest, with polished teeth like headstones in a well tended military cemetery.

'No, I've come to see Paol Houghton. I didn't realise I needed a pass to see my brother.'

'You could just call him?'

'It's very important, personal and urgent...but your suit, its fits you so well!'

The woman swept her hands over her jacket and skirt. 'Oh, this old thing!'

'And your pearls, so lovely...are they real?'

'No, of course not, I'm just a lowly admin!'

'For Paol Houghton?'

'Well, yes. What was it you needed?'

'Well, I just need to catch him quickly, do I need to make an appointment?'

'He's in meetings all morning, can I help?'

'Oh, I just need to see him quickly. I'm his sister, aren't I?'

Katie was pulled by the arm into a quite corner of the mess deck, or what was more commonly known as the collegiate common room, in a college, which this was, apparently.

'I'm Natalie. So, you're his sister, Katie? Can I ask you something personal?' Natalie was short but well formed with wide eyes of light blue. 'Can I ask you for some advice?'

Uh, oh. 'On what? Paol? I don't know if I should, it's a bit close to home isn't it? I'll do my best.'

'Good. I get on very well with Paol, but I was wondering...'

'If he'd go out with you on a date?' You're what we matelots classify as 'split' aren't you? Tick!

'Well, yes, so I was wondering how I could...ask him to go out for a drink, maybe?'

'Of course you can!' You have a sizeable pair of doops. Tick!

'What do you suggest I do?'

'Oh, anything'll do.' You're not a one-eyed gronk just out of prison, are you? Tick!

'Does he do any sports? What does he do in his spare time?'

Need to pull a discrete veil over his extra-curricular activities. He doesn't play tennis or badminton, he's not very good at darts or bar billiards either, based on the crushing defeats Katie had inflicted on him previously. Best not to comment on some of his other interests outside of work also.

'Well, you could invite him out for a drink, but it would have to be a pub, not a wine bar. There would have to be at least four real ales on tap or he'll get grumpy about his lack of options.'

Natalie seemed to be absorbing all this because she was taking notes on her mobile device. 'The older the pub the better but he might bore the pants off you with the social history of pubs.' Katie smirked at her slight indiscretion.

'No, please carry on.'

'Now, this is confidential' said Katie in a whisper, 'but wear a white blouse, top two buttons undone, long sleeves and a showy bra, because he likes breasts but you need to flag 'em up.'

Natalie's smile retracted slightly at this information but she still seemed to want more.

'I don't know how far you want to take it? Do you want to be just friends or do you want to, um, I don't know how to say this, bed him? Because, if you want to bed him, I've got a couple of deal clinchers, if you're interested?'

Natalie was nodding urgently, but she was flushing pink and her breathing had quickened.

Katie drew confidence from this and so she took a deep breath. 'Wear a long skirt with a split up the middle, the higher the split the better. When you're sitting down chatting with him, cross and uncross your legs in front of him. Paol's a bit of a connoisseur of fine legs' said Katie looking under the table, 'and you have fine legs. Look, you will tell me if this is too much, won't you?'

Natalie was shaking her head in such a way that it might fall off at any moment.

'Drop something into the conversation about comic books with female super heroes and say that your fantasy is to dress up as one. If you can convince him that you're game for that, you should be home and dry!'

Natalie seemed incapable of speech at this moment.

'Are you feeling all right?'

'Yes, yes, you seem to know an awful lot about...what he likes?'

'Well, we're sister and brother, aren't we? So where do I find Paol?'

Natalie's eyes roved around to her right and back along the corridor. 'But...you're relationship?'

'I know what you mean...all I can say is that we're...related.' And then she stopped talking because she had seen a thick-set man, dressed like a gorilla in a pale coloured suit, standing at the entrance to the common room, staring at her. 'Oh, shit!'

'I beg your pardon!'

'That man there! I bet he doesn't have a pass!' It was Ulrich Letsch, in his summer-weight suit and a yellow waistcoat with a yellow handkerchief sticking out of his breast pocket. The red cravat around his neck set the whole thing off quite badly.

'Miss Talog, how fortuitous!' Ulrich gently gripped Katie's arm and guided Katie to her feet and moved her away from the table where Natalie seemed incapable of movement.

'Oi! I'm in the middle of something here!'

'I'm sure it's just meaningless tittle-tattle.'

'Oi, arsehole, let go of me!' She twisted and tried to look behind his eyes but he was wearing those sodding shades again.

'We can have a scene here or we can discuss this in a civilised manner.'

'Civilised! You! A gorilla!'

Katie twisted round to look to Natalie, who had gotten up, straightened her clothes and now asserted herself. 'Let her go, or I will call security!' Ulrich relented.

'What are you doing here, you ape?'

'Enough, Miss Talog. I'm here on business. What are you doing here?'

'I'm on business too. Now excuse me!' Katie walked quickly out of the common room and turned right and then left along a glass lined corridor. Ulrich was close behind. She ran down the corridor to where she imagined Paol's office was located. And there was a door, with a name written in black pen on an oblong piece of sticky, yellow paper and it looked like Paol's name. She tapped on the door urgently and pushed it open. Ulrich was just behind her. Katie shut it behind her. There was a staccato tapping on the door behind her, like a hammering woodpecker.

Paol was inside, sitting in a chair looking inquisitively at a monitor. He looked up in shock. 'Katie!'

'Paol, Paol, there's a bloke at your door with a funny shaped head!'

'So what did you say to him?'

'I said, I said... you've already got one!'

'Oh, how absolutely bloody classic...if I had ten quid for every time you'd done that to me!'

'And he wants to show it to you himself!' Katie stepped to one side of Paol's desk as Ulrich strode into the centre of the room, his head set on his neck, like a rugby ball set on its tee, ready to be kicked. It was difficult to say where his head ended or where his neck started.

'Bloody hell, Katie!'

'Ah, brother and sister together, how opportune? How apposite!' He did a little pirouette in the centre of the room and ended up looking at the other, threadbare, fabric covered chair in the room.

Katie stepped across nimbly and pushed the chair so it sat in front of Paol's battered, wooden desk. 'There you go!' She stepped back to the other side of the desk, nudged Paol's shoulder with her hip and then nestled down on his left thigh. 'So, Paol, this is Ulrich, Ulrich, this is Paol. Paol and I are brother and sister, he's my brother and I'm his sister. We all seem to know each other.' He had no back-up medical team with him this time, so she felt safe. She stared at his eyes but they were fixed on Paol's.

'Enough of this tomfoolery' Ulrich said, 'I will explain to you the position you are in and how you can resolve it. Now please listen very carefully.' Paol and Katie pressed their ears forward with their index fingers in unison, in the general direction of Ulrich. Her right hand clawed at Paol's side and he wriggled in his seat to mitigate the urge to laugh.

'So, Mister Houghton, if you persist in your attacks on my organisation, you will force me to take legal action.'

'It's free speech, get used to it.'

'The comments on your blog are libellous. I will pursue you through the courts until I get satisfaction.'

'What does he want?' Katie prodded Paol's ribs.

'Your cooperation. You must consent to help our research, or I will make your situation very uncomfortable. If you do not cooperate, I will look at the potential amongst your close blood relations. Am I making myself clear?'

'So, Katie is the one who best meets all your requirements. It should be Katie.'

'Eh?'

'And the blog?'

'Herr Sankt will close it down.'

'Eh?'

'Excellent. Our business is concluded. Miss Talog, we look forward to your visit. Herr Glaus will accompany you. Good day to you.'

As Ulrich Letsch left the room, Natalie entered with a tray of coffees. 'What happened?' she exclaimed.

'Buggered if I know!' exclaimed Katie.

Paol arrived back at his flat and entered with trepidation. On the coffee table there were five heaps of white petals and in the cut crystal vase, a clutch of giant daisies, shorn of petals. Katie had thrown herself back into the armchair in a fit of desperation. 'What's the matter, Katie?'

'I couldn't find him, could I?'

'Who, Udo?'

'Yes, he'd left college to meet his so-called girlfriend.'

'Ah, and what's all this mess about?'

'Your sodding daisies don't work. I'm trying to tell if he loves me, and they keep giving the wrong answer.' She finished peeling off the petals of the last daisy. 'See?'

'He's in a relationship, I told you. You can destroy as many of my flowers as you want, but it won't change that simple fact, will it?'

'What am I going to do then?'

'I'll tell you what you're going to do. I'm going to go out and then come back in again. In that time you will clear up this mess and you will then treat me with the civility and politeness that I deserve.'

Katie looked at him with her jaw wide in disbelief then she pushed it back. 'Are you serious?' He sodding well was as well. As he turned towards the door she swept the petals into the metal waste bin, adjusted the stems in the vase so that they flopped over in a pleasing way and poised herself on the edge of the seat. As he left the room she crossed to the door and eased it shut behind him. As he came back in she would take him down and put him in an excruciating neck lock.

The door opened. 'Katie, get out from there!'

So, he could see around doors then? She took three paces, curtsied then threw herself on the sofa, face down.

'Katie! Do not abuse the furniture!'

'Eh?'

'Go and put the kettle on.'

'Oh, all right then.'

'And bring out the fancy biscuits.'

'Oh Paol, not the fancy, individually wrapped chocolate ones?'

'Yes, the very same.'

'Oh Paol!' She hurried to the kitchen and switched the kettle on. Ceremoniously, she place the tin of biscuits in pride of place on the coffee table. 'This is a big moment, isn't it?'

'Always! The ceremonial opening of the fancy biscuits!'

Katie unsealed the tin, and took off the protective layer and then sniffed. 'I'm almost as happy just to suck up the smell and not actually touch any of them!'

'All the more for me!'

'Almost I said. Who's going in first?'

'You can.'

'I'm having the blue one and the red and the...'

'Katie, remember the rules...'

'Oh, no, not the stupid two biscuit rule?'

'Yes, one's nice, two's just right and three is greedy.'

'I am greedy!'

'My rules!'

Katie settled herself next to Paol on the settee and unwrapped the first biscuit. 'Yummm!'

'Enjoying that?'

'Mmmmm!'

'Feeling better?'

'Mmmmm!'

'Well, here we are, both in the same boat, no significant other in our lives.'

'Mmmmm!' She had unwrapped her second biscuit and started to chomp at it. 'I may have some good news for you, on that front!'

He paused for a moment. 'Katie, if you were to write six words about me, that I could post on a lonely hearts site, what would they be? I'll do the same for you.' Katie felt sufficiently relaxed to put her bare feet on the table: Paol swept them aside. 'Behave yourself' he admonished. He separated a page of A4 paper and gave half to her. 'Write down your six words, I'll do the same, then we share. Okay?'

'You actually want me to write six words to describe you? To a potential other?' She chewed on the end of the pencil and looked anxiously at Paol. Within sixty seconds, he had finished. She agonised for a further three minutes and then wrote down six words in her haltering, left handed script. She wasn't satisfied with the result, but folded the piece of paper in two. 'I'm ready. You start.'

Paol seemed very pleased with himself. He read out, 'Navy girl, well fit, totally weird.'

'Totally weird? That seems harsh. I'm not weird, am I?'

'It's not a criticism. It's one of your endearing characteristics, weirdness.'

'Oh, I didn't really understand the rules...'

'Don't worry about it - let me see yours.'

'Oi Paol, don't be rude!'

'I meant, I want to see your words of wisdom, Katie!'

'Oh, I don't think I should show you, because...' She screwed up the paper into a ball and held it tightly in her left hand. 'Let me try again, Paol.' Katie got up and walked behind the sofa, so it was a physical barrier between them.

'Katie, show me. That was part of the deal.'

She walked towards his bedroom. He followed her and grasped her wrist. His hand was quickly shaken loose and she stuffed the ball of paper down her pants. 'It's not for you to see' Katie hissed as she mounted the bed.

'Just let me see. I won't be angry.'

'Oh, I think you probably will!'

He grasped her feet and pulled hard on her toes - her feet lashed out but she over balanced. He went for her toes again.

'Paol, not my toes. PLEASE, ANYTHING BUT MY SODDING TOES!' she shrilled. Katie lashed out with her right foot but it caught between the rails at the end of the bed. Her leg was trapped.

Paul loomed over the side of the bed and looked down smugly at her predicament. 'Give' he said sharply.

'Don't you dare sully me. I'm your sister!'

'You don't even know what the word means. Give it to me or the toes get it!'

'Piss off Paol, I've been trained to do fighting!'

'You don't do fighting! Your job is to look decorative on a boat!'

'Oi, I'm not a decoration! And it's in a ship Paol, not on a boat, so that shows how little you know!'

He pulled on her toes again. She wriggled vainly. Katie delved inside her trousers and retrieved the ball of paper and held it away from him as far as her arm could stretch. But Paol set upon her. Their hands wrestled. He had the paper. Katie twisted her leg and wrenched it free.

Paol slid over the bed and out of the room. Katie vaulted over it and dived after him. Her arm wrapped around his ankle and he tumbled to the living room carpet. She scrambled onto his back but he had opened the paper. Her thumbs and index fingers seized the paper and pulled it away from him. She scrunched the paper in her right hand and squeezed hard but too slow, much too slow...

Paol got up as she rolled away and walked across to the picture window that looked down to the busy street below.

'You say you're not weird - what was that?' Paol turned and watched as Katie snatched motes from the air with one hand and tried desperately to compress them back together in her balled fist.

Katie stopped when she saw he was looking. 'I'm sorry Paol, I've made a bit of a mess with my paper.'

'You've obliterated the paper, Katie! And you still claim that you're not weird?'

'No, your right, that was a bit weird, wasn't it? And it was not good...'

'Spontaneous combustion?'

'Yes, whatever. Listen Paol, I'm not going to lie to you, I panicked...'

'So, your six words that describe me: 'Histry nurd, crap at all else.' There's an 'o' in 'history' and 'nerd' is spelt with an 'e' Katie.'

'Oh, and you're so good at correcting my spelling!'

'And that's supposed to make me feel better, is it?'

'Oh, didn't it work? Well, let me try a bit more.' Katie's hand came up to cover her eyes so she could think and avoid his glare. Her left arm stretched out to settle on his shoulder. 'I think you'll be all right because there'll be lots of girl history geeks at your college who are on the lookout for older gits.'

Her arm came back to cover her eyes for a further thought. That's not enough, must keep thinking. Why not try that? Her arm stretched out again to him. 'Other kinds of geeks will go for you!' She considered again and her arm reached out again towards Paol. 'Nerds, girl nerds. There must be loads of them! All those girls at your college, wearing specs and clothes that don't really go...'

Paol's head was resting against the window as if he had lost the will to exist. 'That's you trying to make me feel better, is it?'

'Yes, isn't it working? But those nerdy girls, they'll go for you, won't they? They need their father figures, don't they?'

'For pity's sake, Katie, that's all you think about me?'

'No, well, yes. Well, you look too old to be my brother, but dad and daughter, divorced dad, no, wait, widowed dad! That works!'

'You're unbelievable' he muttered, still staring out through the window.

'I am aren't I? Thank you! Look, let's go out on the pull together. Let's go to that pub just around the corner?'

'I don't think so, I'll probably get mugged' Paol replied.

'I'll be with you, so you'll be fine.'

'That's what I'm worried about.'

'Oi, I'm not going to mug you, am I?'

'Really? Have you got any money?'

'Not much. All right, I'll make some tea and cakes. What's your poison? Something with lemon in?'

'Lapsang souchong.'

'That's not a cheering up tea though, is it?'

'This is definitely a lapsang souchong moment.'

'All right, give me an hour. Lapsang and soda bread.' She switched on the oven as high as it would go and emptied the cupboard above the kettle. 'Nice galley you've got here, Paol!'

'It's a kitchenette.'

'P-lease, it's a galley, isn't it?' She stepped out and saw that he was still propped up against the window. 'Sit down Paol and put your feet up.' Katie looked around the room and her eyes settled on a ship that he had built out of small pieces of wood that took pride of place on his self-assembly Welsh dresser. 'I think what you've done there is utterly brilliant!'

'It's the Andrea Doria, built out of balsa wood.'

'Is it? That's amazing!' She went to examine it closely. 'All those oars and all that rigging! It must have taken forever!'

'It did.'

'We're both unlucky in love aren't we? I wonder why? Why don't you show me this Zella - what's she got that I haven't got?'

Paol carried out a quick sequence of transactions and displayed the required information. 'Here she is.'

'Oh, she's quite pretty, if you like that sort of thing. Brown hair, blue eyes, pairs of legs and doops. She's fully rigged, then, but a bit of a grizzly though.'

'Well educated and well travelled' Paol commented.

'So, she's just like me then except for the well educated bit.'

'In a relationship with you know who. You may have to concede defeat, Katie.'

'I've got one last shot. I might have to use all my native charm.'

'Well, good luck with that. I'll go out and get some food. What do you fancy for supper?'

'Anything'll do. Can I come with you?'

'No, you may not. I remember the last time we went shopping together.'

'And?'

'You embarrassed me so much.'

'How did I embarrass you?'

'Let me see. It was either the fact that everything I put in the trolley, you took out and replaced with something cheaper.'

'I was just trying to help you save money!'

'Or was it at the check out when you insisted on negotiating the price down with the manager? Yes, it was that one, wasn't it?'

'I was just trying to save you some money, wasn't I?'

'I've never been so humiliated in my life. The cat-calling from the others, waiting in the queue, while you haggled.'

'I was negotiating. Anyway, you should be focussed on all the money I saved you...'

'A trifling two quid.'

'There you go then!'

'You're not coming with me. Why don't you make a start on that pile of ironing?'

'That doesn't sound so exciting.'

'No, but it needs to be done. Can you remember how?'

'Yes, I do, you sarky bugger.'

'And what mustn't you do?'

'Wind the iron up to maximum?'

'Correct. Anything else?'

'I'm not to touch any of your gadgets?'

'Exactly. That's very good. I'll be about an hour. Just follow the rules and you'll be fine. That would be a good life message for you Katie, wouldn't it?'

'I suppose it would, you piss-taking bastard!' She was resigned to her fate. As the front door slammed closed, she went to the galley to shut down the oven, set up the ironing board in the living room, plugged in the iron and examined Paol's record deck and the shiny black boxes that drove it. In her left hand was a sausage of re-shaped paper with little patches of green ink still embedded in it.

Chapter Forty-Nine

Thursday 26 May 0815 - Pigs Bay Essex

'Hello, I'm Katie Talog. What's your name?' It was her first day at HMS Hawkins and she had just caught the shuttle bus to the site with moments to spare.

'I'm Leonie.'

'That's nice.' It was strange that she and Leonie seemed to be the only staff in the right kind of uniform.

'You don't really think that, do you?'

'I'm sorry, it's just...'

'Your face gives you away. I can read you like a book...'

'Oh, crap.'

'You're the new girl aren't you? You'll need to watch out for Old King Coles, he's a bit of a stickler. And you'll have to do better at hiding what you're thinking, or you'll be walking around the site with a permanent scowl on your face!'

They stepped off the shuttle bus together. There seemed to be a lot of artificers and sparktricians in their civvies. Katie looked left along the boundary fence and saw a gap. It was a big gap where the razor wire had been bowed down. While the crowd walked in through the main gate, Katie walked quickly to the gap followed at a distance by her new colleague.

While Leonie pouted with her arms doing a double teapot, Katie jumped over the wire into the site and then back again. 'That's easy, isn't it?'

They stepped back into the site and followed the fence back to the security gate. Katie walked into the rickety, paint flaked hut and recoiled at the smell of cigarette smoke. Coughing, she stepped out and then took the plunge back in. She found the emergency call button and leant hard on it. A klaxon sounded satisfyingly in the building that was the length of a rugby pitch away. It was a single storey in a panorama of unrelieved flatness, rank vegetation and isolated concrete and metal fortifications. To her south there was a freighter heading up the Thames, proceeding serenely over the landscape; to her east was a man in dark blue uniform running frantically towards the guard hut.

'What's happened? Just popped out for a minute!' he shouted.

'The security fence is breached!' There's no point in you being on guard here if the local gronks can get in down there!'

'Eh? It's been like that for months! There's no point!'

'Because the gronks will move in and they'll have all the metal away and before you know it, there's nothing left, just a load of gronky wagons and gronky dogs and horses. That's why!'

The image of a lot of gronky wagons on the site seemed to trouble the security man. 'What do you want me to do about it? No one'll pay!'

'Raise a chit to get it fixed. I'll get it paid.'

'Who are you anyway?'

'Leading Hand Talog.'

'Who?'

'It's my rank and name. You should be expecting me.'

He unfurled a very long run of printer generated paper which had hardly anything printed on it. 'Ah, there you are.'

'Raise the chit, bring it to me, I'll get it signed.'

Leonie and Katie walked towards the squat, concrete-faced building.

'What's all this shit?' Katie had wandered into a yard that contained a shambles of wooden boxes and rusting metal equipment, some adorned in grey tarpaulins.

'It's waste, it's a mixture of...'

She kicked a wooden crate 'I need to see whoever's in charge of this shit heap.'

Leonie tutted and banged on a window so hard that it shook. A face appeared and then the window was flung open.

'What is it?'

'It's the new girl...she wants a word.'

'Oh does she?'

'Hallo, it's Katie Talog!'

'Uh, Talog?'

'Yes! Can I have a quick word?'

He closed the window and disappeared into the building.

'I think this is going to be a big brew day' murmured Katie.

Leonie sighed. 'I'll put the kettle on.'

'Good, mine's a mug, milk, three sugars!' After what seemed half a lifetime, a bloke shambled up to her side with one hand scratching inside his trousers and the other scratching his barely thatched head. He was wearing some kind of blue overall with grease highlights. 'What's the problem, mate?'

'It's all this shit. Is this general shit? Or is it special shit? How do you tell what sort of shit this is?'

'It's just waste. I'm dealing with it...'

'How? How can you deal with it if you don't know what shit it is!'

'I know what it is.'

'So, what's all this shit here?'

He tapped it with his right foot. 'Core samples.'

'Core samples? No shit? So some scrote is coming to collect these core samples?'

'Correct.'

'Get it labelled, get it separate so the dirt doesn't get mixed up with the shit.'

After ten minutes, she had agreed with her new colleague how it was going to be sorted and segregated. 'This all needs to be sorted. I want the general shit separated from the special shit and I want it all labelled up and I want it done now.'

He called himself Andy and he seemed a lot happier now that he had been given some direction. She gratefully accepted a mug of tea from Leonie and Andy accepted a mug of coffee.

'This is all going to be brilliant, once it's all sorted.'

'Coles won't like it.'

'He'll love it, no one want's to fall tit over shit, do they?'

'So you want a chit?'

'Yes, raise me a chit for separating out the shit.'

'Listen, they won't like us spending any money...'

'Don't worry about that. It's to do with safety. If I can't get it, it can't be had. You just need to know how to work the system, don't you?'

'They won't be happy...'

'It's just a negotiation. The initial position is: I say what I want, they say they can't do it, then we talk a bit...'

'I don't see how that works...'

'...then they realise that what I want is actually what they want as well...'

'Eh?'

'... and everyone's happy. There! That's how it works!'

'I don't believe it' muttered Leonie, 'she's going at a chit a minute!'

They were all gathered in Old King Coles's office. He sat behind a large, expansive and cluttered desk, as if he was the local magistrate, about to serve justice on a lowly a knave. Spry stood to one side, smiling grimly. Katie was standing to attention, feeling like the knave.

'Talog has already upset everyone here, in the twenty minutes she's been on site. This must be some sort of record.'

'How did you manage that, Katie?'

'Ma'am, there's a gap in the perimeter fence. I'm getting it mended. There's a big pile of site waste in the compound and it's not safe. I'm getting it all sorted out so it can be removed from site.'

'It sounds like these are things that should have been sorted out before we found them, Mister Coles. Why wouldn't we get them fixed?'

'It needs to be done in the proper way. Talog is taking short cuts. She needs to respect the line of command. She needs to respect me or there'll be shit to pay.'

'I see. What do you say to that, Katie?'

'I could have taken more time to get it done ma'am, I'm sorry if I've jumped the gun. And I should have come through you, sir, you're absolutely right.'

There was a knock on the door and a technician pushed his way nervously into the room. 'Apologies, I need to get a signature on this. Who is Talog?'

'Yes, that's me.' She stood and moved to the door and picked up the sheaf of papers. 'Can you read this bit back to me?' He did. 'That sounds good. Where do I sign?'

'Here and here.'

She scrawled her chop onto the form.

'Are you going to use your own rank? The system reckons you're a petty officer?'

'Yep, if that's what the system says...if there's any problem, get back to me.'

'Hold that!' barked Coles.

As the door was closing, Katie gave a wink to the technician and a nod.

'This is unbelievable' shouted Coles, 'who the devil do you think you are?'

Spry looked at Katie quizzically and then back to Coles. 'Step out for a moment Talog.' She did as she was told but leant towards the door in such a way that she could hear all that was being said.

'How long have you been here, Geoffrey?'

'Much too long.'

'I've had a rethink, show me the organisation again.' There was a rapid tapping of finger nails. 'I'll move her to my administration team and you keep the engineering and technical team. How does that suit you, Geoffrey?'

'Just keep her out of my way and we'll be fine' he muttered.

'Good. I'll just have a huddle with the supervisors and you can give her a quick brief.'

'Talog!'

'Yes, ma'am?'

'In you come...'

'Mister Coles will fill you in, Talog.'

'Yes, ma'am.' Spry marched out and made her way down the corridor.

'I don't know what you overheard, Talog, but take no notice.'

'Do I need to get Spry back in here, sir?

'I don't give a toss about what's just been said. You don't do anything until you clear it with me first. You don't use the toilet until you clear it with me!'

'Let me reassure you, sir, if the toilet is anything like the rest of this place, there's no way I'm baring my arse in there!'

'How bloody dare you!' he rumbled. 'I warn you Talog, you're just digging a hole for yourself!'

'Yes sir! You're right, that's probably my best option, out on the range somewhere...'

'Your insolence is intolerable. I warn you, Talog, if there's any more of this, I'll have you out of here so fast your nipples will be spinning!'

'Oh sir' she exclaimed as she looked down at her chest, 'so, you've heard about my spinning nipples?'

'What the hell?'

'Listen sir, you shouldn't believe everything you read in the Navy News...'

'You're just digging a bigger hole for yourself, Talog.'

'Yes, it looks like I'll be needing one, sir. Is that all sir?'

'Remember what I told you. Everything is to come through me. Everything!'

'Yes, sir. Listen, it'll be all right, we've started off on the wrong foot but it will get better. You'll learn to appreciate me. Everyone else does!'

'Talog, get out. I've seen your kind before. They're ten a penny. You need to realise there's a chain of command.'

'Of course sir.'

'And cut the back chat!'

'But sir, I love a bit of...'

'STAND OUTSIDE!'

'Sir?'

'STAND OUTSIDE!'

She saluted, as correctly as she could, left the office and stood outside. She stood at ease but completely uneasily outside Coles' office.

There was a passage of people going the extra yard to go past her, to smirk at her, giggle at her or shake their head at her. Now, it was Leonie's turn. 'You've got a lot to learn.' She shook her head disparagingly, but sympathetically.

'Can I have a mug of tea please, three sugars?' Katie whispered.

Leonie said nothing but walked quickly in the direction of the kitchen. Spry passed by and entered Coles office. They departed together and left her standing to attention.

'You're coming with me Talog. Can you handle that?' It was Andy Prosser, with a mug of tea.

'Yes, Andy, where are we going?'

'Site tour.'

'Got anything for me?' She swigged back the tea.

He presented a form in triplicate which she signed quickly on a spare desk.

'You seem to be right up there in the requisition system.'

'I know mate, I'm all over it! Got a map?'

'Yep, but we'll only go around the perimeter...'

'Good. Anything else I should know?'

'Yep, I'm bringing a pad of requisitions - I think I'm gonna need 'em!'

'Good, bring 'em with you. Are there any areas that we can't go into because of unexploded shit?'

'No, most of it should be clear. Anything that isn't, is taped off.'

'Spare tape?'

'Here.'

The long wheelbase Land Rover bounced along the track just to the north of the seawall. Lapwings and redshanks and skylarks ascended every few paces and their calls rang through the still air.

'What's that Andy?' Katie cried out. She pointed to a flat, overgrown concrete shelf faired into the seawall. Coles and Spry had already jumped out of their vehicle and were poking about the concrete walled entrance way.

'It looks like a blockhouse for watching the fall of shot into the river...'

'What's the point of that?'

'It keeps the observers safe from stray shot.'

'They shouldn't go in...'

'Why?'

'It's taped off!'

'Shit!' Andy's fist hammered on the horn. Spry and Coles stepped under the tape; Spry waved at them and then disappeared from sight.

The Land Rover halted and they scrambled out into the dust. 'Ma'am, ma'am, we need bomb disposal to check it out, ma'am!' Katie's heart pulsed disconcertedly.

A long, concrete walled corridor led to the bunker, overshadowed by bushes and brambles, but behind all this, there was the smell of rotting steel and the whining of a pent-up energy waiting to be released.

'Come on Talog, what's the matter with you?' shouted Spry as she took the lead and thrust her way through the vegetation. Coles followed.

Katie saw scattered boards of compressed, grey-blue fibres and thick, damp and acrid soil below her scrambling feet.

'Anyone got a torch?' laughed Spry. There was red and white striped tape covered the doorway and two grimy, red lettered signs decorated the brick walls. Spry swept the tape away with her arms and pulled at the metal door - it creaked open. Spry stopped, looked up at Katie and laughed again.

'Get back ma'am, we need bomb disposal...tape and signs...there's danger!' Katie ran back to Andy, gasping for breath. 'I've stopped 'em. Get onto bomb disposal team at Barking!' She pointed to the red lettered number in her notebook. He dialled the number. After a few seconds, a voice she recognised came on line. Katie took the receiver, 'Ron, Ron, it's Katie Talog, I'm at HMS Hawkins and I've got a...'

'Good morning Katie, and how are you?'

'Ron, Ron, I've got something that needs your team's urgent attention!'

'Katie, I'm fine thank you, how are...' There was a sudden grating of metal against concrete and then a slow rushing and hissing and whistling, a piercing scream of pain and a long groan.

'Pissing hell! It's all gone off!'

Katie stared at Andy and he stared back. White smoke was billowing along the brick tunnel and it was slashed through by white, spitting flares.

She nodded and he nodded back. They wrenched a fibre board out of the brambles and ran along the top of the entrance wall; it was dropped into the stream of smoke; then another and another, all piled up.

Katie jumped alongside Spry, prone in the gully. Her arms clutched around the wounded woman's chest and heaved and they were moving! She crashed into Andy: 'Pull her back through, mate!'

Where was Coles? Katie ran back into the white smoke, her arms spread over her face. Her left foot was stamping on a limb. It belonged to Coles. He was big! She dug her heels in and heaved, like she was heaving a ewe out of a thicket. Now they were moving! 'Water Andy! We need water! All the water we've got!'

They were out on the track. She beat at Coles' smouldering uniform until it stopped smoking, then bent down to tend to Spry. There were bubbles on the right side of her face and burns on her arms and legs. 'First aid kit!' She held Nicola's left hand - the right hand was burned. 'Nicola, it's Katie. You've been burnt badly. We're getting the medics. You're going to be fine.'

'How bad?'

'It's bad but you'll live. Andy, get the fucking air ambulance now! White phosphorus!'

'You knew...' Spry mumbled through burnt lips.

'How could I?' Andy had a red first aid box but it looked pitifully small. He handed her a water bottle.

'Something inside...'

'Look after Coles, mate' she muttered.

'...exploded.'

'It did, didn't it?'

'My face...'

'It's a bit red on one side, let me irrigate your mouth. You'll be fine, they can do wonders now.' Nicola seemed calm, despite what had happened. Katie called out to Andy: 'When will the ambulance get here? How's Coles doing? Katie turned back to Nicola: 'Where does it hurt?'

'All over. I feel cold.' Katie spread her jacket over the shivering body.

Spry's uniform was blackened, but not melted. The smell of phosphorous pervaded everything, clothes, skin and the air that Katie heaved in. 'You've been very brave.'

She trickled more water over Nicola's face so some entered between her burnt lips.

'Stupid, you mean.'

'Yes, that's what I mean! Where's that fucking ambulance! Get the rest of the crew down here! Water! Blankets! First aiders! Get 'em all!'

And now she was surrounded by a fluster of people in their navy blue work clothes, all staring at her.

Katie shouted another set of directions. Andy passed her a cell phone. Buttons were pressed in a sequence that she had used before, when she had been in trouble, when there was no way out, no hope of restitution.

'Uncle Alec, Uncle Alec, it's all gone tits-up!' She subsided onto the ground.

'Katie? Is that you?'

'Yes! Didn't you hear me! It's all gone tits-up' she shouted. She clamped the phone to her ear with both hands.

'Slowly, Katie, slowly.'

'I keep telling you Uncle Alec, its all gone tits-up!'

'Leading Hand Talog, stand to attention when you're talking to me and address me properly' he roared.

'What!' She stood to attention, her left arm shaking. 'But, Uncle Alec?'

'What's so desperate that you cannot address me properly!'

'I was spraying in Spry's mush!'

'You're doing what?'

'Spry! You must remember Spry! I'm spraying her down!'

'Is there someone else who is better suited to do that while you talk to me?'

'Er, yes, just about anybody sir!' Katie beckoned to the two figures by her: they responded.

'Well, Talog? SitRep?'

'SitRep, SitRep, SitRep. SitReppppp...'

'Take ten paces, turn around and tell me what you see...'

Katie did as she was told. She tossed the phone to her right hand because her left arm was playing up again. 'Bodies and they're all just staring...'

'Any casualties?'

'Two. Spry's on the deck, twenty to thirty percent burns. She's being looked after. Coles is on the deck, out cold. He's being looked after. The blockhouse is still blowing out white smoke, like white phosphorus. Andy is cordoning it off. Helicopter just coming in now. Looks like it's the air ambulance. Touch down point marked out. Fire appliances coming, coming...'

'So two casualties being looked after. Air ambulance about to land. Emergency services arriving. Who's in charge?'

'No bugger is.'

'You are. They're looking to you for direction, Talog, now direct them.'

'I can't.'

'Lead them - you're going to have to hold the fort for a couple of hours. Make it safe. I'm sending the emergency team.'

'Just a moment, sir.' Katie barked a set of instructions to the crowd. 'We'll need bomb disposal' she barked into the cell phone.

'I'll contact Ron Lightfoot...'

'No need, he knows, sir. I'll give him a bit of a hurry-up.'

Her breathing was approaching normal now. The fingers of her left were still flittering but her lips had stopped chittering. She waited for Uncle Alec to give her direction.

'Well done Talog.'

'Eh? I didn't do anything, sir.'

'Yes, you did. Look around. You're in charge, they will follow you.'

'In charge of what, sir?'

'This situation and your fate - call me on this number if you need anything else. Just hold the fort for now. Lightfoot will take command when he arrives.'

'Oh! Thank you sir.'

The air ambulance seemed to take an eternity to settle on the track. A fire engine and a big, official looking car were coming down the track. Katie wondered what had to be done next. There was a girl tending Spry. 'What's your name mate?'

'Mercy...'

'Oh, that's...nice.'

Leonie scowled her. 'Mercy, are you all right to stay with Coles and Spry? Call me when you get there and then every thirty?'

'How?'

'Call Leonie.' Another scowl.

The two casualties were lifted into the helicopter. The medic looked Katie over: 'I think you need treatment too. You're hands are burned.'

She ripped off her gloves. 'It's these. They're all fucked.' She looked ruefully at the tattered leather. 'Those two are the priority right now' she said, nodding at the helicopter. 'Get this lot cordoned off and make sure the fire fighters stay clear! This is a right cake and arse party, isn't it!'

A large, boxy silver car churning up pebbles was speeding towards her. It pulled up in a whirl of gravel. There was something about it that troubled her. Katie walked up to the driver's door and tapped on the window. 'Oi, you can't go any closer. This is a serious incident.'

'And who are you?' asked the civilian in the passenger seat. He was smartly dressed in a grey suit with red pinstripes, a red tie and a mop of tightly curled hair. He had the air of an administrator about him and it was apparently too much trouble to turn his head to look at her.

'Leading Hand Talog. I'm in charge here. Who are you?'

He pursed his lips as he scanned the scene in front of him. He had a name badge that said, 'Gibbons'. His conference must have been interrupted, she reckoned. There was still white smoke billowing along the brick tunnel, behind the black and yellow tape cordon. The crew of the fire engine had stood to and were having a brew.

'Not any longer, you're not. This is MoD property and we're taking it under our control!'

'All right Ron?' Katie asked. They were looking at the blockhouse; the burning had long expired and it squatted like a child, who had just had an explosive tantrum, but now all it wanted to do was sulk.

'Yes, ma'am.' Ron had the hangdog expression of a bucolic spaniel and his expression seemed to have worsened at the thought of having to take charge of this incident.

'Ron, I need your help, mate.' They ducked under the warning tape and strode together towards the blockhouse. 'What's the point of this?' she said pointing at the concrete structure.

'Obvious, isn't it? It's for spotting the fall of shot into the River Thames...ma'am.'

'Isn't it odd then that there's phosphorus inside the bunker? The inside of bunkers is for people, isn't it?'

'Yes ma'am.' She vaulted on to the roof of the bunker and gave Ron a hand-up.

They walked across the lichen and saxifrage spattered roof to the seaward side. A barbed wire fence framed the mudflats and the salt marsh out towards the wide, muddy river. She could see the anti-aircraft forts on their stilts in the middle of the estuary and the brown cliffs of the Isle of Sheppey. 'I need to find out what's inside and how I can make it safe. We'll need to get a wide angle camera inside and some lighting.'

'When do you want this done, ma'am?' he asked.

'As soon as' she replied, 'so I can sort out what's inside and then get out of this fucking shithole.'

Ron looked startled. 'I didn't think swearing was allowed in the RN, ma'am, particularly from lady wrens who aspire to being lady officers.'

'Oi, will you stop calling me ma'am! I'm not a sodding officer, am I?'

'Sorry, ma'am.'

'Anyway, swearing is allowed - it says so in the manual, doesn't it?'

'What manual is that, ma'am?'

'It's the manual of the Royal Navy, available in paperback and hardback.'

'I'm sure I've read it and there was no mention of 'fucking' or that other thing.'

'It's in the glossary at the back - no one reads the sodding glossary' she grumbled. Katie drew out her note book from her back pocket. 'Let me show you.' She riffled through the pages to the section concerning notable calendar dates. 'Here it is, definition of 'shithole' - 'HMS Hawkins, and other shitholes like it.'

'And what does the manual say about 'fucking'?'

'It's a word, commonly used to add urgency and emphasis to a command' she bluffed.

'That's all right then.' He thought for a moment. 'Won't it be dangerous if there are phosphorus bombs inside?'

'Probably, but we must have flooded it with air when the door opened, the phosphorus should have all burned off now. Give me a shout when you're ready and we'll go through the permit.' She looked askance at him. 'What are you thinking about now, Ron?'

'Why don't you open the flap?'

'What flap?'

'The flap at your front?'

Frowning, she looked down towards the crotch of her trousers. 'Don't be disgusting!'

'No, I meant on the bunker' he tutted. They walked to the front of the bunker and Katie bent over the edge and started tapping on the rusty flap covering the embrasure. 'Yep' he said sarcastically, 'that should do it, ma'am.'

She grimaced at him. 'Have you got a tool I can use?'

It was Ron's turn to look puzzled.

'To get my flap open?'

'Ah, I see what you mean, ma'am. A crowbar!' She stuck out her tongue at him but he had already jumped off the concrete structure.

He was back at her side, levering the rust encrusted embrasure. It slowly groaned open. They pulled together until it rested against the pitted concrete. 'That smell, it's phosphorus, isn't it?' Katie declared.

'Yep, all oxidised' Ron replied.

Then something occurred to her: 'I meant to ask Ron, what happened to your ears?' She looked at the pink device lodged in his left earhole.

'I was too close to a four point five inch gun when they fired it.'

'Weren't you wearing ear muffs?'

'I was, but there was too much 'bang' for them to cope with.'

'I've always thought there's too much 'bang' at the release end. You really need all the 'bang' at the other end, don't you?'

'You're absolutely right, ma'am. All that training you've had on weapons and munitions has certainly paid off!'

'You piss-taking bugger! Anyway, all the stuff I deal with tends to go 'whoosh' rather than 'bang' so it's a lot easier on the ears.'

'That must be really reassuring for the people at the receiving end' he commented. They strolled back and jumped off the back of the bunker. 'Anyway, let's get dressed up and see what else we can find.' They retreated to the mid sea-grey Land Rover and Katie helped him put on a full bomb disposal protective suit.

'If we set off a real bomb, will I be protected?' she asked.

'No, put on a helmet and visor and boots and stay behind me.'

'Okey-dokey, but I won't be able to sense anything if I'm wearing a visor though, will I?'

'Just stay behind me and you'll be fine. We'll use the detector and we won't rely on your hyper-sensitivity, or whatever they call it?'

'Okey-dokey, Mark One eyeball only.' They traversed the shore line to the boundary fence on the east side of the site, without finding anything. They approached the creek that formed the boundary and were challenged by a redshank perched on a wooden rib sticking through the mud. Close by were six petrol drums embedded and rusting through in the creek.

'World War Two vintage' commented Ron. They followed the creek inland and Katie caught sight of a ruined building. 'Stay behind me, Katie, we're not in the clear yet.'

As they approached, the red brick walls came into focus as a sad, burned out shell of a one storey building.

Katie froze: 'Something bad happened here a long time ago' she muttered as her gut churned over. She waited for Ron's prompt and then tip-toed into the middle of the main room. The remains of a small fireplace were still evident on the East wall. No wood in the structure had survived the fire.

'Looks like a wave of fire came in from the shore side. It wasn't an explosion.'

'Can I borrow your pen?' she asked.

'Sure, if I can find it.'

'It's in your fag bracket.'

'Oh yeah, there it is' he said as he retrieved a pen from behind his ear and passed it to her.

Even through the solid rigidity of her helmet, and the padding of her suit, she could feel the presence of the two souls that had been burnt off the face of this world. Her sigh misted the visor. Katie decided she would have to update her planner - two arms of the spiral had been hitched but would the whole thing now collapse? She scribbled on her wrist and handed the pen back. 'Do you know what happened here, Ron?'

'Someone had the bright idea of setting the Thames alight, if the balloon ever went up...desperate days.'

'Bit of a panic, then...'

'Big panic...'

'And it all back-fired?'

'It did - too many imponderables, like changing wind direction, but you'd know all about that, wouldn't you Katie?'

'Eh?'

'Changing the direction of the wind - that's the kind of thing you do, isn't it?'

'I think you think you're being really clever, but you're actually not, are you?'

'Eh?'

'You heard - anyway, we're all done here and there's no need to report back on something that happened back then, is there?'

'Well, ma'am...'

'What would be the point?'

'Natural justice, ma'am...'

'I can't though...there's no time.'

'Still...' Katie took off the helmet and shook it - her hair cascaded about her shoulders. Ron gasped 'You've changed, you're...a woman!'

'Blimey. Is it that obvious?' She quickly rescued her hair with a leather clasp and re-secured it above her head.

'You know, if I was twenty years younger...' he wondered out loud.

'You would still be a dirty old scrote' she said, as they stretched out tape to show the area had been checked and was clear, 'and I wouldn't have been born, would I?'

'Oh, bugger! I've blown it haven't I?'

'Yes, you have, you pillock.'

'But what about all the jobs I've done for you! What do you reckon my chances are now?'

'Less than zero, mate.'

They walked quickly back to the blockhouse, swinging their helmets in unison. He wasn't a bad looking bloke, just totally life weary. They sat down on the riverside of the seawall, outside of the taped-off enclosure and prepared to have their picnic. After the tumultuous events of the morning, the team had dispersed back to all their stations. There was no one else about.

'Are you still eating fish paste sandwiches Ron?' she asked.

'You can't beat a bit of fish paste' he replied.

'Have you got anything else I can swap? I've just got ham, cheese and pickle?'

'That's not a fair exchange. You can't beat a bit of fish paste, can you?'

'I'll try the fish paste. Is fish paste actually with fish?' They exchanged sandwiches. 'I can't think of any fish that smells anything like this. Is it the stuff that no one wants to eat?'

'No, it's bloater paste.'

'Bloater?' she replied. She puffed up her cheeks and mimicked a large fish sucking in water. 'Sounds, like a big, fat, ugly bastard of a fish.'

'No, it's smoked herring. It's the prince of fish pastes.'

'I see.' Katie took a bite out of the sandwich. 'Eurghh! That's disgusting!' So, she removed it from her mouth and threw it skywards - a gull seized it and settled down on the seawall to gulp it down. She laid back to confront the sun. Carefully, she brushed crumbs off her shirt but then realised she had made a terrible error.

There was one particular crumb that was taking a bit of dislodging.

Ron was watching her intently.

Katie pulled back her shirt and looked down her front. 'Oh, no!'

He slid alongside her. There was a frisson of sexual excitement emanating from her colleague. 'I can see your bra. It's black' he observed.

'That must be very exciting for you' she replied. 'Listen, turn around, I've got something stuck in it.'

'Two things' he corrected.

'One thing that doesn't belong. Look away now.'

He turned his back to her. She looked over her shoulder, hooked away the shoulder of her shirt and pulled at the right cup of her bra. Still no joy.

Now, he seemed eager to offer assistance. The catch on her bra was unhooked and the contents fell away, including the crumb. The bra was proficiently secured and her shirt covered her shoulders again.

'Better?' he enquired.

'Much' she replied.

'So, what do you reckon?' he asked.

'About us? I think we make a great team. I find stuff for you to do and you come along and you do it. Thanks ever so much, mate.'

'No problem, any time.' Ron Lightfoot looked up and down the seawall and then back to Katie. 'So, how about you and me? How about a little kiss and cuddle? No one can see us here.'

'Piss off, you dirty old scrote.' She unfolded the works order and presented it to him for his signature. 'Anyway, I think you need to keep your mind on the job, Ron. Sign here.' She indicated where his chop applied.

'Pen?'

'Fag bracket.'

He signed quickly and dismissively. 'So, what about after? Me and you? Let's go out for a drink together, for old times sake.'

'Is your missus invited?'

'Who?'

'Your missus. You remember, when you woke up, there was someone else next to you in bed. That was your missus. The one you married for better or worse, makes you your dinner, irons your shirts, lets you have a shag at the weekend, if you've been good...'

'All right, all right, just keep it clean will you...'

'She's probably a big lady, so I wouldn't want to upset her' Katie interjected.

'For your information, we have a very open marriage and if we want to go out with a member of the opposite, er, inclination that's not a problem.'

'Well, it is for me. And just to be clear, there's no way I'm having any more of your fish paste stuffed inside me, so there.'

'You've become a hard-hearted woman, Katie.'

'And you're a soft-headed man, Ron. So, what about this work requisition then? Shouldn't you be calling your little blokes and getting them out here?'

'No, there's plenty of time for that - let's just enjoy our picnic in the sun.'

'Did you read the requisition before signing on it, Ron?'

'Of course not, I trust you Katie.'

'Oh. I think you'd better read it again then, Ron.'

'Have you stitched me up?'

'No, I haven't! See here where you've signed and just above that, the work needs to be done now, not any other time!'

'You're a hard-headed woman, Katie.' Ron made a call on his cell phone. 'Dave, yes it's Ron, I'm with Katie Talog. Are you on your way? She wants the team out here now!'

The reply was indignant, loud and prolonged. Katie heard her name mentioned twice and she wasn't happy with what she was hearing. Ron wasn't happy either. 'Dave, Dave, Katie Talog is with me - she can hear everything you say!'

Katie beckoned for the phone. 'Dave, Dave, she wants the phone!' Ron covered his eyes, turned away and cringed as she placed the phone to her ear.

'Hallo Dave, it's Katie.'

There was the noise of a diesel engine and the bouncing of springs.

'Thanks for your concern about my health, Dave, I'm really touched by that, but, for your information, I'm not 'on the blob' as you put it, but I am getting a bit irritated, because I need you here now, so I really hope you've got your motor running.'

There was a laugh down the line and a comment about someone called 'Stefan Wolf' or something like that.

'If you can get your Mister Wolf down here now, and he can do everything I want, I will be ecstatic' she countered.

There was lewd laughter down the line. She mouthed the name to Ron but he still had his face buried in his hands and he was whimpering. 'No, I didn't mean ecstatic like that. I meant, very pleased.' She heard the sound of banter in a vehicle. 'Anyway, I would have thought that a bloke like you would have been quite attached to his bollocks...'

Katie quit the call and handed the phone back to Ron. 'He's on his way. Dave's a good lad but he's a bit slow on the uptake, isn't he?'

'Good, so we're all good now, are we Katie?'

'Are you trying it on again, Ron?'

'Of course not' he replied, 'so...do you have a boyfriend, Katie?'

'I have several on the go, but no one's come through quite yet.' She looked above the parapet - there was a mid-grey vehicle bouncing its way along the track.

Ron sniggered. 'But what about me?'

'What about you?' The mid-grey vehicle had arrived. She breathed a sigh of relief.

'But what about you? You think that half a fish paste sandwich is all it takes? You cheeky bugger! So what happens when you treat your missus? Does she get the full fish paste experience?'

'She doesn't like fish paste.'

'Don't blame her!'

'So, what do you reckon?'

'Well, come and have a go if you think you've got it in you.' She settled back, resting on her elbows and staring him in the eye.

He hesitated. 'Why are you clutching onto that pen?'

'I'm going to poke you in the eye with it if you try anything on, Ron' she answered sweetly.

'What do you think the MoD are up to, Ron?' She looked across to the squat main block, now surrounded by vehicles. All Katie had to work with was a makeshift tent and a table just outside the taped off area and no idea when she would be leaving. Andy emerged from the tent, cradling a mug of tea. Bomb disposal Dave and his mate were now similarly equipped.

'How do you know this mob?' asked Andy.

She paused. 'It's because of what you do Ron, Ron, isn't it?'

'We've known each other for nearly five years, haven't we Katie, Katie?'

'Um, I suppose so' Katie replied cautiously. He was going to trot out the story about his fish paste sandwiches again.

'She's very coy about how we first met.' There were sniggers.

'Can you tell us all what happened?' said Dave. 'I don't think I've heard this one?'

She shuffled her feet uncomfortably. 'Well, I was a trainee rate and Ron, um, Captain Lightfoot gave us a class on bomb disposal.'

'At Pompey. And what did you think of it?'

'It was very good, wasn't it?'

'And what happened?'

'You put your lunch box on the table in front of me and said it was an explosive device.'

'And when she says lunch box, she actually means my sandwiches. So, then what happened, Katie?'

'I just picked them up and threw them out of the window, as you would.'

'As you would. And, where did it land Katie?'

'In the harbour.'

'And then what happened?'

'You said man overboard, go and rescue.'

'So what did you do then?'

'I did a quick roll call.'

'And then?'

'I had to fish your lunch out of the harbour.'

'Ugh!'

'And then you kept moaning about your wet sandwiches.'

'And then what happened?'

'I had to buy you lunch, which was very expensive when you're a new rate and you're having to buy all the most expensive stuff on the menu.'

'And what did you learn from that experience?'

'Fish paste is evil.'

'Anything else?'

'Not to toss sandwiches in the harbour.'

'Anything else?'

She gave a big sigh. 'Evacuate quickly and calmly, check everyone is clear, secure the area and get help.'

'And the next time we met?'

'Oh, yes. I reckoned there was something else big, brooding and dangerous in the harbour at Portsmouth, but not fish paste sandwiches this time...'

'And how did that go?'

'Much better. It was a sodding, great big parachute mine so...'

'It had to be a controlled explosion. Great bang.'

'Jesus Christ!'

'Katie seems to have the knack of sniffing out these things. In my section, we always breath a huge sigh of relief when she's overseas, as she is no longer part of our jurisdiction.' There was a pause. 'Find anything good on your last tour, Katie?'

'Just a Chinese sub...'

Ron brought out what remained of his sandwiches and tossed them casually on the table. Katie picked them up, pivoted her body around twice, swung her left arm back and launched them like a discus over the seawall.

They were about to get a summons from Mister Gibbons.

CHAPTER FIFTY

Thursday 26 May 1830 - Shoeburyness

Katie, Andy, Ron and Dave had been summoned to the mess room in the squat main block by a stern looking military policeman. She now stood nervously in the round and it was Gibbons in the middle, who insisted that he should be called Dominic as he was their friend and his door was always open.

'This is how I say we will do this. Lightfoot and his team will map all the containers in the blockhouse, assess them, clean them, open them and check them for any explosives. They will then be numbered and transferred here. Is there anything to add to that Captain Lightfoot?'

'No, once we've cleared what's left of the munitions and there are no more explosives or inflammables in there, we'll certify the site as clear. I'll stay nearby in case I'm needed for the investigation.'

'What investigation?' asked Katie, jabbing Ron in the ribs.

'The one that will determine who was responsible for this shambles!' replied Gibbons.

'That could take some time' murmured Katie.

'Have you got anything better to do?'

'Well, actually, yes!'

'So who's responsible for the site overnight?'

'Not me! I've got an appointment!'

'Change it.'

'Huh?'

'Change it.'

'Bollocks!'

'Or you'll be on a charge, Talog!' He had two men with him who had the bearing of military policemen.

'Katie!' hissed Ron Lightfoot.

'I really can't! I made a promise!'

'Talog! I'll see you in my office!'

'He's got an office? How the fuck did that...'

'TALOG!'

'Fucketty, fucketty, fuck!' she muttered. All the pillars of her plan were falling apart. She looked around. No support from her colleagues. She withdrew from the circle and made her way to Coles' office. She wondered how he was doing. She wondered how Spry was doing. Probably a lot better than she was.

The door was closed so she opened it slowly - inside the office there was just the one seat so she settled in that one, behind the desk. All of the personal bits and pieces owned by Coles were now piled in a metal waste paper bin.

'Now, listen, all of you' continued the briefing outside. Gibbons then rattled on about two ratings missing in action at Shoeburyness in June 1940. This she knew - the men had been consumed by oily flames when they set the River Thames alight.

So that was it.

Katie spun out of the whirly chair and threw open the windows. She climbed out, snorted in the dirty, sea-weedy air and looked along the line of the seawall, saw the boxy tops of the forts in the river, the mound of the Isle of Sheppey and the smoggy haze over the city. There was a surge in her stomach and then a burning in her gullet. She heard a faint cry of 'au secours'; Nana had been here an age ago, fighting her way up the river, battling through the flames and then...

Someone had entered the office. It was Gibbons. Leonie followed closely. A tray was placed on the table with undue ceremony.

'No cups?'

'Just mugs sir' Leonie answered pointedly.

'Where the hell is Talog?'

Katie stepped back in the office and made her way to stand in front of the desk.

'Not heard of doors, Talog?'

'I needed some air.'

'Take a seat.'

There wasn't one. 'I'll stand.'

He waited impatiently as she took the mug that had the spoon. Three sugars, good.

'I don't know what's been going on here. The plan was to close down this site. Now there's this mess and if the media gets hold of it...'

'I've kept the top brass in the loop all the way through, ever since I landed here.' He avoided her stare. She kept her fingers crossed as she said this - Uncle Alec must count as top brass, mustn't he?

'I'm going to undo all this mess and get the closure back on track.'

'That's good - how are you going to undo what happened to Spry and Coles then?'

'They're being looked after. Why the hell they went in there I don't know, stupid, stupid, stupid.'

'They were unlucky - it was going to go off as soon as some mug forced the door open.'

'You Talog do not have the rank, experience or authority or knowledge to deal with this.'

'I don't take orders from civilians, you charmless scrote - who are you anyway? What's your rank?'

He looked at Leonie. 'Perhaps you can advise her...'

'He's a very senior civil servant in the M.o.D, Katie.'

'Oh, is he? That's not really helping.'

Gibbons looked through the papers on the desk and then consulted his mobile device. 'This can't be right?'

'Nothing's right about this shithole!'

'You are the most senior RN staff member on site?'

Yes, I'm not quite sure how that occurred...'

'And you seem unwilling to take orders.'

'It depends who's giving them to me!'

'You will take charge of security of the site overnight and hand over responsibility at oh-nine hundred hours tomorrow.'

'I'm sorry, I can't do that...I'm out of here now, my CO is...' There were now two military policeman either side of her.

'You're such an idiot!' muttered Leonie as she cast her eyes upwards, turned and left the room.

Katie sighed. 'So, that's how it's going to be, is it?'

'Here are your orders...' Gibbons pushed a piece of paper across the desk. 'They're addressed to Leading Hand K.E.Talog.'

'Just spell 'em out.'

'Keep the site safe and secure. These men will assist you.' The one on her left turned and gave her a wide smile.

'Fantastic. Where am I supposed to sleep?'

'Sleep? Sleep? You're on watch all night!'

'There's no way I'm doing a double dog!'

'You'll do as you're ordered.'

She sighed again and the papers on the desk fluttered to the floor. The top page seemed to have the seal of an official looking Admiralty signature.

'By the way, there is to be an enquiry into the conduct of operations while you were serving on board HMS Albany during the last week of April of the current year. Your presence will be required.' He picked up a sheet of paper and put it in her hand. He paused as she attempted to read the fine print.

'This can't be right?'

'You will be required to attend a hearing at Portsmouth, on dates to be confirmed. You may resume your leave, but you must ensure that you can be contacted at short notice. You may not leave the country. Subsequent to the outcome of the enquiry, your pay and conditions will be reviewed. Any questions?'

'Why are you doing this?'

'This country needs public servants who do as they are told and can be relied on. We can't afford to have people who think the armed forces are their own private enterprise. This is not a despotic, third world country, this is Great Britain!'

'Instead of that, why don't you find out how my CO got incinerated?'

'We will Talog, we will. None of that is any of your concern. If you have anything pertinent to this case you will hand it to me and someone will deal with it.'

She looked at Leonie. What could he possibly want with a pile of chits and a hastily put together SitRep? Leonie handed a file to Katie and Katie handed it to Gibbons.

'What's all this?'

'It's a load of chits.'

He grimaced. 'Anything else?'

'Nope.'

'We will need to be able to contact you, so where will you be?'

'Am I on a charge?'

'No, not yet.'

Katie scribbled down the address and a telephone number for Clun Farm. She tried to picture how Gwen would react when she got the call. Not well, that was for sure. Katie screwed up the paper, threw it at the bin and started a new sheet with Paol Houghton's details instead.

'And who is this?'

'He's my brother.'

'And he's reputable?'

'Of course he is, he's a senior lecturer in Politics at the North London University.'

'Oh, my good god, a Marxist. Any more misfits in your family?' Gibbons turned to nobody in particular. 'I think we had better contact him, check him out and make sure he understands his responsibilities.'

Katie felt an upwelling from her core and a surge in her heart and lungs. She focused on Gibbon's organs, underneath the silk shirt and tie, starting with his stomach. He continued to speak and she could hear his voice but not the words. His stomach wall now secreted bile acid and the acid grew and grew until he stood suddenly with a look of shock on his face. His hand was over his mouth and his cheeks were puffed out. 'Bin!' he spluttered. He turned and threw up out of the window.

'Is that all?' Katie asked. She assumed it was and so she left the room with Gibbons gagging out of the window.

Katie kept walking until she reached the taped off blockhouse. All was quiet apart from the chipping of the sea birds. She could see the ruins of a building to the east and all the way to her right was the western flank of the site.

There was a man in orange trousers, shaking the fence by the entrance gate impotently, the fence she had made sure was repaired. Two figures ran purposefully towards him.

Robert Glaus stopped his assault on the fence, strode back to his mighty stallion of a car, revved the engine fiercely and drove away in a spitting fury of gravel.

Under the tape she stooped and then quickly, mounting the top of the bunker, she screamed and waved furiously at the back of the rapidly retreating car but it made no difference. It didn't stop.

She subsided onto the top of the lichen and saxifrage spattered roof and gazed up at the sky until she was dreaming.

CHAPTER FIFTY-ONE

A huge advance in Damage Control Operational Training

There were five of them, standing in a line on the top of a huge metal box, whipped by westerly rain, all garbed in light-buff waterproof (supposedly) overalls and fitted with rubber boots and breathing apparatus. But the rain didn't matter, because soon they would descend into the bowels of this huge box, be shaken, flushed and then made to mend all the battle damage that the control room could inflict on them. It would be like fixing a broken toilet from beyond the bend she thought.

Ah, Instructor Ledbetter was about to give them some final instructions. Katie trembled in anticipation. It was her turn to lead this bunch of trainee rates.

'Right - Atiq, Talog, White, Whitworth, Woods. You will assemble in the corridor of the middle level and the exercise will commence when you hear the warning to brace yourselves. You will then receive instructions pertaining to where to go and what to do when you get there. Clear?

'Yessir' they all chorussed.

'I will be in close proximity all the time to witness what goes on and to throw the odd spanner in the works. All clear?'

'Yessir' all but one of them chorussed.

Katie had had a worrying thought. 'Sir, what are the rules on this?'

'Do as your told. And thanks for the prompt, Talog. You will lead the damage control team. Clear?'

'Merde' she muttered to herself.

'Was that an epithet, Talog?'

'Not at all sir! It's a curse!'

'Brilliant. Brilliant. Follow me!'

As they descended the stairway, Witless jabbed her in the ribs. 'If you can't hack it Talog, tell me now. No boots, no respirator on him, this'll be a piss in the park!'

Witless was right. Ledbetter was sporting black pumps and no breathing aid, other than a pair of over-sized nostrils that by rights should belong on the face of a walrus. But she couldn't quell the nagging ache at the base of her gut. They were now in the middle level and the huge box was swaying gently and there was a crackling over the sound system. Ledbetter was now waving at the two operators in the control room. 'Action stations' blared the tannoy. The nightmare was about to start.

'You'll be fine, my Shazia' murmured Atiq, 'we are all trained as leaders...'

'I'm not your Shazia' she hissed back.

'Princess Shaz! That's priceless' crowed White, 'that almost rhymes with my favourite word! Shag!'

'No, it doesn't Baz, you big pillock!' she retorted.

'Keep focussed Talog' bleated Woods.

'Pez is right, let's have a bit of hush' she shouted.

Water was speeding up from the sump to the storage vessel high above their heads. She could hear the whir of valves activating and the pent up forces of water rushing behind the bulkheads and above them. And, there was something else. A sound that did not belong. The sound of tiny, fizzing bubbles, fizzing inside of solid metal, eating it from within.

'Shhh, can you hear that?' She hushed them with a finger across her lips and then indicated with both forefingers the void below the deck. Somewhere below, metal was being consumed.

'Brace, brace, brace!' shouted the tannoy. They seized what handles, shelves and frames they could as the walls of the corridor shook. 'Shrapnel damage starboard mess deck!' announced the tannoy.

'Which one is starboard?' she shouted. Water was now swirling around their ankles.

'This side, you twat!' shouted Witless. He turned the wheel and the bulkhead door pushed in. Water rushed over their calves.

'Get the tools and wedges, Pez. Ghak, get two bracing beams!'

'Bracing beams? Talog, you do not need bracing beams!' shouted Ledbetter.

'Yes, we do!' she shouted in reply. The bulkhead door closed. Water was now rushing about her knees. She shuddered. There was something very wrong. 'Witless, Pez - get wedges in there' she shouted and pointed at the jagged cluster of ugly holes in the vessel wall.

Now there was something about to burst from behind the locker on the outside wall. 'Ghak, Baz, lever that bastard off the wall, something's coming.'

'Whoa, whoa, do not damage the unit!' shouted the instructor. He was too late, wedges had been hammered in and it was levered off the wall. There was a large jagged hole behind. No torrent as yet, but she sensed it was coming.

'Wedge a mattress against that' she shouted, 'and batten it down!' Water was swirling around her thighs and it was so cold.

'She's lost it!' shouted Witless at Ledbetter.

'The floor's coming up, can't you feel it?' she shouted back.

'Get a grip Talog!' shouted Ledbetter.

'Can you feel it? Can you feel it? No, we can't!' shouted Baz.

The instructor waded up to her, struggling against the flow. 'Get a grip Talog. Deal with what you can see and not what you...'

Metal ground harshly against metal. 'You heard that, didn't you?'

'Talog, stop this now...Whitworth, take over. Talog, stand down!'

Ledbetter waded to the bulkhead door, the only escape route, and wrenched at the wheel. It didn't move.

'Ghak, Baz, get the beams up, there and there!' she shouted. Ghak positioned one in the centre of the floor and she shoved it home with her backside. 'Get those sodding wedges in, top and bottom!'

The deck dipped suddenly and water rushed past them and then back again. 'Everybody, grab something quick. The floor's coming up! It's coming up now! Ledbetter, that includes you! High as you can! High as you can!'

The huge box suddenly dropped. Water rushed upwards and took its passengers up with it, like flotsam. Her back slapped against the ceiling. She sank, tried to haul in a breath and coughed water. Her face emerged into air. A massive fist had her suit in a grip, pulling her up again. It was Ghak!

'Breathe, princess, breathe!' he shouted. Her mouthpiece was thrust in her mouth. She sucked in a breath and ripped it off. There were just four heads bobbing on the surface.

'Where's Ledbetter?' she cried out.

'I've got him!' shouted Baz. He cradled a gasping body in his massive arms.

'What's he saying?'

'Abort! Abort!'

'Great idea!'

'C'mon, take stock. Remember your training' spluttered Pez.

She had to get out. She saw that the ceiling was crumpled between the struts. Rivets had popped. 'Ghak! Me! On your shoulders!' She swung through the water, sat on his shoulder, gasped in air, swung back, coiled her legs and thrust upwards. But it was useless, too much resisting, too much hurt. She stared at her Pathan, as she gulped in dirty water and air.

'Again Princess, again' roared Ghak, 'it will yield to you!'

'But it's metal!' He swung her down. She coiled again, felt his power channelling through his hands, his arms, his shoulders, her core. Katie's body uncoiled upwards, legs smashing through and bursting beyond the roof. Her legs were caught, in an unyielding grip! They were being tugged up! Her body was through, flopping onto the wrecked roof! Two emergency responders, steady on the top, calm, strong, asking her if she was okay.

'Get Ledbetter out! He's in a bad way' she shouted.

'We've got him Princess!' It was Baz.

Ledbetter was out, out of the tank.

'He needs help' she shouted.

A medic worked on him and he was now breathing, they said, calmly and unflustered by the chaos around them. The buzzing of distraught electronics, roaring of mechanical saws, lights flashing blindly.

'He didn't have the proper kit, did he?'

Ledbetter was strapped into a stretcher, lowered with a sling, down the side of the tank. There was an ambulance, flashing at her. 'Get him an ambulance!' Now, more arms waving for help. 'It's Pez, get him out' Now Baz and his massive arms were hauled up and out. 'Get Ghak, Ghak's next! No, not Witless, Ghak! Leader's last out!' Witless was out, remonstrating with her. 'Ghak, get Ghak!' Ghak was out. Her Pathan seized her around her waist and hoisted her up. Katie's core surged and a wave of relief rushed over her skin, across her shoulders, over her crown and along her arms. Must get composure back, high-ups about.

They were so sodden, the water drained from their overalls like rain pattering on the upper deck. Rain still poured down from the leaden sky. She watched as Ledbetter was lifted into a flashing ambulance. He was safe. She was not.

There was now a flurry of mechanicians around the box, which was canted at a sorry angle. They were making checks, they wanted to know cause, to know what had happened. The last of the little tremors through her body had now evaporated away. All that was left was a heavy feeling in her stomach which presaged trouble, a large dose of it, bringing consequences that she could not quite imagine, a turn of fate that would bring a bitter taste bubbling up her throat. She gulped to quell her nausea.

There were now two new high-ups in front of her and her team, on the tilted deck. Better get her retaliation in first. 'Someone could have been killed in there, sir. It's a sodding deathtrap!'

The officer looked at her sternly. Witless nudged her in the ribs. 'Nice one, Princess!'

'Piss off!'

'Quiet!' There was hush. 'Who was leader in there?'

She made an offering: 'We're all trained to be leaders!'

'Talog!' said Baz, Pez and Witless in harmony.

'It was Instructor Ledbetter, until he was half drowned in that sodding deathtrap...'

'Knob-head' whispered Witless.

'Until Witless took over...'

'I can't tell a lie sir, it was definitely Talog, Sir!' announced Witless.

'Wanker!' she whispered behind her palm.

Her colleagues were dismissed and they were told to attend a debrief in an hour after they had got out of their wet kit and were dried off. Meanwhile, she was still there in the wet. A high ranking officer had now arrived in front of her and he was having an animated conversation with a civilian in a bright yellow high-visibility waterproof. She guessed the civilian was a high up because he was shouting at the officer.

'Dismissed, sir?' she offered to the officer. With a start, she realised who he was. It was Captain Crichlow, the silent assassin, head of the Raleigh Damage Control Training Unit. Oh fucketty, fucketty, fuck.

'Stay where you are, Talog!' he replied.

Katie moved a sodden lock of hair aside and listened to the state of play. The civilian was upset because his equipment had been used inappropriately, he said. She couldn't imagine how. Crichlow was trying to placate the civilian, claiming that the damage could be fixed. She couldn't imagine how. She just wished they would get on with it so she could get out of her wet clothes and get warm.

'I'll show you! Come with me!' shouted the civilian. His name was President Doherty, apparently. Now in tow was one of the operators who she had seen in the Control Room. He seemed eager to whisper in Doherty's ear at every opportunity, which she thought was very rude. He kept pointing at things and using words such as 'impossible', 'improbable' and 'inconceivable'.

Katie hung back. Unfortunately, she was needed. Crichlow told her to compile a snagging list. When she protested, she got a stern look. So when the clipboard and the pencil were thrust at her, she took them and followed the party down into the tilted and crumpled box. The stairway was quite tricky to negotiate.

The bulkhead door could not be opened easily. 'Needs adjusting by the mechanician' suggested Crichlow as he gave a curt nod towards Katie. When she had regained her composure, she made a quick sketch of a box and its various twisted levels. 'SCARP' she scribbled down, which looked about right.

They forced their way in and stopped in awe at the sight of the two vertical pieces of four by four that supported the crumpled ceiling and propped down the buckled floor. There was a square-sided gap in the roof, where stars twinkled through. At least it had stopped pissing down with rain. 'Floor needs beating out' said Crichlow, 'and ceiling panel replaced.' She wrote down 'SCRAP' with a curly arrow pointing to the top of her sketch.

'Where the hell did these come from?' accused Doherty, pointing at the pieces of four by four.

'Um, the store' she replied.

'Rubbish!' he replied.

'You're probably right' she commented.

Doherty glared at Crichlow, who now had a half-smile etched across his face. 'How the hell did this happen?' he growled pointing at the wavy ceiling with a big, square hole in it.

She shrugged. 'We made an escape panel right there...'

They left this level and climbed back out of the void. She just drew a line across the sketch and wrote, 'SCRAP'. Yes, that looked much better.

Next, the tight-lipped party climbed out and down the side. It was cold and crisp outside and she shivered. 'Sir? I need a hot bath!'

'Just wait Talog, we're nearly done.' Now, here was the sump, rippled over with water gushing in and above it, the smell of metal that had sheared away. 'What happened here, Talog?'

'It broke, sir.'

'Please elucidate...'

'Eh?' She frowned. 'Well, that support there, it's rotten with little holes, sir. Probably will need more than a drop of sticky to fix it.'

Doherty was swelling up, ready to explode. 'This...this was a huge advance in damage control operational training, now look at it!'

Katie and Crichlow shared a glance. Crichlow asked for the snagging list. 'Very pictorial, Talog' he said and nodded in tacit agreement.

'Oh, thank you sir. You're not so bad yourself!' she replied.

'So, in summary...'

She highlighted with her index finger the one word summary that she had written diagonally across the form.

Crichlow glanced at it. 'Got it. Oh, by the way Talog, there's an 'e' in fucked!'

'Oh, sorry sir.'

'Overall assessment, Talog?' smirked Crichlow.

'I think that says it all sir, but as I say, I'm not really an expert' she whispered.

'I think it's reasonable Talog...let them know your opinion.'

'Who me? Well, with all due respect, I think it's a total crock and...it's fucked beyond repair!'

Crichlow guffawed.

She turned her attention to Doherty and shuddered - now there would be a super, huge outburst. Doherty and his lackey looked shocked, as if they had both been slapped hard across the face with a big, wet, oily fish. Perhaps she should help translate, as at least one of them sounded like a colonial cousin. 'Or, if you prefer guys, it's a complete and utter cluster-fuck.'

CHAPTER FIFTY-TWO

1025 Thursday 23 May 1940 - Leaving Paris

"Your turn" murmured Rozenn. They both had a fan of playing cards in their hands.

"How did you do that?" the man replied gruffly. He was portly and English but he had some command of the beautiful language.

"I may have cheated."

"So, what do I do now?" he muttered.

"Play the next card!"

"But I cannot win, there's no point?"

"There's always a point. Or are you saying you capitulate?"

"Never!"

"So, you are in charge of the British and their Empire. What will you do then?"

He searched her face intently and she was forced to blush.

"Fight on. We will never surrender."

"Then, you must do as I suggest..."

"Sell my soul?"

"Ya."

"To the devil?"

"If necessary."

"And we both know what that means."

"We are living through the most desperate of times..."

"The Bolsheviks?"

"You must do whatever it takes to prevail. I fear that this means... unnatural alliances."

"Mademoiselle Abgrall, you are being very...evasive."

"I do not know everything, I just know that there is a... misalignment...a twisting of the spirals...a malevolent conjunction."

"So what do the cards tell you?"

"They tell me I win, but this is just a game of cards."

"Your Christoph, is he the key?"

"Ya, I fear he may be, in part."

Sandy McPherson intervened. "We are flying teams of saboteurs into Belgium to slow down the Hun, and we can fly you in too."

"But not to where Christoph is..."

"Not quite..."

"But Monsieur Sondee, you cannot fight this evil with bullets and bombs and saboteurs, you will need to strike at the tipping point, le point de décision, and Christoph is at that point, and I know him and you need me and you will need all of my clan!"

She fell silent, tight lipped, as she had said much more than she had wanted to say.

"All your clan? Do you mean the Britanni, Rozenn?"

"Who the hell are the Britanni?" grouched the leader of the Britons.

"Ah, the sea witches" said McPherson, "you've not heard of the sea witches, sir? And you a former sea lord!"

"What the hell are you talking about, McPherson?"

"The sea witches - the clan of witches that has protected our sailors and our marines and our shores from those that would attack us for a hundred years or more."

"Assuming they're not a figment of your imagination McPherson, how do I recruit these so called sea witches?"

"I think you just did sir!"

Chapter Fifty-Three

0526 Wednesday 29 May 1940 - Approaching Dunkirk

Rozenn ran just behind the pilot and the Welsh officer. They were panting from the midday heat and the weight of their back packs and the pouches slung around their waists.

And then she saw the aircraft that was to be their transport. She slowed and then stopped in horror at what she saw before her. It was a monoplane but the wings stuck out of the glasshouse of a canopy and were propped up with large struts. The whole machine pointed at a ridiculous angle up to the sky. There were spats over the front pair of wheels and there was mud and grass caked inside them. It looked slow and ungainly like a giant stork.

"How will this get us all the way to the les Pays-Bas?" she shouted at the pilot. The engine had been started, the propellor was whirring and the mechanic was standing proudly to one side indicating the ladder where she and the Welsh officer would climb into the rear of the canopy.

"We have a range of, ooh let's see, over four hundred miles" he shouted back.

"The Germans have planes that look like they were designed to fight, not to fall out of the sky!"

"This is an artillery observation plane, it is not designed to fight, but we have machine guns for our defence. It will meet your needs. We will fly close to the ground."

"Zut alors! I am not getting into that!"

"Why not? Would you prefer to walk, lovely?"

"What do I do if we are attacked?"

"We have two machine guns that can be operated from the observer's seat. Do you see? You will see off any attacker." The pilot had now climbed into the front seat, making himself busy with the panel of controls in front of him. He was no longer listening to her. The Welshman was making himself comfortable in the observer's seat.

"I don't want to end up in a mangled heap inside this wreck" she wailed as she was hauled up by the Welshman. The mechanic beckoned to her and assisted her awkward climb into the rear seat. She would be sitting on top of him, amongst the plethora of packs.

At least the weather was fine so that would not be a problem. She nestled into his lap and secured the safety harness with difficulty - she was confronted by the obstacle of twin machine guns, jabbing into her chest. This was all she could see. After much fussing, she felt as comfortable as she could get. Goggles were placed over her eyes and she received a complimentary pat on the top of her leather helmet by the Welshman.

"Should we introduce ourselves, lovely?" he asked.

"Ya, I call myself Rozenn and I am your liaison officer."

"Ah, bonne, Rozenn, what a lovely name for a lovely girl, isn't it?"

"Pas de bavardage, if you please..."

"Oui, oui, oui, but of course, lovely."

"What can I do with these?" she asked, wiggling the butt ends of the machine guns.

"Well, lovely, you shoot down any Messerschmitts that chase us, don't you?"

"D'accord. You will show me the tits now?"

"Ah, but there's no time, even for the basics, is there?" he shouted as the engine kicked into life.

She prayed that she would not end up in a bonfire of wreckage somewhere in the fields of Picardy. They were now bouncing their way forward and the plane bucked and swayed its way across the turf. In a few yards they were airborne, flying over the scattered roofs and trees of the Paris suburbs and then over the Palace of Versailles. Rozenn settled back in the lap of the Welshman and felt around inside the fuselage for something to feed the machine guns - there was nothing. If they were attacked from the air, they would be completely defenceless. The outcome would depend on the skill of the pilot. "Merde alors" she muttered, "I am doomed!"

The aircraft descended slowly, like a kite on a string, knocked back by the smallest eddy and then the wheels thudded into the field and skidded, first to the left and then to the right. Rozenn breathed a huge sigh. They were down. Then the plane tipped forward. The propellors cut into the mud and the engine whined like a stuck calf as the plane tipped on to its nose and teetered on the brink. And then it fell. Her brain shuddered in its brain case and cut off like a gaslight being snuffed out.

Her eyes opened to reveal a new, glass canopy-bound world that stunk of petrol and metal and leather and mud, a world that was dark above and ghostly pale below.

The Welshman wriggled. "We've got to get out, lovely" he whispered, as if a loud voice would wake the pilot from his slumbers. The Welshman's arms extended beyond her as they slapped at the confines of their glass and metal cocoon.

Rozenn extended her arms and the fingers of her right hand wriggled their way into a gap and she heaved. The canopy slid apart. She released the buckle that was digging into her waist and she gradually slithered into the gap below her like an imago emerging from its brittle case. Rozenn fell to the ground and he fell on top of her and they wriggled underneath the metal sheet of the wing and stood up, free. The world righted.

In front of the plane, through the bent propellors Rozenn could see a round top of a hill which must be significant because it was the only top for leagues - everywhere else around them was flat and sodden and her feet were sinking in. The sun emerged gradually in searing pink and orange streaks. She suddenly became aware that her leg was thumping in pain. Tentatively, she pulled up the leg of her trousers. It was dark so there was nothing to be seen. “Merde alors! My leg!”

“Yes, that is a leg, my lovely!”

“Not any more it isn’t - I have pain!”

“So, that’s blown your chances of modelling stockings for Dupont, hasn’t it lovely!”

“You imbecile!”

“Now, now, lovely, we’ve got more important fish to fry, haven’t we?” He was now checking through the pouches that adorned her waist and his waist and now in the pack that he swung back onto his sloping shoulders.

Christoph and the Grey Sea must be many leagues from here, Rozenn sensed. Meanwhile, she was in this sodden field hemmed in by high banked waterways. Rozenn walked to the front end of the plane and looked in. The pilot looked back at her, smiling inanely, his head at a curious angle - curious because his neck was not positioned where it should be and the look on his face had no meaning. A speck of blood developed in his nose then a fleck of blood in his eye. He had the look of a man whose neck was severed - the look of a man who was completely indifferent to what he was looking at - the look of the recently passed.

The Welshman was still fiddling with his pouches.

“Our pilot is dead - we must return him to the soil” murmured Rozenn.

“No time for that lovely, we’ll have to set the plane alight.”

“Non, he must be returned to the soil!”

The Welshman prepared to fire a flare into the body of the plane.

“Non! You will bring all of hell down on us!”

“You damnable woman!”

“Ah, bien entendu. And you are a very rude Welshman.” After a great deal of straining the pilot’s body was free of the plane.

“You infernal woman!”

“Ah, we have a contretemps, n’est pas?”

“Arrrghh!”

“So, you agree with me. We consign his body to the soil but we do not destroy the aircraft.” They hauled the body onto the embankment and dug a shallow grave. Rozenn thrust a strut of metal into the soft soil but took the pilot's identity tag. "Now we may depart."

The Welshman ignited the fuel from the plane with a flare and it roared into flames. "Now we depart, lovely."

"You imbecile!"

The Welshman glared at her. "Now, we need to get a shift on, lovely!"

They followed the whispering-tree lined embankment. Above the whispering of the trees, all was quiet save for the grunting of cattle munching grass and a distant banging and a whirring of vehicle engines. But above all this, there was the sound of foot falls coming towards them and the clinking of metal. There was a dark figure approaching, a boy in a helmet and some kind of uniform. He was of ordinary height (for a man), fresh-faced (as a woman) and excited as a boy. She gazed at his features, his chest, then his hips, his legs then back to his face. The British were sending boys to fight in a man's war.

"British?" asked the boy.

"Yes" answered the Welshman.

"Better get out before the Germans show up. They're all around!" Rozenn's body lurched downwards and her face grimaced in discomfort. She was cold and wet and her leg hurt. "Is she your bit of stuff, mate?"

"She's my assistant. Do you know where we are?" The Welshman had pulled a map from inside her bodice and pointed somewhere in the middle of it. She punched him in the arm.

"No idea. I'm just going to head down this track and join up with anyone I can find!" The Tommy gave Rozenn a queer look as she hauled her way up into the crook of a tree, inhaled deeply several times and decided. "This way, Welshman."

"What's that, lovely?"

"Attention, your first target." She pointed along a dyke that headed northward, towards a distant sea. It was just grey and shadowy.

"Is she doo-lally? Has she bumped her noggin?"

"We've got work to do. She's my liaison officer, aren't you lovely?"

"Yes, but then I find Christoph..."

The Tommy started walking again. Rozenn wondered if he would be saved. She closed her eyes and let her mind wonder. Probably not.

The Welshman was leading the way. Water seeped out of her trousers and her socks and her boots but then reached an acceptable equilibrium with her sodden skin. Soon, the discomfort in her calf had gone but she was so cold. Her brain seemed numb but a voice inside was shrieking that she was in great danger. And where was Christoph? Many leagues away, and out of reach. She grasped the Welshman's arm and pulled him down the bank. "Boche!"

"What, lovely?"

"Boche!" They listened together to the sound of wheels and caterpillar tracks and boots rumbling across the dyke and decided that whispering was unnecessary. They waded along the dyke, slowly and forcefully, like they were wading through molasses and now they were crouching below the bridge. Rozenn shrugged, what now? He removed a pack from her waist and pushed it into the rotting brickwork. Now, he brought out a torch and in its light, pushed in a shiny metal tube. He signed that they should hurry away from the bridge. Her eyes widened in horror. They would have to wade in full view of the Boche! Their legs worked hard but there was splashing. There was a shout then a volley of shots that splashed alongside them. They flattened their bodies against the bank.

"Explode. The. Bomb" she mouthed.

"I can't lovely."

"Explode. The. Bomb" she mouthed again. A salvo of bullets slashed their way into the reeds above them.

"I can't - it's a chemical detonator!"

"So?"

"It's set for ten minutes..."

"Dix minutes!?!"

There was a flash and a deafening eruption and a bow wave that plunged over them. Rozenn and the Welshman scrambled up onto the bank and ran into the dark followed by bullets. They collapsed inside a ruined shell of a building. "That was a close thing, lovely!"

"That was never ten minutes! Never!"

"Closer to two minutes, I reckon. A little tweak needed, that's all my lovely."

She felt the cluster of pouches that adorned her waist. "You have made me into a bomb, Welshman."

"No, no, no, lovely, they can't be detonated without a detonator."

"What happens if I am shot?"

"You will not explode..."

"How do you know that?"

"I know about such things..."

"But I will be furious..."

"I meant..."

"What if I am shot with a cannon?"

"You will be dead anyway!"

"And every living thing within a league of me..."

"I don't think that will happen."

"But how do you know?"

The earth shook as a series of blasts sent shrapnel singing through the trees. "I don't know, but let's not put it to the test just now, lovely..."

Chapter Fifty-Four

1020 Sunday 02 June 1940 - Dunkirk perimeter

It became impossible to move down the street without attracting a hail of bullets or a storm of shellfire. The barricade of vehicles at the top of the street was no barrier at all and it would be a matter of minutes before the Boche smashed their way through. Rozenn sat with her ears covered with her hands while her left leg shook; the Welshman sat and fiddled with two packs of explosive and what looked like a brass pencil. "Two minutes, Welshman?"

"Less, my lovely. Get in tight." She squeezed into the fireplace and the flash was accompanied by a shower of bricks. They squeezed through the hole into the next building. "Keep moving lovely, they're close behind." There was another explosion and a scream. The Welshman ran, pulling Rozenn along by the arm as she hobbled through cratered gardens. A group of uniforms came out of a cellar waving a white flag tied to a baton, but they ducked submissively back into shelter. "Quick lovely, towards the smoke!" The Welshman pointed at the huge oily pall above the wreckage of the town.

By this means, they traversed the ruins until the sea was close but the sweet scent of the sea was overwhelmed by the smell of burning oil and petrol, burnt cordite and the thick, swirling clouds of dust. Everywhere around her was the scattered remains of a beaten army. *"Ceci est l'enfer!"*

It was an impossible set of choices she was confronted with - flee to the sea with the Welshman or stay and surrender to the Boche, or hide below ground until the fighting was over. She stumbled towards a large, marble faced building that had somehow escaped damage. Pushing her way through the double doors, she came upon a hatch. There were hushed voices below and the clinking of metal and the rubbing of leather. But, most importantly, it was shelter from the hail of bullets, the shrapnel and the thick, enveloping clouds of choking dust. Rozenn edged her hand between the sides of the hatch, unbolted it and threw it open. The voices sounded louder. She stepped down into the dark passageway and called out. There were echoey replies from below. She hobbled all the way down the steps towards the acrid smell of rotting fish. It was then that she realised she had made a terrible error.

CHAPTER FIFTY-FIVE

1207 Sunday 02 June 1940 - The Dunkirk fish factory

Rozenn clambered back up the passageway and out through the hatch. She dropped the hatch cover and dragged a concrete lintel over it. In a few steps she was back out in the avenue, where the midday sun and the swirling dust burned her eyes. She gasped "Plant big bombs, shortest fuse, now!"

The Welshman started to do as he was told with admirable alacrity. "Why, my lovely?"

"Alors, I have stirred up a giant ant's nest."

"What's that, lovely?"

"Soldier ants. Many, many soldiers. The head soldier shouted at me to go to the harbour or along the beach. They're coming now to make sure I go."

"They must be able to squeeze the two of us in?"

"Alors, there's a problem. They are not Frenchmen."

"So, what are they? British or Belgian?"

"None of those. I think they are Germans and they are coming up the passage!"

He was transfixed for a moment. "Jerries! How come? How many?"

"Many hundreds" Rozenn replied curtly. "Vite, vite, vite!" She opened the double doors.

He took two large charges and placed one each on either side of the entrance hall, by the hatch. "Well, they'd better stay down there then. So, why do you believe they are Germans, Rozenn?" He trailed wires out into the street, behind a massive slab of tumbled concrete.

She slammed the doors closed and pushed her back against them. "Their equipment, it's too new and it's too clean..."

"What if?"

"That's not all. I spoke to a man - they addressed him as an officer, but he wasn't in an officer's uniform..."

"Is that all, Rozenn?"

"The officer - he did not make a pass at me, he wasn't interested at all, that simply cannot be..."

"That's not enough Rozenn, what if he just didn't fancy you?"

"Don't be absurd - I gave him my best smile!" Rozenn snapped.

They both turned and stared at the entrance way. There was a quickening clacking of boots on the concrete steps and then thumping of shoulders against the hatch.

"And because he wasn't attracted to you and his kit was clean, that makes him a Jerry? Is that all?"

"No, there was something else."

"What was it Rozenn?"

The double doors were flung open, throwing Rozenn aside into the street. She scrambled to her knees amongst the broken bricks and the dust. A large figure in the grey-green uniform of the Armee de Terre filled the doorway but he was no Poilu. He had two equally large companions. He aimed his weapon at the Welshman and his finger tightened on the trigger. The Welshman just stared at Rozenn.

"Jackboots!"

Rozenn scrambled to her feet and flung her back at the door. A shot rang out. The soldier fell backwards with a roaring curse, tumbled over and took the two men behind him down. Rozenn got up and again threw her back against the door. There was a shrill scream. Fingers were jammed between the doors. A volley of rifle shots ripped through the door. "Welshman! Fire the bombs!" she screamed, but he just sat immobile in the dust, his head poking just above the concrete.

"Feuer, feuer!" came a shout from behind the door.

Rozenn saw the plunger, took three desperate strides and dived on it.

The door erupted into splinters and the concrete structure collapsed into the void below.

There was no building left above ground, just a thick, spreading pall of choking dust.

"We cut that one a bit fine" muttered the Welshman. He lifted Rozenn off the plunger, coiled up what was left of the wire and put it back in the pack that girdled her chest. He was shaking.

Rozenn stopped rubbing her chest and looked down. Curiously, there in the dust, was a freshly amputated finger. She tried it for size against her left hand but it was much too big.

"Now, let's you and me go down to the beach and see if we have better luck there, my lovely!"

But she wouldn't move. "Pourquoi? There is no reason. I cannot go on."

"No Rozenn, never, I will get you out of this."

"How?" She ducked her head as shrapnel flew over their heads. "If I survive, Welshman, there is a chance, if I die, the spiral collapses and there is just chaos and despair!"

"Come with me my lovely, and I will make a home for us in the heart of Wales, in the Cambrian Mountains!"

Rozenn gasped: "The hallowed land!"

"Land of my fathers, my lovely!"

"Land of the witch-mothers!"

"So you must trust me, Rozenn."

"But how?"

"You must, my lovely!"

"It is so far to swim! And I cannot swim!"

"Then...I will tow you across the channel!"

"You are an idiot, Welshman!"

There was a blinding flash, a roar and another building collapsed into a plume of all enveloping dust.

"Rozenn?"

She wiped away the dust that caked her face. "This is your promise to me, Welshman?'

"Yes, Rozenn, I promise to get you out of this."

She shook the dust out of her hair and replaced her helmet. “Then Welshman, I accept your terms. Now, we go to the beach!”

“Just keep still will you!” the Welshman spat through mouthfuls of oily seawater. She adjusted her position on his shoulders so that his frame tipped to one side and then to the other. “Be still woman!”

Rozenn jumped and seized the scrambling net and then clung on tight. She was pulled roughly up the netting and over the bulwark onto the upper deck of the boat.

“Sorry mate, next time!” shouted the matelot. The old tug reversed it’s engines and the water boiled. It moved away from the line of soldiers, standing chest deep in the sea. And he could breathe now because Rozenn was safe. They all watched the tug turn to port and ease its way towards the open sea, to confront the swell and the channel. And she was away and he felt warm inside, despite the chilling cold of the sea, because he had decided he would search for her when he was back in Blighty and when he found her he would court her and she would fall in love with him and they would be married and share a proper bed together and she would have to do as he told her. Rozenn had said that their spirals would entwine and that neither of them could help that, because that was their fate. She called him an imbecile again.

He heard twin aircraft engines roaring above - the roar of a diving German airplane. It had twin engines and it released a stick of bombs.

The Welshman shouted, “No, turn to port, turn to port!” He watched in mounting horror as the distant tug leaned to one side, gradually at first and then more quickly. There was distant shouting, a belch of oily smoke from the long funnel, and then the tug healed over at an impossible angle. It was capsizing, its hull like the red carapace of a beetle flipping over. And then it disappeared below the seamless sea, as if swallowed by a sea monster, and there was nothing on the surface of the water but gushes of bubbles and steam, and a spreading surge of ripples.

“Rozenn” he shouted, “Rozenn?”

And then he realised what an idiot he was, because she was gone, his forever sweetheart, below the grey, angry sea.

CHAPTER FIFTY-SIX

0131 Monday 03 June 1940 - The Mole

Spirals of black, oily smoke spewed over the shattered buildings along the coast, pierced by flashes and flames in the town itself. The company of HMS Eager was entering this inferno for the fifth time. There were many hazards to navigate: sunken ships of all shapes and sizes, violent dive bombing attacks and crowds of soldiers pushing their reckless way along the wreckage of the East Mole.

HMS Eager pulled into the harbour at 01:30 hours local time and her screws were reversed immediately. She drifted purposefully towards the harbour mole. Captain James Houghton reckoned he could get between the French and British destroyers already docked against the mole, even though there was a bare thirty yards clearance either side. During ship trials, no one could manoeuvre a fifteen hundred ton destroyer like he could. And this was his ship. “Get ready gang planks fore, midships and aft.” HMS Eager drew in to the wooden structure and came alongside smoothly. “Tie her up fore and aft” he ordered.

There was a line, four deep of soldiers, many in the grey-green uniforms of the French army, leading towards the shore as far as he could see. He could hear small arms fire but no heavy artillery. “Get them aboard as soon as you can, midshipman. Check what weapons they’ve got.”

The gangplanks were laid across to the mole and secured. Soldiers shuffled across the planks and were directed to the port side of the destroyer. Houghton ordered the look outs to pay attention to anything flying in. "Count the men in midshipman" he ordered. He couldn't believe that the Germans weren't firing on his ship, as they did at Boulogne. What were they playing at?

Tonight, he was tasked with bringing out as many of the last ditch defenders as possible, right under the eyes of the enemy. This would be their last chance. The line of soldiers petered out. There were three hundred men aboard. Houghton ordered the mooring lines to be cast off and HMS Eager swung out bow first into the harbour. The engines ground forward and they were making way to Ramsgate. They cleared the harbour and the engines went to quarter speed. The bow wave curled slowly back to the harbour. He wondered how many men had been left behind; he guessed it was thousands. He wondered what fate awaited them when the Germans realised they had been cheated of the main prize.

He set a course north-east and HMS Eager edged into the swept channel. "Captain, captain, there's another one!" Rating Richardson pointed to a body clasped around a spar, half a cable away, bobbing along with the pitching waves, passive but in harmony and seemingly lifeless.

"Engines in reverse!" The engines whined in protest and the destroyer slowed to walking pace. A rating descended the scrambling net with one hand holding the boat hook. His arm stretched out with the hook like he was at a fairground attraction. At the fifth attempt, it snagged on the trouser waistband of the soldier. He pulled it close until it opened one eye. It gulped and water sluiced out of its mouth.

"Get down here! Give me a hand!" shouted the rating. They pulled the body, rung by agonising rung up the net and hauled the body onto the deck as the destroyer's engines were grinding into action again and gathering momentum. The boat hook was released and the body was free.

"Get her in!"

"It's a girl - what's she doing 'ere? She a fuckin' mermaid or somethin'?"

"It's a girl in a soldier's uniform - there's somethin' very wrong here if you ask me!"

"No one's asking you Lunny! The first lieutenant turned the body over and sat astride her back. His hands pushed firmly and rhythmically against the bottom of her shoulder blades. Water spewed out of her mouth onto the deck. She coughed.

"It's a girl, sir!"

"I can see that! Help me get her into the officer's quarters!"

"Sir?"

"Just do as I say!"

A gang of sullen French soldiers blocked their way.

"What's the matter with 'em? We've just saved their necks, haven't we sir?"

"Yes, but as soon as we unload them, they'll be shipped back to France to continue the fight. There's no respite for them!"

"Surly bunch, aren't they sir?" They dragged the coughing body up the stairway into the captain's cabin.

"Not surprising is it? Not after what's just happened to them!"

"What? Pusser's cheese sarnies, sir? Mug of Pusser's char!"

"You know what I mean!"

"We got to her just in time, didn't we sir?"

"We did, Lunny, we did."

She was laid out on the captain's bed. "Can I do anything else sir?"

"No, that'll be all."

The first lieutenant poured out a tot of rum. Her nose twitched and her eyes opened. She sat bolt upright. "Sacre bleu" she coughed, "sacre bleu! I died twice!"

"Please" he said as he passed her the tot. "Are you French?"

"Non, Breton."

"Same thing. Who are you? What're you doing in British Army uniform?"

"I am liaison."

"Liaison?"

"Ya, liaison officer in the B.E.F."

"Really! Who for?"

Rozenn frowned. "The Welshman with the bombs. Is he here?"

"No one with that description. Drink?" He offered a metal flask.

"Ya" she said as she took a gulp. "Aaah!"

"Be careful" said the first lieutenant, "you were almost a goner back there..."

"A goner?" she asked.

"Be careful" he warned, "it's navy rum."

"Navy rum - like kerosene, n'est ce pas?"

"Do you need a ready supply?"

"Ya. I have cold."

"Here you go." He poured rum into a metal flask. "This'll protect you from the cold and anything else!"

"Merci. Also, I have wet." She tucked the flask so it nestled close to her heart.

"Yes. Let me see what spare clobber I can rustle up."

"Later. I must find my Welshman. I made a promise to him."

"Try on these oilskins."

She put them on but they dragged on the floor. "These will suffice. Now we find the Welshman."

"Follow me."

They pushed their way past a line of soldiers on the gangway and they had descended back to the deck. The ship had gathered speed and was vibrating with a tight rhythm.

"They're mostly below decks..."

"These men? Where are they from?" she nodded at a group of men standing along the port side of the foredeck.

"I've no idea? You tell me!"

Their mood was different to every other evacuee on the ship. "You have taken their weapons?"

"Of course!"

"Do you have men with guns?"

"Some, but..."

"I need to speak urgently with your captain, vite, vite!"

"Why?"

"You have Boche on board."

"You what?"

Rozenn nodded at the huddle of men on the port side of the forecastle, enduring the sea spray, as if they were enjoying it. "Ici, the Boche!"

The first lieutenant beckoned to Captain Houghton, who was leaning over the bridge railings. He disappeared out of sight. She turned for'ard and tapped her foot impatiently.

"What is it Number One?" The captain had arrived with admirable speed.

"The girl we rescued - she thinks we have Jerries on board!"

"What! And why does she think that?"

"There were Boche in the uniforms of the Poilu in the ruins of Dunkirk - I can smell them" she said.

"Who is this girl and what does she know?"

She turned so she could stare into his face and her eyes flashed at the captain but he was looking at his subordinate. "I call myself Mademoiselle Rozenn Abgrall. Maintenant, your armed men?"

"On this ship, girl, I am the captain, not you." And they were standing near the bowsprit, pretending to look nonchalantly in the direction of these soldiers, alongside the ship's crew that manned the long-barrelled gun pointing over the bows. It now traversed so the barrel was above her head. "So you can smell Germans? What do they smell of?"

She snorted. "Fish! Alors, these men are tense, alert, their hands are covering small guns and knives, they are bulky."

"Because of German uniforms underneath? I can't have a fight on board, I don't have the marines..."

"Your gun - tell the crew to point it at me, and follow me step, step..."

She walked quickly away from the narrow, long barrelled gun towards the huddle of soldiers. They all stood, tensed and tight, staring at her voluminous oilskins.

"Bonjour monsieur. Fumer?" Rozenn directed this at the man she guessed was their leader - it was the way that the other men deferred to him. She glanced about the group - one of the men looked away and something inside made her scalp tingle.

"Madam?" He searched through his pockets and eventually found a pack of cigarettes. Gauloises, she observed, in a full, pristine pack. The man fumbled with the pack with his left hand so she took it off him, opened it adeptly and placed one between her lips. So, he would favour his right hand to strike at her.

"Feuer?" she asked. There was a sudden alertness and then a strained silence in the huddle of men and a shuffling of hands through pockets. Slowly, she turned her right shoulder towards him.

"Non, Madam."

She sighed and her hands went to her hips. "Monsieur, what is your unit?"

"Ach, Première Armée..."

"Huh. They surrendered to the filthy Boche."

"We escaped...from the filthy Boche."

Rozenn frowned. "No, you did not." Despite the vibration of the engines, the surge of the sea and the babble of the seamen, she felt hearts jump in front of her, start pounding and then a long, silent moment as hands moved stealthily towards concealed weapons.

"Monsieur, there is a long gun pointed at you and your men and it shoots shells that will make holes in you that are this big." Rozenn made a circle with the thumb and forefinger of her right hand and took the cigarette out of her very dry mouth with the other and held it high in the air. "When I drop my arm, the shooting starts." She took a deep breath and held it in.

The fingers of his right hand crept inside his jacket. The knife was out and tearing into oilskin. She was felled, knife embedded in her chest, no breath, just her panicked eyes, staring skywards.

A hole exploded through the German's head. He flew over the railings. A volley of shells flashed overhead. And then silence, other than the vibration of the ship's engines and the splashing of the ship's wake and the wailing of the girl.

"Jackets off, now!" shouted the Captain.

"Merde alors" Rozenn yelled, "I am stabbed!" She stared in horror at the knife embedded in her chest.

The Boche removed the grey-green coats of the Poilu to reveal the grey-green of the Wehrmacht and the insignia of the Gheist Regiment. Her captain was standing over her with a pistol pointed menacingly. Six men with rifles were at his side and a horde of Poilus pushing just behind.

"Blimey" muttered one of the Marines, "where did they spring from?"

"Search them properly this time and get them in the hold!"

"Kill them!" shouted Rozenn from between the captain's legs. "I am stabbed!" She was staring up at a forest of restless legs.

"Into the hold with them!"

"Did you hear! Over the side!" she shouted again. "They stabbed me!"

"You use witches to do your fighting!" spat a Gheist. "You have no hope!"

"Captain?"

"Lock them up in the hold. Two of you on watch, all the time!" The pistol was shaking as he looked down. "Are you hurt, girl?"

"YES! I AM STABBED!" she gasped.

"Too late Englanders, too late for you." The Boche turned and led the march below deck.

Captain Houghton bent down to tend her. He wiggled the handle of the knife and pulled it up; he waggled the bent metal flask attached at the tip. He pulled aside her clothing and sniffed inside.

She protested: "Captain Houghton!"

"What a waste of navy rum! You're going to have a bruise there, but otherwise, no harm done!"

Rozenn pulled open the slash in her oilskins and felt inside. There's something not quite right - why wasn't she badly hurt? All her under-clothing was cold and sodden. "Alors, navy rum! It protects all from hurt!"

"Get her back into my cabin and watch over her! She's not to come out again unless I say so!"

Captain James Houghton was fretting - not only did he have three hundred exhausted and surly French soldiers aboard and a crack squad of German stormtroopers held below deck, he had been ordered to change course for Sheerness and this course took his ship north-east into a minefield and there were reports of 'E Boat' activity along his route and into the River Thames. And his ship was in the minefield following a narrow, swept channel in darkness. He had two look-outs ahead of the bow chaser, but one mistake could be his last...

He accepted the mug of tea that was put into his open hands and thanked his steward who always knew the right time to bring it. He cradled it in his hands to warm them and wondered what he was waiting for - a tip?

"Captain, I exist to serve you and your crew." It was the Breton girl. She too cradled a mug of hot steaming liquid and a look of concern.

"I thought I told you to stay below." He watched as she pulled up her duffel coat so it covered her neck. A sea breeze was buffeting the huddled figures on the open bridge.

"I told your man that I needed air."

"You need to learn to do as your told."

"But, I owe you my life Captain Houghton..."

"Yes, you do."

"And I will repay this debt..."

"And how do you propose to do that?"

"I will protect you and your crew..."

"From what?"

"Through all your travails."

"How can that be possible?"

"All my strength, I will use, all is possible, even our salvation, despite all the dangers, I will bring you to safe harbour!"

"Poetry never saved anyone, girl!"

"That was not poetry, captain, that was my promise...to you!" She turned, and ran between the captain and the helmsman and clattered down the stairway to the deck.

"Follow her!" he shouted to his Number One. "Keep her out of trouble!" She was caught by the shoulder as she reached the deck, but she just flashed her eyes at him. "Monsieur, what do you call yourself?"

"Watson."

"Watson what?"

"Jimmy. Jimmy Watson."

"Ah, Jimmy Jimmy Watson. C'est bon!"

"No, no, just Jimmy the once."

She was now on the foredeck, standing on a capstan, her hands on her head and then she turned suddenly, screamed at the helmsman and Captain, with her arms thrust to the port side. The ship lurched to port.

"Mine!" shouted a rating. He was pointing at a dark, metal canister that bobbed menacingly down the starboard side of the vessel.

"Alors, there is danger below, you must use all my senses..." Rozenn took the rating's hand and perched alongside the bowsprit. She felt very chilled but tugged the duffel coat tight around her shoulders and pulled a woollen cap down over her ears. "Your helmsman must watch me very well - I will signal each notch he must make to the wheel."

The destroyer eased forward and the wake glistened in the moonlight. Two ratings were at her side, holding her steady by the waistband and reinforcing each of her signals. She felt alive and then, in one moment, she did not, below there was a brooding evil, waiting for an impulse, to detonate and release an explosive force. "Arrêtez!" she shrieked, her arms waving high in the air at the helmsman.

"What the devil is it now?" shouted Houghton.

"Reverse!"

"Reverse? This is a fifteen hundred ship! We can't just throw her into reverse at the whim of a girl!"

"But you must! Danger below!" The destroyer lolled uncomfortably in the swell. There were many eyes looking at her in the strained silence.

She couldn't think of the English words. *"Tournez à gauche, très, très doucement."*

"Port, very, very slowly!" shouted Watson.

"Ah, c'est ca!" The engines of HMS Eager grated and the destroyer's screws ground forward again.

"Wish she'd make up her bloody mind!"

"Ah, c'est bon, allons y!"

And now the ship was headed north, at speed, in the best direction to make a rendezvous, a coinciding of journeys, and a battle in the burning sea and the oh-so slow descent to the sea floor. Rozenn shuddered so violently that the rating holding her left arm asked if she was about to jump overboard. Not just yet, she replied.

Rozenn accepted a second mug of the hot, sweet steaming liquid, known as 'char'. Its main virtue was the way it warmed your hands, your gullet and your stomach as it made its way downstream. She had returned to the bridge, now that the minefield was in the ship's wake, but over the horizon there was more trouble and now she had to get Houghton and his crew ready. She stared at the indeterminate line between the lightening sky and the brooding great, grey sea and became certain that there was danger just beyond it.

"North Foreland" muttered Captain Houghton.

"Monsieur Captain, traverse your weapons to the right..."

"The correct term to use is starboard, and this is my ship and I issue the orders!"

"Ah, d'accord. Monsieur Captain, you should traverse your weapons to the starboard, and alter your course slightly to the left, if it so pleases you."

Rozenn held out her left arm at an acute angle.

"Port twenty" ordered Watson.

"Is she one of them sirens, sir?" the helmsman asked.

"Good God no, why would you think that Boult?"

"Well, is she going to lure us on to the rocks then?"

"How's she going to do that, Boult, she's already on board!"

"Worst luck" muttered Captain Houghton.

"Well, I hear they're very cunning sir, them sirens..."

"She's not a siren, she's...a girl with certain powers and intuitions."

"For Christ's sake! I'll be in my cabin. Rouse me when we're off Warden point, Number One."

"Aye sir."

"A witch sir?" said Boult in alarm.

"Not a witch Boult, just a... sea sprite."

"I reckon she's a witch, sir."

"She's not a witch. There's no such thing!"

"You've not met my mother-in-law, have you sir?"

"No, I haven't had that pleasure, Boult!"

"So, what are we going to do with her?"

"Your mother-in-law? Steady ahead! I don't know, all I do know is we mustn't lose her!"

Rozenn nodded in agreement. She inhaled loudly, coughed and spat over the side. "Monsieur Jimmy, the Boche are close! You must be ready!"

Watson scanned the horizon with his binoculars. "I see no ships."

"Huh? You must!"

"Maybe...a fishing boat? Three fishing boats, maybe more...no, they're not rigged for fishing..."

"Boche! Boche! Boche!"

"Sir, I'll get the captain!"

"Monsieur Jimmy. Prepare your ship for battle!"

"I don't believe it! In the River Thames!"

She stared into his ear. "Monsieur Jimmy! Prepare for battle!"

He swallowed loudly. "Ring up full speed! Enemy ahead! Director, find me the range! Get Captain Houghton!"

"Ah, dix minutes, then we shoot."

Captain Houghton was back on the bridge. "What the hell has she done now?" Watson passed his binoculars to Houghton. "Jesus Christ, what are they? Engine room, full speed ahead. Clear the decks!" He looked to the stern - there was just the one set of torpedo tubes as the rear set had been removed to bolt on two Hotchkiss anti-aircraft guns. All weapons were now trained to starboard and their lines of fire were clear. "Hoist the Battle Ensign!"

Rozenn curled into the far corner of the bridge with her duffle coat pulled tightly around her and one and a half forefingers placed in her ears. "Monsieur Captain?"

"Get below."

"D'accord!"

"But how did you know?"

She shrugged. "Alors, I have special sight..."

"Better than binoculars?"

"Much better - I have far sight."

"How come?"

"Your man Boult said it - I am akin to his mother-in-law!"

CHAPTER FIFTY-SEVEN

0620 Monday 03 June 1940 - East Nock, River Thames

HMS Eager bucked against a wave, settled and then surged forward again. Rozenn disentangled herself from a crush of soldiers and pulled her way along the passageway. Someone was following her - it was the captain's number one. "Hold on!" he shouted.

"Oui, monsieur, forward hold, I interrogate the Geists!"

"No, you don't!" He stopped as there was a pair of explosive cracks and the ship swayed. He listened carefully. "Short, up one hundred!"

"Alors, I interrogate the Geists" she announced to the Royal Marine guard outside the metal door.

"Nobody to enter. Captain's orders!" There was another pair of explosive cracks and another sway.

"Over, one hundred!"

"Monsieur, I am the special emissary of the captain!"

The guard looked at Jimmy Watson.

"No, she isn't" Four loud cracks. "Broadside!" There was the roar of an explosion. "Poor sods!"

"Ah, les pauvre connards! But we must interrogate the Boche and learn their plan!"

"No entry!"

"Uh, that is stupid! I shout through the door then!"

"Wait, that's rapid fire. We must be very close!"

And now, the cacophony of explosions was broken by the rhythm of brass cases clanking against metal above her head. "Maintenant, I go see Captain Houghton again, he needs me!" Rozenn pulled her way along the crowd of cheering soldiers and then hauled herself up the companionway and the metal rungs back to the bridge. "Monsieur Captain!" she gasped. Over the side, there was the grinding and tearing of metal, and the shrieks of the maimed and drowning. She gasped at the carnage streaming past the flanks of the destroyer. "Non, non, non!" But it was no good, the fingers planted in her ears could not shut out the screams.

"Poor bastards, but it's them or us!"

Rozenn ran to the rear of the bridge - there were two burning vessels a league or so to starboard and closer, acrid fumes of burning metal. "Monsieur Captain! Your ship is hurt!"

"Just splinter damage" ruefully poking his finger into a cluster of holes in the metal screen, "and a bent bow but we can still sail and fight! Engine room, half speed! Check the damage to the bow!"

"Monsieur Captain, the danger is not past! Tout droit!"

"Ahead? What is it?"

"Oh, my God! Port twenty!"

HMS Eager slipped closer to the blackened skeleton of a ship floated backwards with the tide, back to the east.

"Monsieur Captain, there are men inside and they need our help!"

"How can you possibly know?"

"I reckon she's one of them blimmin' witches, Captain!"

"I cannot afford the time or the men!" he snapped, turning to where the girl should have been, but she was gone. He walked quickly around the bridge. And now that infernal girl was down below, coiling a rope, getting ready to cast it over the railings at the hulk.

"Have that damnable girl arrested and throw her in the brig! Mister Cundy, go to the telegraph room and contact Sheerness. Tell them all hell has broken out along the River Thames!"

"Aye captain. She's a bit of a handful, isn't she!"

"Who is she?"

"You remember those tales about the Britanni? The sea witches?" said Cundy.

"But those are just tales, Cundy?"

"But did she make the promise, sir? To you!"

And then Houghton's mind was whirling. "You know, I think she did!"

"Now Madam Abgrall, it is madam, isn't it?"

"Mais non, it is mademoiselle."

"Mademoiselle?"

"Oui, mademoiselle."

Rozenn agonised over what she was going to say to Christoph's mother.

"I see, Mademoiselle Abgrall, this...agreement you have with Captain Houghton, I believe it should be formalised, as a contract."

Rozenn closed her eyes. Could Christoph have been in one of the shattered and burning vessels along the river or... "I have made my promise to Captain Houghton and that should be enough."

"That's as maybe, but you promised to protect the crew of his ship...and I need to get through this, no matter what happens."

"Ah, d'accord." She would have to search the river's edge, from one side to the other for any sign of Christoph. Her soul lurched downwards leaving a hollowness that could never be filled.

"Now as it happens, I have drafted a contract..." His hand made a flourish towards the papers trapped in the typewriter. She rubbed her grimy hands vigorously and sniffed them but all she could smell on them was blackness. It was a vile and persistent odour that filled her nostrils so that nothing else could be smelt.

"Monsieur, what do you call yourself?"

"Cundy. Sub-Lieutenant Cundy."

"Alors, you Englanders call yourself by some interesting names."

"That's as maybe..."

And all she had left were the receding memories of their bicycle rides in the hills and swimming in the lakes and rivers and picnics in the forest. "Alors Cundy, what qualifies you to prepare this legal document?"

"I am a solicitor for oaths."

She gazed into his beady eyes, the eyes of a weasel. "D'accord. So, these oaths, you have much experience in dealing with them?"

"Indeed, on Civvy Street."

"I must visit this street. Many Englanders reside there. Now, let me hear it once more." She listened through the narration from the page of typewritten foolscap. "Cundy, it is very demanding for my side."

"It's exactly as I stated."

"Alors, it is not balanced. May I?"

"What are you doing?"

Rozenn sat down and dictated a new paragraph. "Alors, it is a clause of reciprocation" she explained, "and it balances the duties, for my side and for your side, for the duration of this conflict."

Cundy read what had been typed. After some consideration he murmured that it appeared to be acceptable. He removed the sheet from the typewriter with a grand flourish. "Now we can sign."

"So Cundy, you have the full authority to sign on behalf of all your clan?"

"Of course. I am a solicitor for oaths. I'm as good as any lawyer!"

"As good as your captain? And do we have witnesses?"

"Yes, I have found two colleagues who are prepared to sign this as witnesses."

She signed the bottom of the document with a long, languorous flourish. "Voila! And now you will sign on behalf of your clan? And these men..."

"Commissioned officers, of course. They will sign..."

"Mais, oui. And you have read and understood what you are signing for?"

"Of course!" Cundy signed with a flourish. After some hesitation, the document was witnessed by Petty Officers Connor and Welch.

"C'est bonne! May I keep the top copy?"

"No. I will keep that. You will have the bottom copy. Let me just check that the bottom copy is legible. And it is! We have a contract!"

"Yes, we do. You will need to share this with all the leaders of your clan."

"Yes, yes, yes. Of course." He frowned. "What...exactly does that mean?"

"Alors, this is what I told you. It's the reciprocation clause. It ties me and my sister to your clan, your navy, your nation, all the British and all of your empire. I will do all I can to protect you and your people. Your clan, the British, and your allies, will do all you can to protect me and my clan. If you fail in some way or allow me to be killed and I have no issue, then the promise is null. It's all there in this dossier that you have signed."

And then her soul collapsed into itself, because she realised that her Christoph, in all probability, had left this world and she would no longer have this painful but beautiful longing in her heart, no more gentle swoons from his sweet caresses to her ears and to her neck and all that was left was the salty etches of bitter tears streaming down her face. And Zutter was responsible for all of her pain. "Maintenant, your enemy is my enemy and my enemy is your enemy..."

"Ah! Vice-versa..."

"Indeed. We have two terrible conflicts: the first is with the petty tyrant Herr Hitler and the second is with Herr Zutter, his evil paymaster."

"Eh?"

"Alors, it's all in the contract you have signed. Read it and issue it to all your leaders immediately. I will need to call on your clan, your navy, your nation, all the British and all your empire and all your allies to aid me in my war with Herr Zutter."

Rozenn stood to the port side of the prow of the destroyer and snorted in the air. "There is a river to the south-west, n'est ce pas? Is that where our course now lies?" She turned around and realised that Captain Houghton was chewing his lip and wasn't going to reply.

"You must join your fellow countrymen" said Cundy.

"But we have a contract?" said Rozenn.

"Off you pop love" said the helmsman "you'll be in the care of the boys in brown now! We're slipping off to Chatham!"

Rozenn was pushed down the steps and along the companionway. She looked up to the bridge, because something had changed that had put her in peril. Her heart dropped as she caught the eye of Captain Houghton and he immediately jerked his gaze away. A sailor with a rifle pointed it threateningly at her. He pushed her into the seething mass of soldiers on the quarterdeck. "Monsieur, what is happening?" she asked. There was no answer.

She turned to the bearded man next to her. He removed the cigarette from the corner of his mouth. "Madam, this ship has changed course, that is what I know, to a prison ship or to an encampment, who knows, not I. The Englanders think we are traitors and spies, do they not? And you madam, know one of the Boche, so in their eyes, you are a spy, do you not see?" He pointed his smouldering cigarette towards the orange layered mud cliffs that slumped into the sea. "Voila! There is our destination, the dark island!"

Rozenn saw a settlement that fell away to the sea and a harbour, defended by three, tall concrete-clad blockhouses, leaning together, standing on a peninsula which was surrounded by a dockyard, with cranes and a long straight pier, tucked away inside the mouth of the river. She shuffled her feet and squeezed her shoulders into the mass of grey-green overcoats that surrounded her. The air that she snorted in through her nostrils was an unpleasant mixture of muddiness, oil fuel, brick, tar and rotting seaweed. Their course was now south or south-east towards the dark island.

The ship's tannoy blared out a message. They would all be off-loaded at Sheerness docks and be escorted by armed guards. There was a howl of disapproval from the grey-green coated masses and then a grumbling acceptance. The engines of the destroyer were rang down for speed so that the ship could coast into the river and then edge towards the dockyard. The ship was now amongst the cranes and inside the straight arm of the pier. A flurry of shouted activity at the prow and the stern meant that the ship was being secured at the quay. She tried to shoulder her way to the front of the file but with no success. Her neck craned behind as she tried to find a face that she recognised but there was none. She was in a shuffling, stumbling procession heading off the ship along a wooden gangway to the concrete of the quayside. Armed, uniformed men guarded a hastily made route with barbed wire coiled on one side and a long drop into the dock on the other.

Her heart lifted when she saw an officer on the other side of the barbed wire - one of Captain Houghton's subordinates! She shouted and he shouted back in reply. No, they would not let her go, because there were orders from the top that must be obeyed. There were fifth columnists on board and they must be isolated, interrogated and trialled, for the safety of all Britons.

"Bring Captain Houghton! Immediately! Vite! Vite! Vite!" she shouted. She was pushed along in a stream of soldiers, huddled and shuffling to an unknown place in an unknown country. "That man Cundy took my promise and made me sign a contract! He would have me tied to the ship's mast!" She screwed her copy into a ball and threw it. "You must save me, or we all lose!"

He caught it adeptly, glanced at it and pushed it into his jacket pocket, He started to walk quickly along the line of the wire, looking, always looking at her, walking, stumbling now running. "Rozenn! We'll get you out of this!"

A man ahead of her, turned and stared and then threw off his helmet and dived into the dock. He came to the surface and gasped for air. Three rifle shots killed him instantly. His body floated alongside the concrete, bobbing up and down with the gentle rhythm of the ebbing tide. The column stopped, soldiers turned. Two shots in the air persuaded the column to resume their slow shuffle. A man ahead cursed again and again.

"Reste calme" she shouted, *"reste calme!"* But the man behind her did not. He stared wild-eyed at her, dropped his knapsack and ran at the barbed wire. A shot rang out. He stuttered, fell across the wire as another shot burst into his back. Two British soldiers ran to him, pulled his body off the wire and dragged the body away to a black, plank-built building.

She recognised Captain Houghton's number one - he would get her out of this! He was shouting at her.

"What shall I do?" she shouted.

"Just keep your head down. We'll get you out of this."

"How, in a wooden box?" she shouted back.

He had gotten ahead of her, shouting, but it was shouting that made little sense. "Just stay calm Rozenn, stay calm and you'll come to no harm!"

"What if they decide I am a spy, what then?" she shouted back.

"You will be treated fairly, you are in England now and a prisoner of war!"

"What if they decide I'm a spy? What will they do to me? Will they have me shot?" She pointed accusingly at the killed soldier whose toecaps were now scraping parallel, winding trails through the dockyard grime.

"No of course not, we are not barbarians!"

"So, they will cut my head off?"

"No, a spy found guilty will be..." he paused as he cringed at what he was about to say,"...hanged by the neck until dead!"

"Non! Non! That is barbaric! That is inhuman! This is not a civilised country!"

"But it will not happen to you" he shouted back, "we'll get you out of this Rozenn!"

"We? We? You! You!" She tried to get one last look at him, to gauge his strength, his commitment to her. "Make sure that you do, Monsieur Jimmy. Tell Houghton that if I die, the promise dies with me!" She was pulled away by the shuffling mass of soldiers, and their sullen faced guards and thrown into the back of an open-backed cattle truck.

Chapter Fifty-Eight

0735 Tuesday 04 June 1940 - Chatham dockyard

Rozenn clutched hard at the metal tags that hung around her neck - they felt cold and hard, just like the faces of her Englander guards. Her journey to the Medway dockyard in a truck had been long and uncomfortable and now she was cold, shivering and alone; all her erstwhile soldier companions had remained in the carriages of the train. She wondered which of the metal tags could help her in her current predicament and concluded that none of them could: Christoph was gone; the Welshman was gone. The Englanders would probably have her killed anyway. She was thankful for the Royal Navy duffle coat but cursed the man that had stolen her woollen hat.

Rozenn's arms were seized by two men in British army uniform and she was dragged along another long sheet of concrete that ran alongside the dark and still mast pond. Her toe caps ground relentlessly along the concrete until she decided that she had better scamper along with them. They stopped in front of a wooden carcass of a building that seemed far too huge to hold a lone prisoner. A scruff of a boy, in shirt and shorts, pulled the double doors aside and they were inside the dark, cavernous space. She winked at the boy in desperation and mouthed a plea for help.

Rozenn was dragged five big strides forward and she was in front of a man dressed as a civilian but he had the stiffness of a military man. "Bonjour monsieur! Who do I address?"

"Stay there" she was ordered.

In this immense space, she could discern two other figures standing apart, a uniformed woman with folded arms and a non-uniformed man, enjoying a cigarette. This immense barn of a building smelt strongly of timber and rope and was large enough to house a wooden wall battleship of a different, much older generation. But now, above and behind her she sensed a gallery floor where hundreds of coils of naval rope were hung from the sides. Rozenn gasped - the Englanders had brought her into this place so they could break her neck.

She heard herself gabble: "Monsieur, I need to tell you something. It's very urgent. It concerns the security of this country - are you a decision maker? Or do I need to find someone who is? I am a personal friend of your highest leader."

"Tell me what it is."

"Monsieur, but who are you?"

"All you need to know madam, is that I am the person who will determine how comfortably you spend your last minutes on this earth and how painfully you depart."

Rozenn gasped and her legs collapsed under her. The woman officer grasped Rozenn's arms and hauled her back up. "Merci madam" she gasped. Her arms were bent agonisingly tight.

"Thank you Major Fitt. You caught her just in the nick of time."

"Monsieur, I call myself..."

"Rozenn Katerin Abgrall, nineteen years of age, French national, traitor, Nazi collaborator, saboteur and fifth columnist. I know all of this!"

"Non, non, non. I have made my promise to the Britanniques, but all I know regarding the plans of the Boche, I will tell a senior officer only."

"As far as you are concerned, I am the most senior officer you will ever encounter in this land."

Her satchel was wrenched off her shoulder and thrown to the floor. He looked down at the spread of clutter with a sneer. He was tall, but there was nothing of him, a drawn, stale face, lank, dark hair that he kept smoothing over his scalp, a neatly buttoned jacket that enveloped his chest. "Now, what have we here..." His brown, shiny shoe manoeuvred her possessions around in the dirt.

There was her porcelain encased mirror, now cracked.

"For signalling purposes?"

There was her stubby, palm sized blade, triple spiral crowned.

"Assassin's weapon?"

There was a small silvery ingot of precious metal.

"Curious. Why not a gold ingot or a stolen cache of British sovereigns? Hey, ho."

There was her leather bound book of poems. He picked it up and flicked through the pages.

"Ah, the code book. How quaint. Note the many impromptu page markings, Fitt, this is evidence of a cipher in play, I believe."

A letter dropped out. He caught it and brandished it in Rozenn's face. "The infamous love letter from the boyfriend - how absurd." He lit a corner with his cigarette, dropped it and let it burn at her feet. "All the paraphernalia of an incompetent - where's the wireless transmitter, Abgrall?"

"I have no such thing..."

"But we have the aerial, madam." He lifted up the string of garlic bulbs and twirled them. Hollow laughter circled around the empty building.

"Your Prime Minister is a personal friend of mine!" Rozenn sensed he had been an army officer, a man used to giving commands and getting everything his way.

"So?"

"Ow! The Germans are already here" she shouted as the bones in her elbow grated together.

"Do you mean the Royal Family?"

"Aagh! Non, the Geists, in the uniform of a Poilu. You're bringing them to England, in your ships! Please stop, I will talk!"

"Can you prove this?"

"Ugh! Do nothing for three days then see!" Her neck was now pinioned at an unnatural angle so she could not move.

"You foolish girl. The motto of my department is 'The Truth Today'!"

"Ow! That is the truth!"

"Rozenn Katerin Abgrall...'

"Aagh!"

"You are in a very serious predicament!"

"I know this! Release me, then I talk!"

"Why should I believe you?"

"Why? Aagh! I am arrested as a spy - the fate of spies is death! I do not want to die. I want to talk!" Her body was twisted in pain.

"You are convicted as a spy, the sentence is death by hanging." He looked intently at her but she couldn't meet his gaze: "You will be hanged by the neck until you are dead, Abgrall. You are wearing a dead man's uniform - do you have any idea how that looks?"

"Ugh! A la mode?"

"This is deadly serious."

"I know, but you have already decided."

"Do you have anything else to say before you leave?"

"Agh! Get Captain Houghton! Major McPherson! Mister Churchill! They will tell you! I am Britanni. I could be your saviour!"

"Fitt, take her away and extract a confession. If she will not confess, dispose of her anyway." He nodded and Rozenn's wrists were tied together behind her back by the soldiers. A rope was pulled over her head - a rope secured behind her left ear with a hangman's knot.

The army woman pulled Rozenn away, stumbling through the great, cavernous hall. "Monsieur, I have a letter, I have a letter!"

"I shall stop for tea. We will have a resolution today, mark you well, Abgrall! I will have your confession and we'll be rid of you!"

And there was that scruff of a boy, staring wide-eyed through a crack in the wooden walls and their eyes met for a moment. But he was gone. Her fingers clawed at the raw fibres of the noose. "Au secours" she gasped, "fetch help, boy!" She was dragged up a steep wooden stairway to where ship ropes are strenuously twisted together into seaworthy lengths, her knees scraping and scratching, her throat crushing and the breath squeezing out of her. All was lost, all lost.

The boy was at the foot of the stairs.

"Run boy, you must not see!" But her wrists were now free.

He winked a wink at her, like they were conspirators and gave a little grin and ran away.

She was being dragged along the ropeway, splinters scraping through her rucked up clothes, her feet scrabbling amongst the wooden beams to get purchase. Her hand was trapped inside the noose.

The army woman continued on her way, tugging at the rope, every time it snagged, she gave a curse but did not look back, she just redoubled her effort. Rozenn's arm was trapped in the noose, raw fibres tearing at her wrist. All was not lost, not yet.

Both arms trapped, screaming in pain, but the noose was worked loose. Her boots pushed desperately against a rough, wooden pillar.

Her executioner turned and swore but the executioner's face collapsed into a mask of shock and then despair, eyes white and staring. The hangman's noose was around a bollard of wood; a twine was spiralling above her head, like a halo, falling over her shoulders and being pulled tight, so tight, no scream could come out of her throat.

CHAPTER FIFTY-NINE

0759 Tuesday 04 June 1940 - The Ropery

The tall wooden doors were slid open by the dockyard lad and two Royal Marines, allowing Jimmy Watson to stride into the wooden cavern beyond. There were two civilians sat down drinking tea and two private soldiers standing and chatting, their rifles leaning against the wall. The two men put their cups back on the table when beckoned to, by the rifles held menacingly by the marines. The two soldiers already had their hands in the air. "Where is she?" Watson barked.

The senior of the two civilians nodded his head towards the gallery. "Ah, the Royal Navy - you're too late!"

Watson ran up the broad, wooden stairs - in front of him were yards and yards of rope strung out, twisted and stretched to the far ends of the gallery. He could see a figure at the end. He drew his service revolver and ran.

There was a figure standing at the very end, wrapped in a fawn duffle coat and wearing a cap. The figure turned to him, arms folded tightly across her chest, concealing what was below. He saw army battle dress and underclothes at her feet, and this pile was being moved surreptitiously to one side with the aid of her left foot, towards the edge. He took stock, for a moment, of this unique girl, with her flashing greeny-blue eyes and her auburn, ratted hair under the green captain's hat.

"Mademoiselle Abgrall" he gasped, "you look...quite well."

"Ah Monsieur Jimmy" she gasped in return, "you have found me, but where is your..."

"Captain? He's organising emergency repairs for the ship." He was not quite sure what situation he had found himself in and he cursed, under his breath, while his face flushed suddenly in embarrassment: she had few, if any, clothes on underneath the duffle coat.

"D'accord. I have had a bit of a time of it over the last few days as you can imagine. Please take me away from this trou de merde, now!" The nozzle of his pistol was pushed to one side and then she pulled the duffle coat tighter around her body. She kept glancing at the tarpaulin that was teetering over the edge of the drop.

He put his weapon back in its holster. "I think we're on first name terms now, don't you Rozenn?"

"Cher Jimmy" she continued, seemingly unnerved, "I think I need to explain your duties under the terms of...our contract." She seemed very anxious to depart this place.

"What contract?"

"Cundy's contract - the one that binds my clan with, you the Britanniques and all your colonies and your flotillas, fleets and armies - it translates the promise into written English words."

"Yes, but hold on a minute, what happened to your...captor?"

"Qui?"

"The officer who brought you up here. What have you done with her, Rozenn?"

"Ah, you mean my torturer?" Rozenn cast her eye about the wide, echoey space and when she had scanned all parts, she just shrugged her shoulders.

"Yes, the British officer, I think her name was Major Fitt."

"Alors...I think she may have popped out on an errand."

He had noticed the tarpaulin. "What have you done, Rozenn?" he asked anxiously. His heart sank. He knew there was a body underneath, still and unmoving. He pulled the sheet away.

"Ah voila! There she is!"

Major Fitt was bound and suspended on a chair, hanging in air but tilted back so that two chair legs and two naked human legs were sticking out awkwardly above the void. Her hands and ankles were knotted with a rope and a ligature was around her throat, seemingly drawn tight against a hook mounted in the wooden wall. Fitt's eyes were wide with terror, a terror that came from knowing that the consequence of moving the wrong limb, in the wrong way, would result in her being suspended by the neck...

"Rozenn, you must help me to free her!"

"Pourquoi?" Rozenn swung her leg towards the chair but Watson caught it and pulled it away. "She hurt me!" He cursed as he tried to lift the body. "Non, non, Jimmy, that will not work!"

"You must help me, now!"

She folded her arms: "Non, non, non!"

"You must - or there'll be consequences!"

"So, you will hang me?"

"I promise you that will not happen! Not on my watch!"

"D'accord." Rozenn looked closely at her rope work. "Alors, it is a bit of a puzzle, is it not?"

"Rozenn!"

She slipped her hand inside the ligature and pulled it over the victim's chin and into her mouth, and in the same movement, rocked the chair back. Watson cradled the body and lowered it to the floor. Major Fitt made her first tentative gasps. "She's alive, thank God!" They stood to confront each other.

"I made a vow to your captain..."

"I know, for better or worse, but this is...worse!"

"Jimmy, let me remind you, what you in turn promised..."

He stood up as close as he feasibly could to Rozenn so he could shout quietly at her. "I know what has been promised..."

"I don't think you do, so I will tell you now, so there are no more misunderstandings."

"But I do understand!"

"You promise to care for me..."

"Yes of course, but...'

"So, when I need your help, you must come immediately."

"I came as quickly as I could." he snapped.

"And I have been in this trou de merde for a whole day now" Rozenn snapped back, "or at least, I think it's a whole day."

"But I came as quickly as I could, I've had a devil of a time, trying to find you...wait, Major Fitt is coming round!"

Rozenn swung her leg at Major Fitt's head but Watson caught it. He felt her calf in his hand and pulled it tight against his hip so all she could do was hop.

"Laisse-moi partir!" He threw down her leg. "You saved me from the sea, and I am grateful for that, but..."

"You looked like a drowned rat!"

"I was nearly drowned! And still you saved me, so I made my promise...and you made your promise, and now we are bound by a promise that is so, so, venerated that nobody has seen for hundreds of years!"

"Rozenn, it's kept safe in a locked drawer, Admiralty House, London."

"Non! C'est impossible!"

"It is. I've seen it! All officers serving in the Home Fleet are obliged to read..."

"Merde alors!"

"It's written in the old Brittonic and English languages, but it's there all right and it has been archived there for over a hundred and fifty years!" He bent down and tended to Major Fitt - her breathing was ragged and uneven.

Rozenn gasped and waved a hand in Watson's face. "There are men!" She had seen officers in the uniform of the British army, advancing towards her. "Ici, Monsieur Sondee, Welshman! I was at the tipping point but Christoph was not. We must search for his body! I fear he is lost!"

McPherson looked up and frowned: "For Christ's sake, get some clothes on that girl! She can't meet the P.M. like that!"

CHAPTER SIXTY

0543 Wednesday 05 June 1940 - The wolds

When she awoke, Rozenn was curled up on the front seat of an automobile that was being driven ever so slowly in the pitch darkness. The military man driving the automobile was very familiar to her, hunched over the wheel, staring over the windscreen and cursing (in Welsh) at the intricacies of the road ahead.

"Welshman, I must rest!" she announced.

"You have been asleep for three hours, lovely, are you not rested now?"

"Non!"

"I'm not surprised lovely, you've been having a nice conversation with yourself, haven't you?"

"Jamais, jamais, jamais!"

"So, who would Christoph be?"

"Alors, Christoph was my dearest friend in all the world, my angel."

"And Kirk?"

"Kirk? My trainer in the art of artillery."

"And Sandy?"

"Sondee? Alors, my patron."

"And Houghton?"

"Alors, my captain and my confidante."

"And Watson?"

"Alors, my saviour."

"Jenkins?"

"My paymaster."

"You know too many men, my lovely."

"C'est vrai, I have many followers."

"And, how is that, Rozenn?"

"Alors, I am so charming..."

"So I see. Well, we're nearly there."

"Welshman, are you one of my followers?"

"Well lovely, I think I am!"

"No, you are not, you abandoned me to the sea!"

"I did no such thing! There was nothing I could do, lovely!"

"I shouted to be saved! You never came!"

"I thought you had drowned!"

"I had! I was drowning like a rat and I was screaming for you to save me!"

Behind them, the sky was becoming a paler grey. Ahead, the road seemed even more difficult and blurry. The Welshman was staring ahead and making ever more erratic direction changes. "There were so many screams for help that day, my lovely, the wounded and the drowning."

"I have a very special scream, Welshman!"

"So, how am I supposed to know when it's your scream, my lovely?"

"You will know it's me when I scream for you. You will know by the voice you hear. I will not scream for you if I need no help."

"Scream for me, but how?" And then he realised. As the oily salt sea washed over him, he had dreamt a face and imagined a voice - not the voice of an angel, but a girl calling for him, and now she was curled up by his side. In that moment he had known they would be saved, but for what?

"Welshman, I forget, you are just a man and you have no sense of what is vital, do you?" The automobile had come to an abrupt halt. The rising sun had illuminated the end wall of a stone building, with three wooden framed windows, one above the other. Rozenn tugged at the handle and impatiently, stepped over the door onto the ground and with her eyes closed and her nostrils flared wide, she sampled the air and it tasted good. She examined the building in front of her. "This is very old, n'est-ce pas?"

"Yes, lovely it's a very old coaching inn, very old." He wrapped his arm around her shoulder. "We will be safe here."

"But the Boche?"

"We will stop them coming, with the help of your clan and with the help of the battalions of the free nations and the British empire..."

"Alors, where are these battalions, Welshman?"

"Ah, they're on their way, lovely."

She scanned the rolling hills of the Cotswolds with the flat of her hand shading her eyes. "Best they hurry then, Welshman, but now I must rest."

He surreptitiously clasped her hand. "If that is what you want, lovely!"

"Ah, Welshman! That is what I need!" The slabs of stone that formed the walls glowed golden in the light of the ascending sun.

The door at the front of the cottage was swung open and a woman leaned out. "Owain Rhys Talog! Well I never! And who have you got there?"

"Alors, I call myself..."

"Bessie, my lovely, we need lodging..."

"Of course you do, of course you do. Now how many beds would that be?"

"Two, my lovely."

"Two it is. I'll get them ready and I'll heat up plenty of hot water."

"Yes, we're going to need it!"

Rozenn's fingers traversed the golden stones to the door and then she wriggled her body past Bessie's into the parlour.

"Sheesh! Someone needs a bath, so they do! Do you have any clean clothes, dearie?"

"Non, these are all I have." Rozenn's wafted the duffle coat to show the service dress below and the army boots. Then, she rested her hands on the big black stove that was slowly warming. "Madam, I feel warm and safe in this place."

"You're not English, are you dearie?"

"Non madam!"

"She's Breton, Bessie, and so she's...different!"

"Maintenant, I take off these clothes and I bathe in hot water. I may be some time. Then I will need to eat. Then, I will rest with you, Welshman!"

"Oh my goodness me!"

"No, no, no! We've had a rough journey, Bessie my lovely, and we both need to rest - in separate beds mind!"

"I need to bathe, madam!" Rozenn took off the duffle coat and sat on the stove. Bessie picked it up, shook it and hung it up behind the door.

"I'll show you where the bath is dearie and I'll bring up some hot water. Where on earth have you been?"

"Madam Bessie, I died two times!"

"Ah, that would explain the whiff, then! Follow me! Owain, brew the tea dear!"

They climbed the narrow stairs to the next floor and walked along the uneven and creaking corridor. "This is madam's room" Bessie stated as she pushed through an old oak door to a room with a large bed with stiff, clean white sheets. "Please make yourself comfortable, dearie. Mister Owain, I will put him at the end of the corridor, overlooking the downs. I hope that will be satisfactory for you both."

"I need a bath, madam" Rozenn announced.

"I will warm some water for you. The bathroom is opposite your room. You will need to sing while you are in there. There is no lock!"

"C'est bon. I am a good singer" she noted as Owain arrived up the stairs.

"Oh, what happened to your finger?" Bessie asked, "I meant to ask before, but it looks..."

"Ah! Sometimes, when I am nervous, I chew my nails. One time, I was very nervous indeed..."

"Oh, my goodness me!" Bessie tried to chuckle but it stuck in her throat. "I'll get the pitcher." She bustled past Owain and scuttled down the stairs.

"Welshman, if you don't find some clothing for me I will get very cold. I may have to bite off the rest of my fingers." He seemed transfixed, something inside telling him to look away but then a stronger urge to follow the flow of her hair, the lines of her face, the haunting eyes, the elegant neck, the rise of her breasts, the curve of her waist and the legs that led all the way to her booted feet. "Attention! Clothes, now, please" she demanded.

"I'll see what I can rustle up, lovely!"

"Is she all right?' wondered Bessie out loud.

"Je reste là-bas, madam!"

"Are you all right, lovely? We were worried about you?"

"Je vais bien, Monsieur Welshman!"

"Have you finished in there, Rozenn?"

"Oui, oui. I will need some clean underclothes. Do you have any for me?"

Owain walked back to his room and opened the stiff, battered, leather case. There were cream coloured vests and underpants but he wasn't sure if these would be suitable. He took one of each, anyway. He was back outside of the bathroom door, tapping tentatively. The door opened slightly and her right hand appeared, waving frantically. He placed the smallest woollen vest and pair of underpants in the hand and this seemed to satisfy it. The hand disappeared back inside. After three moments, the garments were pushed back outside the door, being waved in annoyance. He pushed them back. After three separate bouts of pushing, they remained inside the bathroom accompanied by a plaintive groan.

The hand came out again. "Gown, please."

He went back to his room to retrieve his midnight blue dressing gown. He wondered what she would make of the gold embroidered nymphs that danced all over it. The gown was taken inside with another plaintive moan and she emerged at last, her hair coiled in a white towel turban. "Merci" she stated perfunctorily as she stepped into her bedroom, firmly closing the door. He firmly pushed the door open and went to stand with her by the bed.

"It's a queen size bed" he declared.

"She was a plus grande queen, n'est ce-pas?" Rozenn replied. She glanced meaningfully at the door. "I think it is time for you to depart" she announced. She walked to the door and opened it wide for him.

"I was wondering..."

"What were you wondering, Welshman?"

"Owain, my name is Owain..."

"What were you wondering, Monsieur Owain?" He seemed to be hiding something behind his back.

"I was wondering if you would like to...have a chat?"

"A chat? What is that?" After a moment had passed, she removed the midnight blue gown, placed it on the linen box and walked to the side of the bed. She smoothed out the vest with her palms so that it covered her underpants. "What would you like to chat about, Monsieur Owain?"

"Anything you like, lovely" he offered. He produced a bottle of Pastis from behind his back and a box of cigarillos.

She opened the pack, beckoned for a match and he lit it for her. She sucked in deeply and blew a smoke ring towards the ceiling. To her annoyance, the circle could not form properly due to the lack of headroom. She removed the cap from the bottle of Pastis with her right hand and took a quick swig from it and gasped at the shock as it passed down her gullet. "You would like to chat about...laying with me, am I right, Monsieur?"

"Yes, it's a very big bed and I thought you might feel...lonely in it."

"Lonely, you say?"

"Yes, lonely, needing company, the company of another person, a human person, a human body..."

"You mean, your human body?"

"Um, yes, if you would like..."

"D'accord. Then remove your clothes and let me see."

"I'm sorry?"

"I said get your clothes off, soldier."

He motioned towards the curtains at the window.

"Leave the drapes as they are. I will need to see."

Nervously, he removed his clothes, leaving his vest and underpants and socks on.

"D'accord." She sucked deeply on the cigarillo, felt its effect throughout her body and coughed violently. She methodically stubbed it out in the ashtray on the bedside table and then took another swig from the bottle of Pastis. "You are perfect" she announced.

There was squirming at the front of his underpants. She turned away to look at the plaster and lathe wall. He came to her and placed his hands on her shoulders and turned Rozenn so she was facing him again. There were tears in her eyes. She pushed him away. "I am not perfect" she said as she presented her left hand, "in fact, I am imperfect, in fact I am disfigured."

"Ah yes" he replied as he massaged her left hand, "dis-fingered!"

"Alors, your great big British sense of humour." Rozenn turned her back and lifted her right foot so he could see two of the branding marks on her body. "And there is another in a very private place."

"I'm so sorry, lovely" he said, "I forgot." He wiped her tears away with the vest she was wearing. Irritably, she smoothed it back down again over her chest and stomach.

"No matter, I get into the queen's bed now." She slipped from his grasp, flipped over the sheet and sat on the bed. "Maintenant, what do you propose?"

"I shall...slip in beside you!"

"I see, well here is a line. You must not cross this line." She indicated a line midway down the length of the bed.

"Ah, yes the Maginot line!"

"Idiot!" she replied.

"The Maginot line, not very effective was it, lovely?" He traversed the bed to the window side, smiling to himself.

"The Boche came up behind" Rozenn commented, "but I will not allow this to happen to me. I will take precautions." She looked at him quizzically. "Have you got all the right equipment, Welshman?" she asked. She looked him up and down.

"Ah, let me check" he replied. She groaned, covered her eyes and buried her face in the pillow as he scampered out of the room and along the corridor. When he returned, he looked very pleased with himself. "Rozenn, I have a French letter for you!"

She looked in horror at the object he presented. "What will you do with that?"

Owain motioned the action of drawing it over his erect member. Rozenn shook her head. He traversed the bed again to the window side, left the object on his bedside chair and nervously removed the rest of his clothes, while plumping up the pillow and slipping under the sheet. He stared up at the ceiling and realised that the hair-line cracks made a shape that was reminiscent of the pre-war borders of France. "Do you see that my lovely, a map of France on our ceiling?"

Rozenn stared at him. "Attention! There is a method where you go most of the way and then pull out at the last possible moment. You British are used to this. It's the way you conduct your foreign policy."

"How does that work?"

"It relies on skill, judgement and diplomacy."

"I mean..."

"You will know because I will kick you off..."

"That will hurt!"

"Yes, but I must ensure that none of your..."

"Spunk?"

"Spunk? Spunk? None of your bouillabaisse is to enter me..."

"Bully baste?" he asked alarmed.

"Fish stew" she explained.

Rozenn turned onto her back and muttered, "My soul, my mother and all my mothers passed, forgive me for what I am about to do!" She jerked her underpants down and wriggled and kicked them off. Resting on her side, she got ready to engage with him. Her hand channelled it's way up his leg until it fitted snugly in his crotch and she palped the warm, moist organ there, softly at first and then more insistently. She released him, grasped his arms and climbed aboard him.

"You crossed the Maginot line!" he exclaimed.

"That is my prerogative!" She tugged the vest off, over her head. "I will take charge now! This must be done with finesse!"

"But, what do I do?"

"Nothing, just lie there and think of the queen..."

"That sounds like treason!"

"Then think of England!" she panted. Her hips started to work him, slowly and rhythmically.

"Aaagh! But, I'm Welsh!"

"Then think of Wales!"

His mind wandered to the land of his fathers, and to his beloved Cambrian mountains. As his body surged upwards, in rhythm with hers, he heard a guttural roar, the roar of a Merlin engine, high above. He gazed through the window up to the far away sky, a small vapour trail fluffed towards the south. He heard the rugged harmony of a whole formation of fighter planes and their rhythmic thrumming was in tune with his. Rozenn shouted to him and there was an insistent banging from below and a rhythmic gasping above, but none of this deflected him. Then he released and she was cursing under her breath. This much he heard.

She continued to rock slowly, to and fro, but throttling down in speed and intensity until she fell off the bed, cursing: "Merde alors! I did wrong" she exclaimed, "I did wrong!"

"No Rozenn, no, you did so right!" He was sore and spent but relieved, joyful and exhausted.

With much gasping and swearing, Rozenn hauled herself up so she could peer at him accusingly over the lip of the bed. "Welshman, you filled me up with...spunk! And now I am awash with it!"

The top sheet was torn from the bed and wrapped around her body. The posture of her whole body seemed to accuse him.

He gazed in awe at her with a stupid smile on his face. "But I thought gravity would save us, with you being on top and me below! It has to go upwards!"

"Idiot! Gravity is not a method of contraception! That is a pump you have between your legs! It doesn't cut out when I'm on top! Haven't you heard of fuel injection pumps!" She mimicked his grunting and his inept thrusting.

His esteem for her grew and grew. She was such a technician, even when she was cross. "What happened about you being in charge, lovely?"

"I got carried away, Welshman!" She waddled two steps and cringed. "Oh, no, no!"

"All your fault then, lovely!"

"I will have to deal with this. This cannot happen! You know this! It cannot be!"

"What are you talking about, Rozenn, what's up?" He realised that all was not well, despite the massive feeling of elation he had, and the sore tenderness below.

"You know this!" she said pointing at her belly, "Your seed! In me!" Rozenn grabbed the vest and underpants, leapt over the bed and took the neck of the bottle of spirit. She burst through the door out into the corridor, stepped through the door opposite and slammed it closed. There was the sound of water gushing through the bath taps. Owain rose slowly and pulled his clothes on, wondering what he should do. He cast around the room. She had the bottle of Pastis. He had to know what she was doing with it.

Owain knocked tentatively on the bathroom door; she told him to go away. He walked back to the bedroom and returned a moment later to knock again. A stream of what he could only imagine were Breton curses came from behind it. And then there were howls, sickening howls like a vixen in heat. He opened the door. The bath water flowed around her kneeling body and the tears flowed down her face and neck and soaked into his vest. And in the stream of bath water a thin stream of vermilion, wending its way to the plug hole and the overpowering smell of aniseed.

"This cannot be" she yelled, "this cannot be!"

Chapter Sixty-One

'I've got my own ship!'

Katie's boots tapped a bossa nova beat on the grey, grimy paving stones. Her near neighbour nudged her in the ribs. 'Pack it in, Talog, there's cameras on us!' Katie stopped, frowned and focussed on the weapon that was resting lightly on her shoulder. The low respectful droning by the poppy clad monument had ceased. With any luck they would be marching back to barracks and she could get on with something more productive, such as resting or feeding. The two minutes of silence were interminably long.

Then, her rank turned in unison and started the march back. The precise clip of the marching boots was accompanied by Katie's off-beat skipping. She winked at the rating marching next to her and then gasped - Captain Mann was looking at her intently and he looked distinctly displeased.

'Talog, stand easy' ordered Captain Mann. She stood easy. He shared an office with two other officers and his corner was neat and precisely laid out. There was a black and white photograph of a warship above his computer, twin funnelled and with twin turrets fore and aft. 'Do you know what you're looking at Talog?'

'It's an old photograph, sir.'

There was silence as he processed this response. He looked quizzically at her, trying to elicit something more.

So, he still saw her as a silly, young girl and not as a young fighting woman. 'It's an old warship, sir, I don't know which one. The freehold looks low so she could be a yacht!'

'Freeboard, Talog, freeboard. She's a battlecruiser, HMS Hood, the pride of the Royal Navy between the wars, Talog. Have you heard of the wars?'

'Yes, sir!' Her body stiffened. She could anticipate the place where this was headed.

'So, what does Remembrance Sunday mean to you, Talog?'

Oh, crap she thought, I've been caught out. 'It's when we think about all the people who have died, or been hurt in service...sir!'

'Very good. And what made you think it was appropriate to dance a jig on this solemn occasion?'

'I was cold sir.'

'Were you, bollocks!'

'Sorry, sir.'

Captain Mann was looking her up and down. He then decided to stand up, pick up a large, brown envelope from his desk and turn to the door. 'Come with me Talog.'

They walked briskly along a wood trimmed corridor which resounded to the co-ordinated clacking of their synchronised steps. They entered a broad room through a set of panelled oak doors. There were photographs of ships all along one wall. Old ships she presumed, as the photographs were sepia tinged and faded, framed in old oak.

'Which ship is this Talog?'

She was confident of her answer. 'HMS Hood, sir.'

'Do you know her story?'

'No, sir.' Another long pause as she thought carefully. Her forefinger traced the line of her bow and then along her foredeck to the forward gun mountings and then the bridge and mainmast. 'She looks a little low in the water sir, could be wet on the quarterdeck in a bit of roughers' she said as confidently as she could. Keep this professional, she thought, show him what you've learnt and show him that you're not such a silly girl.

He nodded. 'Very observant, Talog.' He pursed his lips. 'Britain is at war, two big enemy units, trying to get through the Denmark

Straits, through to the convoys into the Atlantic, what are you going to do?'

'I see a screen of ships and planes, looking for them, tracking them, we're concentrating all our big hitters...'

'Its foggy, Talog.'

'We've got radar, haven't we sir? We've got planes?'

'It's 1941 Talog. Just a few ships have radar, that's all.'

'Whatever. Let me find them, bring up all my big hitters...'

'You've got sight of them. They're heading on a course that takes them into our convoys. They're Britain's lifeline. You've got your two big units only.'

'Screen them off. Get my big units close...'

'If you lose them, it'll be like wolves descending on the sheep fold...'

'You mean, like bears at a picnic, sir? I see us attacking now, full speed ahead!'

'Their shooting's better than ours...you're taking hits on your lead unit.'

'I see us getting closer, getting closer quickly, all balls out, must damage them...'

'You're hit, the magazine's burning...'

'I see us getting closer, getting closer...'

'Headless bodies flying through the air...your control top's been wiped out ...a column of burning gas goes up that's as high as the ship is long!'

Katie's hands now vibrated hard against the wooden panelling. 'I see it all...we keep going, I see us getting closer, now we ram them!'

'She's gone, blown to pieces!'

She stared down at the wooden floor, pushing hard: 'No, no, no!'

'Your flagship is lost...'

Her breath raged in an out, in and out. 'We're pulling back, out of their range, but we must stay in contact, give 'em no rest' she gasped.

'Your one remaining heavy unit, churning through the wreckage, so many bodies...'

'Captain Mann, you had blood on HMS Hood, didn't you? Your blood...I'm sorry, so sorry! She's gone, all in pieces, all hands lost, all lost!'

'And that's the story of the Hood - the mighty, gallant, tragic Hood!'

'I think I've got it sir, I've got it now!'

'I think you have Talog, I really do.'

She turned her tear stained face to him. 'I promise you this. This will not happen to my ship's crew, I will not allow it!'

'I hear you. So Katell Ebrill Talog, you solemnly promise, that you will use every part of you, all of your senses, all of your powers, all of your strengths, to protect your ship and your crew!'

'Of course I will!'

'And you promise, that if the ultimate sacrifice is needed, if your captain demands it, you will bring the heavens down!'

'Yes, yes, yes!'

'Fire and brimstone, raining down from the skies, silver-headed dragons rising out of the seas!'

'Yep, yep, yep, all that and more!'

'Then, Katie Talog, I believe you.' He held the envelope high above his head. She jumped to snatch it from him. 'Here are your sailing orders. You will join HMS Harpy in three days, out of Guzz. You will report to...'

She seized the envelope. 'Aaaahhhhhhhh' went the long, ascending, shrill scream, that started from her core, pushed through by her lungs, modulated by her mouth. It reverberated around the room and along the corridors in all directions.

Katie grasped his hand and shook it vigorously up and down. There were footfalls closing in from all directions.

'What the hell's up?' a newcomer shouted.

'Was that the fire alarm?' demanded a female officer.

'Where's the fire?'

'Katie Talog? Was that you?'

With the envelope waving in her hand, she turned to confront the fluster of junior officers that arrived at the double, junior officers that she knew, because they were all her instructors. 'I've got my own ship!' she cried out.

'Ah, you told her, sir!'

Captain Mann addressed the crowd that had gathered around. 'I did. Let your family know, Talog.'

'I will! Thank you sir!' She skipped out of the hall, along the oak lined corridor, through the door of yew and out into the bright and gleaming world outside. Time to feed and celebrate!

'Race apart, aren't they sir?'

'Who's that?'

'The Britanni!'

'They certainly are!'

'You did explain to her that she's just a rating on board and not the captain of the ship, sir?'

'Of course, she knows, and she made the promise. She made the promise to me! And she will make us all proud!'

CHAPTER SIXTY-TWO

Friday 27 May - Chatham Dockyard

Feet bouncing on the thick wooden planks, dirty grey sea to the left and a busy, smart, railway line to the right, she made steady progress until she couldn't make any more, and she found herself poised above the middle of the river. Katie looked about her and saw the gentle chop of the waves against the pier and the clutch of clucking and fidgeting wading birds on the encrusted structure below.

She was drawn by an echo of a voice to the north-west, over the flat lands and she shuddered - it was the voice of someone she had known to the bones and was now passing away.

Down the river there was a cluster of whirring wind turbines, across the river there was a wide-mouthed estuary dotted with islands of mud and in her nostrils there was that stench of rotting seaweed and shit. It was a flood of sensations that made her sinuses throb, her crown twitch and her back tingle, all the way up and down. Her heart beat ever more quickly.

She would have to cross this dirty, grey-green river, and allow sensations and sights, smells and intuitions, to lead her - not from toot to toot and top to top, by line of sight, as was the way in the hills, but by finger tip touch and by tongue-tip taste and by snorting in each whisp of scent.

The cluster of turnstones leapt as one, gliding above the cushion of air atop the waves, clucking and flitting their way ahead of the boat. It was the river taxi, 'Upnor Castle', arriving for passengers. As the ship approached the boarding ladder, she whistled to get the attention of a crew member. 'Ahoy there, you need a hand?'

'Take this, and be quick about it!' came the shout from the foredeck. Katie grabbed the hawser that was thrown at her and looped the loop over the bollard. The stern was also quickly secured. She received the gangway onto the pier and shackled it. A score of passengers made their way aboard the taxi, with the help of Katie's guidance, until there was just her left.

'You coming? We're about to cast off!' She unhooked the gangway and swung it across to the boat. Then she cast off the two hawsers and jumped onto the deck.

'I'm Katie! Where are we headed?'

'Chatham dockyard!'

'Thought so!'

'Return? That'll be ten pounds.'

'No it won't, I'm crew!'

'You're not wearing uniform!'

'Yes, I am!' She took off her beret and flourished it along her navy blue trousers and shirt. 'Don't be silly! Royal Navy, leading hand! See, that's my killick!'

'I'll check with the captain.'

'You do that. I'll organise a brew - galley this way?'

He nodded, looked confused, turned away and looked back at her, even more confused. 'Um, I don't know, let me check with the captain.'

He was just a lad, in his white shirt with epaulets on his wide shoulders and his black trousers and shoes.

Katie made her way to the forecastle and mingled with what looked like an old lag's jazz band. They must be thirsty. At least they looked old and had various strangely shaped black cases with them, like a Prohibition style gangster hit squad. She enquired what they would like to drink and made her way to the galley. The captain was in the wheelhouse and was concentrating on manoeuvring the vessel, while the crew boy lurked uncertainly by his side. Katie negotiated the crowd in the galley and returned with a tray full of clinking glasses.

He was back. 'There's no discount for the armed services. But if you're a pensioner, war veteran, disabled or a child under 16, it's half price - are you any of those?'

'No, but I'm crew, aren't I?'

'I haven't seen you before!'

'When did you start?'

'Today!'

'There you go! I'm new crew, too! How do you do? I'm Katie!'

He nervously shook her hand. 'Are you sure?'

'Sure, I'm sure. And your name is...Scott!'

'How did you know that?'

'I'm crew, mate! I'm supposed to know!' And, it was written large on his lapel badge.

'And you are?'

'Katie, mate. Katie Talog. See?' Her forefinger underlined her surname stitched large on her shirt front.

'Oh, you must be legit, then!'

'Course I am! Now, I'll just extract some cash from these gangsters and we can have a brew - mine's a mug of tea, milk and three sugars!'

'The queue's over there.'

'Don't be silly - we're crew and we should be getting it free...' Her arm was trapped in a vice like grip from behind.

'Excuse me young lady, can I have a word?'

He looked like the chief engineer with his full set and sharp, alert eyes. His shirt sleeves were rolled up to show some pretty impressive inking.

'Oh, crappetty, crappetty, crap' she muttered.

'A little word in your shell-like...'

She was guided to the railings opposite the cabin and just ahead of the slushing of the steam powered paddle wheel. 'What's up chief?'

'You Andrew?'

'Yep. Mob?'

'Yep.'

'Bugger. Just needed a lift to the other side of the river.'

'Don't see your name on my roster?'

'Are you sure, Chief?'

'I'm sure...so, which ship are you?'

'HMS Albany.'

'Huh? Type 23? You seem to be a little off course.'

'Here's your tea' said Scott, offering her a mug.

'Ta!' Katie took a sip. 'Very nice, just right - so what now?'

'Time for the safety demonstration.' He turned, marched to the centre of the forecastle and hollered for attention. All the passengers turned and listened attentively. 'Listen now, what I'm about to tell you is very important for your safety.' He beckoned to Katie, whereupon Katie turned, looked behind her, looked back to Scott, pointed at her chest and mouthed, 'Who me?' He nodded. She walked to the Chief's side, stared into his ear and tried to make him feel as uncomfortable as she was feeling. It was fascinating how his ear flexed to his different jaw movements.

'This is, err...'

'It's Katie' she whispered from behind her hand.

'This is our newest crew member, Katie.' A short appreciative round of applause followed.

'I'm Welsh' she confided.

'And she's my lovely, Welsh assistant today.'

'Nice improvisation" she whispered to him, 'I like it!'

'And she'll demonstrate how to put on a life jacket.'

'Will I?'

'Now, some of you might think she is already wearing a dual chambered buoyancy aid...'

'Oi, you cheeky sod!' she muttered and folded her arms deliberately across her chest. He offered her the yellow life jacket and she snatched it from him.

'This is an important piece of equipment. Use it properly and it won't let you down' said he.

Katie methodically demonstrated each step of securing the life jacket in synchronisation with the Chief's speech.

'So, Chief, when do I put it on?' Katie asked.

'The captain will make an announcement over the tannoy' he replied.

'And where do I find one?'

'Abaft the bridge and the funnel.' Katie pointed out the locations across the ship in air steward style.

'And if I have any trouble getting them loose or putting them on, what then?'

'A member of crew will come and help you.'

'Is there anything else I should know?' Katie asked.

'No, I don't think so, I think you've covered everything.'

'Good!' She glanced across to where the estuary broadened and to the white swallow-tails as they screamed and plunged vertically into the sea.

'Chief? Who do I talk to about wartime records in Chatham dockyard?'

'No idea. What are you looking for?'

'A destroyer, HMS Eager, came in for repairs in June 1940?'

'After Dunkirk? There was a skirmish along the river. Give me a minute and let me think. Someone in the engine room will know.'

The river taxi came into the Triumph pier at Chatham Dockyard. Katie jumped on to the quay, put a rope around the bollard and manoeuvred the boat in. There was one name she had been given - it had to be the right one. She found a public telephone booth close to the dock. 'Paol, it's Katie!' The inside of the booth was smothered with business cards promoting all the night time attractions available in the Medway Towns. 'I'm in Chatham Dockyard, I've been slung out of Shoebury 2.'

'What did I do? There was an...incident!'

He wanted to know what kind of incident.

'Yes, one of those. I can't say.'

No, I can't tell you what happened but I did not cause it.

'Yes, I may sound calm, but I'm not really.'

'My plan? I'm heading back to Clun but I'll have a stop-off at yours and one in Cambridge.'

'I'll be back at yours, late tonight or early tomorrow.'

'Yes, I've got a key. I'll rouse you when I get in.' This seemed to have created a frisson at the other end of the line.

'No, not like that, you dirty git! I'm your sister, not your tart!' And now he started rambling on about their sister.

'Oh, so Gwen called? What did she want?'

'Oh.' She covered the mouthpiece and fell back against the door, gasping for breath. This made things a little more difficult.

'Am I all right? Not really. Everything's in the balance so it could all tip over, in one of many ways.'

'I don't know. Anyway, I'll see you tonight or first thing tomorrow. Bye!' Katie held the receiver tight against her forehead so it made a mark. She flicked through her planner and all the images blurred into one - all was unravelling, like a double helix in its death throes.

Katie looked at the huge shed in front of her. Supposedly, this was known as 'The Ropery'. She joined a party of Italians on a conducted tour of the shed and nodded and murmured 'Bella, bella!' at appropriate parts of the commentary, provided by a very mature, stooped woman.

And then she saw it!

Hanging from a hook, a grimy length of twine, tied in a triple spiral!

Katie looked up and down the tramways of stretched rope and crocodiles of visitors and then reached up to grab it. She quickly dusted it off and when no one was looking slipped it into her pocket. It was the handiwork of someone who knew of the old ways, was highly skilled and had long dextrous fingers and the eyesight of a scoul - her nana! A shudder worked outwards from her core and along her fingers and toes. Quickly, she left the party, descended the wooden stairs and made her way out of the shed. To her right, there was an old brick-built house and the door at the front was wide open. Carefully, she made her way into the dark interior.

'Oh, hallo, I call myself Katie.' He must have been in his eighties, be-spectacled and wearing a black beret, and wasn't the quickest of movers.

'Hello, I'm Dave, and who are you, miss?'

'I'm Katie.'

'Who's that?'

Before they ended up in a never ending loop, she thought she had better break out. 'Katie Talog, I serve in the Royal Navy, and it's just...I was told there was someone here who could help me?'

'Come in, come in. Take a seat. Would you like some tea?'

'You sit down, I'll make a brew. Just point me at the kettle.'

'No, that's all right, I'll go.'

'No, please let me go.' Too late, he was shuffling off to the back of the building.

Another man appeared, who looked like he was a younger version of Dave. 'Hallo love, who are you after?'

'Listen, I've just met Dave. He's gone off to make the tea. I don't know when he'll be back.'

'I'm Colin.'

'Of course you are. I call myself Katie. Can you help me?'

'I dunno. What was it you wanted?'

She sighed. 'HMS Eager was docked here in early June 1940, what records have you got?'

'Well, probably just the ship's log, but you won't find that here. You might have to try the Kew archives.'

'What have you got then?'

Two full mugs arrived on a tray, balanced by Dave on two hands, swimming in spilt tea.

'Ta very much' she muttered.

'Did she come in for repairs?' asked Colin.

'Who, Katie?' sniggered Dave.

'No, no, no' replied Colin.

Katie frowned. 'Why would I need repairs? Look at me, I'm young and in my prime!'

'You might need your bottom scraped...'

'Oh, really? Are you some sort of expert, then?'

'I've done a few in my time - frigates, destroyers...'

'Anyway, just to be clear, my bottom doesn't need any scraping, thank you very much!'

'It's a very nice bottom.'

'That may well be, but...'

'P'raps you need a rebore?'

'Oi, are you calling me an old boiler now?'

'No, of course not, but when did you last have it done?'

'Excuse me, that's a bit personal, isn't it? And who are you, the ancient mariner?'

'I'm not that old!'

'Yes, you sodding are!'

'You cheeky madam!'

'What are going to do about it then?'

'I'll put you over my knee and spank you!'

'Ha! You'll have to catch me first!' She took a slurp of tea. 'Oh, this is horrible. What happened to the sugar? Are we on rations here?'

'Anyway' said Colin, 'regarding HMS Eager, if she was repaired here, there ought to be a record, oughtn't there Dave?'

'There ought to be' said Dave.

'And the record ought to be here, correct?' asked Katie.

'Yes, it should.'

'Good, let's go and find it.'

'That's okay, let me see if I can find it, I'll just finish my tea...'

Katie looked up at Colin. 'I'm in a bit of a hurry...'

'Finish your tea Dave, I'll take Katie. Now let me see...'

Colin led her to the back of the building and then down into the cellar on old, decaying stairs. In the basement, there was a feeble lamp and rows and rows of metal racking, covered with dirty and grimy boxes.

'Is there a filing system? How do I find anything?'

'You don't, it just gets left here to rot.' Colin kicked out at a box and kicked the racking instead and it shook. He started to hop on his left foot.

She walked along to the end of the cellar and back again. 'Intuition it is then!' She brought out the tied knot of the triple spiral and sniffed at it. Pausing to concentrate, she pictured the ship and Captain James Houghton. She looked at the ceiling for inspiration and then wished she hadn't - There were cobwebs adorning the cobwebs and all the strands of gossamer were ten times more prominent then they should be, coated as they were with black grime.

'What are you doing?' Colin wanted to know.

'Shhh' she hushed, walking along the length of the first rack with her right forefinger trailing along the boxes. She looked ruefully at her dust encrusted finger. 'I'm going to need some household gloves. And a torch. And a step ladder.'

Colin returned with a step ladder and Dave. 'I need to go back up, we have visitors.'

Katie looked disapprovingly at Dave. 'Are you going to behave yourself? I won't stand for any nonsense, not when I'm up a ladder!'

She ascended the first rack.

'Nice rear end' he commented, 'reminds me of Betty Grable's!' Katie looked down at him.

'Who?'

Dave seemed to be in a dream like state, as if he was asleep on his feet. 'Betty Grable. She had blond hair, all piled up in a bun. She was lovely. She had a nice rear end, like yours.'

'Oi, that's enough!' He let go of the step ladder, ambled off and trudged up the stairs. Katie was by herself in the dark but despite this, she found five boxes that interested her. The first box opened gave her no feeling of connection. She ran her finger tip across the corrugated tops.

Still nothing.

The first sheaf of papers was withdrawn and she guessed it was from the fifties. She pulled the last document.

Still of the nineteen-fifties.

She closed the box and opened the second.

Still no connection. It was the fifties again. She tried the next three boxes with the same outcome, but with no sense of connection and the timelines were all wrong. She returned to the next rack and the next rack. Nothing. With a sigh of resignation she reached the last rack. Nothing. This wasn't working. But, in the farthest corner of the room, where there was no light, sat a chest. Katie grasped the edges, bent her knees and heaved. She dragged it under the lamp. It was a tea chest but the cover was torn. Papers were jumbled inside. Covering her eyes with her hand and holding her left hand above the papers, Katie felt a pricking sensation in the middle of her back that proceeded up her neck and over her scalp. Her arm dipped involuntarily into the chest and she pulled out a sheaf of papers. She opened her eyes and saw a typewritten sheet of foolscap paper with dark grey and intermittent print. It had a date that she recognised - it looked like June 4th, 1940.

She turned to see Dave shambling towards her. 'I need to get this chest upstairs - I reckon this is the one!'

'Yes, you've got a tatty old chest there, haven't you?'

'Oi! It's an old tea chest but it's got papers from the war in it. Where's that sodding sack trolley?'

An old photograph was pressed into her face. 'Here's my bit of stuff from the war' he said, showing her a photograph of a young woman in a light coloured swimsuit, looking cheekily over her shoulder. Her blond curls cascaded about her face.

'Ah, I see what you mean, she's a bit of a sweetheart, isn't she?'

'Yes, yes she is. We all had pictures of actresses and singers but she was my favourite.' He looked wistfully at the photograph.

'Yep, I can see why. So, where's the sack trolley?'

'Mmm, I wonder how you would look?'

'Eh? As a pin-up? Bloody embarrassed! Anyway, I need this chest shifting upstairs, and then another mug of tea and a sandwich.'

'Well, Katie, why don't you come with me, and I'll show you what we've got?'

She sighed and wiggled the chest until it was outside of the racking. Dave had found a sack trolley and with some faltering directions, they managed to get the chest upstairs and outside. Her eyes flickered as she got used to the bright light. Colin moved a table and a chair outside and set up an umbrella to shade it.

Katie looked again at the paper she had retrieved. 'What does this say?'

Colin squinted at it: 'It's a chit to record the repair work needed to the warship, HMS Eager. She had a bend in her bow and a gouge in her starboard side that needed fixing and splinter holes in the bridge. Dave rested his hands on her shoulders. 'What do you want in your sandwich, love?'

'What have you got?'

'Not sure, I'll go and check...'

She raised her eyes to the heavens.

'The assessment was completed by Master C.R.Edwards and approved by Captain J.F.Houghton.' She traced the lines of the Captain's signature with the tip of her little finger; it was elegant, authoritative and decisive.

Dave went back inside and returned two minutes later with a mug of tea. 'We don't have tinned tuna or salmon.'

'But what have you got?'

Dave shrugged and started to walk back. Katie decided she would have to shortcut this process. 'You sit here and I'll sort it out.' She ventured inside, turned to her right and followed the corridor. Here she found the kitchenette. She shouted 'Looks like it's ham or ham.

Which one do you want?' Sod it, it would have to be ham from a tin after all. There was a cork noticeboard by the sink and several photographs pinned precariously into it. She guessed these were mementos of Dave's life in the dockyard. Here she found a black, white and grey photograph of a destroyer, alongside at Chatham, well thumbed. She unpinned it and looked at the back. Scrawled in green ink on the back of the photograph was a short message inside a triple spiral. Katie's heart started to pound. She dashed outside, balancing a pile of sandwiches on a plate, and then stopped to compose herself. She didn't want to shock him. 'Dave, who gave this to you?'

He looked at the photograph in his hand and shrugged. 'It was a long, long time ago. I was just a lad, helping out in the yard!'

'That's HMS Eager' said Colin.

'HMS Eager? That's Captain Jim Houghton's ship! Who gave this to you, Dave?'

'Who?'

'Yes, who? That's my nana's mark!'

Dave turned the photograph over. 'No, it can't be! This is from my Rozenn! That's her mark, can't you see?'

'Rozenn? Who is Rozenn?' she asked as calmly as she could.

'She was the girl the police were torturing...'

'What?' Katie took the triple spiral of rope out of her pocket and squeezed it tight to her breast. 'How can that be?'

'Which means...Rozenn must be your nana!' said Colin triumphantly.

'Who the fucketty fuck is Rozenn?'

'She's your nana!'

'But how?' Her jaw sagged in complete incomprehension.

Colin stood in front of her and gently eased her jaw back together. 'You can do this Katie!'

'I helped to rescue her!' Dave exclaimed.

'You did what?'

'I ran as quick as I could to HMS Eager - I got the navy to come!'

Katie's left hand scrunched the spiral, in and out, in and out. Her brain felt like slush being lifted and rolled and turned over. This was the owner of the voice that had been calling her from afar, her nana! How could she not have realised that? And how was that even possible?

Chapter Sixty-Three

Saturday 28 May 0235 - Paol's place

It was still dark as Katie reached the main entrance to the block of flats where Paol lived. She negotiated the card entry system and walked into the concrete area at the base of the stairs where the bicycles were stored. Paol's bike was present. She decided to climb the three flights of stairs to Paol's flat.

Here she would need a key. She looked under the mat. No key. She pushed the letter box open and the flap popped back into place. 'Shhh' she whispered to the letter box. No key. But, the door swung open eerily. Not locked. She stepped stealthily into the passageway to the living room and kitchen. There were clothes strewn everywhere; there was a red headdress on the armchair and a red cloak strewn over the coffee table and a red leather boot just outside the bedroom. She pushed the door open slowly. She could hear the breathing of two people. She peered through the gloom - there were two people in the double bed, asleep. The nearest had a shock of blond hair protruding above the quilt.

'You dirty dog' she muttered to herself. She crouched and then slivered silently across the linoleum covered floor until she was alongside the bed. There was a flicker of awareness on the brows of the first body and a slight cough. Katie's hand picked up a note pad and a pen from the bedside table. The pen worked. She wrote a brief message in capital letters on the first empty page and edged her way on her back to the bedside. She touched the hand of the first body. Natalie looked over the side of the bed - her eyes flashed open, her mouth ajar. Katie quickly put her hand over Natalie's mouth and raised her finger to her lips. 'Hush.'

She flashed the note book in front of Natalie's eyes. It said 'U BIG SLAG!' Natalie frowned and then smiled a warm and satisfied smile. Katie wrote on a new page, 'SKWEEZ TO CHAT?', and her hand settled next to Natalie's.

Natalie squeezed. Katie wrote on a new page.

'HOW GOOD? 1=BAD, 3=GOOD'. Natalie gave five little squeezes. Wow, Katie thought, very good.

She wrote again. 'HIT SPOT? 1=HIT, 3=MISS'. There was a deep sigh, then five squeezes. Wow, thought Katie, Paol's actually a sexual marksman. Who'd have thought it?

She wrote some more. 'DO AGAIN?'. There were six little squeezes.

She was quickly onto the next page. There was a name and address on this page.'1.MAKE TEA? 2.SOD OFF?' There were two squeezes, but the second was long and lingering. Katie took this as her cue to caterpillar her way across the floor out of the bedroom. She switched on the lamp by the door and flitted through the rest of the pages of the pad. There was a name, it began with a 'U'. She stared at it until it came into focus. There was an 'L' and an 'R'. Yes, it was an Ulrich. She closed the pad quickly. Katie wiped a tear from her eye and then picked up her roll bag and quickly and quietly left the flat.

Katie kept watch over Paol's flat until the early hours of the morning. As the rays of sun percolated onto her face through the leaves and twigs of the scabby trees, she got up from the bench and started to walk quickly in the direction of Dorina's place.

CHAPTER SIXTY-FOUR

Saturday 28 May - The Hen Night

'Yes, my friend?'

'Dorina, I need your help.' They were conducting the conversation through the medium of Dorina's shabby flat door.

'Let me place a call now.'

She called. There was shouting. After three placatory sentences, the voice returned to a more everyday timbre. Dorina slid the phone through the gap between the door and the frame. There was a confident female voice at the other end, with a latin accent. It was Christina.

'It's me, Katie. I need your help.'

'Huh, how was your dress?'

'It did the job but I need your help again.'

'Another dress? That makes two! Are you sure?'

'Yes, Christina, I've got a mega night, tonight, and I'll need the works.'

'Why? Are you Cinderella?'

'Who?'

'Cinderella! You want to win the prince!'

'Yes, something like that. I need a complete and utter make up and over.'

'You do realise what this means?'

'I don't know, what does this mean?'

'You will have to do exactly as I say. If I ask you to do something, you must do it, no question. You will have to trust me.'

'I'm not sure I like the sound of that.'

'Your choice. If you want my help, these are my terms. You must accept them. I have friends, they will help. Do you accept my terms?'

'I suppose so, but you just have to realise...'

'I realise how you are. You will need to be primped, trimmed and buffed. It will not be a parade in the park...'

'All right, all right, I trust you. I put myself entirely in your hands.'

'Okay, good. How long have we got?'

'Half a day...'

'Crap! Where are you? Get yourself to my place now. Do you have a dress in mind?'

'No!'

'Crap! Are you going out for dinner?'

'Er, yes, and riding a bull and Salsa dancing, then a long journey and I'm wearing pumps.'

'And the dress?'

'It must cover everything, and it will be black and a bit swirly but not so anyone can see through it...'

'Ah, I am realising - you will need underwear?'

'Oh yes, totally.'

There was a big sigh. 'Get yourself here now.' Then there was a long silence.

'I know what you're thinking, you're thinking, I cannot polish a turd, that's what you're thinking, isn't it?'

'No, I wasn't thinking that, I was thinking what I could be doing this day, instead of this.'

'I'll be very grateful.'

'Of course you will. Get here now!' Katie slid the phone back to Dorina, took note of Christina's address and dashed back down the stairs, three at a time. Some rest and relaxation would be good, before the unfolding of events this eventide.

Katie jogged along three tree-lined streets and arrived at the address of the salon at the run. There were stone balustrades leading up a short flight of steps to a glass pained door, adorned on the inside with hand-written notes on scraps of paper. She tapped on the door and it swung open. A set of stairs led steeply upwards and she pushed past clothes on hangers until she reached right to the top and started to bang on another glass door. It opened as if someone was waiting immediately behind. She was greeted by Christina, eyes shaded, coffee in one hand and a cigarillo in the other.

There were two men with her. This was not what she was expecting.

They were immaculately dressed and coiffured with precision.

They had the kind of eyes that might be found on an animal searching for prey. No, not a rodent, more like the eyes of a pair of weasels hunting down a rabbit and she was the rabbit. Katie put on a slouch, with her hands on her hips and a pout on her lips, defying them to touch her, and looking as un-rabbit like as she could.

'What do you think, Marcel?' asked Christina of one of the two men.

'This is an impossible task' he answered, 'I will have to mow, shave, exfoliate, sluice down, trim, buff and polish in like, no time.' His posture mirrored Katie's but he massively out-pouted her. He was short, tanned and wore a Paisley shirt. This was teamed with a purple pair of trousers which seemed to match his open chested shirt, but didn't really.

'Oi, I'm right here in front of you and I'm not having any of that' replied Katie.

The man turned to Christina and grimaced. 'Hmm, a little bit feisty.'

'Marcus?'

Marcus stepped forward. He was also a product of the tanning salon and randomised clothing. 'Let me take some measurements and see what we've got to work with. There is potential here.'

'Oi!' What kind of people are these? They didn't sound like any kind of people she had met before. Their clothes, though, were the kind of clothes she may have seen in a circus or a pantomime. 'Listen to me, I have rights...' Were they circus performers? Her body gave a quick shudder.

'What happened to my right to enjoy a kiss and a cuddle on the sofa while watching a romantic movie on a Saturday afternoon?'

Katie tried to recall her training on human rights. This was a new one to her. 'I'm sorry, I don't actually know what to say to that.'

They approached Katie from both flanks so she was hemmed in.

They started to examine her closely.

Her arms dropped to her sides and she tightened up her body and her left arm started to wobble. She wondered what they would do to her. The tutting started slowly and built up to a crescendo of volume and frequency.

'What's the matter, haven't you come across a pair of queens before?' said the one who called himself Marcel.

'Um, yes, when I'm playing poker?'

'Oh dear, poor navy girl!'

'And what does your experience inform you about pairs of queens?'

She hesitated as she wasn't sure where this was going. 'They beat a pair of jacks?'

'Very amusing. And in life?' asked Marcus.

'Do you do...special dancing?' asked Katie.

'Aww, how sweet!' said Marcel.

'Ooh, oh dear, oh dear' tutted the one called Marcus.

Marcel came to her front and pulled out the front of her denims and peered inside. He gave a low whistle.

She pushed him away. 'Oi, get out, you've not been invited!'

'Oh dear, we're going to need anaesthetic and industrial machinery for this one!'

'You cheeky sod! That's rude!'

Marcus was behind her. He blew on his hands to warm them and then expertly ran a tape measure around her chest, below her breasts. 'Oh, yes' he exclaimed. The tape measure was then run across her breasts and round to her back. 'Oh, yes, yes.' Katie bit her lip. The tape measure now curled around her waist. 'Oh, yes, yes, yes.' The tape measure was then run over her backside. His hand followed the line of her thigh and then playfully slapped her bottom. 'A little bit large down here, aren't we?' He squeezed her buttock - she quickly removed his hand.

'They're muscles, pal!'

'Muscles indeed!'

Marcus turned his back to Katie. 'Hmm, what was the brief again?'

'She's Cinderella, she will go to the ball. Katie is a bit prim, doesn't like showing skin, do you? She will need sensible shoes for dancing, no heels, sensible knickers.' Christina showed them a sketch she had made on the back of a brown envelope.

'So not these ones that last saw the light of day in the Middle Ages, then' suggested Marcel.

'Oi, there's nothing wrong with these' exclaimed Katie.

'Deluded?' queried Marcel.

'I'm afraid so. I spoke to her brother, he will contribute funds for this make-over. He wants a picture of Cinderella when she's ready for the ball.'

'Oh, bollocks' muttered Katie.

'Let's get started then. Marcus, take her to the sluicing station. Marcel, come with me to the costume department. We find a dress. You have all the measurements you need?'

'It's a big ask. We need to start immediately with body, hair, nails, pits. Come with me Katie.'

'Good. We should reconvene in...let's say two hours?'

'Good. Roll the 'miracles to perform' music.'

Dorina attempted to lace the dress up. 'We may have to sew you in my friend' she commented.

'It's a good dress and it looks good on you, but you need to wear it like a woman, not like a man' said Christina.

'Oi, what's that supposed to mean? What's the matter with the way I wear it?'

'You walk like a matelot!'

'What? So, what do I need to do?'

'Think of a lady who is graceful and walk like her.'

'Gwen said think of a Royal princess and walk like they do' said Katie, brightly.

'No, much too horsey - think of someone more lady-like.' They paused for thought. 'Think of...a fairy tale princess?'

'Who?' Katie walked her normal walk across the room.

'She walks like a matelot' giggled Marcel.

Katie walked back with a pronounced swing of the hips.

'You walk like a female impersonator, my friend!'

'Try balancing something above you while you're walking.'

'Like your head' giggled Marcel.

'Like a pint glass? I don't think that'll work, it's all I can do to keep my head on straight.'

'So, you're going to wear those pumps?'

'Yes, I have to - I'm going dancing. I can't wear heels, I'll topple over.'

'No make-up?'

'She wouldn't have it' muttered Marcus.

'And that bag?'

Katie checked through her satchel - everything that she was going to need, that evening and the following morning, was present.

'Strike a pose, my friend'. Dorina took two pictures, one front on and one with Katie looking over her shoulder. 'We have achieved the impossible my friends! And Paol has the proof!'

Katie bustled her way past the two bouncers guarding the entrance to the Mornington Crescent drinking establishment and her ears were immediately assailed by the high pitch of women's chatter. She immediately caught sight of Flick and her circle of hens. Her heart sank. They were all in heels and impractically curtailed dresses. So, she had stumbled into a beauty pageant - all that was missing was the tiaras and sashes. Oh, hang on...

'KT, KT, KT!'

'Hallo, it's me, Katie.'

Flick gave her a quick hug. Wants to travel the world and save interesting people. Judging from her heavy breath and slurred speech, Flick had already got a head start in the drinking stakes. 'What have you got in store for us?'

Katie wiped the smear of cow grease from her cheek. 'So much!' She extracted a sheaf of papers from her satchel and distributed them.

'Hello, who is this?'

'Katie, this is my mum, Penny. Penny, meet KT. KT is my best friend in all the navy!'

'I'm pleased to meet you KT - what's that short for?'

'It's short for Katie.' Penny wants the world back to how it was when she was head girl in a private school.

'Katie Talog? I see. So Katie, I need to talk to you about the arrangements for Felicity's hen night. They seem very, um, unseemly to me.'

'It's all been arranged. We're expected, all over town.' Katie looked around at the eight participants. 'There is a plan for this evening, girls, and we need to be tight on the timings.' No one here would be any use in a fight, if it all kicked off, which it all would, as there were a couple of coming flash-points...

'I don't think this works for me' said Penny, as she tore the sheet of paper from top to bottom with considerable ceremony.

'But, it's all arranged!' exclaimed Katie. She scowled at the other girls who just looked down on her. In contrast to all the others, she probably looked like she was on her way to a wake.

'I don't care...I know a beautiful Italian restaurant, it's not far from here and...' Penny stabbed triumphantly at her mobile device, 'they have room for us!'

'But, we can't...'

'Yes, we can. I just said...'

'Mum!'

'Sounds good to me...' Carly, a vet, loves animals but would never sink to shoving her arm halfway up a cow's arse.

'Can't beat Italian. The waiters...' Emma, professional man-eater.

'Bella, bella!' Victoria, edits a magazine, can't form a whole sentence though...

'All right listen up girls, listen up' shouted Flick. There was a hush right across the pub lounge and then normal, casual chatter resumed. She slipped off her heels, stood up on a stool and surveyed her troop. 'Before we decide anything, I want to say something...'

'Speech, speech!'

'No, no, this will be like a eulogy, a eulogy to KT. Friends, relations and colleagues, lend me your ears!' There was a barrage of hoots and laughs and catcalls. 'I come to praise KT, not to bury her!' There were more laughs. 'Although, under a different set of circumstances, I could have been burying you, couldn't I, KT?'

'I don't know what you mean, Flick.'

'You know exactly what I mean. I asked KT to do this for me, and to be with me this evening, and I just need to explain...'

'There's no need, Felicity.'

'KT, you have given me great cause to worry about my decision...'

'You didn't need to...'

'You volunteered for a posting while at sea so I had no idea when you'd be back...'

'But, I'm back now!'

'And you are a nightmare to get hold of!'

'My phone died!'

'You keep leaving me little messages and I can never get back to you...'

'I've been busy!'

'Then KT decided that she would go hand to hand with a bunch of hostiles while she was off Madagascar so she could rescue a squad of French commandos...'

'But, I had no choice!'

'Yes, but you could have been killed, couldn't you?'

'Ah, but I wasn't, was I?'

'Then I heard a rumour doing the rounds that you were going to fight my husband-to-be. I don't know what you were thinking KT, but just so there's no confusion, if there's any fighting of my husband to be done...'

'But that was never going to happen!'

'...if there's to be any fighting of my husband, I will be doing it, not you!'

'But there was never going to be a fight!'

'Hmm. I realise that I'm taking a big risk, I'm going to marry a man who...' This drew a round of sympathetic applause. '...a man who is a Royal Marine' she continued, 'who will inevitably suffer from male pattern stupidity. So KT, dealing with my husband, that's going to be my job going forward, not yours...'

'But it was...'

'Quiet, Katie. I wrung the truth out of him...'

'Noooo! Which bit?'

'So I know what you were up to!'

'Noooo! Really? All of it?'

'But despite all that, she's here now and I trust her. I trust her, and here's why. When you're a pilot in a helicopter, on a rescue mission, a Liberian tanker needing help, foundering in a tempest...' Felicity paused and surreptitiously wiped a tear from her right eye, '...in a tempest.'

'Take your time Flea.'

'When was this, Felicity?'

'You're hundreds of miles from land, you're running out of fuel and some well-meaning twat of an officer comes on line and says you're going to have to ditch...and the waves are so tall, you know they're going to swamp the chopper...you know it's not going to end well...you start praying...getting ready to meet your maker...then this little girl's voice comes on line... and she's got a plan.'

'That's enough Felicity, we've got it...'

'So, we're above the survey ship...'

'My first ship, HMS Harpy' added Katie.

'We can't see anything, the sea's raging, the winds throwing the chopper about, KT got us down on deck. We bounced, we bounced three times, the matelots got us secured. And there's this girl, this girl here, in her Sou'wester, a red flare in her left hand and a green flare in her right hand, she's all miked up...and she got us down.' Flick stepped off the stool. 'Now, come here, you.'

Katie edged cautiously up to Flick.

'Closer' she was ordered. 'So, she's calling me all the...under the sun. You didn't like my landing, did you dear?' Flick paused.

'You did all right, Flick' Katie noted as she pulled out a cloth bag, 'and by the way, this is the Swearing Bag.' She offered the bag as Flick pulled out a note and placed it inside.

'Sliding scale, KT?'

'Of course, five pounds for the really nasty ones; two pounds for the not so nasty ones; one pound for blasphemers and general curses.' She was pulled tight to Flick but just managed to free her arms.

'I should have done this years ago.' She squeezed tightly as Katie gave her tentative 'you're crushing me' taps on her back.

'It's all right Flick, it was me doing my job.' She eased Flick away.

'So, if this girl says turn fifteen degrees port, that's what I will do. If she says drop twenty and get in the lee of the hangar, that's what I will do.' There was a tentative ripple of applause. Katie watched as Penny turned and walked quickly towards the lady heads, her neatly manicured hand clasped over her gagging mouth.

Flick held up a sheet of paper and started reading. It was Katie's (No, Paol's) hen night plan.

'So, if KT says 'Raging Bull' at 6pm, that's where I will go. Raging Bull, KT?'

'Yes, we take turns riding a mechanical bull and the winner is the one who stays on the longest. We'll be matched up against a bunch of dicks.'

'Complementary jugs?'

'Yes'

'What does that mean?'

'Rum cocktail, first three jugs are free. We said we were bringing a team of fit girls...and we have these.' She flipped up her dress to a chorus of gasps to reveal what she was wearing - running shorts. She held up a pack of shorts. 'I have spares in case anyone's worried about showing off their stuff.'

'I see, then we eat at this place in Islington, called 'Nuts'? Is this a vegetarian place, KT? Because I will be needing red meat tonight.'

'No, it's not...'

'Please explain...'

'It's a restaurant. We'll be served by blokes in tiny pants and bow ties and not much else.'

'Sounds awful, but I'm game' noted Flick brightly.

'And then, Salsa City at twenty-three hundred sharp.'

'What's this?'

'We dance the Salsa with fit, Latina blokes.'

'I don't know the Salsa, Katie.'

'No worries, we spend the first hour learning the dance, step by step, with more, fit Latina blokes.'

'I see. And complementary jugs?'

'Margaritas, yes, I said I was bringing a team of fit girls.'

'There seems to be a theme here, KT?'

'Yes, it's your hen night Flick. It's very important we get there on the dot each time.'

'I think we can do that. Well, I'm going with KT. Anyone else?'

'In which case girls, I just need your money. Flick, we're shipping out in ten, make sure everyone's ready. I'm going to catch up with your mum.' She walked quickly to the toilets and pushed her way in. There was one cubicle closed but there was the sound of retching inside. Katie banged on the door, and after a moment the door was pulled open. Penny wiped her mouth with a tissue and stepped to the washbasins. She checked her face and wiped away the smears that had appeared below her eyes with another tissue.

'Is it true, you saved the life of my daughter, the most precious thing to me in the world? And she's never mentioned it until now!'

'No, no, Penny, I just saved her from an early bath...'

'I don't believe you, I saw the way that Felicity embraced you, she's never done that to me!'

'And the helicopter, we needed that back otherwise that was a sodding fortune down in the drink!'

'That is nothing compared with the life of my daughter. Nothing! And she said nothing. Nothing! And you? You? You're just a girl who...'

'Listen to me Penny. Flick's had a couple of drinks, and she's a little bit emotional. That's all it is. We drag the fly boys and girls out of the drink all the time.' And there it was, the lie; the little lie, designed to avoid the pain of the truth; to divert attention away from the hurt, by making a joke of it. Katie swelled in relief that she had been able to take the heat out of a situation, to protect her and Penny from any further pain. 'That's why they've all got webbed feet, isn't it? Look, they just like to make a drama out of every crisis...' Katie paused. 'Did I say that right?'

'I never wanted her to join, it's just not worth the risk. She could have a high powered job in the city, earn ten times as much and she's marrying a squaddie! A squaddie! He's not even an officer, he has no prospects...'

'Penny, they're in love. They're properly in love. Mad Dogs...'

'Mad Dogs!!'

'Sorry, I meant Lance Corporal Maddocks...he has prospects. And he's properly in love with your daughter, Penny!'

The boy tumbled, hopped over the mattress and fell into Katie's arms - she pushed him away indignantly.

'Beat that!' he crowed.

'Where's your champ!' came another shout.

'Come on Julie Bloody Andrews! What have you got?'

Penny and Katie scanned the room - Flick and the other girls were in animated and loud huddles around the bar, shouting discordantly with no interest in riding the bull again. Penny looked to Katie. 'It's all down to you, KT, I nominate you as our champion!'

'You'll have to match the stake, Julie Andrews, match it!'

'I'm not sure about this, Penny?'

'I have it covered, KT, just don't let me down!' Penny counted out five notes and put them in the pot that was being waved under Katie's nose.

'That's a lot Penny!'

'There! Go KT!'

She gathered up the skirts of her dress and approached the operator. 'Remember what I said, switch it down to the special setting.'

'No! No! Turn it up! Turn it up!' came the chant, 'Turn it up! Turn it up!'

'Listen, I'm a girl, put it on the girl's setting!'

'There's no such thing!'

Katie grasped the rein and mounted the bull. 'All right boys, turn around, there's nothing to see! No photos, no glimping!' The mechanical bull cranked into motion, gathering momentum; she slid to the left and then to the right, her thighs squeezed tighter, her left hand set on the neck of the beast, her right wrapped with the rein. Her shriek, was echoed by the beast's insides, now bucking up and down and rearing upwards. She was vertical, squealing continuously, like a rabbit in the jaws of a weasel, now in discordant harmony with the shrieking bull. Surrounded by bodies shouting and screaming at her and the operator, she and the bull reared again and the bitter and choking smell of burning metal and rubber filled the room. She was edging down, despite the friction provided by her shorts.

'I've switched him off! Just leave him alone!' shouted the operator.

She was sliding down. 'Sorry mate.'

Feet now firmly settled, arm now settled.

'He's had it! I've tamed it!' Katie stroked the nose of the beast. 'I've tamed the big bollocked beast!' she whispered in awe.

Penny took the stake money and pushed it at Katie. 'You utterly, amazing girl! How did you do that!'

'Penny, I just clung on as hard as I could!' Katie grabbed the notes and pushed them into her satchel. 'I think that should buy us all the cider we can drink and more!'

'How...did...you...do...that!'

'I...just...clung...on...as...hard...as...I... could!'

'You are totally amazing!'

'I know, it was amazing! Now we go eat!'

They plunged out through the doors into the street, singing a song about a little bull that was quite different from all the others. They saw a sleek, white ambulance outside with a triple spiral on the doors, crowned with S.I.K.S. in red letters and with some other hieroglyphics in black. Katie recognised the driver and his passenger. She walked across the street and tapped on the driver's window - he turned to look at her. Despite his clean, white overalls, the mess of his thin, black hair and the thin, messy beard, suggested that she would not be getting the best medical care from him.

The ambulance screeched away but at least she had made contact.

Penny tugged at the shorts of their table assistant called 'Tiberius' and pushed her empty glass at him. It was filled with red wine.

'Why aren't you drinking, Katie?'

'I am, look!' she said as she thrust the pint glass of lemonade towards Penny.

'Have a glass of wine, this is a particularly fine Pinot Noir!'

'No thanks, Penny, I need to keep my shit together!' She slipped a couple of coins into the penalty pouch. 'Oh, bollocks!' She slipped another coin in.

'Just one sip!'

'No thanks!'

'Why, Katie?'

'About three years ago in Malta, I got completely hand-carted, that's why.'

'What happened?'

'It was a run ashore, wasn't it? Someone dosed my blackcurrant with the local red wine...'

'Ah, Felicity told me about this!'

'Oh, no!'

'You took on the local ladies of the night at their own game!'

'No, I didn't! It was just dancing, that's all, on the tables mainly, and on the bar. I ended up rolling all the way down to the bottom of Strait Street. The local police had to fish me out of the harbour!'

'Then what happened?'

'I was in loads of trouble. They had to pump my stomach out! Never again!'

'So, no more good times for you Katie!'

'Yes, good times, but I mustn't get shot away. Tonight, I need my head together, like never before!'

'Just a little one?'

'All right.' Katie took a sip. 'That's not a bad drop, Penny!'

A waiter named 'Brutus' came between them and didn't resist when Penny pulled at the gusset. 'Whoa, not bad, if only I was a few years younger!'

'You're a bad Penny!'

'And what is happening with you Katie? Why is it so important to be on time?'

'We're booked in at eleven, if we miss that we'll miss the training and we'll be rubbish...'

'But that's part of the fun, isn't it?'

'We're not going to be late, Penny, this has all been planned with naval precision.'

'What's the real reason?'

'I've told you Penny!'

'Tell me again, this time the truth!'

'I always tell the truth!'

'The real truth!'

'Oh, bollocks. Buggery, buggery bollocks.' Katie looked around for inspiration but there wasn't any, just a sequence of old photographs of old fashioned bars full of old fashioned people. She slipped some more coins into the pouch. 'I made a promise to my nana...and when my lot make a promise, it has to be kept.'

'And?'

'The Swiss stole something from her a long time ago...and I've just worked out how I can get it back.'

'The Swiss? And your nana keeps reminding you?'

'Yes, but the only problem is, she's probably dead now.'

'I don't suppose she's missing it? Whatever it is?'

'I have to get it back to her, or she cannot pass to the other side.'

'Is she haunting you?'

'Yes, something like that!'

'You poor girl!'

'What? What do you mean? Anyway, it doesn't matter. We need to get going...there's fit Latina men waiting for us!'

Katie manoeuvred her way along the queue heading through the double doors of Salsa City, all about to descend to the dance floor below. A sleek white ambulance passed by the queue slowly, but the crew did not respond to her wave and they sped away. Ahead of her there was a head that she recognised, despite it missing its little piggy tail. 'Udo, it's me Katie! I knew you'd be here, didn't I?'

'Katie! You look very nice!'

'I do, don't I? It was a big team effort though...and who's your friend?'

'Katie, this is Zella - she's my... fiancee.'

'Ah, your lobster! Hallo Zella, I call myself Katie and I'm...'

'Zella, this is Paol's sister, Katie...'

'Oh, yes, I'm Paol's sister, which is how I know Udo. I'll catch up with you later, when I've got my girls in.' Katie beckoned down the queue and the members of Felicity's hen party came into line and followed her to the entrance. She waved a ticket at the gate keeper and they were inside.

They descended to the basement of the club. The floor was planked with wood but despite this, there was a queue of people hoping to be shown how to dance the Salsa on it. 'Let's get in the queue and register - I used to think Salsa was just something zingy you eat.'

'Actually Katie, it's a mating ritual, like that thing praying mantises do' replied Penny.

'Praying mantiseses? Isn't that where the boy gets eaten by the girl?'

'Yes it is, but fortunately for them, I've already eaten.'

'Me too, let's get registered.'

With registration complete, Katie headed back to their assigned trestle table with three jugs swinging in her hands and a stein of lager.

'Yay! Margaritas!'

'Absolutely. Save me a drop, I'm just going to a little chat with my boyfriend.' She collected the stein of lager and her own glass.

'Don't be long! We're gonna need you when the music starts!'

Udo's party was just two trestles away so Katie pushed her way in between him and Zella. She seemed a little annoyed about this, but no matter.

'Oh my, you're wearing a dress Katie!'

'I am aren't I? Like when we first met. I wonder how long it will stay on this time?'

'Udo!' exclaimed Zella indignantly.

'Anyway, this one's yours, for old times sake' she said, as she pushed the stein his way. 'I've really been looking forward to this moment.' They clinked glasses. 'So, is Paol talking to you again?'

'He seems to be doing everything he can to avoid contact.'

'Me too, he gets in a bit of a sulk, doesn't he?'

'Not to worry, prosit!'

'Iechyd da! He was very critical of you, wasn't he? I think there's a bit of jealousy there, because of...what we did together.'

'Udo?'

'It was nothing!'

'I thought we were good together, weren't we?'

'Zella, it was nothing!'

'Oh Udo, you are naughty, not telling your lobster about us!'

'Katie, I think you had better leave!'

'You mean Zella doesn't know about us? That's very sneaky of you, Udo!'

'Katie, please leave!'

'Yes, leave!' said the young woman opposite, in a very tight fitting red dress.

'Are you hoping to dance in that? Can't wait for your floor show!'

'Pardon?'

'Granted.' She was face to face with Zella. They were of similar height and build, both with brown hair twirled into a top knot and long black dresses. 'Blimey! You're me, only German with it!' But she had proper Cuban dance shoes and a steely expression. Katie turned to Udo. 'I'll meet you on the dance floor Udo, and we'll have a chat in private.' She turned on her soles and walked away, feeling Zella's glare burning the back of her head.

'Trouble?' asked Penny.

'Yes, he's got this fräulein bint who's the spit of me!'

'Is there going to be a fight?' asked Felicity.

'I don't think so, I'm done with him for now. Let's dance.'

'Well shot of him!'

'Good looking lad, though!'

Katie took stock of the situation, while draining her glass. 'Right, we're beginners so we're on first. You'll have to listen well to the calls.'

'I've never done anything like this before. Won't it be embarrassing?'

'Don't worry. The instructor told me that it's the bloke's job to make us look good; if we don't look good then he doesn't look good. You'll get a whole lot of different blokes, so if they don't make you look good, that's all right, but it will mean that he won't look good, and he won't get the hottest girl so he'll...'

'Get eaten' said Penny.

'Exactly! So there's no pressure on us!'

It was slow going and not at all challenging, except for the posturing of a whole succession of male partners and then she was counting them down until it was Udo's turn. She could see Zella, four couples away, coming in her direction and she was not concentrating on her partner; she was concentrating on her and Udo.

'What's the matter, Katie?'

'Nothing's the matter, Udo, just show me your stuff.'

'Please don't say any more to Zella.'

'It's just...I want you for myself and I can't share you with anyone!'

'Oh my god, Katie.'

'And I do get insanely jealous...'

'But I can't Katie...'

'But I do need to be loved, I need to be put on a pedestal above all others...oh bollocks! We've started!'

'I do like your dress.'

'Good! Nice shoes, by the way.'

'You are such a good dancer, Katie.'

'And so are you, now lead me like I'm the only girl in the world...'

Udo smiled back.

She nestled her face against his neck: 'I'm yours, I'm yours, I'm yours, I'm yours...' she whispered in his ear.

There was a shout and the instructor was waving his arm at her.

'What's up now?' she wondered.

Zella came up behind Udo: 'My turn!' Her arm encircled his waist and she pulled him away.

'Zella!'

'You haven't been leading this poor girl on, have you? That's so wicked of you!'

'We haven't finished yet!' Udo departed to her right and he was gone. 'You know what happens to Hamburgers, don't you!' she shouted after them.

'Katie, don't be so idiotic' Udo called out, above the music.

'And you will be sunk without trace, pal!' The man in front of her was trying desperately to attract Katie with his best, Salsa moves. 'Piss off you idiot!'

Udo was being led away by Zella, away from her and up the wooden stairway. They ascended with arms entwined.

And now her arm hurt where it was being pulled. It was Penny. They were heading back to the trestle table. She was sitting astride the bench, fingers itching, mouth and throat dry. And now she gazed through the glass jug and considered emptying the green, mushy dregs into her mouth. 'Why aren't you dancing Penny?'

Penny was talking to her, a vision in shocking pink. 'Just forget about him Katie, don't go chasing him. He's not worth it.'

'You're wrong' Katie hissed back, 'we have a blood pact. He has to be mine, he has no choice. He has to be mine!' She drained the jug, spat out a mouth full of mint leaves, slipped off the bench and marched to the stairway.

Here, there was a tall girl in a red dress barring her way. It was so tight, it was almost obscene. 'I'm Zella's friend' she stated, 'so do not get between her and Udo, or else!'

'Or else what?'

'I'm sorry?'

'Are you threatening me?'

'I don't understand?'

'Let me help you understand, if you don't get out of my way...'

'I've studied Taekwondo for five years and I am a black belt in karate!"

'So?'

'And I have a far superior physique!' she said proudly, her chin set at the perfect angle to receive an uppercut.

'That's not going to help you when I melt your kneecaps and rip your soul out...'

'You do not frighten me!'

'Then you must be very stupid!'

The girl in the red dress slumped suddenly to the floor, her face contorted in pain.

'Katie, Katie, what's the problem?'

'There's no problem, Penny!'

'Just stop what you're doing!' said Penny firmly.

'I don't think I will...'

'Do you think this is helping?'

'It's making me feel better. When her soul screams out, I'll feel even better!'

Katie turned and ran up the wooden steps, two at a time. It felt fresh outside. She steered her way to the right of the building but suddenly felt uneasy. There was a sleek, white ambulance and two ambulance men in white overalls with Zella's arms held taut between them; Udo was scrunched on the paving stones, holding his stomach in.

Katie took three quick steps and dived to tackle the nearest man. Her shoulder thudded into his stomach and he collapsed, winded. The other man swung his arm, but missed as her leg sweep knocked him off his feet. Zella was free. Katie turned and knelt by Udo. 'Help needed here!' she shouted out into the street.

A man barged her away and there was a flash of metal between them. Udo gasped and spluttered. Katie pulled the man down and his knife bounced under the ambulance. 'You useless fucking pricks! You've got the wrong girl!'

Udo sprawled on his knees and palms. 'Man down' she screamed. 'Get me some help here!' A small spot of blood appeared on Udo's shirt half way down and expanded rapidly. Katie ripped off the tail of his shirt and wrapped it into a bandage and pressed down on the neat hole in his stomach. He was gasping for breath, like he was having a baby. She pushed the wad down again. 'Udo, remember to breath, remember to breath, now what are you feeling, can you feel me here inside of you?'

'Are you an angel?'

'Of course, I'm just a bit shit at it!'

A thick sheaf of her hair was tugged sharply upwards and she scrambled up with it. Katie swung her knee towards her assailant's groin but it impacted against bone. She tried to grasp her assailant's arm with her hands. His other arm was swinging towards her and she bobbed to avoid the blow but it caught the back of her head. She swayed as her eyes tried to re-focus. And then her legs buckled beneath her as another blow took her on the side of her face. The ground teetered and then came up in a rush to meet her and now that was all that filled her mind.

And now the grimy paving slabs moved past her eyes as she was dragged to a sleek white vehicle with an open boot door. Over his shoulder she went and she was flopped into the back of the ambulance. The door came down and there were urgent voices. No light, just cold unyielding metal around her and the banging pain in her head. And there was the uncontrolled sobbing of Udo and Zella and more distressed shouting. The vehicle accelerated and the tyres screeched.

'Felicity, It's Katie! She's leaving. She's going after Udo!'

'So what mum? Leave her to it, she's mad...but wait, she's got all our money!' Felicity got up and rushed with her mother up the stairs.

'But she's your friend!'

'No, she's not, she's no one's friend!'

'But she saved your life!'

'No, she did not!

'You said she did!'

'She changes the rules. That's what she does. With her long, fiddly fingers and witchy muttering, she gets everything she wants and if the rules are against her, her eyes go funny and she changes them! That's what she does! She's a nasty, mean bitch!'

'Why did she save you? Why did she step out into a tempest and bring you in?'

'She wanted a crack at my man! That's what it was!'

'How does saving you, help her with that?'

There was a long pause as Felicity's mind tried to link up the neural pathways into a coherent answer.

'Oh, crap. It doesn't mum!'

They were now outside and the freshness of the night air was abrupt and sobering. Penny saw a figure lying on the pavement, clutching his belly. There was a dark red stain in his shirt. He was attended by a girl shrieking in her own shock. It was the German girl, Zella.

'Katie's gone! She's gone with our money!' came a pathetic, child-like wail from the stairs below.

'Tess, take them all downstairs, get them a coffee, sober them up. Mum and I will sort this out.'

'Zella, Zella, what happened?'

'It was Katie!'

'What was Katie?'

'Katie came. They wanted her!'

'Who were they, Zella?'

'I don't know. There were men, in white uniforms!'

'Were they medics?'

'No, not medics. They had a knife! They stabbed Udo!'

'What were they driving?'

'I'm not sure. An ambulance?'

Felicity rang the emergency services. Calmly and precisely, she spelled out what the situation was and where the ambulance and police needed to come.

'Katie talked to an ambulance crew, a few blocks back' murmured Penny, 'she seemed to know them.'

'Can you remember anything about them, Mum?'

'I can! Let me talk to the police!'

Felicity gazed down the High Street. 'KT's mental, but she wouldn't stab anyone...curse them, maybe.'

'How can you be sure, Felicity?'

'I can't. Something's changed, she's gone right off the rails. KT, what in the name of God is going on with you?'

CHAPTER SIXTY-FIVE

Sunday 29 May 0011 -
In the SIKS Laboratory, Cambridge

'Stop that, or you'll be sorry!' shouted the ambulance driver. The ambulance halted so Katie stopped kicking at the metal panels around her. The rear door opened slowly. Standing there was the man with the thin messy hair and the thin messy beard.

Katie twisted so her feet could perch on the road. 'It's all right, you can drop me here - I'll walk the rest of the way!' She could see that the back panel had bowed outwards under her kicking and the white paint was cracking. He was now rubbing the cracks with his moistened finger but it did nothing to conceal them.

'Get that door shut! Get her back in!' was the shout from the front of the vehicle. Then he made a radio call. 'We have the subject but she's extremely agitated - what do we do with her?'

She tried to identify the deep, muffled voice that responded. The man's tone was irritable but business like and impatient and it was a voice that she knew because of the tremor inside of her.

'You're lucky, if it was down to me I'd teach you a lesson!' said the messy haired man.

'What? How to do kidnapping! Don't make me laugh!'

His slap to the side of her head caught her off guard and the sharp thing that was stabbed into her thigh stopped her caring.

There was no dreaming now, just a continual agitation inside, because she had no control over what was going to happen to her and she had been beaten and now she was going to be sucked dry, like the prey of a spider, withering on the web.

The car stopped. There were animated voices outside. The boot was flung open and she was dragged out, with her head and body bowed. The smells were the smells of the open country and not the city and the whinnying was a horse and not a drunken party girl. She was supported on either side as she was dragged down cold, chipped steps down to a door below ground level. The door in front of her was steel, very solid and very forbidding. The clanking of bolts on the other side culminated in the door being dragged inwards. She was pitched inside to a cold grey painted corridor, the kind of walkway that could be found in a large warship. There was a clinically clean, white coated individual waiting with a cold steel wheelchair.

Katie was picked up, dropped in the wheelchair with her satchel, spun around and pushed quickly up a ramp, through a set of banging double doors into a large, pale grey room with coated ceiling, walls and floor. It was coated in such a way that it could be easily cleaned, with a brisk flush of water from the hose and brisk brush with the broom hanging in the corner.

There was a cab rank of yellow bins, all waiting to have their contents tipped in to the furnace, and transformed to a black sooty smoke, spray rinsed and then spurted out as particles bereft of life.

Now, she was in a cold, clean, lift, heading upwards. When the lift door opened, her nasal passages were assaulted with the stench of disinfectant. Her senses started to waken.

'Nearly there' said the male nurse as she was propelled into a cold, clinically clean white room with no windows but a substantial steel bed. He lifted her up and placed her on the bed and clipped her ankles in place. She tried to sit but with a click, her wrists were restrained. 'They'll be along in a moment to take care of you, so just relax.'

But she couldn't relax because she was stretched out wide on a cold, hard rack and could barely breath. Two people entered the room and the door closed quietly behind them.

'Here she is' said a female voice. 'How are you copin', still a bit drowsy? I expect so. Oh, you have been in the wars, haven't you? Let's take a look, shall we?' The female pulled at the shackles and concluded that they were safe and secure.

'Is she awake?' said the male voice that made her heart palpitate in fear of what he was about to do to her.

'I can't be sure. I'll hoist the frame so she's more comfortable.' A motor whirred and the frame pivoted upwards so the shackles got tighter and tighter and her wrists and ankles screamed in pain. Her satchel slipped to the sparkling clean floor.

'They should've blindfolded her and cuffed her hands behind her back! That would've been a bit easier! She can't do anythin' now, see, the shackles are tight.' There was a female voice and a male voice. The male voice she could put a name to. It was Ulrich Letsch.

'Let's get on, we'll need her processed before the early morning flight.'

'She doesn't look particularly dangerous, does she?' laughed the female.

'Those idiots have beaten her' complained Letsch, 'look at the state of her face.'

Katie's eyes flittered and closed again. *'Pwy wyt ti? Ble ydw i??'* She understood she was in danger.

'What was that?'

'Did you hear that? Was that Welsh?'

'She's coming around, I think. Doctor Letsch, why don't you take a look under her eyelid?'

'Dylech rhyddhau fi a gadewch i mi fynd.'

'There it is again. Makes no sense to me!'

Letsch approached cautiously and opened her right eyelid. He gasped and stepped back. 'She stared straight back at me!' He took a deep breath. 'So, you are conscious. That's probably a bad thing for you.'

'You can't do this to me!'

'You surprise me Miss Talog!'

'There are rules about this!'

'I'm aware.'

'And you have to follow them!'

'Indeed we do!'

'You're not allowed to do anything to me or you'll be in deep dwang!'

'Why?'

'I don't give my consent!'

'Ah, but you have. Nurse?'

She had a plastic wallet which she now opened. 'Consent form?'

'Yes.'

'Here.'

'Ah yes, co-signed by Herr Glaus - this is your signature, is it not?'

'It can't be!'

'It is. And your doctor's agreement...'

'Would that be you, Doctor Letsch?'

'It certainly is, nurse.'

'You're never my doctor!'

'It says here that I am.'

'Noooooo!'

'It does.'

'So, what you have agreed to is...'

'I never did!'

'A set of procedures...'

'Never!'

'...to remove organs and tissues ostensibly for a major transplant procedure...'

'Noooooo!'

'...that could save the life of at least one child, and many other children...'

'You're not having my stuff!'

'...and you have led us a merry dance, Miss Talog, and now it is time for you to repay your debt to society...'

'But I'm still using it all!'

'...to the benefit of our research studies, and possibly for all of humanity too, by allowing us to isolate and characterise certain materials and tissues.'

'You can go and whistle for it!'

'I beg your pardon? I don't think you realise the importance of this to mankind!'

'You want to use my body as a body part factory? Go fuck your nanny!'

'In your position, after all the trouble you have caused, I would have thought you would be a little more conciliatory!' The nurse pulled in a steel trolley that had metal equipment rattling on it and Katie's body trembled in response.

'Herr Zutter wanted to see you, ah well, for he and his family have been avid collectors of human specimens. The family have held onto this romantic notion of an ancient race of fine and noble people whose heroic deeds became the inspiration for poets, writers and story tellers throughout the age of enlightenment...'

'Hold on, can I say something?'

'Please do not interrupt. And then these people disappeared from the record and became the inspiration for legends. The Zutters believe that these people never died out and therefore, their descendants still walk amongst us. Herr Zutter believes that your female line is of pure descent from these people - the Britanni!'

Katie gulped noisily. 'Oh no, there's been an almighty cock-up!'

'What on earth do you mean?'

She tested the metal of the shackles with her wrists. They were going to be difficult to defeat. 'I'm not Britanni...I'm not a witch!'

'Don't be ridiculous!' But the frown betrayed him. 'Your grandmother and your mother...'

'Maela? My mum? She's not the witch!'

'I have science on my side! I have the entire genealogy of your family!'

'She's not the witch!' Katie's shoulders twisted in their sockets and she felt the veil of darkness descending over her. 'She's just some tart from Rhyll!'

'Nonsense!'

'But Doctor Letsch' said the nurse of no knowledge, 'what about the good science, what about the swab sample tests?'

'Huh, it could be contaminated! She had a mouth full of kebab!'

'Please! Maela's not the witch! It's Alain! He's the witch!'

With her eyes clenched tight, she felt the stirring in her clenched core.

Letsch pauses for a moment. 'It's irrelevant, I will secure all the materials I need from you' he said as his arm waved towards the trolley of sharpened, shiny tools, 'and I will store them securely and anonymously, what will be left will be just clinical waste. This will be burned to atoms and you will cease to exist. And what is so poignant, is that no one will care! Not your family, not the institutions you work for, nor any of your acquaintances. You will just cease to be!'

The shackles around her wrists were tightening. 'I'm not going to lie to you, mate, we're in a bit of bother here' she hissed, 'and if you give a tinker's toss, you'll get me out of this!' She pushed her finger tips into the metal surface and they burned. Her body started to shake.

Something awful was about to happen.

In the labyrinth of cells within Katell Ebrill's long bones, a handful of signalling proteins assembled and spiralled their way to the special cells whose job it was to martial her body's response to any threat. They locked, kissed and made their way to find more of these special cells in the brilliant micro-caves of her marrow.

The cells that had been kissed, sprang to life and curiously, each of them gave birth to another signalling protein. In this way, from small beginnings, the exponential rise of the storm began.

Her organs started to swell and mobilise for action; her heart, lungs, liver and kidneys. Along the titanium-lined neural pathways of her long bones, energy flowed and channelled it's way to nerve endings. Her skin started to tingle, her veins and muscles pulsed and energy flowed across her skin, reaching the wrists and fingers of her hands. Tiny particles passed energetically into the metal that bound her and consumed it. The particles in the shackles were bouncing up and down, like springs in a mattress, enduring an epoch making shagathon!

Katell Ebrill shrieked as the metal flashed bright and sparked. 'Oh sod, I'm coming, I'm coming!'

Her eyelids flashed open and the shackles sparkled and fizzed and tiny glowing fragments flew. Ulrich bobbed as a piece of metal sang past his forehead - a slice of skin and hair flapped over his right eye.

Her arms now free, Katie bent double, seized the shackles around her ankles and screamed, 'Oh sod, oh sod!' A flash of blinding light sparked another maelstrom of metal shards. The shattered pieces span across the floor and the legs of the frame collapsed.

Blood dribbled down Ulrich's face: 'What in the name of all that's holy are you?' he cried. He grabbed a scalpel from the trolley but with a wave of his arm it flew to the ceiling and embedded itself there.

'You don't know me' she hissed, 'and you will never know me!'

She approached him, as he cowered in the corner, her palms outstretched. She sensed the uncontrolled pounding of his heart and his convulsing lungs. A flap of bloodied scalp hung over his face, so she lifted it carefully and replaced back on his head. She lifted his right arm pityingly and placed it on his head to keep his scalp in place.

'I have mapped your DNA, I can trace your bloodline back thousands of years, a whole line of witch-mothers going back into pre-history!'

'Ah, you still think my mum's the witch...'

'But...'

'She's not...!'

'But she must be?'

'Its Alain - he's the witch.' Her bloodied hand rested on the door handle and it was thrown open.

'Impossible!'

'So all of your research - not worth a sheep's fart, is it?'

Katie picked up her satchel from the floor and put the strap over her shoulder. She was through the door and she was through with the room and through with Letsch. Facing her on the wall was a plan of the facility. On the opposite wall was an alarm button - she hit with her elbow. Down the corridor a steel trolley was coming, clanking with cups and saucers.

'Cup of tea, love?'

'No, ta. There's a man in there...'

'I can't go in there, love.'

'...who needs an ambulance.'

'Oh my! What's happened!'

'He was careless.' Katie turned and ran the other way down the corridor. She needed to ascend a floor and run through the laboratories, negotiate several doors protected by keypads and locate the vial, to the accompaniment of incessant ringing alarms banging through her head.

Up a flight of stairs, along a corridor and now for the keypad. She keyed in '2905' and the doors swung open and she was running alongside clean, white benches stacked with instruments and glassware and into another room with a keypad, which took the same code and she was in a dark space, faintly lit by emergency lights, full of cold, metal vessels. Through a set of large white glossy doors, protected by keypad (Ha!), she found the sliding racks and wrenched these apart. And there was the location of the vial that made her shiver inside - the one that looked like it had a glowing sea anemone inside.

But there was another vial that she was drawn to - one that looked like it contained a yellow sea slug. It made her insides squirm but took this one too. Turning on her heels, Katie ran back to the laboratory and closed the door behind her. There was a yellow, biohazard suit hanging by the door and she stepped into it. Still the bells rang. Her arm swept along a bench and bottles smashed on the floor. Acrid fumes billowed to the ceiling.

Katie looked back to the room of mobile racking beyond the white door. Thousands of disembodied souls must be trapped inside and some were crying out to her, not just the two in her satchel. Something nasty was bubbling up from her stomach and up her gullet and left arm started to swing to and fro despite her restraining right hand. Coming up through her feet, up her legs and through her core and her arms was a surge that had to be released. Her fingers tingled and her index finger extended. She watched in awe as a blue arc leapt from her tips to the big black box in the corner of the room and then cascaded to all the other black boxes.

There was a flash and random streaks of light fizzed and bubbled around the laboratory. Katie waited, and her right foot tapped impatiently. Outside, a vehicle with blue flashing lights arrived in a hurry.

The stacked machines started to rattle; glass vials in the samplers scratched and scraped in a hideous cacophony; liquid spewed out of the vials.

'Haaaaa' she shrieked. Printers clattered into life and reams of fan folded paper fluttered towards the ceiling like white stairways. Digitised data scrambled and then unwound along cables chased into the walls to a flickering black box in the basement. She skipped amongst the aisles and orchestrated the chaos along the length and breadth of the room. She paused, brought her hands together and a ball of energy engulfed the room in a single pulse. She skipped back to the airlock door and eased back the hood of her overall. A wall mounted camera focused on her and scanned her up and down. She looked coyly at the floor and she pictured in her mind the image of an overweight slob sitting on his leather lined chair working the camera with one hand and working his prick up and down with the other. A ball of energy leapt up from the floor and smothered the camera. The camera shuddered and dropped down limply. She dashed through the airlock, sliding each door open in front of her. Two emergency staff ran past her and did a double take - they came back to shout at her for direction.

'It's all gone off' she shouted in reply, 'back there!'

She quietly entered through the door they had vacated. Inside there was a clear plastic tent with a little girl inside, on a bed, lying in quite repose, such a pale, fragile girl in such a clinically clean and orderly landscape. 'I don't know what Letsch promised you, but he was wrong and I am so, so very sorry for that.' Katie meticulously unpicked all the cables and tubes that came in and came out of the bubble and then opened a hatch. She placed a vial in the hand of the little girl. It had a typed label that stated on it: 'Seznec: Britanni.'

Katie closed the hatch and left the room, closing the door carefully. There were footsteps reverberating along the corridor. Not hers.

She made her way through the door of the fire escape. The steps down the outside of the building were traversed quickly. Two angry guard dogs were racing towards her - she would have to calm them.

'Down boy!' she commanded. The first Rottweiler subsided submissively to the ground, paws forward. She directed her hands towards the other dog: 'And you!' It also subsided passively.

Katie rushed to the entrance gate - a security van with two blue uniformed officers was blocking her way. She laid her hands on the bonnet and pushed down hard. It bounced upwards and shuddered downwards. As she ran away along the perimeter fence she heard a crunch - the kind of crunch you might hear when a vehicle's wheels crumpled outwards.

Katie seized two hands full of security fence and shook it vigorously. 'Bah' she shouted in frustration. The security guards could not get out of their van. She shook the fence again and it rattled. She felt a deep pulse of energy, pulsing away from her and working quickly around the edge of the site and then reconnecting in front of her. Curiously, each section of the fence shook in sequence until her section shuddered. 'Just fall down will you!'

There was a curious fizzing where the fence panel connected with the vertical steel supporting poles. She shook the panel again and there was a creak from both sides. She kicked it and it toppled.

Katie took a hop, skip and a jump over the prone section in front of her. She was free of this hateful place.

Katie padded down the road feeling exhilarated for a moment but then a feeling of oppression caused by the soreness of her body and the exhaustion of spent muscles came over her.

And she didn't know what needed to be done next.

She sniffed at the air and it was fresh and clear. The land around her was level and covered with waving grass fronds and hedgerows that whispered to her in the light breeze. She could hear distant alarm sirens and alarmed shouts but none of this made a response in her.

At first, she was not aware of the police car that had come up alongside her, or the young officer who leaned out of the open window and asked who she was and wanted to know if she was in any trouble?

The police car stopped ahead of her and an officer got out and approached her slowly. He seemed very young, fresh-faced, cap in hand, tall and still eager. Katie stopped walking and pushed her arms towards him with her wrists uppermost and together. They were red raw and she cursed because the red was blooming under her finger nails again. The police officer asked her name again, how she was and where she was going.

She answered that her name was Katie and that she thought she may have done something really bad. She couldn't be sure what it was she had done, but there had been some kind of storm spiralling around her in the building behind her. Which building? The one back up the road, owned by SIKS, the one with all the body parts, stored in anonymous vials that had typed script on a white label that denied the possibility of a human soul, because without a given name, how could a soul exist? Her left hand reached across to where she had secreted a vial in her satchel. It was still there.

Katie felt her head bow, her knees fold and her body crumple into a ball at his feet. Her arms were together and outstretched, imploring somebody, anybody, to save her from herself.

Chapter Sixty-Six

Sunday 29 May 0115 - In the cells, Cambridgeshire

The desk sergeant picked up his pen and started filling in the form in front of him. 'So, based on the information we have gathered, is she human, a mutant, a vampire, a demi-god, a werewolf or an extra-terrestrial?' He frowned to himself and wondered if it was possible to have female werewolves. Although she was wearing a yellow one-piece suit over a black dress, she was more than likely to be human, he thought. So human then, sub-species Welsh? Wearing loud clothing in a built up area is no longer considered a crime. He awarded himself a small chuckle for that one. 'And, what's she supposed to have done?'

'We found her wandering around after the attack on the SIKS facility, Sarge. She seemed lost and disoriented. Claimed she had something to do with it!'

'Any evidence?'

'We've asked for CCTV but their system has gone down. She's got burn marks on her wrists and ankles and her hands have got blood on them. There was one casualty in the facility who's got a nasty cut on his head.'

'Who's blood is it, love?'

'His, Ulrich Letsch, he had me shackled to a bed and he was going to carve me up. I stopped him.'

'Someone had better get to A&E and have a little chat with our Mister Letsch then. Any witnesses, love?'

'He's got a female assistant, but she left in a hurry. And there was a tea lady. And there was a bloke on CCTV watch but he may have had a bit of a shock. And two security guards. And two emergency responders.'

She looked up through a gap in her fringe, one eyed. His eyes watered, and so he wiped them discreetly. His daughter was about the same age and she was on a gap year and spending it in Australia. He resolved to call his daughter as soon as he was done here. He had to know if she was safe and that she was not in any trouble.

'What's your name, love?'

'I call myself Katell, Ebrill, Talog.'

'That's...different. Katell, can I call you Katell?'

'Call me Katie, please. Listen, I am not a killer and I am not a thief' she pleaded as she searched into his soul, 'and I am not a liar and I am not a cheat! And that's all there is, that's all there is.'

He sat down next to her and gently parted her fringe. 'We'll need a bit more than that when you're ready.' He whistled when he saw the wound on the side of her head. 'I'll get the duty doctor to look at that - have you been in a fight?'

'The scrotes who kidnapped me - one of them clumped me on the side of my face.' She lifted her hand to feel the side of her face but couldn't bear to touch it.

'Are you Navy?'

'I am, how did you know?'

'It's the way you talk. So you must be a Wren - where are you based?'

'Devonport, but I've been seconded to HMS Hawkins - or at least I was. I'm on leave now.'

'Anyway, these are serious charges you've documented here. Are you happy to sign?'

'Yes, give me the pen.' She scrawled a triple spiral in an awkward, contorted left-handed scrawl and put her initials in it.

'Is there anything else you would like to say?' He wiped away a tear when he thought she wasn't looking.

'They mistreated and abused me, but you've been very kind.' She studied the state of her hands as they resided in her lap. 'Very kind.

Can you get me some tea please, three sugars?' She smiled a smile that creased its way across her cheeks and then she grimaced with pain.

'You could do with a change of clothes. Let me see what I can find. Is there anything else I can do for you?'

'Can you give me something to get rid of this bastard headache of mine?'

'I'll get the Duty Doctor to have a look at you.'

In that moment, she felt a wave of nausea. She needed to lie down, but she couldn't get down quickly enough. The cold, unyielding floor came up to meet her. She was switched off like an unwanted light in a cold, unknown, windowless room. And she dreamt and dreamt and dreamt.

CHAPTER SIXTY-SEVEN

'You're mistaken, the LZ is in French territory. It must be...'

'All right Testy?' Katie took her place in the last rank of those shipmates who were about to be physically trained. Thirty minutes of gentle exercise she thought would set her up nicely for her special breakfast treat, which would set her up nicely for a solid eight hours of off-watch hammock action.

'No Talog, you're late!' bawled out the instructor.

This would in fact, not be fine, not at all. 'Only by a few minutes Testy, but Number One wanted a SitRep...'

'In this place, at this moment, I am your number one!'

'Bollocks! You're just a sodding club swinger!'

'Get down Talog, and give me thirty press-ups!'

'I'm not ready to do press-ups!'

'Get down there Talog!'

'Bollocks to that!' Everyone turned. They were all looking at her. 'Oh, all right.' She dropped, got her self set and completed two. Testy was now above her. 'Those don't count!'

'That's bollocks, Testy!' She stretched, dipped and she was stuck. A hefty trainer was pressing down in the middle of her back. She rolled and swept it away. 'Sod off Testy!'

'Get on your feet Talog! You're coming with me!'

She got up. 'You just think you're better than everyone else! Well, you're not!'

'With me Talog! And take this!'

Testy thrust the exercise mat at Katie. And that's when the serious shoving started.

'What's up?' said the chief petty officer. They were standing to attention in the cabin that acted as the court for dispensing of justice - his cabin.

'Cat fight, these two, up on the hangar deck.'

'Ceeps, it wasn't a fight, it was a just a little spat' Katie replied indignantly.

'Looked like a fight to me!' Gurney clicked the heels of his training shoes, turned and marched out of the cabin, chuckling to himself.

'Pillock!' Katie muttered as his white sport shirt and shorts disappeared out of sight. 'It was just a bit of friendly shoving, that's all Ceeps, nothing to it, just like the wardroom dash for the drinks cabinet!'

'Watch it, Talog!'

'Shut it, Talog' muttered Testy.

'Clubs, what's your side?'

'She's late, disrespectful, disrupts class...and insolent to boot!'

'Talog? I thought you were Princess Punctual!'

'Sorry Ceeps?'

'That's sarcasm, you fool!'

'Oh, I was in a briefing, I couldn't get away!'

'Who with?'

'Watch handover with Irma. And Number One wanted a word.'

'I see, that makes it all right, does it?'

'Yes, I think so Ceeps!'

'Absolutely brilliant Talog, blame the officers!'

'No, I'm not' Katie replied, 'look Testy, I'm explaining, not blaming.'

'Chief, just give me ten minutes with her, I'll teach her respect. I challenge you Talog. I'll give you a lesson in MMA. What do you say?'

'You can't be serious Testy!' Katie's left arm described a slow spiral to her side. She held it back with her other arm. 'What's MMA, anyway?' The whole of her left side felt agitated, and her fingers tingled as if charged. 'Anyway, respect has to be earned, doesn't it Ceeps?'

'Do not call me Testy!'

'Everyone calls you that!'

'Only because you started it!'

'Ah yes, fair point!'

'So Talog, what do you say!'

'To what? What's MMA anyway?'

'So that's a no, is it?'

'No, it's a no thank you Ceeps.'

Clubs smirked and clucked like an apprehensive hen. 'Chicken!'

The light in the room blinked twice. To her left, the computer sighed and the screen died. The chief petty officer's mug jolted in his hands and then he cursed. 'Jesus' he cried as he dropped the mug and howled.

Number One bustled into the cabin. 'What's up Chief? Is this a kangaroo court?'

'No, no, just a minor disciplinary matter!' He wrung his hands in pain and tried to dab up the mess on the floor.

'You'd better get yourself to the sick bay, Chief, and get some treatment for that' said Number One. Ceeps left, wringing his hands.

Number One turned his attention to Katie. 'Talog? Hands down to your sides.'

'Sorry, they're down now Number One.'

Her left arm settled to her side. 'Arms clasped behind your back, Talog. That's better. Well?'

'It's all settled Number One. Just a little disagreement. We'll sort it out between us, and I'll get an officer to oversee matters!'

'Good Clubs, good. Talog?'

Katie whispered to Number One. 'Listen, she's massive, and she's got muscles and she can handle herself and I don't even know what MMA is anyway?'

'And?'

'Well, I don't want to be a spectacle...'

'So?'

'Well, the dicks will have a good laugh, I suppose...'

'And?'

'Number One, just let Talog and I go head to head, and we'll sort this out, once and for all.'

'All right Talog, what do you say?'

'Well, if I think I'm going to be late, I'll send my apologies and rebook. Are we all right now Testy?'

There was a shout over the tannoy. It was for Number One. He was wanted in the war room. He frowned and got ready to leave.

'Clubs?' he asked. She shook her head.

Katie made as if to shake hands. Clubs didn't move and just stared ahead. A bead of sweat made its way down her forehead and trickled ever so slowly down the bridge of her nose.

'Clubs?' asked Number One.

'Testy?' asked Katie.

'All right Talog, what should you be doing now?'

'Scranning down and then racking out, Number One!'

'Go and do it. Dismissed.' She glanced towards Testy, turned and slid into the corridor. She stilled her breath and listened.

'Right, she's gone now. Clubs, a word to the wise.' It was Number One's authoritative voice.

'With the greatest respect sir, that was a mistake. Get us in the ring together, I can sort this out, once and for all.'

There was a long pause. He would be studying Testy's face intently. 'I know Talog looks like she just fell off the top of a Christmas tree, but she didn't. Don't back her into a corner or...you'll end up going to hell in a handcart!'

'Sorry sir?'

He gave a deep sigh. 'I've not seen it first hand and you don't want to. It's reputed to be like your insides all unravelling at the same time. It's not pretty, Clubs.'

'Sir?'

'Dismissed, Clubs. Remember what I said. Don't back her into a corner!'

Katie waited until Testy emerged into the gangway. 'Are we all right now, Testy?'

'No, we're going to settle this in the ring tomorrow, ten hundred hours.'

'Eh?'

'You heard. And if you don't show, I'll make sure everyone in this ship knows how gutless you are!'

'I've got loads of guts!'

'And I'm going to spill them. Ten hundred hours tomorrow, Talog, in the ring and I'll get your CO to officiate!'

'Cutie to officiate? Right you are.' Katie turned and made her way to the mess deck shaking her head. What on earth is MMA, she wondered?

She caught up with Rating Miller. 'So what's MMA, Mulch?'

'It's a chewy bar, isn't it? Try the galley.'

'It can't be that. How can you demonstrate a bar of chewy?'

Next she found an officer from the medical team. 'Doc, what's MMA?'

'MMA? It's a kind of sticky, isn't it?

'Can't be, Doc, it's being demonstrated on me, isn't it?'

'Falling to pieces, Talog? Try the Clankies.'

Katie caught up with Colin Dale, by pulling urgently at the sleeve of his shirt. 'Hey Dingley, hold up, have you heard the buzz!'

'What's up Ket?' They moved aside so as not to impede the flow of blue clad humanity heading to the mess decks.

'I'm having a bout with Testy tomorrow!'

'A bout of what? With Testy? Do you mean Clubs? Our genial physical training instructor? How come?' The questions came at her like a spitting Gatling gun.

'Yes, we just had a spat, I don't think she likes me very much!'

'Come on, Ket. A bout? Official? For real?'

'Yes, it's all arranged, in the hangar, ten hundred, tomorrow.'

He seemed to be doing some quick calculations as his jaw sagged open. 'A bout of what, Ket?'

'I said, didn't I? About the fact she doesn't like me, that's what it's about!' His visage had suddenly turned very quizzical. 'Oh, I see what you mean, Dingley. Well, I think she's settled on MMA, whatever that is.' She suddenly realised that she may have made a terrible mistake, judging from the change of expression on Dingley's face.

'Ket, do you actually know what MMA is?'

'MMA? I don't know. Is it...musical movement arts? Is it like oriental gymnastics?'

'No, no! It's fighting! One on one! No music!'

'Bugger? But it's arts! You can't get hurt doing arts, can you?'

'What the hell do you think you're doing, Ket? You don't know what you've signed up for! She'll bloody murder you!'

'But, we're only sparring, aren't we? That'll be all right won't it? Helmet, lots of padding, no problem!'

'You actually don't know what MMA is, do you Ket?'

'It's just sparring, isn't it?' she blurted out loud, not really believing it. She was now very concerned. 'Or, is it?'

'It's punching, kicking, grappling. It's brutal if you don't know what you're doing!'

'Oh, bollocks, that sounds really serious, doesn't it? No padding then?'

'No padding. It's deadly serious. And with Clubs? She'll massacre you!'

'You think so?' There was now a hush between them as she pondered what to do. 'What are the rules on this, then?'

'It's like boxing, but you can hit, kick, wrestle on the deck, until one of you submits or is knocked out cold!'

'So it's not how many points you score, then?' Her heart went cold and a large void formed in her belly. 'Crappetty, crappetty, crap. So Dingley, what do I do? What are the odds?'

'The odds against you? One hundred to one. Clubs is massive, massive, odds on favourite...have you seen her sparring with the super fit?'

'Oh no, that doesn't sound good. What are we going to do?'

'What are we going to do? Well, we could start a book. Get all your supporters in there.'

'Good. That sounds good. Everyone can see me getting massacred!'

'Ah, but starting a book is a no go. No one's gonna bet against Clubs! Unless, you have a plan?'

'No plan but I've seen the wrestling on the telly, haven't I? So what do I do then?'

'Wait, wait, let me think, Ket. I know what we'll do, we'll start a sweepstake, one pound a go, how long do you think Ket will last against Clubs?'

'How many rounds, do you mean?'

'No, how many seconds! It's not going to last a whole round! I'll take stakes on every ten seconds you can last out, starting with nought!'

'Nought? That's bollocks! She's not going to knock me out in less than a second!'

'Let me see your guard, then?'

Reluctantly, she put up her fists.

'Ket, you won't last half a second!' he said, shaking his head sorrowfully.

'Listen Dingley, I think you think you're trying to help but you're really not!'

'Like this' he said as he adjusted her fists so that her right covered her chin and her left presented a vague threat to an attacker.

'Is that all right? Will you spar with me, Dingley?'

'When? How? Your best hope is to keep your fists up, cover your face, and take what's coming to you! Who's refereeing?'

'Cutie.'

'Cutie?'

'I mean Big CIS is going to officiate!'

'Big CIS! Oh, good God, Ket!'

'She'll make sure there's fair play, won't she?' She paused as she considered what she had just said. 'Oh, my soul, I see what you mean! She won't be happy with a knocking out' Katie muttered to herself, 'that would be too easy. Testy'll come at me like a killer zombie, throwing bombs and then when she lands one, she'll either choke me or try to break my arm off. Bugger! They won't be happy until I tap out, will they?'

Dingley shook his head and gave a sympathetic smile. He had already collared three passing ratings and given them a quick bulletin on tomorrow's big event. 'Throw a punch at me!'

'Eh?'

'Throw a punch at me!'

She jabbed a left and it hit him squarely on his nose. 'Like that?'

'Bugger, I wasn't ready!' he howled, clutching his nose.

Breakfast was calling. She turned to head for the mess deck. 'Don't worry, Dingley, I'll fetch you a bag of frozen peas, then I'll scran down and rack out. It'll all seem much better after a bit of shut-eye, won't it?'

'Let me see if I've got this straight, Muddy' murmured Katie to the blue shirted rating alongside her in the galley queue, 'basically, you want to shoehorn me into a ridiculous, shiny, tight-fitting bathing suit and then get me to parade my stuff up and down in it.' His name was Walters, his trade was marine engineering technician and he was the most diminutive member of her Communications and Information Systems department, and therefore the most irritating. 'All in aid of HMS Albany's Theatre Afloat?'

'Absolutely, in a silvery, sexy, slinky leotard' he replied. He seemed to be salivating at the prospect of this; or it may have been the automatic, human response to the smell of grilled bacon in the morning.

'Yes, what you said, Muddy. You want to get me in this tiny, tight-fitting suit made out of turkey foil so I can prance up and down...'

'Dance along to disco funk!'

'Yes, whatever that is, while I point a big tool at Flight Commander Hodge, in a smutty and disgusting way...'

'In a sexy, alluring way!'

'And sing at him at the same time...'

'Yes! That's it! You've got it!'

'Really? Sing? So you only want me to squeeze, prance, dance, wave and sing all at the same time...' She waved away the offer of a bread roll but took the red plastic tray.

'But don't worry, we'll be right with you, done up to the nines, your very own personal dance troupe!'

'I was afraid of that, so you'll be right behind me, ogling my arse!'

'No, we'll be dancing alongside you. Here's the words you need to learn!' He presented her with a multi coloured page of paper and true enough, there were words there. The words of the song and the picture of a high-stepping silver-clad bint built slowly in her mind. 'Brilliant' she said as she accepted a mug of tea from across the stainless steel counter and scanned the patterns on the page.

'Don't worry, I'll run through 'em with you!'

'So, what in the name of funk does this all mean?' she wondered out loud, nudged him sharply in the ribs and sniggered. 'Did you see what I did there, Muddy?'

'Yes! It's going to be hilarious!'

'Yes, I can see why you might think that...'

'Well?'

She looked him carefully in the eyes. 'Luckily, I've stopped leaking blood, until tomorrow morning anyway, so it could be a goer. So, just to be clear, you want me to squirm like a ferret into this shiny condom suit-thing, dance so I broil in my own juices like a Christmas turkey and give him the full Devonport disco gronk experience?'

'Exactly! Are you in Ket?'

She considered the handsome authority of Scotty, his knee weakening grin and the reassuring squeezes he gave to her shoulders and arms that sent pulses shuddering through her core: Touching; squeezing; pulsing; releasing. Oh, she was so in, she was so in...

'Ket?'

'Of course I sodding am! But you do realise what this is going to cost you?'

'Beer ration?'

'No, beer rations. So, when do we rehearse?'

'Rehearse?' He gave a double 'thumbs-up' to a table of colleagues nearby. A loud cheer roared across the canteen from one table followed by jeers from all the others.

'Yes, you monkey, when do we rehearse? It's not going to be another of those half-arsed efforts where we rip the piss out of the management!'

'No, of course not, we know they're all personal friends of yours...'

'Well, I really look up to them and...'

'They really look down on you?'

'Yes, that's the one' she said as she clocked the familiar, rotund figure of a man of authority approaching. He looked like he had something on his tiny mind. 'Listen Muddy, give me thirty, we'll wear overalls, I'll sort out the steps then we'll rehearse the shit out of it.'

'Talog, with me. Now!' called out the Chief.

'Oh, not you again! I've still only just finished my watch' she replied, 'don't I get a break Ceeps?'

'Just swallow your tea and come with me, Talog.'

She gulped from her mug and pushed it back across the stainless steel counter. 'Buggery, buggery, bollocks, Chief. So, where are we going?' She gave a little reassuring wink to Muddy the mechanician.

'Follow me. The Old Man's worried that we've taken our foot off the gas, we're back pedalling, we're not buckling down and cracking on.'

'I had no idea Chief...it must keep him awake at night.'

'So, CPO's rounds. With me, Talog.'

She led the way out of the canteen, they descended to the lower deck and headed for'ard. 'So where are we headed, Chief? Who are we doing over?'

'So you know the form, Talog?'

'Of course I do, Chief, strike hard and fast and scare the living crap out of them.'

'Hmm, you still haven't quite got the hang of this, have you Talog?'

'Oh, I think I have Chief. So, where...?'

'Your mates, the marines, in the barracks.'

'Oh, come on Chief, give them a break, they're only just off mission!'

She came to the last door forward on the starboard side. 'Are you sure, about this Chief? This seems really unfair.'

'Just get on with it, Talog...'

'Your call, Chief. Oh, how's your hand?'

He looked at his bandaged hand. 'It's fine. I'm getting the electrics checked out in there.'

'Oh, good idea.' She knocked timidly at the bulkhead door. 'Hallo, is there anyone at home?' she enquired politely.

'Piss off Talog' came the reply from within and then jeering.

She waited for three moments, wrenched the handle round and pushed the bulkhead door open. She strode into the constricted space and shouted: 'CPO's rounds, by your lockers, now.' She reached the far end of the space, scrambling through and stretching over a chaos of bodies and clothing and cursing. In a few moments the chaos had resolved to a row of panting bodies lined up and standing by grey painted lockers.

Marine Scott's legs writhed up and down as his pants caught midway across his thighs. 'Oi, Marine, you only need to dance a jig for the Old Man!' She paused sympathetically and then announced, 'All right mate, just take a deep breath and haul up your keks!' She waited patiently before continuing. 'That's better! You keep still for me and Ceeps!' she confided to the marine. She now looked about her and addressed the ragged row of undressed soldiers. 'Oh, bollocks!' she moaned in dismay.

'Come on Ket, you must have seen naked men before!'

'Want to see my old chap, Ket?' leered Spud Gun.

'No ta, not such a limp one as yours, anyway' she said as she flicked a glance at Ceeps. 'Anyway, when I finished my watch this morning...'

'The sky was awful grey' chimed Ryan.

'No, actually it was awful blue again' she replied, 'which is how I'm feeling now!' She walked along the rank looking at each face and the space behind. 'I felt proud at the start of my watch. I thought, here I am on Her Majesty's Ship Albany, the best ship in the finest navy in the world. Then I arrived down here and I thought, bugger me, we've been shipwrecked!' She paused to take her cue from the chief petty officer. He nodded to her. She advanced to the first rank of marines and confronted Marine Boyle. 'What have you got in your locker, marine?'

'Just my stuff.'

'Open it.'

'I'd rather not...'

She stood back and sucked in a deep, hiss of a breath through her teeth. 'Oooh!'

He cringed and then turned to the locker and jabbed at the lock with the key. Finally it opened.

She pushed past and gasped. 'Who's this?' she asked, pointing at the lurid poster inside the locker door.

'It's...my mum.'

'Your mum? Blimey, big girl, isn't she?'

'Never noticed before...'

'Even when you had your chops around her doops, mate? Is that how she sends you off?' She cut the sniggerers along the line with a quick glare. 'So, is this all yours?' she asked, pointing at the pile of lewd magazines in the base of the locker.

'No, I'm keeping them for a friend' he replied.

'It's a wanker's paradise in here' she observed.

She moved to the next in line, Spud Gun, who was chomping down on a sausage. The door of his locker was already open and all she could see was a large expanse of snap shots - the theme of the snap shots seemed to be girls in various stages of undress. 'Allo, doll, see that space there? That's for you!'

'Oh really? Were you born a fucking idiot or have you been eating your stupid brain again?'

'She can't say that - that's discrimination!'

'Can I just check the rulebook about this, Ceeps? What does it say about idiots?'

'Zero tolerance' chimed in the Chief.

'Thought so...'

'No, no, doll, you can't say that - I know my rights!'

'Legend!' shouted Boyle.

'So, how about it doll?' leered Spud Gun.

'You must think you're a bit of a cult, Spud Gun' said Katie as she moved on to the next marine, 'well you're nearly right!'

Maddocks was shuffling his feet uncomfortably, she thought.

'Open it.'

'I'll get you for this, Talog' he muttered in reply.

'If you were a higher form of life, I'd be worried, but you're not, are you? Now open it.' Reluctantly he turned and grudgingly inserted the key in the lock. 'Wait, do I need breathing apparatus?'

'No!'

He turned back to the locker and the door creaked slowly open.

'Hard hat?'

'No!'

'All right, just open it carefully...' An avalanche of knotted clothing spilled out. She strode back to the door, and turned back to address the roomful of squaddies. 'This is a trou de merde!'

'No, it isn't!'

'And you've got sixty to get it fixed!'

'Minutes?' asked Maddocks.

'SECONDS!' she shouted. She and the CPO walked out. There was a flurry of movement inside as they stood outside. They turned and walked silently along the navy-grey metal corridor. 'Sorry Ceeps, you shouldn't have had to walk into that' she said as she paused to check out his crisp, knee length white shorts, 'especially not in your Sunday best!'

'What's that you said, Talog?'

'Trou de merde? It's a polite way of saying 'shithole', isn't it?'

She sensed the ship's tannoy system coming to life. Help was needed. It was Benoit, her Benoit. 'I've got a shout. I'll leave you to it.' She ran back along the corridor heading aft. She would have to go topside and take the deck to the hanger at the stern of the ship. In ten jumps up the ladder she was outside again. It was barely light outside. As she ran along the deck heading aft, a pod of dolphins breached the sea below her to her right, whinnied, and then dived sharply away from the grey hull of HMS Albany. The Lynx helicopter was ahead and below her; it's two midnight blue goggle eyes, the four long straight limbs above, the bulbous body and the narrow tail tapering away, made it look like a giant, brooding dragonfly, poised on the helicopter apron. A jump carried her over the last set of steps and flying into the arms of a man in pilot's overalls. 'What's up?' she whooped as she was whirled about, straddled over his shoulder.

Scotty dropped her reverentially to the deck. 'We've got a shout' he replied, 'apron side briefing in five.'

She drew a quick breath to stop the swoon. 'Ooh Scotty, I reckon you're going to need...a winch girl!'

'Which girl?'

'Me! I'm your winch girl! And I can do the lingo!'

'Not the French again! What've you heard?'

'They've got themselves in trouble and we need to bale them out again!'

'What is it this time?'

'I don't know, the usual, a breakdown, just routine, I reckon it's Benoit, he's got himself into bother again.'

'What happened to their support, Tally?'

'The Strawberry? Dunno, they're probably all having le petit dejeuner on the upper deck!'

'The Jauréguiberry? Get yourself suited and booted then and I'll get the mission bulletin.' He dropped her on her feet and she scampered towards the hangar and took the spare overall with the name 'TALOG' on it and grabbed a helmet. She checked the microphone system. It was working. Two mechanicians were standing arms akimbo, gazing at the flank of the Lynx helicopter. She was going to have to deal with them again for the second time in a few hours, which meant she would have to talk Clanky. As she approached, she recited a little rhyme of all the swearing words she knew - there were at least twenty-four of them at the last count.

Katie was ready. 'All right you tossers, what the fuck's up?'

'She failed the bloody pre-flight checks, KT. There's something up with the bloody avionics!' replied Ray Knights.

'Shit! Not the avi-bloody-onics, Bogey? Where? It's not where you had the fucking covers up?'

'We don't bloody know where, we're still trying to fucking track it down!'

She tutted. 'Oi, Bogey. Did you fucking find it, mate?'

'What KT, the fucking trouble?'

'No, you twat, my fucking pendant!'

'Oh, that little thing. No, we fucking didn't. That's the third fucking time we had all that shit out!'

'Where the fuck has that gone, then? I've looked all fucking over for that!'

'Well KT, let's try this. When did you last have the little fucker then?'

'It was when I was chasing that Chinese submarine, you big, hairy twat!'

'You don't even know what that means!'

'What? Yes, I do, there's a big fat hairy one right in front of me!'

'Just can it Talog, or there'll be trouble.'

'What are you going to do, breathe on me?'

'Oi, be nice KT!' There was a short pause while he considered what to say next. He must be thinking, she thought. 'I think I've got a solution for our little problem.' Bogey ambled off to the workshop in the hanger.

'For fuck's sake! Let me get in there.' She swarmed under the console and arranged her body so she could look underneath the panels.

'Can you get this bastard cover off?'

'Which one? This one?'

'Yes, that little bastard there!'

'Look, just give the swearing a rest will you! It's not clever, it's not smart and I feel abused when you carry on like this!' complained Thick Crust.

'Just shut the fuck up, you big tart, and help me get that fucking, bastard cover off now!'

'If you were a bloke, I'd deck you!'

'If you were a bloke, I'd think, there's no fucking point!'

'Oi! What's that supposed to mean?' He levered the cover off. 'All right, KT?'

She peered inside and followed the sheaves of cable under the console of the helicopter from her prone position. Her legs fidgeted amongst the belts and buckles of the co-pilots seat. 'I think I can feel it now' she called to TC in the next seat as he operated the controls of the Lynx helicopter. 'This lot leads to the avionics and this lot to the control surfaces and this lot to the hydraulics...'

'Tally, on your back again?' exclaimed Flight Lieutenant Scott Hodges as he peered down at her through the open door.

Her heart fluttered for a moment. 'Oh, yes Scotty, what can I say, I'm a hands-on girl and I'm getting stuck in!' Her heart settled down. Maybe it was indigestion or a consequence of being the wrong way up in a confined space.

She rolled out of the cabin and jumped to her feet. 'Let's get that fucker off down there' she said as she pointed to the starboard flank of the machine. 'Wait, you...didn't shove a...fish up here, did you?'

Bogey had returned. 'No!' he said, 'you didn't did you, TC?' he confided behind his hand. 'Come on girl, what's up?'

'I've been pissing blood - that's what's up!'

TC shouted at Katie: 'What's happened to you KT? Why has my darling turned into a hell bitch?'

'Ah, word is from below, she's on the blob, first time ever, and she doesn't know what's fucking hit 'er! It's knocked her sideways, poor cow!'

'Oi, Bogey, don't be crude!'

The cover was removed with alacrity. 'Gauntlet, KT?'

'No, wanker, let me see if I can get my sodding arm up there and give it a bloody feel.'

Bogey motioned to unbutton his trousers.

'Don't be dirty, you scrote. There's no way I'm shoving my bloody arm up there, unless I'm ripping your fucking bollocks off!'

'Oooh, KT!' he minced.

'I don't believe it, the sheaf has come adrift again' she moaned and eyes shut tight, it was clipped firmly back into position. Her breathing returned to something approaching normal. 'Get the fucking cover back on, fire the bitch up and run the fucking diagnostics again!' She re-entered the cabin and squirmed under the console again. The auxiliary rotor fired into life. 'Thank fuck for that' she shouted, 'let's re-run the pre-flight checks and get moving!'

'Yes, Captain KT!' they saluted back.

'Oi, you piss-taking bastards!'

'Feeling better, Tally? What happened?' asked Scott. He took her by the arm and steered her to the end of the apron.

'Not really, I'm just off watch, I've missed breakfast and I've been pissing blood' she shouted, 'and Clubs wants to beat the living crap out of me, just because I gave her a bit of banter!' The Lynx was now behaving as she should be.

'Just take a few deep breaths and calm yourself.'

There was that heart flutter again. 'Mission briefing, Scotty?'

'In two, on the apron. How's my mount?'

'Oh, I'm fine' she replied, 'oh, you mean Nerys? She's fine too!'

'That's good enough for me. You'll do our communications and liaise with the French.'

'D'accord, Scotty.'

Number One was by the helicopter, leading the briefing.

'Right, Scotty, co-ordinates have been programmed in for the LZ. French Lynx, five French servicemen, helicopter malfunction. Talog, talk to them en route and find out what's the latest. Descend by winch and check the LZ before landing. Nutley, check their machine, just check that they haven't put in the wrong fuel or lost the ignition key. If you can get it going, good. Get them to follow you back to the Albany. If you can't, airlift them back here. Any questions?'

'En route Number One? Blimey sir, you're a bit of a linguist on the quiet, aren't you?'

'Very funny, Talog. Any danger, anything that looks wrong, just abort. Don't put yourselves in danger. Talog, have you got that?'

'Oui, Numero Un' she replied, but she was frowning.

'What's up Talog?'

'Sir, they don't seem capable of using Nato protocols...'

'Use your native charm, you know them and you've worked closely with them. You're our negotiator-in-chief, remember. Stay in continuous contact. Anything you don't like, get out. Got it?'

'Yes, Number One, I'm just there to sex things up, aren't I?'

'You really need to get some leave Talog. I'll have a word with chef. We'll have eggs, gateau and your own pot of tea ready for you on your return...'

'Are you sure you're not French, Number One? It's called chocolate cake where I come from!'

'And where would that be, Talog? Jail?' At this, Number One turned smartly and walked away.

Katie noted the co-ordinates and put up the electronic map on the navigation tablet. She looked across at the entity on the flight deck - it was like a giant dragonfly, with huge shining blue eyes set together, four out-stretched shafts stretched above into the sky and a long, slender tail. The bulge of the sensing devices under the nose was like the feeding appendage of the dragonfly, coiled, ready to strike. She shook her head - no, it was a Lynx helicopter, waiting to be ridden over the Great Blue.

'You, me and Nutter, the dream team. What could possible go wrong? We just need you to charm the pants off the French, we'll be back in time for le petit dejeuner. It will be a cake walk.'

'It's just that the landing zone isn't on French territory, is it? If they were on an exercise, why aren't we landing on French soil?'

'You're mistaken, the LZ is in French territory. It must be. Show me.' She showed him the screen.

'Look, Froggy land; Non-Froggy land' she said pointing to the map.

'Let me remind you Tally, Your job is to follow orders, not to challenge them.'

'I know that, Scotty.'

'Just do your job and you'll be fine. Think about that breakfast they'll have lined up for you.' They separated and walked around the waiting machine and reconvened back where they started. 'All fit?' Scotty asked.

'Yes, smoke, flares, two collapsible stretchers and two side arms only. So, nothing that's going to be useful in a fight' she said brightly, 'apart from me, that is!'

'Let's hope the French are in a good mood, then. Anyway, you'll have us?' Scotty replied.

'Yes, but that's what I was worried about. You're the pilot, Nutter's the co-pilot and you're going to have your hands full, aren't you?'

'You'll be fine.'

Katie stood looking at the nose of the helicopter. That girl was still there, throwing thunderbolts from her outstretched left arm towards an unseen enemy.

'So, this girl painted on the nose, who is she?'

'It's a woman we respect and admire greatly.'

'She looks nothing like Her Majesty!'

'No Tally, it's not Her Majesty, it's someone else we respect and admire greatly.'

'Whoever, she is, she's an idiot!'

'Why, pray tell?'

'If I was throwing around thunderbolts, I would make sure I was wearing a Mark 5 Flame Retardant Suit, I wouldn't be doing it in my keks, would I?'

'Well, that's interesting, because...'

'Because, what?'

'Well, it is someone we all know pretty well and whom we adore' Scotty announced proudly.

'Is she?'

'You've got to allow for artistic licence...and imagination.'

'That's never me!'

'Why not?'

'Noooo!' She traced the outline of the girl's torso and legs with her index finger. 'It can't be?' She looked back at the fuselage and tried to comprehend the stencilled markings that filled the expanse of the flanks. 'Oh, Ultra Mare!'

'Just like your cap badge!'

'She must be a big mare then?'

'No, its Latin, isn't it?' he teased.

'All right then, clever dick, what does it mean?'

'Over and above the sea' he replied.

'Very good, so she's not a big mare then?'

'I didn't say that!'

She jabbed him in the ribs. 'It's not really me, is it?'

'Get yourself strapped in girl, we have a go!'

'Nice one! You really had me going, there!' Katie climbed aboard and settled herself in her specially customised bucket seat, the one just behind the pilot's seats and ahead of the benches in the main cabin.

'All right then, so who is she? Is she one of your groupies?' Katie asked.

'She's a girl we all admire greatly, that's who she is' replied Nutley.

'So she's some bint you picked up at the gronk-o-mat?'

Scott made the preliminary checks. 'We have a go.' The secondary engine kicked in and the tail rotor whirred into life.

'So, how did you get her to pose? Did you get her drunk or did you bribe her?'

'Main rotor, go. All ready for lift off.'

'When her old buffer finds out, he'll have your bollocks for baubles!' She looked intently out of the main door window towards Flight Deck Officer Wilkins and his outsized orange gloves, standing in front of the hangar. 'Fido has given you a twirl, you're good to go Scotty' she shouted.

'Now come on, you tired old bitch, get up in the air!' said Nutley.

'Oi, don't be rude to her!' Katie pulled her hands against the bottom of her seat, willing the helicopter to rise. 'Don't listen to the nasty man, Nerys, you can do this!' Slowly, the helicopter yawed to port, then starboard then gained height. 'Come on Nerys, you can do it!'

'That was bad, she needs a complete overhaul, poor bitch!' The helicopter levelled out and pulled her way along the port side of the frigate.

'Well, she's twenty years old, which is, um, let me see, sixty years old in helicopter years. Right, Nerys has gathered up her petticoats' announced Katie over the radio, 'and she's up and running.' She checked the onboard computer and her own calculations. 'At one hundred and twenty knots, course ninety-five degrees, we'll be at the target in twenty minutes. I'll now hand you over to your pilot for this flight, Scotty Hodge and his co-pilot, Nutter Nutley. I'll going off-line to frat with our French friends. Over.'

The aircraft controller came on line. 'I'll remind you to maintain normal communications discipline, I know this is a milk round, but keep it professional, team. Over.'

'Roger that, Duke One' replied Scotty, 'normal service is now being resumed. Over. That was directed at you, Tally.'

'Sorry Scotty, but I had breakfast all lined up' moaned Katie, 'the galley was going to knock up Benedict eggs for me and my own pot of tea. Then I was going to the hanger, slinging up my hammock and getting a solid eight hours of kip before my next watch!'

'Well, good luck with that. Now, let's get a fix on these Frenchies.'

'Sure thing, Scotty, just leave it to me.' Then there was a pause. 'So, who is that daubed all over the nose?'

'Yes, who is the girl, Nutter?'

'It's just nose art. It keeps the flight team amused.'

'So Nutter, what was the brief?'

'We wanted a good looking girl, but with a certain 'je ne sais quoi'.'

'Got it, but maybe we shouldn't have gone with a girl who exudes so much sex...'

'Ugh!'

'Sexy girls, I'm thinking she must be French, a bit of Ooh La La!'

'French girls?' sniffed Katie. 'Smelly!'

'Yank, then?'

'Tacky, you'll end up with gum on your dick.'

'Ouch!'

'I've always fancied an Asian girl...'

'Yeah, but one's never enough is it?' commented Nutter.

'Italian?'

'Pushy...'

'A girl from Brazil...'

'Wobbly.'

'Moscow girls...'

'They sing and shout!'

'Bolshy.'

'English?'

'Snotty!'

'Swedish?'

'Muscley!'

'A fräulein?'

'Arsey.'

'What?'

'A Scot?'

'Mushy!'

'A Greek?'

'Grizzly.'

'You know what, I'm going to give up on girls, they just don't sound very nice any more!'

'Well, have you thought about...' murmured Katie.

'An Irish girl?'

'Getting warmer...'

'A Welsh girl?'

'Um, a little too witchy!'

Scotty seemed to be searching the remotest reaches of his mind. 'A girl from the Welsh Marches, maybe?'

'I think you've cracked it, Scotty! Not too witchy, not at all snotty, a lovely, chippy, mesmerising girl...'

'So where do we find this Goldilocks girl?'

'Eh?'

'Yeah, who'd have thought it? A girl from the Marches? Do you know anyone who fits the bill, Tally?'

'Yes, I think I do' she said quietly.

'Wait a minute! Where are you from Tally?'

Her hand went to her mouth. 'Blimey! It's me! Hold on, incoming message. Please repeat, over?'

'Ultra, Ultra, situation update. The French chopper is U/S! Are you in contact? Over!'

'Tally's talking to them now, over.' Her exchange started in English and then in faltering French. She made a quick signal to Scotty: 'There's someone tapping in on our transmission, Duke One, over.'

'Who the hell could that be? Over' came the reply from the control room.

'We don't know, but Tally has a plan.' Scotty waved to her. 'What's the plan, Tally?'

She resumed the exchange in French and then switched suddenly to a throaty, more guttural tongue.

'Tally's talking to them in another language, it sounds, out of this world to me. Over.'

Katie switched channels. 'Benoit's from Ushant, Brittany. Correction, Lieutenant Seznec, but I'm having trouble with interference and it's all garbled. Over.'

It wasn't garbled at all. She was being told to turn back and save her soul.

'Who are they?'

'They're the bloody French, aren't they?' Katie flicked him a quick look and briefly considered punching him on the shoulder. He would have to quickly juggle the yaw pedals to keep the Lynx on an even keel. No, best not to do that, not now.

'Come on Tally, I need to know what the situation is.' Nutley turned and stared as she ran through an array of nervous hand and finger signals as she spoke loudly on the radio link and looked out of the windscreen; she signed them again when he shook his head. 'Get a grip, Tally, what's going on down there?' The sea was still brilliant blue but there were now white crests on the flourishing waves and a spiral of smoke over the land.

'I've got it, there's five of them, one casualty.' She signed again. 'There's also civilians...'

'What's that Tally? Civilians, where did they spring from?'

'A boat on the other side of the island.'

'Above the LZ now, looks calm, not much to land on, over.'

'Winch me down Scotty, I'll do a quick recce.'

'You sure Tally, can you trust them?'

'I trust Benoit with my life...wait there's more.' Another stream of panicked chatter. She signed again. 'There's more coming in. There are four civilians. But we've only got room for two occupied stretchers and just smoke canisters fitted? We have no weapons apart from side arms, not even a GPMG.' She looked at Nutley, then back through the windscreen.

'Let's hope we don't need to do any fighting. What are they saying?'

'We need to get a casualty out. He's wounded - he's taken a bullet in the leg.'

'A bullet? How? Did he shoot himself?'

'Their Lynx is grounded - some sort of electrical fault. Winch me down close to their Lynx. I'll assess the landing zone while you do a holding pattern, Scotty.'

'They've marked a spot. Have you got that Scotty?' They were hovering above the stranded helicopter.

'Ready Tally?'

'Ready. You got me Nutter?'

'Got you. Out you go.'

Her legs flailed as she went over the lip and she was juddering her way down the cable and down into the overwhelming heat and dust below. There was a cluster of shitty, concrete dwellings inland and a crowd of people looking up and pointing at her. This was going to end badly, she was sure. Two packs landed in the dirt next to her.

Katie watched Nutley peer down from the main door of the chopper. 'Harness released, winch retracted and she's down on the deck. Over!'

'Tally, how's it looking?' called out Nutley. 'Over.'

'Landing space just east of their chopper, to the seaward side. No sign of anyone yet - they must be keeping their heads down? Over.'

'What's happened to Talog? She's gone off air, over' There was a quiver in the Air Controller's voice.

'There was a stream of invective, Controller. The gist is, she's going to have your knackers on a plate when she gets back, over!' Scotty had completely missed it.

'Urgent, where is Talog? Over!'

She pulled up the First Aid pack and the stretchers. 'Scotty, I'll get the casualty back here, you get ready to land on my signal? Over.'

Katie slung the pack over her shoulders and carried the two rolled stretchers towards the French Lynx. There was a casualty being tended by a soldier in khaki overalls and black beret. 'Comment ca va? Ca va bien, monsieur? C'ette homme, est-il walking wounded?'

'English, please' he implored.

'D'accord, ce n'est pas un problem. Can he walk?'

'No, his leg is broken.' She looked down the casualty's frame and sure enough, his right femur was shot through. She dropped a stretcher.

'Merde' she cursed. 'Alors, so you've got him comfortable and stopped his bleeding. Can you quieten him down, he's making a lot of noise?' Her eyes scanned inland. 'What's the position of the rest of your team?'

'Do you see the buildings? They are coming. You must be careful, we are being watched. Keep your head low and run fast!'

'Got it, get your casualty on the stretcher and keep him happy. I'll scamper over to your mates and see what's occurring.'

'You are a beautiful woman. Benoit is very lucky!'

'D'accord, and what's your point, mate?'

'There's no point. I'm just saying.'

'Alors, you must concentrate on what needs doing now! A bit of focus now will save spilt blood later.'

'D'accord. When will you rescue us?' he asked.

Katie looked to the sky where the navy-grey Lynx was circling many meters above the shore. She heard a whoosh and then a projectile flew out of the cluster of buildings heading skywards. She shouted into her mouth piece 'Scotty, rocket heading your way, up, up, UP AND AWAY!'

The Lynx climbed sharply upwards and the projectile looped lazily past and then plummeted into the sea where it exploded with an impressive plume of water and white smoke.

'Scotty mate, did that spill your cappuccino? Over.'

'Tally, yeah, I've got froth all over my pants! Over.'

'Scotty, story of your life, mate. Listen, one casualty comfortable, he's getting packaged ready to go. I'm going inland. I'll call you in when we're ready. Civilians coming in, family of four. It's going to be two lifts, isn't it? The casualty first. Is there any more air support available? Can we put out a call? Over.'

'Roger that Tally, two lifts. Negatory support in this part of the ocean. Be quick and be careful, over.'

'Scotty, got it. Over and out.' There was a gun shot and shouts of alarm. 'Blimey, where did that come from?'

Time now to absorb, assess, assimilate then advance and overcome...all of the signs, all of the sensations, all the vibrations and energies must feed into this one thing. It was now all about Benoit, and he was all that mattered. Everything must be brought down to this one, simple thing.

'Tally's got company and they don't sound too friendly! Over.'

'Urgent, Ultra One. Abort. Get Talog out of there! It's a trap! It's her they want! Over!'

All incoming babble now cut - she was on her own.

Katie set off inland, with her pack and a stretcher. She found a half-dug trench with a French marine half-sitting in it.

'Bonjour fella. Comment ca va?'

The marine looked at her incredulously. 'You are a girl! We need a squad of your marines!'

'Quelle affaire, huh! Well, you've just got me, mate.'

'Do you see? They're coming in.'

She could see. A man, a woman, two children ran quickly towards them, stooping and soundlessly screaming across the hard dirt. They were shepherded by two soldiers in khaki camouflage and berets. The civilians rushed past, followed by the first soldier. The French lieutenant, her Benoit, turned and stepped behind a building wall, a wireless pack on his back. There was the crack of a high velocity weapon overhead. Thankfully, it was a miss.

He stepped out of cover, their eyes met and he waved frantically at her but it was a wave that said run and save yourself.

Get back! Get back, BENOIT!

He slumped backwards to the wall, rigid and straight. As he toppled, a blood red streak described a perfect arc on the wall.

He was on the ground, out of her sight, cursing.

Katie's heart and lungs surged with panic. She looked to her right. 'Merde, where did that come from?'

'They are close, we need to get him. They are upon us.'

'Who's close? What's occurring?'

'The hostage takers come.'

'What? What hostages? No one said anything about that! I'm not here to fight!'

'It's all changed. We're in trouble. You must attend to Benoit!'

'Yes, I must attend to Benoit.' Another anguished curse came from behind the concrete.

'He's shot, did you not see? You can see that building across there?' He pointed a tired, tanned arm inland towards the collection of sun bleached buildings brooding in the relentless heat.

'Just follow the red rainbow' she muttered to herself. Katie could see the shattered concrete walled building. 'I see it' she admitted. It was about fifty paces away, fifty paces across dust and gravel and no cover. She heard a deafening throat gulp. It was hers.

'Do you see that gap?'

It was barely man-sized. 'I see it.' Her stomach did a flip as she understood the direction the conversation was taking.

'I think you can get through there and save him. I need you to do this.'

She removed her helmet and swept her hair back from her eyes. 'I can see a gap, but I can't see how I'm supposed to get through that.' She regretted the amount of cake she had been eating recently.

'We will distract our opponents. You run with your medical kit and stretcher, throw them over the wall and squeeze through. You must see how he is and rescue him and we will then come and rescue you both.'

'But that's crap! That's never going to work!'

'It's our only choice. We need a squad of marines, instead we have you. Can you fire a gun?'

'No, I was thrown off training - I was a menace to my own side!'

'D'accord. Understood, no gun for you! Now compose yourself. Tell me when you are ready. We will provide you cover with bullets.'

She brought one of the stretchers to her side.

'Benoit needs your help now. He is shot. You are our most important piece in the game. You are our queen!'

'So if I'm the queen, what are you then? The sodding joker?'

'I am the white knight! You must rescue our king!'

It was now all about Benoit, and he was all that mattered. Everything must be brought down to this one, simple thing. 'You're right, I'll go and rescue Benoit! Cover me!' She would soon be with him and make the rescue and he would be in her debt for ever and ever.

Katie took several deep breaths, waited for another high velocity round to fly overhead and sprinted across the ground, accompanied by a flurry of automatic fire and dived headlong into the gravel. Her helmet thudded against the wall.

Over the wall lay Benoit. There was fresh blood in the dust. She edged her way snake-like to the gap. 'Comment vas-tu, Benoit?'

'Katell! I told you not to come!'

'I had to!' He seemed surprisingly chipper in the circumstances. 'It's my duty!' She was now squeezing through the gap.

'Get your backside in' he spluttered. She thought she could see a bubble of blood at the side of his mouth.

'Pardonnez-moi?'

'Get your backside in' he spluttered again, 'and please, no French. So, a girl to do a man's job. Ha! You English!'

'British!' She pulled apart the buttons of his shirt. 'All right, lets get this patched up. You'll be right as rain in no time.'

'I can see by your visage' he gasped, 'it's not good.'

'So what seems to be the problem then?'

'I'm shot through.'

'Can you see the medical kit? Crap, it's sodding yards away. Why did I throw it all the way over there?'

He stretched his neck back and grimaced. 'You will need it.'

She reached across, grabbing the strap.

'Slowly, very slowly, Katell.'

She inched it across the soil.

'Keep your backside in.'

Now, she could reach it and rip it open. 'I'm not going to lie to you Benoit, we're in a spot of bother here!'

'Now, no mess, no noise or loose wrappers. They must not know you are here, my Katell, so very, very slowly.'

She unwrapped the biggest sterile bandage she could find. It made a deafening noise in the silence.

His eyes were closed and he was mumbling. 'Are you a Valkyrie, carrying me to Valhalla on a mighty black steed?'

'Nope. I'm a Wren and I'm taking you back to my ship in my little grey helicopter.'

'Let me see your face.' She flipped up her visor. 'Ah, my demon angel, Katell!'

'How's that?' She worked the bandage into place and secured it. 'I'm going to have to strap you into the stretcher then drag you out of cover. I don't know how that's going to work, we'll be in full view of the shooters!'

She winced as a high velocity bullet flew over.

'It does no good hiding from those -- they've already gone. It's the one that you cannot hear that will kill you.'

'So ducking the bullets is no good. I'll stop doing that, then.' Katie unravelled the stretcher by his side and manoeuvred him carefully onto it. She gave him a little hug when he was strapped in place.

'Your blood runs hot' she heard whispered in her ear.

'It bloody does, doesn't it? It's all a bit bloody hot about here, isn't it?'

'And the elixir of life runs through your veins, child.'

'I think that's probably just cider, isn't it? Have you taken a sneaky shot when I wasn't looking?'

'You heal with your hands. You are a healer.'

'How much morphine have you had? Now you're talking utter bollocks. Just save your breath.' He didn't seem to be talking but thankfully, he was smiling.

But now there was the booming of a sarcastic voice through a megaphone. Katie stopped still to listen. 'What are they saying?' Despite the man calling out in a language she was not fluent in, the tone of it suggested it was not morning prayers. 'I got bits of that. That doesn't sound good.'

'They know you're here' said a voice.

'That's good, is he on the welcoming committee?'

'They know you are...the woman.'

'That's also good? Do they know I'm unarmed? If I put up a white flag, will they let me go through?'

'No, it's you they want.'

'That isn't good. Why do they want me?'

'They think you are a witch and so they will take the parts of you that make you special. They will... emasculate you!'

'Eh? But those are my best bits -- what's the matter with them?'

'A white witch, a white witch, that's what they think you are.'

Benoit cursed for breath as he pulled a pistol out from its holster. 'Take this. Kill yourself before they take you.'

'I failed small arms training twice. I can't handle these things, can I?'

'Take it. One shot in the mouth. Don't let them take you alive.'

'Sod that!'

He subsided back into semi-consciousness. 'Maman, maman' he moaned.

'I'm giving you a shot of morphine now, stay calm!' She stabbed the needle into his arm. He gave a little grunt and there was that unnatural calm that heralds a sudden change in circumstance.

In the silence, as she strained to sense what was happening, there was the sound of slow footfalls in the gravel from two directions; the sound of leather straps straining against clothing; the sound of the catch on an automatic weapon being pulled back, ready to fire. The smell of male sweat, leached into their clothes, sweating, breathing, moving towards her, stalking her like they were stalking a prey animal. She took the pistol in her two hands and pressed the barrel so it was tight against her cheek, took a deep breath and stood to confront her stalkers.

There they were, two willowy, loose limbed boys, in shorts, brilliantly coloured football shirts and worn baseball caps. They froze as if the animal they were stalking had stuck its head out of cover.

Katie levelled the pistol to the boy to her right and then the one to her left. 'All right lads, listen up, I need your help.' They looked at each other and smiled. The lad to her right winked at the other. 'This way lads' she called out and moved backwards. They followed her, but put themselves between her and Benoit. Boys with guns and knives; guns strapped to their backs and long bladed knives tucked inside leather belts. She frantically tried to recall her combat training - do not turn away, face them, keep your arms up in front of you. 'All right lads, just wait there and help me get my casualty out of here.'

They turned and chuckled at each other. She couldn't work out what they were saying but she knew it was about her. Do not turn away, keep facing them. She held the pistol up to the sky and pulled the trigger - it clicked harmlessly.

They were upon her, pinioning her arms against the concrete wall, smiling and chuckling at her. The boy holding her left arm twisted it. The bones in her elbow joint grated together and she yelped in pain. Katie held onto the pistol desperately, but her arm was bent back so that the barrel was pointing at her head. The pistol's safety lock clicked - her heart jumped and her body pulsed quickly in fear. The barrel was hot on the skin of her face. She tried to wrench it down out of the boy's grasp. A shot, the sound of metal searing through flesh and muscle. A gasp of shock and pain. The three figures froze in their tight embrace. The boy gripping her right arm stared down suddenly, alarmed. A shriek and then his body splashed into the gravel. A pause as he felt down his right leg. He shrieked again, a long shrill shriek as he clutched his lower leg. Blood trickled down his leg - hot, restless, bubbling blood, disappearing into his bright blue training shoe.

Her left arm came free as the other boy pushed her away and stared screaming at the pistol in his hand. He cast it away, furiously shaking his hand, scrambling backwards. She heard his breath rasping in his throat in uncomprehending fear.

He was scrambling in the direction of Benoit, staring back at her. What to do now? His assault rifle was still slung across his back but the long knife was held in hand. She steadied herself. Her hands were stretched out towards him at the ready, but they could only make puny little fists. Keep facing him, don't turn away, watch his eyes. His eyes will tell you where he will strike.

His other hand darted out and seized her collar. She was pulled to the ground, despite her scrabbling legs, trying vainly to get some purchase in the gravel. The knife was at her stretched, pulsing throat and she was helpless, like the prey of a giant ant, to be dragged away and dismembered. She took a last look at the soldier she had tended; it was too late for him and too late for her. Her hands unclasped and her fingers stretched out towards him.

A bullet flashed past. The tip of the knife spiralled in front of her eyes and jagged towards her and she grasped it. The handle was in her hands and she was on her feet. A sphere of light flooded her sight and burst away. Her core and her lungs expelled a scream that roared through her throat. 'LOOK...WHAT...YOU'VE...DONE!'

There was silence. The boy's hands fell dumbly to his side. His eyes flared; her eyes glared. Her leg came up, poised between them and landed in the centre of his chest. He fell over backwards and his body bounced in the gravel, his eyes wide and swivelling about, begging. Her legs straddled his body. A babble of sounds came rapidly out of his mouth, in time with his thumping heart.

'No, no, you will not go to heaven! You won't go to heaven, because you did this!' She raised the knife high above her head ready to strike; it would penetrate his eye socket, sever the orbits of his brain and plunge into the bone at the back of his skull. She arched her back and readied herself to stab him through.

'Look...what...you've...done to me' she hissed, 'look...what...you've... done!'

'Child, your blood runs hot - don't do it!' It was a cracked voice, calling out to her. She looked around her but there was no one there, just her and this boy who had attacked her and now he was writhing in helpless terror, in his red devil football shirt. He was still jabbering but she couldn't make any sense of it.

Her body was coursing with the fuel to fight, still poised to wield a weapon and strike. The knife paused as she removed her right hand from the grip and wiped it clean of blood on her chest. And then the knife came down sharply, slicing through...

Chapter Sixty-Eight

'Raise the red ensign, Lieutenant Nail, we're going into battle!'

'You'd better listen to this' Lieutenant Jenny Nail announced to the team on the bridge of HMS Albany.

'What is it, CIS?'

'It's the running commentary, from Ultra, but I can't make any sense of it.'

He listened to the conversation going on over the radio. 'Come on old girl, what's up with you?'

'Wait, wait, I was in Rennes last summer, that's how the locals spoke. She's talking to them in Breton!'

'Clever girl. No bugger will get that!'

'What exactly did we get from the MoD?'

'Bugger all as usual.'

'Lieutenant, lieutenant, shall I rouse the captain?' called out the steward.

'No, no, I can handle this' blurted out Jenny Nail. She had said the words out loud but she was not sure she could deliver. Talog had got herself into trouble again and it had to be during her stint as officer of the watch.

'She's on her own and surrounded by hostiles' came the message from Flight Commander Nutley 'and they've got guns and knives!'

An image appeared in Jenny Nail's mind. They would form a circle around Talog and lunge at her and she would hiss and spit back. Hiss and spit against guns and knives!

Jenny looked behind her. There was the captain, who had ghosted in, wearing the dishdasha procured by Talog in a Somalian souk two months ago, his peaked cap at a steady angle and a mug of tea cradled in both hands. He gave a gentle nod of encouragement towards her. The multi-striped dishdasha looked ridiculous on him but it was his preferred off-watch garb now - it had now become a tour of duty of record length but discipline in the ship was not all it should be.

It was Talog, with that wide grin creasing her cheeks, always pushing at the boundaries, the source of incessant ribbing on games night, the continual chatter on the mess deck, the blessed moments of peace when she dropped, in a feline, foetal ball to sleep, in the most ridiculous and damned inconvenient places. She wasn't the heartbeat of the ship but she was surely the soul of it - HMS Albany's very own sea-witch.

'Set a course for the landing zone, full speed, rouse the bootnecks, get me the best time to launch.'

'Well done, lieutenant. Hail the Jauréguiberry and I'll speak to their captain. They must have some idea of what their countrymen are doing. I'll give the MoD a heads-up on this one. My team in the War Room in two minutes. Maintain the con, get Scotty to maintain station and feedback constantly. Talog's one of ours and we'll fight to get her back. Raise the red ensign, Lieutenant Nail, we're going into action!'

CHAPTER SIXTY-NINE

'I am! I am the bloody witch! Look at me!'

The knife came down at an angle and sliced through the leather strap that crossed the boy's chest.

'You...don't ...even...know...me!' She pulled off her helmet.

The voice came again. 'You are the life giver child, not the life taker. Don't do it.'

'Still!' She turned back to the boy between her thighs. 'I will lay you out on the ground' she hissed as she motioned with the knife from his diaphragm to his groin. A dark, moist circle spread concentrically from inside his trousers, tiny at first then and spreading quickly. Then there was the tang of ammonia in the hot, fetid air. 'I will lay you out bit by bit and we will see how long you can survive with nothing left in you, no body no soul. I will show you what is inside of you. I will show you all of this!'

'The pulse of life - it flows through your body! Set the boy free' the other voice pleaded.

Katie looked around her again. It couldn't be. She started to rise and her prisoner tried to wriggle free. The boy edged away tugging his shorts up. Then he stood up on loose legs and scrambled desperately back out of the shell of the building. He fell to one knee. Getting back up, he scrambled another ten paces, fell to both knees, looked back at her and then scrambled away again.

Katie lifted the knife above her head. She turned and charged at the wall behind her and buried the blade hilt deep into the concrete until it bit into the iron frame. Her body shuddered as the wall shuddered. A scream reverberated around the space. The wall shook, cracked and exploded into a thick pall of choking, acrid dust. The shroud of dust settled on her and around her. The wall was gone. She could see the shoreline and see the acacia trees. She could see the helicopter high above, her only hope of salvation.

Wiping the thick layer of dust from her face and ruffling her hair, all caked in blood and dust, she muttered: 'You didn't see any of that did you?' There was no response. 'You saw nothing and you heard nothing, and you weren't talking to me, were you?'

She thought she heard him cry 'Maman'.

'We can't stay here. We're going to have to get out.' She pulled the rope taut where she had lashed it to the stretcher and screamed to the French marines. 'Smoke and rapid fire now, I'm coming in!' She crouched as a hail of bullets flew over her head, put her lid back on, then stood and pulled the rope around her shoulders and dug her feet in. Painfully and slowly she gathered momentum. The stretcher and its passenger were dragged many paces until willing arms grabbed the rope and pulled with her. The stretcher skidded over the ground in a shower of dust and gravel and then it shuddered past a concrete bollard and then into the shelter of a concrete outhouse, out of reach of bullets, out of reach of the searing sun. She collapsed in a gasping heap.

'Mon dieu, what in the name of all that's holy are you?' yelled the marine.

'Bloody knackered, that was never fifty paces, more like a hundred!' She found the bent mouthpiece and hailed the helicopter. 'Ultra, come in please, over.' The French marine tenderly wrapped her bloodied hands with bandage. There was room on the beach for the helicopter to land but there were two stretchers and a family of four to evacuate. The mother and the son were still sobbing, the father was remonstrating with a marine and the daughter was drawing a bead on Katie with a long stick.

'Tally, got you. Where's the LZ? What's your situation? Over.'

'Next to their Lynx, seaward side. Two casualties to evacuate. Both stretcher cases. One life threatening injuries, he's a T1, I think we may be too late. The other's a T2. All balls out Scotty, over.'

'Get them ready. I'm coming in. I asked, what's your situation? Over.'

'Alive, over.'

'Have you been fighting, Tally? Over.'

'Sorry Dad. All balls out, remember? We'll cover you. Over.'

'Good?' asked the French marine.

'Good' she replied. There was just the right thickness of bandage to allow her to flex her fingers. The angry man on the megaphone had started to broadcast again. 'He really doesn't like me, does he?'

'What happened to the wall? Grenade?'

'I used a bit of leverage, that's all. Cowboy builders, huh?'

The Lynx descended and then landed in a pool of dust and a shrapnel of gravel and a wall of pressured air.

Her patient's voice crackled in his throat.

'Benoit, it's me, hold on, I'm with you, we're lifting you out.' She knew she was losing him. His dressing was checked and she re-assessed the amount of morphine she had given: the limit had been reached. She laid by his side, her hand over his wound and pumping a plastic bag over his chest. Her lips touched his ear. 'Benoit, its Katell, your little angel!'

He grimaced. 'Demon!'

'Oi, behave!' He seemed to be easing away...but he was hanging on to something. He moaned again. She laid across his body, pressing firmly against the pressure bandage with her chest, but nothing could be done to arrest his passage to the next life. Her mouth was close to his left ear and she whispered 'Feel my strength, feel it. Take what you need, take it, anything you need from me, take it, through my touch, my hands, my mouth, my body...just take it.'

Nutley was standing above her. 'Tally, it's time. You alright?'

'Yep. Broken leg first then Benoit.' As his stretcher came to be lifted, she heard the death rattle in his throat. She pressed her face to his but he seemed to be going. Katie gently pinched his eyelid with her lips and eased his right eye closed. She moved softly across his face and her lips pinched the left eyelid and pulled it gently closed. 'Listen Benoit, our souls are eternal, our souls are eternal, when we pass over, something better begins.' She kissed him lightly on each of his eyelids.

'I'm sorry Benoit, I'm the last thing you will ever hear, I'm sorry I couldn't save you for this life and we didn't lie...'

There was a jolt as their bodies parted. The French family were already in the cabin and Benoit's stretcher was loaded in front of them. The mother started screaming.

'Room for a small one?' she jested.

Nutter replied: 'We'll be back as soon as we can, Tally. Just keep your head down, stay behind the marines and no more fighting!'

She shook her head slowly as she drew her finger across her throat, the signal to say finished, no more. The Lynx climbed off the ground slowly in a turmoil of gravel and sand and shrieking. They were hovering above, climbing slowly.

'Tally, what have you done?'

'Everything I bloody could.' The screaming reached a new crescendo as the helicopter paused in its climb upwards. 'But it wasn't enough, was it?'

'Tally, Tally!'

'Get out of here. Get him back home. I'm staying behind!' And the helicopter was gone.

Her head spun as she tried to make sense of what was around her. Her lips and nostrils were bombarded with hostile sensations that made her skin and her nerves twitch. Or was it the thick layer of concrete dust that coated her? So here she was on the shoreline with four French marines and a French Lynx helicopter. One of the marines was tinkering in the cockpit of the helicopter and the other three were attempting the hopeless task of setting up a perimeter around their piece of the waterfront.

They fired occasional bursts of automatic gun fire in the air but people were approaching relentlessly, all armed with something, whether it was a farming tool, a stick, a kitchen utensil, a wooden club or a gun.

Katie climbed into the co-pilot's seat. The French marine had booted the electronics back up but the hydraulic circuit wasn't responding. 'Can you get her started?' He shrugged and continued to flick switches up and down. And then he stopped to stare at her as she reached under the console and probed through the coiled cables. She grasped two coils of cable in her hands and looked upwards to the myriad switches in the roof of the cabin. 'Merde alors mate, you've got a stowaway! Bring the tool box!' Katie jumped out of the helicopter and started banging the panels on the underside. 'Hear that?' Non? Ecoutez-bien. You bang there and I'll bang here and when we collide...' She levered off the middle panel with a screwdriver and shoved her hand inside and behind and to the right side and then to the left side. 'Merde. Avez-vous les gauntlets? Non? Bucket?' Her hands had settled on something that squirmed through her fingers and coiled around her wrists. With her feet placed squarely on the fuselage panel she pulled hard and fell over backwards. Her hands were shrouded in a living mass of excited particles. She shook her hands, cursed and stamped through the mass with her left boot. 'Get me a squirter! Get me something!' It swirled in an iridescent spiral like a nest of new born snakes. Her legs took her far from the helicopter towards the village. It tried to escape but she gathered it up in her hands, raced to a still pool of water and furiously swilled her hands and wrists in it. The pool bubbled and then blew smoke spirals through the surface. She scoured her hands together until the iridescence was smeared away.

It was then she realised that she had a crowd of onlookers surrounding her who were looking on in amazement. Katie stood with her boots still in the pool and removed her helmet and shook out her hair. A plume of dust rose and then settled over the pool. 'I imagine you're all wondering what I'm doing here' she said as she tapped her foot in the pool, to check if what she had pulled out of the helicopter was still alive, 'well, you and me both!' She slowly replaced the helmet back on her head and the crowd started to edge their way back, except for one boy. He looked at her; she looked behind at the sound of the main engine of the Lynx juddering into life.

He was a young boy, with a stone in one hand and a sling in the other. He waved it at Katie, beckoning her to come with him. She stumbled towards him, her feet splashing through the pool. He waved the sling at her head, pointing at her helmet. She paused and spoke to him: 'Now, be a good boy and put it down.' His eyes widened and his smile widened so she could see all his teeth, bared against her and in that moment, she saw the face of disdain and contempt and she knew she was in trouble.

The stone was carefully placed in the sling and it was swung round and round his head and it was released with such force that it smashed through the side of her helmet. She was now face down in the pool, her arms thrashing helplessly and all around her, ripples spreading away. In the corner of her right eye she saw a dark smudge. It meandered slowly down her visor, heading down past her cheek, down her face, a streak of dark, living liquid that used to be inside her head.

Katie looked across the pool of warm, salty water; still, inanimate, solidifying before her. Hexagonal crystals grew upwards at the side of the pool, slowly at first, but now growing more quickly, growing towards her. Salt crystals formed and crusted her face and her lips.

A black, jointed creature appeared at the edge of the salt pool. It waved two long appendages at her and then its articulated limbs moved its shiny, black body towards her, tentatively, probing the salty surface, carefully but relentlessly moving towards her. It reached her visor and waved its forelimbs which now picked at the perspex surface: tip, tip, tip, tap, tap, tap, tip, tip, tip.

Katie turned her head and it hesitated, then scuttled away across the crystalline surface. She was being baked into this pool, her blood now mingling with the salt and the water and the dirt and the falling raindrops.

Suddenly, her body slurped out of the slick of salt and was being dragged backwards. There was another burst of automatic fire. It was the French marines. They had come for her.

Katie was aware that she was rising quickly and it was happening in jumps, like a dodgy lift in a high rise, stopping at every floor. From her co-pilot's seat she could see the marine hunched over the controls. And she was burning up. She tugged at her bandages, but then quickly tugged them back, when she saw how bloodied her hands were. 'I'm calling in, we need permission to land.'

There was a navy-grey shape flying on a parallel course to theirs. She waved at Scotty in the Albany Lynx, tracking their flight from half a football pitch away to port. He gave a thumbs up signal in return. She wished she shared his level of confidence. The deck of HMS Albany was below. The radio crackled into life.

The French Lynx descended hesitantly, level by level until a few yards above the deck. It descended the final ten steps suddenly, bouncing the undercarriage. 'Cut the power to the main rotor now!' Katie shouted. The helicopter lurched to the left. 'Cut the power now!' she screamed. The blades ground on the deck to an ear shattering halt. The pilot looked at her sheepishly and smiled broadly. 'We arrive' he murmured. He unstrapped and pulled her against him and hugged her tight.

This she didn't need, and she couldn't respond anyway, because her hands were sore and her brain was banging against her brain case. 'We did, didn't we' she muttered, 'but you shouldn't be flying a helicopter though, should you? You don't sodding know how, do you?'

'My maiden flight!' he responded triumphantly.

'Oh, my soul, my soul, what the fuck have you done!' The doors of the helicopter were flung open simultaneously but her pounding on the buckle of the seat harness was to no avail. And the straps were cutting into her sides as they strained to hold her in. 'Give me a hand here, I'm stuck!' There were two men waiting anxiously for her, her co-pilot and the FIDO. She settled back in her seat - the buckle was jammed. 'You're going to have to cut me loose!' They set to work. She was slipping into arms that gathered her under her legs and around her shoulders, lifting her out of the seat. 'She's very limp, is she okay?' asked a helper.

'He should not be flying a helicopter' she shouted out, pointing insistently at the French marine, 'he doesn't know how! And look what he did to my sodding flight deck!'

The Frenchman spoke across her to her FIDO. 'Ah, magnifique! Incroyable! She was the queen and she was in the middle of their ranks and she defeated them. She rescued our king!'

'You see him? You see him! He doesn't know how to be a pilot, he could have killed us all!'

'Calm down, Ket, you're in safe hands now.'

'He could have crashed us, we could all be burning in the sea!'

Maddocks took over from her pilot. 'Yes, but the sea would put out the flames, wouldn't it?' he replied.

And now Big CIS joined the throng. 'Look, this isn't a game. She shouldn't have been exposed to fire like that! She didn't have a weapon!'

'Alors, you could have sent in troops but they would have just been pawns in the battle. She was the key piece on the battlefield. The enemy knew that' said the French marine.

'For pity's sake, shut him up!'

'Who were the enemy and what were you doing there?' shouted Ceeps at the French marine.

'It was a rescue mission' was the reply. They lowered her slowly to the deck and she planted her feet tentatively on the apron but her legs would not straighten.

'Ah, she was magnifique! The enemy knew she was our most important piece. They knew they had to capture her. We protected her as best we could, but she beat them, right in the middle of their lines!'

'Let's get that helmet off' said FIDO. They eased the helmet off her head. 'Christ, she's been hit, there's blood down her face!' He wiped it away with his hand. 'Get a stretcher out here pronto and get her to the sick bay!' he shouted.

'What about my poor bloody hands, my poor bloody hands!' She thrust her hands under her arms and squeezed hard to nullify the pain. 'My poor bloody head! My poor bloody head!' Now there were three marines running towards her. 'Where were you when I needed you? I had to fight off their blokes, that's your sodding job, that is! I had to fight off the whole, sodding Zulu nation back there!'

'You're safe, you got back all right Ket, that's the important thing' said the helicopter handler.

'I had to fight hostiles!'

'You're safe...'

'It's not my job to fight hostiles, that's your job. Where were you?' she shouted.

'Look, we're all in the same team...we're one team...you got out in one piece!'

'No thanks to you! My job is to find hostiles then send you to sort them out. When you've finished sorting out their hostiles, then I bring you home. That's how it's supposed to work!'

'Look you're a bit fraught...'

'No, I'm not! I had a fright! And a fight! You should have been there to fight their blokes. If I have to find their blokes and fight their blokes, why do I need you?' They had grabbed her flailing arms but she threw herself free. Another white garbed officer joined the maul that surrounded her. 'Oh great, it's Number One, what do you want?'

'Stay calm Katie, we're all here to look after you.'

Big CIS turned to Number One. 'Talog is one of our key assets, she should not be thrown into hand to hand fighting! That's someone else's job!'

'Oi, I'm not an asset!' She stumbled back towards the helicopter. She had a throng around her, trying to help her, but no one could. 'Get Testy, tell her I'm ready for our fight!' The helicopter was like a giant dragonfly, with it's bulging midnight blue eyes, it's four flying appendages, the mandible concatenated below the eyes.

'Ket, can you walk?' asked a marine.

'Course I can walk, you sarky bastard!' She stopped and looked around with wild eyes. 'But they weren't hostiles, they were just kids. I shot one of them, I wanted to stab the other, why should I be allowed to live?' She took two unsteady steps and she was leaning against the door of the French helicopter.

TC was spouting in her ear: 'What have you done to yourself? What did you do?'

She stopped to shout at him: 'Listen TC, you'll need to manhandle their Lynx into the hanger and break it down, because it won't fly anywhere.'

'Why are you shouting, I'm right here!' shouted TC pointing at his ear.

'That's enough sailor, can't you see she's wounded?' replied Number One.

She pointed at the collapsed undercarriage of the helicopter. 'Only a man would think that something so puny, dangling underneath, would be up to the job!'

'Are you the mechanic now? Are you? Is there anything you don't do now? Is there?' shouted Nico.

'Well, Thick Crust, do what I say then I won't sodding shout at you' she shouted.

'Are you the captain now? Are you?' he shouted back.

She steadied herself and said loudly, calmly and deliberately, 'Just get the sodding helicopter broken down, put it in the sodding hangar, then get out of my sodding sight!'

'Do as you're told sailor' shouted Number One.

'My poor bloody hands, just look at my poor bloody hands' Katie whimpered. She turned towards the stern of the ship, took two more faltering steps forward and two steps back and sank to her knees. She was held before she could fall to the deck. 'I'm so sorry, I'm so sorry. I did something really bad!'

'Don't worry about that now Ket, let's get you...'

'I swore at everyone, I fucking swore at everyone!'

'Ket, Ket, just calm down!'

'But I've just done some really bad things...'

'Look just take it easy, we've got you back and...'

'I sent his soul to hell, I sent his soul to hell!'

'Someone get a shot in her, she's out of control...ah, look at that for timing!' The on-duty medic arrived at the double.

Katie stared at the appendage on the Lynx helicopter, coiled back, ready to strike. She twisted around so she could shout at the Medical Orderly. 'You're not sticking anything in me, scab-lifter, remember what I said!'

'Katie, yes, that's right. We agreed a word, what was the magic word?'

'Abracadabra? Was it abraca-fucking-dabra?' The sky was turning to a boiling red.

'No, not that one. Remember, there's a word that you must use before I take you down. Can you remember what it is?'

'Take me down? Oh, I don't know. Is it frotch?'

'No, it isn't.'

'Is it thatch?'

'No, it's not thatch.'

'Is it...is it snatch?'

'No, it's not snatch. You're on the right track though.'

'Is it bitch?' The sea was now a dark, seething purple.

'It rhymes with bitch...'

'Is it nitch?'

'No. It's not nitch. Come on Katie, what is it?'

'I don't know, you've got me, mate.'

Captain Marriott arrived in great haste. 'Does it really take a dozen of you?'

'Captain, Captain! The big film this week? What was it?'

'I've no idea Talog. Number One, what's going on here?'

'The one where the Welsh got all trapped. In a farm, it was...'

'Zulu?'

'Yes, yes, that's the one! Captain, what I've just been through, it was just like that! There were hordes of them!'

'Get her below deck. Get her some help!'

'Captain? Captain? I bet you didn't realise...'

'Realise what Talog?'

'When you left Guzz, you had all your fancy sonar and your fancy radar and your fancy helicopter and your fancy battle pants...' She looked down to his neatly ironed, white shorts.

'Yes, Katie?' replied the Medical Orderly.

'Bet none of you realised...'

'Realised what Katie?'

'In all your little inspections and your captain's rounds...'

'Yes?'

'You had something else on board, not on the pusser's inventory!'

'What sort of thing, Katie?'

'Ah ha! An all seeing being, that's what!'

'And this all seeing being, is she called Katie?'

'Ah ha! You're trying to trap me! You crafty bugger! Go away and lift a scab!'

'Come on Katie, who is the all seeing being?'

'It's one of the wrens, isn't it?'

'Is it Wren Worthington?'

'No, it's not Wanda! It's not wonder girl!'

'Is it Wren Patel?'

'No! No! It's not Irma!'

'Wren Knowles?'

'No! No! It's not Nicky!'

'Who's left?'

'I don't know, do I?'

'Come on Katie, who is it?'

'Aha! It's me! It's me! I'm the all being seeing. I'm the witch!'

'Who is the witch?'

'I'm the witch!'

'Who is the witch?'

'I am! I'm the bloody witch! Look at me!' She pulled her sleeve up and offered her right arm.

'All right Katie, that's the one.' The hypodermic needle went in. There was a sharp jab of pain in her lower right arm.

'All right Number One, let's disperse the crowd, haven't you all got jobs to do?'

'Did you know she was a witch?'

'Of course, we knew. Every ship needs its sea-witch and Katie is ours' said Big CIS proudly.

Katie turned to her medic but her eyes could no longer see straight. 'I feel whoosy, it's going dark, it's all going dark. I can't...'

'They're not standard fit, but they supplement our radar and sonar systems perfectly. And they're transferable technology too' added Big CIS brightly.

'They're a bit temperamental, and they have special dietary needs, but ours has worked out surprisingly well' said the medical orderly.

'What the fuck are you all talking about' moaned Katie.

'You. Our sea-witch. All our ships should have one!'

'What a load of bollocks.' She staggered but she was held on both sides. 'I'm going, I'm going, I'm going.'

The giant dragonfly lifted into the air by a few feet and hovered in front of her. The appendage coiled in and then struck out, the mandibles snapped closed around her waist and sliced her in two. As the two parts of her collapsed, she heard the chaplain's voice and he sounded concerned. Katie pulled her torso towards him. 'Help me, help me, help me' she whimpered as her world went dark around her.

Katie recalled waking up and seeing the concerned face of her CO, Big CIS at her side. The white, crisp sheets on the clinic bed were so comforting. She turned over to go back to sleep but her hands and her scalp hurt.

'And remember, do not call him Dad or Old Man to his face' Big CIS warned.

'Huh, please, give me some credit' she answered with her back to Big CIS.

'What's the other thing you call him?'

'Last Word, ma'am.'

'Yeah, don't use that one either.'

'Here she is, sir' announced Big CIS. Katie started to rise from her bed but she needed help to get sat up.

'Stay where you are Talog' the Captain boomed. 'We'll be shipping you back to the UK so you can get some additional treatment and some recovery time.' He paused. 'So, how are you feeling now?'

'A bit shaky, sir.'

'Understandable, but I'll need your action report before you leave.'

'I'll need a writer to dictate to, a very large slice of fat knacker pie and as much tea as I can drink, sir.'

'Are you negotiating an order with me, Talog?'

'Certainly not, sir, just trying to improve it. I suggest that to get the task done...most efficiently I dictate my report to someone who's not suffering from the shakes but I will need cake and tea to sustain myself while I'm doing it so I don't faint.'

He thought for a moment and then nodded. 'See to it lieutenant.' She departed quickly to action the order.

'Make sure it's not rubbishy' Katie called after her, 'it will need to have a lot of chocolate in it and I'll have my Benedict eggs now!'

'Well, Talog, there were a couple of errors of judgement yesterday but we got out of it with some credit. The conduct of yourself and your colleagues was exemplary.'

'I...'

'Wait a moment Talog. What I was going to add, was that it is no more than I would expect from any member of my team.'

'Is that a compliment, sir?'

'Accept it with good grace Talog, you will find that compliments are few and far between in the service!'

'Thank you sir!'

'You've have now been at sea now for the best part of thirty months. You've done nearly thirteen months continuously, which is much too much. We'll get you home in a couple of days then posted ashore to develop your skills in managing people. How do you feel about that?'

'I think my managing people skills are already highly developed, sir.'

'So you say. I'm sure we will find an adequate replacement for you, another girl from the Marches, maybe not with your peculiar talents and attributes.'

'Thank you sir - was that a compliment, sir?'

'Er, no, you need to work on your listening skills, Talog.'

'I will, sir.'

'I assume this means that you will have to relinquish your 'Uckers' trophy - so how did you keep hold of it for so long?'

'Skill sir, a little bit of luck and quite a bit of cheating.'

'I see, well I will pretend I didn't hear that. I must say that I won't miss your unionisation of the lower deck, Talog.'

'Sorry, sir?'

'You know very well what I mean.'

'I think it's important that everyone feels they have a stake in the ship. It's a tribute to your enlightened captaincy, sir.'

'Anyway, get the report ready by eleven hundred today.'

'I'll need tea, cake, writer sir. Then it will be done.'

'Good. And this is a personal letter for you.' He handed her a sealed envelope which she sniffed along the seal and then tucked away.

'Smells good, sir!'

As he headed out of the room he left a final riposte: 'You're best suited to Operations though and working with the Royal. I'll recommend that you are posted to one of our assault ships.'

'Thanks Dad!'

CHAPTER SEVENTY

Sunday 29 May - The Marches

Gwen parked her car in a flurry of gravel and locked it. There was the trickle of a stream from the fold above and the echoing of the hillsides to the guttural 'kronking' of the ravens and the anxious calls of lambs and their mothers in the rough, upland pasture. All else was silent, in and around the old, stone-built miner's pub but she could tell from the vehicles present that she was the last to arrive: there was a battered red bicycle; a Land Rover and an Audi TT convertible. She wondered what the locals would make of this cabal.

Gwen entered through the side door, next to the smoking shelter, and found the others ensconced in the side room. A nod to the man behind the bar had the pleasing effect of a large, glass of cold Chardonnay arriving in front of her. This joined the half of stout, the pint of ale and the fancy glass of designer lager on the table. She nodded to the Vicar, to Mister Pratt and then to Alec Wicks.

'Well? What's happened?' she asked.

'It's Katie, she was assaulted in central London last night. She's recovered but she's being held in a police station in Cambridgeshire.' Alec Wicks took a gulp of ale. Somehow, he didn't look quite right out of Royal Navy uniform.

'I don't understand, why is she in Cambridgeshire? Do I need to go and get her?'

'She's being held there for questioning. The police said they will move her out to a military base in Suffolk for her own safety. We just have to sit tight until they get back to us.'

'Is this something to do with that Swiss organisation?'

'SIKS? Yes, it is - she trashed their Cambridge facility last night!'

'She did, but why?'

'What has happened to your sister? She seems to have gone off the rails' murmured Mister Pratt, as he sipped his stout.

'And you're surprised? Didn't you see this coming? Look, she's a classic sociopath, here, see this, this is what her condition is called, ASPD, antisocial personality disorder, I looked it up.' Gwen waved a sheet of paper in front of his face.

Alec put down his glass: 'Be careful how you label her, Gwen. Katie's pathologically incapable of lying as you know and if she tries to tell a lie, she goes into meltdown. Anyway, both you and I know what actually happened...'

'She's turned, I sensed it as soon as she came back.'

'Katie does seem to have taken on the role of spokeswoman for all of pagankind' muttered the vicar.

'Vicar, please, she was upset...and the verger should watch her step, in the mood that Katie's in, I fear for her life!'

'Gwen, please, Katie's not coming for anyone!'

'I don't know how much she has told you...'

'Just spit it out.'

'In the Comoros Islands, she was involved in a botched operation where she got into an eye to eye fight.'

'I know, and that's how she got those injuries to her head and her hands.'

'Indeed, and it was a miracle she got away.'

'But her little demon would have protected her...'

'Her what?'

'Listen, we all have a little demon in her heads, even you, but some of us have learned...how to control ours.'

'And how do you control yours, Gwen?' asked Mister Pratt.

'This isn't about me...'

'You're her closest living relative.'

'You mean, apart from our mother?'

'And her grandmother...'

'Don't be ridiculous!'

'I think this is about your nain, Gwen!'

'She's must've been dead for years!'

'Katie believes she is alive, or at least...'

'That's ridiculous!'

'Hear me out. Katie believes she has a promise to fulfil, and when our clan has a promise to fulfil, we do it, no matter the cost!'

'Jesus Holy Christ!'

'She thinks...the women of the Elenydd are holding the body of our nain.'

'But why?'

'So Katie has to come back and deal with them.'

'Jesus Holy Christ' exclaimed Pratt, 'witch wars!'

'But our nain needs something before she can safely pass to the other side...or she'll be in eternal stasis.' Gwen took a deep breath. 'But, what is it, though?'

'Witches, what rubbish!' The vicar took a long draft of lager.

Gwen gave the vicar a steely glare: 'The naivety of the Anglican church astonishes me some times!'

'Go on Gwen, how do you control that demon in your head?'

'This isn't about me, it's about Katie - she's turned, but she's so immature, such an ingénue...'

'I think this is pertinent.'

'I have learnt to keep tight rein...'

'This is ridiculous - how is it possible to have a demon living in her head?'

'Ah, but it's only a little one.' Gwen's finger circled the top of her glass until it sang to her. She looked through the brilliant, pale-yellow fluid, now swirling in the glass. 'Katie, Katie what is your plan?'

'Gwen, what can you see?'

Her right hand swept through her gathered hair and unfurled the neat and practical bunch that she had adopted for her veterinary duties. It fell around her shoulders.

'All right, I'll give you a moment - Mister Pratt? What's your assessment of Katie?'

'Katie's always had fantastic endurance but now she's filled out, she's like Gareth Edwards and Phil Bennett rolled into one! Only prettier! She's physically adept and strong and she's a natural leader!'

Gwen snorted. 'Being able to kick a rugby ball the length of the pitch isn't going to help her now!' She got up, walked to the stone lined window and gazed out to the hills and sky. 'So, what is it, little sister?'

'Vicar?'

'As I say, she's mentally strong and focussed and absolutely clear of her identity.'

Gwen's palms pressed hard against the cold, stone flags. 'Come on sister, what is it?'

'What's the matter, Gwen?'

'I told my husband that he had to destroy his flock this morning. Rampant disease.'

'I'm so sorry Gwen.'

'No matter. It's done.'

'But there was an incident last Sunday' continued the Vicar, 'I have a Somali refugee under my wing and he knows of Katie...'

'Katie's done much of her work along the Horn of Africa' noted Alec Wicks.

'Of course! She's lost the triskelion! She wasn't wearing it when she returned!'

'My Somali believes that Katie tried to pull him from the sea and he heard her use an exhortation to her gods...but it failed!'

'Katie doesn't need any gods. She's quite capable on her own!'

Gwen looked out of the window and scanned the sky. There was a kettle of red kites above, circling, soaring, crying. 'But Katie, you had a conversation with Papa? But how? I'm the only one who can get inside his head!'

There were two ravens, leaping from the crags and switch-backing across the valley. She gasped through her fingers. 'That's it, that's it! They're waiting for her!'

'Gwen, please! Your sister is in a secure unit in a Cambridgeshire police station!'

'I tell you, she's coming back!'

'Gwen, any moment now, she will be in the care of the military and she will be in their protection for as long at it takes!'

'She's coming back' said Gwen as she drained her glass and turned for the door, 'and we had better be ready! Mister Wicks, alert the Royal and get a squad and a helicopter out to Welshpool! Vicar, send the verger away for her own safety. Mister Pratt, just...just...do nothing!'

'When's she coming Gwen?'

Gwen hesitated as she scanned the hills and sky of the outer world and then each of the faces of Katie's cabal. 'Tomorrow!'

CHAPTER SEVENTY-ONE

Monday 30 May 0215 - Motorbiking

Katie's eyes blinked open and her eye-lids flickered in time to the staccato beat of the blinking lamp in the ceiling. In the silence, she could hear a voice - it was a sneery, self-righteous voice, not in the cell, nor in the corridor outside, but inside her head.

'I told you this would happen.'

'No, you didn't!'

'Yes, I did!'

'Who are you, anyway?'

'I'm your spirit guide...and girl, do you need me!'

'Oh, it's you. Tosser!'

'Rude girl! And this is what happens to rude girls!'

'What does?'

'They...incarcerate you!'

'Who does?'

'And it gets worse...'

'How does it?'

'Well, let me see - yes, they will impale you by your core, on the high altar!'

'Noooo!'

'Then, they will spill your innards on the chapel floor!'

'Noooo!'

'And then they will toss your empty cadaver to the beasts of the moor!'

'Noooo!'

'And lay your giblets out on hallowed ground!'

'Noooo!'

'Then burn them! Burn, burn, burn what's left of the little witch' cackled the voice, 'then damn your blackened bones, and scatter them to all points.'

'But, why? What's the matter with them?'

'And then your disembodied soul will wither in hell, you contemptible little witch. Wither, wither, wither!'

'Which bunch of born-again scrotes is doing all this?'

'The exceedingly pious of course, those who think they are above all else, so repent before it's too late!'

'I'm not repenting - I didn't do anything!'

'But you must! Look at the ledger of sins you have committed!'

'My conscience is clear, you moronic, self-serving twat!'

'Ooooh!'

'You heard me!'

'And who was it who tried to murder that poorly, little girl?'

'Not me! She was living on a false promise!'

'Your blood runs hot...'

'Oh, just fuck off out of my head, you abject moron!'

'Ooooh!'

And then the voice evaporated away, leaving her alone in this empty box of a cell. The bars across the window framed a moonless sky and the white walls were the canvas for wild, unintelligible scratchings from a soul in torment.

The door opened into the corridor now that the lock was impotent and ruined. Katie rose and felt her way along the cell walls and pushed the door further open. She was not in a chapel nor on hallowed ground - she was in a police cell.

'I've got to get going!' she shouted down the corridor.

A policewoman came to the open doorway. 'All right love? Would you like a brew?'

Katie gasped. 'You gave me a shock! Yes, and a slice of cake. I've got to get going now!'

The policewoman turned and walked away briskly and Katie followed her. 'Bad dream?'

'Oh yes, that's what it was, a bad dream, in a bad time, in a bad life.'

'Look, there are people coming to help you. It might look bad at the moment but in the morning, it'll all be fine. You'll see.' They walked together to the kitchenette for the tea making ceremony and chatted about how warm it was for late May and what a busy night it had been in the south of Cambridgeshire. She filled the kettle, got the carton of milk out of the refrigerator and searched the cupboards. 'Lemon drizzle okay?'

'Hmm, have you got anything with chocolate in it?'

'Er, no.'

'Lemon drizzle is fine, then.'

'How do you take it?'

'The tea? It's one milk and three sugars, isn't it...'

'Three? That's a big sugar hit! I thought I was bad...' Her voice tailed away. '...but that's no problem whatsoever.'

Katie watched the Desk Sergeant pour over a written document, as she slurped tea and ate lemon drizzle hungrily. 'I'm sorry about your cell, Sarge!'

'Don't worry love, I've raised a work ticket, I'm sure someone will be able to fix it!'

'Miss Talog's in the canteen, having a mug of tea with the early shift. And some cake' announced Policewoman Hicks in that brisk and business-like manner of hers. 'I'm going to join her. What a bloody night!'

The door to her cell was wide open, the lights were flickering down the corridor and the digital lock was clicking to a hypnotic, bossa nova beat.

He looked through her signed statement. It was written in a faltering, non joined-up script that could have belonged to a primary school child, and a young one at that, but this was a primary school child that could recount a cold, clinical and detailed account of an assault, an abduction, an imprisonment against her will and a destructive electrical storm that had ebbed and flowed around her.

The scribbles in her notebook told of inexorable and alarming changes to her body and mind in the last few weeks of her life and the scribbling had become bolder and more colourful by the day. She was a very disturbed soul.

Two minutes later, he called the duty officer and briefed him. 'There's been an attack at the SIKS facility near Cambridge. I think it may have been one of those cyber attacks. A lot of damage has been done, apparently. The owner is flying out a team from Switzerland this morning to sort out the mess and they should be on site about six o'clock this morning. Firefighters and paramedics are in attendance.'

The duty officer wanted to know if there had been any injuries.

'There was one chap with a head wound but he couldn't tell us what happened. He seemed to have lost his mind, and he was getting attention in A&E at the city hospital. We've had to transfer fifteen patients to the hospital. There was one very poorly child but she's in isolation in the critical care unit. There were two traumatised private security staff who the fire brigade rescued from their vehicle. We've called out the duty vet to attend to two very sleepy guard dogs and the duty doctor's had a look at the main suspect, Miss Katell Talog.'

He confirmed that she was indeed from the Marches and was in all likelihood, part Welsh.

'She's got a bruise on the side of her head and a black eye which ties in with the description of how she was abducted. She still seems very drained - we're not sure what part she had to play in last night's extravaganza. She originally claimed she was a witch when we picked her up. The doctor's checking that out and we're seeing if anyone can corroborate what happened. She says she did it, but she's just a slip of a girl and talks a bit of Welsh and she's a serving member of the Royal Navy - make of that what you will. I think we'll get CID in and let them sort it out. Yes, there are CCTV cameras in the building but we can't recover anything from the system. And, we've had a call from Special Branch, they seem to want her in their own custody.'

He wanted to know where.

'They wouldn't say. I reckon Mildenhall. Where is she now? She's having a mug of tea with the early shift. Why isn't she locked up? The electronic security system has gone down. Handcuffs? Yes, we tried those but we've had two sets fail. The metal was rotten. How? It was full of air bubbles so they must have been part of a duff batch. Are you coming in?'

Yes, he would.

He looked at the possessions they had recovered from her - there was a ring bound notebook, with crumpled and wrinkled pages; a strawberry flavoured condom still in its wrapper, a phone card which still had some credit on it; a public transport card that had been issued to a Paol Houghton and over one hundred and fifty pounds in cash. Miss Talog insisted that this was the kitty for the hen party she had been leading. There were two sewing needles, with cotton streaming out of their eyes, inserted into a cork and a chain of seven safety pins and four buttons, all linked together. Not the paraphernalia that you would expect a young woman to carry, for a night out on the town, he thought. She had a cell phone in her possession but the innards were melted and there was verdigris oozing out from under the cover.

And then there were some items that made no sense at all: an ingot of what he guessed was tin; a liquid-filled vial which seemed to contain a preserved sea anemone; a piece of very old blackened leather. There were characters inscribed in the tin and in the leather that he could not interpret, no matter what he did to view them. The leather collar had an old piece of bone inserted through it.

He picked up the phone and called Sergeant Charles Otterburn. 'Sarge, I've got something very interesting here. One of our customers...'

'Do you know what time it is?' came the response.

'No, that's another thing that's happened on my shift. All the bloody clocks have gone down!'

'Well, for your information, it's three o'clock in the morning. This had better be good!'

'Well, let me describe what I have in front of me. We've brought in a girl and her hair was tied back with an old leather fastening. It's old. It's got hieroglyphics on it. But this is the interesting bit. It's held together with a piece of what I reckon is very old bone. Have you got your video connection up?'

'Give me a second.' There were thirty seconds of grumbling and fumbling. 'I'm ready, shoot it up.' There was silence while the desk sergeant rotated the piece in front of his video camera.

'Well?'

'I'm not sure. I know someone at the British Museum who is going to be very excited when he sees this, and the leather fastening. And what's that?'

'I reckon it's a nugget of tin. Can you hear this?' He pinged it and it sang down the line.

'Bloody hell! I've never heard that before!'

'That's not all! See this?' He rotated the vial in front of him.

'Bloody hell! What's that?'

'Dunno, it's labelled an 'Abgrall' but it looks like a sea anemone to me!'

'I'll see what I can find out.'

'You must have some idea what this all means?'

'Look it's three in the morning. They're all extraordinary. I don't want to go out on a limb, but...'

'Go on...'

'I reckon that pin is a penis bone...and she is...something else!'

'A penis bone!' he manipulated his prick to check that it was still in one piece.

'Yes, judging from the size and the shape, it's the penis bone of an otter.'

'Bloody hell! What's she doing with that?'

'You need to talk to her. We need to find out where she got this from. It must be a museum piece.'

'No, you need to talk to her.'

There was a long pause and a silence for intense thought.

'I'm coming in. Make sure she doesn't go anywhere.'

'Make it quick, an officer from Special Branch is coming to pick her up.

'I'm on my way!'

Katie replaced the phone in its holder - the lady at the Middlesex Hospital, London had confirmed that Mister Udo Sankt was critical but stable. His girlfriend had been released after treatment.

'That's one blessing, the phone's still working, love!'

There was a commotion at the front desk. A new visitor had arrived. Katie followed the desk sergeant to the desk and peeped out from behind him.

'Leading Hand Talog, I'm taking you into protective custody' he said abruptly. He was dressed in a grey pinstripe suit, with a tight waistcoat, a red tie and had the bearing of a military man.

'Who are you protecting?' wondered the desk sergeant.

'Her and the general public. I'm taking her to a secure unit at RAF Wyton.'

'Why Wyton?'

Katie whispered 'You need to get me out of this! He looks quite stern!'

'You can't lock her up, she should be in hospital!'

'I have orders...'

'You'll need a lead lined bunker, buried a hundred feet underground' said the desk sergeant under his breath, 'otherwise you have no chance of holding her!'

'We know what we're doing.'

'You have no idea what you're dealing with...'

'I'll behave' said Katie. The bulge under his jacket suggested that he had a powerful weapon under there. 'I'll get my things.'

'I'll get them, love' said the desk sergeant. He went to the back office, surreptitiously placed her belongings back into her satchel and returned to the desk. 'There you go.'

She looked through the contents - all present and correct. 'Thanks for having me' she said sweetly.

'You're welcome, it's been our pleasure, love. You've kept us entertained all night. Wait till I tell my wife what happened on my shift!' He was frowning.

'What's up, sarge?'

'There was someone I really wanted you to meet - but he's going to miss you...'

'I'm sorry about that and I'm sorry about your clock...and all the other stuff that got broke.'

'Don't worry about it...but if you know anyone who can fix it all.'

He made to book Katell Ebrill Talog out of his care, to the man from Special Branch. The clock, which proudly stated that it was linked to the Harwell atomic centre, was clicking as it jumped backwards through the years. 'Bugger this' he mumbled and then reverted to his wristwatch. 'How do I report all this? And what's going to happen to you?'

'Don't you worry about me, just worry about your daughter' she said, winking at him.

The man who was taking charge of her was fair haired, craggy looking, about forty years old she thought. She tried to picture him with his clothes off. His jacket and his waistcoat were now open as he waited impatiently and through his ever so tight shirt he seemed to have firm stomach muscles. Very nice she reckoned and neatly compact, too.

'Can you positively identify her?' he asked of the desk sergeant.

'Hallo, I call myself Katie and who are you?' she asked and offered her hand.

'Did she have any ID on her when you picked her up?' This seemed very rude and he needed to be shown some manners. Maybe, it was the nature of his job, but here she was right in front of him, asking a perfectly civil question, and he was simply ignoring her.

'Not exactly...'

'So no positive ID then?' Now, he turned his attention to Katie. 'Turn around.'

She sighed noisily: 'Nope. You didn't say please.'

He gripped her by the shoulders and turned her firmly. He then slipped the left shoulder of her dress down her arm. 'So that's something, the triple spiral tattoo on the shoulder blade. I want to see the others...'

'Piss off!' she hissed.

'I'll settle for the right foot - sit down' he ordered, motioning with his arm. Reluctantly, she settled in the seat in the reception area and offered her left foot. He pushed it away and lifted the other one, removed her shoe and there was the spiral tattoo. 'There, that matches the description I've got. So, you're Katell Ebrill Talog?'

'Yes, I've already said, haven't I?' His hands were coolly masterful but not in a particularly tender way. 'So, is this...foreplay? I can't say I'm impressed!'

'Let's have your other leg.'

'Nope. You didn't ask properly.'

He lifted her foot and quickly attached an ankle bracelet. Her hands went to pull at it but she couldn't remove it - she fell back into the seat. 'I hope you don't think this means were engaged?'

'We've had a great deal of trouble tracking your movements over the last few weeks. I'm not sure if it's something you do deliberately, or if you're trained to be elusive, but it's been frustrating keeping tabs on you - so which one is it?'

'Maybe it's something else - maybe you're a bunch of useless tossers?' He let this pass but she could tell she had rattled him. She pointed to the ankle bracelet: 'So, what does this mean? Are we engaged now? This is all a bit sudden - I normally expect to be wooed first.'

'No, it means we can track you, if you get away again...'

'Oh, so you're expecting to lose me then?'

He sighed. 'I'm taking you to RAF Wyton. You'll be held there for your own safety. Your commanding officer will visit you there.'

'She's in hospital with severe burns.'

'Your new commanding officer, then...'

'Who's that then? And what about my family?'

'They're probably all still asleep in bed.'

'So, why can't I go home, what am I supposed to have done?' Policewoman Hicks handed her the yellow bio-suit and gave her a respectful salute.

'The powers that be haven't worked that out yet.'

'They need a bit of a hurry-up then.'

'Hmm, the Swiss business that owns the facility isn't pressing charges yet but the HPA and the police are crawling all over it.'

'That'll be SIKS, then.'

He shepherded her out of the doors and they trotted together down the steps towards a sleek and powerful motor machine.

'By the way, do you know what happened to their server?'

'Do you mean their super computer? I think it all got muddled up.'

'Muddled up?' He gave her a strange look. 'We've seized computer equipment...never mind that, get in the car.'

'Are you going to put cuffs on me?'

'You're not under arrest.'

'Good, so I can go home then...'

'Get in the car.'

'Please?'

'Get in the car.'

'Hold on, I'm going to wear this.' She stepped into the bio-suit and pulled it on. 'That's better.'

'Is that contaminated?'

'Don't be rude! Course it's not!'

The passenger door was closed with a ceremonial and solid 'thunk' and she made herself at home in the passenger seat.

'It's quite a pretty car, isn't it? Rented?'

'No, it's my car.' A button powered up the engine and made the panel with all its controls light up. He donned leather driving gloves and handled the steering wheel and controls with smooth assurance.

'It makes a nice, growly sound when you do that' she commented, as the car accelerated.

'Pah! Have you got stomach ache?'

'No, it's the smell of your aftershave, it's a bit overpowering, isn't it?' He seemed to find the upward lilt at the end of each sentence quite excruciating, judging by the way he gritted his teeth and grimaced each time she spoke. It was his attempt to block out her continual chipping - which was never going to work.

'What are you doing down there? Please do not pleasure yourself in my car!'

'I'm not! It's this coverall, It's making me feel a bit squelchy down below, isn't it?'

'Get your hands out and put them where I can see them!'

She placed her hands on her lap and then started stroking her legs down to her knees. 'I just find this so comforting, especially when I'm in a bit of jeopardy.'

'You're not in jeopardy, we just want to make sure your safe. And stop playing with yourself? Fold your arms - no, I mean it, fold your arms!' She now started to nonchalantly massage her chest and trace around where her breasts should be.

'Sit on your hands!'

She pouted and then slowly and deliberately slipped her hands under her legs.

'You're just a silly girl. I can't believe all the trouble you've caused.'

She stared at the side of his face sullenly. 'I'm no trouble, am I?'

'And with that overall on you look like a teddy bear!'

'Well, you look like a stuffed twat.'

'Shut up!'

'So, are you Special Brunch? All special lunches and bugger all else? Where's the job satisfaction in that?'

'It's not Special Brunch...'

'Military Intelligence then? I've always thought that was a bit of a contradiction...'

Silence. Just the sound of leather on leather on the steering wheel as the car was steered quickly through a sequence of tight bends.

'Put your hands where I can see them! And stop fiddling with them!'

She placed them on the dashboard and massaged the control panel. 'So, how's your career going? You seem to have ended up being a chauffeur? That must be a bit of a let-down?' He seemed to be getting agitated and maybe a blood vessel was about to explode, judging from the throbbing she could see on his temple. Maybe she should back off on the banter a bit.

'Are you all a bit gay in Special Brunch?'

'I'm not gay' he muttered through clenched teeth.

'Transsexual then? Because, I'm okay with that...'

'Quiet!'

'Because, you could be my sex toy!'

'Silence!'

'Listen, I think we should talk, because I'm a little bit worried that this isn't going to work out...'

'What the hell are you talking about?'

'Hmm, our engagement to be married, of course.'

'What?'

'Listen, it's not going to work out if you're gay or transexual and you won't even talk to me about it...'

'I'm not!'

'I'm sorry, but I want to cancel the engagement - you can have your ring back.'

'WILL YOU SHUT UP!'

There was a pregnant silence. 'Ooooh! If I was your boss, I think we'd now be having a very, very serious conversation about your anger management issues.'

'I don't believe this!'

'Oh, my soul!' She placed her left hand carefully over the dashboard and then quickly withdrew it. He suddenly became concerned and his eyes flitted quickly over the control panel.

'What the hell is that?' Several vehicle alarms had started to flash in unison. After a few moments, he pulled over into a lay-by and parked behind a line of five lorries. 'Stay there while I check the tyres and brakes.' He exited the car and stalked to the rear. Katie opened the passenger door, rolled out of the car and then underneath. He ran back to the passenger door, looked inside and then wildly in every other direction. As he jogged down the rank of lorries, Katie rolled out from under the car and rolled under the lorry parked five yards ahead. She scrambled above the rear wheel wells and then stretched herself so she couldn't be seen. He jogged back to the car. He was shouting into his mobile phone.

'Yes, activate the tracker. She can't have gone far!'

He now ran farther down the rank of lorries.

'What do you mean it's not working? What do you mean there's no signal? I fitted it on her just minutes ago!'

As the starting motor of the lorry above her whined and the engine coughed, Katie rolled to the ground, climbed up to the off side door, pulled it open and slipped inside. She reckoned the driver was probably French and quite alarmed.

'Bonjour Monsieur, je travail dans le Ministry du Transport. Parlez vous Anglais?'

He shook his head.

'Non? Je suis désolé. Eyes on the road. Maintenant, j'ai voudrai montez un spot check de votre camion? Oui? C'est ça. Bien!'

He jabbered at her out of the corner of his mouth. He was quite young but his stubble was quite old.

'D'accord.' All she had to do was pepper her conversation with 'd'accord' and he would surely understand. 'Allez vite, c'est bonne monsieur. C'est un tres jolie camion, ne c'est pas?'

He inserted his motorcycle into the location closest to the outside of the all-night cafe, took off his helmet and gloves, locked the panniers and pushed his way through the door and was greeted with the smell of old cigarette smoke, burnt toast and stale cooking fat. He had never got used to the wide gait needed to walk comfortably in leather trousers, so he adjusted himself while he thought no one was looking and then looked around the clusters of off-white chairs and tables.

There was an attractive girl in a yellow coverall sat at a table gazing out through the window towards the road and twiddling with an empty mug. Their eyes met and she gave him a wide smile that made his loins squirm. Although she looked tired, dishevelled and distracted, as she fiddled with her mug with one hand and supported a bag of frozen chips against her temple with the other, he was compulsively drawn to her. She was the kind he yearned to meet on the road: young, alone, needy and desperate.

He decided that she must be the one and so he walked up to her table and tried a joke. 'Is it safe to eat here?' he asked, glancing at her suit and casting his eyes about the place.

She gazed back at him thoughtfully and gave a wry smile: 'Probably not, I'm just wearing this to keep the flies off.'

'Is it working?'

'No, they seem to quite like the colour.'

'My name's Ian, do you mind if I sit with you?'

'No, that's tidy' she replied. A Welsh twang, he reckoned and a long way from home. He placed his helmet and gloves on the chair next to her.

'Can I get you anything?'

'Yes, a mug of tea with milk and three sugars in it.'

'Right you are. Anything to eat?'

She gave a resigned sigh: 'A fried egg, bacon and tomato roll would be lovely.' A girl with a healthy appetite. Ideal.

'I'll see what I can do, back in a mo, that's a load of sugar!'

'And don't forget the tomato ketchup.' She picked up the tomato shaped dispenser and squirted at the table to show it was empty.

He sauntered to the counter and conversed to the lad in control of the hot plate as he smashed two eggs and smeared two rashers of streaky onto the hotplate. The hotplate jockey reckoned he had never seen her before and she had come in with a wagon, like they all do and she must have had an argument because the driver was sitting outside on his own, smoking, disowning her 'cos she was just another long haul runaway.

He returned to the table: 'So what's your story? Are you in trouble?' He slid a mug of well-sugared tea towards her.

She seemed to decide that this was the time to remove her coverall. 'Look away, I'm just going to take this off.'

So he watched her out of the corner of his eye, a mug of tea at his lips, as she rolled it down her body and over her legs and hurriedly smoothed down her rucked-up black dress.

'You looked!'

'I never did!' But he had, because she had the most extraordinary legs but just where it got interesting, all he could see was her black shorts - cycling shorts?

'Anyway, sorry about that' she apologised, 'you must've got a bit of an eyeful there!'

'No, don't be sorry, I really enjoyed that!'

'You dirty, glimping pervert!'

'No, I'm not!' So, was she Royal Navy?

She looked him up and down, and he wondered what she saw: A well-built bloke in his mid-forties, neatly cropped dark grey hair, kind, smiling eyes, slight south-east London accent and a magnet for young, lonely, desperate girls. 'What are you thinking?'

'I'm thinking what happened to my egg, bacon and tomato roll?'

'I'll be just a mo. Sit tight.'

She was watching him as he walked to the grill and came back with two rolls. 'That's brilliant' she said and she beamed widely when she realised he had also remembered the tomato ketchup dispenser. 'Anyway, I call myself Katie and I'm a Wren in the Royal Navy and now I'm...'

'On the run?'

'Um, not exactly.'

'Are you a fugitive?'

'A fugitive? From what?' She took a moment to devour a large bite of her roll.

He thought he would now demonstrate his knowledge of all things military: 'So if you're in the armed forces - does that mean you've gone absent without leave?'

'AWOL? Um, no, I'm actually on proper leave and I'm just trying to get back home, aren't I?'

'Where's home?'

'The Marches...'

'Where's that?'

'It's Shropshire, isn't it?'

'So how do you plan to get there?'

'I don't know - I'm stranded' she muttered, nodding outside to where the driver was fuming.

'You're in luck! I'm headed that way, I've got a pick up in Liverpool. I could give you a ride most of the way, if you don't mind riding pillion.' There it was, the offer, and she would be in his debt and then who knows what might happen? 'Have you got any suitable clothing?'

'Suitable for what?'

'Motorcycling.'

'Oh? No, only what I'm standing up in.'

He pondered for a moment and smiled when he realised there was a spare helmet and spare gloves in the panniers. 'That'll do, but you're going to get bloody cold!'

'I'll wear my onesie and hold on tight!'

He suddenly felt very uncomfortable in his nether regions, whatever they were. 'Excuse me for asking, but why are you wearing a yellow onesie? It looks very fetching, mind.'

'Does it? A bloke from Special Brunch reckoned I look like a teddy bear.'

He was sure she meant Special Branch, which in turn meant she was in serious bother. 'Er, did he? That doesn't sound like the kind of thing Special Branch would normally say?'

'No, I think he was a bit cross with me...'

'What happened?'

'He was...taking care of me.'

'Was he? Didn't make a very good job of it did he?' He decided not to pursue this. 'So, what's your story?'

'Um, how long have you got?'

'All the time in the world...'

'I'll...whisper in your ear if you promise not to tell.' She stood up and hauled the onesie back over her legs. There was something about her look of concentration, and her determination not to show anything, which was almost too much to bear. 'So, eat up and drink up...'

'Whoa, hold your horses...'

The girl paused in mid tug. She popped the rest of the roll in her mouth, licked her fingers and swilled back her tea. 'What is it?'

'I need to know more about you?'

'Hmm, let me see; Wren, on a promise, quick, quick!'

'Is that all I'm getting?'

'I'll flesh it out, en route. Ready? Now, take me to Clun!'

'Clun? Where the hell is that?'

'Head to Ludlow and I'll point you in the right direction, if I can stay awake. It's good of you to take me, but...what are the rules about this?'

'That doesn't matter, I'll think about how we can settle up.' His eyes twinkled, hopefully in such a way that she wouldn't think of him as a dirty, old git.

'And who are you?'

'I'm Ian, and I've got a collection to make at Liverpool University.'

'Oh, good. Are you allowed to give fugitives a lift?'

'No, that's a good point. You'll have to promise not to tell anyone.'

She engaged her little finger around his and declared: 'I solemnly promise.'

She finished donning the biohazard suit and skipped outside while he settled up inside. He left the lad with a conspiratorial wink.

'What do you think of my Tiger?' he said, waving towards his machine.

'I hope he can fly!'

The Flying Tiger? Why hadn't he thought of that? He gave her an ear-piece so she could share his music. 'I hope you like hard, driving rock.' She donned the helmet and gloves and he ensured the helmet was secure.

She was astride the pillion like she belonged there. With a good run they would arrive in Clun in two and a half hours and then who knows what could happen?

Katie was relieved to get off the motorcycle and beat some life into her chilled legs and arms. After two minutes of her warming war dance, she was ready to remove the biohazard suit and enter the cafe. It was barely morning, and the air was very fresh, but despite prolonged inhalations and careful listening, there was nothing new being borne to her on the gentle, westerly breeze. Not a thing.

Ian went to the counter to bring back hot drinks, while she leaned over the juke box, her fingers flitting through the options. She accepted the well-sugared tea and decided it was time to ask the question.

'So, are you married, Ian?'

'Do I look married?'

'Well, no, you actually look like you were married before...'

'Eh?'

'...but now I think you look separated, with no kids to worry about and your life is a little bit empty.'

'Alright, alright, who've you been talking to?'

'Just you, but it's written all over you and your soul...'

'For Christ's sake! What else do you think you know about me?'

'Um, that's it really, but there's a dark spot...'

'A dark spot? What the hell are you on about?'

'The bit where your little demon lives...'

'For Christ's sake! What are you talking about?'

'But it's nothing to worry about...'

'Why mention it then?'

'Because, you need to know...' She could tell he was fretting now so she grasped his hand to try and console him but he pulled it away.

'You know all about me but I know nothing about you!'

'I gave you the six word version! I couldn't give you the long version because my lips got frozen to my teeth!'

'Alright, just calm down. We need to sort out what you owe me...'

'We didn't sort that out, did we? But I've got an idea...I'm going to dance for you, because I know you like that kind of stuff!'

'You're kidding. Here?' He looked around; there were three other drivers in the place and they were all looking her way.

'Yes!' There were three tracks that she felt would be suitable. Katie positioned herself in front of Ian, as he slumped into a chair, and she slapped her hand on the jukebox to start the performance.

And it started: ten minutes of spiralling, whirling, hip grinding motion that became infamous in service station security history; caused the Association of British Ballroom Dancers to be petitioned; defined a radical new style of modern dance now known from this moment as Wild Abandonment.

Her hips rocked to and fro, her arms extended and rotated as she promenaded across a row of tables.

She waved at the juke box and the second track started. 'Gonna get your motor running mate!' She shimmied and she strolled and worked her hips to the beat. 'Is this working for you?' she cried out.

'Oh yes, it's working for me' he said.

She clicked her fingers at the juke box and the next track played.

'Now, I'm going to drive you really crazy!' She raised her hands above her head and clapped to very second beat, stomped on the spot and swayed her skirt to and fro. And now she attacked the solo segment, promenaded to her right and then to her left and beat out a crescendo of flamenco taps.

'More!'

'I'm rockin' in the house of blue light!' she wailed as the rocked to the east and then to the west.

'Come on baby, drive me crazy!'

'Do it, do it, do it!'

'More!'

'I'm a hard headed woman and you're a soft hearted man!' She tottered on the table...

'You've been causing trouble since time began!'

'Gonna rock and roll down to Ludlow Town!' The table tipped...

'More!'

'I'm going!'

He caught her, just as she fell. 'My God you're weird, but you're wonderful with it!'

'I'll take that, though I don't feel too wonderful at the moment!' She sat in his lap gasping for air. 'Oi! Don't prod me!' She swept aside the sweat soaked locks that bounced about her face.

'I'm not!'

She sluiced back her tea. 'Eh, shouldn't we be back on the road again? Everyone's waking now!'

'Give me a minute! I just need to straighten myself out!'

Within thirty minutes they had arrived in Clun, and had pulled over at the foot of the track that led to Clun Cottage. They pulled off their helmets together.

'Ian, basically, you're a good man' she said as she fumbled for a pen in her satchel, 'but you just need to be mindful of your little demon, because they can be right, righteous, little gits and they think they're helping but they're really not.'

'So, what happens now?'

'Well, basically, you piss off to Scouseland and do what you promised, like I have to do...'

'And that's it?'

'Actually, not quite - can I write on you?'

'Eh?'

'I was just going to write that I, Katie Talog, promise to pay the bearer on demand, anything he wants. Then I was going to sign it.'

'No, you bloody well can't!'

'Oh! In that case, I will need something personal from you, something with your essence in. It's probably going to be a lock of your hair.'

'Why do you need it? I'm quite keen that you don't mess me up any more!'

'Well, I don't think ear-hole wax will work or finger nails or toenails, and I'm definitely not going down for your pubes. But, it's quite lush just here.' He yelled as she quickly pulled a pinch of hair from his chest - it left a bit of a gap, but it probably wouldn't show. She scrawled a triple spiral across his wrist then added her initials. 'There you go!'

They patted each other on the back and Ian was on his way. Neither of them had known what else to say, so the parting was short and abrupt.

Katie murmured out a quick incantation to the god that protects travellers and then walked quickly up the track but now her pace slowed to a crawl. An acrid smell was assaulting her nostrils and she could see the cause - a shallow burial of diseased sheep and the scurrying of brown rats amongst the limbs that poked above the soil. She fought the temptation to cry, but the whole flock must have perished.

Onwards she walked until she was near the cottage and listening carefully. She removed the biohazard suit and draped it over the scarecrow and then run at a crouch until she was below the window to Stefan's study. All she could hear were big, man-size sobs that tore at her soul.

Katie crept around the cottage until she reached the cottage garden - it was overrun with nettles. She felt around the lock of the kitchen door and worked it open and she was through. At the foot of the stairs she could hear Gwen punching her pillow and calling out for Stefan to just stop his sobbing. Katie took a deep breath and opened the door to the cupboard below the stairs and pulled out her rucksack. A wave of exhaustion poured over her. She had to rest.

Chapter Seventy-Two

Tuesday 31 May 0625 - The Vicarage

Gwen took two phone calls in quick succession: the first was the Cambridgeshire Police asking for help in finding her missing sister; the other called to say that when Miss Talog arrived, she should call back immediately. Gwen slammed the phone down, tears making salty slicks down her face.

Gwen walked up the stairs and turned automatically towards Monique's room; she opened the door slowly to look inside. Monique was asleep under the bedclothes with Owain the sheepdog and Katie, the witch on top. Gwen strode quickly to the bed and seized Katie's arm. She was awake immediately. 'Come with me' Gwen whispered. She dragged her bedraggled sister, who dragged her rucksack to the landing and then down the stairs into the kitchen. Gwen pulled Katie round so that she could confront her: 'Look what you've done!'

'I've done nothing and I'm not the reason for any of this!'

'And you think you think you can just come back here and put us all at risk?'

'There's no guilt in my heart, Gwen!'

'No, just this stupid, stupid promise!'

'No promise is stupid, Gwen.'

'This one is.'

'I need to rest. I have had a bit of a time of it over the last few days...'

'You don't care about us, after all we've done for you!'

'Of course I care, I took one to protect your kids...oh, shitty, shitty, shit, shit, shit!'

'You did what?'

'Took one...' She popped her satchel into the rucksack, squeezing to make sure the vial was still there. 'But they were after Monique.'

'Tell me what happened!'

Katie's nose wrinkled as she attempted to put together a reply but it was very difficult. 'When?'

'You know when!'

Katie slipped the rucksack over her shoulder. 'Ask the verger.'

'The verger? Our verger?

'Not our verger, your verger!'

'What...happened!'

'She marked me!'

Gwen didn't appear to be shocked by this. 'Is Monique part of this deceipt?'

'No, but Al is.'

'I don't believe it!'

'Well, just think about it and it'll all become clear, won't it?'

'Alexander has said nothing.'

'No, but that's because we made a pact.'

Gwen glared at Katie, her lips were tightly set.

Katie got ready to duck the coming blow. They danced around the kitchen table but Katie's rucksack caught on the cupboard handle. The blow came but Katie caught Gwen's wrist and twisted it away. Gwen twisted but she was pulled flat against the refrigerator and she couldn't move. Katie moved up close and pressed her left index finger to Gwen's forehead.

'Please don't do this Katie, please don't...'

'Realise this. You are blessed with powers. You can read other's minds. You need to work out how to use this to bring your family together!'

Katie paused to let this sink in.

'Realise this. Your daughter is blessed with powers. You need to sit her down and help her through this...and protect her from the verger!'

'Please, Katie!'

'Realise this. I'm doubly cursed. I don't know what I can do about it. No one can help me now, not you, not anybody.'

'But, you're not alone!' Gwen bared her left shoulder.

'Oh shit! You as well!' Katie removed her finger and Gwen fell away from the refrigerator, flopped into a chair and started to cry softly into her hands. 'There's a whole sodding coven of you!'

'Mama! Auntie Katie!' shouted Eek from the landing above. The sky had darkened and there was a storm coming.

'I've got to go. Look after your mum.'

'Auntie Katie, don't go!'

'Nothing's been done here, has it? Nothing! I'm all on my own!'

Katie stepped outside. The sun was blocked out by a dark grey cloud looming above the hill and her body shuddered. She felt the first blob of rain slap her face. It was going to be a monster of a storm. She ran to the scarecrow, ripped off his yellow suit, tugged it on and then tugged her rucksack back on. It was as dark as night. The first flash heralded a thumping rumble of thunder.

She slapped her palms against her thighs. 'I am not a sodding witch! I am not a sodding witch!'

The ground heaved slowly under her feet like she was standing on the back of a massive heaving, monster; the muscles in her legs reacted like she was balancing on the deck of frigate in a heaving sea. What was going on below?

The sky darkened and another golf ball sized blob splattered like a crown on the ground. She shivered as she felt the number of blobs of rain increase. She was hit on the head and recoiled in surprise. There was a shout behind her. Stefan stood outside the front door, looking more and more bedraggled. There was a slight, trembling figure coming to her, it was Eek. Her hands offered a mug of liquid.

'Thank you Eek, what is it?'

'It's water, Auntie Katie.'

Katie took the cup and drained it. It was water. As she held the cup out, it filled again with globs of rain.

'Get inside Eek, find your mum and give her a big hug. She needs you.'

'Where are you going?'

'I'm going to find my mum, and then...'

'Are you going to give her a big hug?'

Katie didn't reply immediately as she thought about the best way to answer that question. 'Something like that.'

Katie arrived at a crossroads in the village and considered which direction to take. She turned right, walked quickly up the road and turned sharply down the lane that led to a rambling, red brick Victorian house. A large oak door with gilt trimmings stood before her. She thumped the door with her fist and listened. Footfalls came to the door. It opened slowly.

She saw deep brown eyes that opened brightly and a brown face that went from curiosity and then wonder in half a moment. 'She's here! She's here! Exactly as you said master! Praise be to god! She's here!'

She offered her hand. He took it, kissed the top of it and drew her further inside.

'I'm sorry, I'm dripping wet. Is the vicar in?'

A woman bustled up. 'Oh my goodness, you are soaked to the skin. Take your things off and we'll get you warmed up!' She was small, with neat, short grey hair, a white pinafore and a bustling air of efficiency.

'Is the vicar in?' Katie asked. The woman seemed to offer better prospects than the boy who opened the door. He was now prostrated before her with his forehead pressed hard against the floor tiles. She bent down to ruffle the hair on the top of his head, her fingers probing the ebony skin between black tufts of hair.

'You came for me! It is you! It is you!' he chanted.

'Yes, it's me!'

'But she must get her clothes off first, Cilmi, she can't come in here dripping water like that!' And she was dripping water steadily on the boy's head.

'I am blessed!'

'No, I'm just dripping on you!' Katie looked behind her. The house was sealed off from view of the village by bushes that sported cream and pink blooms. She removed the rucksack, the biohazard suit, her long black dress and her shoes. Surely, that would be enough, wouldn't it? The vicar's housekeeper considered her attire for a moment, beckoned Katie inside and then instructed her to deposit her wet things in the porch. She was led to the back of the house, though the hallway, through a reception room to the kitchen. The oil-fired stove was alight.

'It has got very cold suddenly, hasn't it, dear?'

'Yes, the storm came down very suddenly. I think the cottage on the hill got the worst of it.' She was now shivering, partly through cold, partly through exhaustion and partly through not knowing what was going to happen to her.

'You poor thing. What name shall I give?'

'Say its Katie, no, no, Katell Ebrill Talog. He will know who I am.'

'Parish business?'

'Not really, it's a bit personal, isn't it?'

'Ah, I see. Let me call the reverend. I think he may have been expecting you. Take a seat.'

Katie was left on her own. Her clothes and the rucksack started to steam and her underclothes started to feel clammy. She opened the rucksack, loosened the inner bag and delved inside to pull out dry ones.

'Ah, Miss Talog. What on earth has happened to you?'

'Ah, vicar, quite a lot and I do need to go through it with you, now.'

'And why me, pray tell?'

'There is no one else! My lot don't do forgiveness, they just do revenge! Your lot do forgiveness, don't they? Only your lot will do that, don't they Vic?'

'Have you breakfasted, Katie?'

'No, does that help? There's not been time. I've just had an almighty ruck with my family and...'

'The Hoflands?'

'Yes, I left Gwen in pieces, and...'

'Let's get you warmed up. Mrs Evans, please can you do the honours? Cilmi, come with me. Let's find towels for Miss Talog.'

'Cilmi? Do we know each other?' murmured Katie, her brow knitted in a frown. A sequence of images flashed by her eyes, images of a raging sea and raging winds.

Clutched tight in his hand was a roll of fabric, the colour of a Royal Navy flight suit. She could see the stitching of letters on it: a capital 'O' and a capital 'G'.

'You came from the sea! You are the sea witch! You saved me!'

'I am not a witch!'

Below and beyond, below and beyond; the light blue sky; the deep blue sea; the verdant green islands with burnt-red beaches; something was surging quickly through the water, stirring the waves, rippling layers of air and agitating the visor and the inner workings of Katie's helmet. She removed it and her palms stroked the shiny, bulb-like surface.

There was something big below, powering through the shallow waters in the channel below and leaving an ugly perturbation behind.

'There's a sea monster, heading east of north-east, going like the clappers!' Katie was in the bucket seat at the front of the helicopter cabin, just behind the pilot and co-pilot seats in the Lynx helicopter. The cabin thrummed from the whirring of the rotor above.

'Adjusting course, twenty degrees starboard. Let's track that' replied Flight Commander Scotty Scott from the pilot's seat. The thrumming of the rotors changed pitch as the helicopter altered course.

'Nothing on the screen - could be a whale' muttered Flight Commander Nutter Nutley from the co-pilot's seat. He prodded buttons in the seat mounted panel to his right side and strained to look at the green screen displays in the console in front of him. 'Jesus H. Christ, would you look at that!' The wake of something big was now foaming through the channel, far too close to the surface to be comfortable. 'It's a sub - look at it go!'

'Nutter, message the Albany. Any blue units in this zone?'

'On it.'

'Collide. They're going to collide, with another boat, it's too fast, too shallow, can we flash 'em a warning?' shouted Katie. 'Course twenty-five degrees, doing twenty knots. It can't be one of ours. My money's on Chinese...'

'Lost it! It's gone deep!'

'That fishing boat has turned into a turtle!' The Lynx slowed and descended.

'It's turning turtle, Tally, fancy a dunk?'

'Sure. I'm ready. You got me Nutter?'

'Got you, lowering now!'

The helicopter hovered above and Katie hovered above the sea. There was a survivor!

The sea slapped and slurped against the hull of the upturned, rough planked, wooden boat. Katie swung about on the end of the wire, in the grip of the freshening breeze that blew in from the dry, reddened wilderness to the West. So close to the coast! As she rocked to and fro, the horizon ebbed and flowed with it. The contents of her stomach were heading upwards.

She burped and pardoned herself. 'I can see a survivor Nutter, drop me five!'

'Abort Tally, abort, the wind's getting up! Too much!'

'Drop me five Nutter, I've got them!'

There was a huge sigh in her ears. 'Make it quick Tally, there's the mother of all hooleys heading our way.' Must get the both of them in one lift - one was clawing the planks of the boat, one splashing wildly in the surf, five lunges away. Her feet scrabbled on the hull of the boat, not getting any purchase. A boy lunged at her, seizing her leg with long, sinewy arms. She grabbed the collar of his shirt and heaved him up. There was screaming below her. One was hooked in the harness, cradled between two yellow, ribbed arms, couldn't fall. She gasped: 'I've got one secure. Forward five, NOW!'

She couldn't see the second boy. Was that a hand rising, above the up and down of the water? Her body, nearly horizontal, every sinew stretching, fingers touching, wrist clasped to a pale brown wrist, his shaking head just there, wide eyed, flailing, flailing. A jump and his pale brown hand seized her collar and wrenched at it, rending fabric. A wave flooded them. She cursed through the wet of the salt, exhorted all the gods to bring him to her, but the vortex was pulling, sucking the boy below. She wriggled and squirmed, clutching for his waving arms as he dropped.

Gone was his face, a mask of calm resignation, to whatever was going to happen to him; he had reached out to her and he was ready for whatever might befall him, swallowed by the great blue.

'Reel me in Nutter, one secure, one lost. Shitty, shitty, shit, shit, shit.' She twisted in her harness. Boy number one was clutched close, they were face to face, his arms hooked through the harness, and they were spiralling together, up through the ripping of the wind and the spray of the frothing sea. 'I've got you, you're safe' she shouted through the visor of the helmet. Still they spun on the wire as they climbed upwards. The mechanical chopping of the rotors grew louder. They were swung into the cabin. 'I lost one, he was sucked down.'

Nutter acknowledged this. 'We got this one Tally. You did all you could. Look at all this shit coming in!' He pointed to the dark boiling clouds coming from the west. The chopper was bucking like a wild horse.

The boy was released from the harness. She sat him in the seat next to her's. His eyes implored her to go again. Nutter shook his head. The Lynx swayed in the wind. 'Get yourself strapped in, Tally. We'll get our lad back to the Albany.'

'Just face it Tally, you can't win 'em all' consoled Scotty.

'Why not? I called on the gods, but they didn't fucking help, did they?'

'Don't call on the gods, Tally, call on yourself. Fuck the gods, Tally!'

'What's your name, mate? Fahmi?'

The boy's eyes were closed - he was praying to the one god.

'Gods are there to help. What's the point of having them, if they don't help when you need 'em? I saw his mate's face as he went down - he thought I was gonna save him!'

'Cilmi.'

'Cilmi? Is that his name? Let's give him a prayer...you never know, you never know.'

There was a long uncomfortable pause, as Cilmi looked in her eyes, looked to her left and then to her right and then at her bare feet. He stroked her feet with the back of his hand, the hand that clutched so tight the knuckles were white. 'You saved me! Now I save you!' The roll of fabric was brought out of his hand, unfurled and the pendant inside rolled into her palm and they held the pendant together, raising it above her head and then placing it reverentially around her neck, so the light danced rainbows through the endless, triple spiral. It settled in place, above her heart.

'Tris!' she shrieked.

'Tris?'

'But what happened to your mate, Cilmi? Where is he? Is he here? What happened to you!'

'No, he's not here Katie, but he's safe, you rescued him, remember?' murmured the Vicar with a ludicrously wide smile on his face.

'But I lost you, I lost you...' She saw Cilmi's face, his staring eyes, staring up at her as she swung from the winch and then he was staring at the wide grey sky, the vortex pulling him below. And then he was swamped, a wild clutch at the neck of her overall and then a resigned calmness as he was taken below. 'I lost you, I lost you to the big blue...'

'But I'm alive, I'm saved, I'm telling you!'

'I didn't save you, I lost you!'

'No, no, no. See, your pendant! I took it and I was saved! It was you!'

'Cilmi, please go now...'

'But, I'm saved. Cilmi and Fahmi are saved!'

'Go now!'

She watched as Cilmi slunk away.

'Listen, Vicar I've done some bad things, vicar. I lost Cilmi to the big blue and a soldier...'

'Tell me about the soldier, child.'

'There was this man, badly wounded, his name was Benoit. I sent his soul on his way, but he came back to life, I don't know how!'

'You saved his life, there is no sin in that!'

'Didn't you hear me? I sent his soul to hell!'

'Although you are not a Christian, I can see you have a good soul. We have the same values, we just go about our business in...very different ways.'

'Eh?'

'The triskelion, is a symbol, just like our Holy Trinity...'

'Really? It just means air, land and sea to me, with the fire at the heart to ignite it all!'

'Yes, whatever.' He laid his palms on her brow. 'Katell Ebrill Talog, I absolve you of all guilt for these confessed sins. In the eyes of our Lord, no crime has been committed and therefore, there is no penance.'

'Thanks Vic!'

'Now Katell Ebrill Talog, go and fulfil your promise!'

Despite putting on clean and dry clothes: a loose fitting shirt and multi-pocketed trousers, a frock coat of many pockets, belted at the waist; boots, socks and a warm rucksack: Katie still felt the damp on her skin and in her bones. But, there was a thermos of sweet tea in the side pocket of the rucksack and a fistful of chocolate biscuits in her hand and so she was as ready as she was ever going to be.

Katie followed the drive to the road, and found a vehicle with big, rubber tyres, waiting for her. A long sinewy arm came out and she gratefully took it and was pulled inside the cab.

'Hallo Ben, how are you doing?'

'I'm wondering what I'm doing here?' he said as he passed her his oilskin.

She wrapped the oilskin around her shoulders. 'I need to find my mum. Follow the road down to the valley and head for Newtown.'

'Where in the name of God did that lot come from?' he said, looking to the rapidly clearing skies.

'The rain? It fell from up above, didn't it?'

'And now it's stopped' he noted cheerfully. And so it had. As suddenly as it had started, the rain had stopped. The ground heaved a sign of relief and started to suck the water away. Rivulets cheerfully chuckled and trickled down the road. The sun bathed the glistening ground in a shiny iridescence. 'So, what happened to you?' Ben seemed to have a keen interest in the way her clothes had moulded themselves to the contours of her body.

'I got changed at the vicar's - so, how come you came?'

'The vicar asked me to.'

'He does work in mysterious ways, doesn't he?'

'I heard an argument between you and your sister, Katie? You never did get along, did you?'

'News travels fast in the valley, doesn't it?'

'It's your shrieking voice that travels...'

'Well, what it is, Ben, is that we're too alike, aren't we?'

Ben laughed. 'No you ain't, you're totally different. You couldn't be more different, you're as different as different could be!' There was a pause that was uncomfortably long. 'So, where to?'

'Take me to...the moon, Ben!'

'Hold on Katie, we're not doing that.'

'No, you're right, you'll need a lot of juice for that.' The tractor had jostled its way down the road and was now trundling through the village. She waved at the puzzled faces they passed along the street. Their faces remained even more puzzled. They followed the valley to the west.

And then there was a another long silence as the tractor careered down the road and trundled out of the other side of the village. 'Thanks for helping me, Ben.' She wondered about how best to bring up the subject of his love life. 'So, how's it going with Sheepy Clara?'

'Just leave it be Katie, please.'

'Are you still seeing her?'

'No!'

'Good. Why ever not?'

'You know why not!'

'Do I? Is it because she's an imaginary girl and she doesn't actually exist, because they're the worst kind of girl, Ben.'

'Yes, that's it.'

'I'm not sorry to hear that Ben. She was never going to be any good for you, being an imaginary girl. But you made me fight for you Ben, what was that all about?'

'I have feelings for you Katie, I always have...'

'I know, but it's been difficult, Ben.' She felt a sudden rush of desire, or was it just lust? It was painful. It consumed her. Her heart bulged in excitement and her breathing became very deep. 'Well, let me tell you what I see, Ben. I see me making a home for us, for me and you and Owain, we will have a squabble of hens and a whinny of goats, we will have two kids, a boy and a girl, and I will make you the happiest man in the world...there, that's what I see. What do you think about that, Ben?'

'What about my mum?'

'What about your mum?' she snapped back.

'You should make room...'

'I'm sorry Ben, but there's no room in my dream for your mum!'

'But she's the only mum I'll ever have!'

A silver saloon overtook them with its horn blaring.

'You need to keep your eyes on the road, Ben' she commented tartly.

'Sorry.'

'Ben, there's nothing I'd like better than to throw you on the ground and do you until your brains come squirting out of your ears, but...'

'You're my fantasy girl, Katie, you always have been. I dream about you every night, since I saw you again...that night in the pub.'

'Oh, really' she thought. Her loins still ached but the moment had passed. If he mentioned his mother again, that would be it.

'Mum will be wondering where I am.' Her desire evaporated away like the last residue of moisture from her damp clothes. The tractor turned into the main street and pulled into the garage. 'I'll get some gas' he commented as he hopped out of the cab. He filled the diesel tank and a spare container. He went to the public phone box and made a long animated phone call. She was ready to discard the oilskin - she was warm now - and she was ready to discard Ben.

He was back in the cab and he was smiling. 'My mum's wondering where I am, so I told her. She's not happy. She says there's a big fuss going on at Clun Cottage. There's lots of shouting and screaming and toing and froing.' She says I ought to take you back.' He offered her a sausage roll and a polystyrene cup of tea. 'So, what am I going to do with you, Katie?'

'Just take me over the border, Ben, to Kerry Hill. I need to find my mum.'

'What about me and you?' he said.

'Let me sort out what I need to do and then I'll get back to you Ben.' She paused for thought. 'These dreams you have about me. What happens?'

'I can't tell you. Katie, they're, they're very difficult for me to talk about, they're private...'

'I need to know Ben, I need to know what's in your dreams...'

The engine of the tractor had kicked back into life and they were now trundling to the West.

'So, where am I heading?' he asked at the junction.

'Left' she replied, and head towards Kerry Hill.' The tractor was now heading along the ridgeway and making the slow climb up to Moat Hill.

'I need to know, Ben, you need to tell me what's going on in your head.' They were on a long straight section of road. She clutched his arm and drew her head into the warmth of his clothes. 'Tell me, Ben.'

'We're flying together over the sea...'

'Oh, oh, what sea is that?'

'It's a very large sea, no land in sight. We don't know where we're going but we're flying...high up in the sky.'

'That sounds nice. What happens?'

'It goes dark, something blots out the sun. Something big, something bad...' They passed the Dog and Duck Cottage and she acknowledged a wave from the apron-wearing woman tending flowers in the garden. They were now over Offa's Dyke. Round Bank loomed ahead of them.

'It, it swallows you and spits you out. You fall into the sea. I can't see you anywhere. You're gone.' He gulped and surreptitiously wiped a tear from his eye.

'And that's it? That doesn't sound good. This evil thing, what's it like?'

'Just big and evil. Let's talk about something else.'

'All right, like what?'

'Do you remember Will Haycocks? He's reforming the village band. He's going to call it 'Isolator'. Are you in?'

'Isolator? Why? That sounds a bit doomy, doesn't it?'

'It'll be all acoustic again, me on guitar, Will on fiddle, Tonny on squeeze box, you on vocals...'

'Well Ben, I'll sing and dance for you and do some raggedy percussion if you want.'

'Will you wear those black shorts?'

'What, the little ones? I think you're really pushing your luck now!'

'If you don't wear them, we'll make you audition!'

'You dirty sod! All right, I will if everyone else will.'

'I think people will come a long way to see you in black shorts, but not the rest of us.' His cheeks had gone a brilliant pink.

'Well, obviously, but I want to see...oh, never mind.' She squeezed his arm and smiled. Then the fragile smile disappeared. She stood up on the seat. The tractor rocked along the road as their route ebbed away into a track. They were in a plantation of conifer trees that crowded their way up to the track and the air was thick with the smell of pine resin. A slow moving, horse-drawn vehicle was being turned around and it blocked their way forward. The tractor closed the gap slowly but surely. It was a caravan, with rubber-tyred wheels being pulled by a tired, brown and white horse.

Katie climbed onto the front of the throbbing tractor engine and crouched. They were now so close that she could step onto the rear of the caravan and edge her way along the frame above the wheels. The tractor engine whined as it slowed and then came to a halt. She slid alongside the driver and pulled the reins tight. The tired, brown and white beastie, responded immediately, neighed, swung his head back towards Katie and came to a halt.

'Alright Mum? You seem to be in a hurry? What are you running from?'

Katie jumped down from the caravan and immediately she was confronted by a boy she recognised. It was the home-help, Dafyd. 'Bore da, princess' he said. He came uncomfortably close to her and then closer still.

'Bore da, Dafyd' she replied. 'If you get between me and my mum you will get hurt, so back off.'

Ben came up and stood just behind her. The tractor engine and the horse were now quiet. 'Mum, I need to talk to you, just me and you, or...'

'Or what, child?' asked Maela. She took the delicate wooden stemmed pipe out of her mouth and tapped it out on the side of the caravan.

'I'll turn Dafyd into food for the trees...' She raised her left hand, palm leading, towards his chest. It touched. Dafyd took two steps to his side and clutched his chest. 'Away' Katie cried. His body lurched backwards and he was gasping on the ground.

'Child, you are troubled' said Maela, 'leave him be...'

'Send him away.'

'Send your pet away...'

'Ben, Ben, leave me now.'

'I'm not leaving you Katie, you need me...'

'I'll deal with this. Tell Gwen what's happened. Tell her I'm dealing with mum. Tell her to be at the field of Camlan, two dawns from now...'

'But Katie...'

'Go now Ben. Camlan, two dawns from now! And tell Gwen to bring Owain, because I will need the both of them!'

The tractor engine fired up. Ben swung it into a slow motion manoeuvre that took it back in the direction of England. The tractor slowly disappeared into the distance.

'I said I would come back and here I am. Are you ready, mum?'

'Just let me tend to Dafyd.' Maela knelt by his side and helped him to his feet. Katie took off her woollen hat and let her hair cascade around her shoulders. 'You've changed Ebrill, and not for the better...' She embraced Dafyd, whispered long and hard in his ear and then patted him on his back as he trudged into the forest.

'You knew all of this was going to happen to me and you did nothing to warn me, nothing to prepare me.' She examined her mum's face carefully. She looked completely calm and rational. Her eyes were dark, closed pools and Katie could not see behind them.

'Oh, I think I did but you kept running, my child...'

'Listen, things have started to happen to my body...'

'Yes, those things can be dreadful, but you're just experiencing growing pains, we all have these. Some of us are better at handling it than others.'

Katie looked behind her. Ben's tractor was now like a shiny green beetle trundling along the track, going about its daily business. Dafyd was now out of sight in the forest. Soon there was the loud 'thunk' of axe against helpless wood. 'They're not growing pains' she hissed.

'Why don't you tell me about them? Whatever your travails, I'm here for you now.' Maela commenced the feeding of shag into her silver-bowled pipe.

'What travels? You're not here for me now, you're thinking about Dafyd! You are the worst mum in the world!'

'You do not know what pain I had to endure, your birth...'

'My birth? You just squirted me out, wiped your fanny and said, job done!'

'Ohhhhh, it was never like that, you vulgar, vulgar child, such pain, such pain. I think you need to grow into yourself, and do it quickly.'

'You never bothered with that, did you mum? So who brought me up? Because it wasn't you, was it? You were too worried about your tits shrivelling up!'

'Ohhhhh, you horrible, disgusting, vulgar child!'

'What? No more denials, mum? Nothing else to say? So, who was my suckle nanny, mum? Who was it?'

There was a long pause while Maela's nose and her lips flittered: 'Your sister.'

'My sister? Not Gwen!'

'Yes.'

'What?'

'Yes, not Gwen. Your sister, Gwenllian, not your sister Gwenaëlle.'

'I don't know a Gwenllian, do I, do I?'

'I named her after the warrior princess...'

'No wait, wait, I've got another sister? Nooooo!'

'All right, she can't be. Have it your own way, this is what you do...'

Katie staggered away towards the trees, thoughts whirling through her mind. There was a solitary oak tree in front of her. She encircled it with her arms and pulled tight because her own world had started to sink away into the soil. In the furrows of the bark, there was a busy, busy world of small crawling animals, going about their busy, mechanical existence. Big, brown ants that stunk of acid, larger, greener, more delicate creatures, with long, gangly legs that were the food of the ants, then there was the call of the yaffle to her side, sounding curious and agitated all at the same time. It hopped over the leaf litter, green and red, wide eyed, strong billed, with a long tongue, snaffling ants. She tried to work out where she fitted in the pecking order of things - it was somewhere below the green, gangly creatures.

Katie felt ready to talk to her mum again. She pushed herself away from the tree trunk and turned to confront her mother. 'So, I have another sister, called Gwen. She must be about Gwen's age, or...'

'Younger...'

'I'm lost, I can't make sense of any of this...you had a child after Gwen, called Gwen, how was that possible? How could that happen? What were you thinking?'

'You have several sisters...'

'I don't believe this...'

Maela started to work along the fingers of her right hand. 'There's Gwenaëlle, she's the oldest, then there's Gwenllian and Morwenna, she's next, then Angharad and...'

'But Gwenllian, she was my tit nanny...where is she now?'

'She's married. She has two grown up children. She lives with her partner in Rhayader. I had other, more pressing duties. I couldn't attend to you.'

'Go on, what could they be, mum? What could be more important? Hold on, none of this makes sense... you had another family? You had two families going at the same time? So who looked after me?'

'Your nana.'

'My nain? But she was...your mum!'

'Of course!'

'But...I thought she had died. I thought you said she was dead?'

'I may have exaggerated a little...'

'I thought you had buried her?'

'She is not buried. We do not bury the living, unless they're very, very bad people.'

'I can't deal with this. Do you mean she's still alive? Why didn't you tell me! Where is she?'

'She's over there' said Maela, pointing vaguely westward in the direction of the Cambrian Mountains.

'Why didn't you tell me!'

'Because you knew. She has been calling you.'

Katie clutched at her chest, not knowing what to do. Her gut was telling her to go quickly. 'How can she be alive, mum?'

'She's in a kind of stasis, trapped between the worlds.'

'Who's got her?'

'You already know this.'

The women of the Elenydd.

'Why haven't you gone to her?'

Maela struck a match and lit the pipe. 'They are powerful witches; they will destroy everything I have. Dafyd has already been poisoned against me.'

'Oh, I am sorry about that mum...but what about nana?'

'She has had her time...'

'What...about...nana!'

'Dafyd is no longer willing, I fear he is attracted to younger...'

'Slebog!'

'How dare you!'

'Slebog, slebog, slebog! You've spent your life whoring. Your life is a crock of shite, you're nothing but a dried up whore!'

Maela's eyes flashed and she pushed the stem of her pipe into the soil.

They paced around each other, looking, sensing, feeling for the moment, Maela turning as if her daughter was tethered, like a spider's prey, wriggling helplessly in her web, being drawn in. Katie extended her left arm and felt a power surging through her arteries again. 'I will return you to the soil as dust, Mum, you will be food for the trees. That's all you are good for!'

But she hesitated, then held back, she could not bring herself to strike.

'You would harm your mother?' Maela wailed.

Katie's arms dropped to her sides. 'No, I wouldn't.'

They were face to face, Katie's arms pinioned to her sides, as if wrapped in the spider's gossamer.

Maela's arms struck out and grasped Katie's neck and squeezed. In the next moment, a tendon was twisted spitefully. Katie shrieked and staggered backwards, she was falling and spinning through the air. She bounced heavily, rolled and lay gasping for air. Maela prowled about her.

Katie tried to move her left arm but she couldn't. She tried to move her shoulder but couldn't. There was a paralysing pain in her left side which meant she could move nothing, not even her ribcage.

She held her breath and waited for what must surely come, the end blow. There was the concerned face of Dafyd coming into her view, as he approached slowly. 'Is she...?'

'No, she's in a quiet repose' replied Maela, 'because I've disengaged her left side but it will pass, after a day or so. The women of the Elenydd will see that she is no longer a threat.' There was a metal cylinder, hung over her shoulder, and the cap was open. Her hands flittered through the contents and withdrew a tattered logbook.

'Have this read to you, before you do anything, Ebrill.' The logbook was thrust roughly inside her shirt. 'If you still decide to find her, make sure she eats this before she goes!'

Katie tried again to move her left arm but couldn't.

'Such a shame, because my daughter thought she had a promise to fulfil, but it is better this way.' Her foot pushed firmly against Katie's arm and she started to roll slowly down the slope.

'My, you were awesome!' replied Dafyd.

'I was wasn't I? There's life in the old women yet!' She kicked at Katie's torso and it rolled more quickly.

The jabbing pain stabbed mercilessly into her left side, over and over.

'But what happens now, my lady?'

'We will lay up over the border, where we will be safe. Her nana will subside soon, I feel it. I will not miss her, she has caused so much conflict, so much distress, so much distress...' The horse whinnied.

'You were the one that they wanted, Ebrill,' Maela cried out, 'they thought you were the special one, the one that they had to take so that the rest of us could live our lives in peace. You were the one, Ebrill!'

Katie's mind was in a whirlpool, spinning round and round and the pain became too much too bear.

And then, Maela's voice was muffled because her mouth was swamped by Dafyd's and they fell down together to the soil, rolling through the heather and the grasses, panting and giggling.

Katie looked up to the sky, because it was the only direction she could look. Her arms were spread into the heather but they were still connected to her. She moved her fingers, first of the right hand and then the left hand. And then the pain swamped her and her consciousness evaporated away.

And she awoke, spread out and cosseted in the depths of the heather, where she could see grizzled plants, hear excitable birds and frenetic bees all around her. As she lay motionless she carried out a quick inventory of her limbs - all seemed present and correct, but she wasn't sure where she was or what had happened.

A shadow came upon her.

She gasped and it hurt down her left side.

A figure knelt close to her side, a young, anxious man, with a riot of tawny hair only partly concealed by the hood of his mid-blue cagoule. 'What happened to you?'

'Fell!' she gasped.

'Out of a plane?' he asked in alarm.

'No!' Even moving her jaw brought a reaction from her chest. She hoped that her terse responses wouldn't drive him away.

'You fell? How?'

'Fighting' she replied.

'Who with?'

'My mum.'

He looked perplexed at this. 'Fighting with your mum?'

'I lost.'

She hoped he wasn't going to repeat everything she said or this was going to be a very tortuous, tedious and tiresome conversation.

'You lost? Why were you fighting? What was it about?'

She ignored all this. 'First Aid?' she asked.

'I have a first aid badge' he replied.

Good, she thought. 'Good hands?' she asked.

'I'm a scout. Yes, I suppose so. What do you need me to do?'

'Lift shirt' she grimaced.

He rolled the shirt up her chest and over her head.

'Can't see!' she exclaimed.

'Sorry' he said as he rolled it back to girdle her neck.

'Left tit' she directed.

'Bra?' he replied.

'Cut off' she instructed.

He stood, went to his rucksack and opened a side pocket. He was the kind of lad who had a first aid pack, she thought. Good! He removed a pair of scissors from the compact red pack and poised over her at the ready.

'Mind tit' she warned. He cut the strap and she yelped at the spasm of pain and then she whimpered pathetically. Her mind swirled as it dealt with the shaft of pain that split the left side of her chest. She opened her eyes. He was still with her.

'Tit muscle' she instructed.

'Oh my god, that doesn't look right?' he exclaimed. Not too quick on the uptake she thought.

'Thumb forefinger' she ordered. He got his thumb and forefinger ready in a pincer grip. This was going to hurt madly. 'Hold, twist on three' she instructed. 'One, no wait.' She would need something to bite on. 'I'll scream. Plug ears' she directed.

He went to insert cotton wool in her ears. 'Your ears!'

He inserted them in his own ears.

'Strap in mouth.' she added. He folded a piece of webbing and inserted it between her waiting teeth. 'One, two.' She clenched her body in readiness. 'Three!' He pulled and twisted.

She spat out the webbing and screamed a high pitched yell. It was such a yell that skylarks and meadow pipits stopped singing in mid-song; a scream that caused small furry creatures to scramble into their underground burrows; a scream that caused her good samaritan to leap and scramble rapidly away on his hands and knees. Her left arm flapped up and down in mindless revolt. She turned her body to squash its rebellion but it still quivered madly. She held it with her right hand until the shaking became a shiver. She flopped flat on the ground and panted like a shocked dog.

He came back towards her, slowly and tentatively, looking about her in palpable anxiety.

'Told you' she said simply, 'just can't deal with that shit!'

'I thought you were very brave!'

'No, I bloody wasn't!'

'So, how are you now?'

She wondered where should she start? No bones broken, but there's something still not quite right. 'Not sure, badly winded. I've just checked and there's nothing broken but, but...' He knelt beside her and used both his hands to check her body, starting with her head and neck and then probing her shoulders and her arms and her chest.

'What's this?' He'd found a logbook inside her shirt.

'It's my nana's.' I'll let this pass she decided, as she was enjoying his air of youthful concern and his air of knowing what he was doing and his long, strong, supple fingers. And the pain in her chest was evaporating, like early morning mist. He started to work on her rib cage. An intervention was needed now, 'Ouchee! That's my tit! There's nothing broken in there, thank you!'

'I'm so sorry, I didn't mean...'

'To feel me up?' she asked. She pulled her shirt back down over her chest. That didn't hurt, so he must have fixed my tit muscle. Good lad! She sat up but she was firmly and gently pushed back down to the ground with his strong, sensitive fingers. Such assured fingers and hands!

He continued with her stomach, her pelvis and her upper legs.

'Ooh, that's actually quite...quite...nice' she cooed as his fingers pushed into her thighs, 'but I think I need a little bit more, right there, yes please.' But, he didn't agree. He stopped abruptly and pulled away.

'Can you sit up for me please?' he asked abruptly. So, he was going to continue with this ridiculous procedure in order to meticulously assess what was wrong with her. She let him continue after a sigh and a deep breath. The skylarks had resumed their song flights and the sound washed over her like a soothing balm. He positioned his rucksack behind her back and drew her into a sitting position. Next, a swig of water was proffered from his flask. She let it dribble down her throat. He drew back. 'So, what really happened to you?' he asked.

'Just now?' she asked.

'Yes' he replied.

'Well, I was just laying here on the ground, minding my own business, when a complete stranger came along and started feeling me up.'

'I did no such thing!' he countered 'I meant before you fell!' He seemed upset by the accusation. 'Anyway, I was not 'feeling you up', as you call it. I was checking you over. I was concerned that you had been badly hurt.'

'I'm better, you mended me. I think I'm fine, thank you.'

'Can you stand up for me please?' She got to her feet unsteadily and she swayed. 'All right, put your hands on my shoulders, please. Does it hurt anywhere?'

'Well, my left tit's a little bit tender where you've been... checking it' she replied coyly, 'but I didn't mind that so much, did I?'

He tutted. 'Anywhere else?'

'My lower back.' He took a deep breath and moved his hands across her lower back and to her buttocks. 'And my front.' His hands moved over her hips. 'No, a bit in from there. He stopped abruptly when he realised she was smirking at him.

'You seem perfectly fine to me' he concluded, 'so I don't know what happened back there, but...'

'That's what I've been telling you' she said as she watched his face carefully and then pursed her lips, 'and you're not so bad yourself, Andy.'

Inside, she felt a compelling urge to ease him down into the heather, delve under his weatherproof clothing and under his veneer of self-control - so young, yet so assured. 'It is Andy, isn't it? I don't know how I know that, but I do.' She eased her nana's logbook into the side pocket of the rucksack.

'It is, how did you know?'

'You look like an Andy' she replied, 'so I shall know you now as Handy Andy!'

He frowned. 'So what's your name?' he asked.

She looked about her. 'Oh, it's...it's Heather, isn't it?'

'Don't you know your own name?' he said looking at her quizzically. 'Amnesia?' he wondered out loud.

'No, it's definitely not amnesia, it's Heather. Heather Moore, isn't it?'

'With an 'e'?'

'Er, no, with, let me think, ah, three 'e's.'

He tutted: 'So Heather, what happened to you?'

'Who? Oh yes. I fell.'

'And what were you doing?'

'I... I was fighting with my mum.'

'Why would you...?'

'Actually, she was fighting with me. We had an argument, didn't we?'

'What about?'

'It's a mum and daughter thing, isn't it?'

'Mum's are always right. They know best.'

'That's complete and utter bollocks. You don't know my mum.'

'You need to go back to her and sort this out.'

'Did you see the state she left me in? She took me out and left me by the side of the track!'

'So, where did you land?'

'About here' she said, indicating the impression in the heather.

'No, no, no, I meant where on your body.'

'On my back.'

'I think I should lead you down to the valley and have you checked out properly. You could have a spinal injury.'

'There's no need, I'm fine, you mended me. Thank you so much Handy Andy. I'll just get my sack and I'll be on my way.' Katie swung the sack over her back, came up to the boy, pulled his shoulders so their bodies came together in a meshing of fabric, inhaled deeply on his scent, nuzzled his neck and kissed his cheek. 'You have a good soul and a good spirit; you will be fine. You will meet a special girl and make her very happy.'

She dropped her hands from his shoulders, dropped her eyes to the ground and turned and started to stumble down the track heading west, giving a last goodbye wave. He stood alone amongst the heather, staring open mouthed at her leaving.

Katie stood tall at the Kerry Pole and looked across the vale to the north-west, her feet planted solidly in the soil and her body stretching upwards. The breeze jollied its way across the serried ranks of rounded hills and buffeted the skin of her face and neck. Behind her, and deep, deep below, massive layers of rock crunched up and down, slowly jostling against each other and high above her, a jet of wind streamed quickly and relentlessly to the east. A straggle of fork-tails, banked and soared in the long, winding valley below her, as if showing her the way to go.

She closed her eyes and concentrated on each breath as it came in and as it was expelled slowly out of her body. To the south were the headwaters of the rivers that would gather their strength and vigour and head out of the green mounds of Powys. The going would be too difficult there, especially with a heavy pack, grinding into her shoulders and hanging heavily on her hips. Instead, she would follow the track to the west, ford the rivers of the Hafren and Trannon and bypass the wilderness of the Elenydd at its northern end. She would find the gap hanging between the uplands and strike towards the farthest point west, where dolphins and porpoises patrolled the coast.

In this place she would find the body of her nana and make her whole again.

Chapter Seventy-Three

Tuesday 31 May 2020 - Ponterwyd

Katie found old, decaying branches on the woodland floor and gathered them in her arms. There was more than enough for a fire, a large fire to dry her and keep harm at arm's length. Satisfied with her haul, she turned back towards the river. It was then that she realised there was something else in the woods with her. Thirty paces to her right, there was a flicker of movement amongst the trunks of trees, amongst the boughs and leaves. She stared but could not see any shape or form that she could translate into a realisable object.

Katie quickened her steps but they kept catching on roots and briers. She took another quick look to her right - there was something moving towards her, about twenty paces away. A kaleidoscopic patch of green, brown and black. Her heart leapt up to her gullet. She ran as quickly as she could through the briers that snagged her ankles and the branches that caught her legs. She leapt between a pair of alder trees and she was at the river, her feet scrunching across the gravel then splashing through the cold, flowing water. The river sucked the warmth out of her body, she was up to her thighs, she stumbled and she was immersed to her shoulders. She was back to her feet and then wading through the water, through the meander and onto the sandbank. She stopped, looked behind her and sucked air into her gasping lungs.

Downstream, there was the long, low cast iron structure that bridged the Hafern. But there was nothing moving, nothing that could harm her. She stared into the wood and scanned to the left and to the right. There was no movement, no sound. As her breathing recovered, there was the sound of a blackbird 'pink-pinking' and the sneezing 'pit-choo' of a marsh tit.

Katie breathed in deeply and blew out in relief. She was safe. It was just her imagination running wild. She dropped her load of wood. As she bent down she sensed there was something very close behind her. As she turned slowly...a soft pad of a foot on the sand and shallow measured breaths. It was there, just in front of her, a green, brown and black being, a kaleidoscope of colour, that blended with the trees. It was tall. It whispered a throaty whisper she couldn't interpret. She stepped back and very slowly, crouched and felt at her feet. Her fingers found a rock, and she clutched it tightly in her hand. She drew herself upright slowly and drew her arm back ready to strike.

A green arm swung and struck her arm and she watched in dismay as the rock flew away behind her and plopped into the river.

She drew herself up to her full height clutching an old bough. She lunged at its chest. 'Get back! I have powers! I can...'

Its hand went to its face and pulled the mask away. It was a man. There were brown smears across his face and it was framed with black curls laced with silver.

'Yes, you heard me. I have powers!'

He seemed to be having a struggle to comprehend this.

She prodded the bough tentatively at his chest and it met with solid flesh. The bough shuddered in her hands as a hatchet smashed through it. She thrust again and he chopped again and again, so there was just a limp two foot left. Then she dropped it because her hands were throbbing so much.

The green man crouched, collected a ball of tinder and struck two sparks with a pair of flints. It crackled and flickered into a spark. Quickly, he gathered material and it burst into a flame. He looked at her and shook his head.

'Look, l do have powers, just don't push me, because you will be sorry.'

He got on with setting a fire on her island.

'You don't believe me, do you?' Her teeth gnawed away at her lower lip. 'You see those birds up there?' She pointed to two huge, black birds perched in the high trees above. 'Well, I command them. I can command them to do whatever I want...' At this moment, one of the ravens chose to swing downwards and hang upside down from the branch. 'I can command them to do...somersaults!'

She sighed, what an idiot of a bird. 'And other things...like peck out your eyes.' The two birds leapt from their branch and flew away kronking to the west. 'Oh, crap' she muttered.

He pointed to the poor embers of her failed attempts to set a fire. He seemed to be asking her what was this? He seemed to be challenging her to demonstrate what powers she had? If you have powers, girl, why can't you set a fire? A show of bravado was needed here. 'That's what's left of the last bloke who tried it on...'

He shook his head dismissively. The flames were now licking shards of dry, rotten wood and they were catching light. He opened his hands to display his handiwork.

'So? You've got all the technology, haven't you? You've got flints and tinder and moss, haven't you?' She moved as close as she dared and warmed her hands and rubbed them. But she couldn't approach quite close enough to warm her wet body though. Flames were starting to lick upwards and the world around her started to darken.

'Turn around' she ordered the man and slipped off her wet trousers and shirt and squeezed them out in the river. 'You peeked!' The accusation fell on deaf ears because when she looked towards him, all she could see was the back of him as he crouched over the fire, tending to it.

Her wet clothes were hanging limply from a line tied between two alder trees. She took ten strides and untied one end of the line and walked back towards the fire. She pointed to the man and signalled to him to hook it over the branch above her head. He stood, made the loop and passed it back to her. She pulled it tight, secured it with a knot and sat down again.

'Why here?' he seemed to be asking with his eyes and his hands.

She shrugged at him. 'I thought if it all got out of control, there was plenty of water to douse it...' And she was out of way of any homestead or byway.

'I see' he seemed to be saying, and he shook his head again, sorrowfully.

Katie was now watching him from a squatting position ten paces away. The flames licked down and the embers glowed red hot. He opened a bag at his flank and pulled out two rainbow flanked fish, shining and still flexing fresh. He slit them, one after the other with a stout, sharp knife. She got to her feet, walked slowly towards the fire with her plastic plate held out, just two paces from him. He looked up and she stretched the plate towards him. He scooped up the innards and put them on her plate. She looked down, bewildered and baffled then retreated slowly back to her ground sheet. She prodded the warm, shiny, bulging organs with a twig and gasped at the way that they wobbled, as if still alive. 'What am I supposed to do with these?' she asked. 'How can I eat this stuff?' She hung the chain of crimson and purple organs in the fork of a long twig and suspended them over the glowing embers.

They were barely getting warm. She lifted the twig out of the sand, climbed up the river bank and stuck it in the ground. There were sinister, shadowy winged creatures looking down from the branches of the trees.

She turned back with alacrity and jumped down to the sandbank and again, confronted the green and brown man. 'Let's negotiate. I will let you use a part of this...place of mine' she indicated with her arm, the outline of the sandy ridge in the river, 'if I can have one of those.' She pointed towards the fish. There was no answer. He put a wooden spike through each fish and suspended them over the embers. They started to sizzle. 'I see, you're being a bit hard nosed about this. Listen, let's do a trade, I've got something you really need, I've got meat.' Katie stepped to her sack, searched through the pockets and found what she was looking for: Cellophane packs of dried meat. She took one pack and approached him again. He watched her approach out of the corner of his eye, still focussed on the fish. She waited patiently and judged her moment to precision.

The fish were now sizzling on the spikes that impaled them. Her mouth watered in response. 'You're not having both, are you? That would be greedy, wouldn't it? Look what I've got' she said as she proffered the pack of meat, 'it's biltong. Yes, that's right, meat! Do you want some?' she asked.

He looked at her quizzically.

She answered the implicit question. 'It's dry, and it's salty and peppery but it makes your teeth think they're eating meat...' He took it and put it in his breast pocket. 'Wait, you're supposed to trade me something for that! You can't do that! You bugger!'

She was aware that her mouth was dribbling and saliva was travelling down her chin. 'Listen, I don't know what sort of meat it is, it could be ostrich, or antelope...' she said as she wiped saliva away with the sleeve of her vest, 'or it could be crocodile, so hand me it back if you don't want it?'

He took a fish off its spike and filled the split belly with a sheaf of soft, aromatic leaves.

'I see, you're going to be tough' she muttered to herself as she worked out what to try next, 'but let me see, I'm a girl and you're a man...creature, probably' she continued, 'with all the needs of a man-creature, so I will show you some skin' she said, gulping again, 'if you let me have that fish.'

She prised up her vest to show her belly button. Her skin was drawn quite tightly across her stomach - uncomfortably tight. Still no glimmer of a response from the green man. 'I see, you're going to be tough. Well, because I'm a girl, I have girl bits, I will show you one of my girl bits for a fish.' She tugged her vest up towards her chest.

At last, there was some movement. He wrapped a fish in a wedge of leaves and passed it to her. She grabbed it and stepped backwards to her groundsheet and sat down. It was hers! Her teeth tore into the blackened flanks of the fish. It burnt her lips and her tongue. She kept biting and swallowing. And then she gnawed the flesh between the bones. She wiped her mouth with the sheaf of herbs and swallowed them greedily. Katie sat back and saw there was just a floppy skeleton in her hand. Katie watched the green man as he ate slowly, deliberately and meticulously, nibbling but not gulping it down. What restraint! She took a glug of water from her bottle, then stood up and approached him again. He hadn't touched the biltong, which she felt was ungrateful. She tossed the fish skeleton away. 'So, if we're sharing this island in the middle of this stream, I think we should get to know each other - what's your name?'

He didn't reply. She kept looking in his eyes to see if they spoke to her. They spoke of a wariness, a distance that she couldn't quite comprehend. 'Listen, I call myself Katie.' Still no response other than a slight wink of recognition. 'Now, this is where you say, that's a pretty name for a pretty girl, isn't it? No? All right, what do you call yourself? Come on, what do they call you?'

The green man was thinking but he wasn't prepared to answer. 'I'm going to call you Mutt...' He was still looking at her in puzzlement. 'So, do you want to ask me why? Well, it's short for Mutt 'n' Jeff. It means deaf. You can't hear me can you? Or can you? Or, are you just being rude? You are listening to me, aren't you?' She sighed heavily. 'Not much of a talker, are you? Um, parlez-vous francais, monsieur? No? Gallic? Spracken sie Deutsch? Nein?'

A thought seemed to spring into the front of his mind. 'Maela's child?' he seemed to be asking.

'What? Maela's what? Do you know my mum?'

He nodded as if in agreement.

'And when I say, know her, do you understand what I am saying?'

The green man frowned and shook his head slowly.

'When I say you know her, I mean, have you shagged her? Did you launch the pink torpedo? Bury the sausage? Ram her? Screw her?' She mimicked the action of a man having vigorous intercourse.

He now seemed to comprehend the question but gave no indication of what his answer was.

'No? Really? You must be the only bloke around here who hasn't!' She walked back to her ground sheet and unfurled her sleeping bag. She needed slightly more privacy. She got up, loosened the rope suspended above so that her drying clothes made a makeshift screen. She wriggled her way into the sleeping bag, propped herself up with her rucksack so she could watch him. It was no good, she couldn't keep her eyes open. She succumbed to her weariness and subsided into sleep. And this time, there were no demons, just a green man who inhabited her dreams, a green man that merged into the woods and trees who could not be seen unless you knew he was there, a green man who was watching over her.

Katie woke. For a moment, she couldn't work out where she was. There was the sound of water chuckling over stones in the river and a grey wagtail, perched on a stone in the river, furiously wagging its tail. She looked across to where the green man should be but there was no one there. The embers of the fire had been kicked over with sand and gravel. She rubbed her eyes as she got up. There was something hanging around her neck. She gasped when she hooked it up to the level of her eyes and saw what it was. 'Buggery, buggery, bollocks!' she exclaimed. It was a tiny leather pouch and it had two flints in it.

Katie looked for the green man, up and downstream and up the flanks of the hill in front of her. He had swept his marks clean from the sand but there were marks in the damp soil of the river bank. She jumped up onto the bank and ran along the footpath downstream then cut into the woods. She climbed, leaping over fallen boughs, pulled her way up past leaning pine trunks and gnarled ashes and oaks until a track crossed her way. It was clear beyond the track, a long view across the serried ranks of verdant hills, sprinkled with sheep and rocks and trees. Her lungs bulged up her gullet as she sucked in the sweet cool air of the morning.

Her senses re-focussed, fuzzy at first but then becoming clearer. There was a movement to the right of her field of view. She re-focussed again. It was moving quickly, gliding so quickly over the ground. She kicked her legs into action and sprinted down the rough track, skipping the tractor cut gouges and piles of dung. The figure stopped. She shouted. 'Come back, come back!' He turned for a moment and then continued on his way. 'Come back, we're the same blood! Come back!' Katie sprinted alongside the hedge to the gate. She vaulted the gate and looked desperately to her left and right. There was a small stooped man, propped up on a shepherd's crook, staring at her quizzically.

'You should get some clothes on dear, you'll catch your death!'

She looked down at her underclothes and brushed away the burrs and the pollen. 'I'm sorry mate, I got up in a hurry.' She scanned the field boundary, there was no sign of him.

'Dad? Dad?' But she was uncertain. Was it him? The figure had merged into the green and brown shape shifting landscape. She closed her eyes and re-focussed - there was nothing, not the slightest perturbation in the eye of her mind.

'Oh my soul! Oh my soul! What have I done?' Katie looked about her. Fortunately, there was no one listening. There was just the lowing of cattle in the pasture to her right and the whinnying of a horse and the bleating of sheep above her. 'I was going to show him my doops for a fish!'

Chapter Seventy-Four

Wednesday 01 June 2150 - The battle of Y Glonc

The skirmish at Y Glonc started slowly in the glow of the late-afternoon sun, as the two opponents sized each other up. A snidey voice came into Katie's head, to make an announcement...

'Introducing first...in the red corner, weighing in at one hundred and thirty pounds (Never!) in her bare feet, hailing from Rhayader, Wales, with a career record of no wins or draws or fights (Oi!), fighting as a southpaw (Eh?), Katie (Tally) Talog!' Katie gave herself a little clap.

'And in the blue corner, something monstrous, unencumbered with vest or trunks, regarded by many as the best British super-heavyweight prospect for many a year...'

'Booooh! So, who is this fool?'

'It's the agent of your death, doom and destruction, little witch...'

'But what is it?' she gulped.

'A ginormous crocadilla-sheep!'

'There's no such thing!'

'And it's going to kill, kill, kill you!'

'Booooh!'

'You can go boo as much as you like, but I warned you!'

In her corner though, were two vocal ravens, kronking from the top of an upright stone and a ragged wave of fork-tails, buffeted by an upsurge of billowing air. The giant windmills of the wind farm turned into the breeze from the east and their blades slowly, but then more speedily, beat into life. Katie stood on a mound, looking eastwards into a clear, cloudless sky but this thing was rising inexorably, blanking out low hanging sky objects. There were no clouds, so the evening star should be visible to her, but it was nowhere to be seen. Her body gave an involuntary shudder and her heart pounded loud in her chest.

What options had she got? Through the filter of her short experience and long training, they were three: fight, run or hide. None of them offered any good prospects. She emptied her rucksack into the rough grass and heather and searched for weapons. Despite desperate rummaging through pockets, sleeves, packs and compartments there was just dried fruit (which she could throw), dried bread and dried meat; a water bottle; a box of matches; a small entrenching tool; a large ground sheet that doubled as a basha; a sleeping bag; an assortment of crumpled clothes - an assemblage of hopelessness, a scatter of clutter that meant her impending defeat.

She wondered if she could outrun it, but no, it was coming quickly upon her, wheezing like a steam train up a steep incline (which it wasn't), bellowing like a distressed cow (which it wasn't) and moving the ground below her like a mutated mega-sheep, born out of the deep, dark, leaden chambers below (which it probably was).

On the plus side, Katie had the triskelion and two shiny, flint flakes hanging around her neck.

But defeat would mean death, doom and destruction.

She would have to get under cover. Grabbing the entrenching tool, Katie scratched desperately away at the thin, dark soil and then clattered into the rubble below. There was now a shallow trench that she could lay in and pull the groundsheet over her. As plans go, it was pitiful but it was all she had.

The whole of the sky to the east was now blacked out. She laid herself in the trench and pulled the groundsheet over her head and waited with her breath pulsing in and out. What if she surrendered? This was the last resort of the Royal. If you had no ammunition, no food and no means of escape, you surrendered - you would live to fight another day. But this was different - would the monster accept her surrender? Had it signed up to the Geneva Convention, particularly the bit about how to treat prisoners of war? She suspected not - this was a monster that probably did not take prisoners. Oh, bugger, bugger, bugger.

And what would the scene look like tomorrow?

If her nightmare was right, her body would be split apart, her organs ripped out, her bones and flesh scorched and scattered. How would she be pieced back together? The ground was now bending up and down and her core vibrating with it like it was being bounced on.

And now it was upon her - a huge brooding creature that stank of goat; that blocked out all light; quelled bird song and compelled creatures to slink away below ground. The thumping built and built inside her until she could bear it no longer.

She jumped out of her burrow, dug her feet deep into the soil and extended her arms towards the darkness, little and index fingers extended and her other fingers coiled back like a trigger. Through the soil, she felt a gush of energy and the flight or flee juice rushing through her arteries.

Between her arms she could see trails of coruscating purple and green bubbling their way north-eastward, twisting and turning into each other with a sweep of her arms.

A scream rasped out of her throat: 'Baaaaaaaaaah!'

A wind whirled around her that gathered force and flattened the plants about her. Two of the windmills reached a terminal crescendo of whining.

The monster seemed to hesitate.

Two giant windmills gave up the ghost.

'Where've you gone?' she screamed. 'Come back here!'

Stars and constellations and planets were now restored to their rightful positions in the evening sky. There was a rush of wind and then silence. With her arms still extended, swaying slowly, dozens of eyed emperors made a constantly moving ribbon that spiralled down and flirted with her fingers and her arms, some dispersing to settle in her hair and on her shoulders. She looked around her at the circle of flattened sedges and grasses and heaths. The skewed and broken stems filled the air with the sweet smell of a summer meadow. At the furthest reach of the flattened plants were stones, all in a ring, with shining crystals pulsing, like there were glow-worms embedded in them.

Her arms returned limply to her sides, her head slumped and she subsided to her knees. She raised her hand which was now decorated with three moths, wings held outright flashing their eyes at her. 'All right boys, you've had your fun, off you go.'

She whirled them away with her arms and watched as they dispersed about her.

Katie heard excited shouts of young men to her left and saw a minibus reflecting the setting of the sun. She would have to move on quickly, so cramming all her belongings into the rucksack, pulling it tight, swinging it over her shoulders she was heading along and then down the valley. Behind her, there were two flaming motors on the giant windmills, belching black, oily smoke to the east.

Katie skirted around the wood on the northern side and walked quickly towards the farmstead of Rhyd. There was a red telephone box at the junction and now within easy reach. She shed the rucksack, propped it up outside and rang the telephone number that she had memorised. There was a click as the phone was picked up at the other end and the sound of two stilted sobs.

'It's Katie, who's that?'

Still silence.

'Is that you Gwen? It's me, Katie, can you hear me?'

'I can hear you, Katie. I'm so sorry, so sorry.'

'That's all gone by now, so listen to me, Gwen. I'm alright. Have you seen the news? Is there something about...an incident at a wind farm?'

'Wait, let me see.' The phone was put down and Katie could hear footsteps clacking away into the distance. Katie tapped her fingers impatiently against the glass of the box. Come on Gwen, this is burning money, she grumbled to herself.

After what seemed like an interminable period of time, Gwen was back. 'There's something about a Powys wind farm where two of the units are burning. They reckon its due to a freak wind. That's not something to do with you, is it?'

'Of course not, Gwen, but I'm going to have to walk through the night to keep on track, heading west, or west of north west. I'll be at Camlan early tomorrow.'

'What's the point of this Katie? What's the point? Why don't you just come back and we'll talk about it and put it all right?'

'Listen, it's too late for that, but it's just...something's following me.' Katie tried to work out the best way to describe her stalker. 'It's quite big and mean and it's behind me now, for the moment but it was a bit of a near thing at the wind farm. I just managed to escape.'

'How's it following you, Katie?'

'Well, it's having to walk, because it won't fit in a car...'

'So, it's quite big then...'

'Yes, Gwen, it's quite big.' So many sodding questions, but no sodding answers.

'Katie, it's all in your head. Honestly, it's not real.' Katie could hear Gwen thinking but there was no sound coming through the telephone earpiece, only a quiet humming. This has happened to me. You get over it, it takes time. It's happened to all of us. It's not real. Your mind is playing tricks on you.

'Gwen, I can't hear you Gwen but I can tell what you're thinking. What's going on?'

'Don't worry.'

'What's happening?' There was a pause.

Gwen seemed to be contemplating what to say next. 'It's all in your head. Get back here and we'll sort it all out somehow.'

Katie could hear the thoughts running through Gwen's mind, thoughts of how to put this right, but there was no way.

'It's all part of growing up, it's something you just have to work through. It's growing pains - it's nothing, it's really nothing.'

'Gwen, I know it's not nothing. You can't hide it - you're lying, I can hear it in your voice.'

'Just don't do anything stupid, Katie. Just take care and I'll come and sort it out tomorrow. I'll come to Dinas and I'll sort everything out. Just keep safe and don't do anything stupid.'

Two beams of light illuminated the telephone box. Katie stared towards them but could not see the source. 'Listen Gwen, there's something up outside. I've got to go. I'll see you at Camlan.'

'Katie? Katie?' The receiver was slammed down. Katie stepped out of the phone box. Her rucksack was missing but there was a white minibus outside and a boy was trying to launch it onto the roof rack. She was surrounded by a band of young people. They were smiling at her and ushering her towards the vehicle.

'Please, give me back my sack!'

'Was that you up on the hill?'

'Up in the middle of that storm?'

'The one that blitzed the wind farm?'

'That was you wasn't it?'

They were all young, eager, full of energy; she felt embarrassed by her own lack of energy.

'And who are you?'

'We're sea cadets!'

'Sea cadets? What are you doing here?'

'We saw you on the hill! You looked like you were in trouble. We've come to rescue you!'

'Oh, thanks.'

'Where are you staying tonight? Where are you headed?'

'I'm headed west, towards Dinas...'

'That's where we're going! We can give you a lift there. And we can put you up for the night! We're staying in the bunk house! That'll be all right, won't it Mr Davenport?' They all looked towards the man standing by the minibus.

He was a mature man, hanging back, with spectacles perched on his nose and a deep, thoughtful face. 'My, you look tired and hungry, my little sausage. You look like you can use a lift' he said. 'My name's Colin. I can drive you to wherever you need to be. Or I could get you to a guest house or a pub. How does that sound, sausage?' He offered a hand shake which she accepted. It was cold and clammy.

'I've got nowhere to stay. I was going to bivvy out, but if you've got a spare bunk' she replied, wiping her hand down her trousers.

'Get inside then. It's a bit of a mess and it's a bit tight inside, but you'll be fine with us, you silly sausage.'

She would have to squeeze alongside Rory on the long folding seat at the front but she was relieved that she didn't have to walk any further or sleep outside. This was all good.

They came to a small village which had an inn.

Katie was persuaded to go inside and join them for a drink. She accepted. She drank long and quickly from a pint and her strength and her appetite were coming back. They all seemed to be in good spirits and chatting continuously about the routes they were going to climb. None of the names of the routes made any sense, in that they all seemed abusive, full of unfamiliar words and numbers.

'So, it's Katie is it?'

'Yes, I'm a...leading hand in the Royal Navy. And, no I'm not on an exercise or hopelessly lost.'

'Are you yomping?' she was asked.

'No, I just needed to get away. I'm on leave, aren't I?'

Back outside, it was a star strewn sky. For some reason, the minibus started off on the main road and then headed onto a back road, where it came to a sudden halt.

'Do you fancy a bit of minibus surfing?'

'I'm sorry, what did you say?'

'Come with me.' Rory opened the door of the minibus and climbed onto the roof. He grabbed her arm and pulled her up top. 'Keep low and hang on tight. It's going to be bumpy up here.'

'What if I fall off?'

'No problem. We'll go back and pick you up!'

'But I need to be kept safe!'

She felt safe once she was clipped to a roof rail with a climber's tape, a rope and two spring hooks.

As they approached the main road to Dolgellau, all the passengers squeezed back inside the minibus. But before Katie dropped off the roof she stood up and listened intently to the west - there was a distant whimpering, like someone aged in the final squeeze of death. She was running out of time.

'No standing and no larking around on top while we're on the arterial roads' shouted Colin, 'the local police are a bit sensitive about roof passengers.'

Chapter Seventy-Five

Thursday 02 June 0007 - Dinas Mawddwy

Inside the bunkhouse, a meal was prepared from tins of meat, tomato sauce and spaghetti. Katie ate quickly and headed for the washrooms. 'I'm going to turn in after a wash. I'm completely knackered. Where do I rack out?'

She was led to a small dormitory with just three bunk beds. 'Take your pick' invited Rory.

'I don't need any special privileges. I'm used to dossing down with a bunch of born-again scrotes, aren't I?'

'I think it's best if you have some privacy. You look tuckered out.'

'Thanks, that's very kind.'

'I'll just heat up some water for you and bring it out. There's none in the washroom.'

Katie followed the boarded corridor along and pushed the door open. It was barely lit and smelled of damp. There were hooks on wall for her clothes. She mashed her vest and her trousers into a basin and hung them up on a line to dry. Wearily, she propped up her body over the washbasin, turned the taps on and tried to trickle out enough water to wash. The face looking back at her was down-turned with fatigue, barely open grey eyes and surrounded by tangled and ratty hair. Her forehead pressed against the cold glass and she closed her eyes.

Katie awoke with a sudden snort. The door was creaking behind her and she tried to push it closed with the back of her foot. 'It's occupied!'

The boy pushed his way in, carrying a bowl of steaming water. She looked at him over her shoulder. It was her minibus surfing partner, Rory.

'Out you get, you cheeky sod, I'm trying to have a wash' she hissed.

'So you are' he replied. He tipped the hot water into the basin and whipped up a lather with his hand. 'There you go.'

Her head was still pressed to the mirror and her arms locked straight, holding the wash basin mounting. 'Thanks a lot, mate, tootle off now.'

'You look like you need a hand?'

'I am a bit stuck, aren't I?' She was turned so she was facing him. He had dark curly hair and a ruddy complexion and a sodding smug grin and a bath sponge in his mitt. Her arms were still holding tight to the wooden counter behind her and it was only this that prevented her sliding down to the cold, damp floor.

He moistened the sponge and slowly and carefully, wetted her hair. Her head leaned back over the wash basin and her slide downwards was arrested by his arm around her back. Then he started to smooth out the tangles, systematically and gently, so it was all teased out and rivulets of water trickled down her neck and her back.

'Huuuuh, I reckon you've done this before, haven't you?'

'I have three sisters, so I have...'

'I think they're very lucky girls.'

'What's this mark?'

'It's just...a brand.'

'I don't understand.'

'I'm marked...'

'But why?'

She sighed. 'It's so I'm marked.'

'But what does it mean?'

'Watch out for me...'

'That's sick, that is. They stamped you with this...thing, like you're cattle.'

'Yep, that's about it.'

'But you're lovely...even with this graffiti on you.' He continued to absent-mindedly wash her hair through, gently pulling out the tangles.

She was very aware that she was getting very, very wet and bubbling inside. 'How can I be? I've got graffiti all over me?'

'You are the graffiti girl, graffiti on your skin, not on a wall' he murmured. Her hair felt clean and tangle free and Rory had wrapped it in a towel. He lifted her onto the counter so she was sitting on her towel.

'My bra and pants are all soggy' she noted.

'So they are, but it's no problem' he said as he un-hitched the bra and removed it.

Katie gasped, 'You cheeky sod!' She quickly crossed her arms over her chest but he placed a bundle of bubbles on her nose. With an upward puff, they were blown upwards so that a shower of iridescent spheres cascaded over them. 'Listen to me Rory, you're just a boy and this really isn't going to work, is it?'

She started to slip, so her arms dropped to grip the counter. He quickly placed two plumes of soap bubbles on her chest. 'I haven't got time for this, stop messing about!'

He eased her hands away in his hands and his warm breath blew the bubbles away very slowly and very gently. Gripping the washbasin behind her with both hands, her back arched backwards and her pelvis pressed gently forwards. 'Oh...my...soul!'

He paused to collect another handful of foam and gently covered her shoulders, her chest and her tummy.

'Rory, this has got to stop...you're getting me all...messy!' Her arms folded around his neck and pulled him closer. She inhaled the scent of his hair. He was descending towards her tummy and her body convulsed again in response. 'I haven't given you...permission.'

Her right leg coiled around his waist and tried to pull him tight. Her body convulsed again from her core. She jumped and encircled his waist with both her legs and squeezed tight.

'Katie! Cool it!'

She couldn't be stopped. Her upper body arched away, her legs squeezed him again. They spun around and her body banged against the door, again and again. She pulled his body to hers and pulled his shirt apart. Her lips parted and then darted towards his, but she couldn't connect and her mouth slid along his cheek to his neck and her teeth sank into his neck; he yelped. They banged against the door again in their embrace. Her surge was coming. Her body shook and then she was enveloped in waves that shook them both. They buffeted against the door, sending rhythmic claps of sound through the whole building. Throughout the building there was a hushed silence.

'Katie! Cool it!'

'I'm sorry, I'm sorry' she panted, 'I totally lost it.' Slowly, she came back to earth. 'I'll behave now.' And suddenly, all her energy had dissipated down into the cracks of the tiled floor.

He lowered her slowly to the ground and crouched before her. He took the towel and softly wiped her body down to her feet and toes. 'There, you are, all done' he said as he stood up.

'I am as well.'

She tried to cover herself up as much as she could with her arms. 'So why did you...why didn't you?' she wondered aloud.

'There's nothing the matter with you that a good night's kip won't fix.' He shrouded her in her towel, gathered her up and swung her into the corridor, pushed through the door into the smallest dormitory. He laid her down on the top bunk furthest away from the door and wrapped her in a blanket. He started to rummage in his jean pockets and pulled something out. It was a fine, silver pendant. There was a tiny medallion suspended from it. He kissed it lightly and then placed it gently round her neck. 'This will protect you from what's to come' he whispered.

She turned over sleepily onto her belly. Her arms and her fingers reached out to him. 'I need a man to protect me, I need to be held... like I've never been held before.' She was losing consciousness so her arm subsided and flopped over the side of the bunk bed. Her right leg was gently moved back onto the bed and tucked in under the blanket. Her eyes closed and she slept a deep, deep sleep.

The greyness filtering in through the dingy, cobweb strewn windows hinted that the sun would rise soon. She swept the blanket aside and jumped down from the bunk. There was some noise at the front of the bunkhouse but the back was quiet. Katie carefully tiptoed towards the kitchen. The debris of the previous night was still there, illuminated by the stark ceiling lights. Colin was stood in the centre of the kitchen with his arms akimbo. He looked around at the devastation and complained to Katie, 'Where do you start?'

'One of us can clear up and one of us can start getting breakfast ready. I'll put the kettle on while you're thinking.' She filled the kettle and plugged it in. 'Is there something wrong with my legs?'

'No, no.' He quickly averted his eyes. 'I was just wondering what all the banging was about last night?'

'Oh. I had a bit of a fit in the heads but Rory helped me out. He's a bit of a lad, isn't he?'

'This is why these trips are a problem. You get a young woman coming along and they all start showing off and playing the fool... whoops, I could have put that more tactfully!'

'Nothing happened, well, nothing much, any way.' She started to scrape the residue out of a large pan. 'Do you always get lumbered with the cooking and cleaning, then? What arse-ache!'

'It's just quicker this way.'

'Even so...'

'Last night, you didn't seem to know where you were going. Do you need any help?'

'I'm trying to...get away from it all.'

'So, you are a fugitive then?'

'I suppose I am.'

They all came to breakfast in a dishevelled queue for scrambled eggs, toast and beans. She slapped a lump of scrambled eggs on Rory's proffered bowl. 'I hope it chokes you' she hissed.

'What's the matter? What did I do?'

'What's the matter? What's the matter? You just left me lying there!'

'Get over yourself! You were knackered out! I just cleaned you up!'

'I thought, you liked me and I thought you would hold me because...I was so ready to be cuddled, to be held tight, to be adored, to be...safe with someone, someone who would look after me, no matter what...'

Katie stopped because there was silence in the room and all eyes were looking at her. All eyes, wide with wonder...with apprehension about what was about to happen. 'Let's you and me go outside so I can shout at you in private!'

He hesitated, looked at Colin who nodded and they went to the main door, jostled their way through it and then followed the wooden walls to the back of the hut. They stood together overlooking the steep fall to a babbling brook, surrounded by trees. The fall was decorated with freshly fallen lumps of soil and rock.

'What was last night all about?'

'You looked like you needed looking after, so I helped you. You looked wiped out...'

'Well, I was, but that stuff you did with me, that's not what normally occurs when you wash hair, is it?'

'You did all of that, not me!'

'What are you saying?'

'You...you went all unnecessary!'

'I had to do all that...because I would have exploded!'

'You're a very strange girl...'

'I'm strange! You give out organisms to your sisters!'

'They're called orgasms...'

'You admit it, then!'

'No!'

'You do!'

'Never. It's just you! That never, ever happened!'

'Well, never mind all that...

'But...did you need it?'

'Need it? Having my hair washed and all that? It was fine.'

'And?'

'But it was the other stuff that did for me, didn't it? The trickling down me and the bubble blowing...'

'I didn't do that! It was you!'

'You're missing the point. You did all that to me, but it was just... washing, wasn't it, because we weren't doing it together. It would be like me watching you cracking one off in the heads, that's what it was like...'

'Oh, I think I see.'

'But that's not even the point, is it?'

'What is the point?'

'I hoped, I believed that somehow, somewhere I could find someone who would care for me, for what I am...'

'And what are you really, Katie?'

Her eyes watered and her lips trembled. 'I'm a sad, lonely bastard of a girl.'

'For God's sake Katie, there must be people who care for you, look at you. And if you don't believe that, you need to see a headshrinker.'

He hesitated, turned away and then walked very slowly away, as if waiting for her to call him back, but she didn't.

Instead, Katie edged her way round to the back wall of the hut that overhung the river. In the brook, on a mound, a tree had grown and then been split asunder. Out of the freshly split trunk, a sappy shaft of wood, thrust upwards, like the shaft of a thick sword. She edged her way along a narrow stone shelf so she teetered above the shaft. The finger nails of her right hand were pushed into the soft putty in the frame of a window, her left hand clutched a piece of plank that protruded through the wall. She eased herself outward from the wall so her belly was above the shaft. Her fall would impale her on the shaft and then they would all be sorry: Rory, Gwen, all of them.

Katie took a deep breath that softened the anxious thoughts that raced through the front of her mind. Release the grip and she would fall, be impaled on the shaft, and then there would be no more promises that couldn't be kept... so she pushed with her left hand and teetered on the edge.

A hand grasped her wrist and pulled sharply. Her right leg swung high above the gorge. It scrabbled for a foothold on the side of the cabin. Her foot found it. Another sharp tug on her arm - she was in the arms of Rory. 'What are you doing, you little idiot?' he shouted.

'Go inside and eat your sodding eggs, Rory...'

'What about you' he replied.

"I don't want any sodding eggs.' Katie took another deep breath. The moment had gone and she was left with the reality of the promise. 'I'm going now. I'm going to find my sister...'

'How are going to do that?'

Katie fumbled through the pockets of her shirt. There was something she had to do, at this moment, when she felt bad about herself. She withdrew an envelope. It was typed with a message. It was for the eyes of her new commanding officer. 'Here, read this for me...' She withdrew the letter from inside the envelope and presented it to him.

He scanned through it quickly. 'Who is Captain Marriott, anyway? Is he your boss?'

'No, he's my old CO. Well, actually he's my CO's, CO's CO. Yes, that's about right? What does it say?'

'It says you performed all your duties as expected. Blah, blah, blah. No difference between the men and the women. But then, you knew that, didn't you, Katie?'

'No, no I didn't. Come on Rory, what does he say?'

'He says you're disrespectful and not very well educated. I think we can all agree on that. He doesn't mention that you're an idiot, which is surprising, isn't it?' He handed back the letter.

She stared at it and tried to make sense of the words. They ebbed in an out of her vision and then her brain started to make sense of them. The letter had an April date on it. Her finger traced the outline of each word along each line and she could hear Captain Marriott speaking to her.

My ship, HMS Albany, has four wrens serving on it. Back in 1990, I swore that I would never have women serving in my ship's company. I would not be able to order them into combat as I could not be confident about how they would perform under fire. How wrong was I! Over the course of two tours of duty, my ship's company has performed all of their duties with great verve, professionalism and spirit. This has included the rescue of a squad of French commandos, the securing of two stricken merchant vessels, weathering a tempest and all the routine activities needed to sail, operate and fight HMS Albany. In all of this, there has not been one iota of difference in the performance of the men and women in my crew in the completing of their assigned duties.

With one exception - Leading Hand K E Talog (Acting)!

Katie gasped. 'With one exception! Me!' She folded up the letter and slid it back into her trouser pocket. 'Oh my soul!

Katie dragged her feet along the crumbling, stony path, as above her, the dripping, dew laden trees, spattered the path in front and behind her. She had left the bunkhouse quickly after stuffing her coat pockets with bread and bananas and filling her water bottle from the tap.

She was very late. Slowly at first and then with increasing purpose Katie jogged down the track. There was a box of a car there with all its lights on and the engine spluttering coughs of gas and drops of liquid. She threw the rucksack down and ran to the driver's door. It was Gwen's car.

Katie hammered on the window - there was no response. She peered inside the vehicle. There was a figure slumped in the driver's seat. It was Gwen asleep inside but the door would not open no matter how much she tugged at it. There was a brick embedded in the track. It lifted easily into her hand and she crashed it through the window glass. A hail of glass shards flew around her - she prised the lock open. Gwen's hands were fixed to the steering wheel.

'Too late' Gwen murmured.

Katie released the buckle of the seat belt and wrenched Gwen out of the car to the ground. She was still breathing, just. Katie listened to her chest - her heart was beating, just. She pumped it six times and then blew into her lungs, a long forceful blast of wind.

Gwen was coughing now. 'I knew you would come for me' Gwen gasped, 'if only for the dog.'

'What do you mean?' Katie looked back to the car - Owain must be in there. She climbed in. A coiled bundle of fur was on the back seat. Katie stepped over the console and lifted the motionless bundle into her arms. She stumbled back out into the cold, damp air. She shook the bundle. 'Owain, wake up!' She placed the bundle on the ground. 'Come on Owain, wake up!' She opened his mouth and loosened his tongue. 'Please, Owain!' She massaged his chest. 'Owain!' There was no vestige of life, no breath, no beating heart. 'Gwen, he's gone!'

'He went so quickly...I heard this whimpering.'

How could he? How could this free spirit just go to sleep? She must be able to wake him. She shook his shoulder. She pulled his right leg, as in the game of paws that they played across the balustrade of Clun Cottage, but no more. 'Bastards! Bastards! Bastards!' she screamed into the air. She hoped that the bastard women of the Elenydd had heard her.

She went across to Gwen. 'How could you let him die?'

'I was dying!'

'But, but...where's your mobile?'

'In my pocket. Why?'

'I'm calling for help.' The phone peeped out of Gwen's breast pocket. Gwen had been trying to call someone called 'Katell'. As Katie prodded the phone to get the emergency number, Gwen stuffed something into her hand.

'You'll need this.'

Katie shouted to the operator, who seemed unbearably calm. There was a scrap of paper in her hand but she just stuffed it away in her breast pocket. The ambulance was on its way, she was told. It would need to get a long way up the track. How is the patient? One just alive and one just dead said Katie in reply.

The police would have to attend. She walked carefully back to the body of Owain - would he spring back to life after playing dead? Not this time. She retrieved the blanket and tucked it around his lifeless body. The first convulsion racked her body.

'You know it wasn't me don't you?'

'Just shut up Gwen!'

'The car stopped for no reason. It was steep, but even so...'

'Just shut up Gwen!'

'I thought you would come here. I thought you would find us, but you were too late.'

The police arrived first, in a Land Rover. There were two of them, very sympathetic about her loss. But you must be relieved to have rescued your sister? She didn't want to answer this. 'So, my lovely, it's Katie Talog, is it? That sounds familiar - wait here, I'll be back in a jiffy.' He jogged back to the police car.

Katie quietly heaved the rucksack over the shoulders, quietly walked to Owain, gathered him up in his blanket and then walked away quickly down the hill, away from the track. The mist soon shrouded them and there was just the muffled calls for her from the track above. Owain's muscles still yielded but he was heavy. She tenderly moved him so he girdled her neck. Her thighs pushed quickly away through the heather and away from Gwen. The mist still eddied in pools around them, just as it did on that fateful day fifteen hundred years ago.

She crossed a stream which had cut it's way through the dark red soil. There was a knoll in the flood plain of Camlan. She pushed her tired thighs until they were on the top of the mound. This would be the place for him. The sun flirted with the clouds and shy shafts of light lit the top of the hill. She placed the dog down softly in the heather and started digging with the entrenching tool. It must be a big bed for him, as he always used to fidget. She placed him in the round hole, with the blanket around him. She removed the dog tag she had made for him at Devonport dockyard workshop and threaded it through the chain around her neck. Slabs of stone were placed around him and then gently over him so that he would not feel them. Finally, she returned the dark soil onto him and then built a small cairn over the top to mark his resting place.

'Here lies Owain Madog, Prince of all Welsh sheepdogs.'

No one was listening. Another convulsion shook her frame.

'He was so loving, so faithful, so trusting, so betrayed.' She promised herself that this would be dignified and fitting for such a noble and loving dog, but the convulsions took over. She took deep breaths but they could not quell the shaking. 'Rhiannon, please look after him in his new life, protect him. Tell him I love him. Tell him I'm sorry I wasn't there to protect him.' The bitter tears stung her eyes and etched their way down her face and down her neck.

All the pillars on which she had based her life had been kicked away. There was still her wastrel of a mother and what remained of her bastard family but everything else she had cared about was gone. She looked with bitter eyes to the east. In her soul she knew that she was heading towards the demise of her existence - all that was left was the sodding promise.

'Goodbye Owain Madog.'

The final rock clacked into place on the top of the small cairn. She hoisted the rucksack onto her back, clutched his dog tag around her neck and then stumbled her way to the west, through the pine woods that hid the valley of Nant Blaen-y-cwm, along the track that looked over Nant Talymiery and then climbed through the wood that shrouded Coed Mawr.

In the clearing, she sat and sorted through the food she had packed; dried meat; dried bread; dried cheese and dried fruit. A smorgasbord of dried delights. She couldn't bring herself to eat any of it. She settled for a slug of water from the canteen, a banana and a bread roll.

But all about her, she was conscious of shadowy shapes that flapped lazily amongst the tree tops, parallel to her path, flashing black, white and russet, still attending her progress. She did not dare to stare towards these creatures, but she sensed that their paths were going to abruptly coincide.

Katie traversed the valley, forded the stream and then ascended the steep wooded path through Ffridd Newydd until the trees thinned out and then stopped. She heard a sound of distress, a sorrowful whinnying. She lifted her head and her sinuses and ears flared. There was a moor to her left, serried ranks of pine trees to the right, and razor wire between. Ahead of her, a cry of pain. She hurried her steps and there was the source of this cry, a wild-eyed doe, impaled on the wire, left flank pulsing rhythmically, but slashed through.

Katie removed her pack and slumped down next to the beast. Her shadowers settled in the trees of the forest around her and waited. She contemplated what had to be done. Her hand settled over the beast's eyes and soothed them closed. The hopeless struggle against the wire and the breathing panic subsided. 'I'm sorry mate, there's nothing to be done. I'll make it quick, I promise you.' She eased the commando knife out of its sheaf and hid it from the beast, the blade resting along her arm. The knife was jabbed sharply into the taut throat and jagged two handedly to the side. The beast gasped, slumped and expired.

Katie gasped and slumped against her pack until her breathing settled again.

'I commit the soul of this beast to your care, Rhiannon.' She paused to see the reaction of the flying creatures, resting in the trees around her. 'The body of this beast I commit to the living world.' The knife was ripped down through the hide and the tissue of the beast, so the chest opened wide. The chest was bared and hung over the wire, an invitation to feed on the flesh. She wiped her hands and blade clean on the hide, re-assembled her pack and threw it over her back. With a bow to the beast, and a skyward nod to her gods, she turned and kicked her way onwards along the path that led north-east.

CHAPTER SEVENTY-SIX

Thursday 02 June 1122- Cader Idris

It was mid afternoon when Katie reached the quarry that girdled the main road heading southward to Corris. Her ever-present companion, the silver flecked fork-tail, hovered ahead of her, leading her on and all his rag-tag followers. And there ahead of her, framing the horizon, was the bulky massif of the mountain, Cadair Idris.

The fork-tail twisted its way effortlessly through the ebb and flow of the breeze up the slope. She groaned inwardly. You heartless bastard. All right, we'll take a break after I've climbed to the top of the crags. The pack was swung back over her back and she started trudging upwards, slowly at first and then quickening her pace.

She ascended the hilltop at Maen Du and then followed the broad ridge that ran to the south-west. The land fell away more steeply to the north and west. She reset her sights to the south and west. The going was slow for her, through the glue-like peat.

Over the toot, into another green valley, she stopped, weary from walking. She opened the contents of the leather pouch that hung around her neck and removed the two flints, struck them together in a shower of lively sparks. The dried moss caught fire and she piled dry twigs and leaves on top. They smouldered slowly. She found a screwed up ball of paper in her pocket. Instead of tossing it on the fire she unfurled it and tried to read it. The kettle on the meths stove was boiling fiercely so now she would warm her hands and gullet before facing the damp cloud again.

It was the letter written by Captain Marriott. Her left index finger traced the flow of characters across the page trying to follow the ebb and flow of the pen on paper. The letters swirled at first and then came together in patterns she recognised in her mind. With trepidation at first she traced her way through the written words but what she saw was Captain Marriott speaking them, directly to her:-

With one exception, Leading Hand K. E. Talog (Acting)! I don't know how they raise these girls of the Britanni in the Marches but I would like more of them in my crew!

She cursed under her breath. 'But Captain Marriott, I'm Brit-ish, Brit-ish!' He continued speaking to her.

Calm down Katie! I could do with at least two more of you so I can cover all watches!

'There's only one of me, Captain Marriott!' Or was there? She thought back to what her mum had said, and thought back to her first few weeks at HMS Raleigh, but she couldn't make up her mind about the two other young girls in her class that looked as lonely and isolated as she felt.

Your ability to know what is going to happen, and then react accordingly, is uncanny. It's like having radar, sonar, Identification Friend or Foe, a crystal ball and the all-seeing eye in one package, which gives my ship's crew an extraordinary advantage.

'I told you Captain Marriott - I'm far-sighted!'

For the day to day operation of the ship, you are willing to take on any task, any watch and carry it out with great verve and efficiency. Your contribution to the pursuit of the Chinese submarine off the coast of Zanzibar by our Lynx helicopter, using sonar buoys, dipping sonar and bluff was extraordinary. This should be presented as a master class at the School of Anti-Submarine Warfare.

'You want me to run a master class, Captain Marriott? In front of a fluster of junior officers? I don't think so!'

The crew of my ship carried out the rescue of the submarine crew after it had rolled over and the Chinese were completely bewildered about what had just happened to them.

Most recently, you were involved in what should have been a routine helicopter mission in the Comoros Islands which went badly wrong. What happened next was witnessed by our French colleagues and reported to me. And what they told me was that by your own efforts, you rescued a French officer, fought off at least two assailants in eye to eye combat while doing so, and got him back to the helicopter for urgent medical attention, thus saving his life. In addition, you arranged the rescue of four civilians and a squad of French commandos in the same mission!

I can't commend the overall performance of my ship's crew too highly but I would single you out, Katie, for special attention. Your written communication is appalling and a damning indictment of our education system. Your verbal communication can be abrupt and colourful...

She giggled at this. 'Captain Marriott! Really!'

...but your general conduct over the past twelve months has been nothing short of exemplary. You should be as proud of that as we are of you.

Whatever that was supposed to mean!

And now he was gone, having said his piece, so Katie folded the piece of paper up carefully and slid it back into her pocket, in case she needed it again. She threw more sticks on to the fire so it burned more fiercely. The cold that had stiffened her limbs was still there and the tracks of her tears were still etched down her face.

And so, on the high altar on Mynydd Moel, below Cader Idris, Katie emptied the contents of a linen bag onto a low, flat stone when the wind from the west momentarily abated. There was a necklace, a photograph of her nana, a leather clasp and pin, an ingot of tin and a signed photograph of HMS Albany. The sun lit the clouds above the sea with a tangerine cream sky. 'This is a special place and a special plea' she announced to the mountain 'and now you show me the way.'

There was no reply, just the moaning of the wind. Katie snorted in the air and watched the ravens cavorting above her. She looked across to the summit as she pronounced, with the vial tight in her hand: 'I am Katell Ebrill, born of Maela, who was born of...Rozenn.' There, that should do it she mused. 'None of this came with a manual. I don't know what I'm supposed to do next, maybe...someone will come to help me?' She heard no response but were the ravens showing her the way?

And then she remembered there was something in her bulging breast pocket, the thing that Gwen had stuffed in. The note was scrawled in a mixture of Welsh and English characters that swirled in spirals and made no sense at first. She moved the note towards her eyes and then away again. The letters started to join and trigger meaning in her head. The realisation of what the letter meant started her heart pounding and her eyes watering. She had to get to the wilderness of Tonfanau, and deal with whatever was in her way.

And then she heard a whimpering carried on the lightest of breezes but no words that she could interpret. She may already be too late.

The sky was covered with purple clouds and a whirling breeze spiralled from the north to the south and then to the west. It had become so dark she could barely see one step ahead of her. Coming down the track was a gaggle of kids, headed by a man wearing white plimsolls - or, at least, the plimsolls used to be white. About one hundred paces away he started to wave his arms in the air, imploring her to take heed. He was shouting. They came together and he remonstrated with her. 'You must turn back, follow us down to Dolgellau...' Through the black and purple billowing clouds, there was a gap above and to the west, and above the gap was blue sky. Around the gap, were feathery streams of bright orange cloud, flapping more and more in the wind. "You must turn back, the heavens are about to open!'

'I've got to keep going. My route goes over the summit. I've got to get west of the mountain!'

'Turn back now lady, all hell is going to break loose!'

'I'm fully kitted, I've everything I need to weather it - I'll be fine. Get the kids off the mountain.'

'Alright, alright' he said as the wind and rain whipped at their grimacing faces, 'I'm giving you two hours and then I'm calling Mountain Rescue.'

'I don't need Mountain Rescue - I'll be fine. Get the kids to safety.' At this, they paraded past at double speed and stumbled down the path to Dolgellau; Katie strode off in the opposite direction to Penygadair. The leader turned and gave one more despairing look towards her and then strode off after his charges.

Katie was at the summit of the rocky massif that overlooked the giant's seat. A succession of clouds scudded over and intermittently shrouded the hilltops inland, but where she stood, above all else, everything was still. As she turned to the next quadrant, she could see that massive scallops of rock had been gouged away and here the mountain dropped away sharply. Around she cast about the triangulation pillar and then she stopped suddenly because the back of her scalp bristled and the fine hairs on her neck and on her arms stood to attention - something was rising towards her. She leaned to look over the scalloped edge - it was steep and fell away sharply to Llyn y Gadair. Nothing could get up here, surely?

The surface of the tarn below was like a mirror but little eddies started to mark the surface, heading in her direction and becoming larger and more and more frequent. She inhaled deeply and there it was, an odour she had learned to fear, the odour of goat. Her left arm swung about until she grasped it firmly with her right. What was she to do?

Katie delved quickly into the body of the rucksack and pulled out a tape, a rope and two spring hooks. With the tape she made a harness for her backside and clipped it tight with a spring hook; with the other spring hook she clipped herself into a rope loop. There were eddies of wind coming up the steep face of the rock below her and loud scraping against steep rock. Katie threw a loop of the rope over a spike of rock, crawled to the edge of the precipice and carefully peered over.

'Aaaagh!' she yelled. Long curled horns embedded in matted white fur jutted up from below! Two amber eyes, black slitted, staring at her! She leapt back. The stench of goat, gag, gag, gag! She gulped repeatedly but couldn't swallow. Two massive horned hooves appeared, scrambling for purchase. With a huge snort it was facing her, its black lips parted, massive shovel bladed incisors and cobble stone sized molars and those two massive, diseased amber orbs.

Katie flung out her left arm to protect herself from the wet and snorting snout and its fearsome gut-churning breath. She coughed and something chewy came up into her mouth. But she could not see anything beyond the face of the beast, just soiled and matted fur, taut black lips those massive molars and those amber orbs. Her tongue and cheeks manoeuvred a gobbet into the front of her mouth - she spat it into the beast's right eye. The beast teetered on the edge and cloven hooves scrabbled against rock!

Katie clenched her fingers and swung a left handed uppercut into its snout. 'Haaaa!' It flapped under her fist and mucus sprayed everywhere. She re-balanced, crouched and launched a drop kick against its left hoof. It gave way!

Her feet were dangling over the precipice but the rope held her. She wiped mess off her face with her sleeve. It was gone! The stench of goat was gone, whipped away by a whirl of wind that whistled about her and sucked away a shower of shards that tinkled down the rock face.

Katie's limbs gradually stopped shaking as the wind ebbed away. She tip-toed up to the very edge of the precipice so she could see what had happened to the beast. 'Haaaa!' she shouted at the cleft a thousand feet below. She punched the air in triumph.

But there was a new and very alarming development! Creaking of rock, below her feet, coming rapidly towards her from her left and from her right. Her body suddenly lunged downwards. The whole rock face under her cracked and then lurched downwards. The slab slipped down two feet, paused and then accelerated down the rock face. She was falling away into space, into the abyss.

To and fro, to and fro, the heels of her boots scraped the freshly hewn rock and her harness sawed into her thighs. Her eyes popped open as her shock momentarily receded. She was just like a pendulum, scraping her way to and fro across this rock face, waiting for the moment, which she felt must come, when the rope gave way or her harness slipped.

Here she was, suspended by a loop of rope over a sharp spike of rock, just long enough to arrest her fall but just too short for her feet to get any useful purchase below. And there was no one around to hear her.

Katie blinked away the tears and tried to reason, but the pain of the taut harness cut through her thoughts.

I could cut myself loose and take my chances sliding down the rock face? No, I will end up in a cleft with that sodding, great beast, all mangled and bloody.

I could wait for Mountain Rescue to come? No, they will be hours yet. I could be well and truly crucified before they arrive.

I could set off a flare, I've got one in my pack! Her left arm reached behind her but she couldn't stretch far enough. Bollocks!

She was going, tipping upside down but by desperate scrambling with her feet she was upright again. Her lungs heaved in several gulps of air and these eased her pain, for the moment. But below, when she twisted her neck, all she could see, hundreds of somersaults below, was a giant- size fissure below, that was sealed by a huge slab of rock. She wondered how many classic climbing routes had dropped into the cwm - hundreds probably. It was a very big slab of rock that had been cleaved way from the mountain - big enough to seal in a sodding, super-sized beast.

Her mind sealed out the pain for a moment, and now she could hear many voices.

'Au secours!' croaked a very distant voice.

'Not now nana, I'm busy!'

'Look at what your stupid promise has done!'

'It's not a stupid promise, Gwen!'

'Remember your training, Wren Talog!'

'I was never trained for this, Mister Wicks!'

'Come back to us!'

'Who said that?'

Noisy wing beats flapped across her face and a huge, black bird settled on the edge above.

'Oh bloody brilliant, now you're going to peck my sodding eyes out!'

As she craned her neck upwards, the raven slipped off the rock, bounced on a lip of rock, somersaulted and landed on the edge above, kronking away.

'Use those ridiculously long limbs of yours!'

'They're not ridiculously long! They're just the right length to reach the ground!' Until now.

Katie looked about her. To her right side there was a lip of rock, just vacated by a raven, that she might be able to reach with her leg. If only my leg was twice as long as it actually is, or I was twice as dextrous, I could reach that lip.

'Use those ridiculously long limbs of yours!' she heard.

She scrabbled to her left and started to swing slowly across the rock face and then with increasing speed and amplitude. She twisted her torso and swung her leg. The sole of her boot gripped onto the lip and she was stuck. Katie gasped in big gulps of air while she calculated the next two or three moves. There was a small crack above her head that she could reach with a jab upwards. But if she missed, she would be on her way down. Her heart pounded against her ribs. It had to be now before her strength ebbed away.

Katie heaved with her leg, swung her left arm upwards and inserted her hand. It slipped until she clenched her fist into a ball. It jammed into the crack. She had to swing her way up to the ledge now. Gritting her teeth and her face and her body she lunged upwards. Her left leg found another hold on the ledge; her right knee mounted the lip; the skin on her knuckles ripped away; her right hand pushed against the rock. She was teetering on the ledge, looking down into the abyss, her lungs and heart thudding against each other. She pushed with her arms and bounced up onto the ledge.

Safe, safe, safe!

Katie pulled herself to her knees and edged her way to safety. There was thc sharp tang of shattered and friction burned rock but no sign of the beast below. By some miracle, the spike of rock and the rope and the harness had all survived the force of her fall. She unhooked the frayed tape and scrambled away desperately from the edge to the summit of the mountain. With her back resting against the concrete pillar on the summit she gulped down air between gulps from her water bottle and fed the rope and the harness and the spring-clips back into the rucksack. There was a gap in the clouds and she could see the sea. She had to get there as quickly as she could. With her rucksack back over her shoulders, she stumbled towards the wide track, flexing her aching thighs and kicking her aching legs back into motion.

She was sliding downwards amongst the sharp shards of rock, down and down, spinning around and until she came to a halt, a way down the slope, balanced on her rucksack, like an upside-down tortoise, limbs waggling in the air.

Katie looked upwards and saw that she was below the line of clouds and here there was sunshine. She felt the angled sun on her face, closed her eyes and came to a complete halt and her limbs stopped waggling.

And now the sunshine was gone, all blocked out, because of the rushing of wind and pounding of air on her face and the jiggling of stones around her. I'm finished, she thought as the noise and the pounding pushed her into the ground. There was shouting above her and then there was a two legged being crunching on the gravel beside her. The clips that held her rucksack secure to her body were released and she was eased away from its comforting embrace. There were strong limbs gripping her so tight, she could not escape.

And now she was being pulled away from the ground and tugged upwards, spinning in the air. Strapping enveloped her and was pulled so tight that her arms and legs screamed in pain. Her body was hanging above the ground, her body arched back in silent supplication. She was in an unnatural embrace with another being that uttered guttural commands above the roaring and chopping of blades.

And now she was pulled upwards into the swirling air and being swung into the metallic jaws of a machine; a yellow, thundering machine that hung in the air over the mountain; a machine that made the air throb and hum around her. Katie was now enclosed in darkness; a space of hard, unyielding metal, glass and leather. The smell of dried leather, sweat and oil suddenly shocked her into a wide eyed and wide mouthed comprehension. She was in a flying machine!

The smells, the throbbing of the rotors, all the sensations brought about by a machine, a machine that Katie knew - a Sea King helicopter.

And then there were arms and voices attending to her - voices that proclaimed and pronounced what she was already aware of; that she was suffering from exhaustion, bleeding knuckles, scrapes on her arms.

A man in dark green overalls, was shouting at her: 'Well lassie, I've never known anyone with such an appetite for destruction, whether it's yer own or others around you.' It was a Scottish voice, a voice that conveyed the stoicism of the Glaswegian from the Gorbals. She kept silent and tried to blank out his voice. The constant thumping of the helicopter rotors couldn't drown out his high-pitched nasal whine.

'I know ye can hear me lassie, I can tell. Yer twitching ears give ye away. Leading Hand Talog, RN, welcome back to reality!'

It was Cummins of the Royal. 'You need to take in some energy, lassie. Just keep still now.'

'Leave me be!'

A thumb traversed the nape of her nose and travelled across her forehead.

'Ach, look at that, will you, it really works!'

'Told you so!' said a voice from the co-pilot's seat. It was Uncle Alec's voice.

A tube was thrust in her mouth - she yelped as her knuckles were treated with antiseptic and bandaged tightly.

'You're to come with us, lassie!'

'I need to rest! I'm done in!'

'Our instructions are to help you get to where you need to be, as soon as we can!'

'We've been following the trail of devastation you've left across Wales!'

'Mad Dogs, Mad Dogs! What are you doing here, you should be married!'

'Yes, I should. Flick said that this was more important!'

'You should be shagging her brains out, not bailing me out!'

'I couldn't agree more!' shouted Flick from the pilot's seat.

Katie sat up and looked through the glass of the fuselage window. She saw an imposing, dark rock covered with dark feathered, hunched shapes, sitting forlornly like sentinels to the other world.

The helicopter was below the cloud line and cruising ahead of a steam train struggling up the valley, leaving tiny puffs of steam against the lush green backdrop. And all along the valley were the light and dark, angular shapes of fork-tails, flapping slowly westward.

'We're to get you to your target, as soon as we can. There's no need to thank me, lassie. I realise that we will always have a mutually assured disrespect for each other.'

'Shit!' shouted Flick. 'Hang on tight, turbulence!'

The helicopter yawed from side to side and the console between the pilot's seats sparked blue.

'We're expected' shouted Uncle Alec.

The Sea King helicopter landed with a bounce on the short turf of the headland and Katie stumbled down the steps to the ground. They were at the place of the waves: Tonfanau.

Chapter Seventy-Seven

Thursday 02 June 2056 - Tonfanau

Behind Katie, a succession of linear waves lapped against the shore; ahead of her, to the right, was a large expanse of sheep grazed turf; ahead of her to the left, were the footprints of old, concrete buildings, wiped off the face of the headland, apart from one. It had red brick walls and a corrugated, metal roof and there was something inside that was drawing her in.

Below her feet there was a flat stone set in the turf - it had the initials C.d.B scratched on it and a date. Katie scratched at it with her foot - it had been set here in the year 1940.

She heard Flick shout: 'Listen all, we won't be flying out of here. The chopper's U/S. Katie, get your hands inside the covers...where's she gone? Where's she gone? Katie?'

'She's gone! All we can do is get digging and wait!'

Katie started her walk to the red-brick shelter. Her legs felt old and achy but despite this, her footsteps became quicker and more determined. The vial was in her hand, the triskelion round her neck and the rucksack on her back.

The red-brick shelter was close but there was a girl hiding inside it and a girl skipping to her flank and this girl started to sing a nursery rhyme as she skipped:

'One: You arrive all bare!'

'Two: You pretend to care!'

She was a plump, freckled girl with a bare midriff and a shiny ring that glowed.

'Three: We all stare!'

'Four: You want to pair!'

Katie stared at the ring and her left hand made a tugging movement: 'Does that hurt!'

'Wha?' She went wide-eyed and panicky. 'No, why would it?'

And now she was staring at it too.

'But it's coming out, isn't it?'

The girl bent double and collapsed on the turf, clutching her belly as Katie kicked open the door to the shelter.

Gum chewing Auburn Scrunch girl, sat crossed legs in front, hair scrunched inside a pink cap. 'Oh my soul, you're here! Get Ceridwen here, quickly!'

'I can't! My guts are spilling!' cried the voice from outside.

'Do it now!'

'I need my nana!' shouted Katie.

'But you can't, she's not ready!' said Auburn Scrunch girl.

'Where is she?'

'She's in front of you, isn't she?'

There were two sheets of wavy, rusted iron in front of her - she threw them aside and gasped.

'Get Ceridwen!' screamed the girl.

Embedded in the soil was a still, naked body. It was the body of a very, very old woman.

Nana! What have they done to you!

There were tendrils coming into the body and back out to the soil, nothing moving or humming, just an infernal buzzing that was now tormenting her brain.

'You've come, we didn't think you were coming, did we?' said the girl. She seemed to be shaking inside from a racing heart.

The body was covered in little welts.

Katie's cheek and palms pressed flat against the body. 'It's me, Katie. It's all right, I'm with you now.' She looked at the girl. 'What did you do?'

'I didn't do anything, did I?'

'I'm taking her away now...'

'Look, she hasn't got long 'cos they just dumped her 'ere.'

'...but I won't leave it too late to come back - you do understand, don't you?'

'No, not really' said the girl, trying to extract a ball of gum from her teeth. 'I'm just going to get someone, aren't I?'

Katie nodded as tears trickled down her cheeks. 'It's all right, I've got her...' The girl's fingers were stuck in her mouth. She stumbled out trying to shout. There was the roar of a diesel engine closing rapidly. It skidded to a halt outside.

The prone figure stirred. 'It's me, Katie, do you remember me?' The being nodded and a short brittle smile came across her face. 'I made you a promise.' The being slowly moved her head. Katie ripped open her rucksack and opened her ground sheet on the shitty soil.

Katie forced on a grin. 'Look, Nana, I've got something for you, can you see!' She held up the glass vial. She swirled the viscous liquid. There was an elongated yellow digit inside, flakes of skin slipping from the surface like the tentacles of a sea creature. The being's eyes widened for a moment.

Nana, how do I get you out of this?

There was anxious whispering outside.

Carefully, stem by stem, Katie unpicked the tendrils. She wrapped her arms under the being's neck and waist and lifted and soil rained down to the sheet. The body weighed very little, as if it was a hollow shell. The triskelion was laid on the body's chest and the vial wrapped in the left hand. Katie cocooned the body in the ground sheet. There was a stir, a creasing of the face and a moan.

'I'm taking you outside, Nana.'

Must get her away from this trou de merde.

'They will not have your body!' she murmured to the still figure in her arms. She carried the body outside but two women stood in her way. Ceridwen, head piled high with silvery grey hair, jabbed Katie in the ribs as she went past. The auburn haired women growled in her throat and started to gag on her own phlegm.

Katie kept walking towards the sea as the sky darkened. She went past the girl writhing on the ground, clutching at her guts. Following her, was a sky full of harpies and a gaggle of walking witches. The sun was well on its way to the horizon.

And there in the neatly, sheep manicured turf, at the edge, a deep, round hole had been dug, a tamarisk bush to one side with its tangled root ball, an entrenching tool and a pile of soil. The body in her arms was frail and splintered. Katie tugged at the sheet so it shrouded the whole body, only the deeply wrinkled face showing. She smoothed the eyelids closed with a pinch of her lips.

There was just the kiss of the wind from across the sea, tropical breeze tainted and a stillness across the bay, broken only by the breaching of the surface, by a pod of harbour dolphins, whinnying in the calm.

Katie laid the body in the pit, still now, and peacefully coiled. An angular shadow passed over them, fleetingly, and again, and then another. They were high above, long, pointy feathered wings and tawny, contra-twisting tails. The fork-tails were all around, blackening the sky, forming a kettle above.

There were hollow shouts from all around.

Katie got up and stamped on the turf. 'I'm here for you, Rozenn!' She stamped her feet again in a rhythm and her arms stretched, alternately punching at the sky. 'You came from the soil, now I return you to the soil! Rozenn! Rozenn! Rozenn!'

Her right foot stomped and her left arm stretched: 'This is not your end Rozenn, this is your passing over!' The fork-tails were gathered above the headland in a ragged flying circus, so many that the ground was a patchwork of elongated shadows, their talons clutched together, dangling below, ready to release their payload.

And then the stomping and stretching broke out in earnest: 'Rozenn, I will come with you to the next world and so long as you have blood in this world, you will be remembered!'

Suddenly, a fork-tail peeled away, plummeted down towards them, talons outstretched, crying out aloud. A load of twigs settled over Rozenn's body. Katie dropped down and pulled the sheet tightly over Rozenn's head. Another payload of soil and twigs landed on them. 'You idiots!' shouted Katie, towards the sky. One by one, and moment by moment, another fork-tail peeled away from the circle, plummeted, dropped its load and flapped away.

She eased herself alongside the body, and coiled herself head to head and toe to toe with the body of her nana. As she sniffed at the loam, energy flowed into her body through the soil and she felt herself calm at last. 'I will stay with you, I will see you on your way.'

This was how it was meant to be. Her head returned to the chest which was still, no anxious rattle of breath, just stillness, a slight residual warmth.

There were footsteps approaching rapidly over the turf. There was shouting and the unfurling of a parachute.

'What do we do' shouted Mad Dogs, 'start shooting?'

'No! Get a 'chute over them!' shouted Flick.

'The fork-tails...they honour our lady!' said Uncle Alec in awe.

'Is she gone yet?'

Nana is passing over.

Katie glanced upwards and saw the shadow of the parachute stretched above, something that might provide some shelter underneath, if it wasn't billowing so much. She rested her head on Rozenn's chest and pulled her tight. She was passing over but her amputated finger had been returned to her and the triskelion adorned her bare neck.

Nana has everything she needs. I'll stay with her, I'll take her the rest of the way, I'm not sure if I'll be coming back.

But with every passing moment, with metronomic precision, more twigs; clods of peat; sheaves of leaves; and fast food wrappers were deposited.

'Child, you don't have to do this, it's not your time!'

Yes, it is, I'm ready.

Through the silk of the parachute, Katie saw the flitting shadows of lanky winged, fork-tailed kites; stiff winged, short-tailed buzzards; majestic, gliding sea eagles, from all directions. A pair of ravens perched on the rotors of the helicopter, giving a running commentary.

Silly sods.

Katie spat out a mouthful of twigs and cursed, but it made no difference. They would not relent. She settled alongside and wrapped her arm around Rozenn, the parachute unfurled above their heads, the thud of soil and sticks making a loose rhythm.

Katie clenched her teeth.

They will not have our bodies Nana, they will not have our bodies.

Under the pile of soil and sticks and leaves, first the thumb, then her middle finger and then the two remaining fingers parted company with the vial, and Rozenn had passed over.

She heard Auburn Scrunch girl wailing because she couldn't understand what was occurring.

She heard the sneering calls of Ceridwen, declaring that the Britanni were finished.

And then there was nothing but the slow tick of her wristwatch, clawing it's way around the watch face, past each of the numerals and the sound of her voice crying, 'Danu knows I tried, I tried, I tried.'

And then with just the roll of the sea, the kiss of the breeze and the growing pile of soil and plant debris, Katie's arms unclasped and she was rising slowly, away from the shell of her nana's body, away from the comfort of the silken shroud, rising above, over and beyond the sea.

CHAPTER SEVENTY-EIGHT

Epilogue

The young RN Wren walked towards the grim, brooding installation know colloquially as 'The Tank'. It was a typically grim and brooding November day, where the clouds formed a uniform sheet of puffy grey across the sky. Her breath puffed voluminously into the cold, moisture and smoke saturated air, like the puffs of a smoke spewing dragon. The double metal doors, coated in old white paint, groaned in protest as she pulled them apart and inside, she marched quickly into the dark void, turned left and marched up to the Royal Marine lieutenant and saluted. She read the name tag on his shirt uniform. It read 'TENNANT'. No! Surely not?

'Kit off' barked the lieutenant.

'What, not even any small talk, lieutenant?' she replied. After a moments pause, waiting for a reply, she put down her towel, and stooped to remove her boots and socks. 'Are you taking your kit off too, lieutenant?' she asked.

'No,' he replied, 'I'm the assessor and you're the assessee.'

'Oh, I see. Then someone needs to switch on the sodding heating, it's bloody cold in here!'

'There is no heating - this is 'The Tank'!'

So, she took off her cap, shirt and trousers and piled them on top of her towel on an off-white plastic chair. She ran her thumbs all round the leg openings of her swimsuit to check that everything that should be tucked in, was tucked in, and nothing untoward was showing. Nothing was.

She looked apprehensively to her right across the surface of the pool and shivered. In the thin, insipid light it was large, motionless and darkly silent.

The lieutenant spoke. 'Do you know why you're here?'

'Yes, it's a date. We're going to sit by the pool, top up our tans and drink cocktails, aren't we?'

He looked puzzled. 'Really?'

'Then I thought, depending on how things go, we could nip round the back for a quick knee trembler' she added. He wasn't bad looking either, no significant other she reckoned, and therefore, totally available.

'You're deluding yourself' he commented.

'Not really lieutenant, they said be here at oh-nine hundred and pack a swimming costume and a towel. So I did.' She picked up the towel and whirled it dramatically around her shoulders to cover her feeling of cold nakedness. 'I did wonder if it was a date, because if it is, it's not shaping up too well, is it?' She paused for a reply. There was none. 'Am I here for a swimming lesson? Because, I think it would save a lot of time, if I just said, for the record, I can't swim and it's pointless learning me how now, isn't it, lieutenant?'

To her left against the grey paint-peeling concrete walls was a boat hook and what looked like an upturned coracle. Above her head was a small, compact but upside down landing craft, tethered to a winch and suspended from rust coated chains. Oh crap, she thought, I'm going under water and I'm going to be drowned. Her body gave an involuntary shiver that sped up her spine, over her crown and along her limbs to the tips of her fingers.

'I'm not going to learn you swimming, as you put it, I'm going to demonstrate to you that you can swim - Flipper.'

'Flipper? Oh, how did you know about that?'

'It's in my notes - Flipper. Here it is.'

'Oh, that's what they called me at HMS Raleigh, isn't it? It was a bit sarky but it's to do with the shape of my feet.' She pointed downwards with her forefingers to illustrate the point. 'It wasn't supposed to mean that I can swim, though?' She peered into the dark brooding liquid mass to her right. 'So, where's the shallow end?'

'There is no shallow end' he replied, 'this is 'The Tank'!'

'Come on, there's always a shallow end, isn't there? How am I supposed to get in? And where's the sun lounger and the bar?'

He didn't respond. He seemed to be intently reading his notes. 'Show me the sole of your right foot.'

She paused for a moment. 'Lieutenant, shouldn't you say please?' she added. There was no response. She then turned away from him, raised her lower leg so he could see the sole of her right foot.

'I see, very good. I can see another distinguishing feature on your left shoulder. Ah, good. And you have another one, which is...'

'I'm not showing you that one, lieutenant, because it's private, unless we have a second date, which isn't looking very likely at the moment.'

'I'll take that one as read. Good system. I think we should make it universal. Makes the job of piecing together bodies much simpler.'

'You what?' She turned her head over her shoulder to gawp incredulously at what he had just said.

'When they get mangled in action.' He quickly seized her by her waist and thighs, lifted her over his head and hefted her through the air. Her leg, chest and head collided with the cold liquid that drove the breath out of her body and shocked her brain into numbness. She flailed deep into the liquid darkness with desperate arms and legs but sank into the gloom. Her legs thrashed out but they could not find a solid surface to push against, there was nothing that her hands could grasp at, just a stream of bubbles that marked her passage downwards. She coughed but more oily water flowed into her lungs. Nothing to breath! Must get out! Her hands thrashed again into the dark water, her legs trailed limply behind. She squeezed her legs together and clawed again. Her head burst above the slick and there was air.

She coughed out water and rasped in breaths that filled her lungs with air and water. With four swings of her arms, she reached the cold, tiled overhang of the pool. Her arms were grasped and she was heaved out. Bending double, she coughed onto the broken white tiles below her and cleared her nostrils. It was then that she realised that her nostrils had been cleared over a pair of shiny, black, parade ground boots.

'You and your kind are known as 'Sea Witches' by people all the way down the coast of East Africa and across the Indian Ocean' he stated, 'can you tell me why?'

'Nope.'

'Oh, I think you can.'

'Oh, I don't think so' she said, still bent double. She stood upright and spluttered: 'All right' she coughed, 'it's to do with the name on the nose of the chopper...it's a bit of a mix-up, isn't it? They're confusing us with the equipment; a helicopter, that's all it is. They...just can't deal with the idea of women in our armed forces, can they?'

'Your particular crew - how many skull and crossbones have been earned now?'

'More than twenty, but...we're a team...and it's not just about that, we do much more, we put in clean water systems...we patrol to keep all seafarers safe.' She had removed the water from her lungs and the snot that had come from nowhere to fill her nose and sinuses.

'Ah yes, you remind me, the infamous Operation Spring Roll. That caused a lot of mirth in the ward room. Chinese not best pleased, are they?'

'No, well they shouldn't have been there, should they? How did you hear...?'

He gathered her up in his arms and threw her back in the pool. She caught her breath before she splashed under water. Her limbs spread out and started pushing, newt-like in the water, suspended between the air and the dark mass, coughing out water. Her arms thrashed again and her legs squeezed together to propel her to the side.

The lieutenant pushed her back under the water with the boat hook.

Her body wriggled and she was back to the surface, gasping and hair hanging over her face. 'Help!' she screamed lamely.

The lieutenant threw the coracle into the water and stepping inside daintily, he paddled his way towards her. He prodded her back under the surface.

She emerged again, gasping. 'I'm cold, get me out!' She tried to thrash her way around him but couldn't - she thrashed her arms again and grasped the side of the coracle - he pushed her deep under the water. She had gasped in a lungful of air this time. She sank vertically in the water, legs and arms outstretched and together, sinking slowly and remorselessly down into the dark. Her feet found the bottom of the tank, her legs flexed and pushed upwards, quickly and strongly.

She surged up and her hands grasped the coracle side and pulled sharply down. A silhouette of a man in uniform described a perfect parabola above her head and there was a loud splash as he smacked into the water. Then he was out of sight in a medley of bubbles.

He was behind her! She was seized her by her shoulders and pushed back under the water. As they struggled together in the dark, they came back to the surface, gasping under the cover of the upturned coracle.

'That's more like it' he said, 'remember to breathe and use those ridiculously long limbs of yours.'

She squirted the accumulated water in her mouth directly into his face. 'Wanker' she shouted. They were holding each other, and her legs were wriggling animatedly but she was barely keeping her head above water.

'So, what have we learned?' he asked.

'You're a sadistic, cretinous bastard!' she blurted out.

'There you go, feeling better now?' he replied.

The wriggling of her legs was keeping her afloat and her nose just above water. 'You, big, ignorant, condescending prick' she spat between spurts of water from her mouth.

He pushed her below the water, grasped her waist and pulled her through the water from underneath the coracle. The light was no better out of the shelter of the boat. He towed her body to the side and lifted her so one leg and one arm rested on the apron of the tank and she could haul herself out as a heaving, panting wreck on the spoiled and broken white tiles. Her limbs shook out of control and she tried to get to her feet but couldn't. He leapt out of the water and lifted her. She wobbled but kept standing. They dripped together on the tiles, his beret sagging over his right eye.

'Pass me the sodding towel' she gasped.

He threw it towards her and she caught it and wrapped her shivering body in it. 'This has been the worst date ever...and I've been on some bad ones!'

He looked as if he was going to make a speech. He picked up his clipboard and a pen and made a squiggle on the printed sheet of paper. Yes, the pen was still working despite everything.

'So,' he looked intently and inquisitively at her to check that her breathing was back under control. 'So, through the dunking test we have established that you don't drown. It was close at times, but you don't drown. Without a shadow of a doubt, you are, therefore, in point of fact, a witch.' He made a laboured note on the printed sheet.

Her arms described a double handled teapot. 'No, I'm sodding not!'

'The evidence is overwhelming.'

'Bollocks! No, it's not! Are you saying that anyone who doesn't drown is a witch! That's just bloody stupid!'

'You have many accusers.'

'Accusers? Who are these idiots?'

'I have a long list...'

'Show me!'

He took two steps to his briefcase perched against the wall. He removed a sheaf of fanfold paper and unfurled it so that it ran for yards along the cold, crumbling tiles.

She swallowed noisily and tried to work out what her response should be. She picked up the long rippled paper and tried to read the names. He noted she was struggling and highlighted some examples for her. 'Ah, here we have Mrs G Hofland and her daughter, Monique. See here, that's the Princess Royal. And here we have the First Sea Lord, the Minister for the Armed Forces and the Archbishop of Canterbury.'

She ran through a catalogue of retorts that she could use but held them back. None of this made any sense. 'Oh, my soul, that is a well sodding long list of accusers. But I am no witch! I'm a good girl!'

'That's as maybe, but we must follow due process.'

'Ask Maela Houghton, ask her, she'll tell you!'

'We did. She says you are a witch. See here!'

'I don't sodding believe it' she moaned as she saw the elaborate signature, 'even she has betrayed me!'

'So, as you have been declared a witch, we are obliged to respond. The evidence is actually quite compelling. See here.' He presented a decision tree that she attempted to follow, step by step.

'Oh bugger, I see what you mean. Now I can see it all in black and white, I don't know what to say. Do you burn me at the stake now?'

'No of course not, this isn't the Middle Ages. We have policies for dealing with people like you. So, what do I need to do to convince you?'

She thought about the incredibly long list of accusers, the infallible logic of the flow chart and her recent under water experience. 'Nothing' she replied grudgingly.

'Good, so, you confess to being a sea witch. Please sign here.'

She ripped the pen from his proffering hand. 'If I sign this, what'll happen to me? Do I get my marching orders?' He was a Royal Marine lieutenant after all. What a prick!

'I'll tell you that in a minute. Just sign here.'

She gulped and scrawled her mark on the damp form. 'I can't believe I just did that.'

He frowned at the unintelligible mark on his sheet. 'Of course the down side to all this is that you will probably burn in hell' he chuckled.

'You seem to think you're utterly hilarious' was the best she could come up with, 'but you're really not.' She shut up and waited for the punchline.

'Right, well done. Incidentally, we have also demonstrated that you can in fact swim, if only to avoid drowning.' He nodded at her to try and elicit a response but she just stood and glowered. She pulled the towel tighter to her body and shivered. 'More pertinently, I'm recommending that you are suitable to work with the Royal as a Marine Wren, rank of leading witch, sorry, that should be leading hand, normal Ts and Cs apply. You will report to Birkenhead on November 30th to join her Majesty's assault ship, HMS Indomitable. Now, what do you say to that?'

'I say, go screw yourself, you moronic, self-serving twat.'

'Ah yes, they did warn me that you had a 'bon mot' for every occasion. I didn't hear a 'no' in there, but would you like some time to consider?'

A spat of hissing and snarling invective came at him.

'Ah yes, that's a good point.' He made a note. 'Fluent in cursing, multiple languages. Any other comments? Apart from the ones that I can't print. No? Well, job done I'd say.' His beret was sagging even more over his right eye so that he had to squint. He turned to leave her but he returned to hear her response.

'I'll do it' she said resignedly. 'I know I'm going to regret this, but I'll do it. Can I go now, lieutenant?'

He looked thoughtfully at her. 'It's interesting you say that the soubriquet 'Sea Witch' does not apply to you. It's evident that Her Majesty's enemies both fear and respect you in equal measure. I don't know anyone else in her Majesty's armed services who has that reputation, apart from us in the Royal. So well done. You're one of us!'

Lightning Source UK Ltd.
Milton Keynes UK
UKHW012341260120
357609UK00011B/42